Himawari House

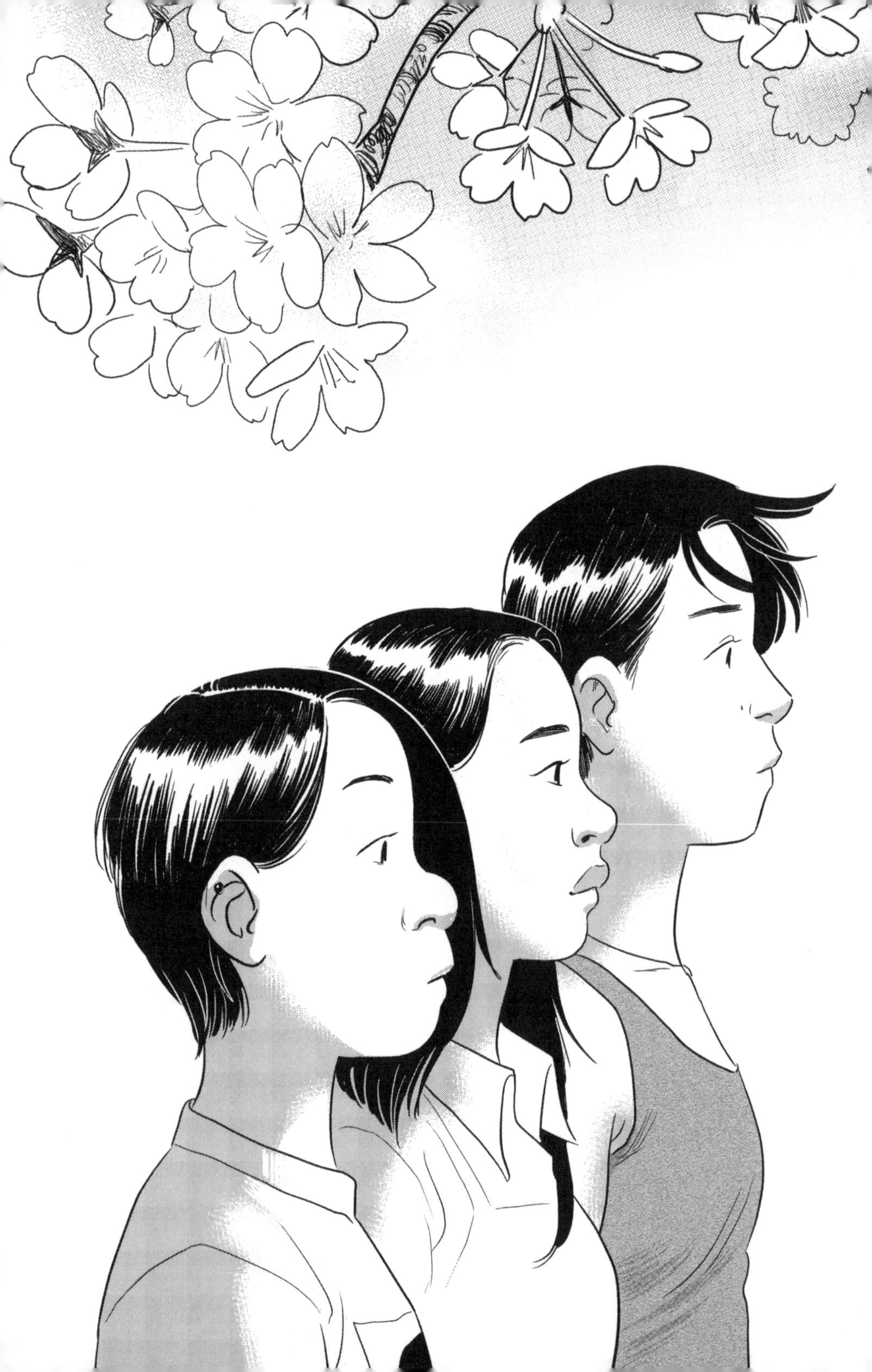

Himawari House

Harmony Becker

:01

First Second

These are the things I remember about Japan.

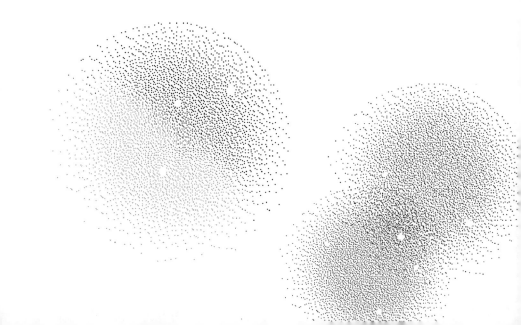

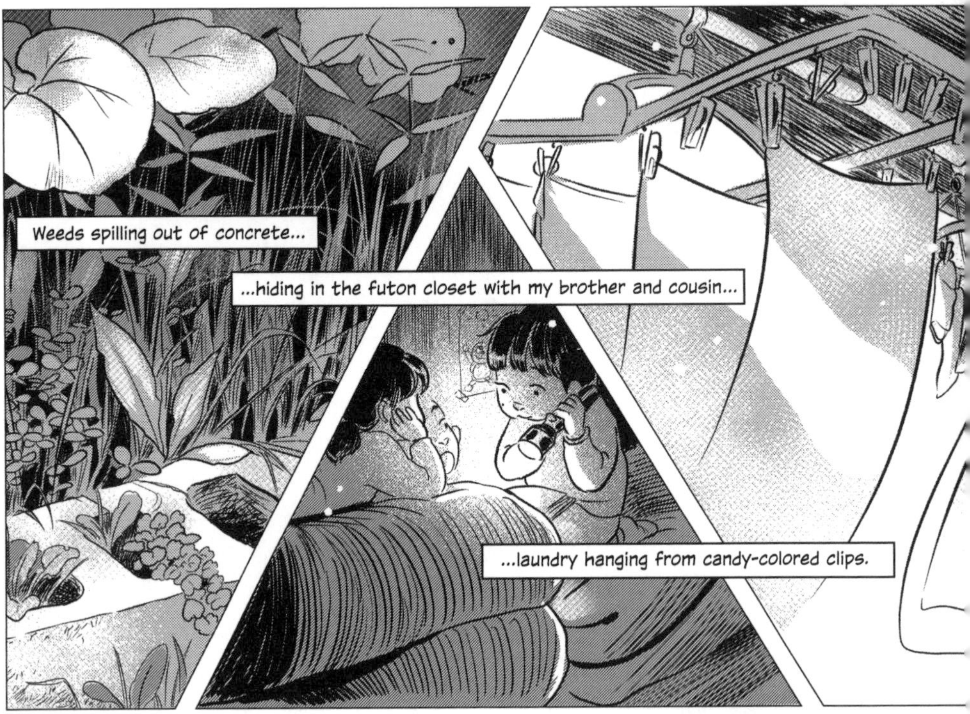
Weeds spilling out of concrete...
...hiding in the futon closet with my brother and cousin...
...laundry hanging from candy-colored clips.

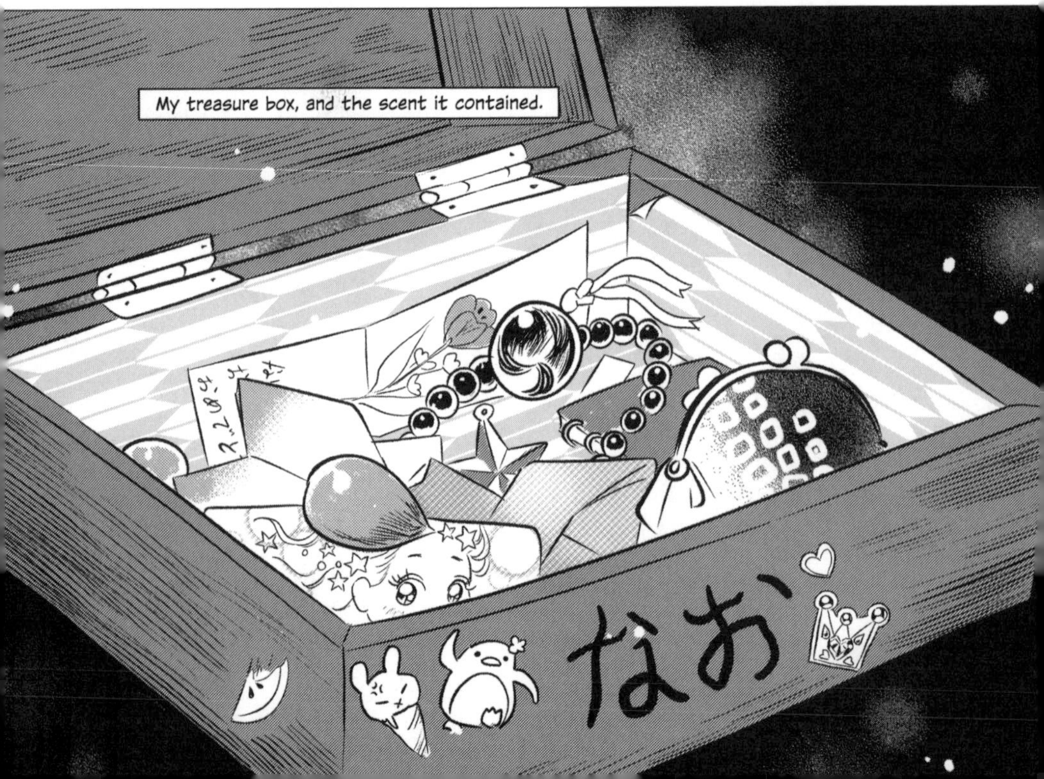
My treasure box, and the scent it contained.
なお

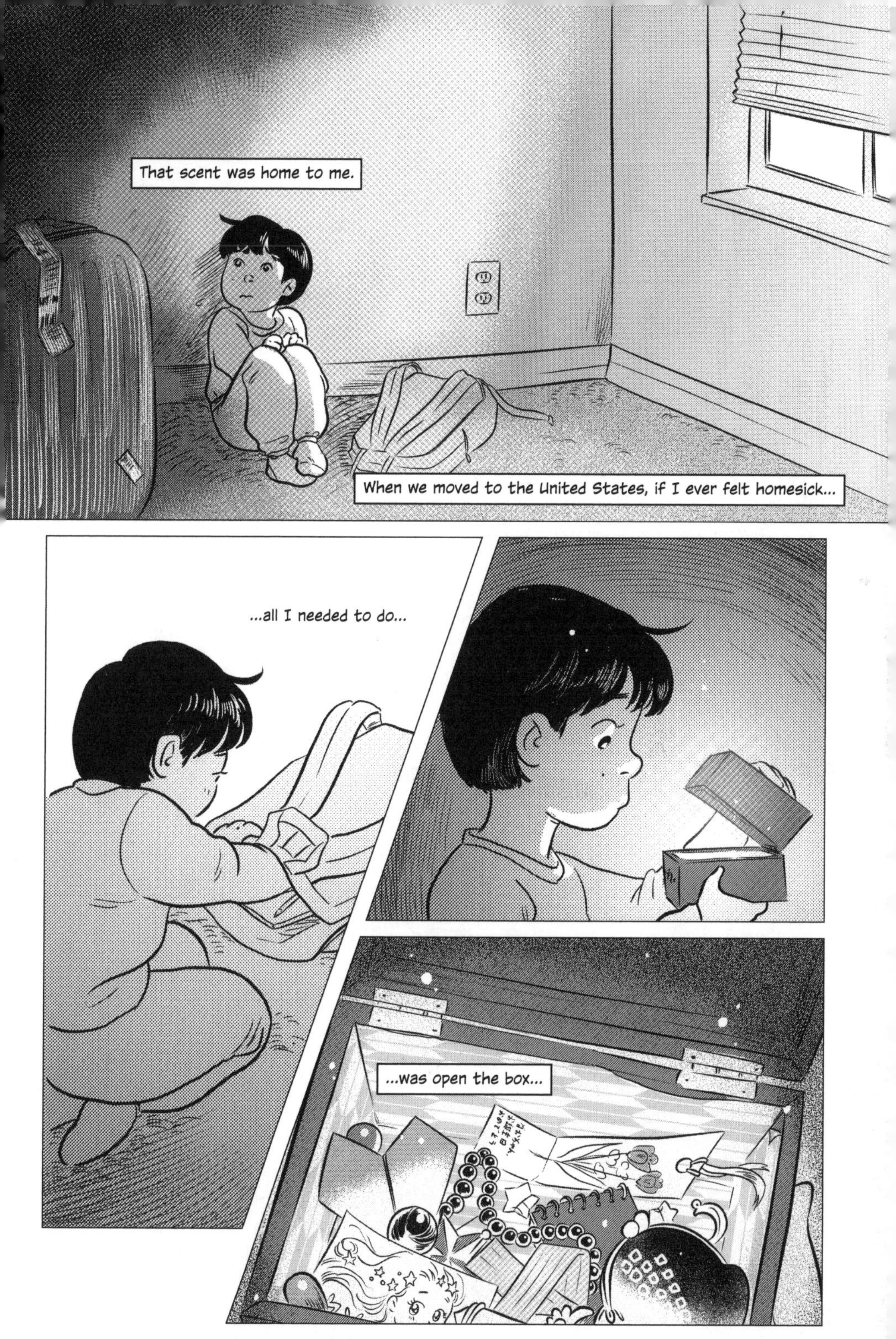
That scent was home to me.
When we moved to the United States, if I ever felt homesick...
...all I needed to do...
...was open the box...

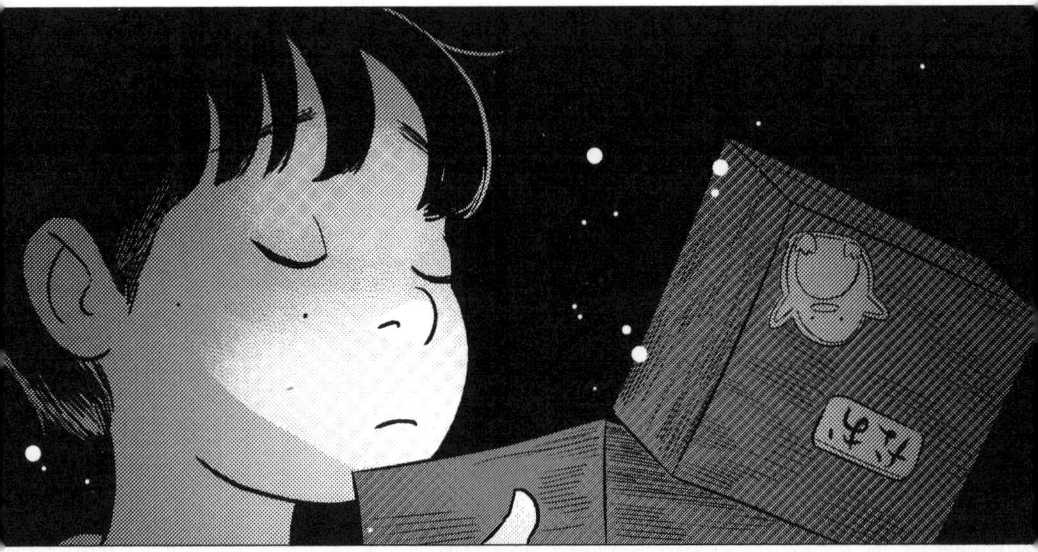

...and breathe in deep.

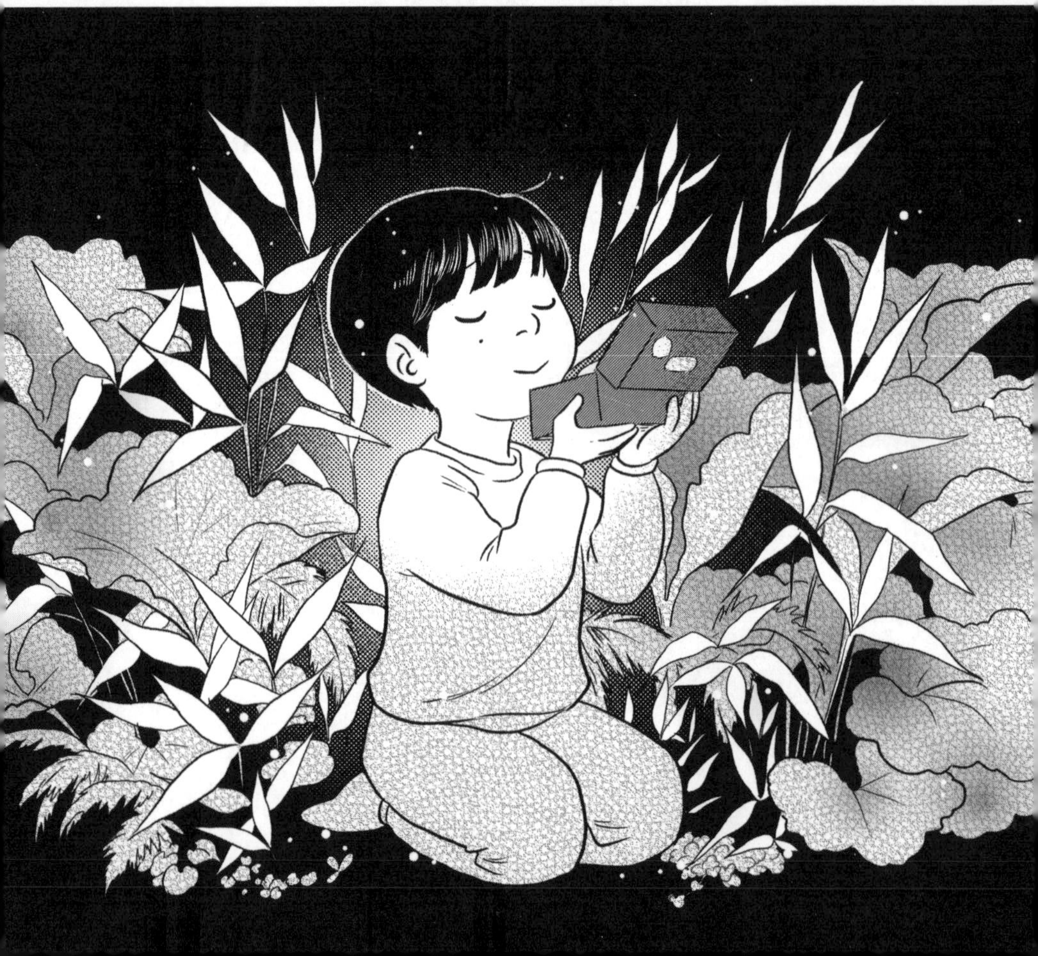

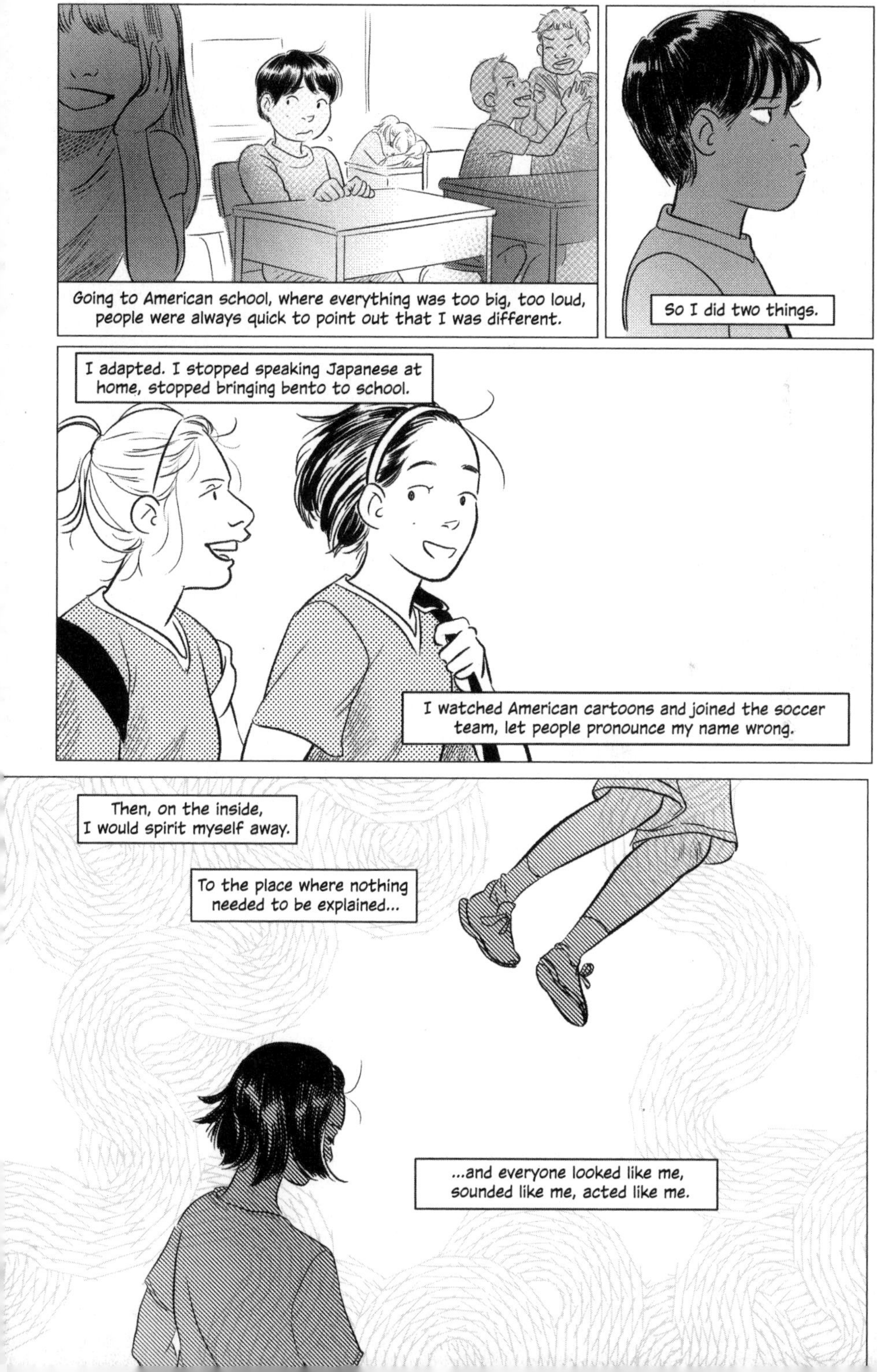
Going to American school, where everything was too big, too loud, people were always quick to point out that I was different.
So I did two things.
I adapted. I stopped speaking Japanese at home, stopped bringing bento to school.
I watched American cartoons and joined the soccer team, let people pronounce my name wrong.
Then, on the inside, I would spirit myself away.
To the place where nothing needed to be explained...
...and everyone looked like me, sounded like me, acted like me.

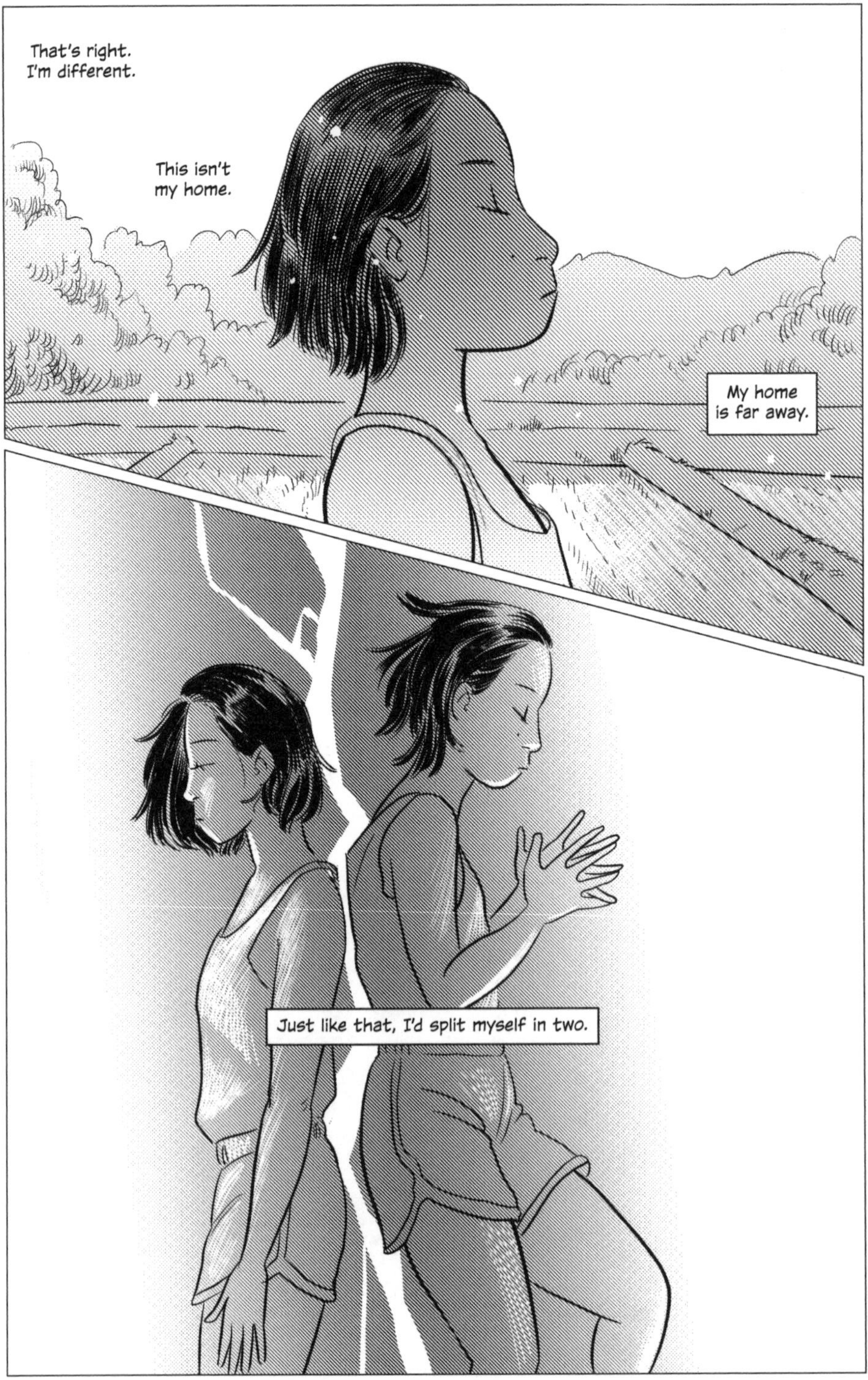
That's right.
I'm different.
This isn't
my home.
My home
is far away.
Just like that, I'd split myself in two.

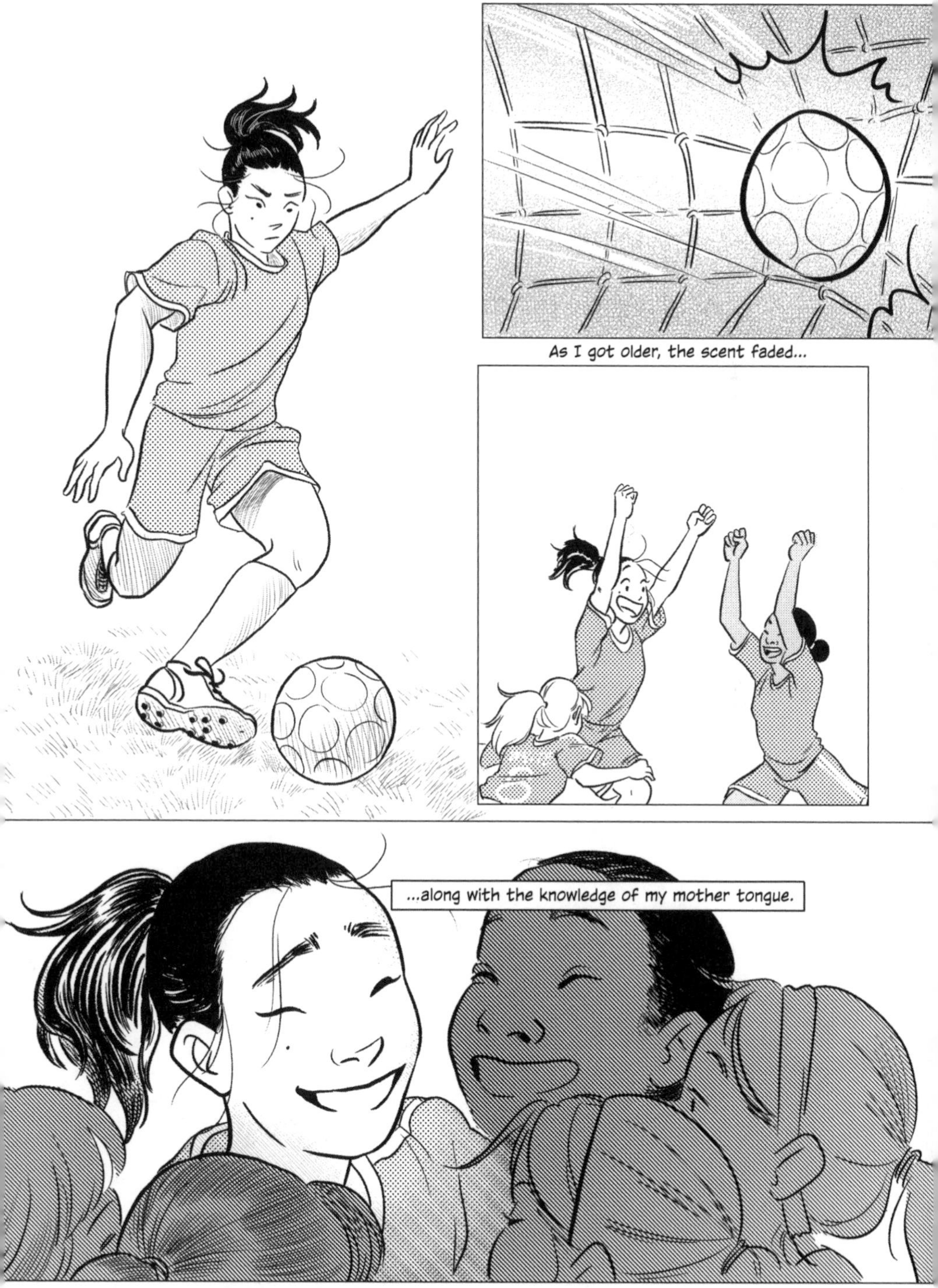
As I got older, the scent faded...
...along with the knowledge of my mother tongue.

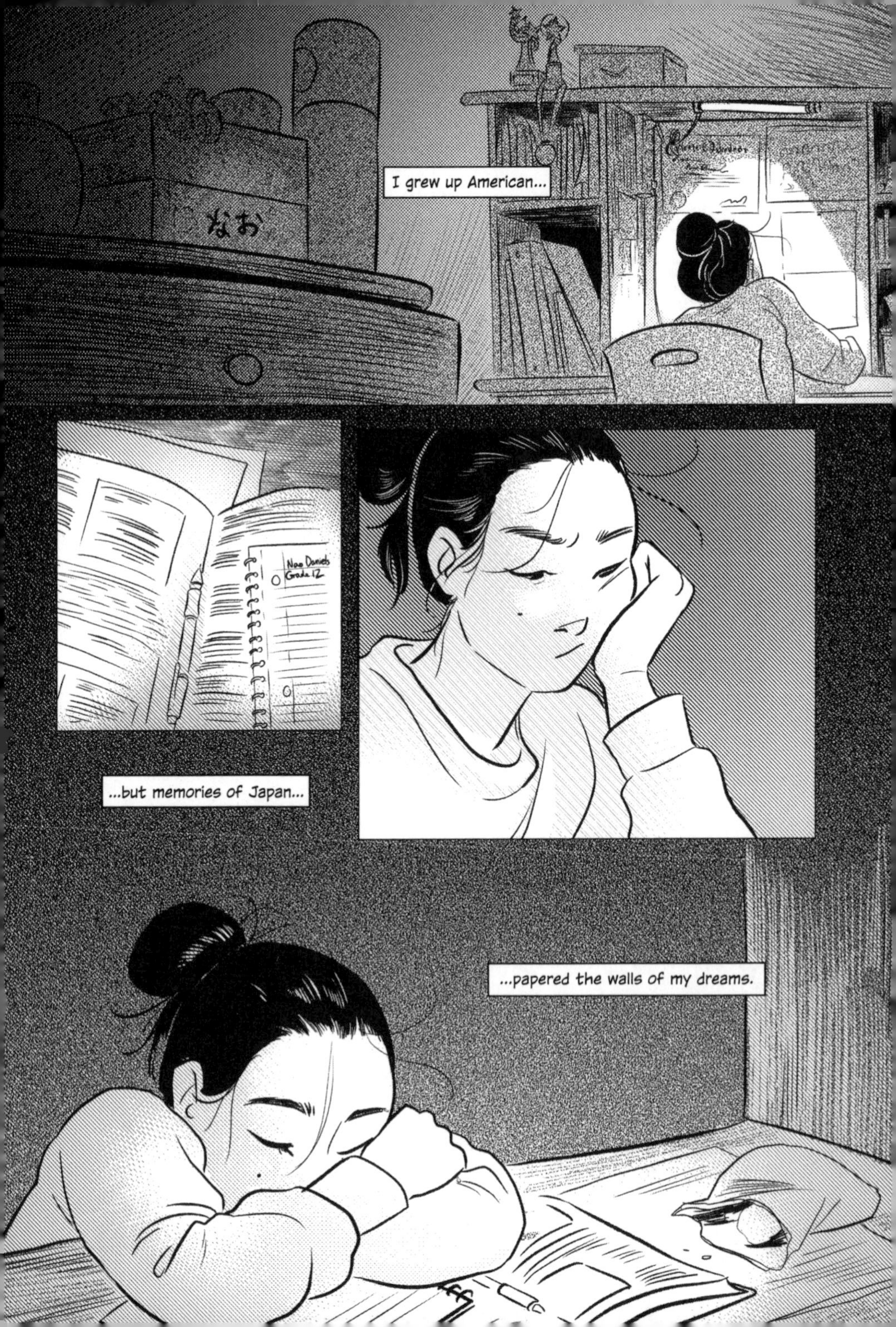
なお
I grew up American...
Nao Daniels
Grade 12
...but memories of Japan...
...papered the walls of my dreams.

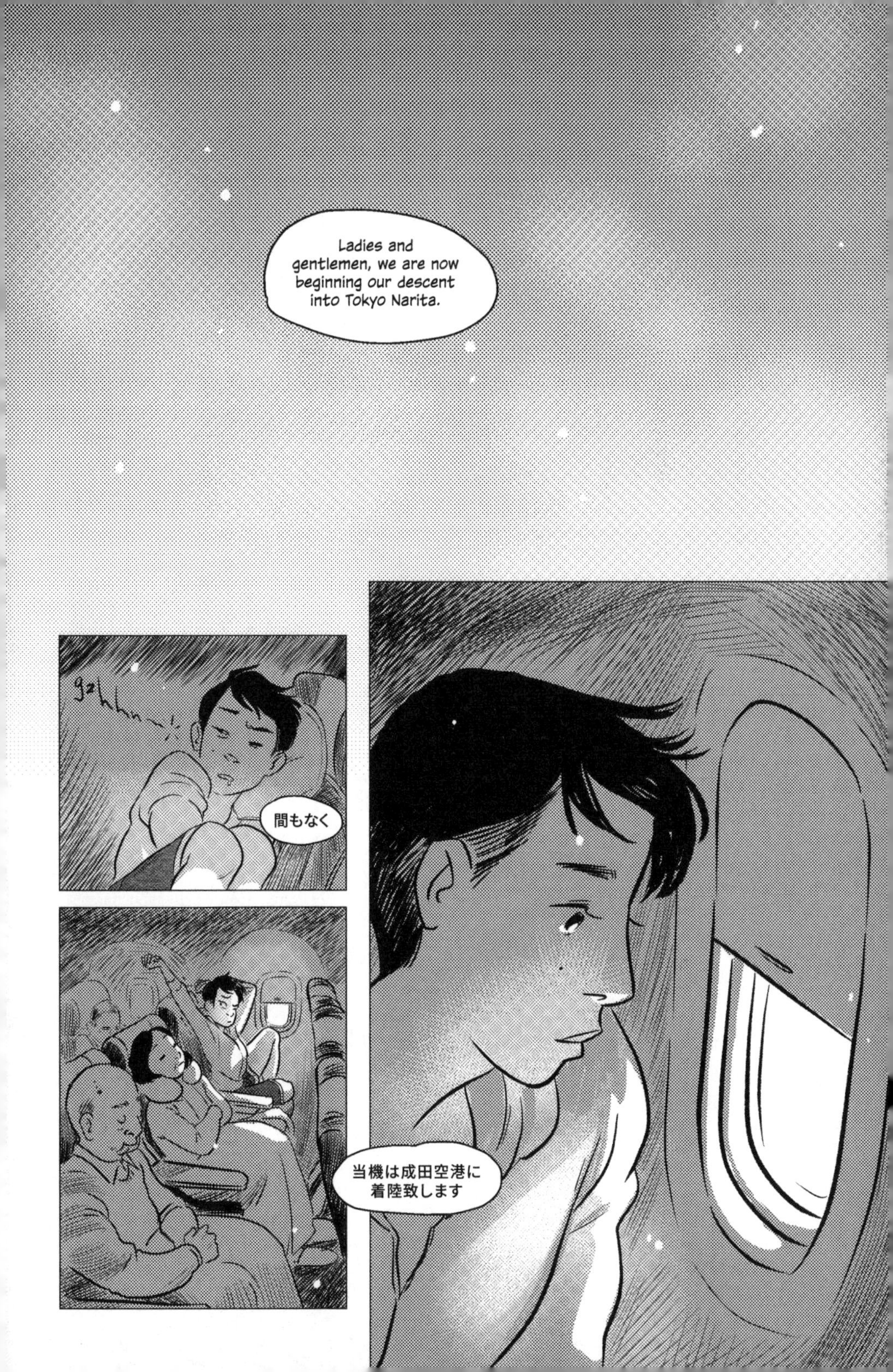
Ladies and gentlemen, we are now beginning our descent into Tokyo Narita.
間もなく
当機は成田空港に
着陸致します

Chapter 1

I don't know where Singapore is

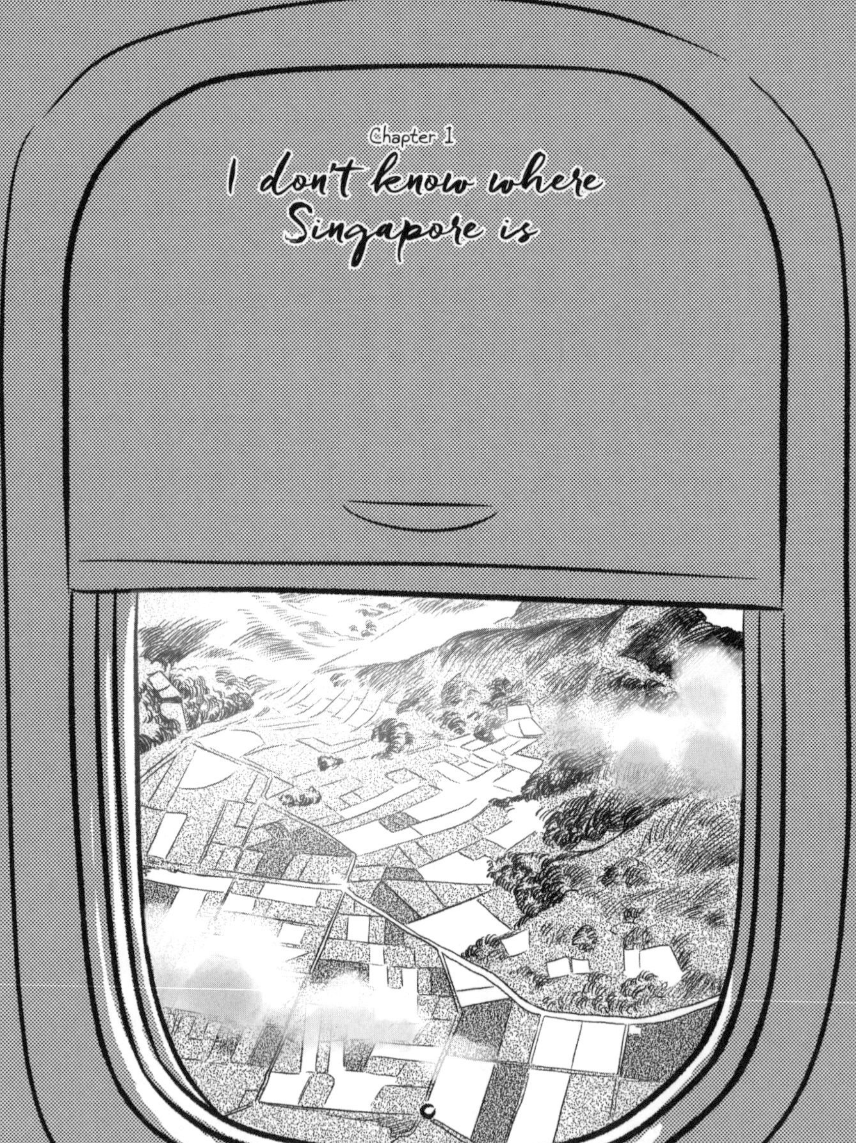

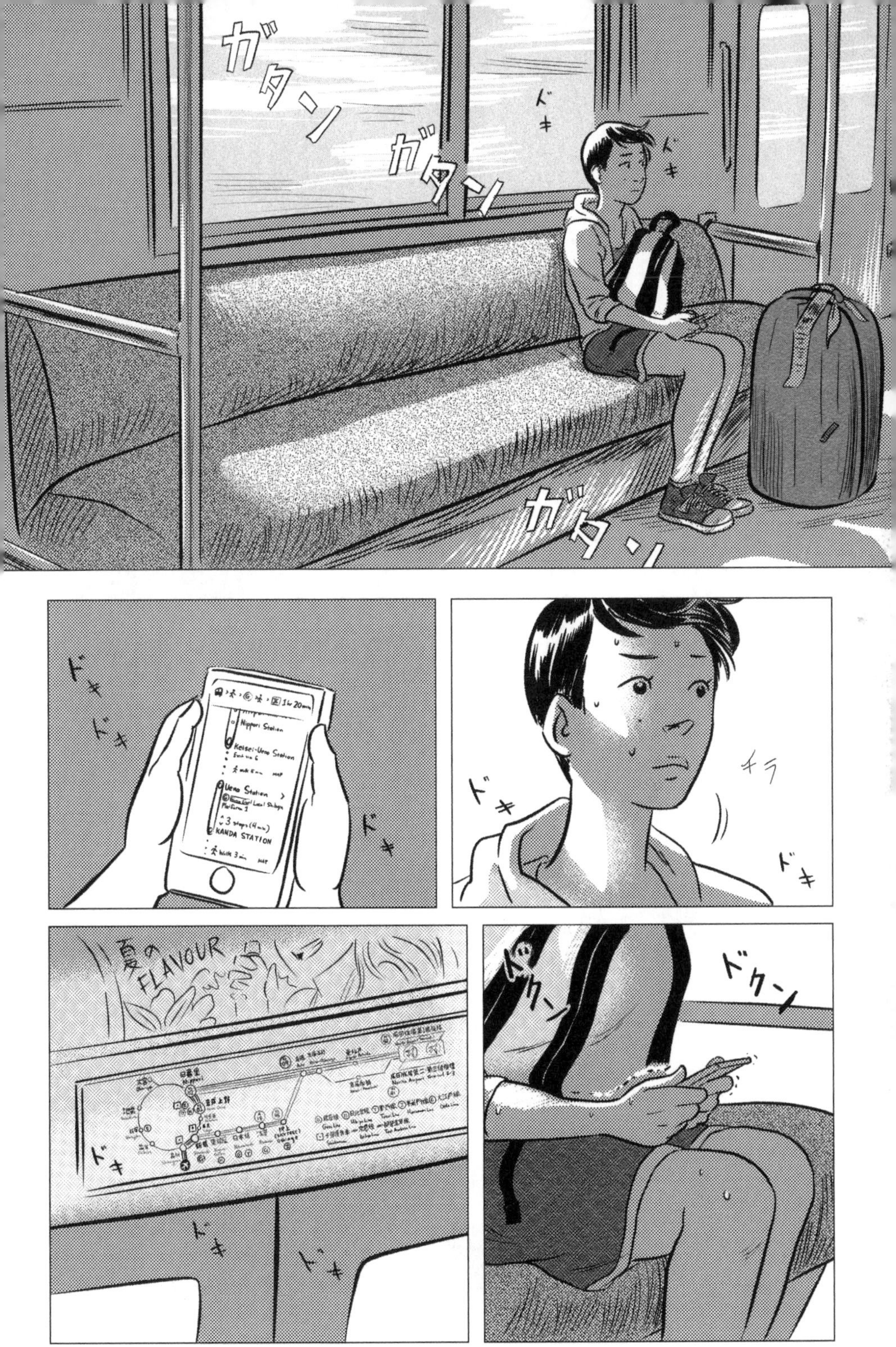
ガタン
ドキ
ガタン
ドキ
ガタン
ドキ
ドキ
Nippori Station
Keisei-Ueno Station
Ueno Station
3 stops (4 min)
KANDA STATION
Walk 3 min
ドキ
ドキ
チラ
ドキ
夏のFLAVOUR
ドキ
ドキ
ドキ
ドクン
ドクン

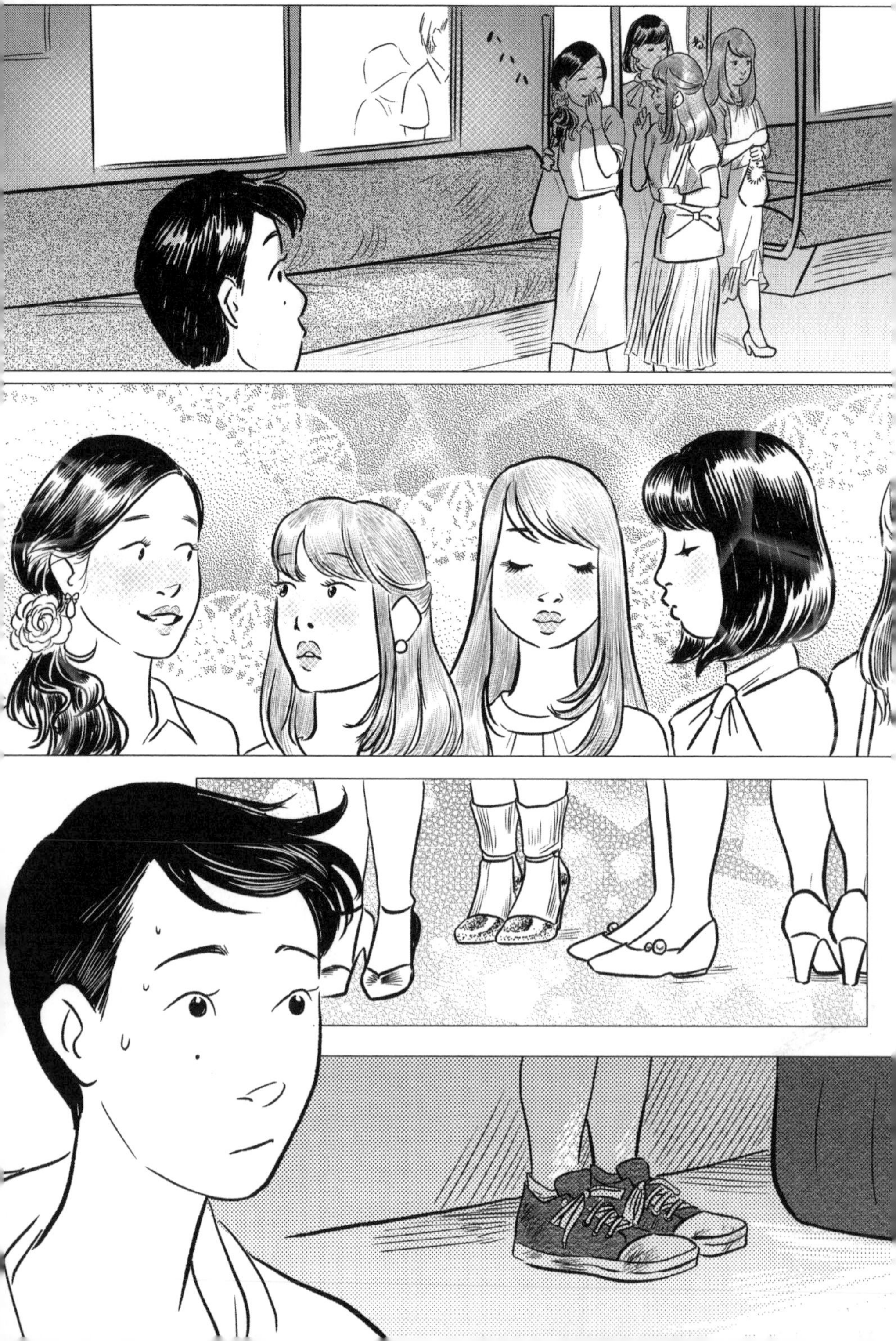

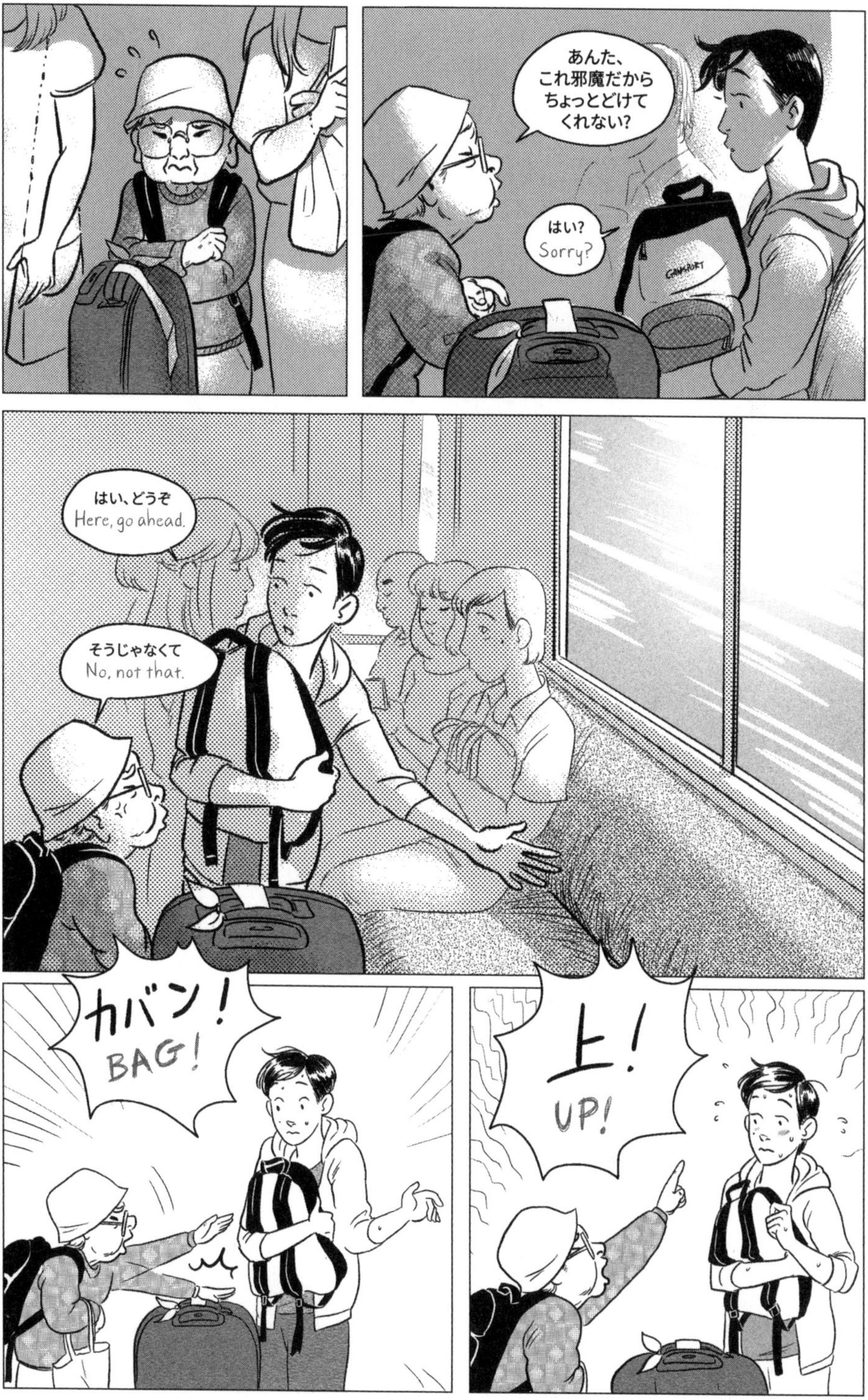
あんた、これ邪魔だからちょっとどけてくれない?
はい? Sorry?
はい、どうぞ Here, go ahead.
そうじゃなくて No, not that.
カバン! BAG!
上! UP!

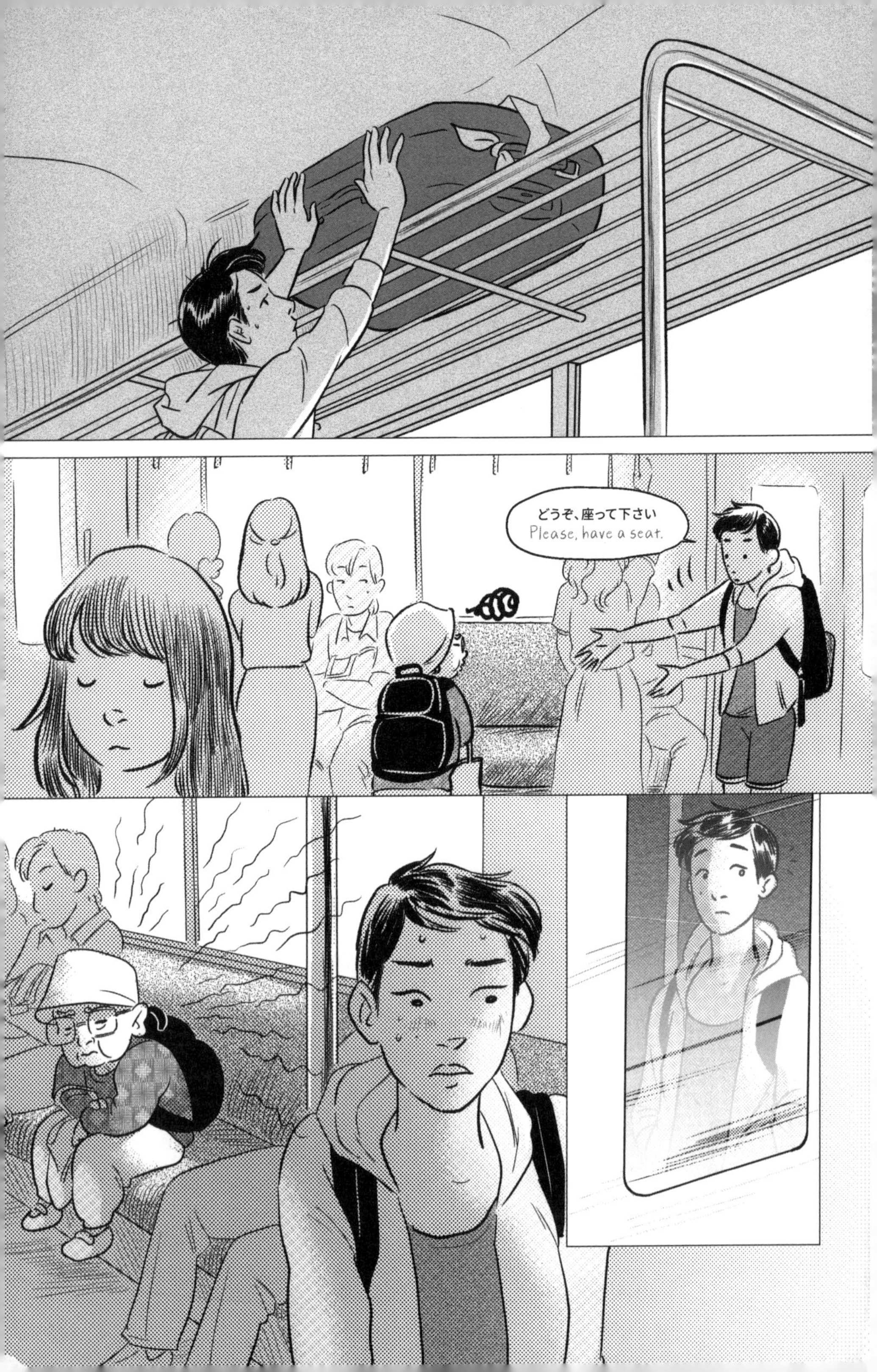
どうぞ、座って下さい
Please, have a seat.

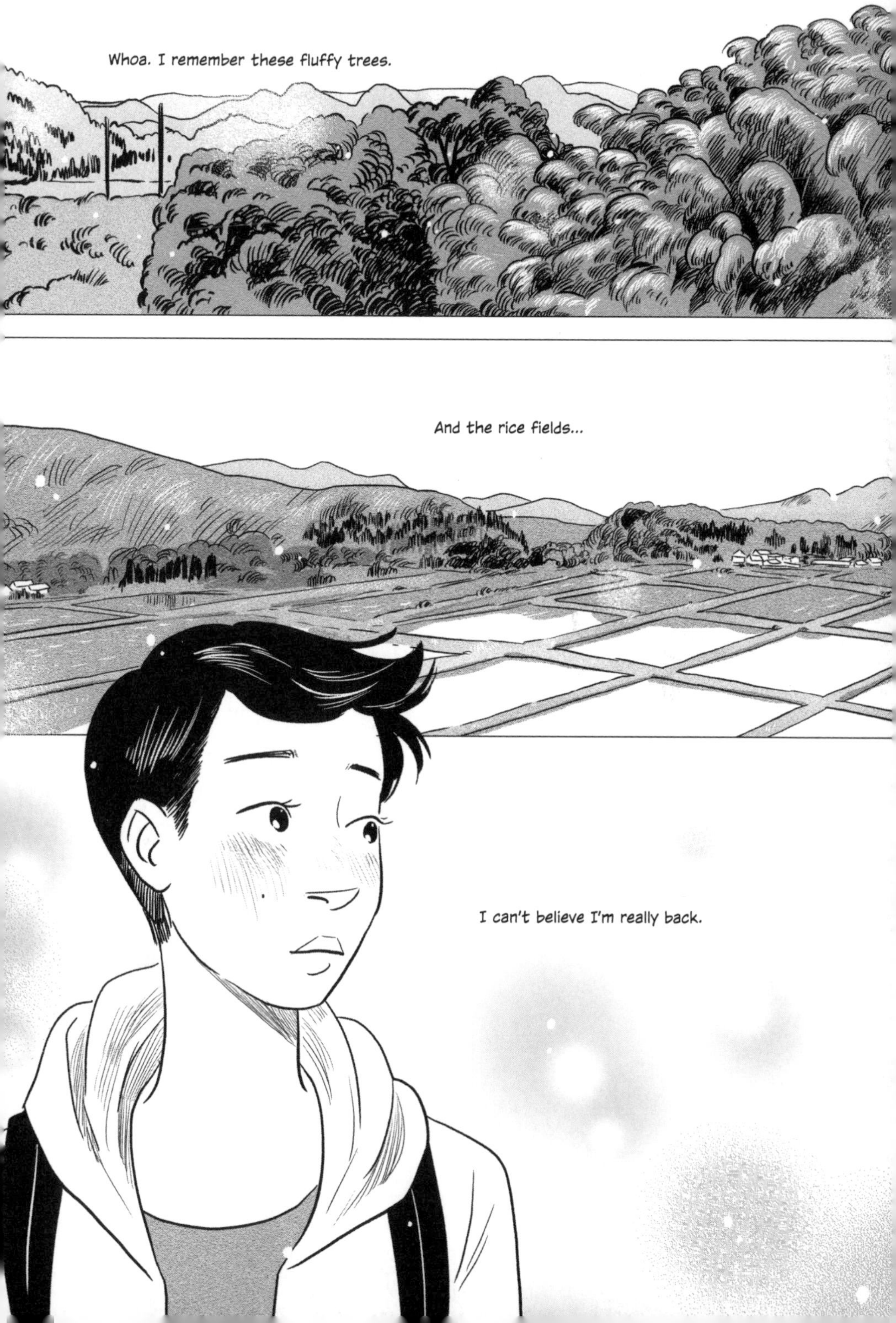
Whoa. I remember these fluffy trees.
And the rice fields...
I can't believe I'm really back.

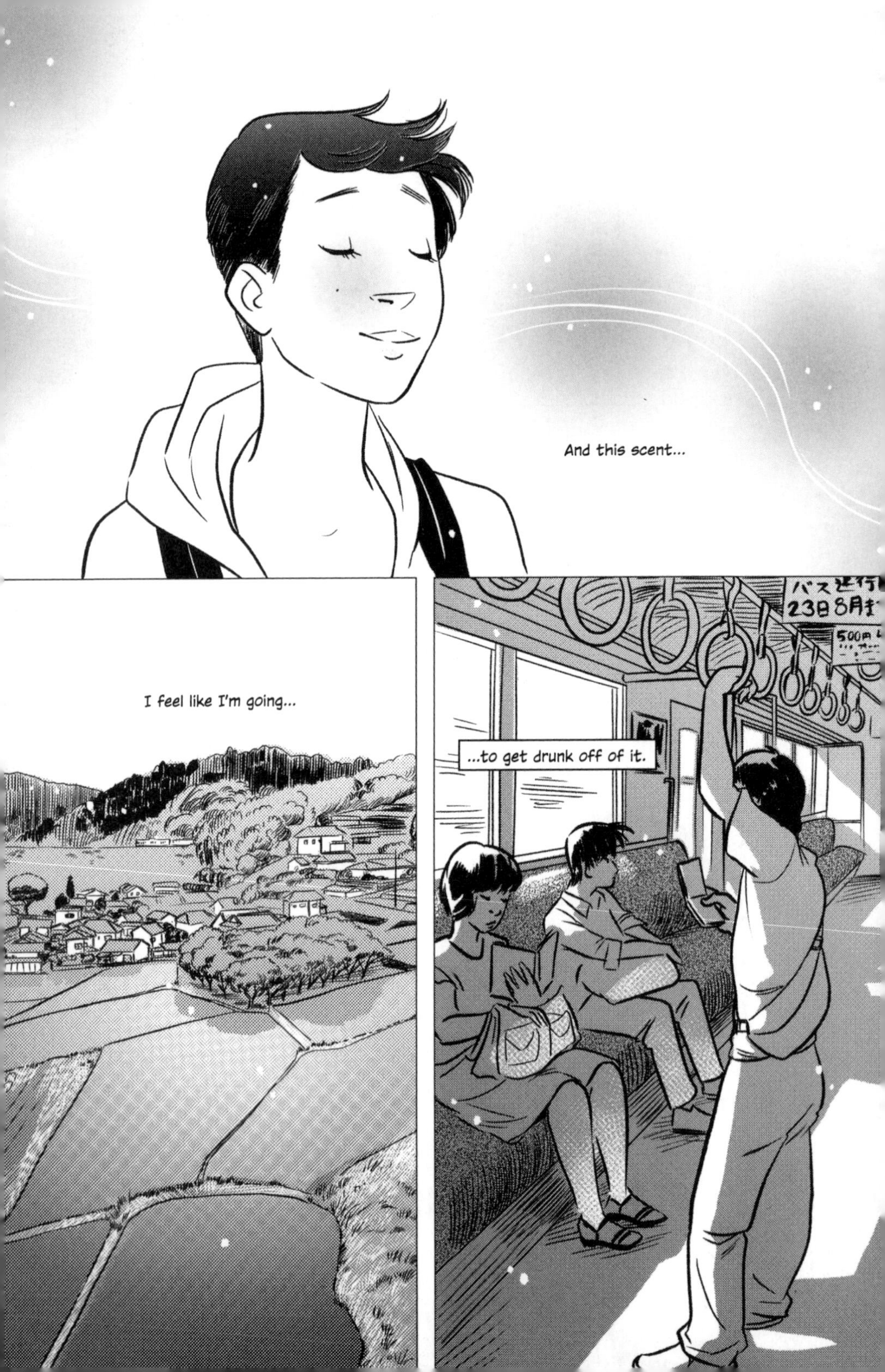
And this scent...
I feel like I'm going...
...to get drunk off of it.

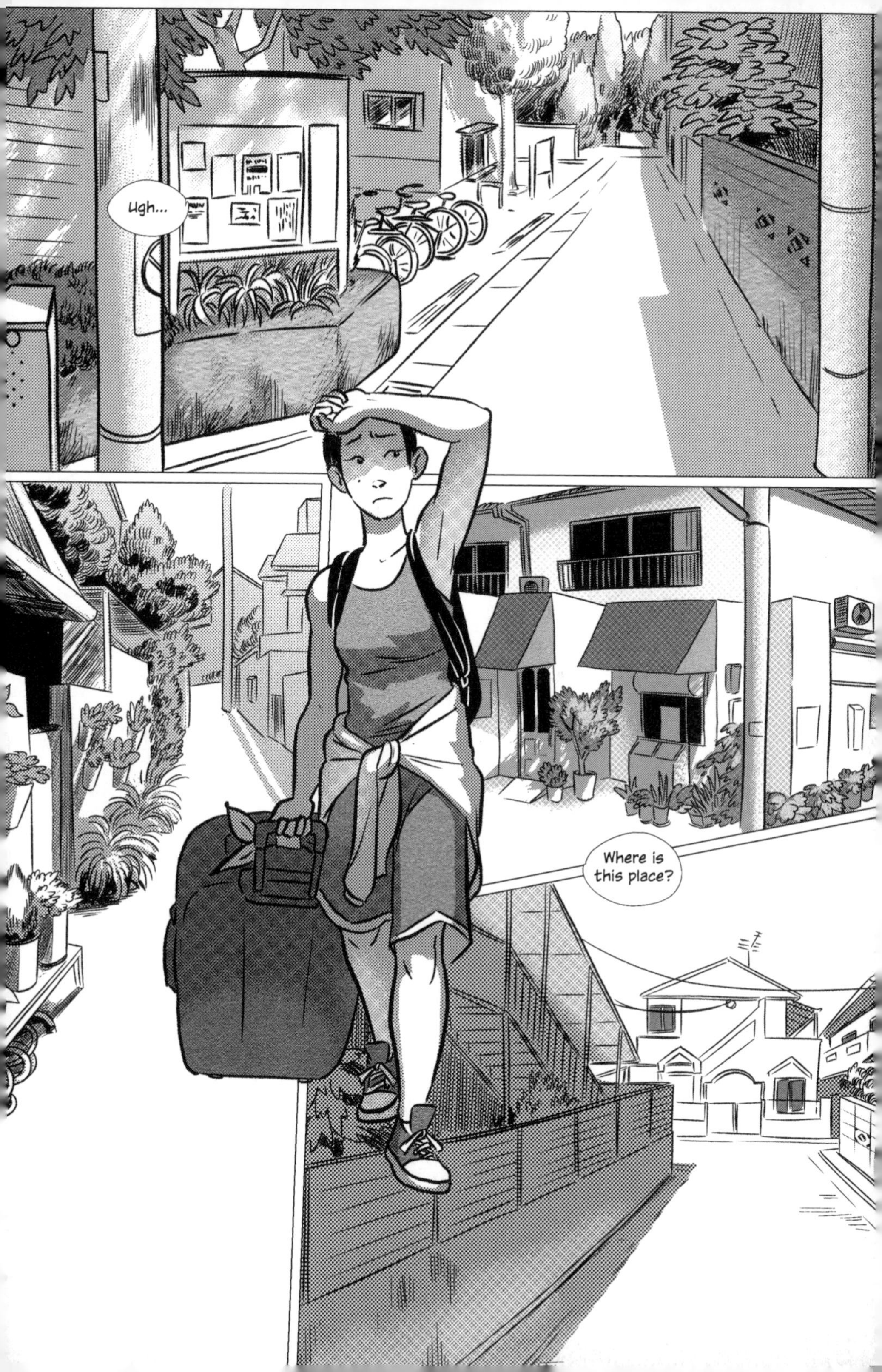
Ugh...
Where is this place?

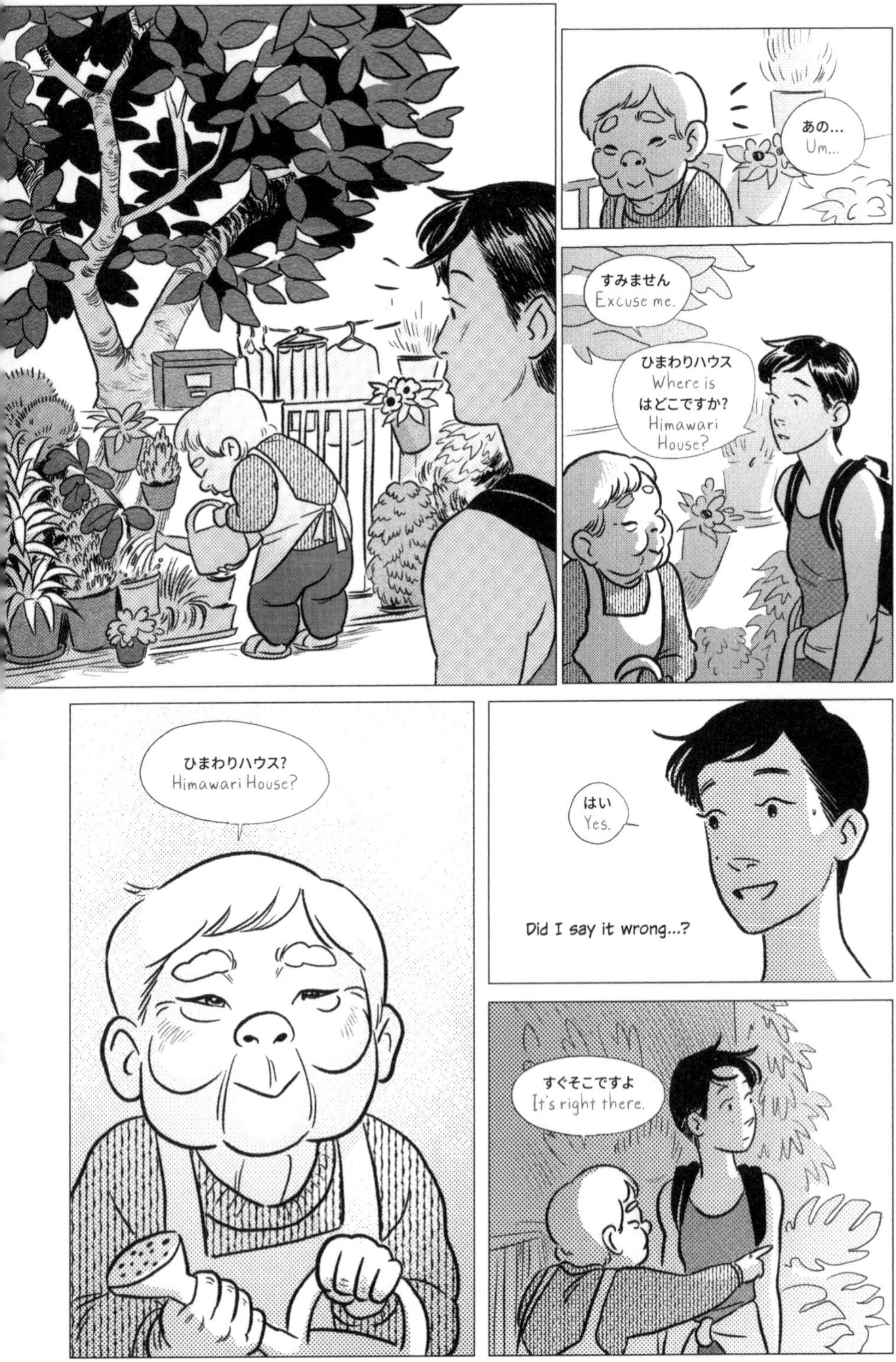

あの…
Um...
すみません
Excuse me.
ひまわりハウス
Where is
はどこですか?
Himawari House?
ひまわりハウス?
Himawari House?
はい
Yes.
Did I say it wrong...?
すぐそこですよ
It's right there.

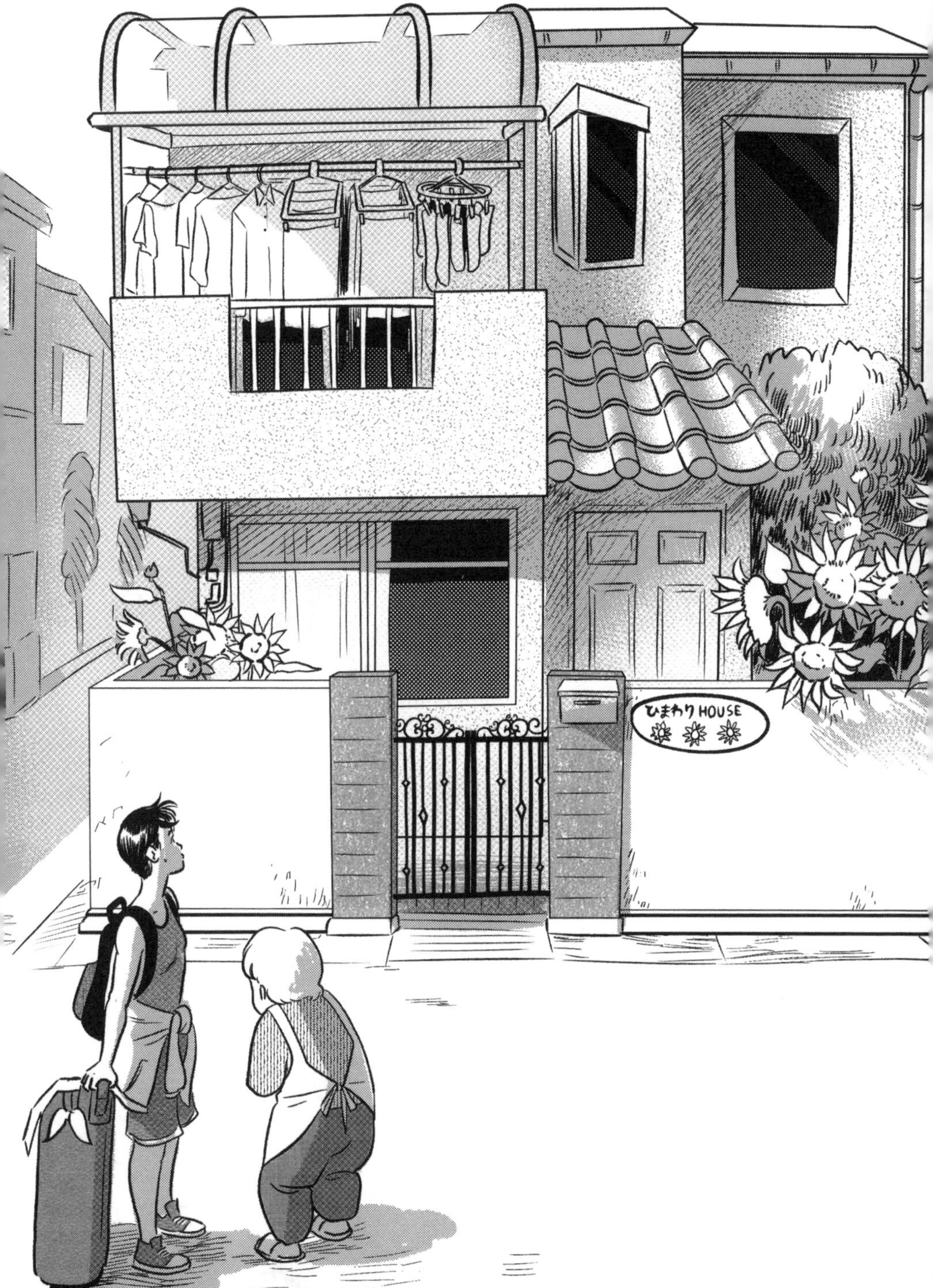
ひまわりHOUSE

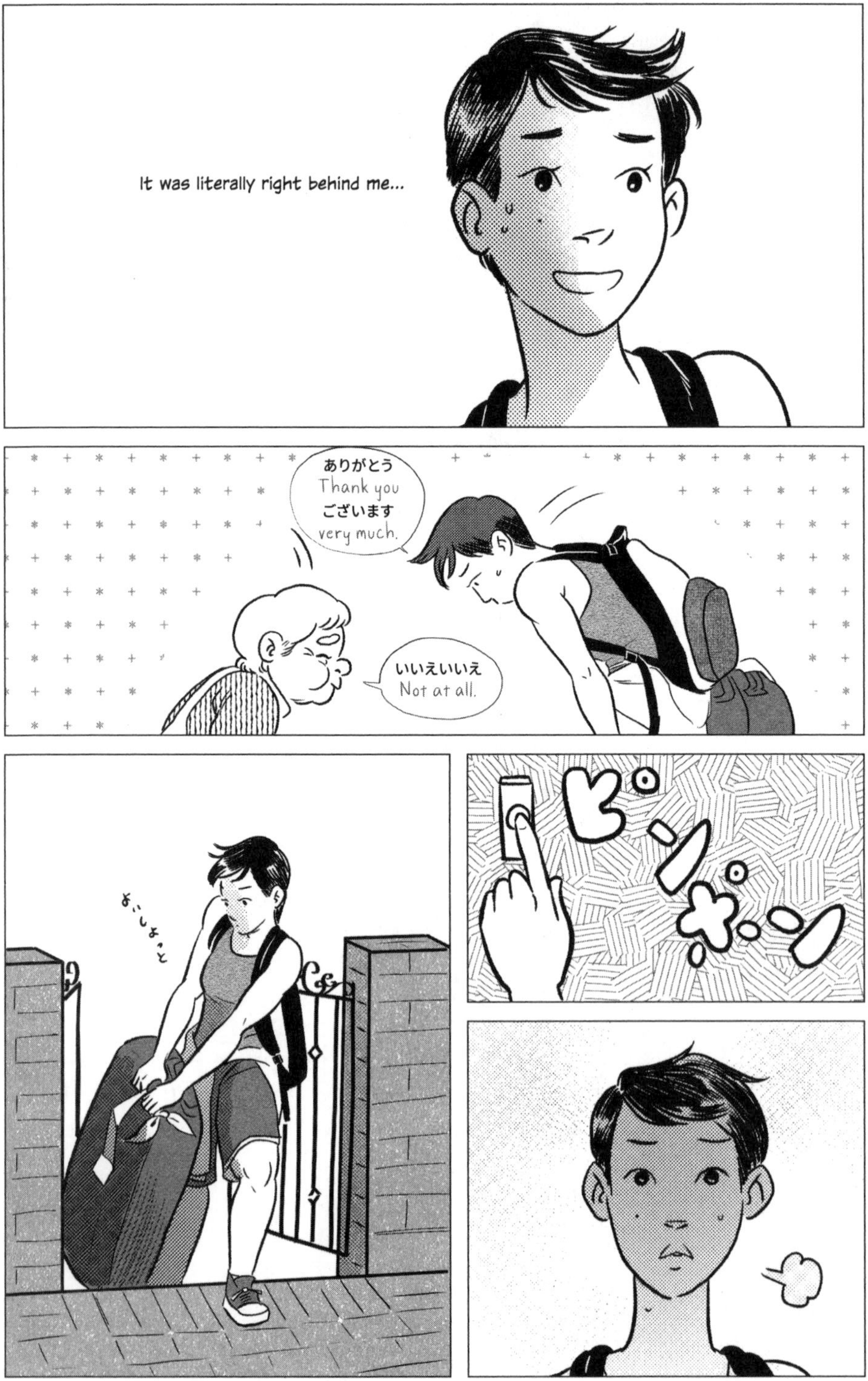
It was literally right behind me...
ありがとう
Thank you
ございます
very much.
いいえいいえ
Not at all.
よいしょっと
ピンポーン

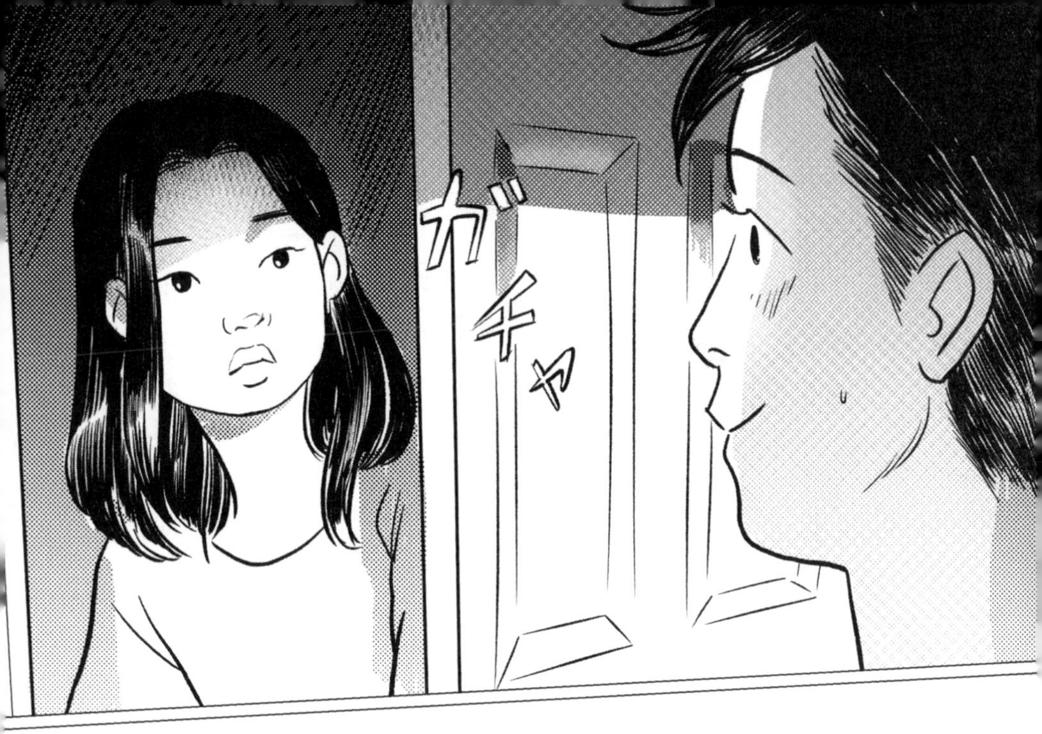
ガチャ

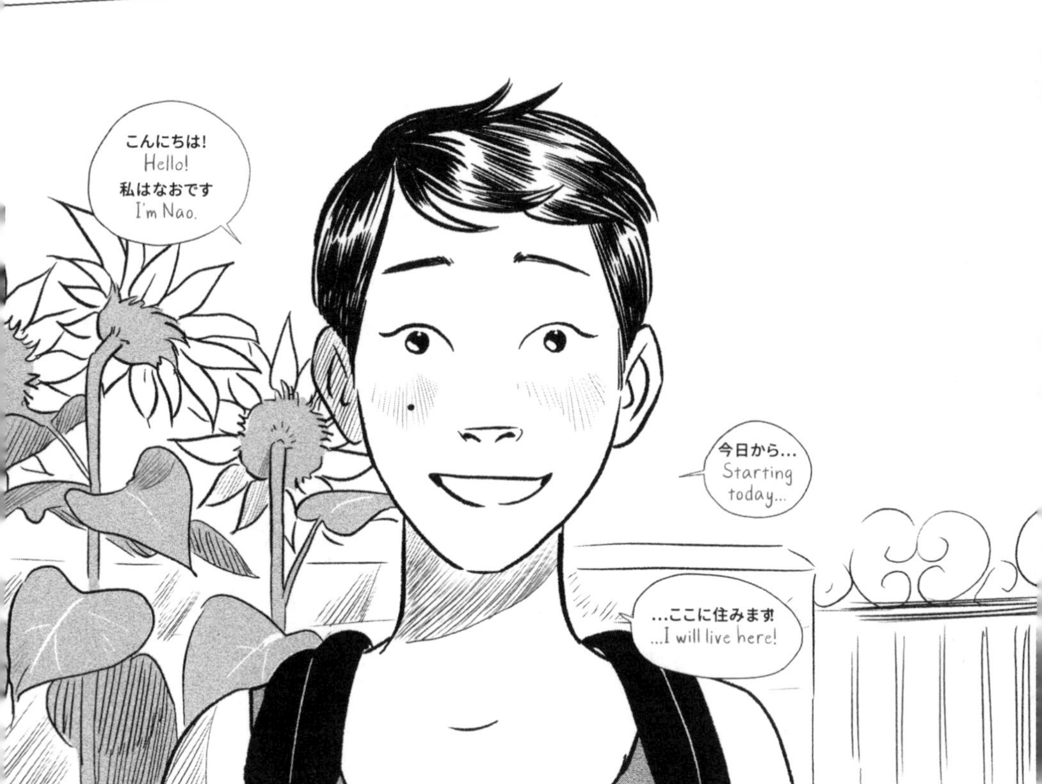
こんにちは!
Hello!
私はなおです
I'm Nao.
今日から…
Starting today…
…ここに住みます!
…I will live here!

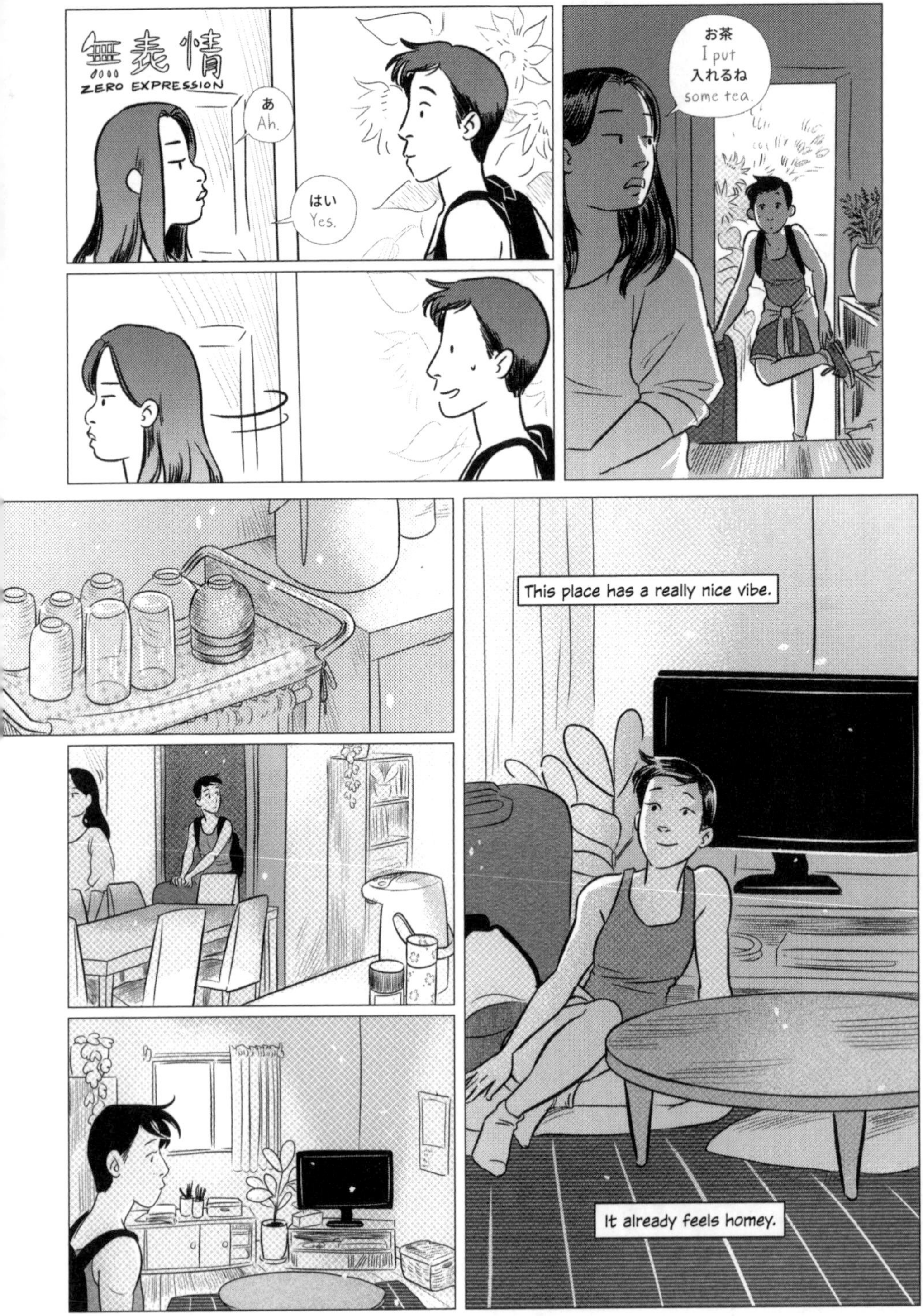

無表情
ZERO EXPRESSION
あ
Ah.
はい
Yes.
お茶
I put
入れるね
some tea.
This place has a really nice vibe.
It already feels homey.

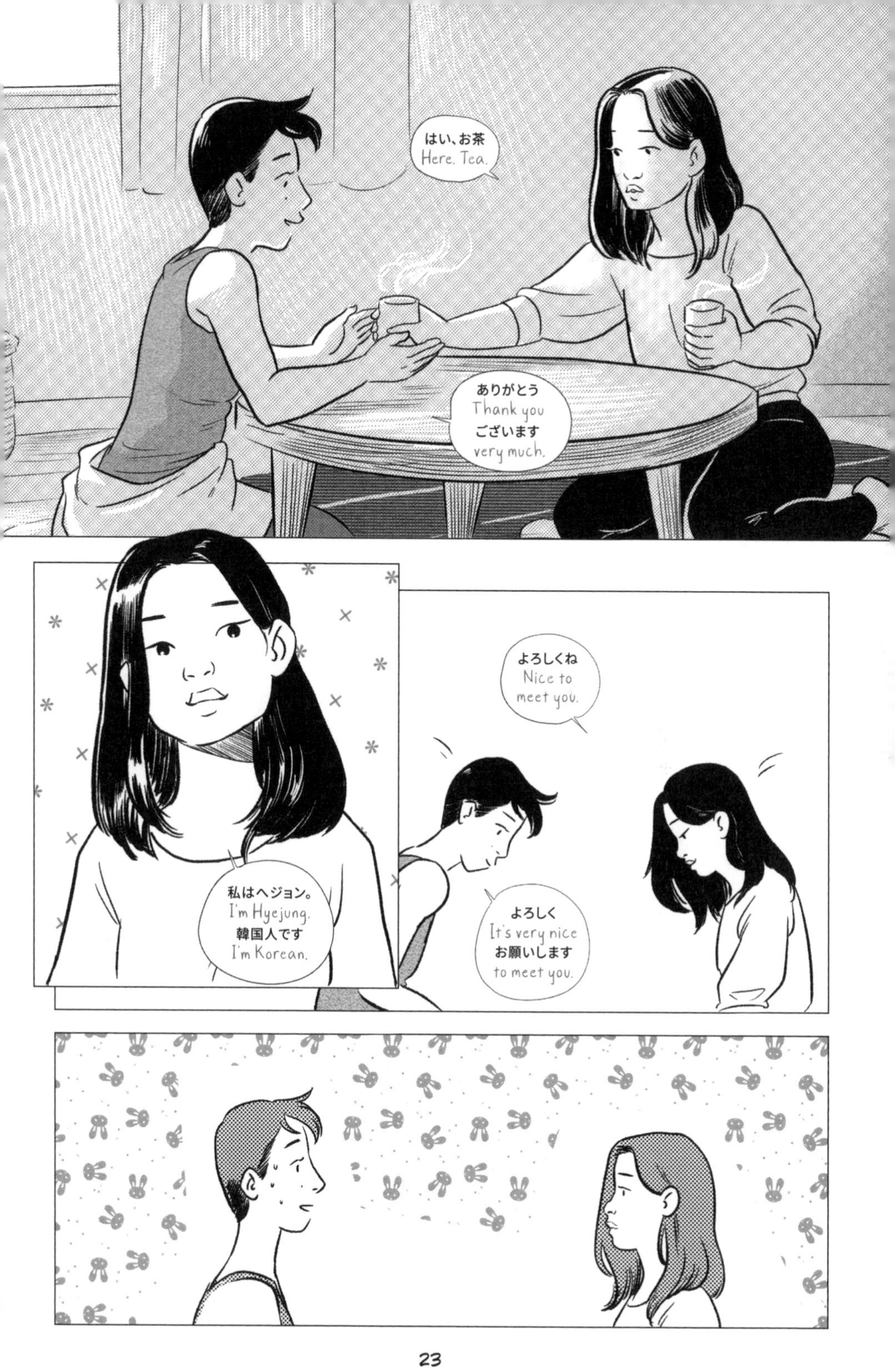
はい、お茶
Here. Tea.
ありがとう
Thank you
ございます
very much.
私はヘジョン。
I'm Hyejung.
韓国人です
I'm Korean.
よろしくね
Nice to
meet you.
よろしく
It's very nice
お願いします
to meet you.

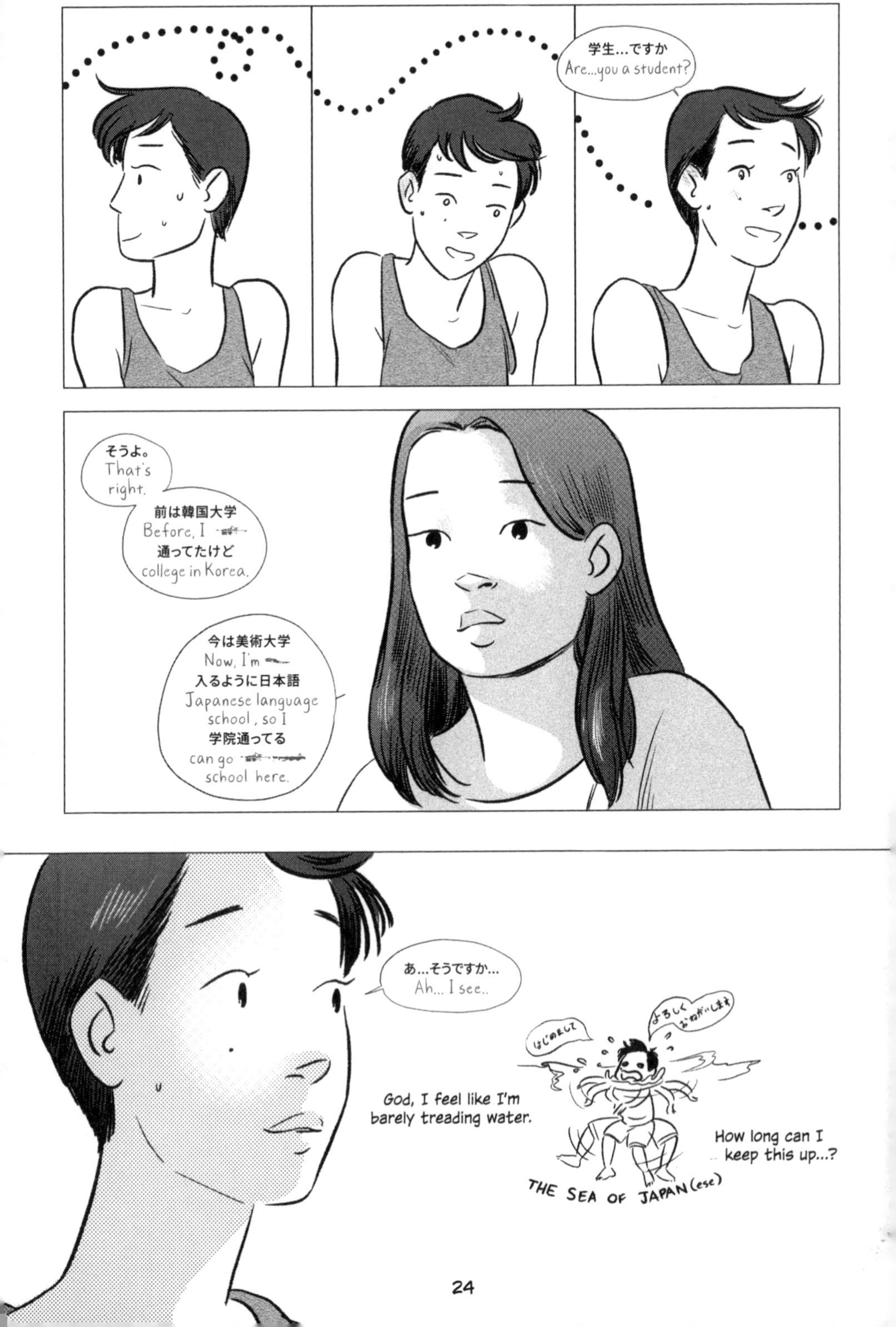

学生…ですか
Are…you a student?
そうよ。
That's right.
前は韓国大学
Before, I
通ってたけど
college in Korea.
今は美術大学
Now, I'm
入るように日本語
Japanese language school, so I
学院通ってる
can go
school here.
あ…そうですか…
Ah… I see..
God, I feel like I'm barely treading water.
はじめまして
よろしくおねがいします
THE SEA OF JAPAN(ese)
How long can I keep this up…?

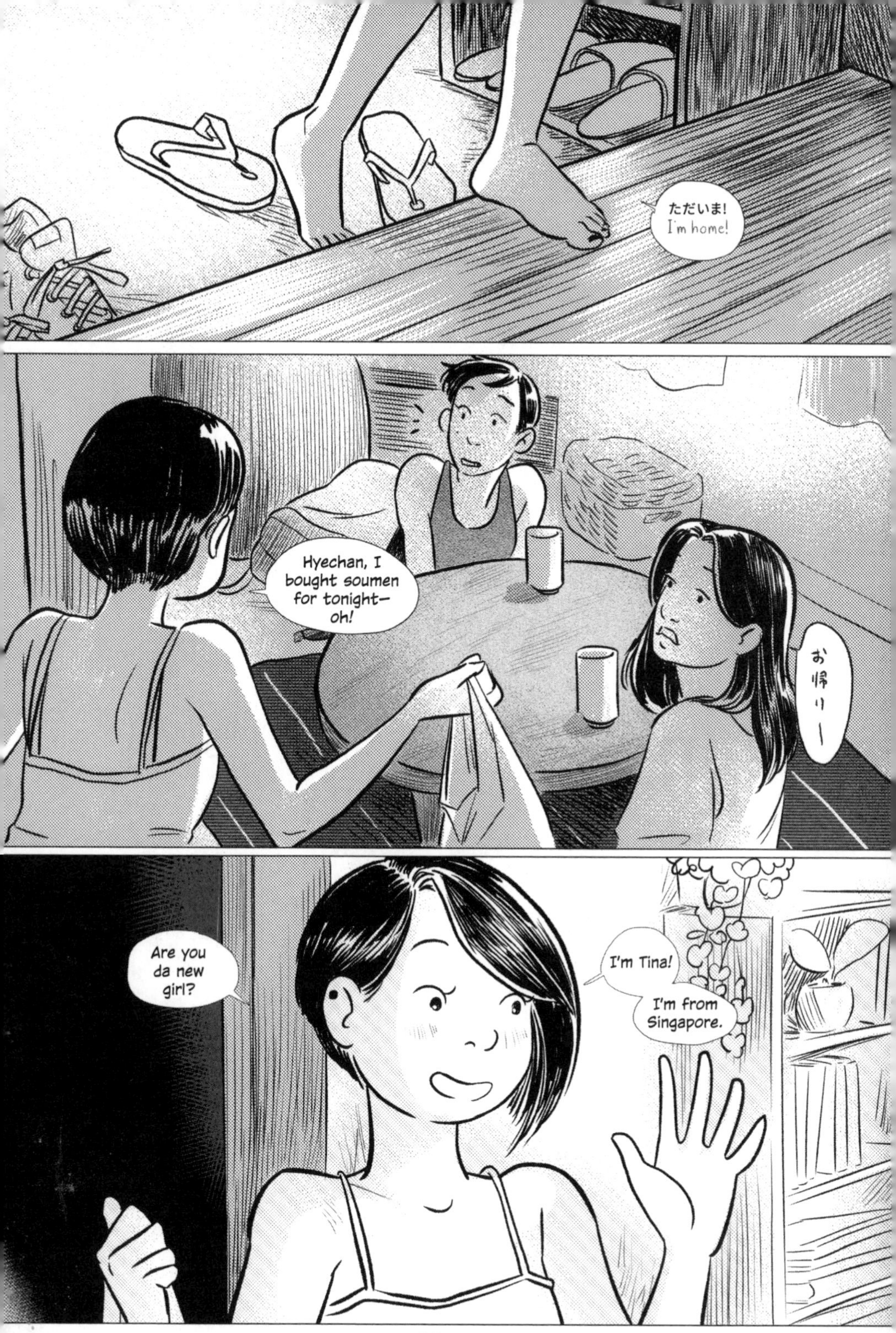
ただいま!
I'm home!
Hyechan, I bought soumen for tonight— oh!
お帰りー
Are you da new girl?
I'm Tina!
I'm from Singapore.

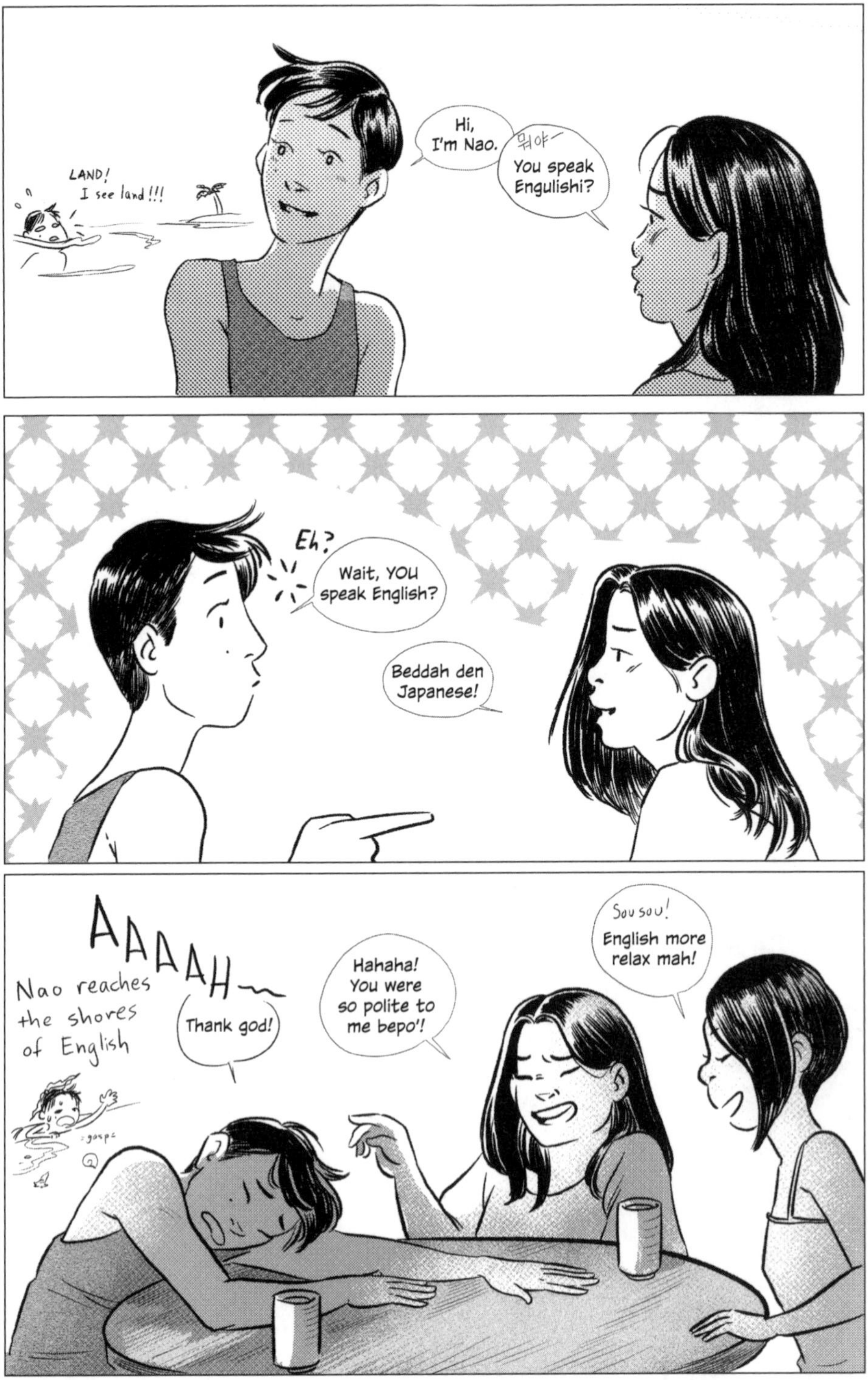
LAND!
I see land!!!
Hi,
I'm Nao.
뭐야-
You speak
Engulishi?
Eh?
Wait, YOU
speak English?
Beddah den
Japanese!
AAAAH
Nao reaches
the shores
of English
Thank god!
Hahaha!
You were
so polite to
me bepo'!
Sou sou!
English more
relax mah!

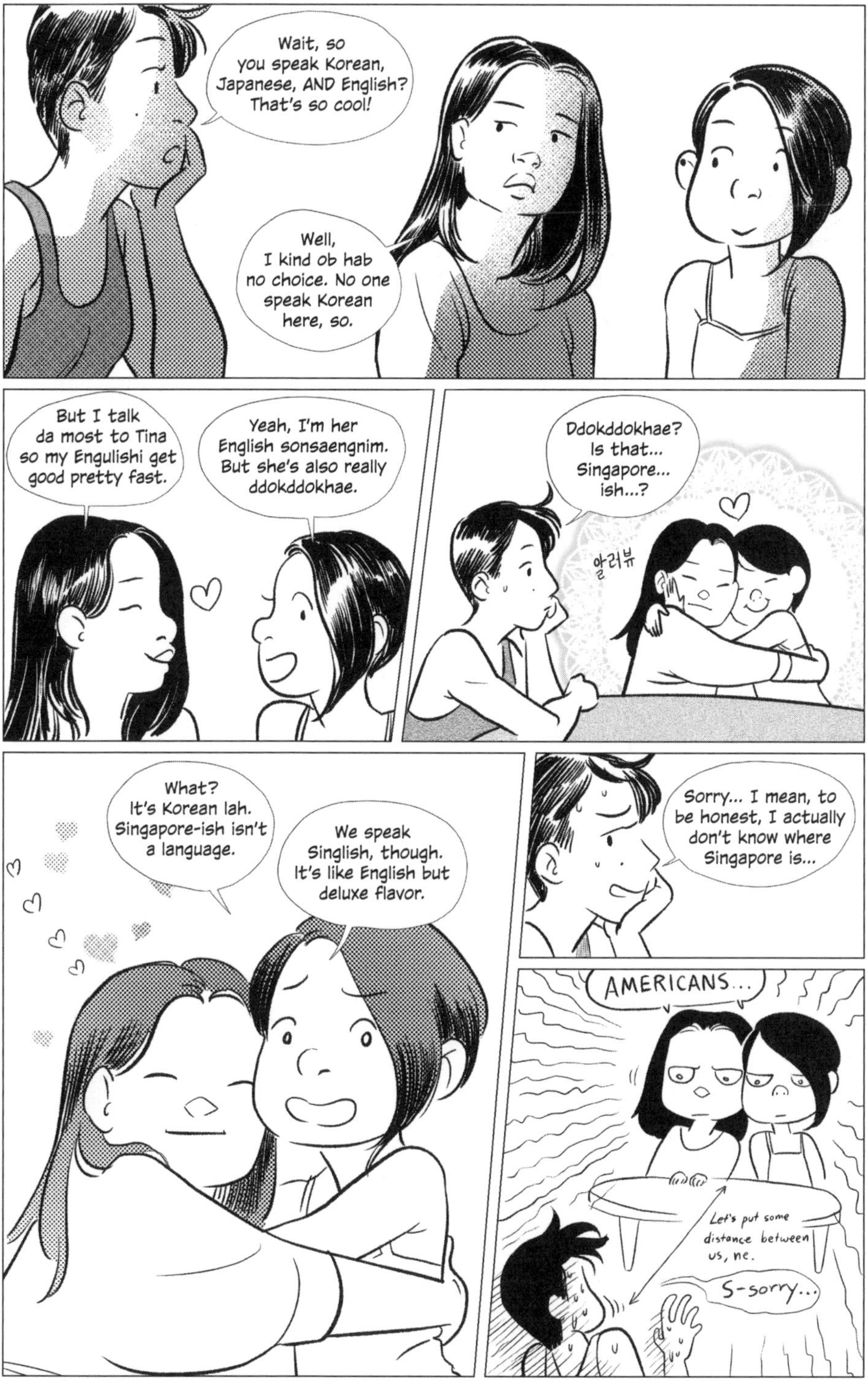
Wait, so you speak Korean, Japanese, AND English? That's so cool!
Well, I kind ob hab no choice. No one speak Korean here, so.
But I talk da most to Tina so my Engulishi get good pretty fast.
Yeah, I'm her English sonsaengnim. But she's also really ddokddokhae.
Ddokddokhae? Is that... Singapore... ish...?
알러뷰
What? It's Korean lah. Singapore-ish isn't a language.
We speak Singlish, though. It's like English but deluxe flavor.
Sorry... I mean, to be honest, I actually don't know where Singapore is...
AMERICANS...
Let's put some distance between us, ne.
S-sorry...

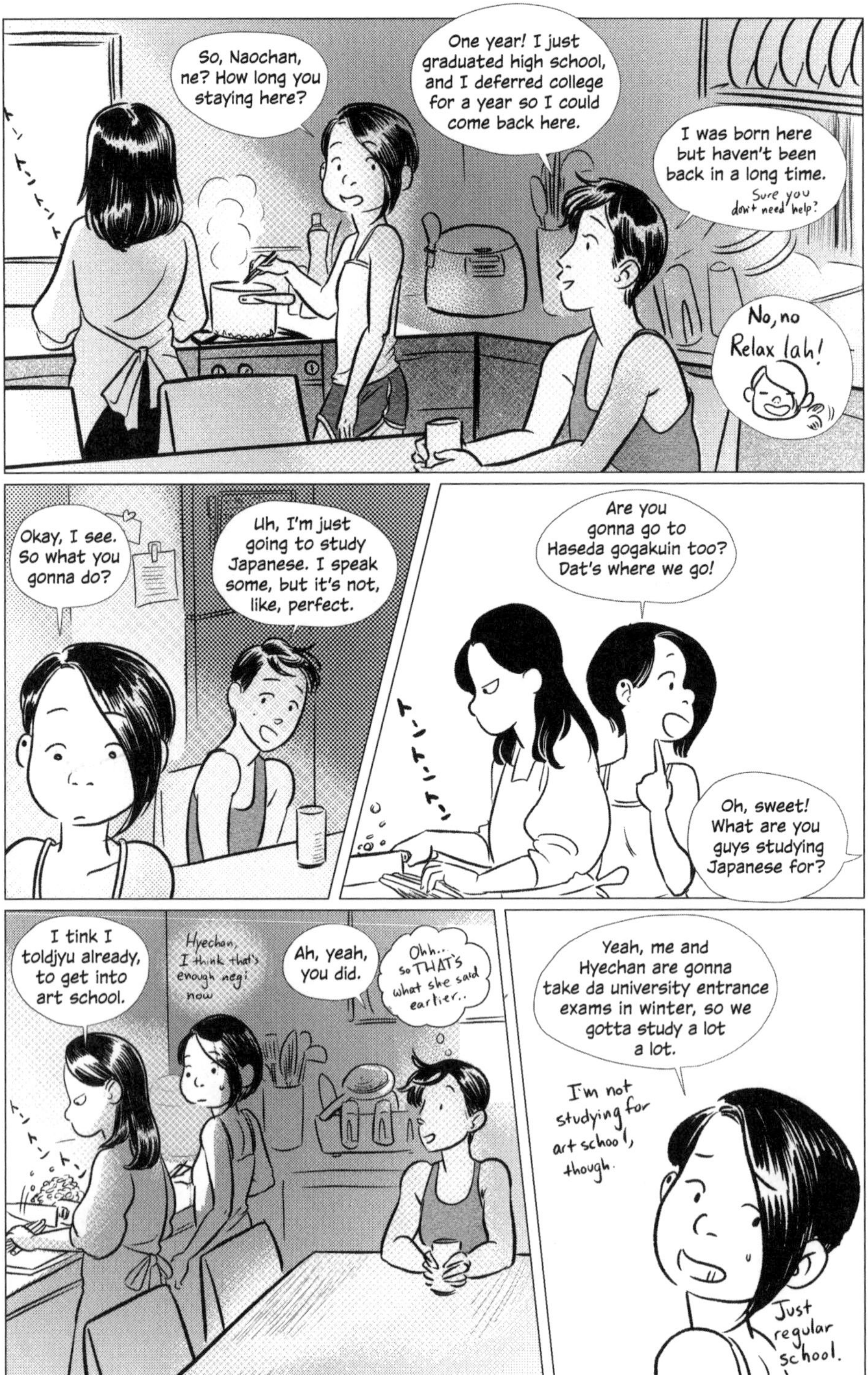
So, Naochan, ne? How long you staying here?
One year! I just graduated high school, and I deferred college for a year so I could come back here.
I was born here but haven't been back in a long time.
Sure you don't need help?
No, no Relax lah!
Okay, I see. So what you gonna do?
Uh, I'm just going to study Japanese. I speak some, but it's not, like, perfect.
Are you gonna go to Haseda gogakuin too? Dat's where we go!
Oh, sweet! What are you guys studying Japanese for?
I tink I toldjyu already, to get into art school.
Hyechan, I think that's enough negi now
Ah, yeah, you did.
Ohh.. so THAT'S what she said earlier..
Yeah, me and Hyechan are gonna take da university entrance exams in winter, so we gotta study a lot a lot.
I'm not studying for art school, though.
Just regular school.

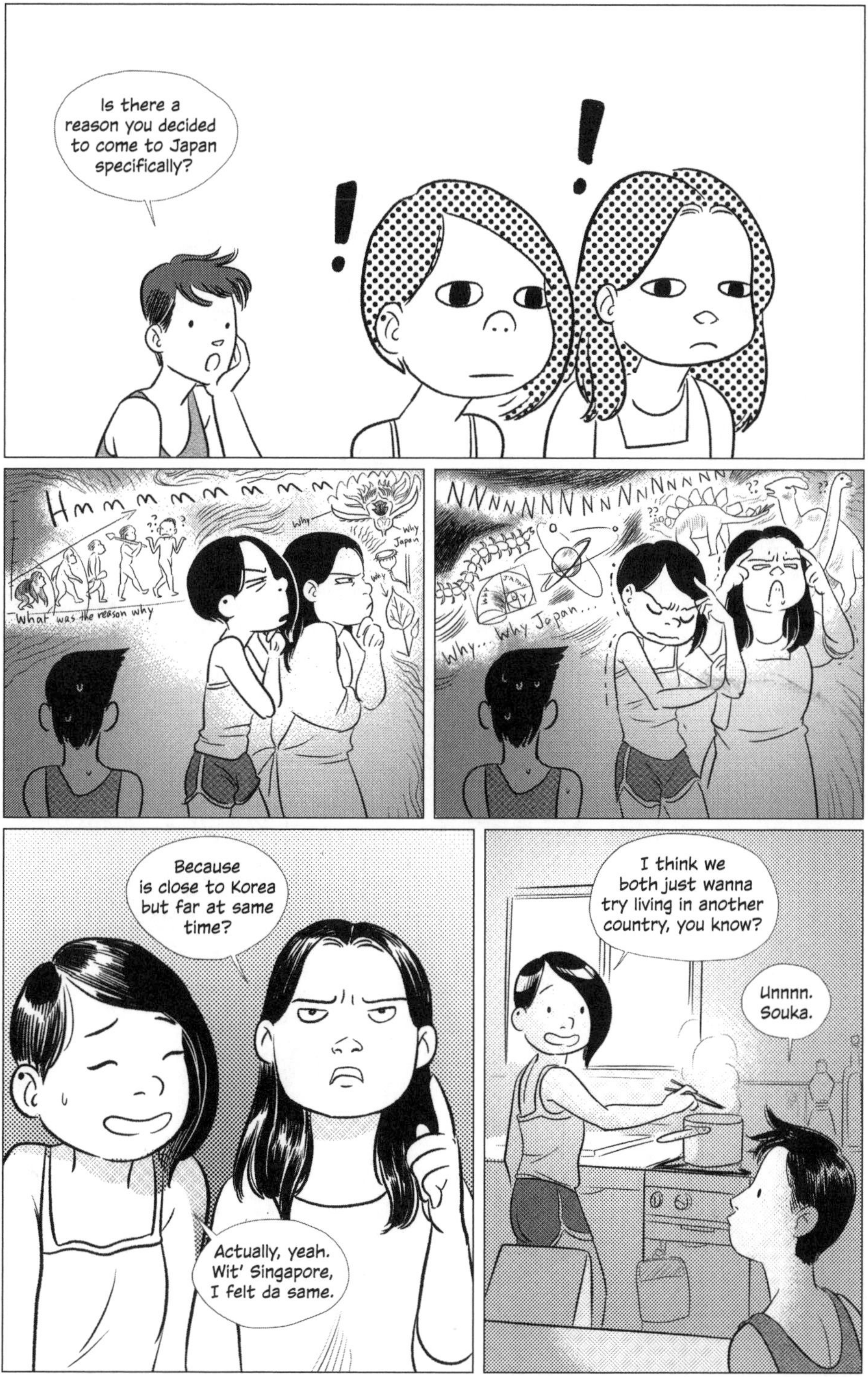
Is there a reason you decided to come to Japan specifically?
!
!
Hmmmmmmmmm
What was the reason why
Why
Why Japan
NNNNNNNNNNNNNN
Why... Why Japan...
Because is close to Korea but far at same time?
Actually, yeah. Wit' Singapore, I felt da same.
I think we both just wanna try living in another country, you know?
Unnnn. Souka.

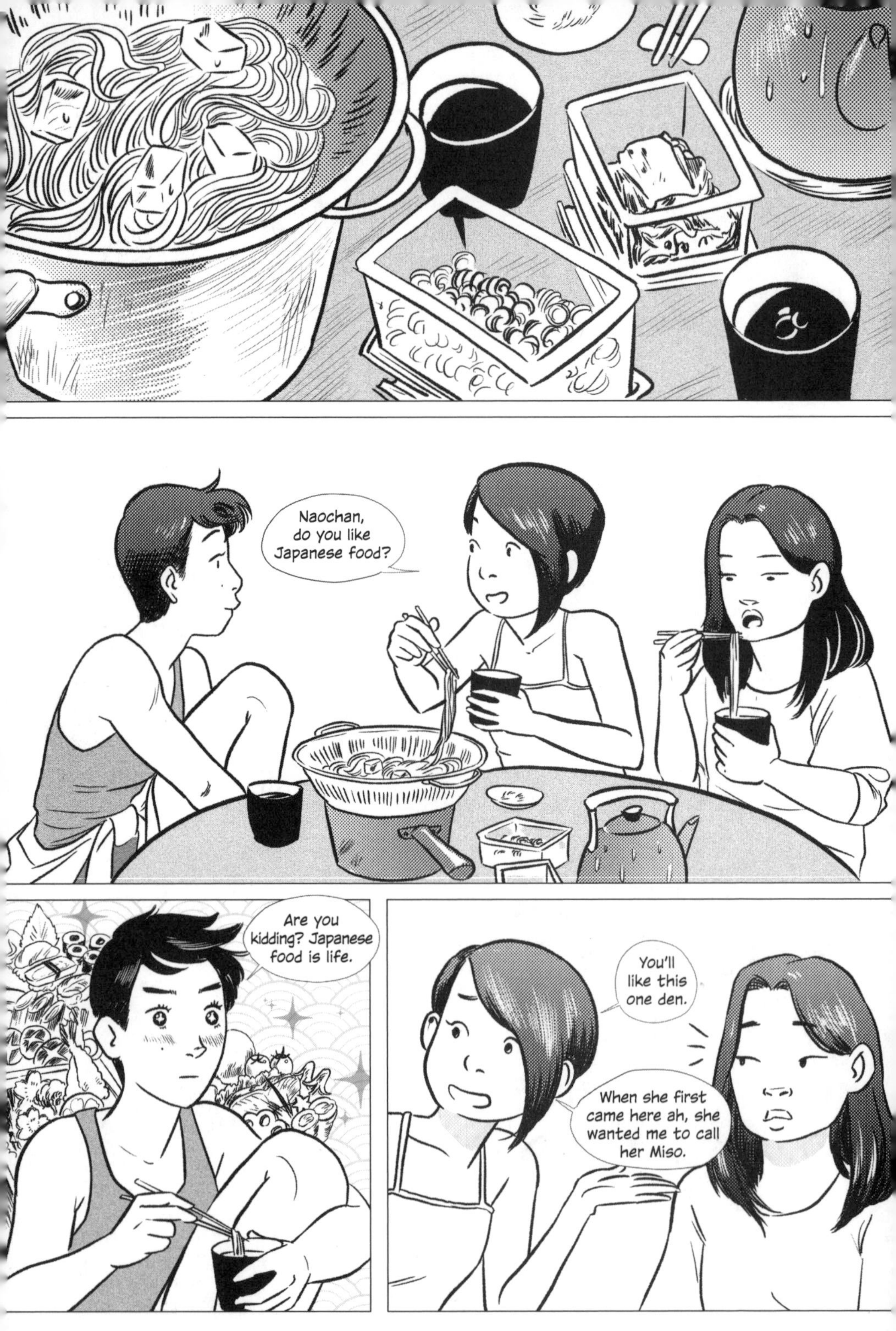
Naochan, do you like Japanese food?
Are you kidding? Japanese food is life.
You'll like this one den.
When she first came here ah, she wanted me to call her Miso.

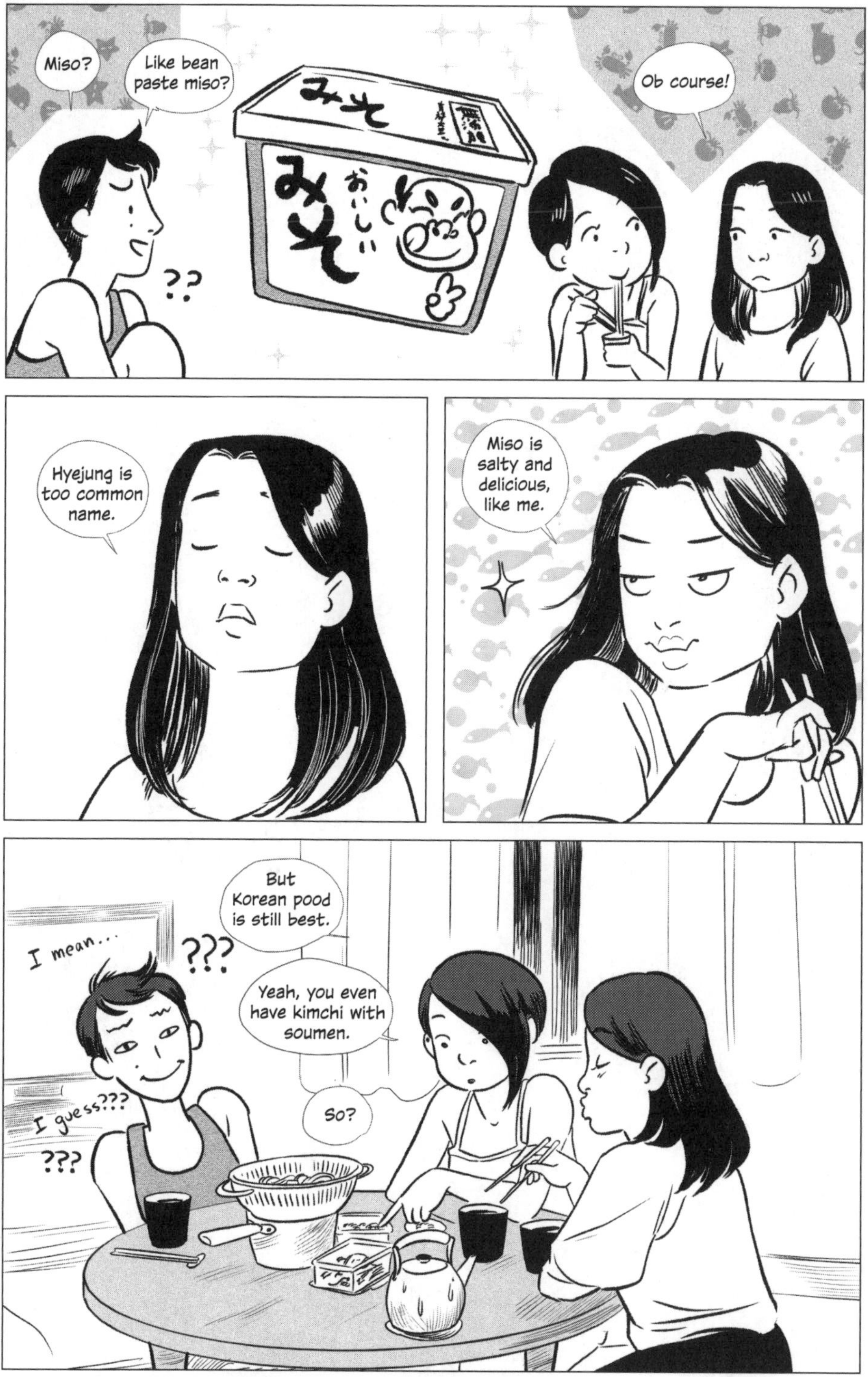
Miso?
Like bean paste miso?
みそ
みそ
おいしい
Ob course!
??
Hyejung is too common name.
Miso is salty and delicious, like me.
But Korean pood is still best.
I mean...
???
Yeah, you even have kimchi with soumen.
So?
I guess???
???

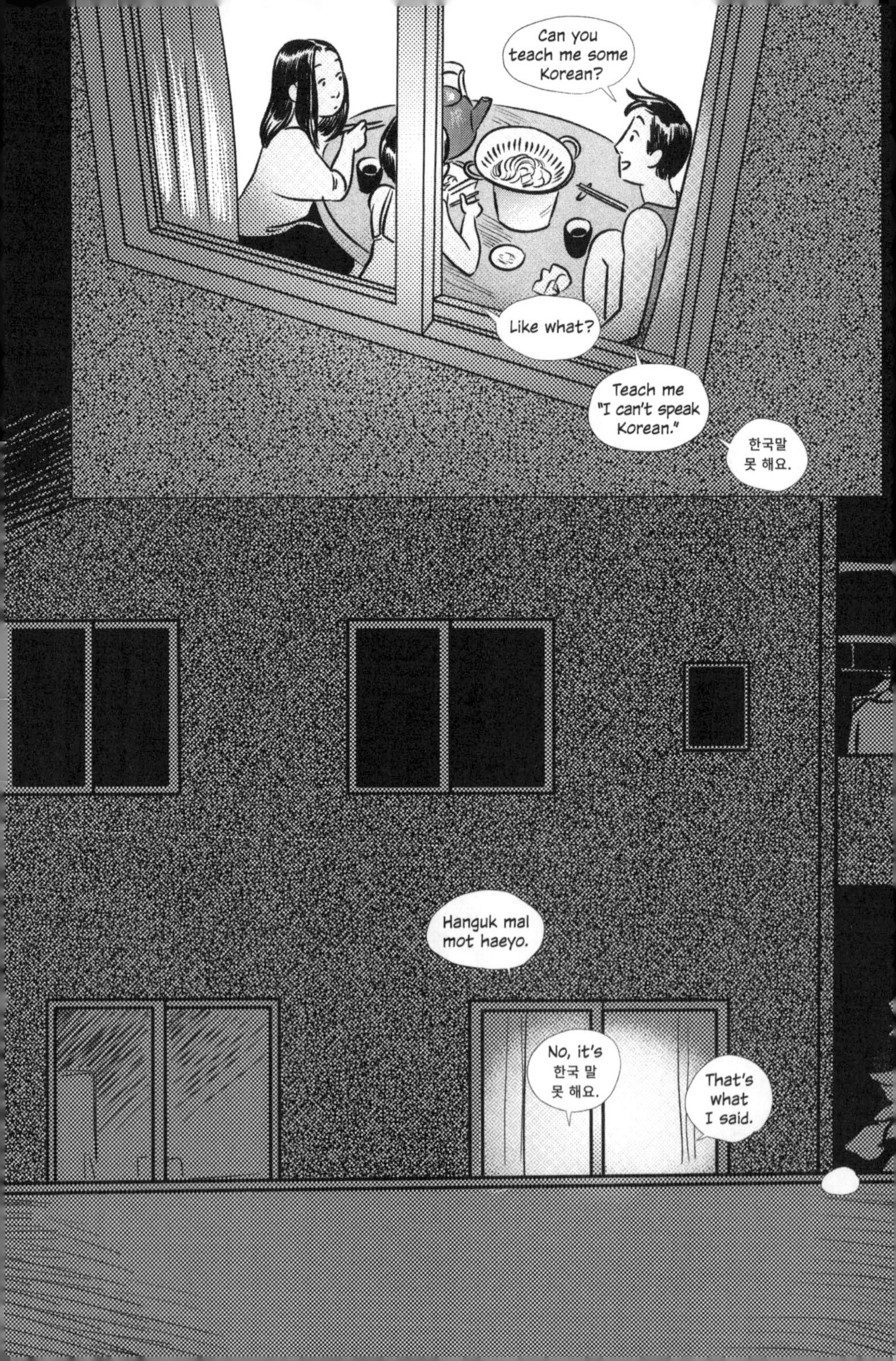
Can you teach me some Korean?
Like what?
Teach me "I can't speak Korean."
한국말 못 해요.
Hanguk mal mot haeyo.
No, it's 한국 말 못 해요.
That's what I said.

Chapter 2

The Road Home

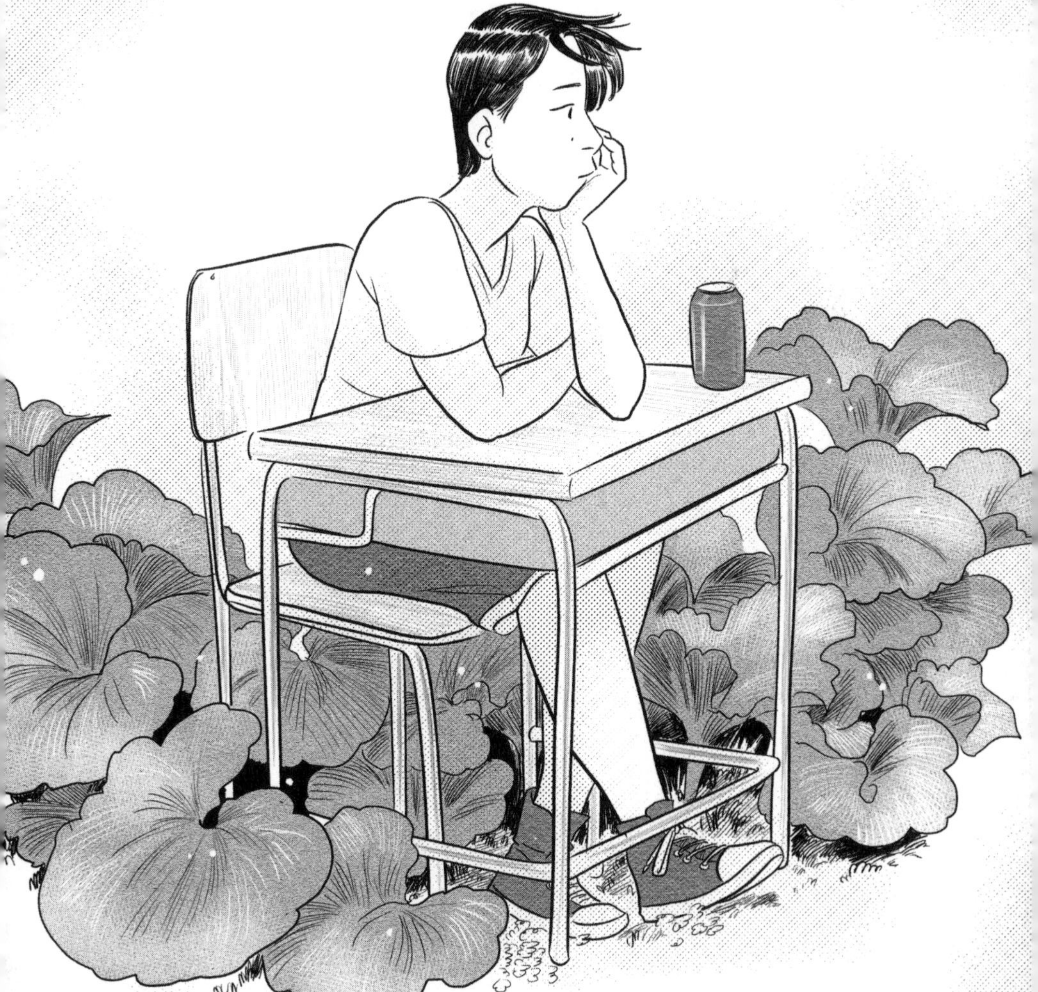

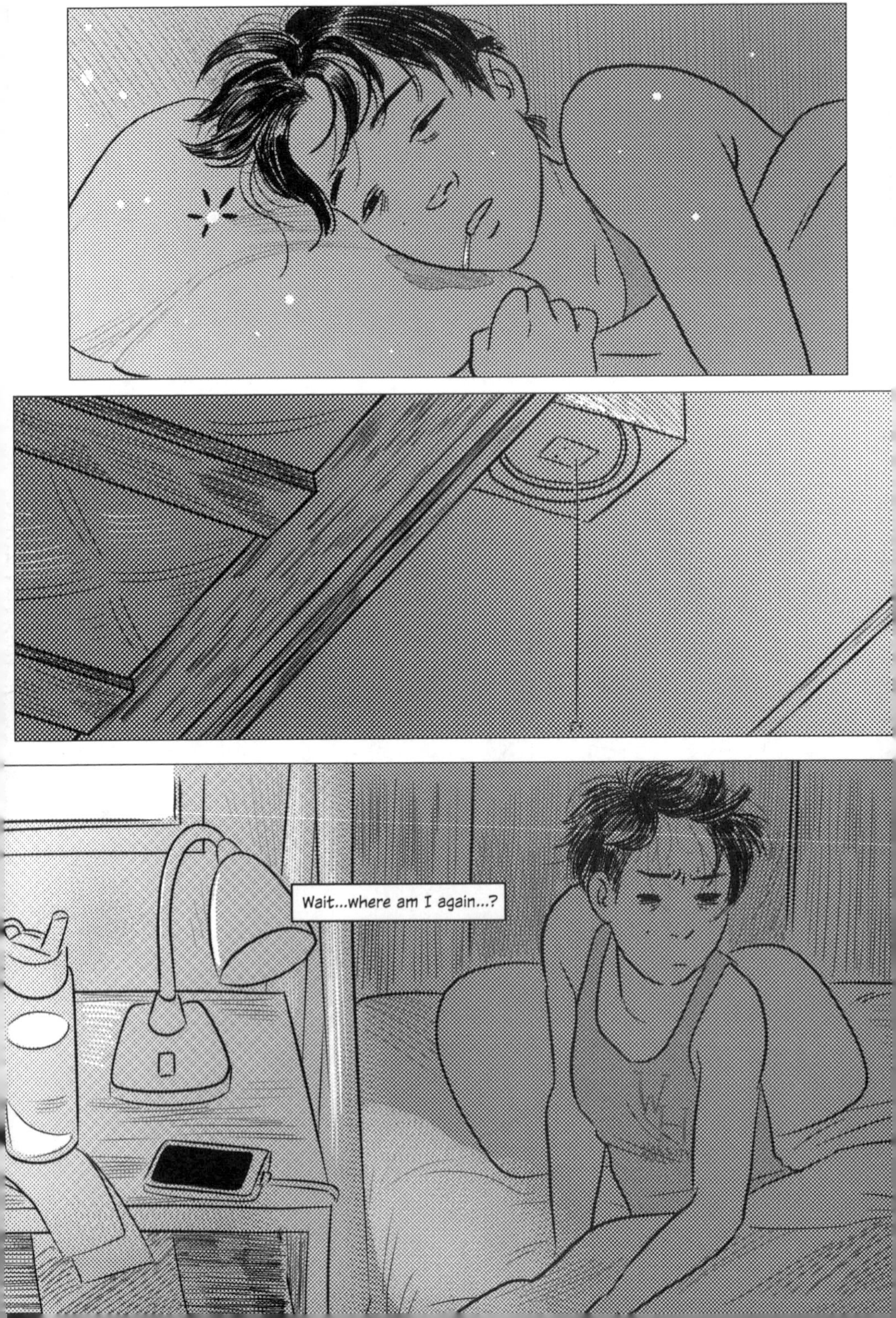
Wait...where am I again...?

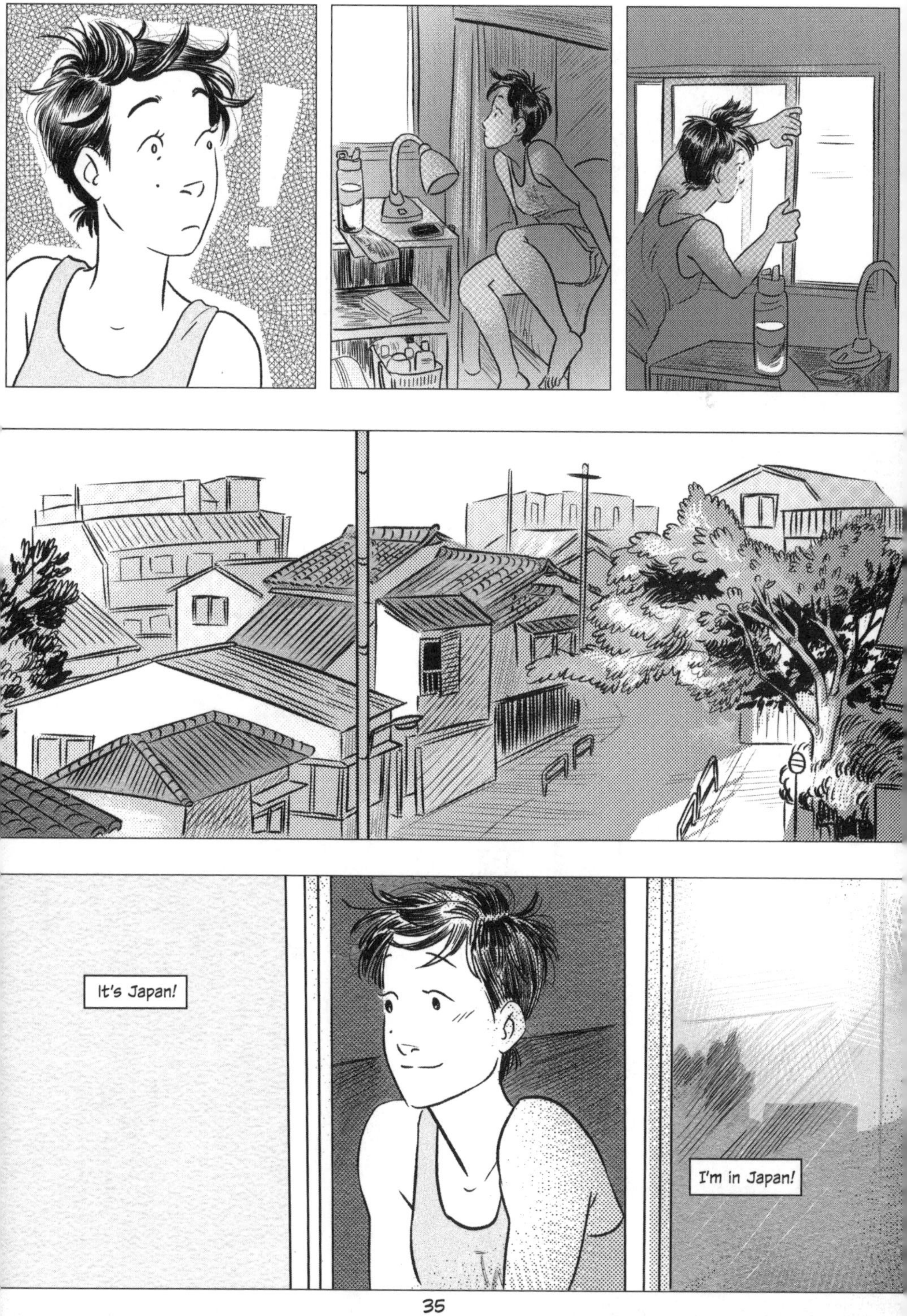
It's Japan!
I'm in Japan!

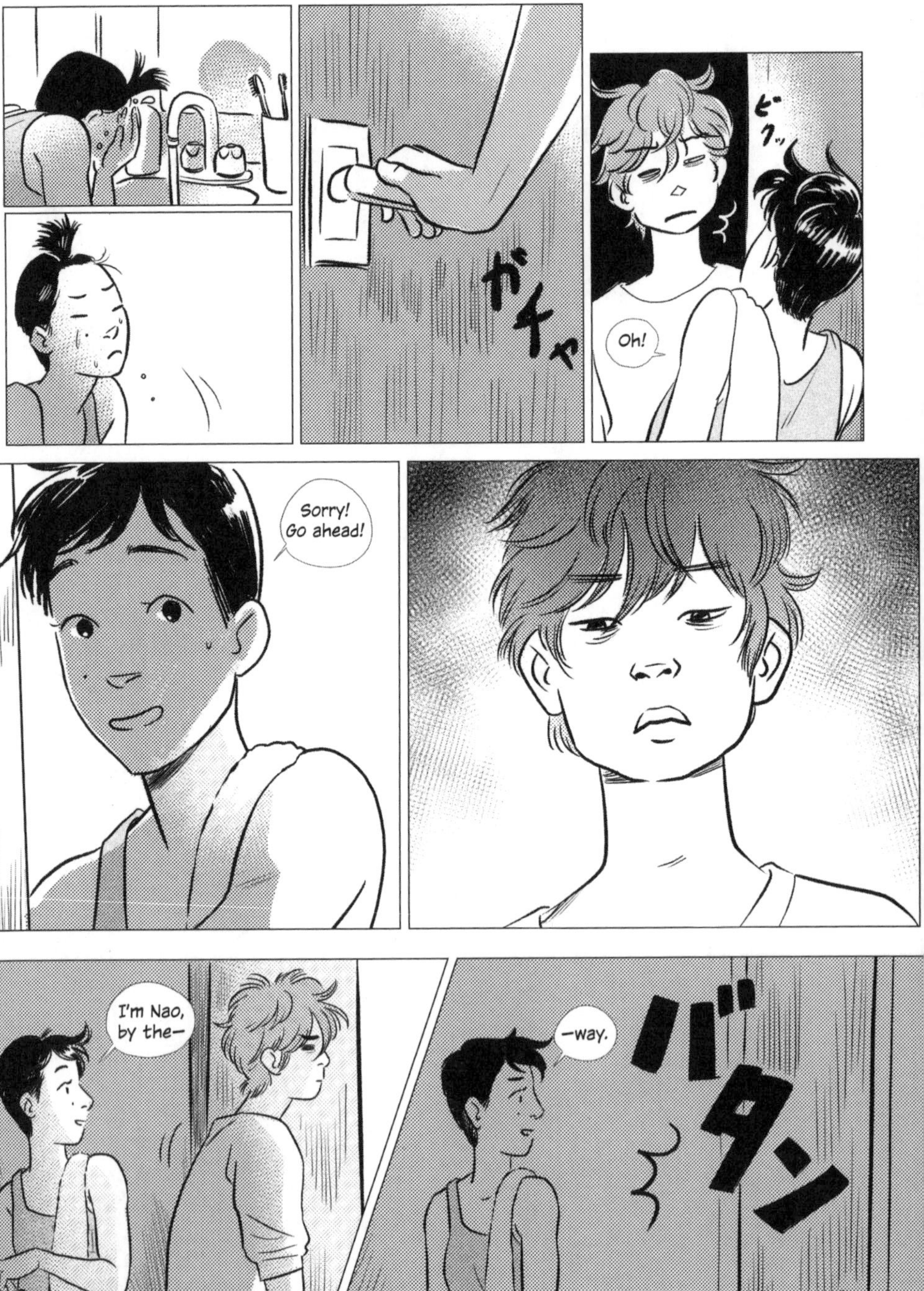

ガチャ
ビクッ
Oh!
Sorry! Go ahead!
I'm Nao, by the—
—way.
バタン

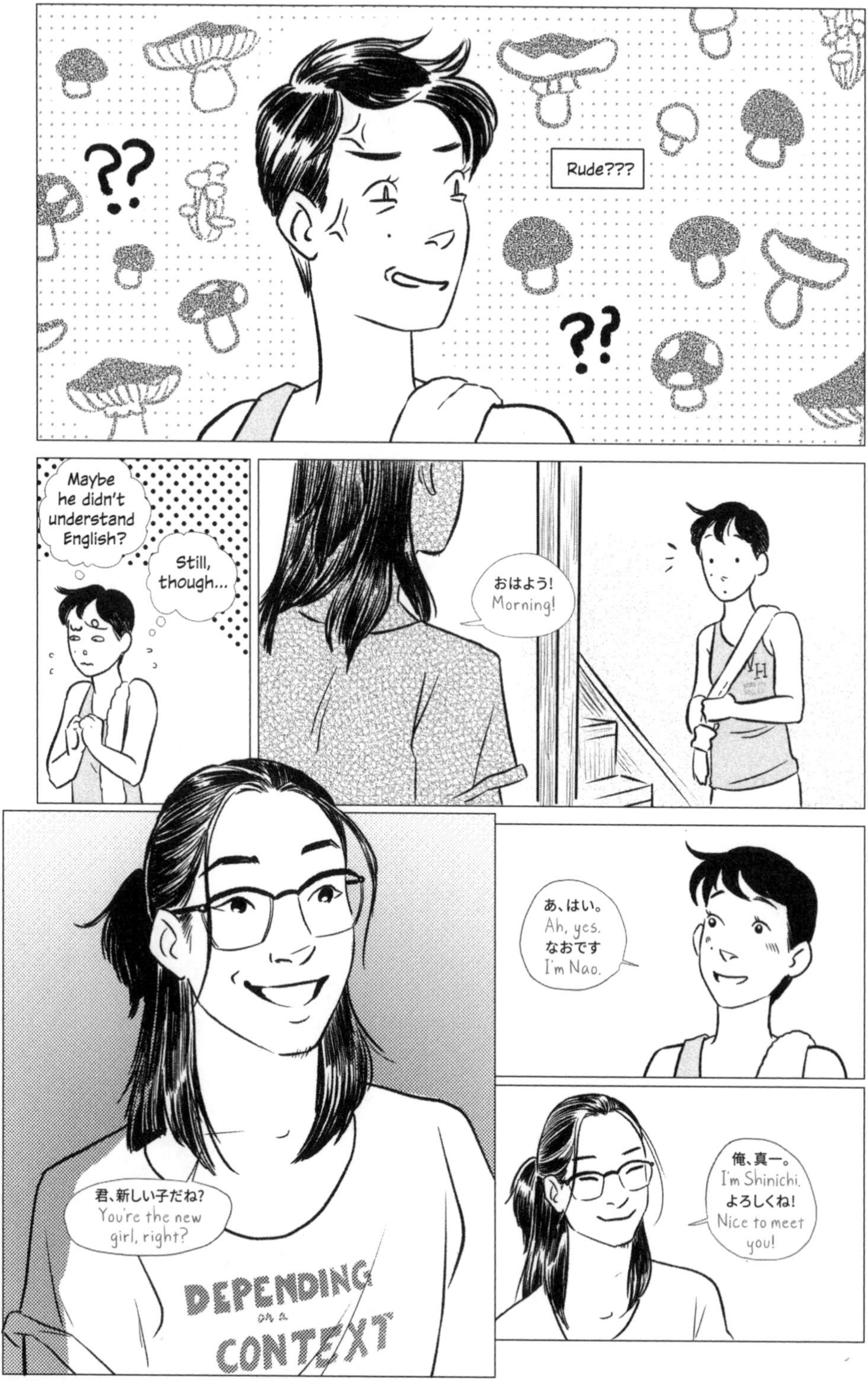

Rude???
Maybe he didn't understand English?
Still, though...
おはよう!
Morning!
君、新しい子だね?
You're the new girl, right?
DEPENDING on a CONTEXT
あ、はい。
Ah, yes.
なおです
I'm Nao.
俺、真一。
I'm Shinichi.
よろしくね!
Nice to meet you!

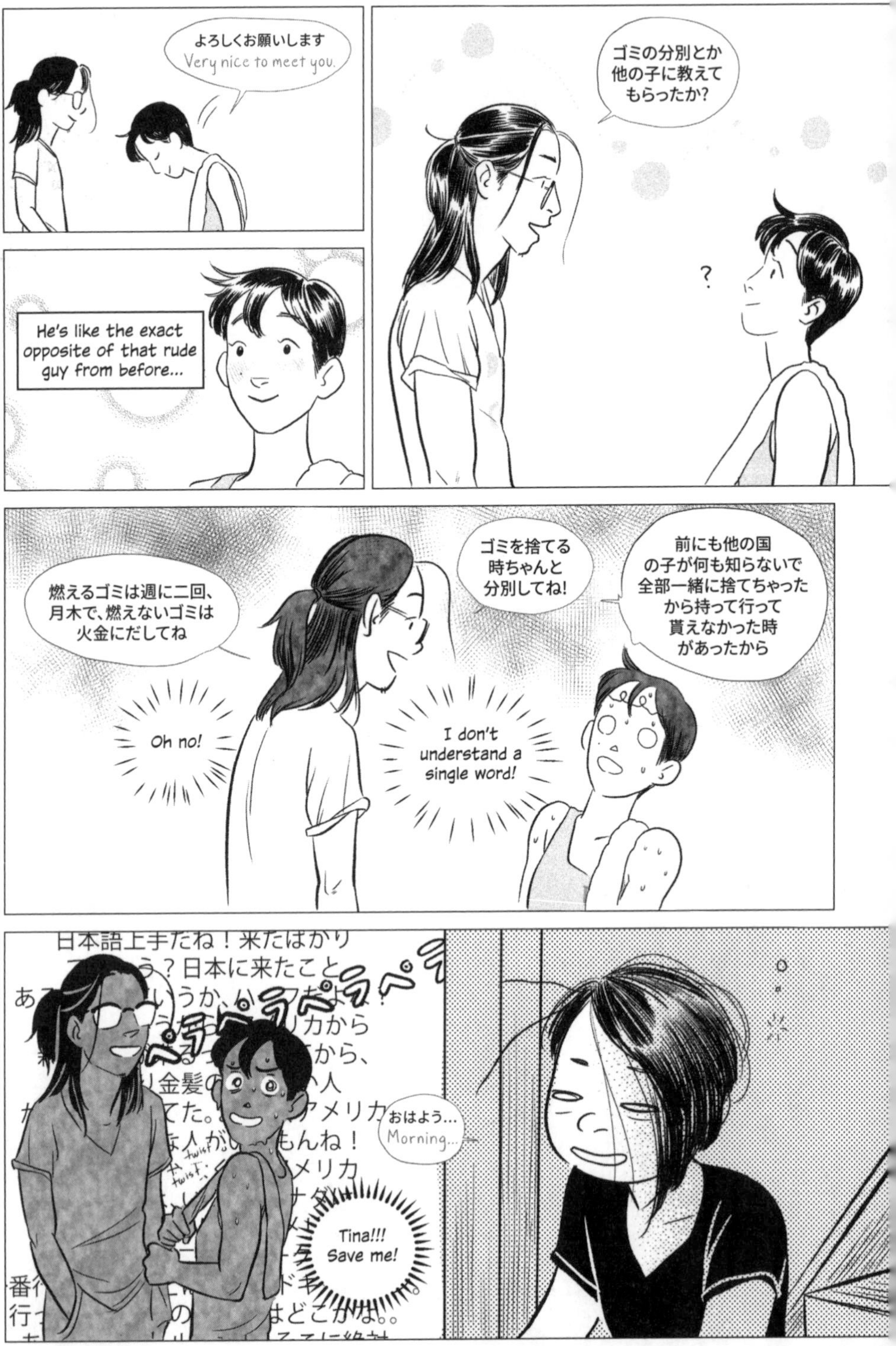
よろしくお願いします
Very nice to meet you.
ゴミの分別とか他の子に教えてもらったか?
?
He's like the exact opposite of that rude guy from before...
燃えるゴミは週に二回、月木で、燃えないゴミは火金にだしてね
ゴミを捨てる時ちゃんと分別してね!
前にも他の国の子が何も知らないで全部一緒に捨てちゃったから持って行って貰えなかった時があったから
Oh no!
I don't understand a single word!
twist twist
Tina!!! Save me!
おはよう…
Morning...

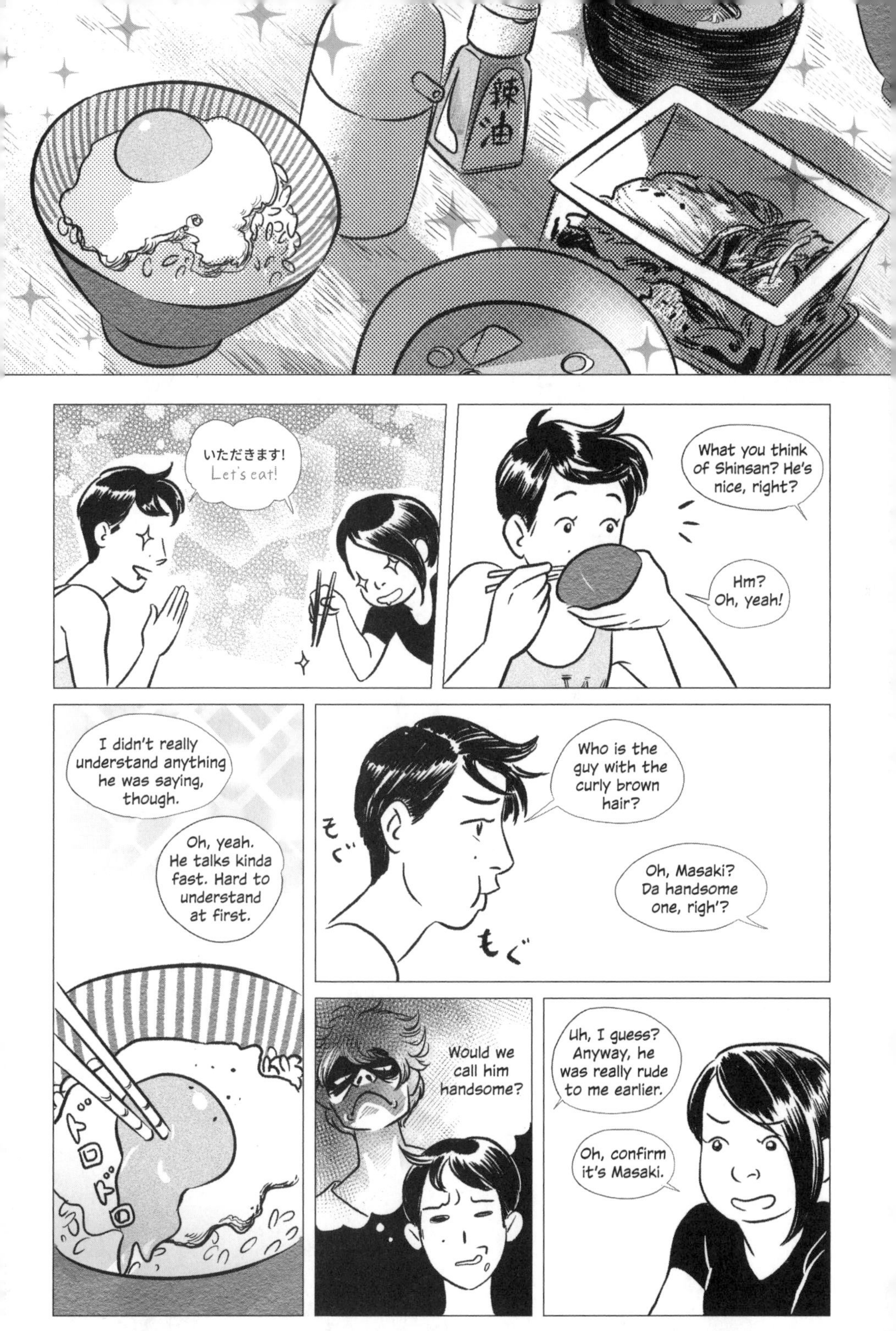
辣油
いただきます!
Let's eat!
What you think of Shinsan? He's nice, right?
Hm? Oh, yeah!
I didn't really understand anything he was saying, though.
Oh, yeah. He talks kinda fast. Hard to understand at first.
Who is the guy with the curly brown hair?
もぐ
もぐ
Oh, Masaki? Da handsome one, righ'?
Would we call him handsome?
Uh, I guess? Anyway, he was really rude to me earlier.
Oh, confirm it's Masaki.

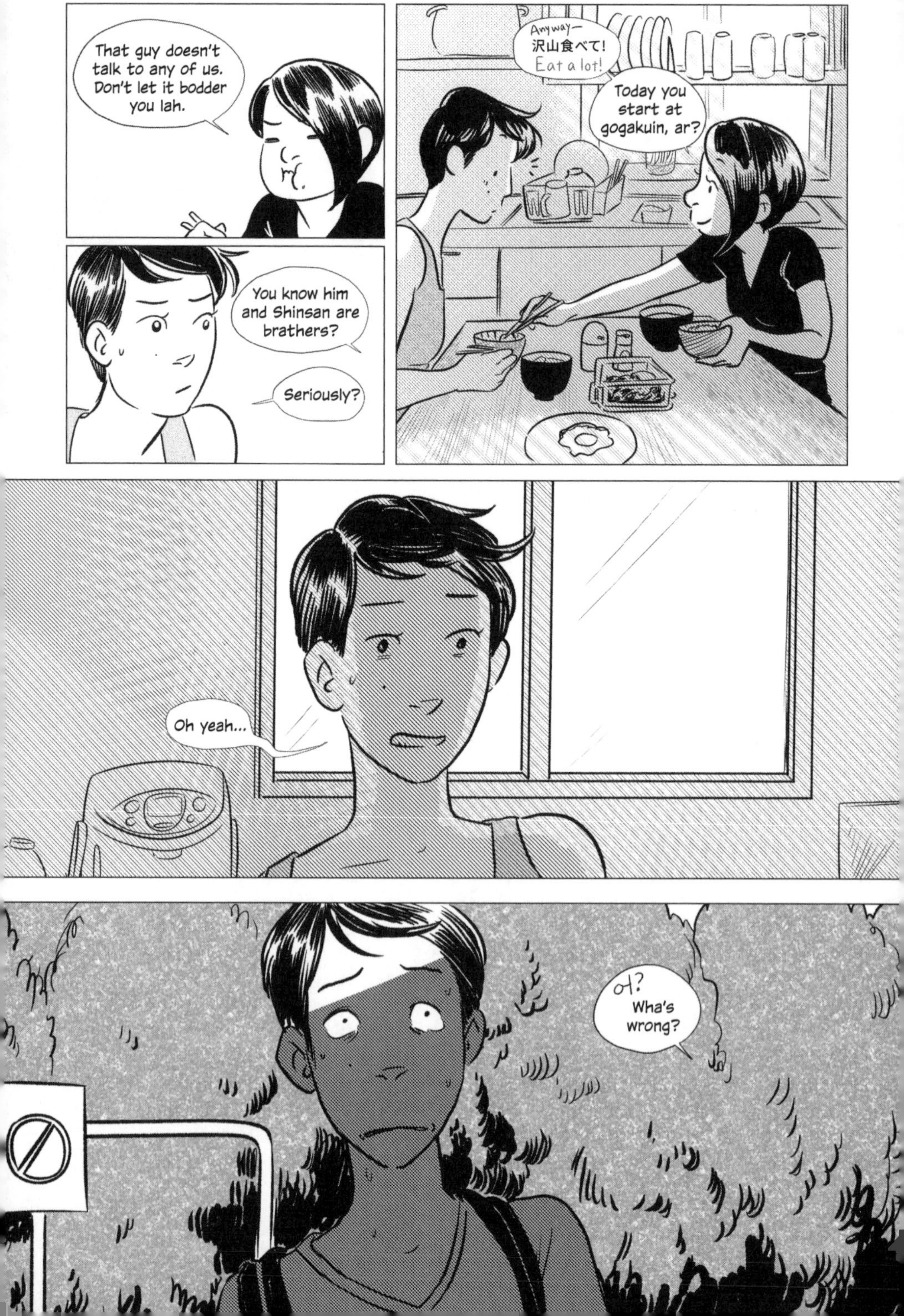
That guy doesn't talk to any of us. Don't let it bodder you lah.
Anyway—
沢山食べて!
Eat a lot!
Today you start at gogakuin, ar?
You know him and Shinsan are brathers?
Seriously?
Oh yeah...
어?
Wha's wrong?

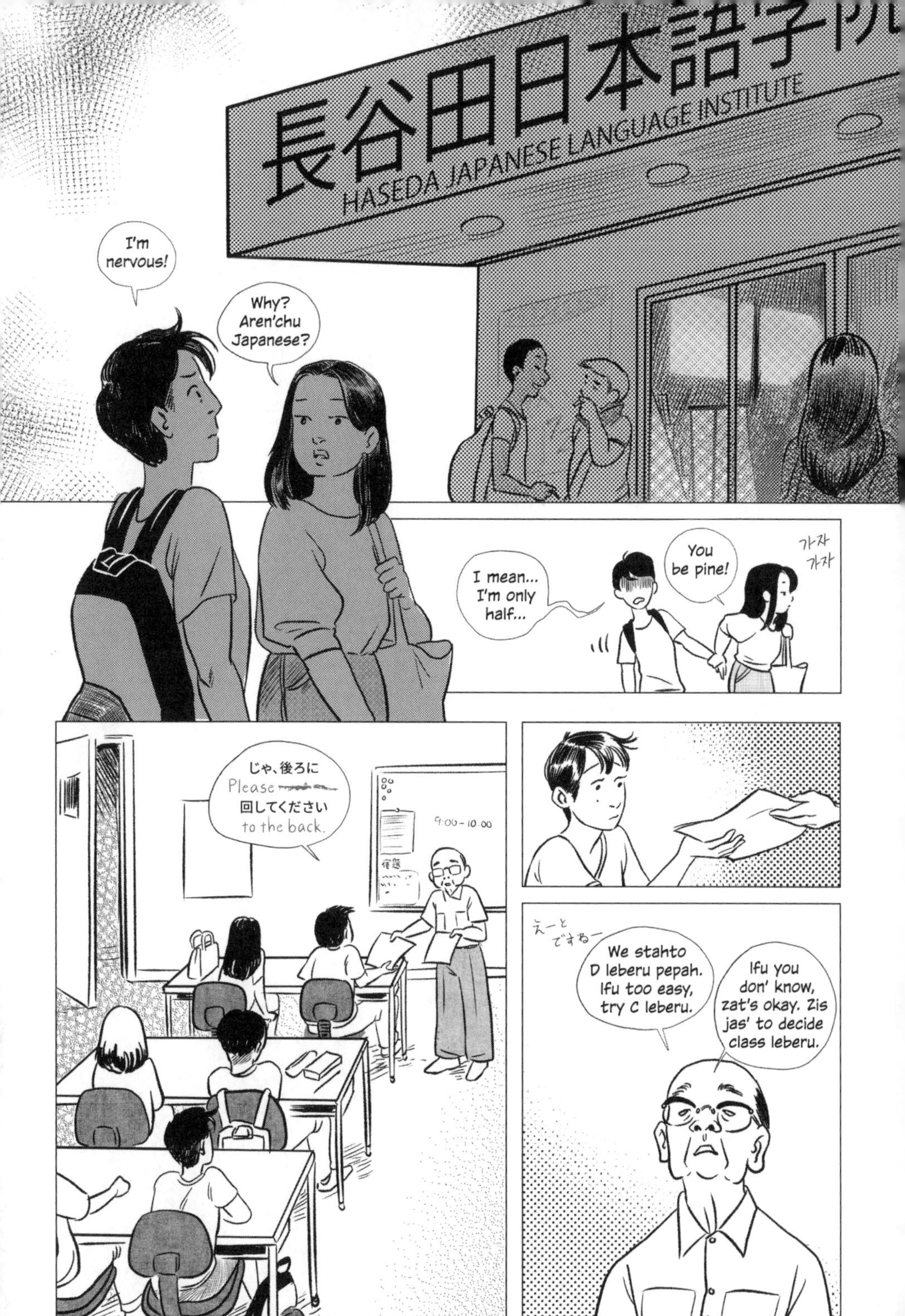
長谷田日本語学
HASEDA JAPANESE LANGUAGE INSTITUTE
I'm nervous!
Why? Aren'chu Japanese?
I mean... I'm only half...
You be pine!
가자 가자
じゃ、後ろに Please 回してください to the back.
9:00 – 10:00
宿題
えーと ですねー
We stahto D leberu pepah. Ifu too easy, try C leberu.
Ifu you don' know, zat's okay. Zis jas' to decide class leberu.

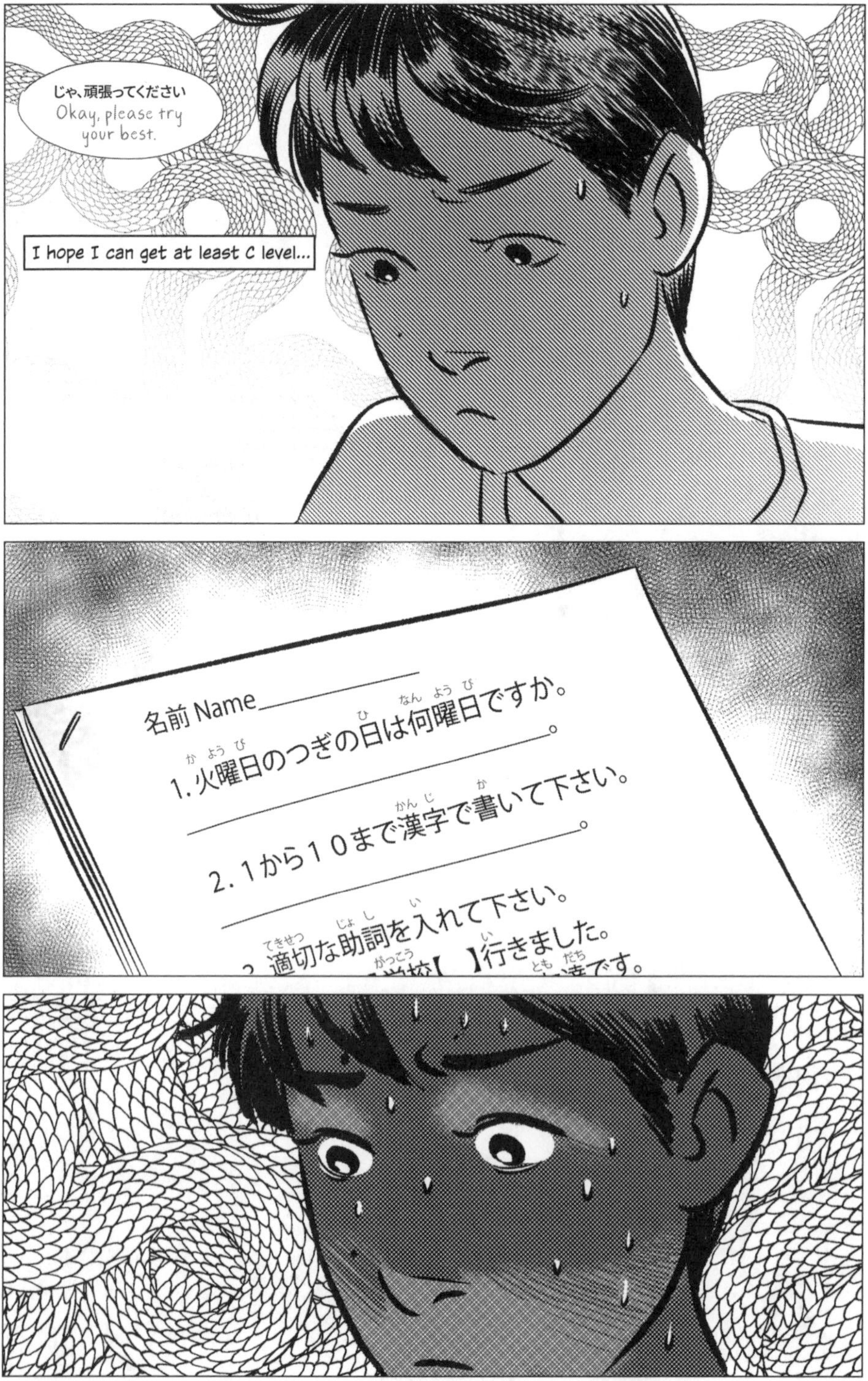
じゃ、頑張ってください
Okay, please try your best.
I hope I can get at least C level...
名前 Name
1. 火曜日のつぎの日は何曜日ですか。
2. 1から10まで漢字で書いて下さい。
適切な助詞を入れて下さい。
【 】行きました。

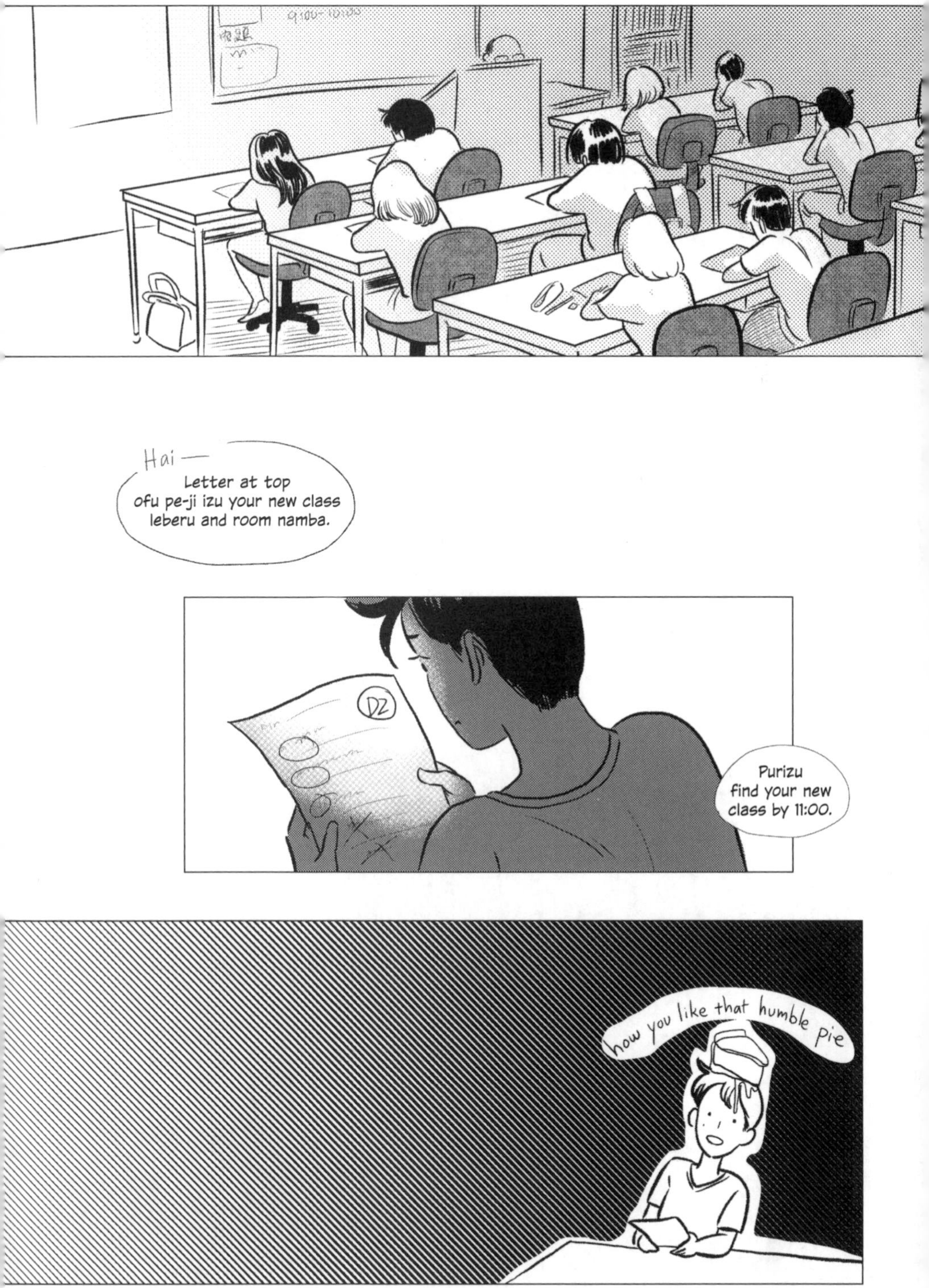
Hai —
Letter at top ofu pe-ji izu your new class leberu and room namba.
Purizu find your new class by 11:00.
how you like that humble pie

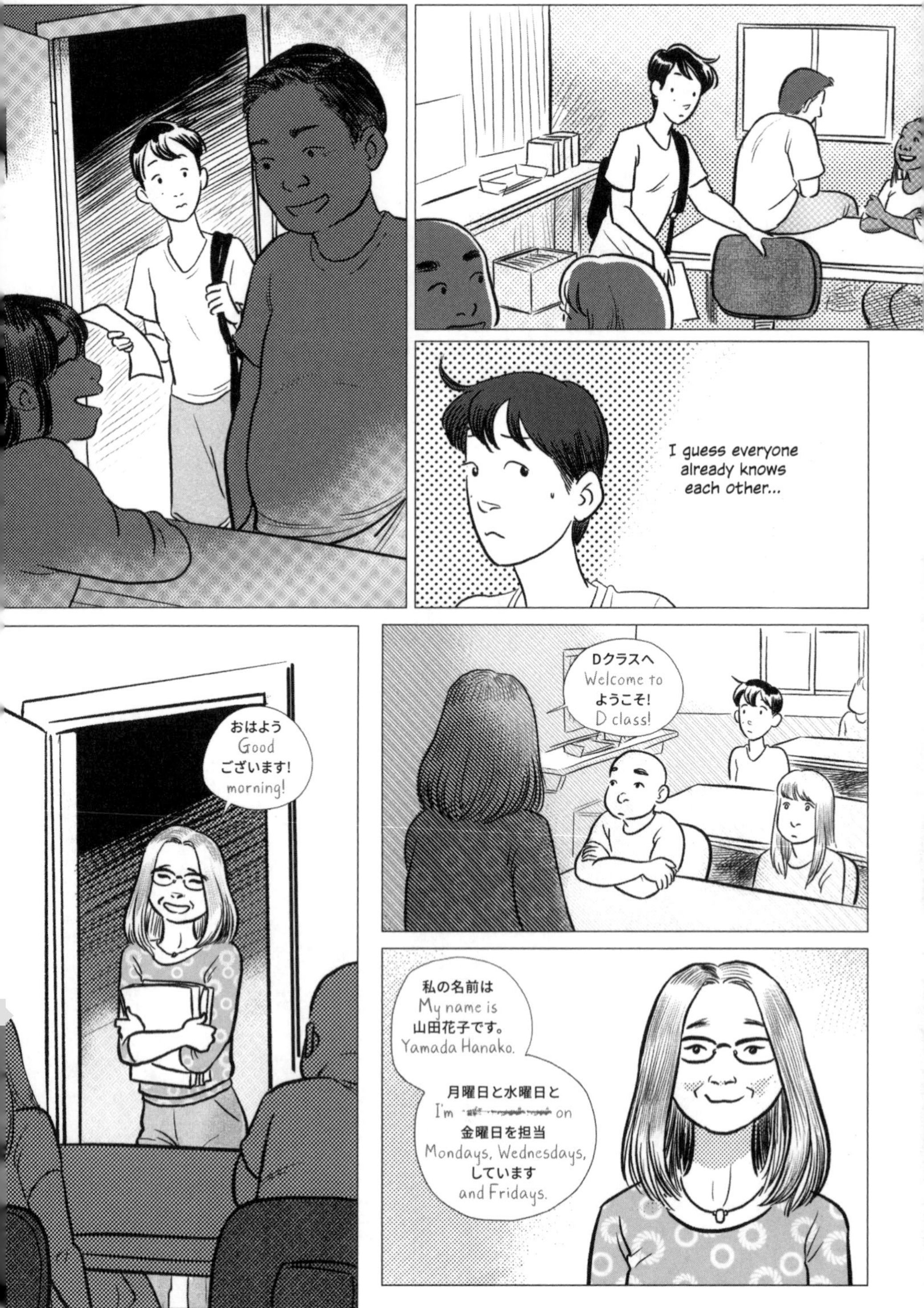
I guess everyone already knows each other...
おはよう Good ございます! morning!
Dクラスへ Welcome to ようこそ! D class!
私の名前は My name is 山田花子です。 Yamada Hanako.
月曜日と水曜日と I'm on 金曜日を担当 Mondays, Wednesdays, しています and Fridays.

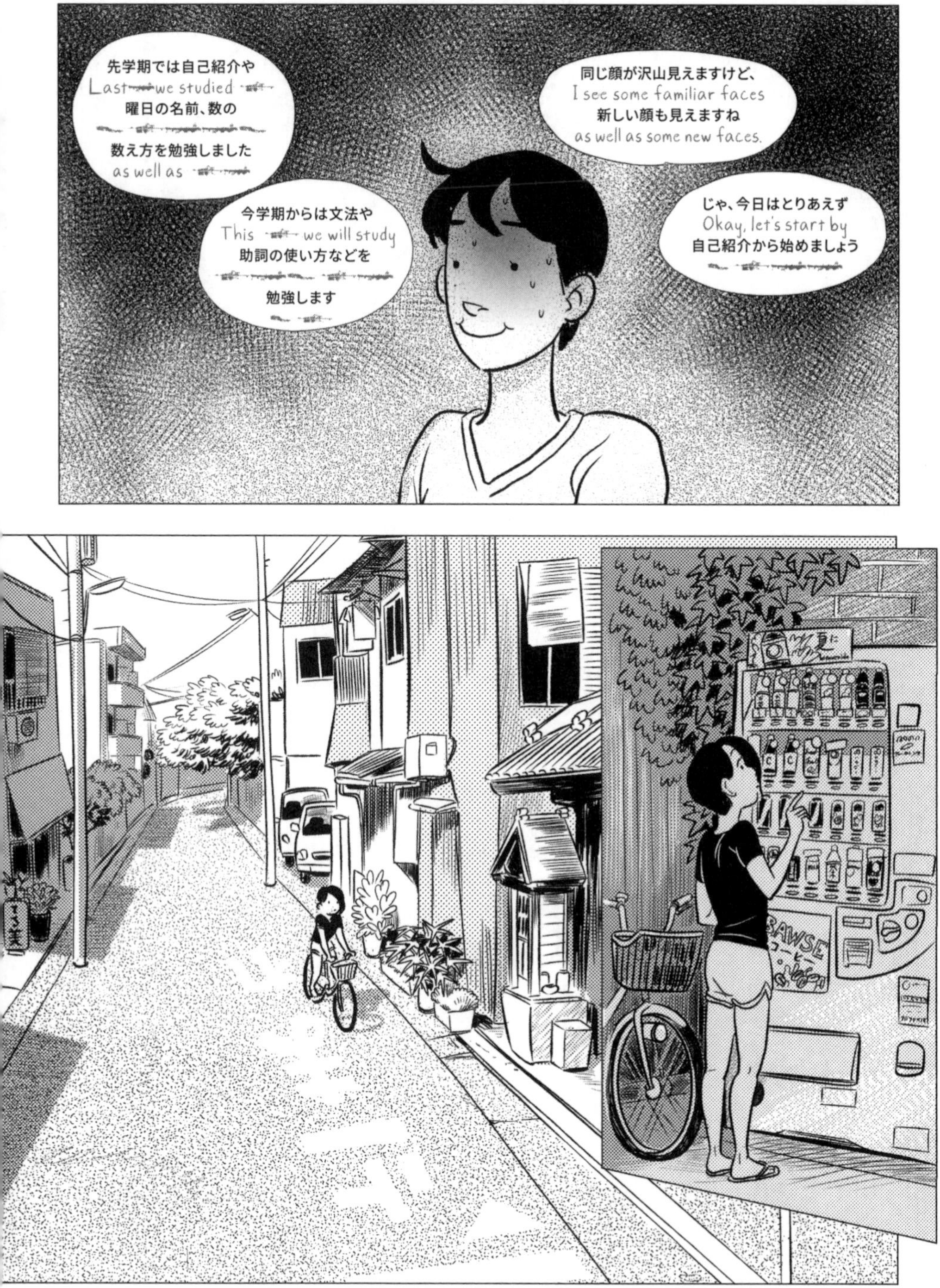
先学期では自己紹介や
Last we studied
曜日の名前、数の
数え方を勉強しました
as well as
今学期からは文法や
This we will study
助詞の使い方などを
勉強します
同じ顔が沢山見えますけど、
I see some familiar faces
新しい顔も見えますね
as well as some new faces.
じゃ、今日はとりあえず
Okay, let's start by
自己紹介から始めましょう

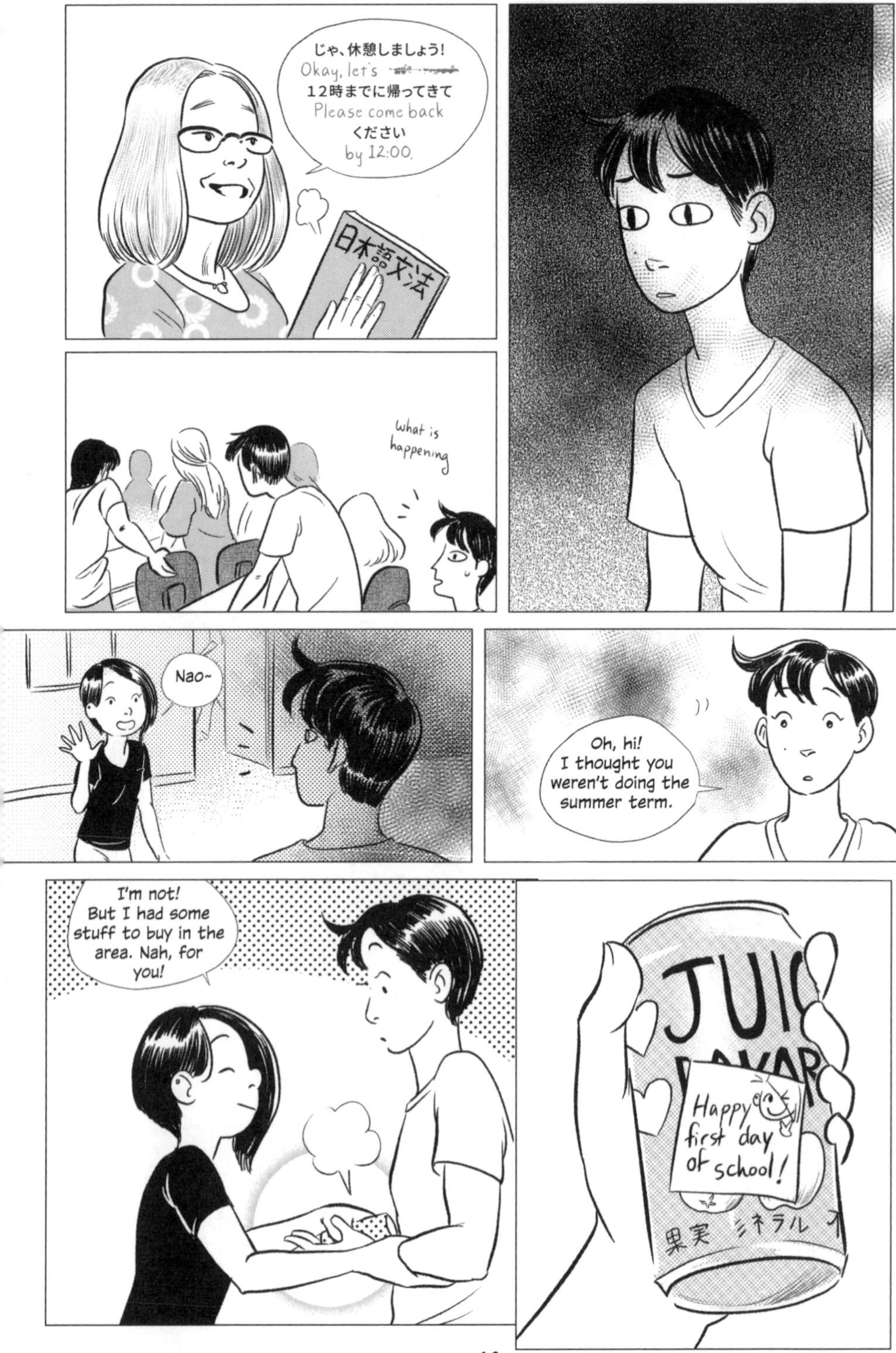
じゃ、休憩しましょう!
Okay, let's
12時までに帰ってきてください
Please come back by 12:00.
日本語文法
what is happening
Nao~
Oh, hi! I thought you weren't doing the summer term.
I'm not! But I had some stuff to buy in the area. Nah, for you!
JUIC
Happy first day of school!
果実

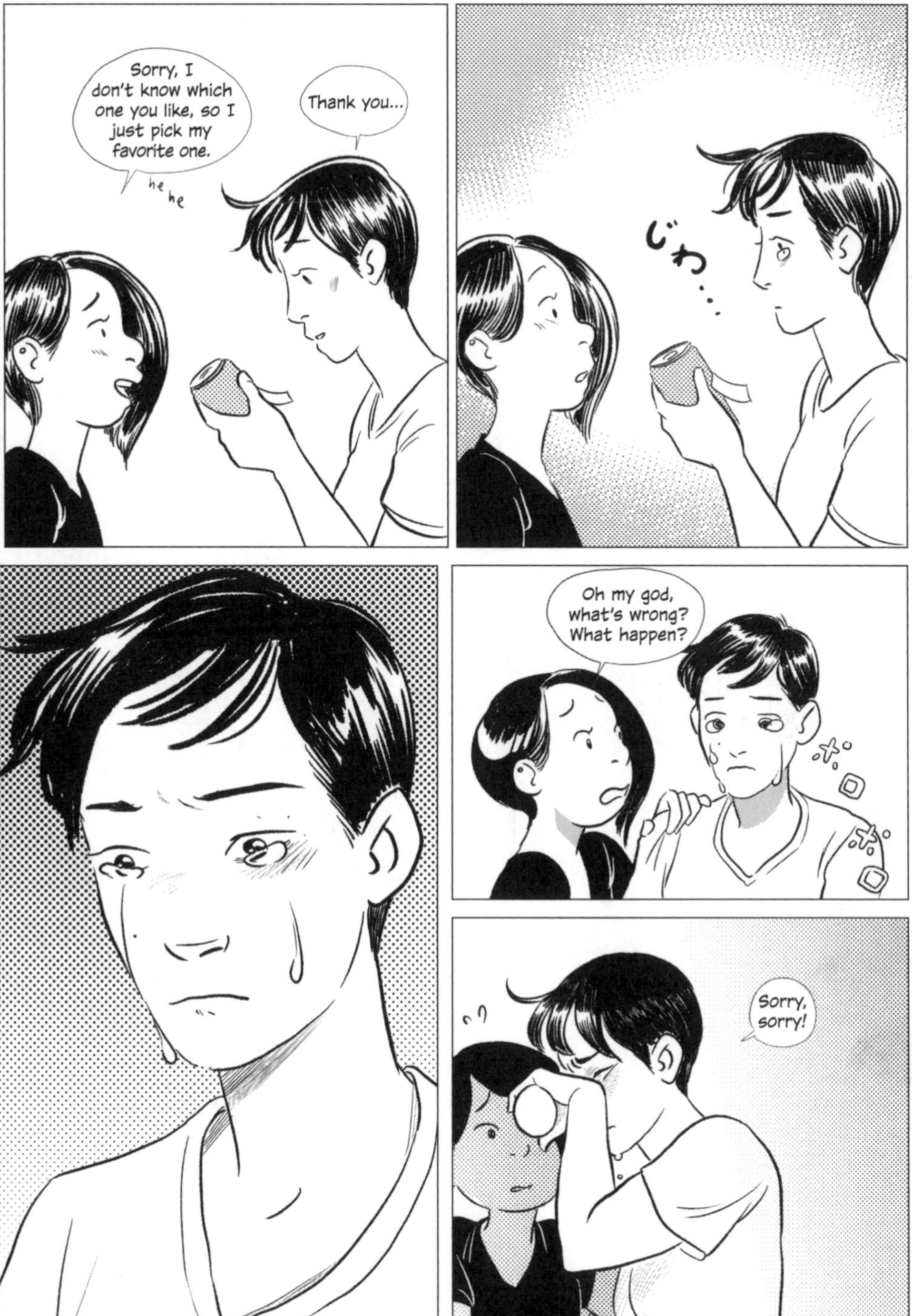
Sorry, I don't know which one you like, so I just pick my favorite one.
he he
Thank you...
じわ...
Oh my god, what's wrong? What happen?
Sorry, sorry!

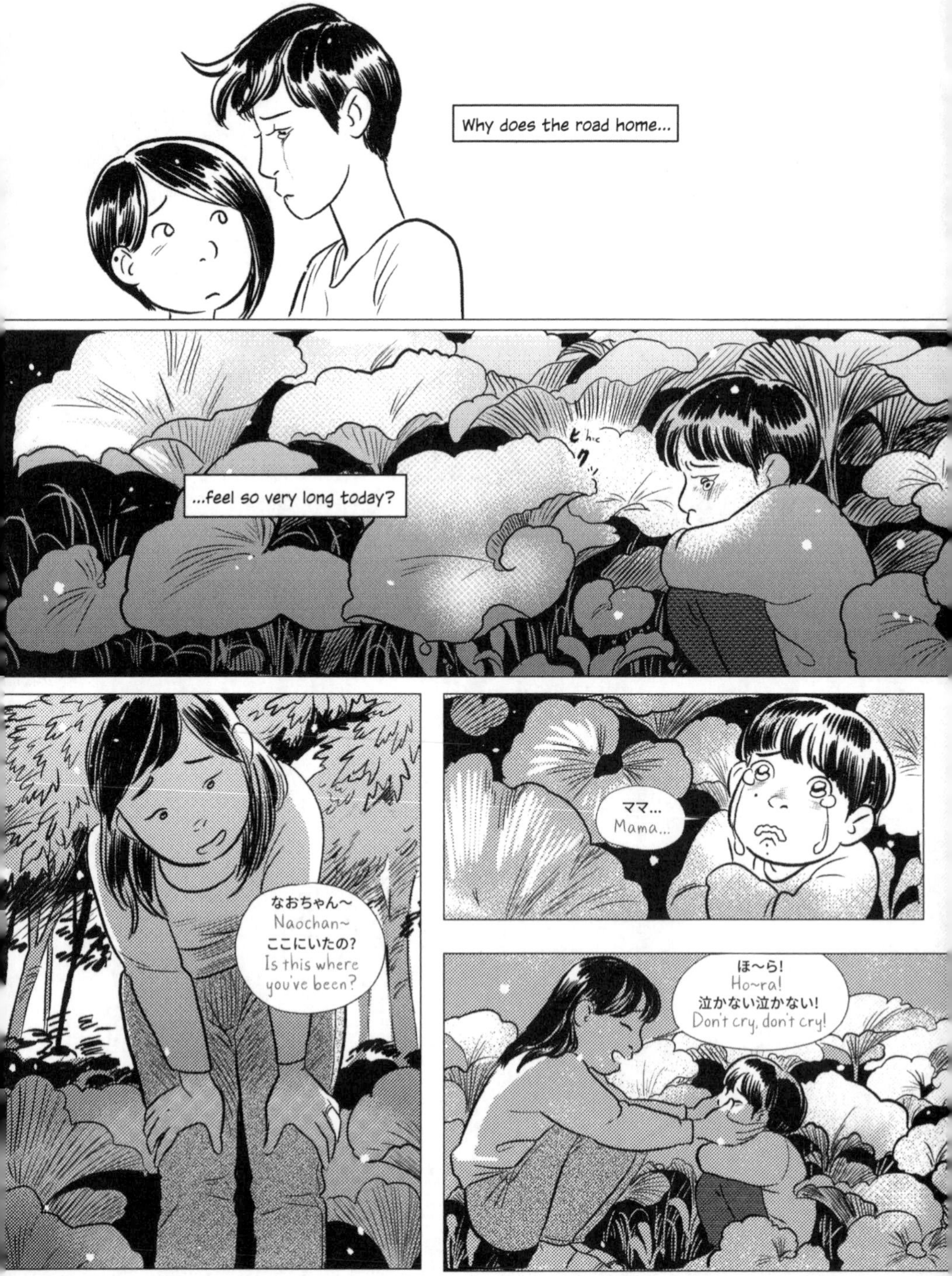
Why does the road home...
...feel so very long today?
ヒクッ
hic
ママ...
Mama...
なおちゃん～
Naochan~
ここにいたの?
Is this where you've been?
ほ～ら!
Ho~ra!
泣かない泣かない!
Don't cry, don't cry!

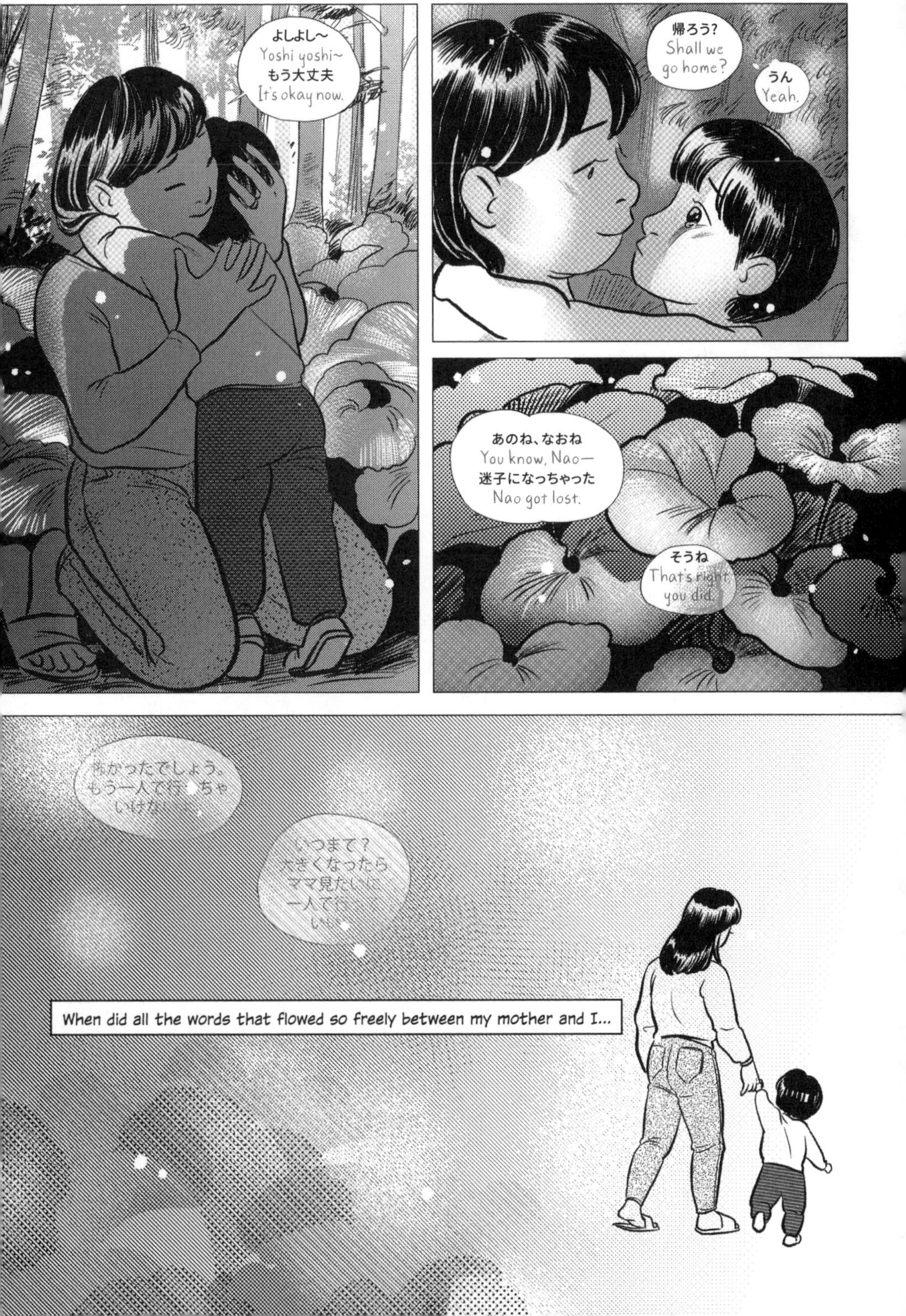
よしよし～
Yoshi yoshi~
もう大丈夫
It's okay now.
帰ろう?
Shall we go home?
うん
Yeah.
あのね、なおね
You know, Nao—
迷子になっちゃった
Nao got lost.
そうね
That's right you did.
いつまで？
大きくなったら
ママ見たいに
When did all the words that flowed so freely between my mother and I...

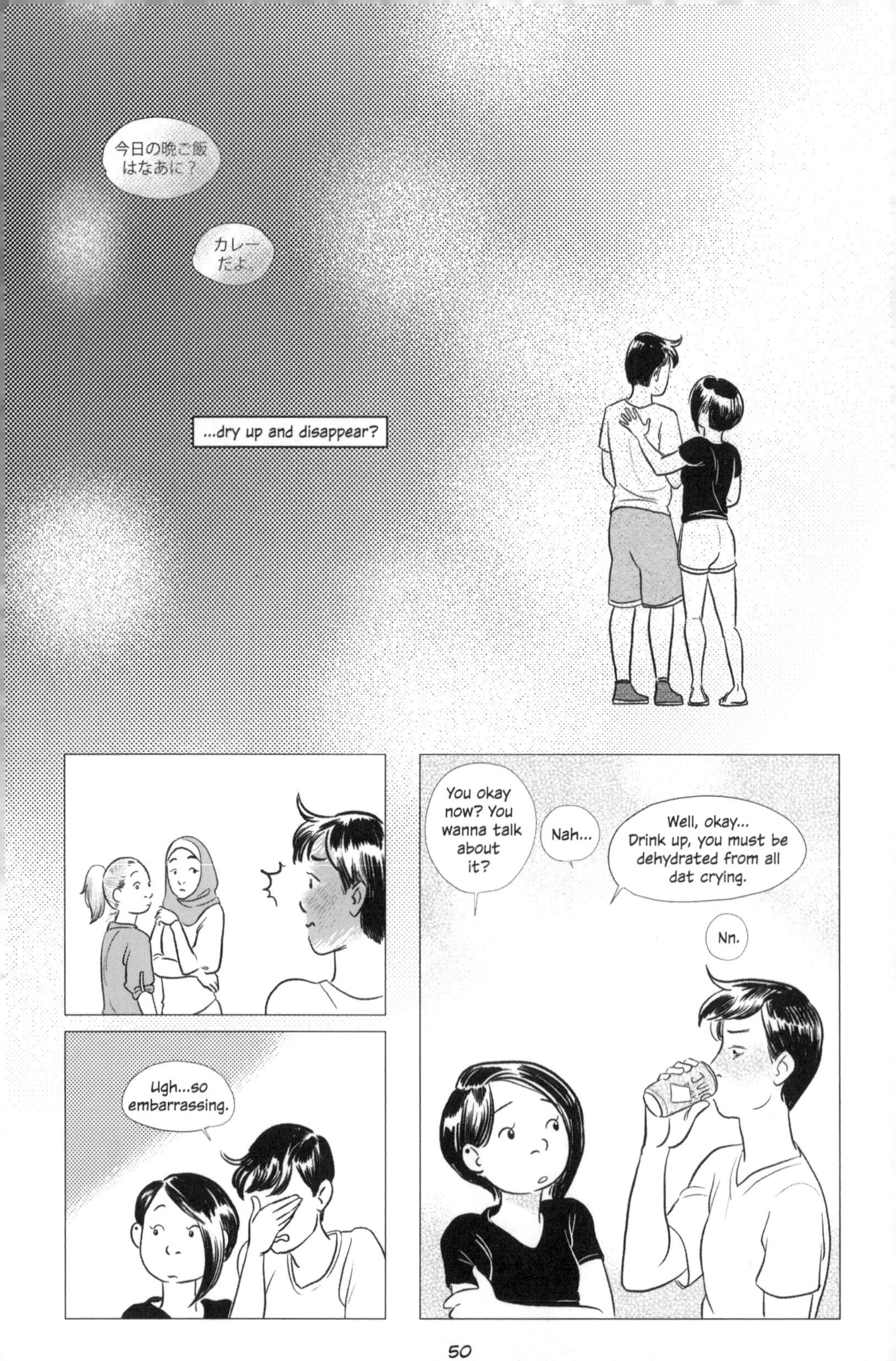
今日の晩ご飯
はなあに？
カレー
だよ。
...dry up and disappear?
Ugh...so embarrassing.
You okay now? You wanna talk about it?
Nah...
Well, okay... Drink up, you must be dehydrated from all dat crying.
Nn.

Chapter 3

Awa Odori

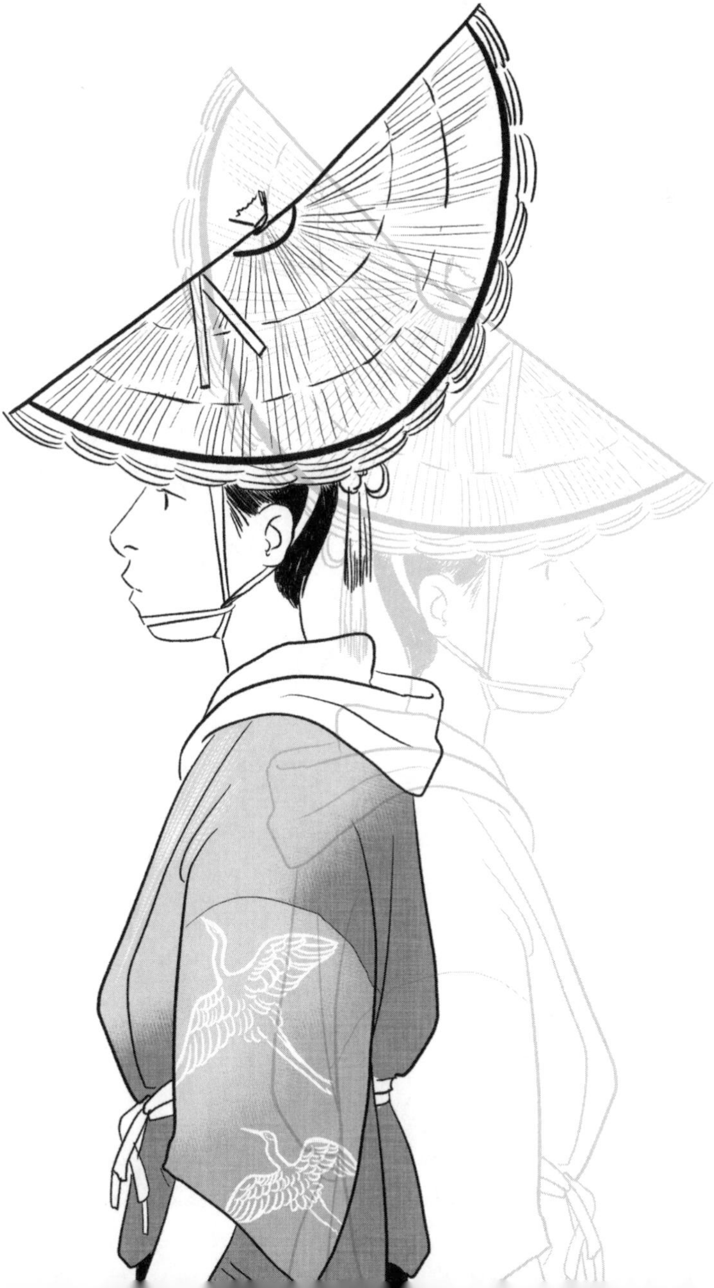

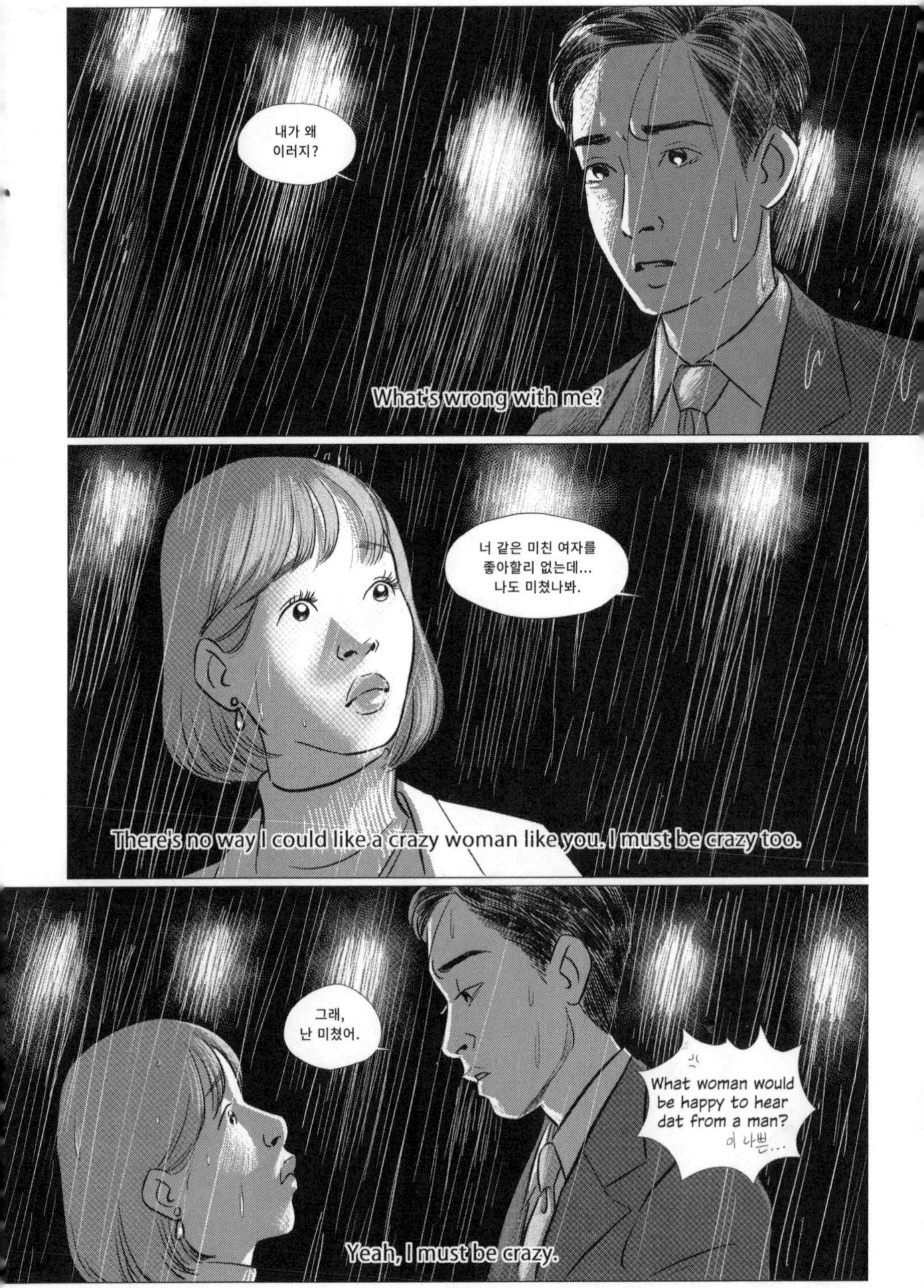
내가 왜
이러지?
What's wrong with me?
너 같은 미친 여자를
좋아할리 없는데...
나도 미쳤나봐.
There's no way I could like a crazy woman like you. I must be crazy too.
그래,
난 미쳤어.
What woman would
be happy to hear
dat from a man?
이 나쁜...
Yeah, I must be crazy.

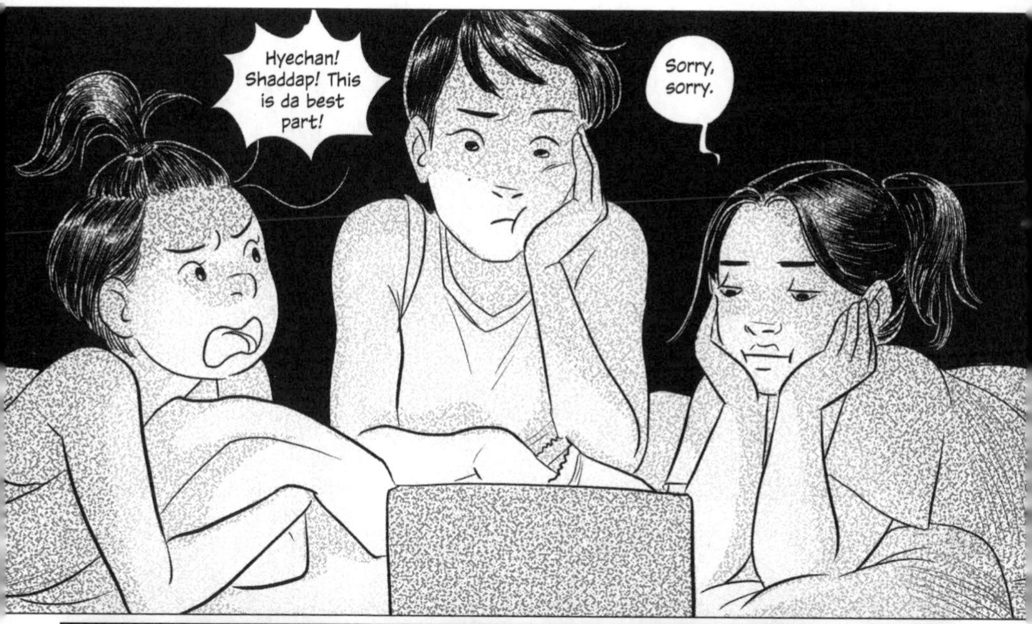
Hyechan! Shaddap! This is da best part!
Sorry, sorry.

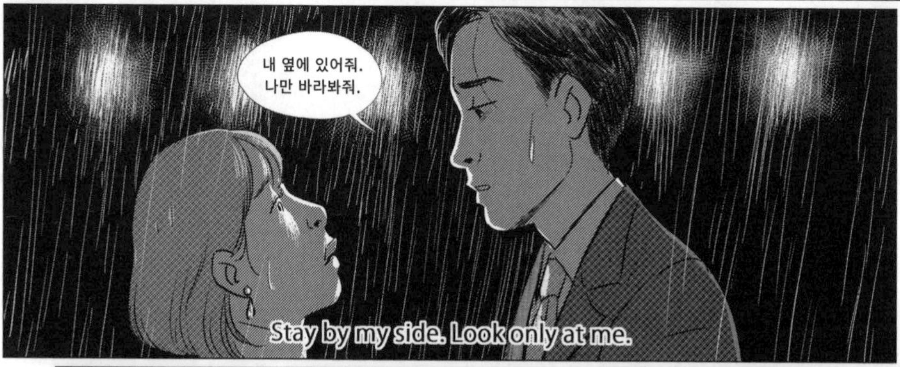
내 옆에 있어줘.
나만 바라봐줘.
Stay by my side. Look only at me.

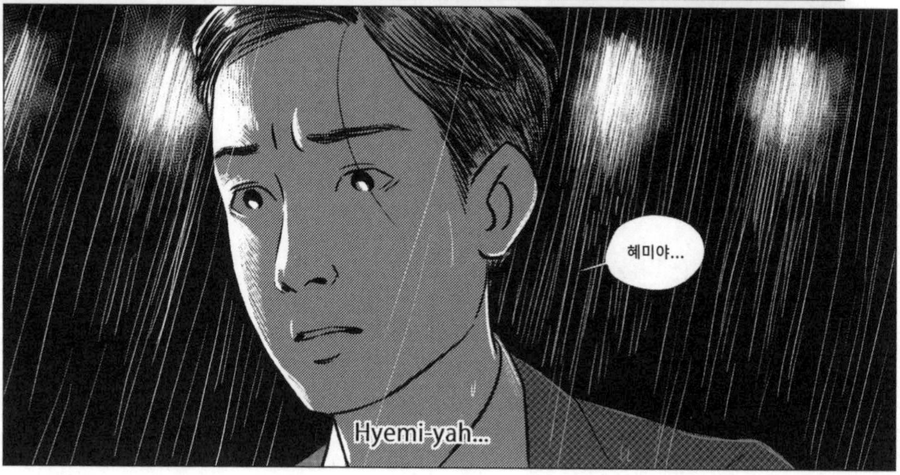
혜미야...
Hyemi-yah...

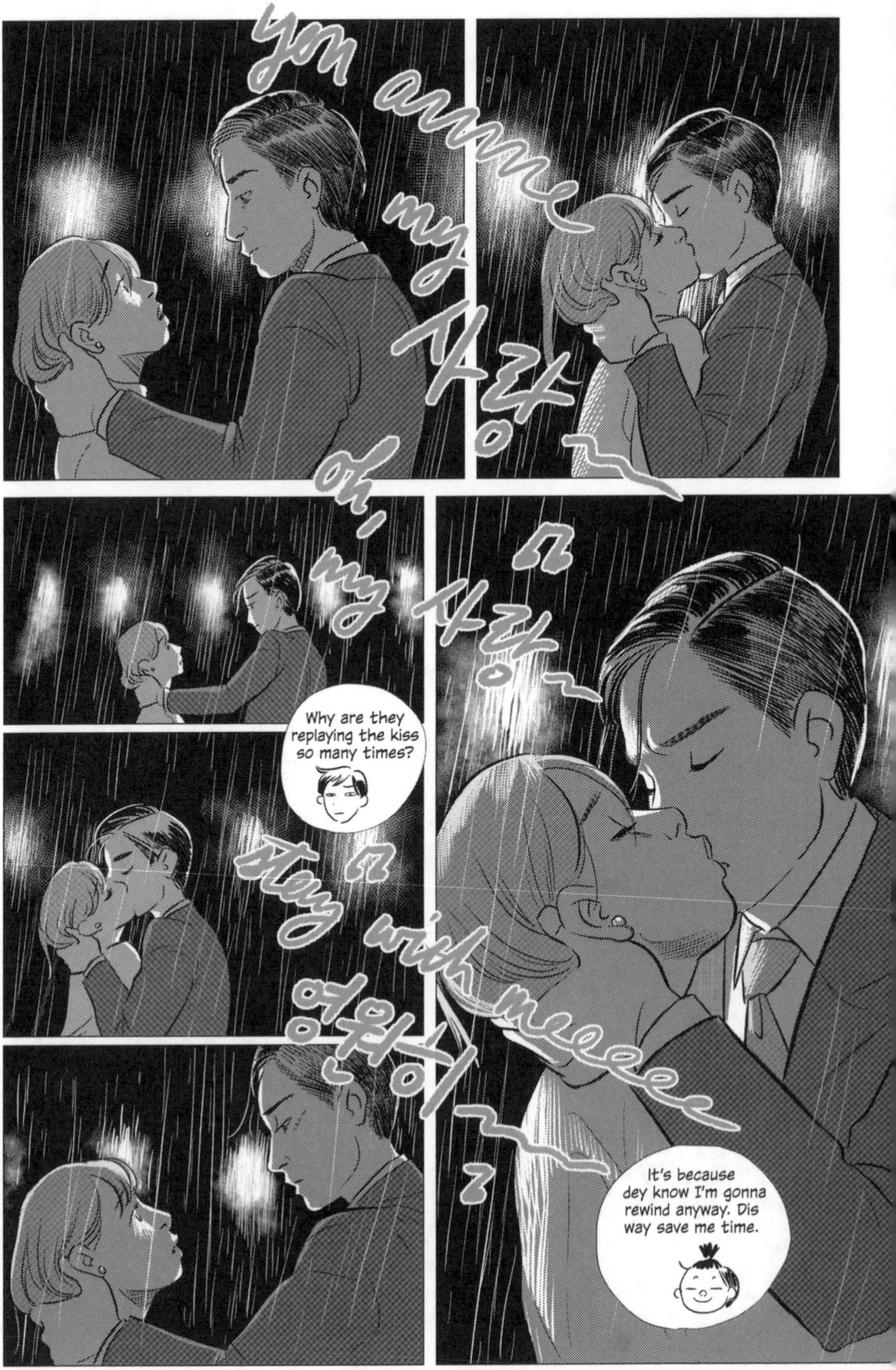
you arrrre my 사랑~
oh, my 사랑~
Why are they replaying the kiss so many times?
stay with meeeee
영원히~
It's because dey know I'm gonna rewind anyway. Dis way save me time.

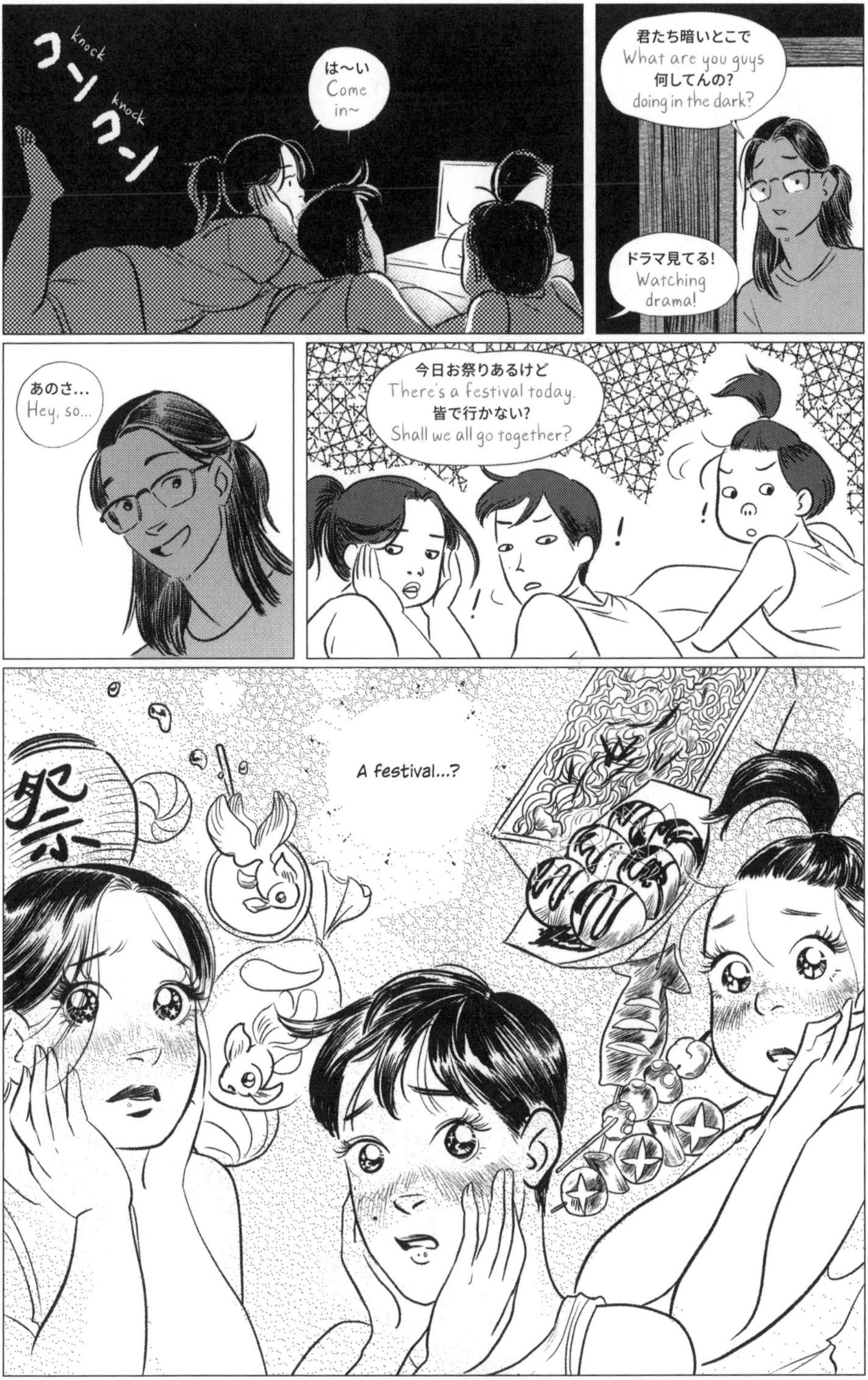
コン knock
コン knock
は〜い
Come in~
君たち暗いとこで
What are you guys
何してんの?
doing in the dark?
ドラマ見てる!
Watching drama!
あのさ…
Hey, so...
今日お祭りあるけど
There's a festival today.
皆で行かない?
Shall we all go together?
!
!
!
A festival...?
祭

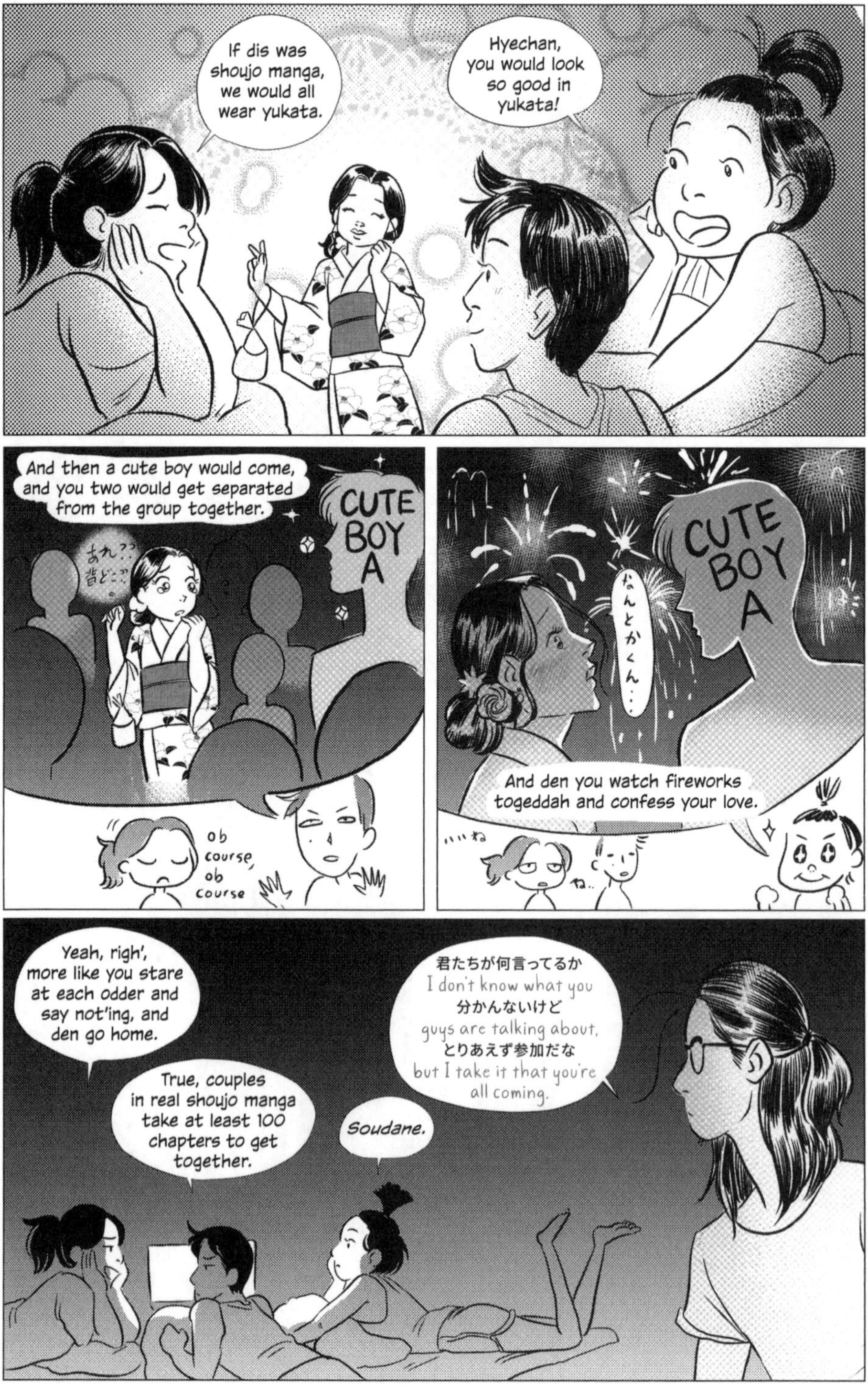
If dis was shoujo manga, we would all wear yukata.
Hyechan, you would look so good in yukata!
And then a cute boy would come, and you two would get separated from the group together.
CUTE BOY A
あれ?? 皆どこ??
ob course, ob course
CUTE BOY A
なんとかくん…
And den you watch fireworks togeddah and confess your love.
いいね
ね..
Yeah, righ', more like you stare at each odder and say not'ing, and den go home.
True, couples in real shoujo manga take at least 100 chapters to get together.
Soudane.
君たちが何言ってるか
I don't know what you
分かんないけど
guys are talking about,
とりあえず参加だな
but I take it that you're all coming.

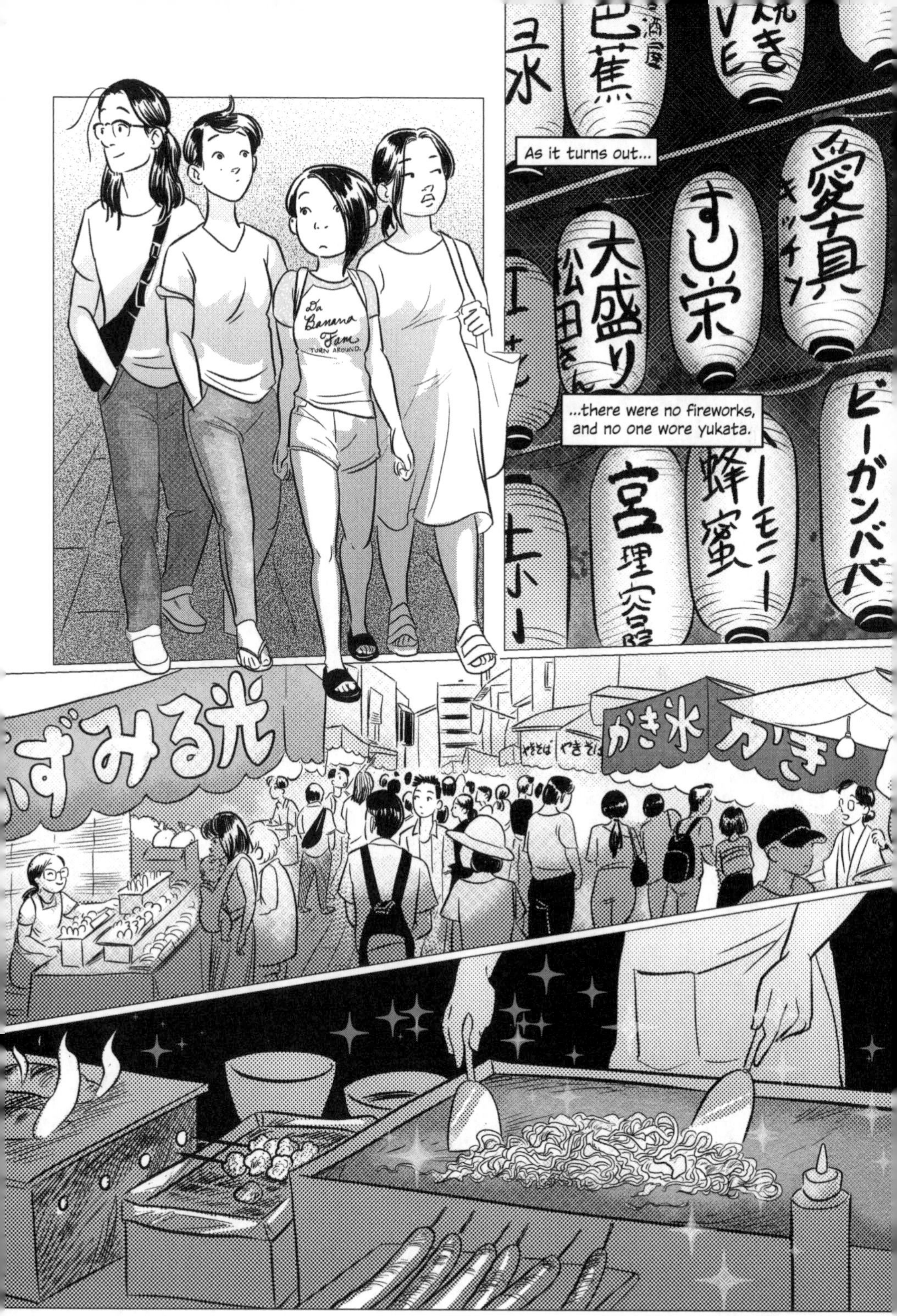
As it turns out...
...there were no fireworks, and no one wore yukata.
Da Banana Fam
TURN AROUND.
愛真
すし栄
大盛り
ビーガンババ
かき氷

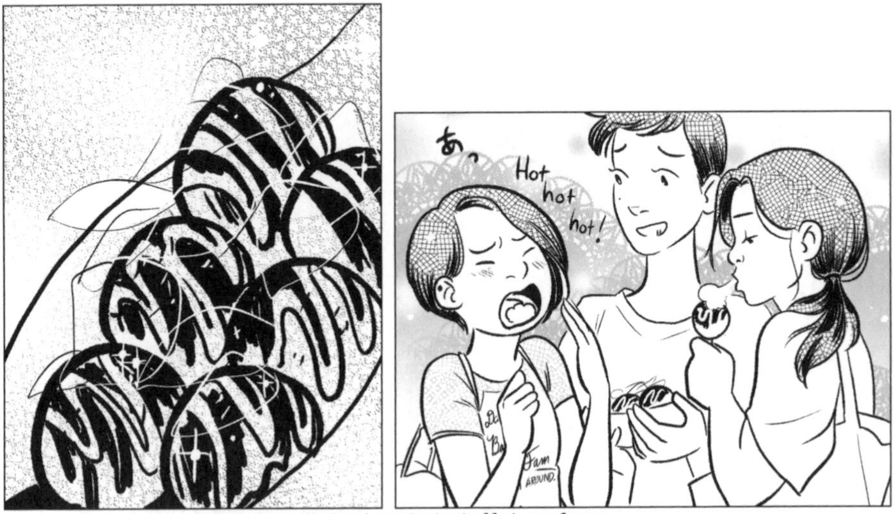
あ、
Hot hot hot!

Instead, we just stuffed our faces.

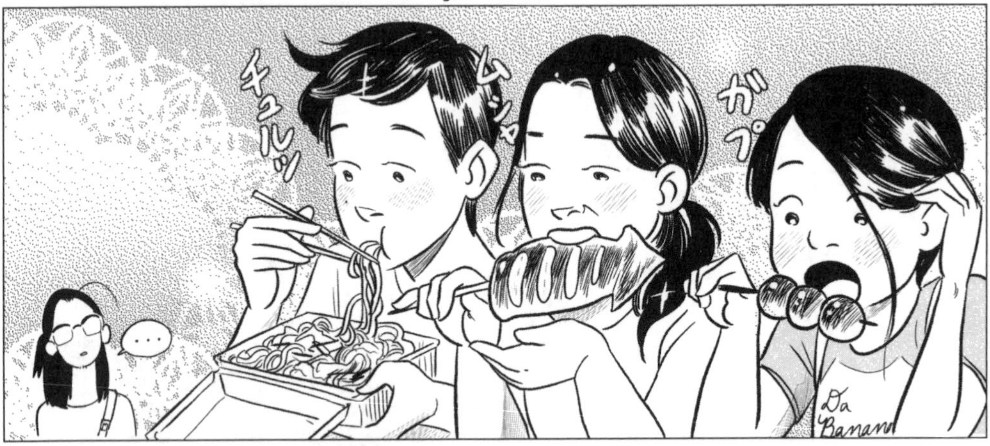
チュルッ
ムシャ
ガブ
...
Da Banana

Which was just as good, if not better, than fireworks with a cute boy.

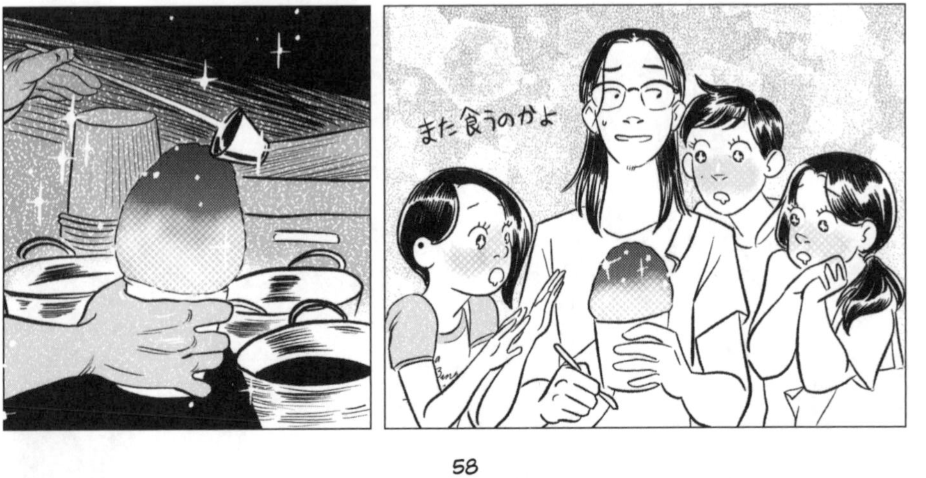
また食うのかよ

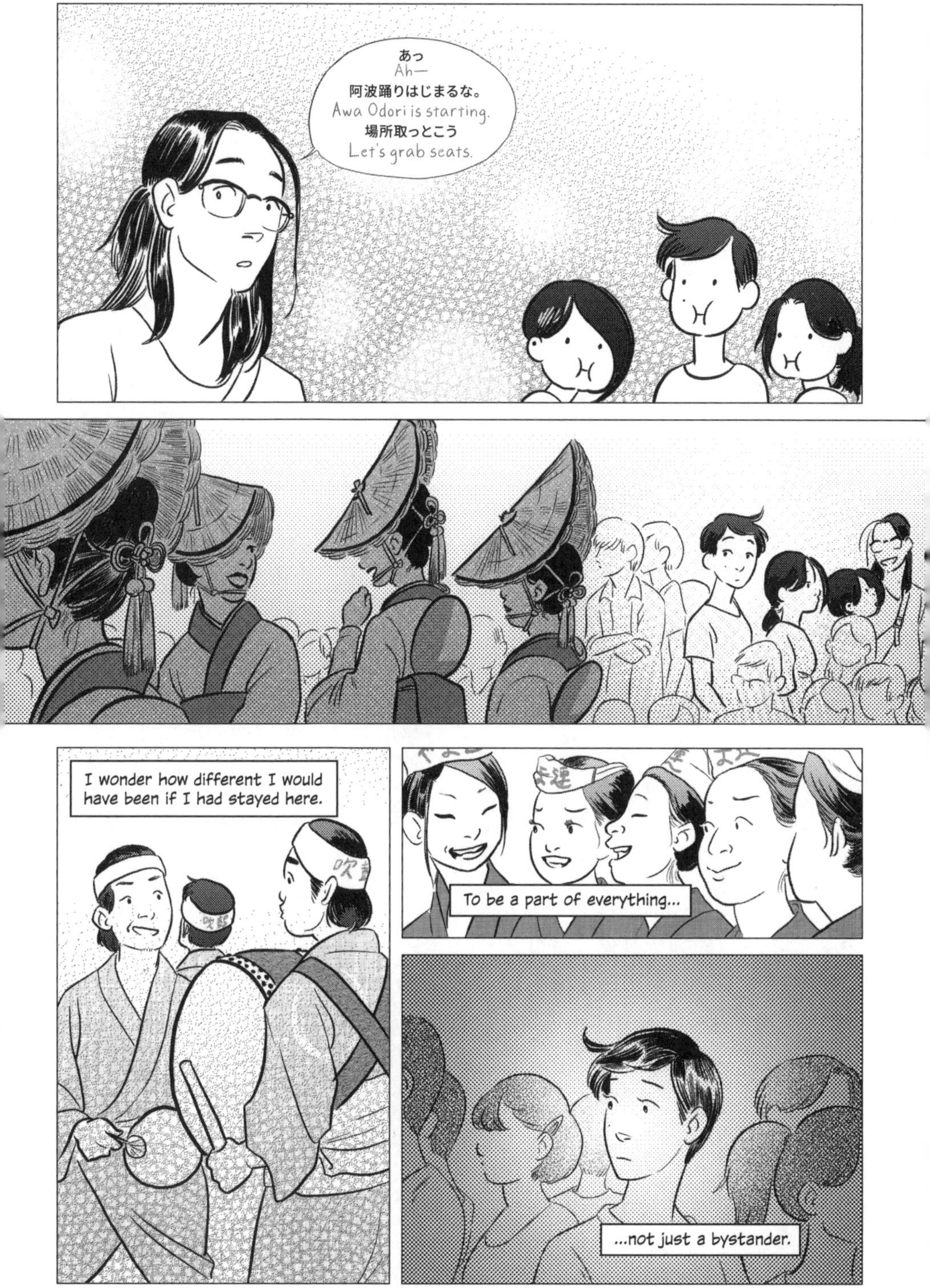
あっ
Ah—
阿波踊りはじまるな。
Awa Odori is starting.
場所取っとこう
Let's grab seats.
I wonder how different I would have been if I had stayed here.
To be a part of everything...
...not just a bystander.

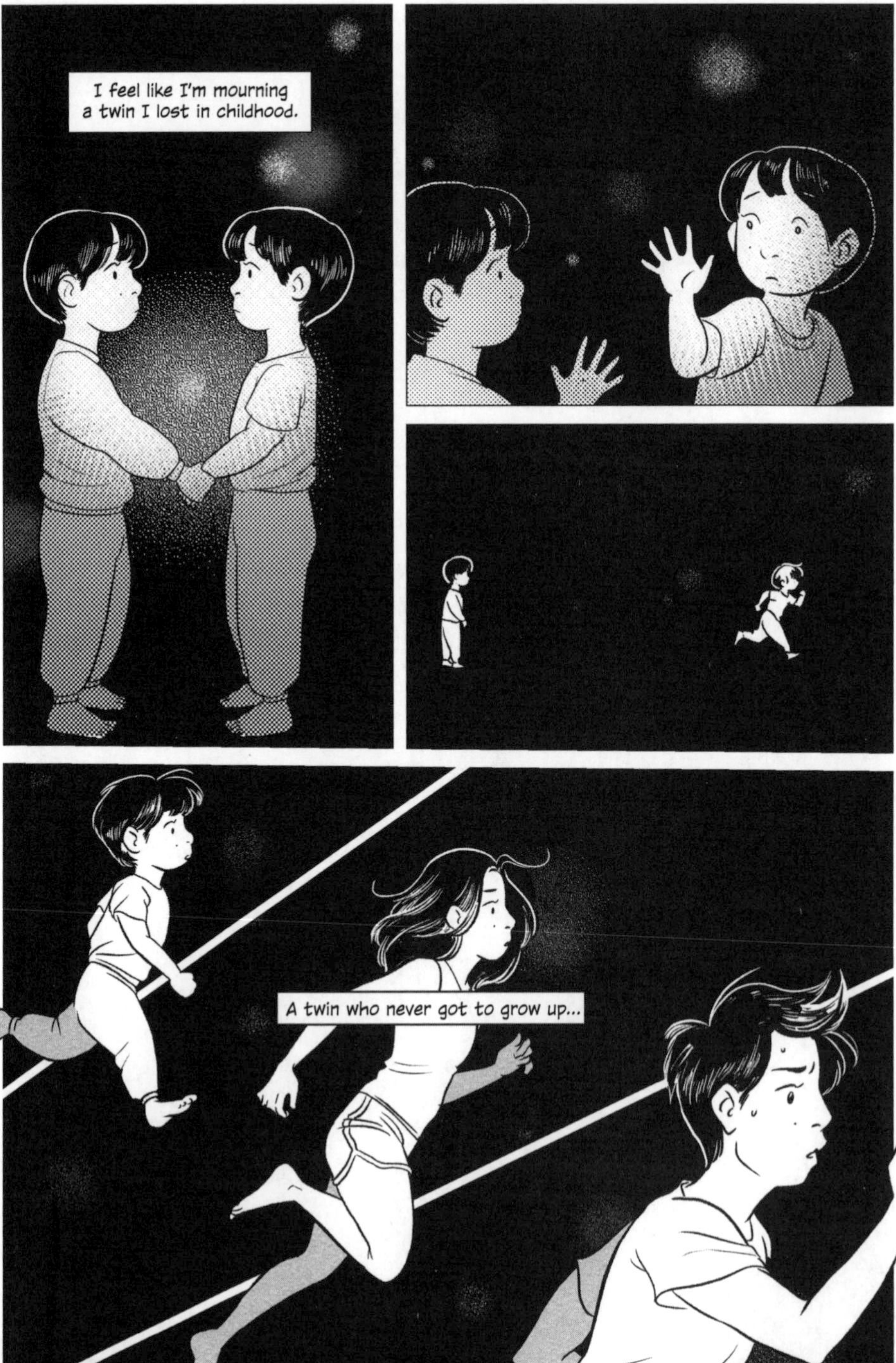
I feel like I'm mourning a twin I lost in childhood.
A twin who never got to grow up...

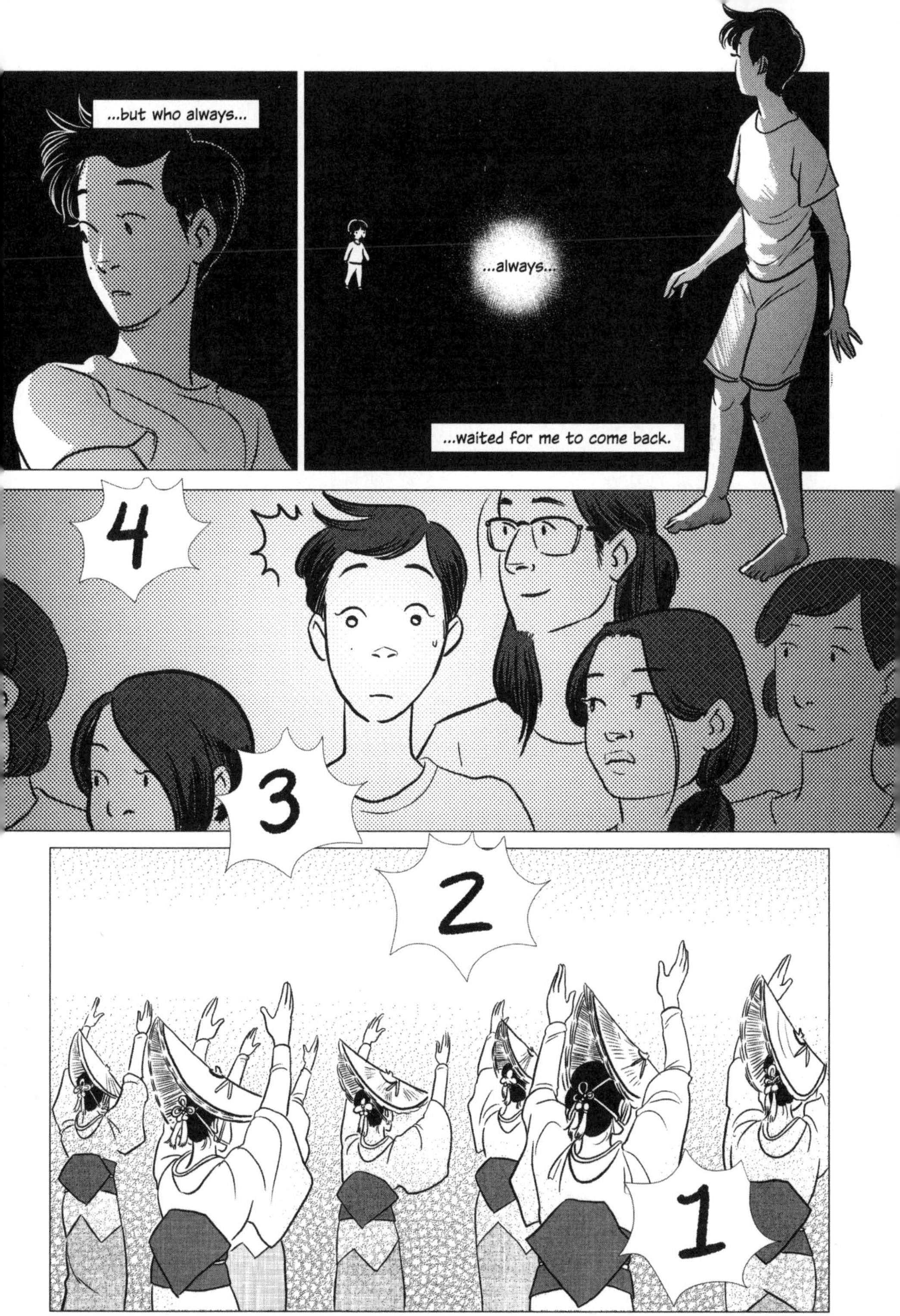
...but who always...
...always...
...waited for me to come back.
4
3
2
1

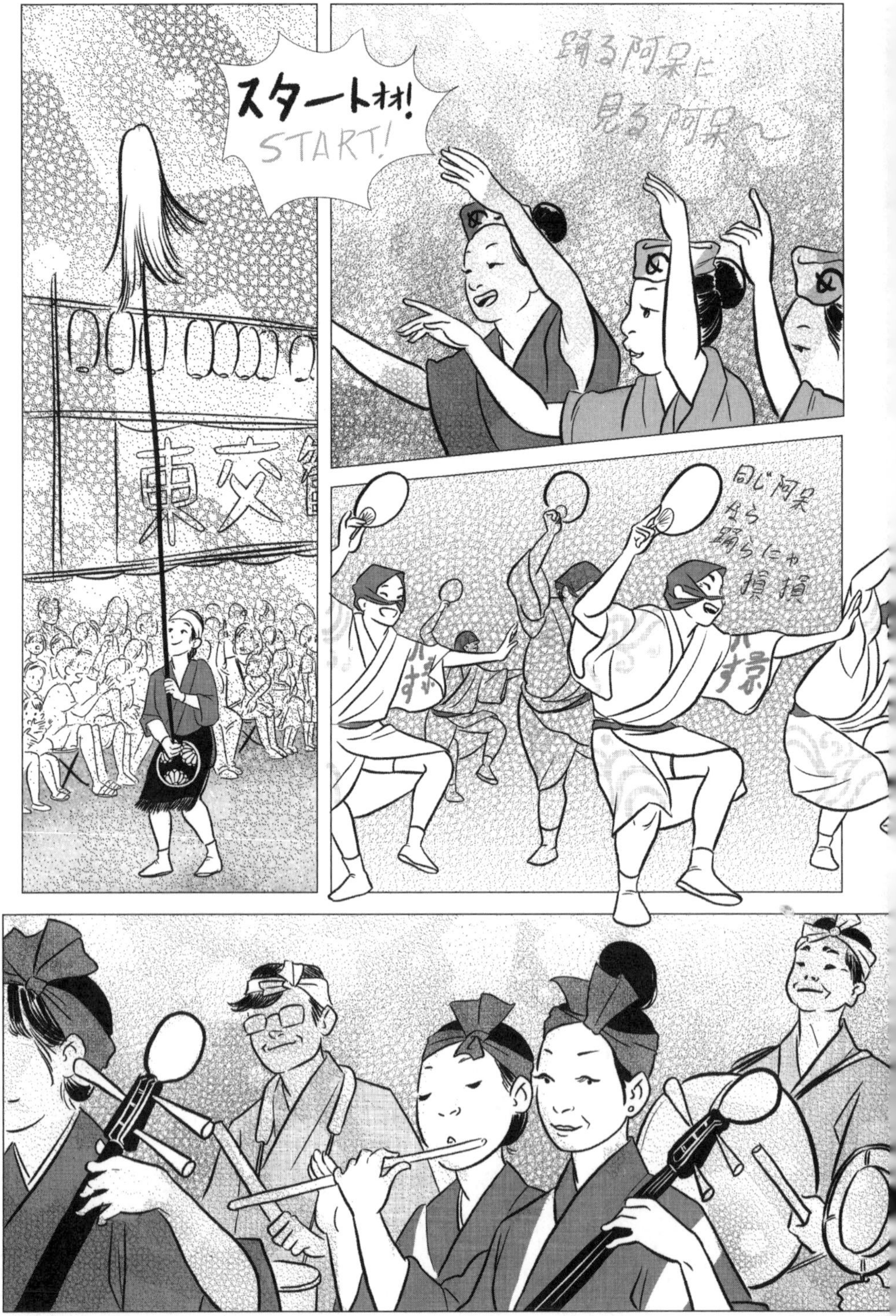
スタートォォ!
START!
踊る阿呆に
見る阿呆〜
同じ阿呆なら
踊らにゃ損損

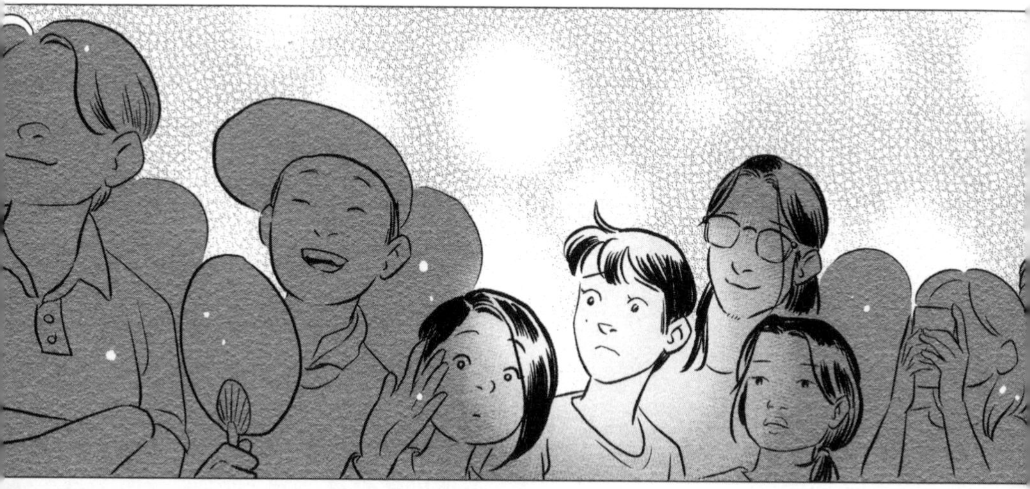

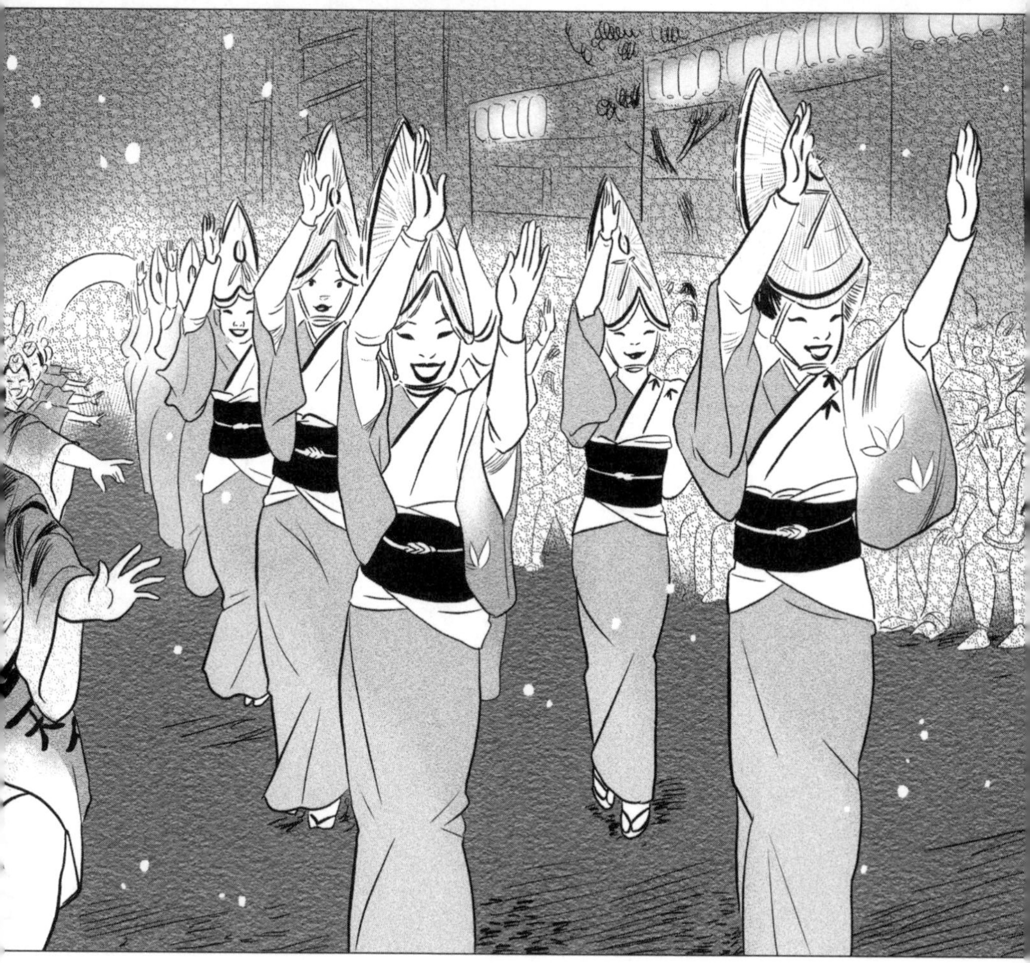

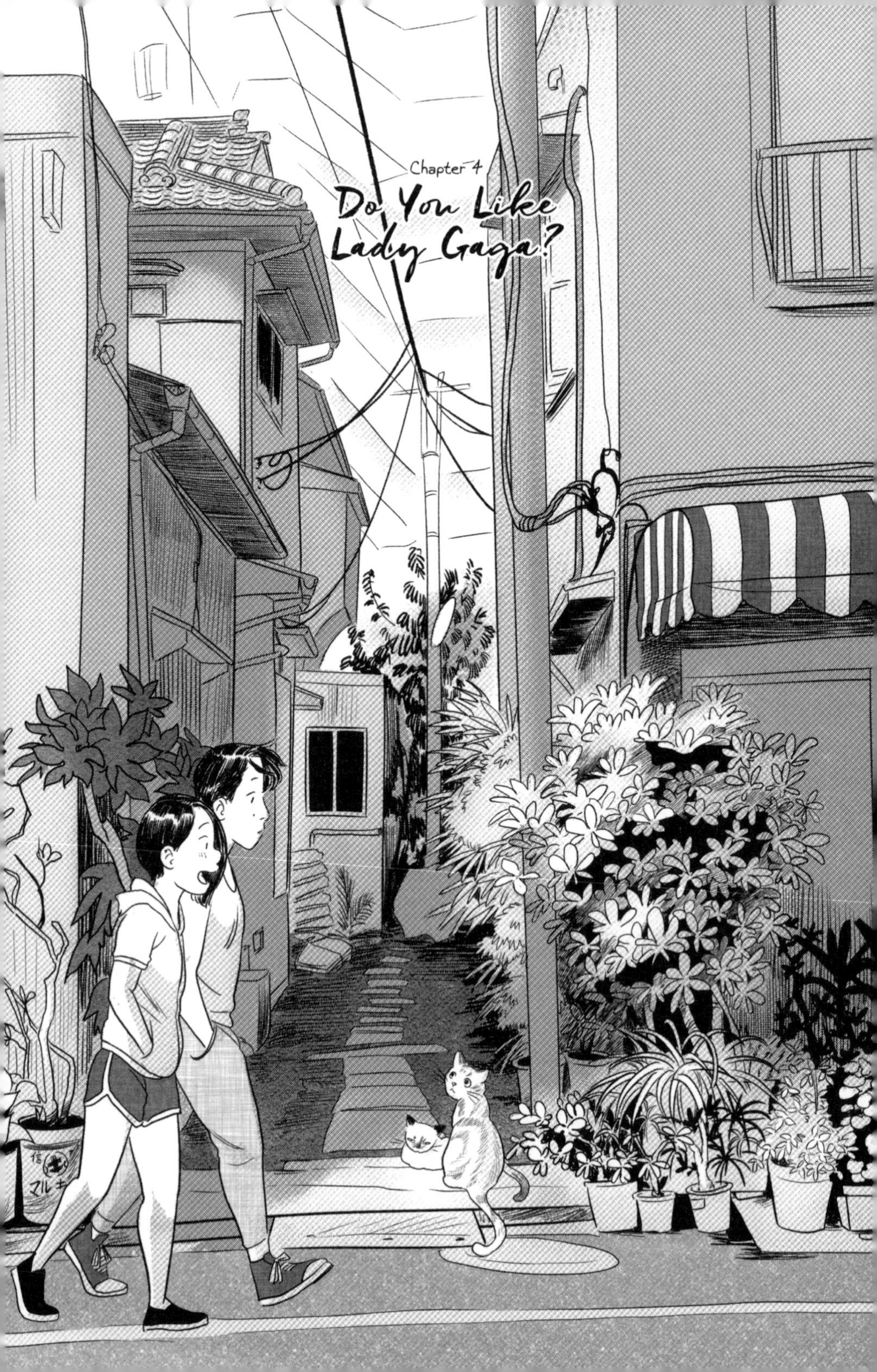
Chapter 4
Do You Like Lady Gaga?

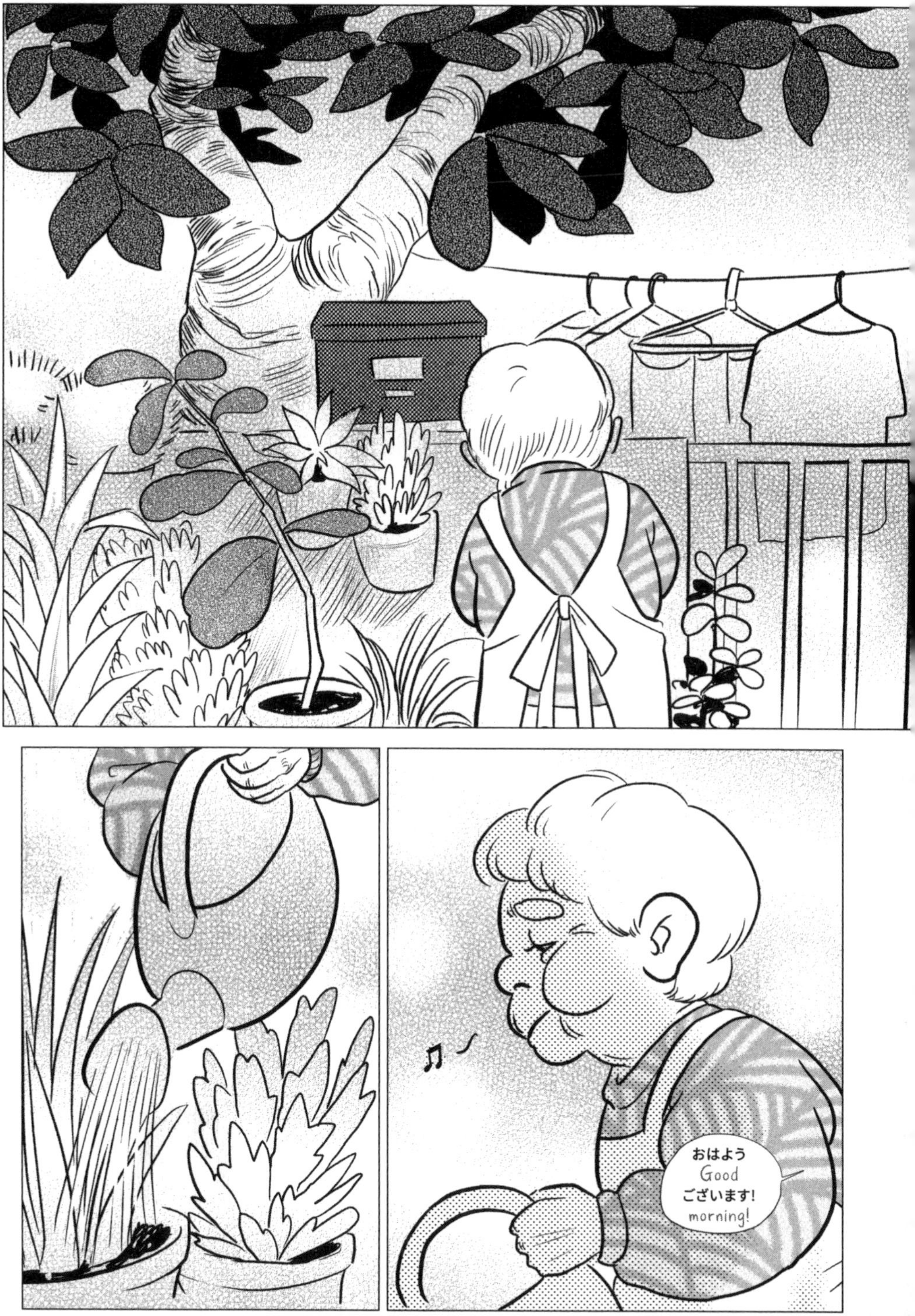
おはよう
Good
ございます!
morning!

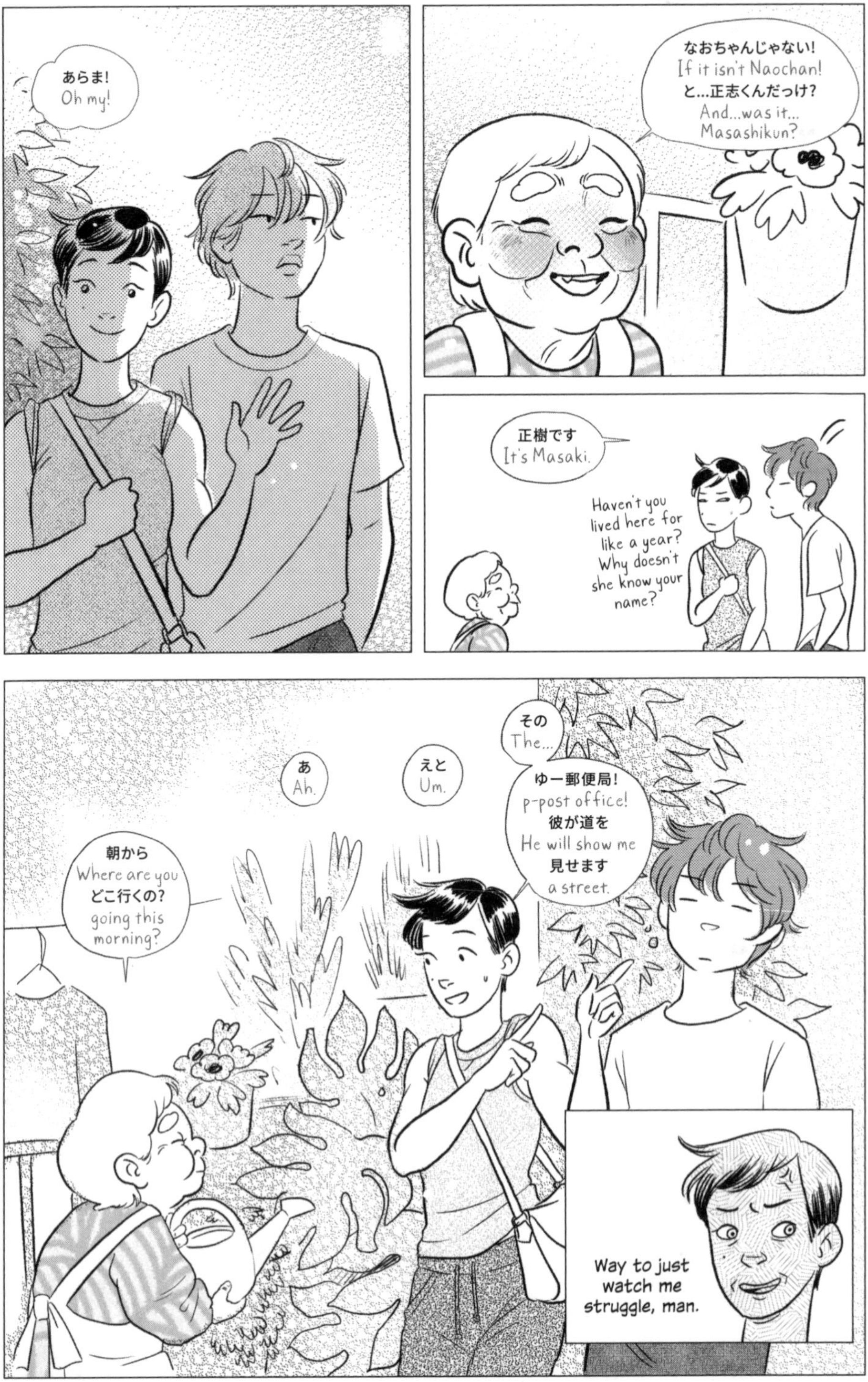
あらま!
Oh my!
なおちゃんじゃない!
If it isn't Naochan!
と…正志くんだっけ?
And...was it... Masashikun?
正樹です
It's Masaki.
Haven't you lived here for like a year? Why doesn't she know your name?
朝から
Where are you
どこ行くの?
going this morning?
あ
Ah.
えと
Um.
その
The...
ゆー郵便局!
p-post office!
彼が道を
He will show me
見せます
a street.
Way to just watch me struggle, man.

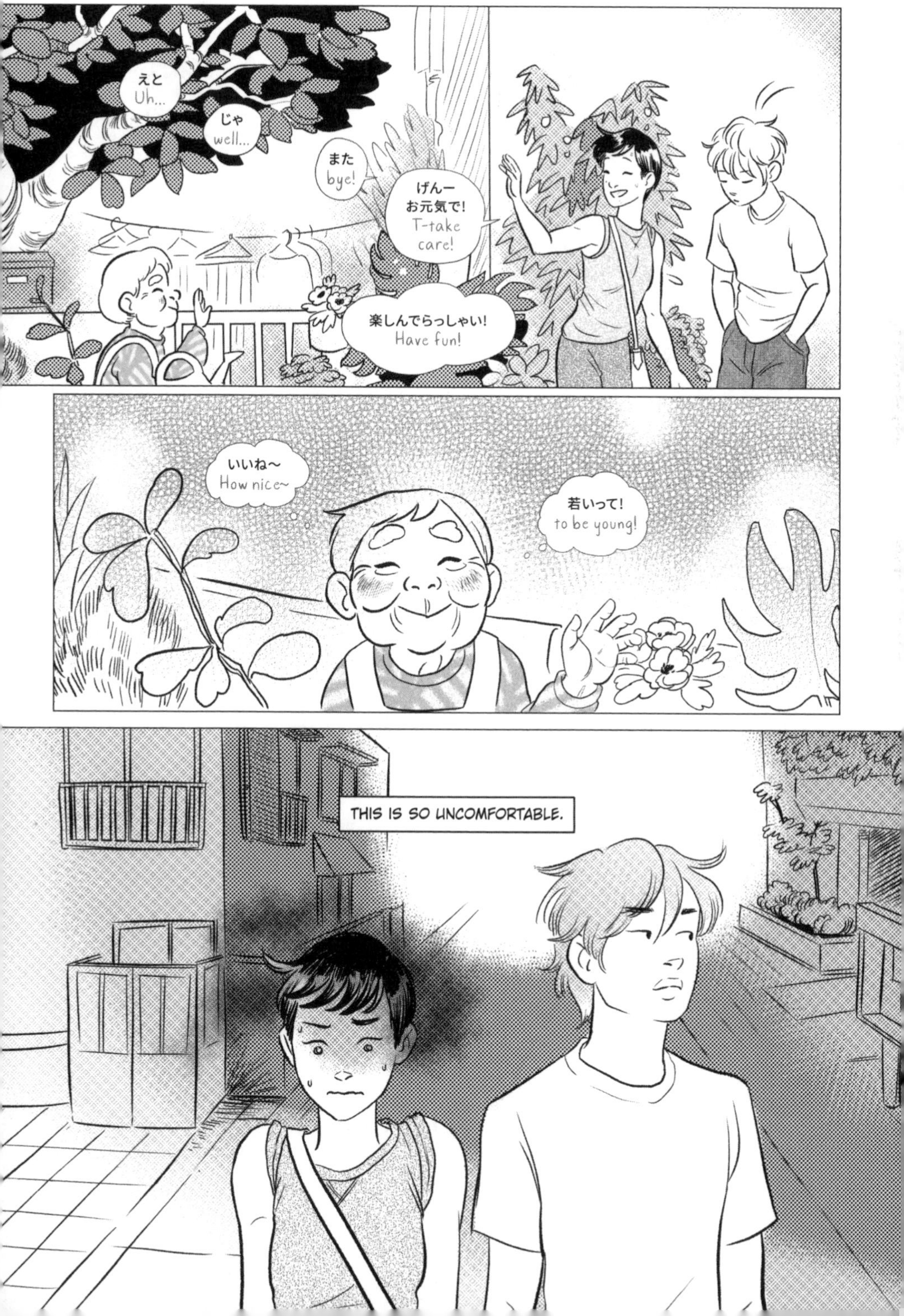

えと
Uh...
じゃ
well...
また
bye!
げんー
お元気で!
T-take
care!
楽しんでらっしゃい!
Have fun!
いいね～
How nice~
若いって!
to be young!
THIS IS SO UNCOMFORTABLE.

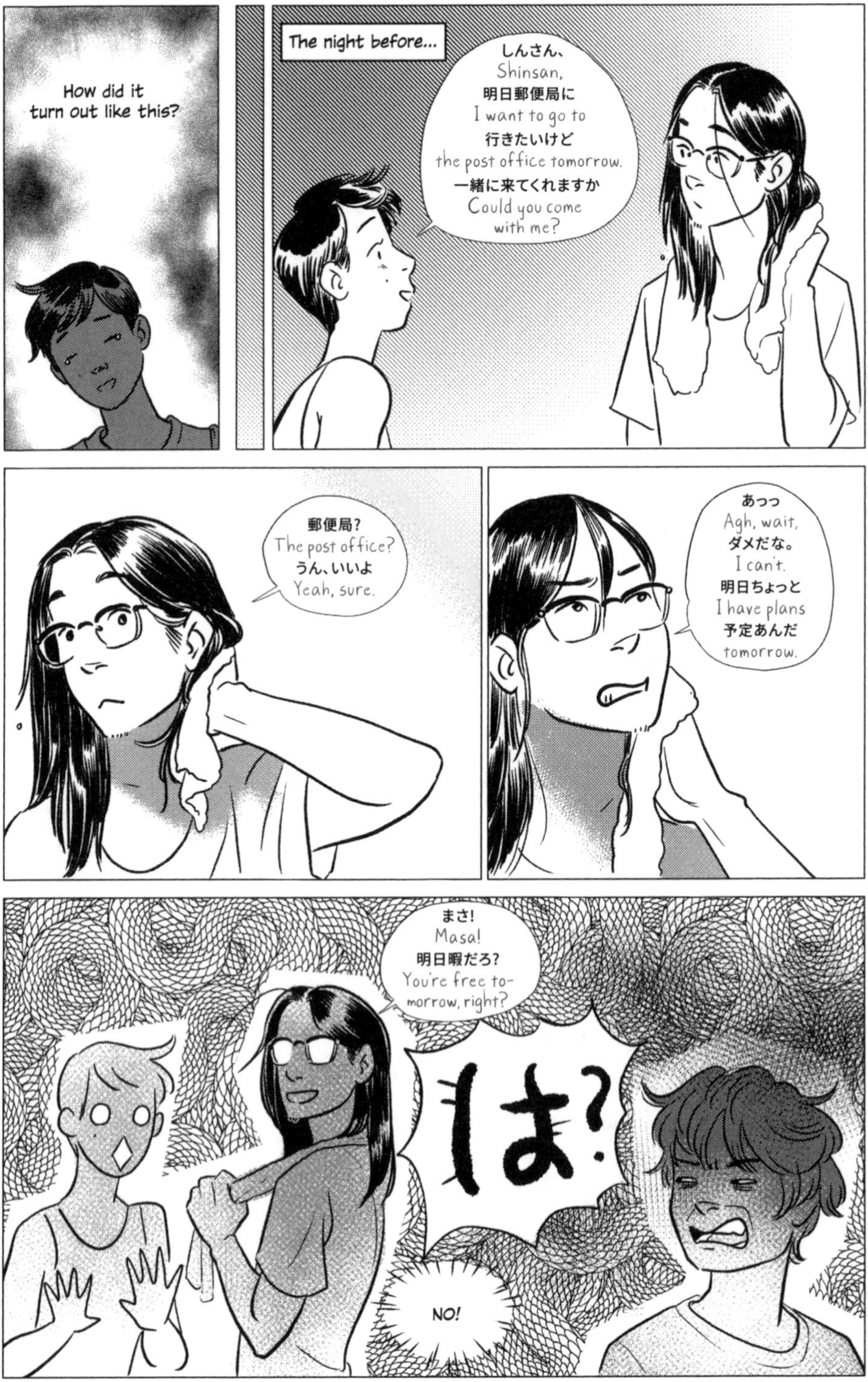
How did it turn out like this?
The night before...
しんさん、 Shinsan, 明日郵便局に I want to go to 行きたいけど the post office tomorrow. 一緒に来てくれますか Could you come with me?
郵便局? The post office? うん、いいよ Yeah, sure.
あっっ Agh, wait, ダメだな。 I can't. 明日ちょっと I have plans 予定あんだ tomorrow.
まさ! Masa! 明日暇だろ? You're free to-morrow, right?
は?
NO!

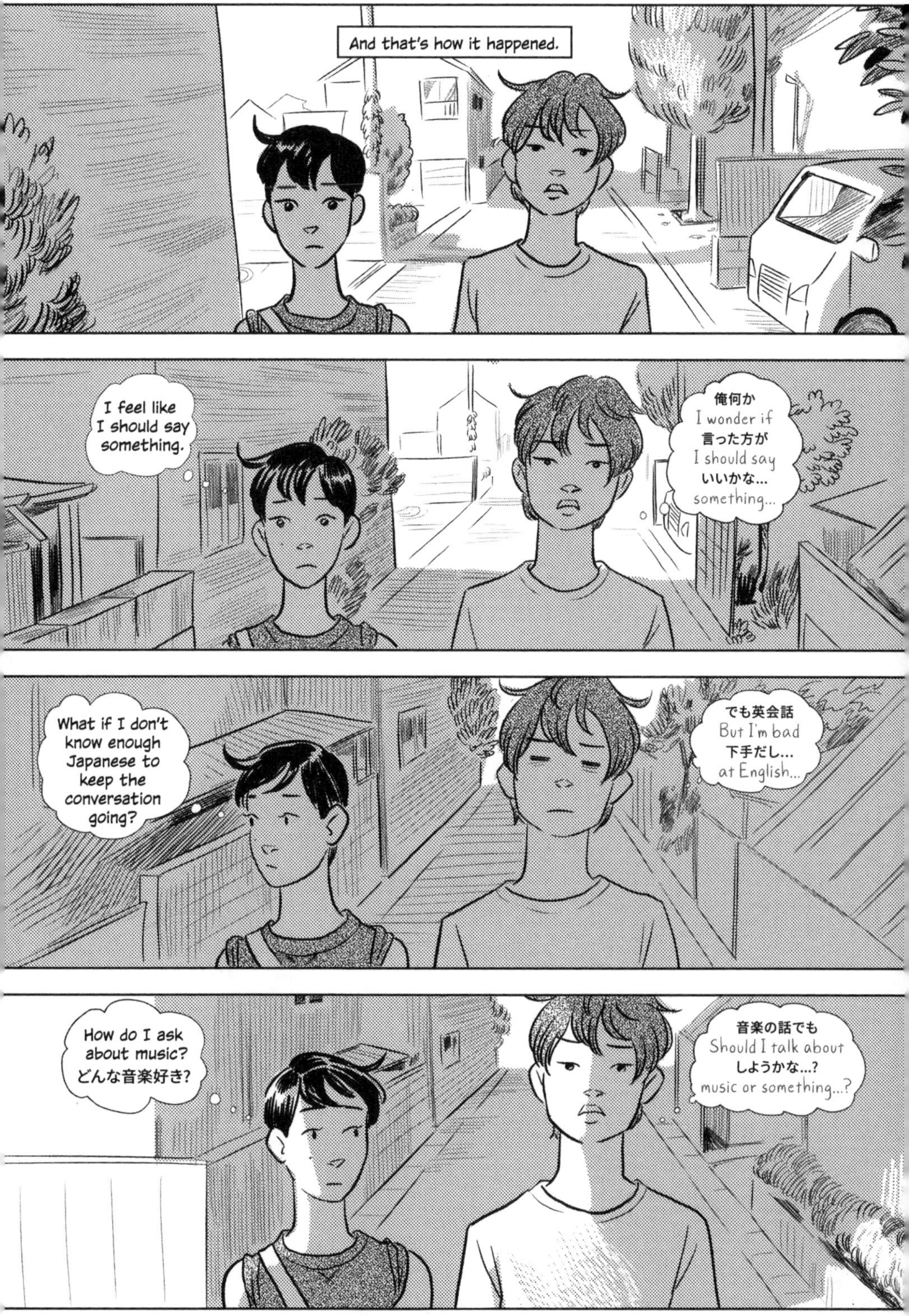

And that's how it happened.
I feel like I should say something.
俺何か I wonder if 言った方が I should say いいかな… something…
What if I don't know enough Japanese to keep the conversation going?
でも英会話 But I'm bad 下手だし… at English…
How do I ask about music? どんな音楽好き?
音楽の話でも Should I talk about しようかな…? music or something…?

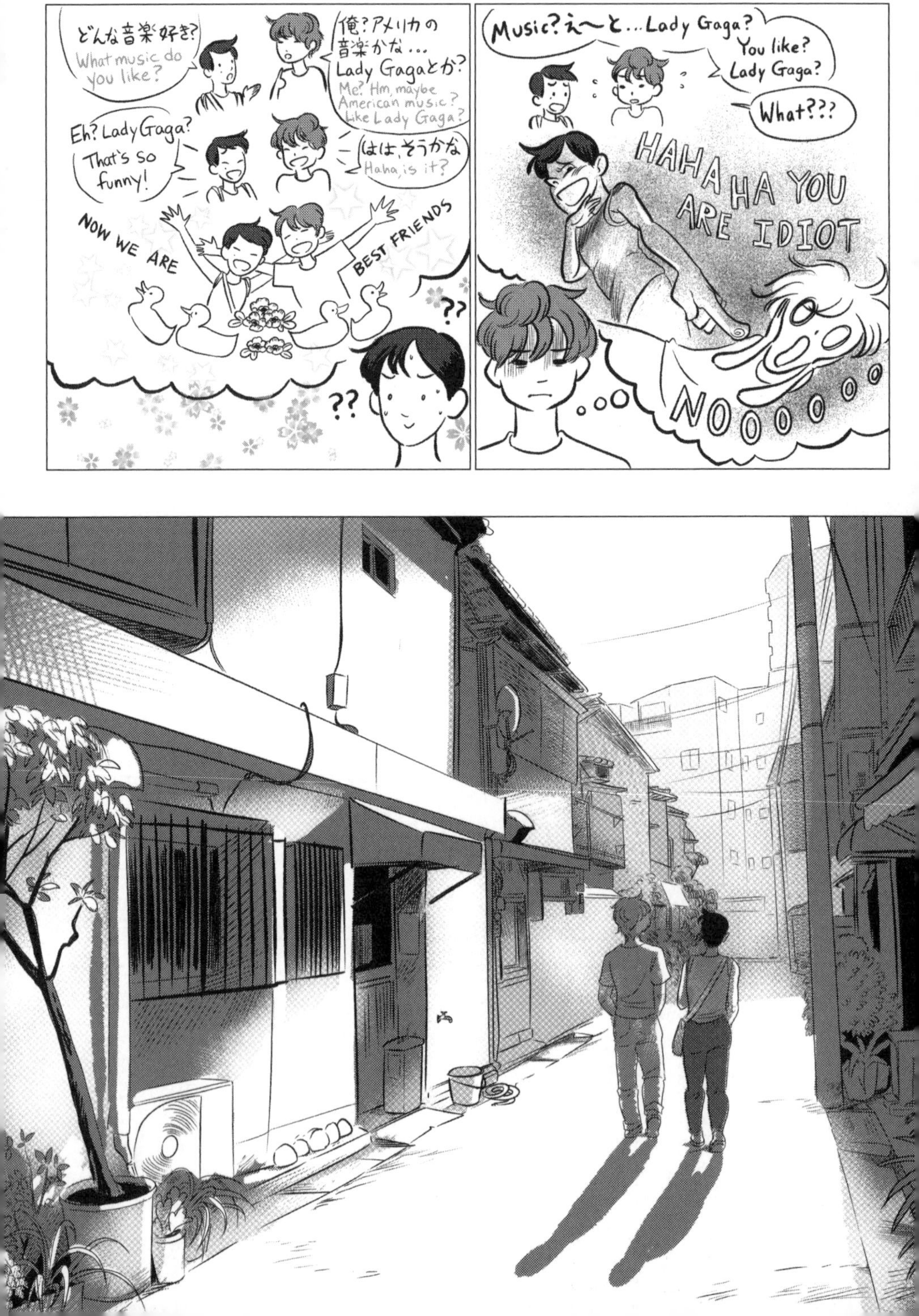

どんな音楽好き?
What music do you like?
俺?アメリカの音楽かな…Lady Gagaとか?
Me? Hm, maybe American music? Like Lady Gaga?
Eh? Lady Gaga? That's so funny!
はは,そうかな
Haha, is it?
NOW WE ARE BEST FRIENDS
??
??
Music?え〜と…Lady Gaga?
You like? Lady Gaga?
What???
HAHAHA YOU ARE IDIOT
NOOOOOOO

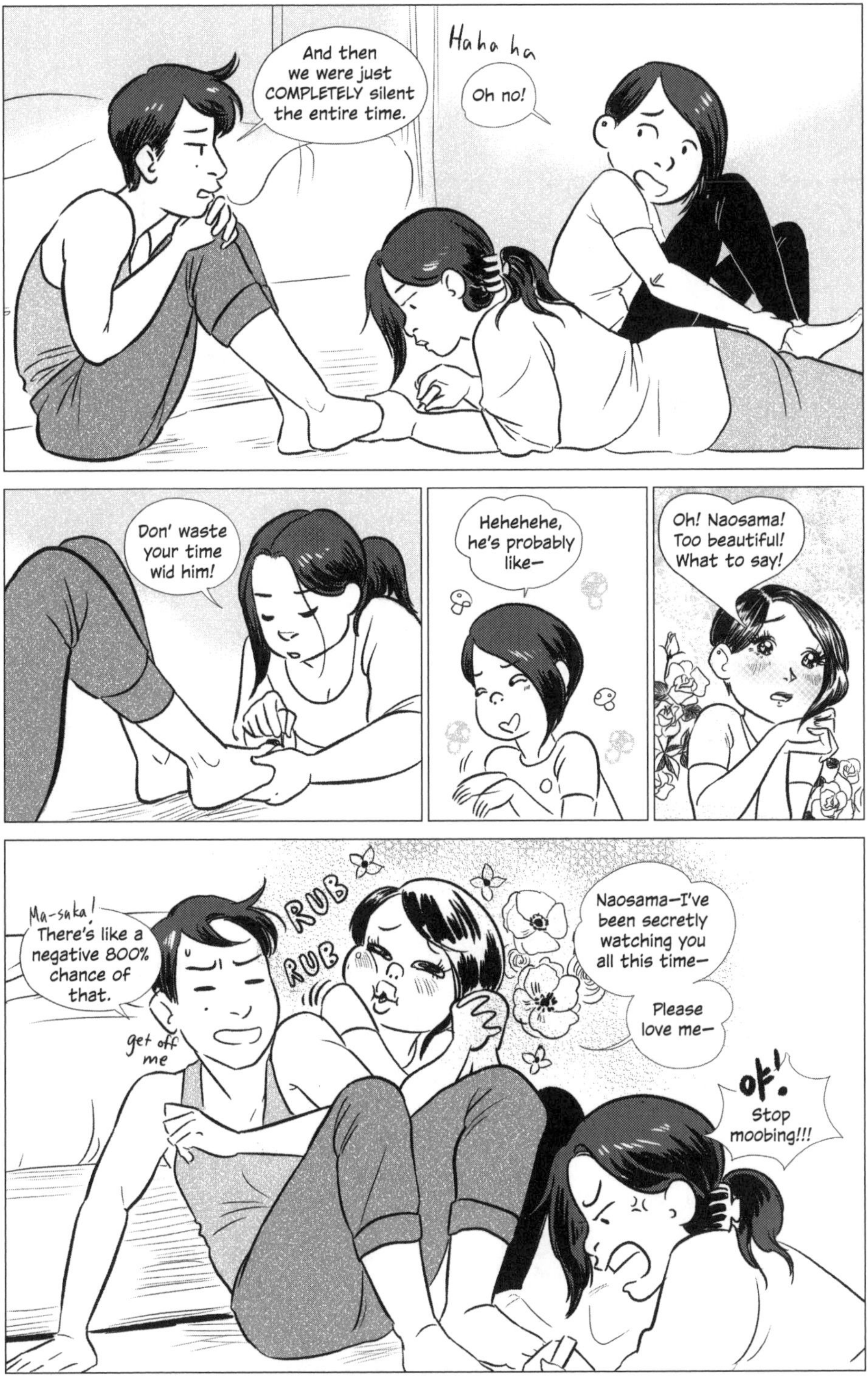
And then we were just COMPLETELY silent the entire time.
Haha ha
Oh no!
Don' waste your time wid him!
Hehehehe, he's probably like—
Oh! Naosama! Too beautiful! What to say!
Ma-saka! There's like a negative 800% chance of that.
get off me
RUB
RUB
Naosama—I've been secretly watching you all this time—
Please love me—
야!
Stop moobing!!!

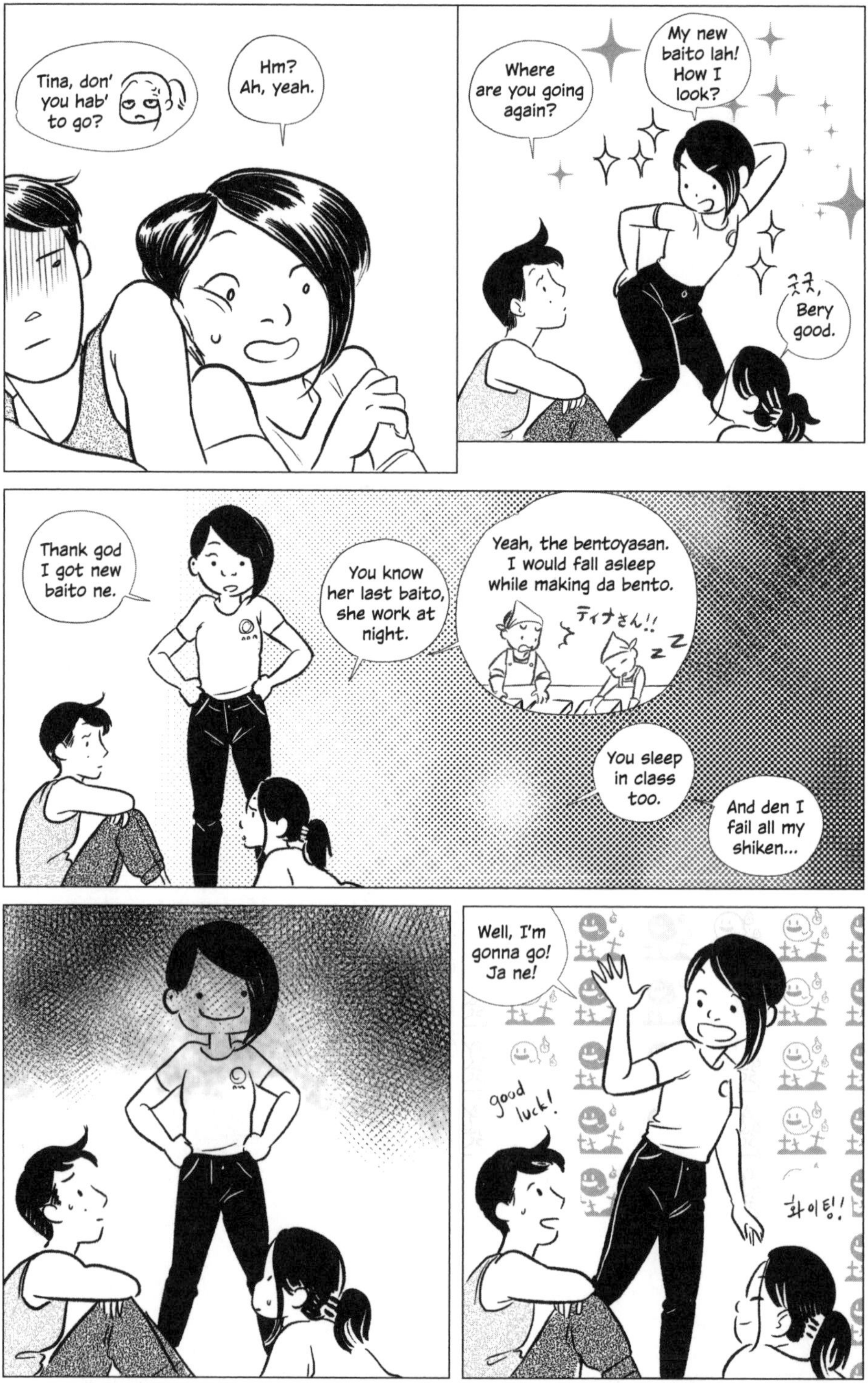
Tina, don' you hab' to go?
Hm? Ah, yeah.
Where are you going again?
My new baito lah! How I look?
굿굿, Bery good.
Thank god I got new baito ne.
You know her last baito, she work at night.
Yeah, the bentoyasan. I would fall asleep while making da bento.
ティナさん!!
z z
You sleep in class too.
And den I fail all my shiken...
Well, I'm gonna go! Ja ne!
good luck!
화이팅!

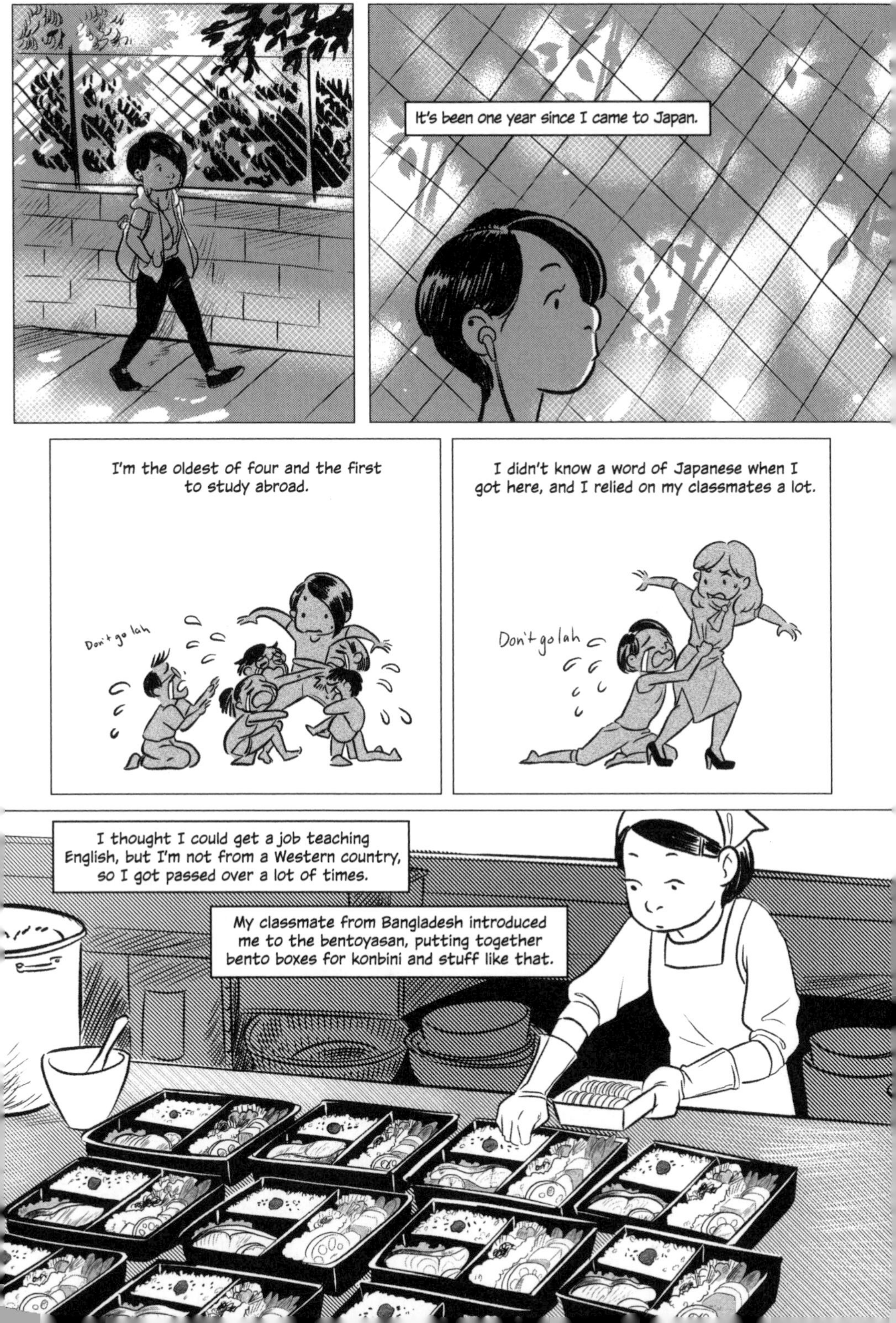
It's been one year since I came to Japan.
I'm the oldest of four and the first to study abroad.
Don't go lah
I didn't know a word of Japanese when I got here, and I relied on my classmates a lot.
Don't go lah
I thought I could get a job teaching English, but I'm not from a Western country, so I got passed over a lot of times.
My classmate from Bangladesh introduced me to the bentoyasan, putting together bento boxes for konbini and stuff like that.

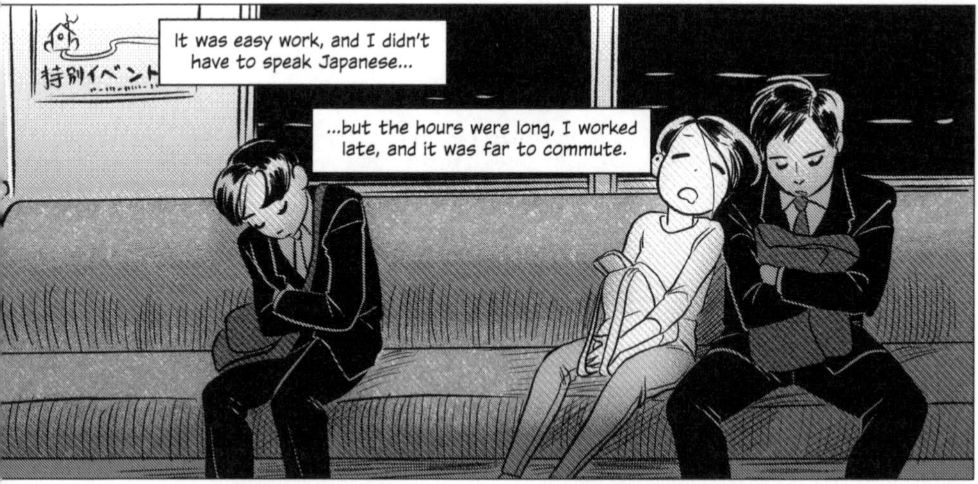
It was easy work, and I didn't have to speak Japanese...
...but the hours were long, I worked late, and it was far to commute.

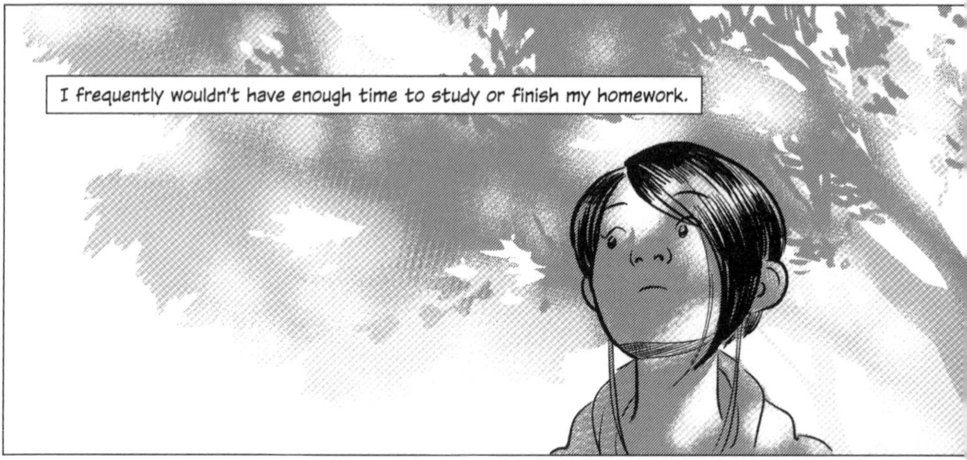
I frequently wouldn't have enough time to study or finish my homework.

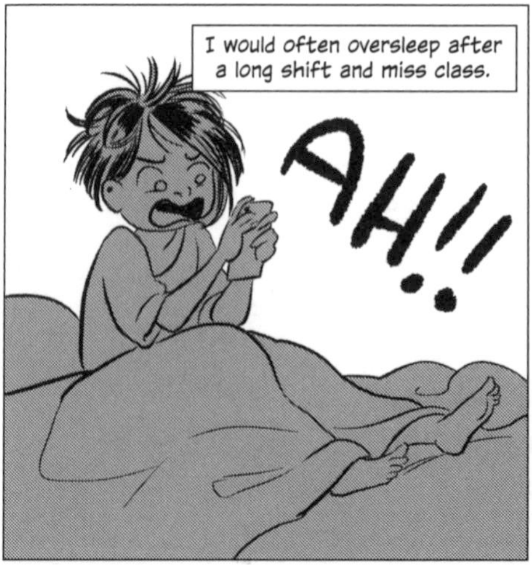
I would often oversleep after a long shift and miss class.
AH!!

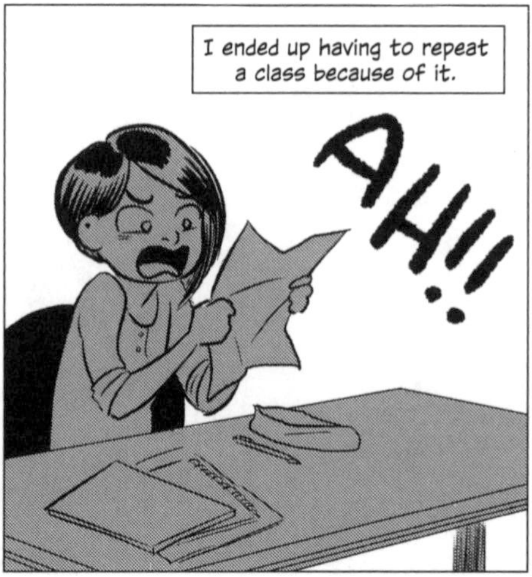
I ended up having to repeat a class because of it.
AH!!

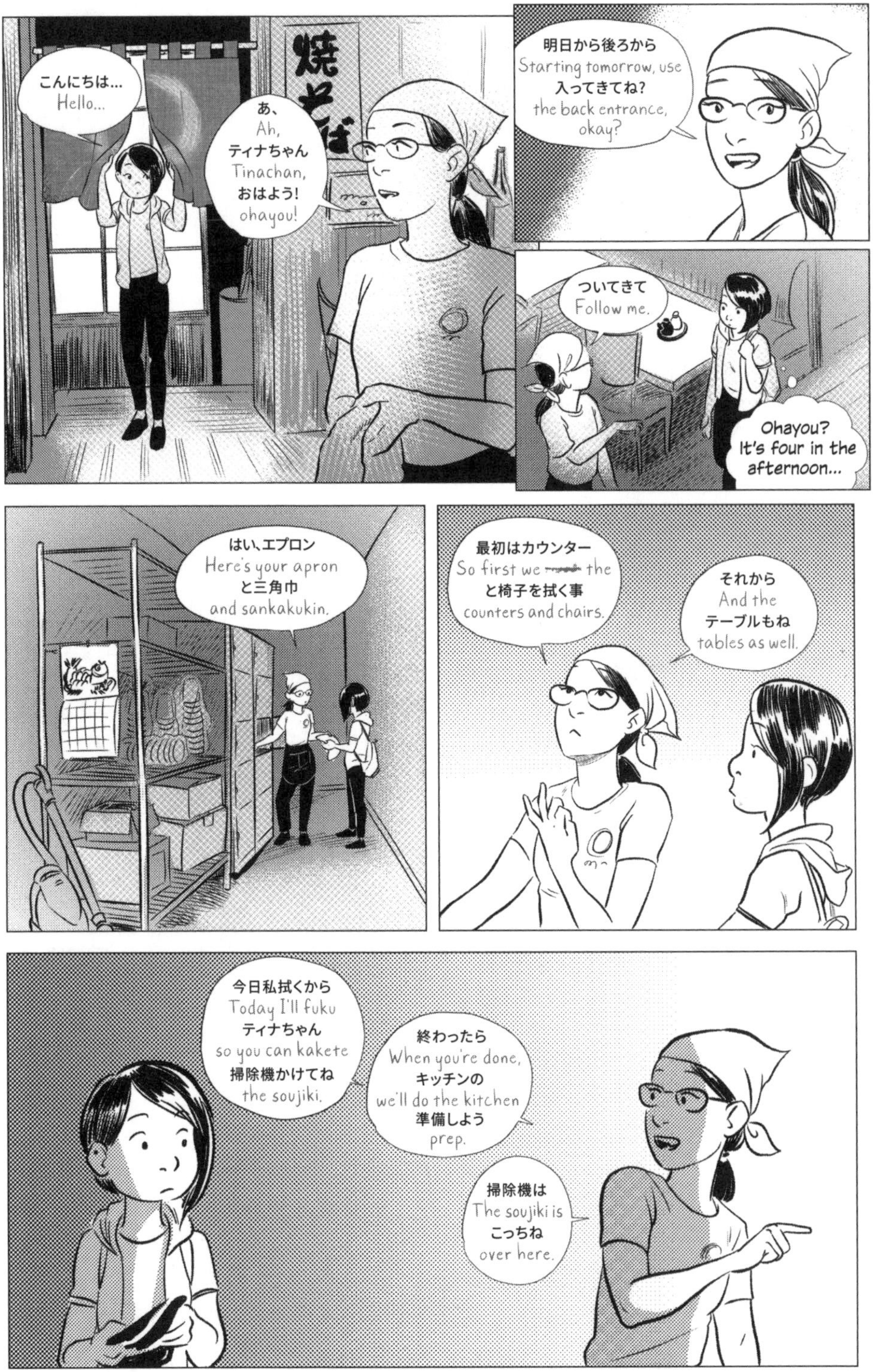

こんにちは… Hello...
あ、 Ah, ティナちゃん Tinachan, おはよう! ohayou!
明日から後ろから Starting tomorrow, use 入ってきてね? the back entrance, okay?
ついてきて Follow me.
Ohayou? It's four in the afternoon...
はい、エプロン Here's your apron と三角巾 and sankakukin.
最初はカウンター So first we the と椅子を拭く事 counters and chairs.
それから And the テーブルもね tables as well.
今日私拭くから Today I'll fuku ティナちゃん so you can kakete 掃除機かけてね the soujiki.
終わったら When you're done, キッチンの we'll do the kitchen 準備しよう prep.
掃除機は The soujiki is こっちね over here.

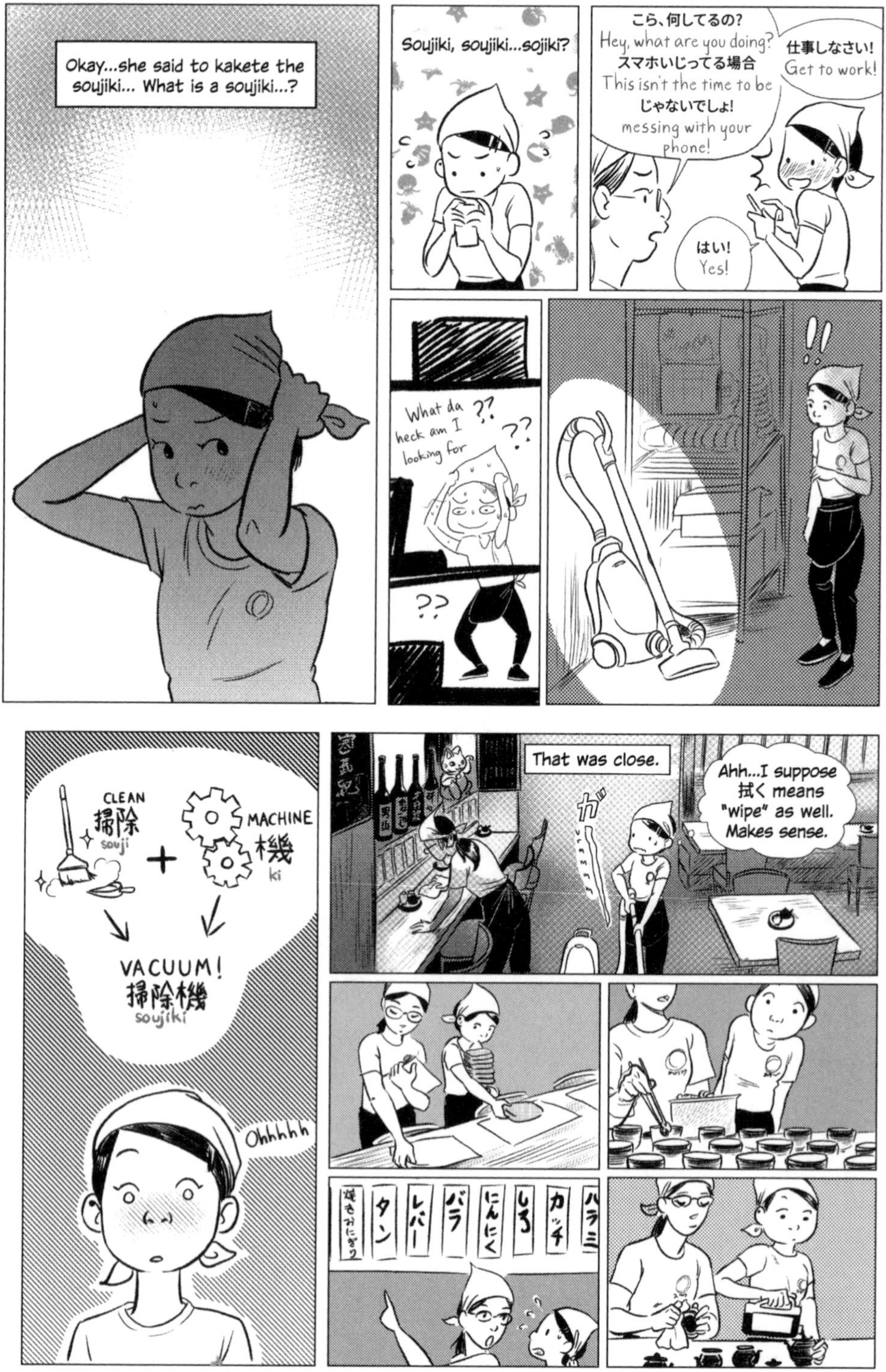
Okay...she said to kakete the soujiki... What is a soujiki...?
Soujiki, soujiki...sojiki?
こら、何してるの?
Hey, what are you doing?
スマホいじってる場合じゃないでしょ!
This isn't the time to be messing with your phone!
仕事しなさい!
Get to work!
はい!
Yes!
What da heck am I looking for
??
??
??
!!
CLEAN
掃除
souji
+
MACHINE
機
ki
VACUUM!
掃除機
soujiki
Ohhhhh
That was close.
Ahh...I suppose 拭く means "wipe" as well. Makes sense.
ハラミ
カッチ
しろ
にんにく
バラ
レバー
タン
焼きおにぎり

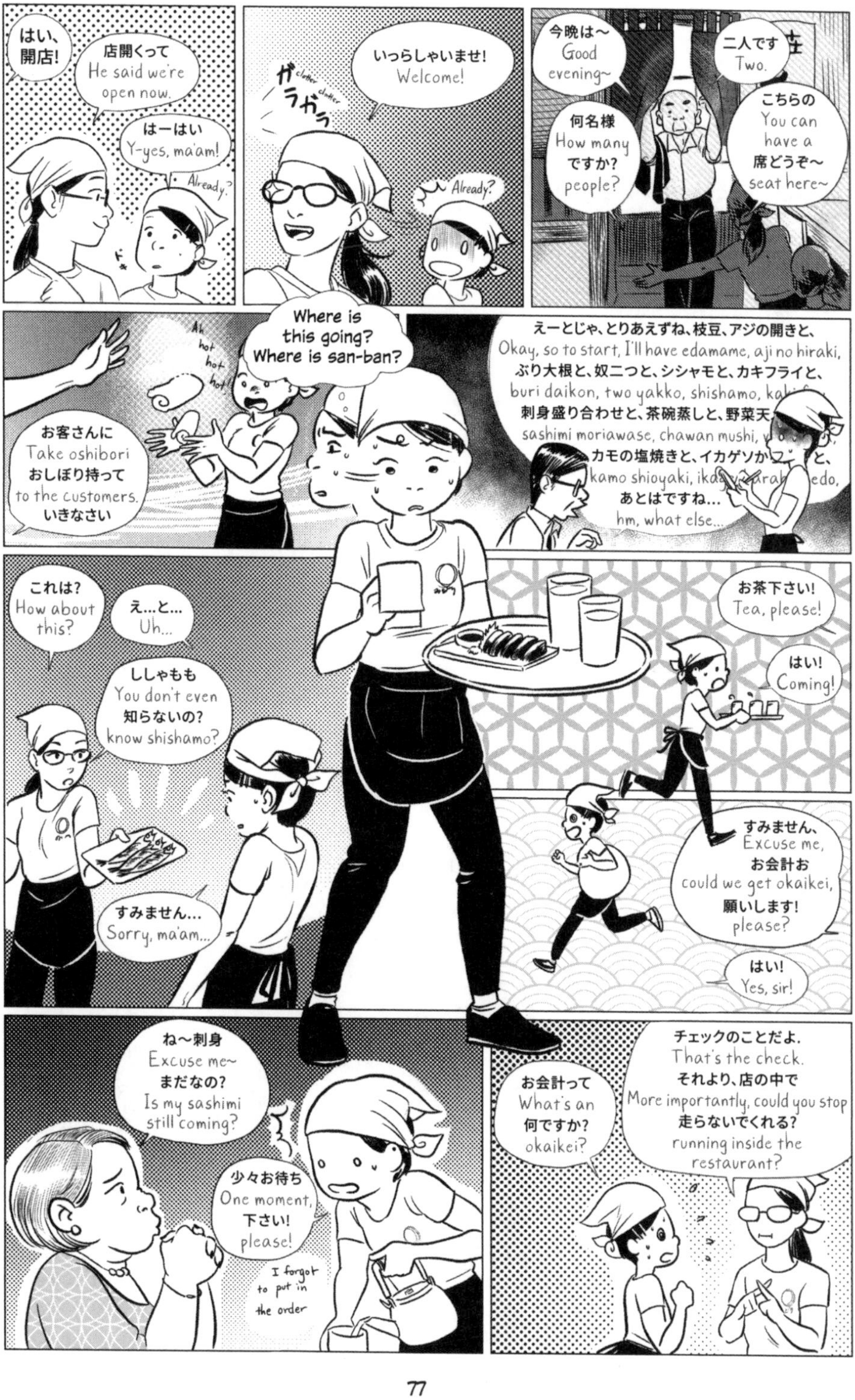

はい、開店!
店開くって
He said we're open now.
はーはい
Y-yes, ma'am!
Already?
いっらしゃいませ!
Welcome!
ガラガラ
clatter clatter
Already?
今晩は~
Good evening~
二人です
Two.
何名様ですか?
How many people?
こちらの席どうぞ~
You can have a seat here~
Ah hot hot hot!
お客さんにおしぼり持っていきなさい
Take oshibori to the customers.
Where is this going? Where is san-ban?
えーとじゃ、とりあえずね、枝豆、アジの開きと、
Okay, so to start, I'll have edamame, aji no hiraki,
ぶり大根と、奴二つと、シシャモと、カキフライと、
buri daikon, two yakko, shishamo,
刺身盛り合わせと、茶碗蒸しと、野菜天、
sashimi moriawase, chawan mushi,
カモの塩焼きと、イカゲソか
kamo shioyaki,
あとはですね…
hm, what else...
これは?
How about this?
え…と…
Uh...
ししゃもも知らないの?
You don't even know shishamo?
すみません…
Sorry, ma'am...
お茶下さい!
Tea, please!
はい!
Coming!
すみません、お会計お願いします!
Excuse me, could we get okaikei, please?
はい!
Yes, sir!
ね~刺身まだなの?
Excuse me~ Is my sashimi still coming?
少々お待ち下さい!
One moment, please!
I forgot to put in the order
お会計って何ですか?
What's an okaikei?
チェックのことだよ.
That's the check.
それより、店の中で走らないでくれる?
More importantly, could you stop running inside the restaurant?

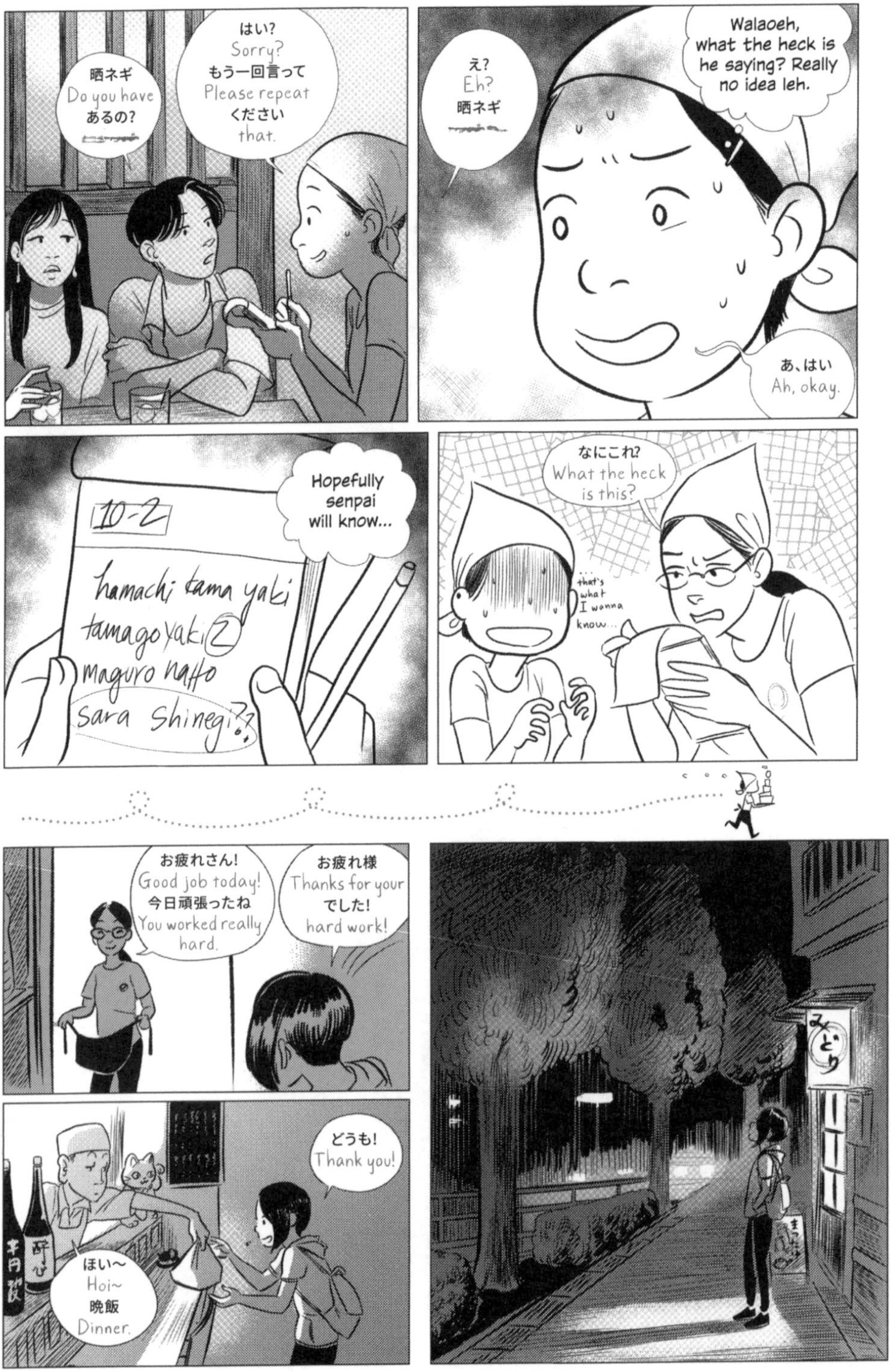

晒ネギ
Do you have
あるの?
はい?
Sorry?
もう一回言って
Please repeat
ください
that.
え?
Eh?
晒ネギ
Walaoeh, what the heck is he saying? Really no idea leh.
あ、はい
Ah, okay.
10-2
hamachi tama yaki
tamago yaki 2
maguro natto
sara shinegi???
Hopefully senpai will know...
なにこれ?
What the heck is this?
...that's what I wanna know...
お疲れさん!
Good job today!
今日頑張ったね
You worked really hard.
お疲れ様
Thanks for your
でした!
hard work!
どうも!
Thank you!
ほい~
Hoi~
晩飯
Dinner.

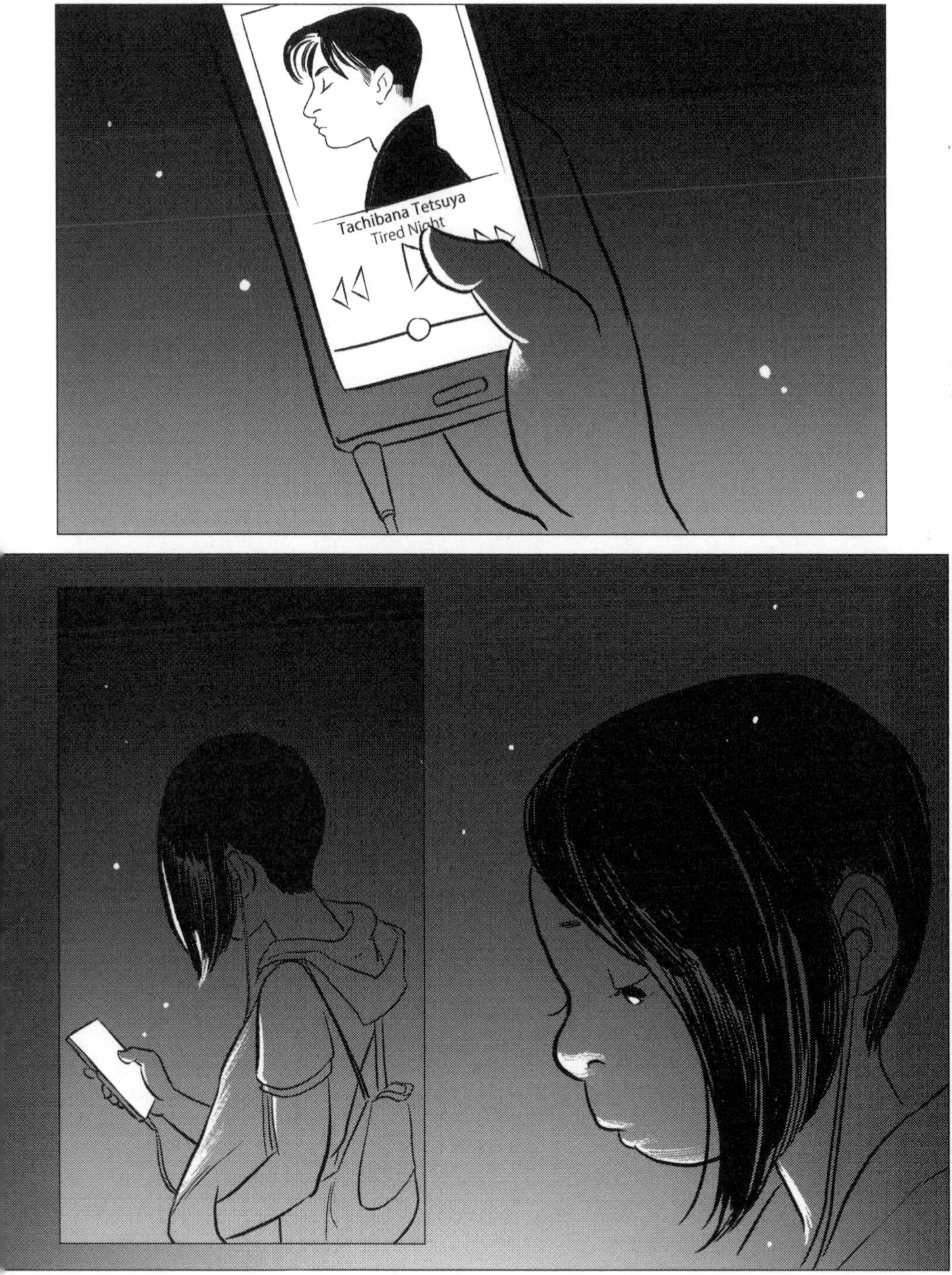
Tachibana Tetsuya
Tired Night

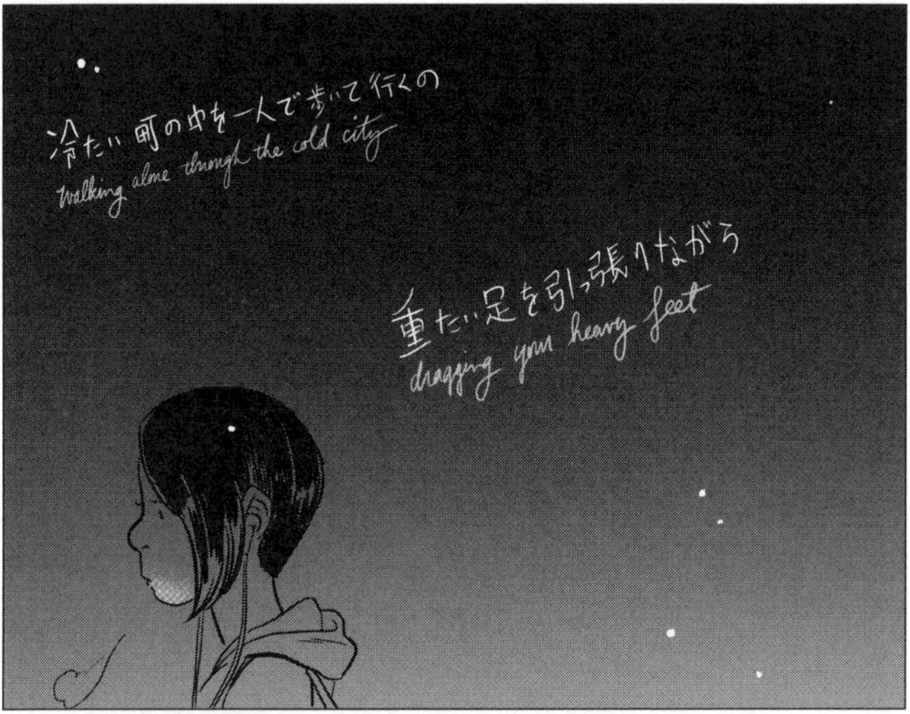
冷たい町の中を一人で歩いて行くの
Walking alone through the cold city
重たい足を引っ張りながら
dragging your heavy feet

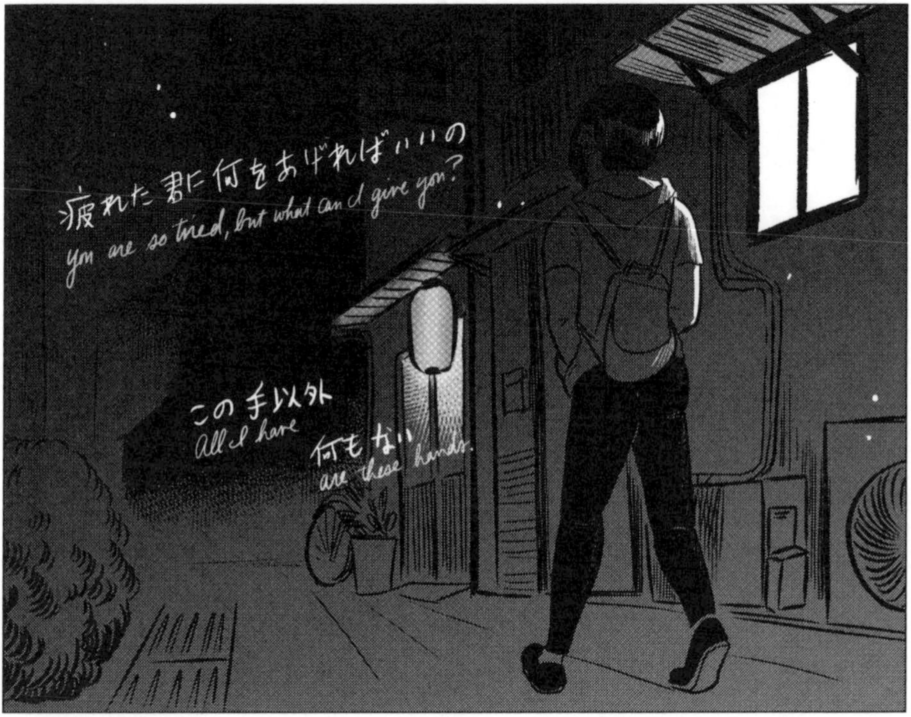
疲れた君に何をあげればいいの
You are so tired, but what can I give you?
この手以外
All I have
何もない
are these hands.

Chapter 5

Appa

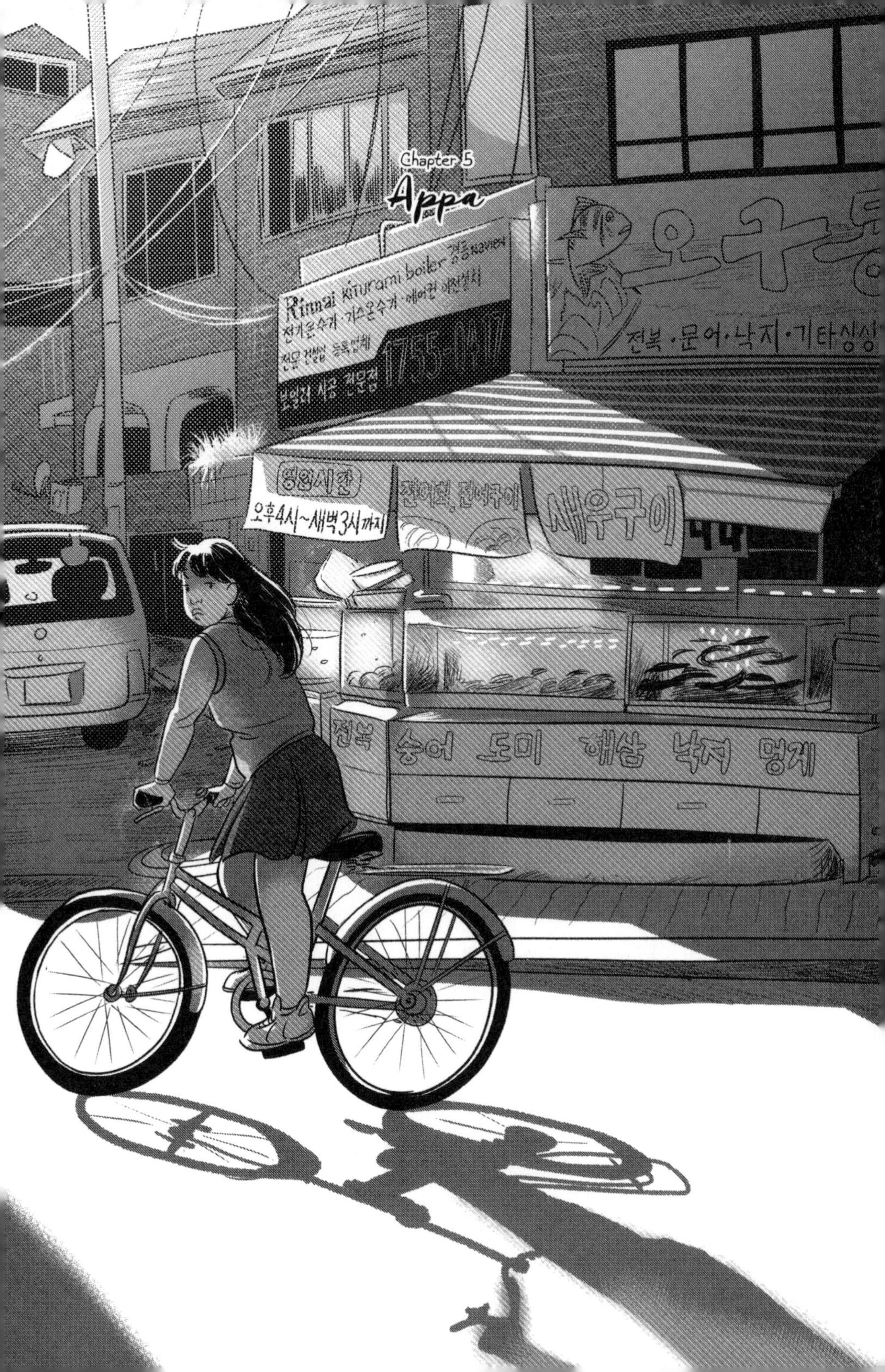
Rinnai kiturami boiler
오후4시~새벽3시까지
새우구이
전복 · 문어 · 낙지 · 기타싱싱
전복
숭어 도미 해삼 낙지 멍게

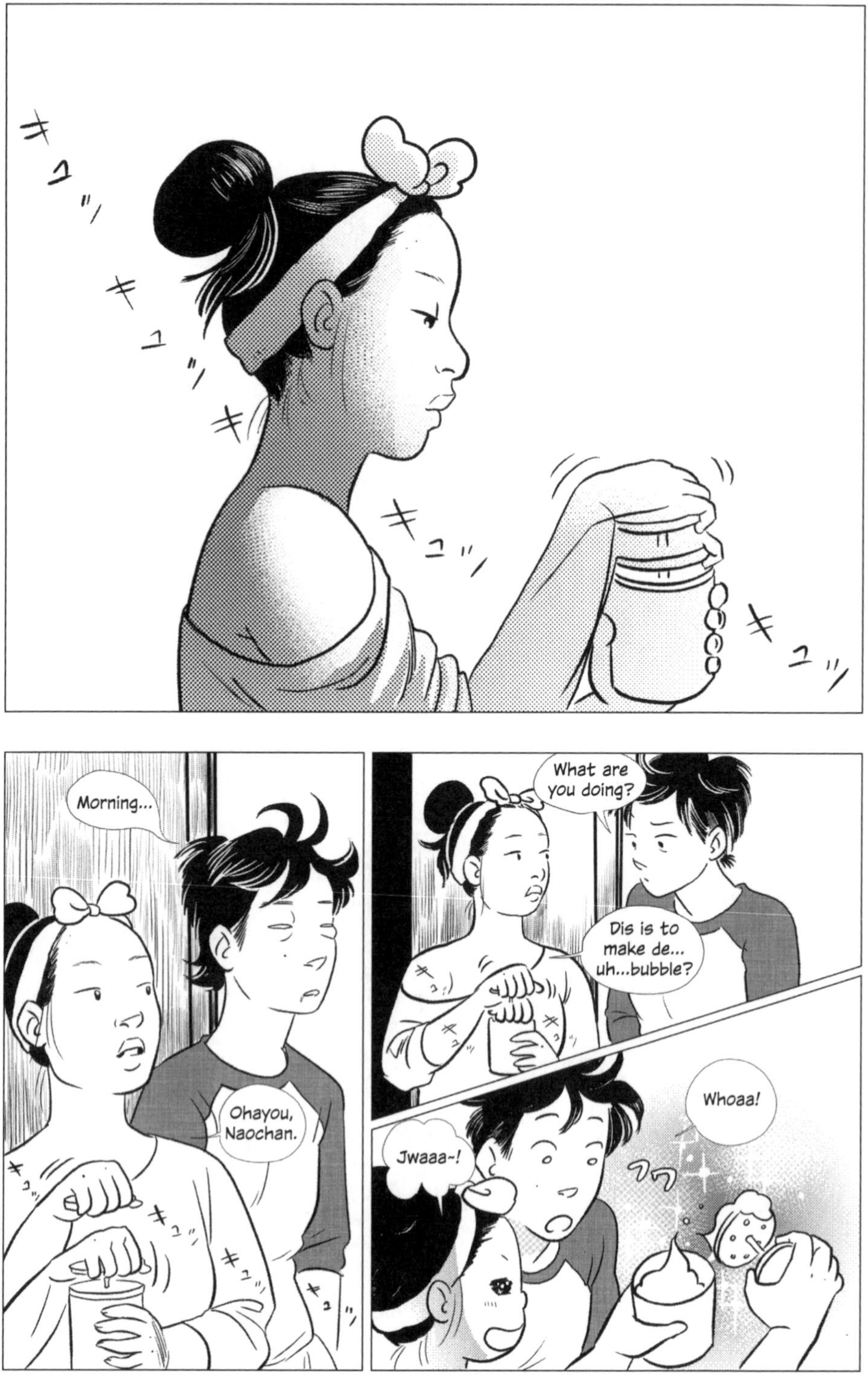
キュッ
キュッ
キュッ
キュッ
キュッ
Morning...
Ohayou, Naochan.
キュッ
キュッ
キュッ
キュッ
What are you doing?
Dis is to make de... uh...bubble?
Whoaa!
Jwaaa~!
フワ

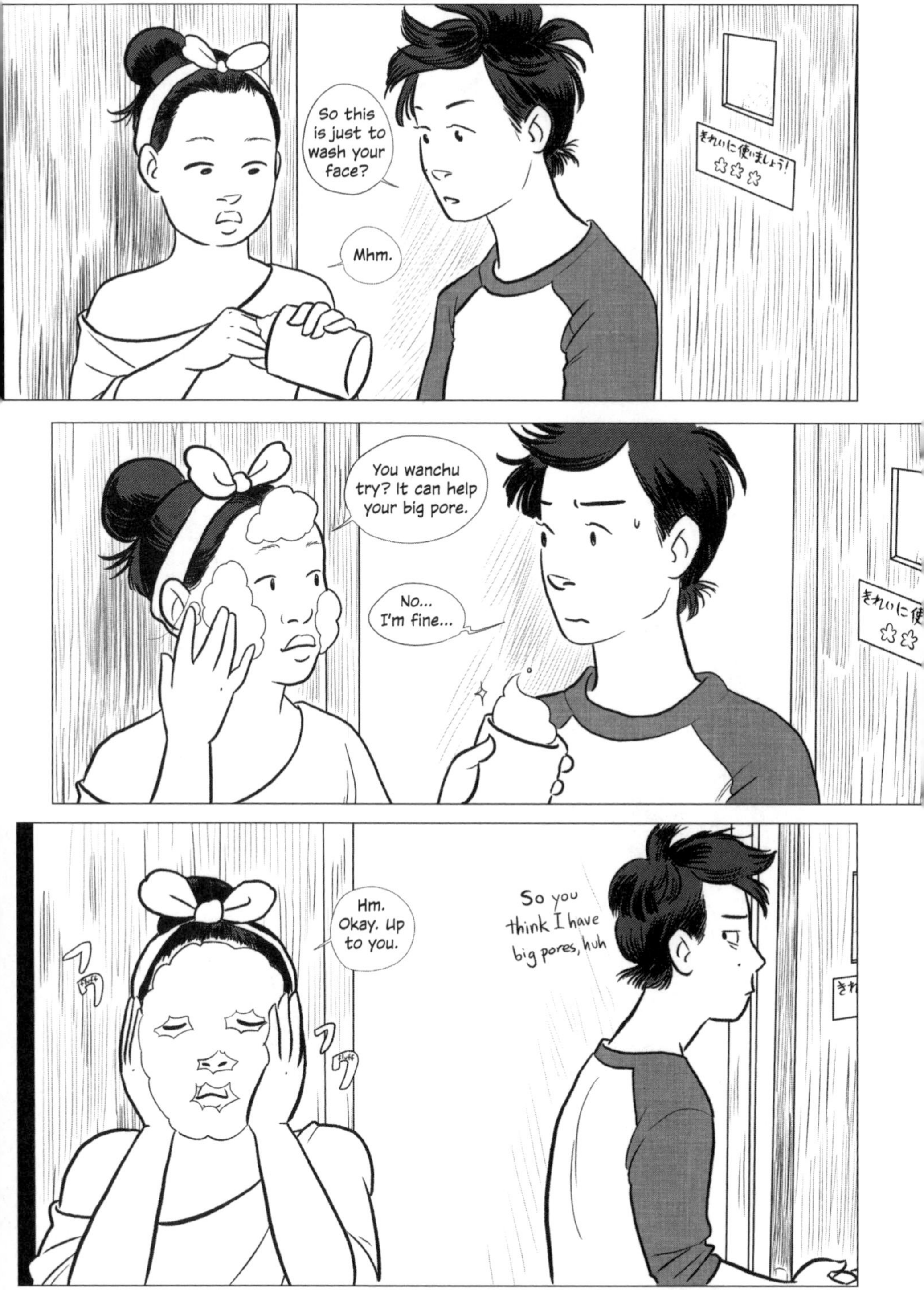
So this is just to wash your face?
Mhm.
きれいに使いましょう!
You wanchu try? It can help your big pore.
No... I'm fine...
Hm. Okay. Up to you.
fluff
fluff
So you think I have big pores, huh

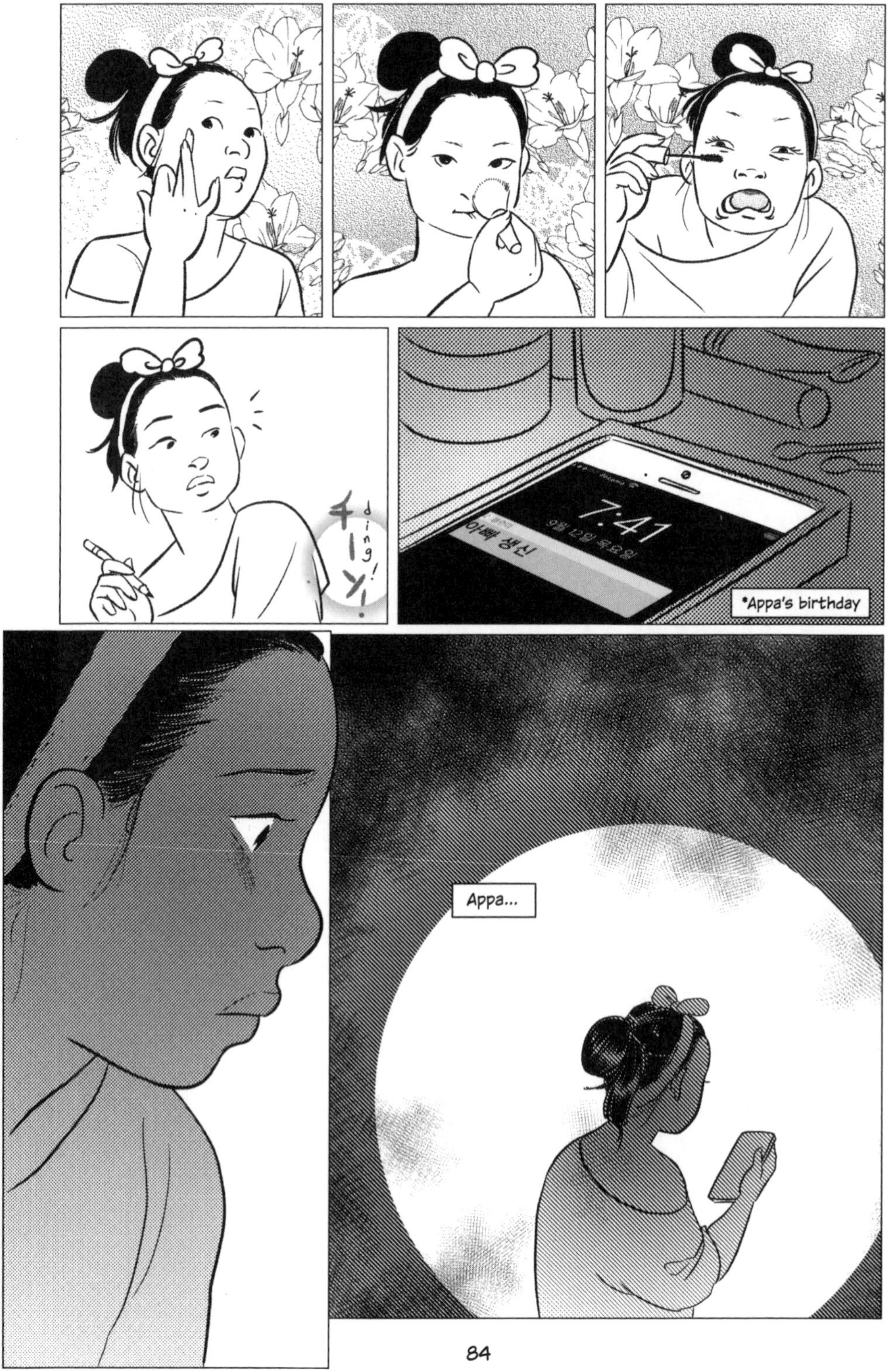
ding!
チーン!
7:41
아빠 생신
*Appa's birthday
Appa...

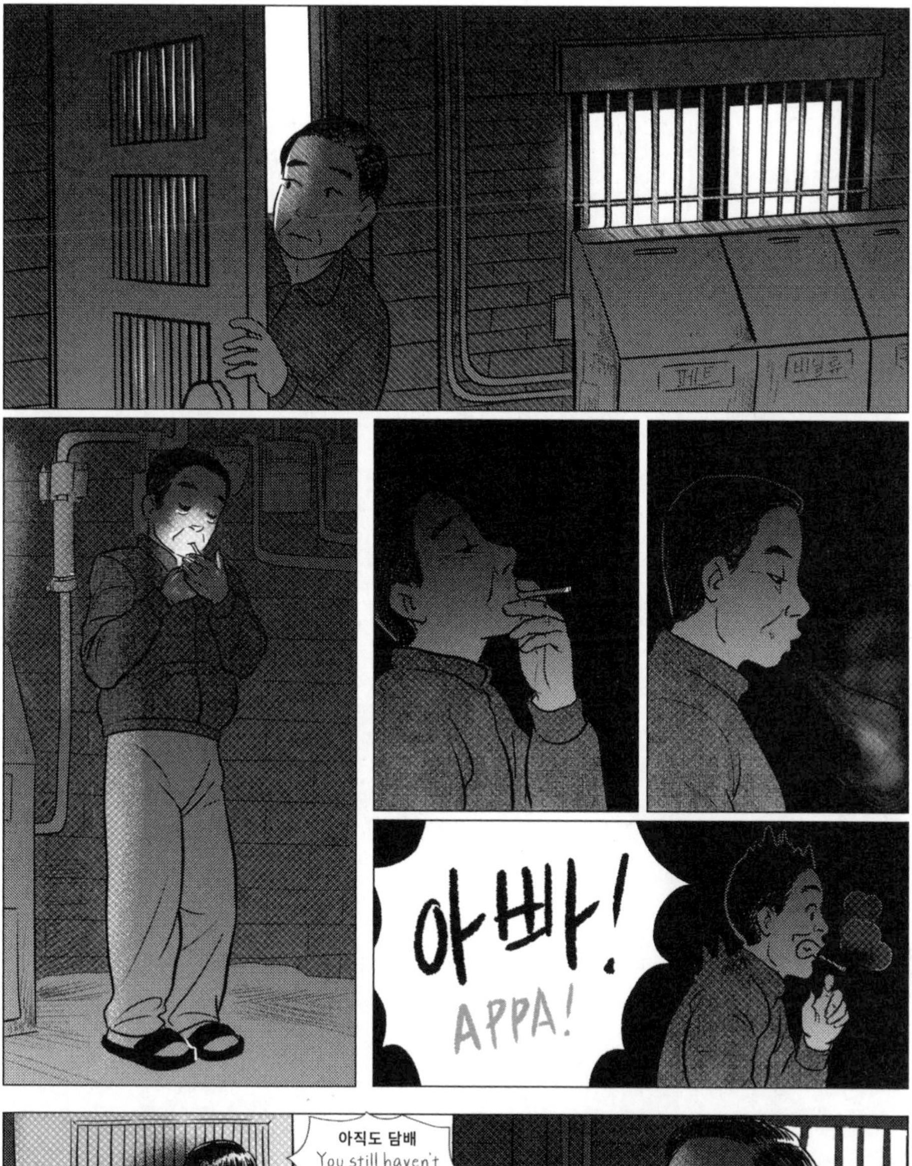

비닐류
아빠!
APPA!
아직도 담배
You still haven't
안 끊었어???
quit smoking???
어, 혜정아!
Oh, Hyejung-ah!

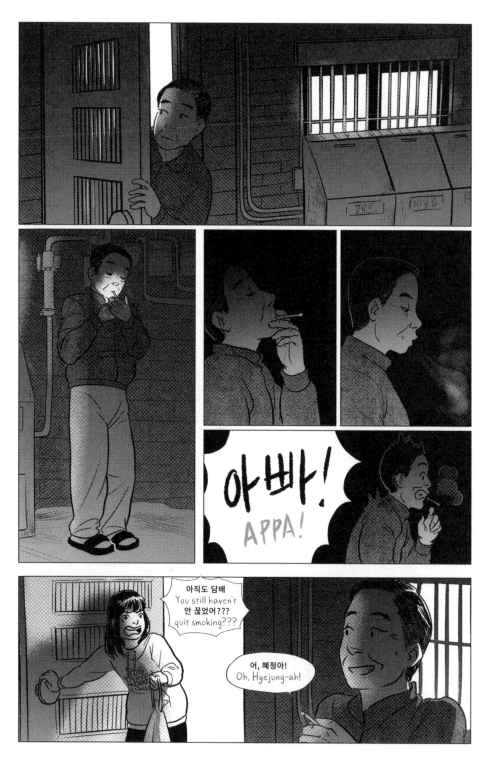

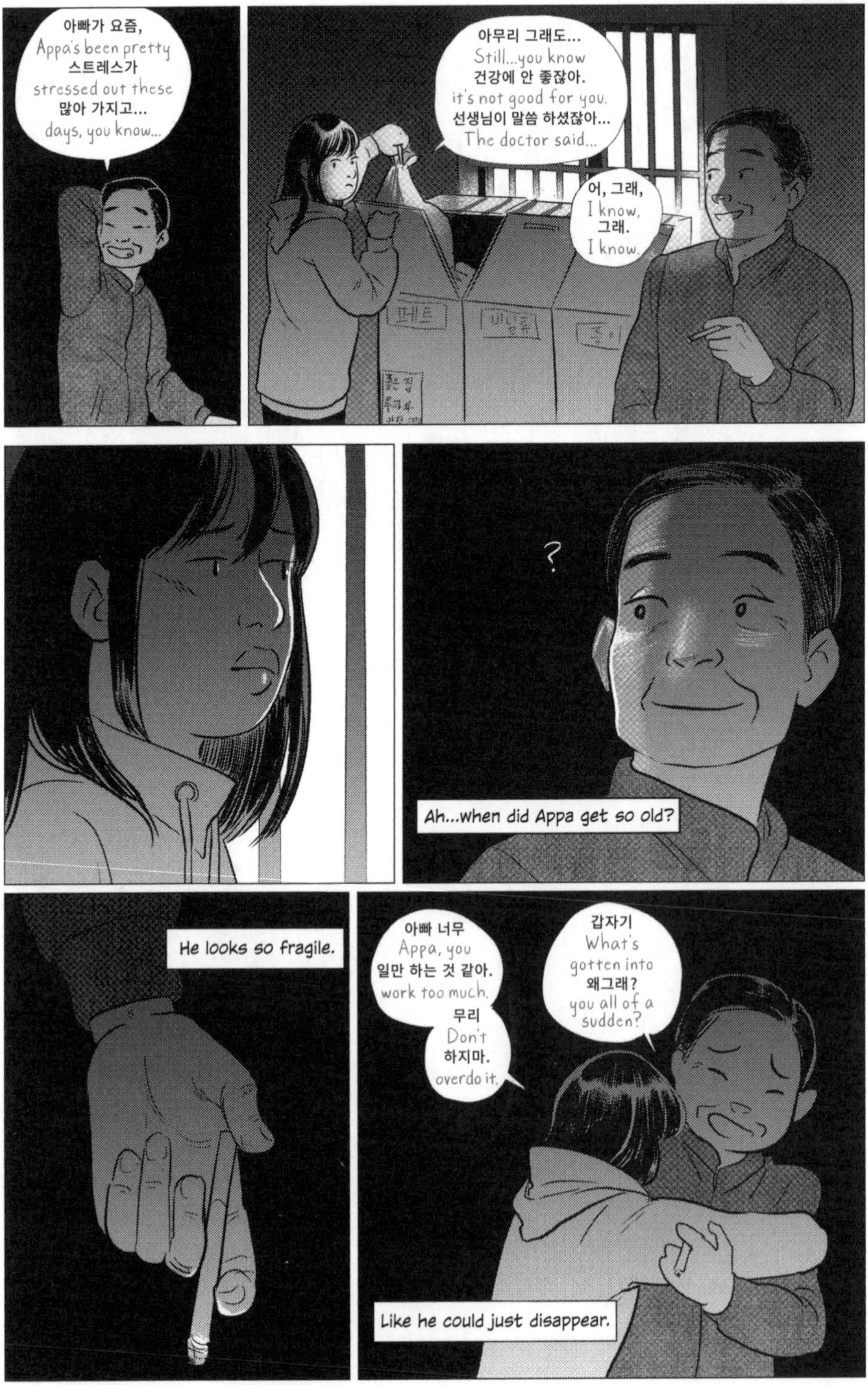
아빠가 요즘, Appa's been pretty 스트레스가 stressed out these 많아 가지고... days, you know...
아무리 그래도... Still...you know 건강에 안 좋잖아. it's not good for you. 선생님이 말씀 하셨잖아... The doctor said...
어, 그래, I know, 그래. I know.
?
Ah...when did Appa get so old?
He looks so fragile.
아빠 너무 Appa, you 일만 하는 것 같아. work too much. 무리 Don't 하지마. overdo it.
갑자기 What's gotten into 왜그래? you all of a sudden?
Like he could just disappear.

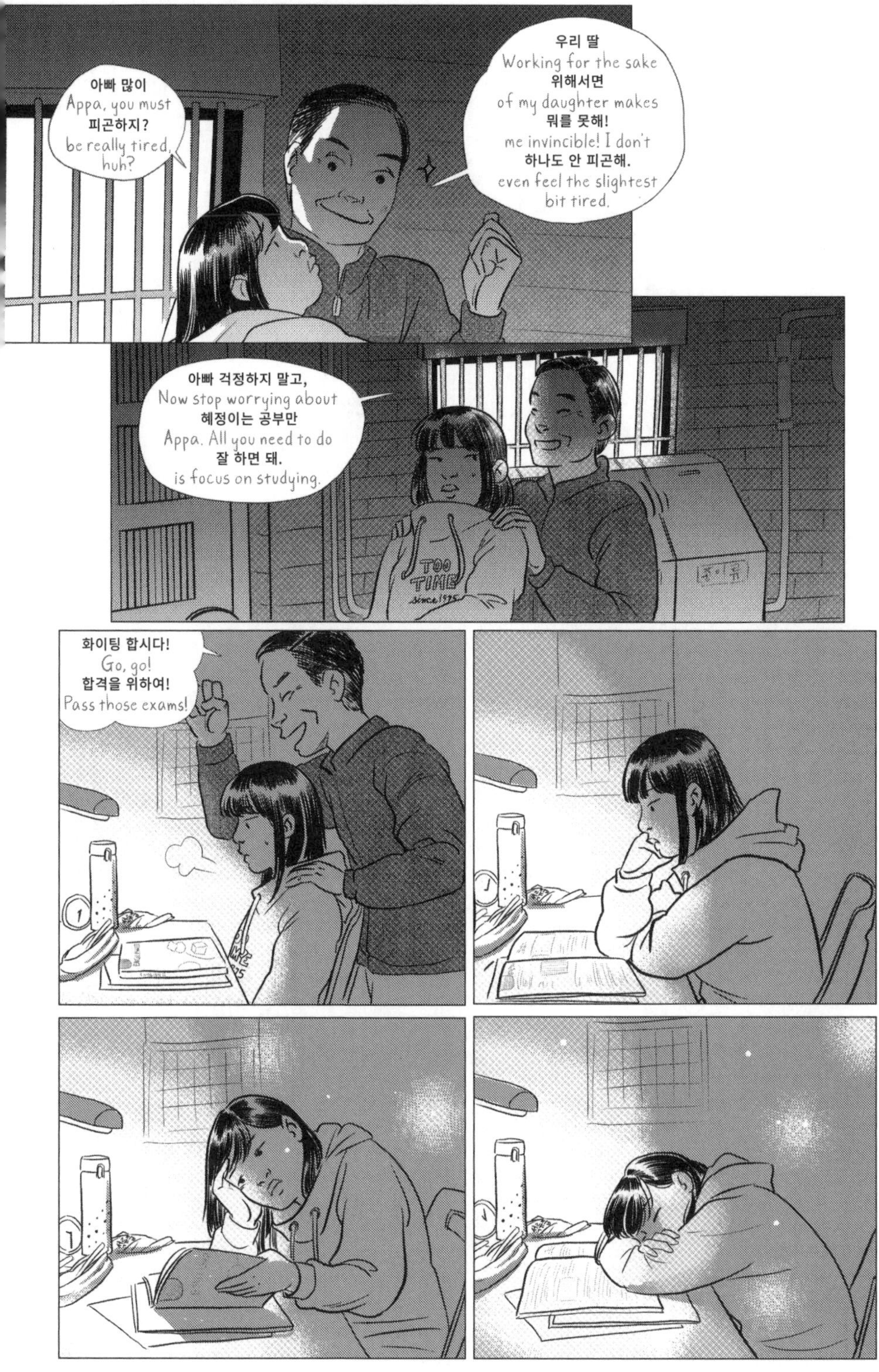
아빠 많이 피곤하지?
Appa, you must be really tired, huh?
우리 딸 위해서면 뭐를 못해! 하나도 안 피곤해.
Working for the sake of my daughter makes me invincible! I don't even feel the slightest bit tired.
아빠 걱정하지 말고, 혜정이는 공부만 잘 하면 돼.
Now stop worrying about Appa. All you need to do is focus on studying.
TOO TIME since 1975
화이팅 합시다! 합격을 위하여!
Go, go! Pass those exams!

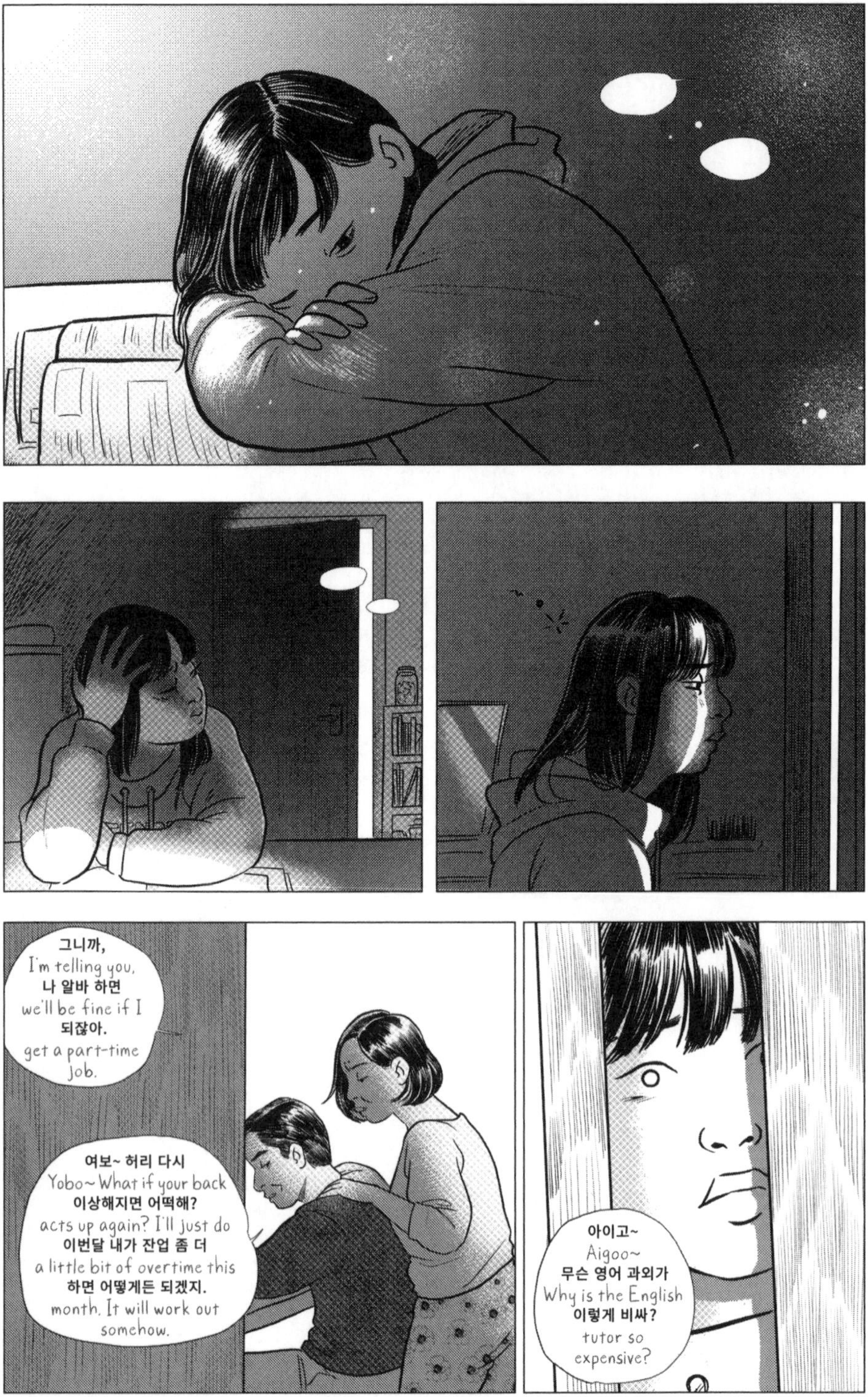
그니까,
I'm telling you,
나 알바 하면
we'll be fine if I
되잖아.
get a part-time job.
여보~ 허리 다시
Yobo~ What if your back
이상해지면 어떡해?
acts up again? I'll just do
이번달 내가 잔업 좀 더
a little bit of overtime this
하면 어떻게든 되겠지.
month. It will work out somehow.
아이고~
Aigoo~
무슨 영어 과외가
Why is the English
이렇게 비싸?
tutor so expensive?

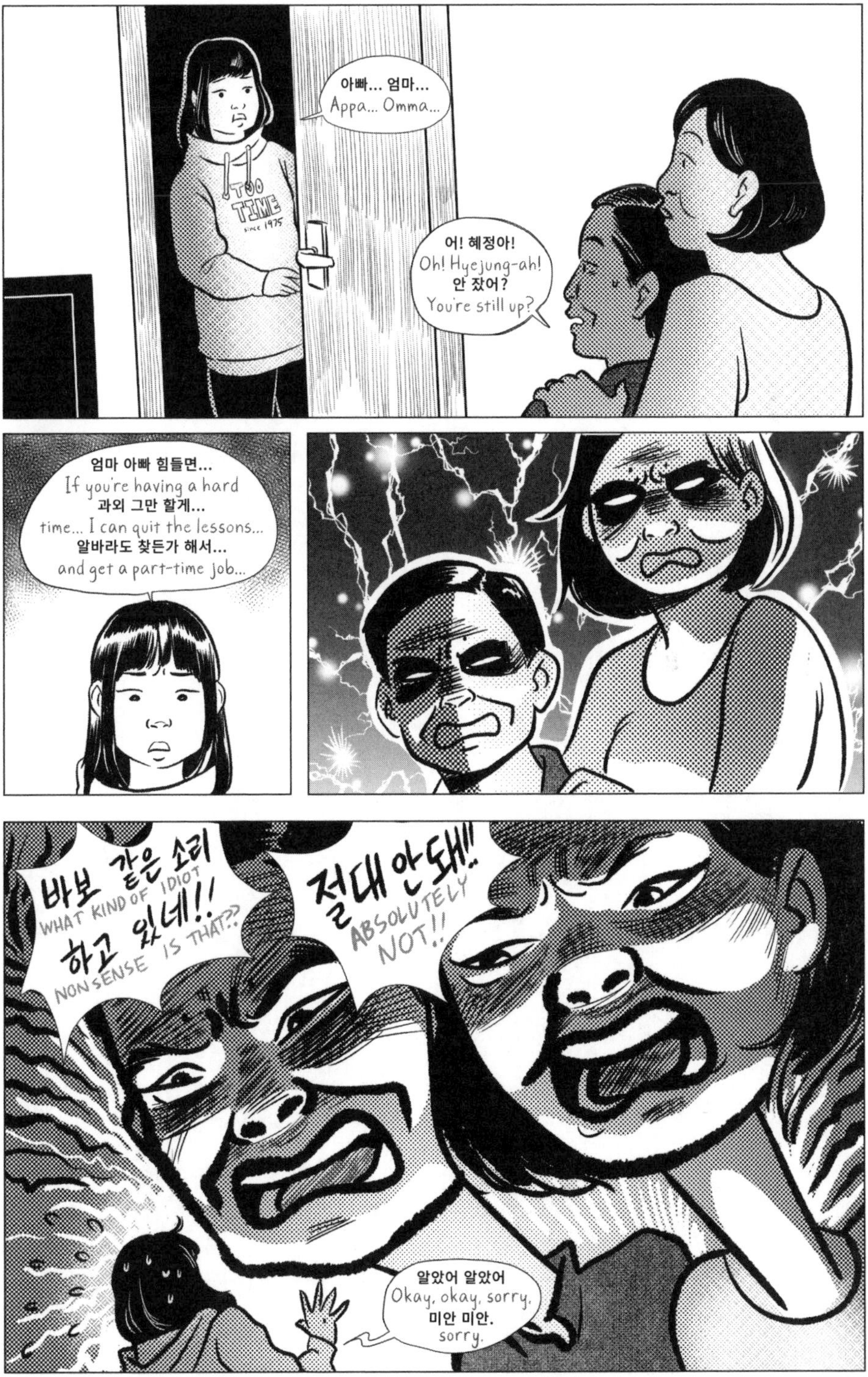
아빠... 엄마...
Appa... Omma...
어! 혜정아!
Oh! Hyejung-ah!
안 잤어?
You're still up?
엄마 아빠 힘들면...
If you're having a hard
과외 그만 할게...
time... I can quit the lessons...
알바라도 찾든가 해서...
and get a part-time job...
바보 같은 소리 하고 있네!!
WHAT KIND OF IDIOT NONSENSE IS THAT??
절대 안돼!!
ABSOLUTELY NOT!!
알았어 알았어
Okay, okay, sorry.
미안 미안.
sorry.

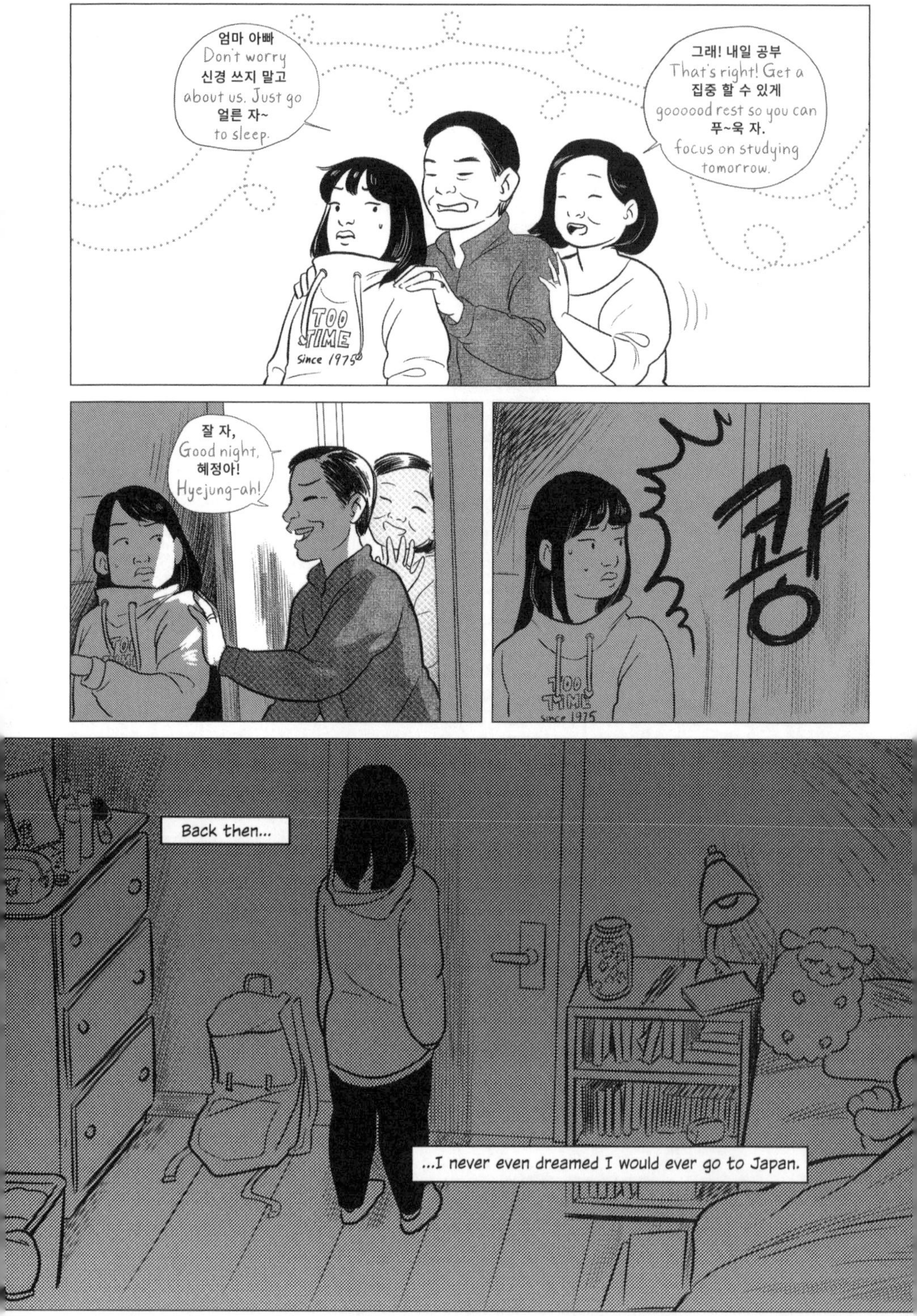

엄마 아빠
Don't worry
신경 쓰지 말고
about us. Just go
얼른 자~
to sleep.
그래! 내일 공부
That's right! Get a
집중 할 수 있게
goooood rest so you can
푸~욱 자.
focus on studying
tomorrow.
TOO TIME Since 1975
잘 자,
Good night,
혜정아!
Hyejung-ah!
쾅
Back then...
...I never even dreamed I would ever go to Japan.

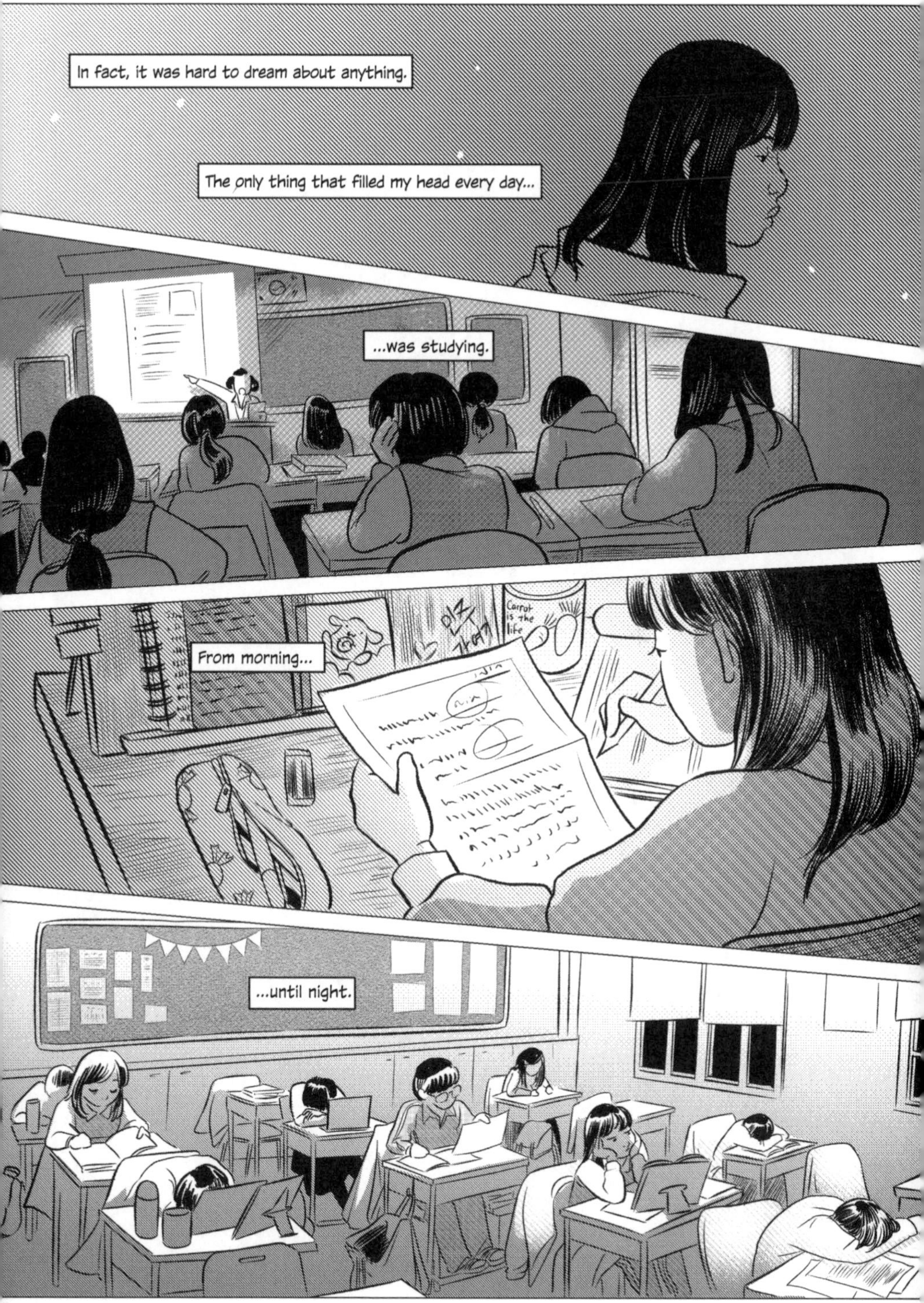
In fact, it was hard to dream about anything.
The only thing that filled my head every day...
...was studying.
From morning...
Carrot is the life
...until night.

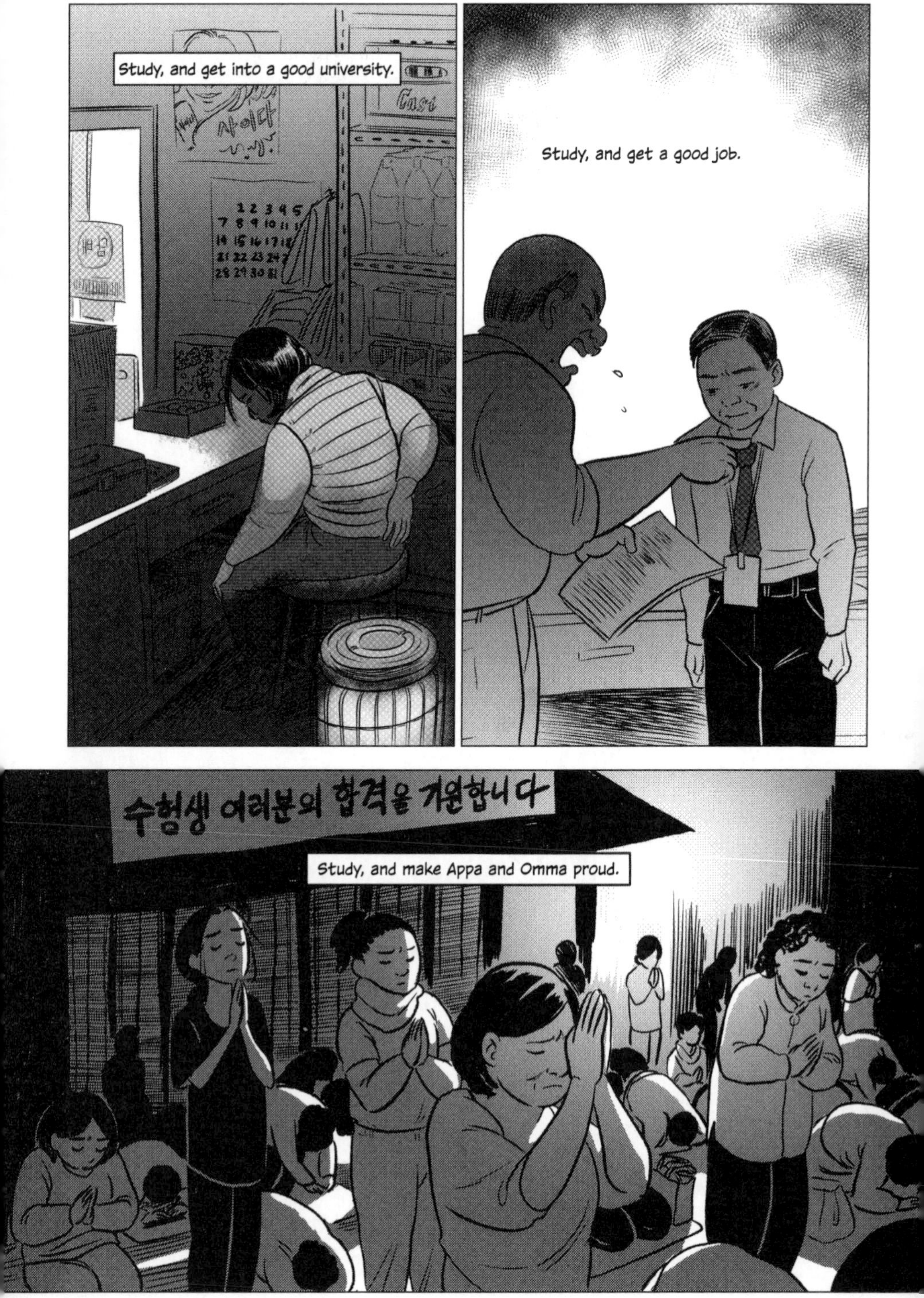
Study, and get into a good university.
Study, and get a good job.
수험생 여러분의 합격을 기원합니다
Study, and make Appa and Omma proud.

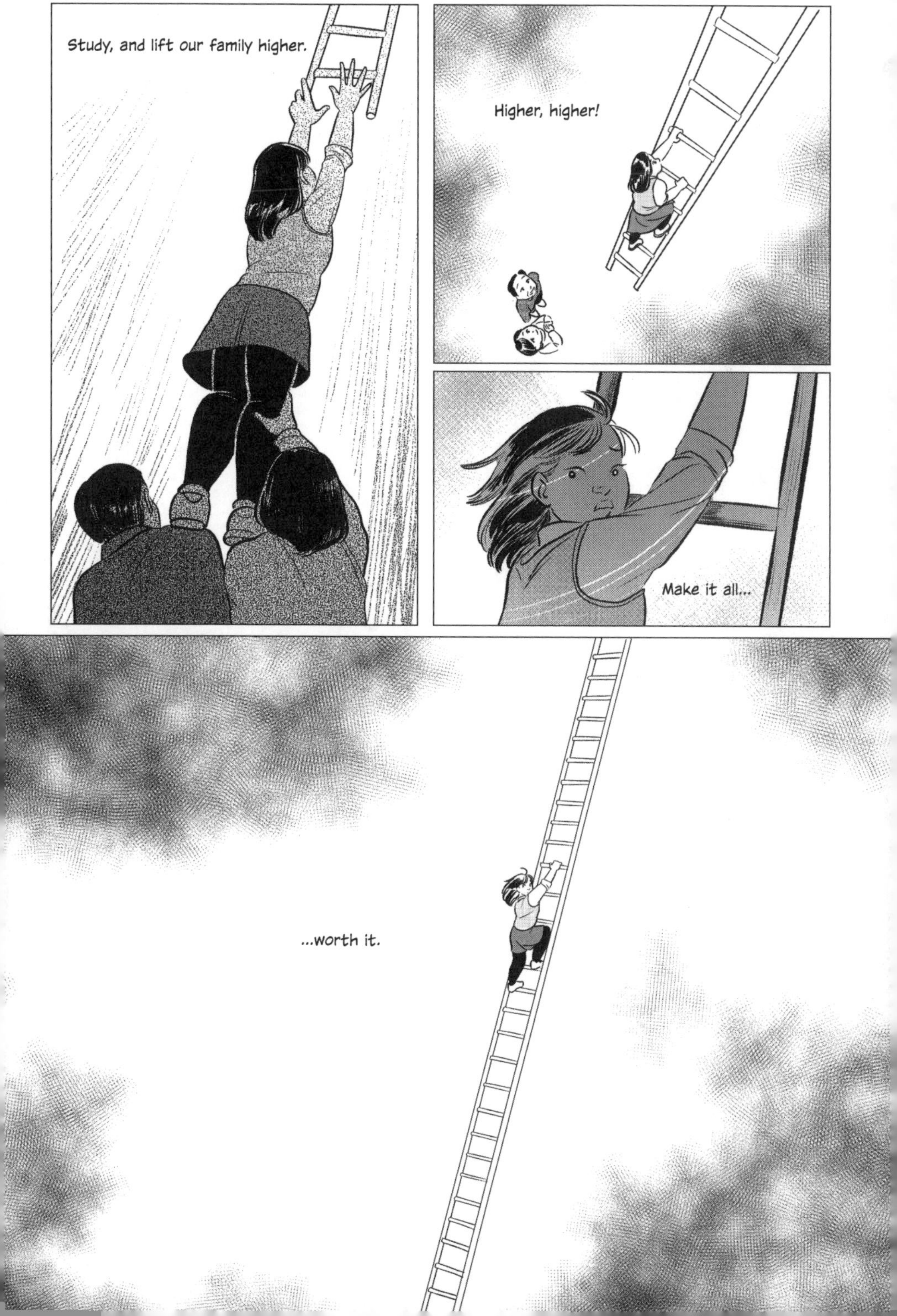
Study, and lift our family higher.
Higher, higher!
Make it all...
...worth it.

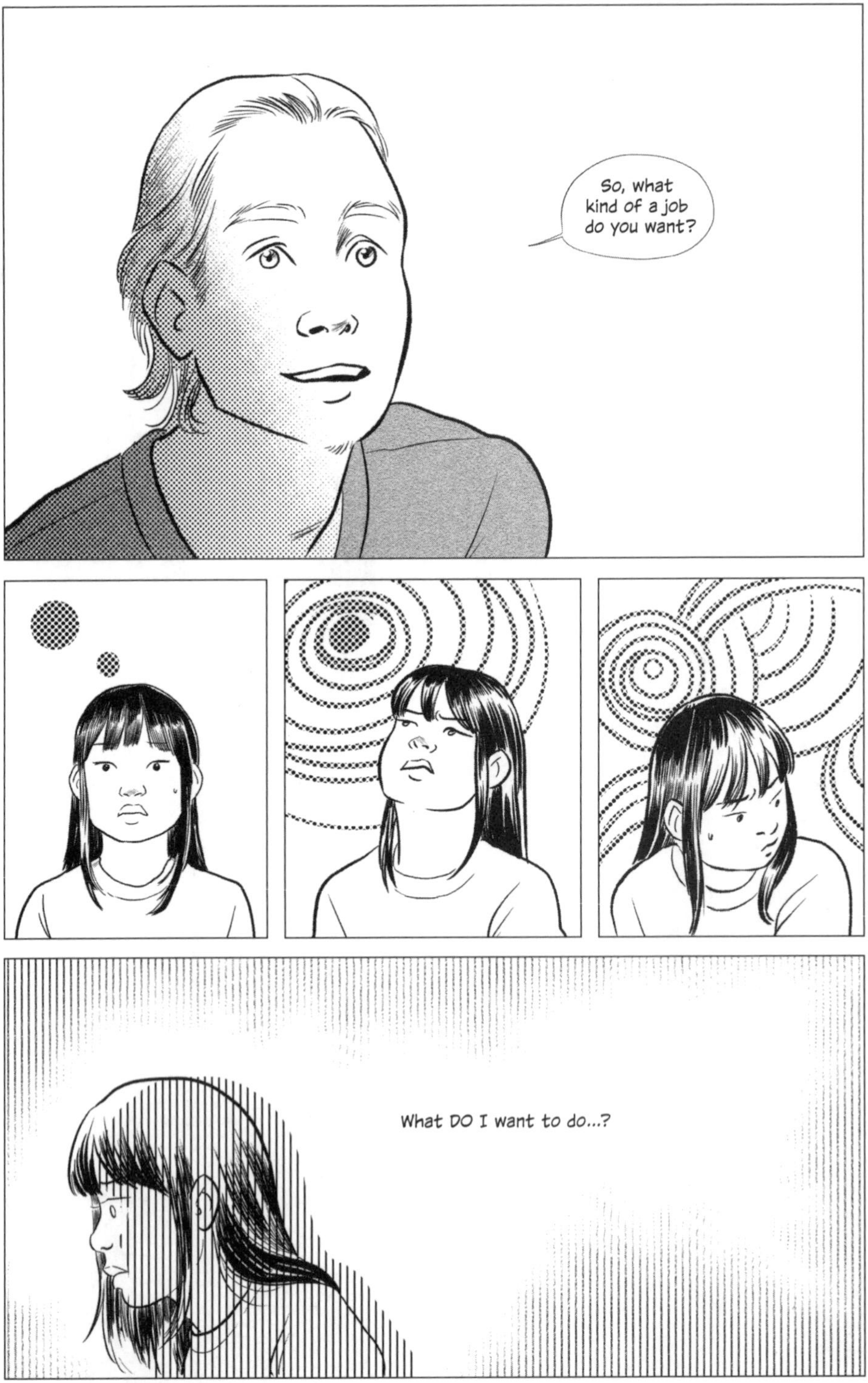
So, what kind of a job do you want?
What DO I want to do...?

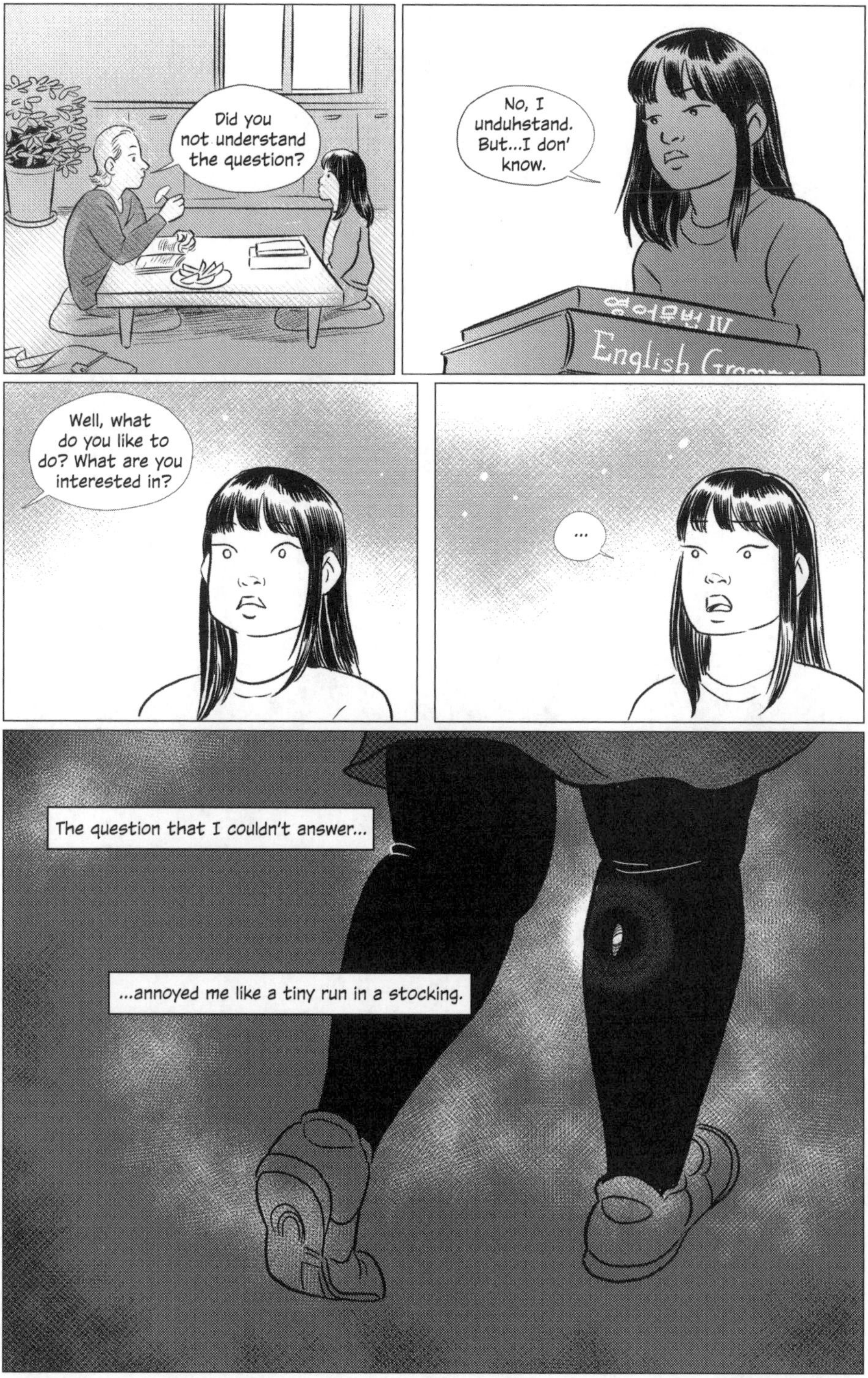
Did you not understand the question?
No, I unduhstand. But...I don' know.
Well, what do you like to do? What are you interested in?
...
The question that I couldn't answer...
...annoyed me like a tiny run in a stocking.

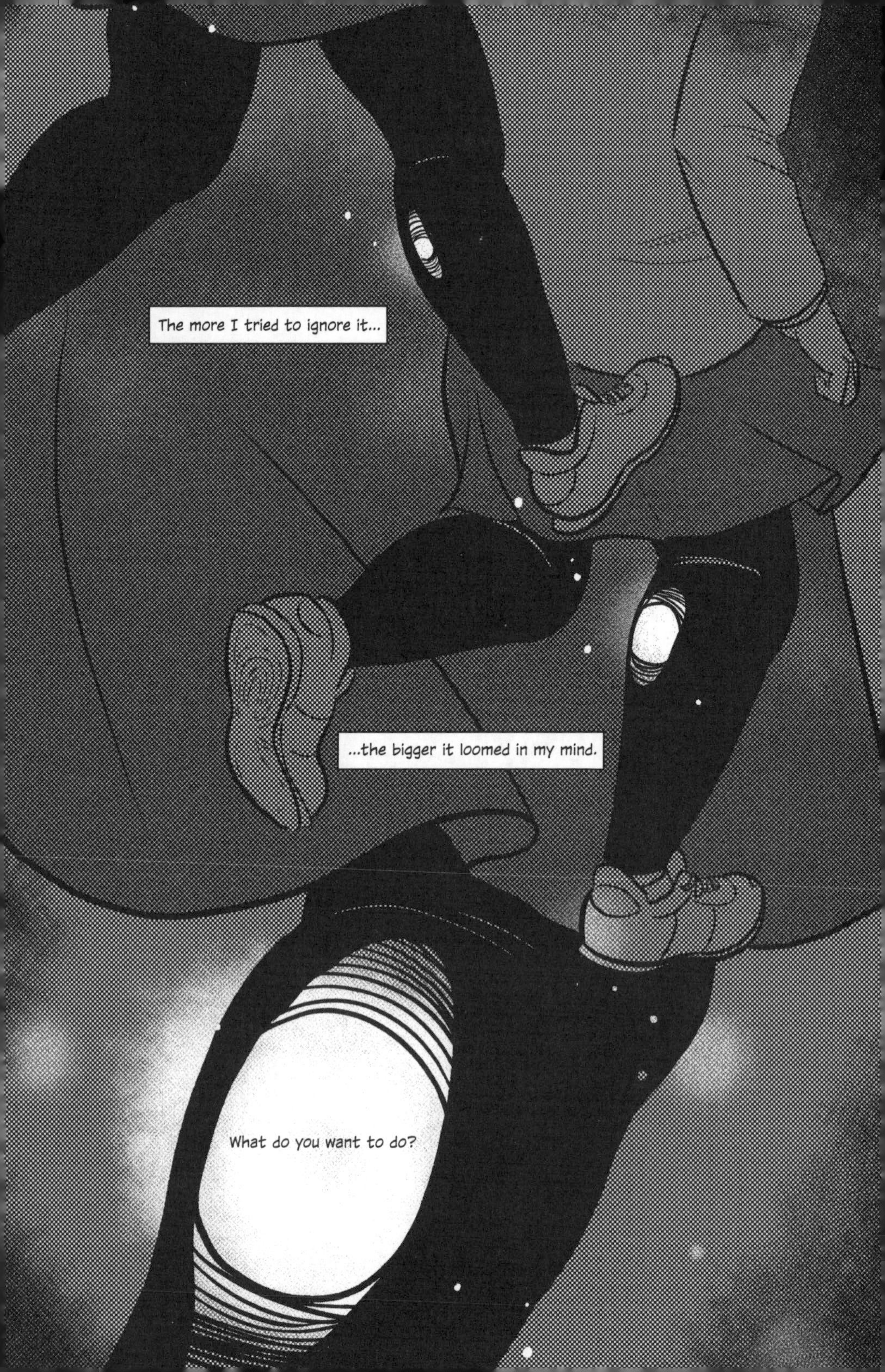
The more I tried to ignore it...
...the bigger it loomed in my mind.
What do you want to do?

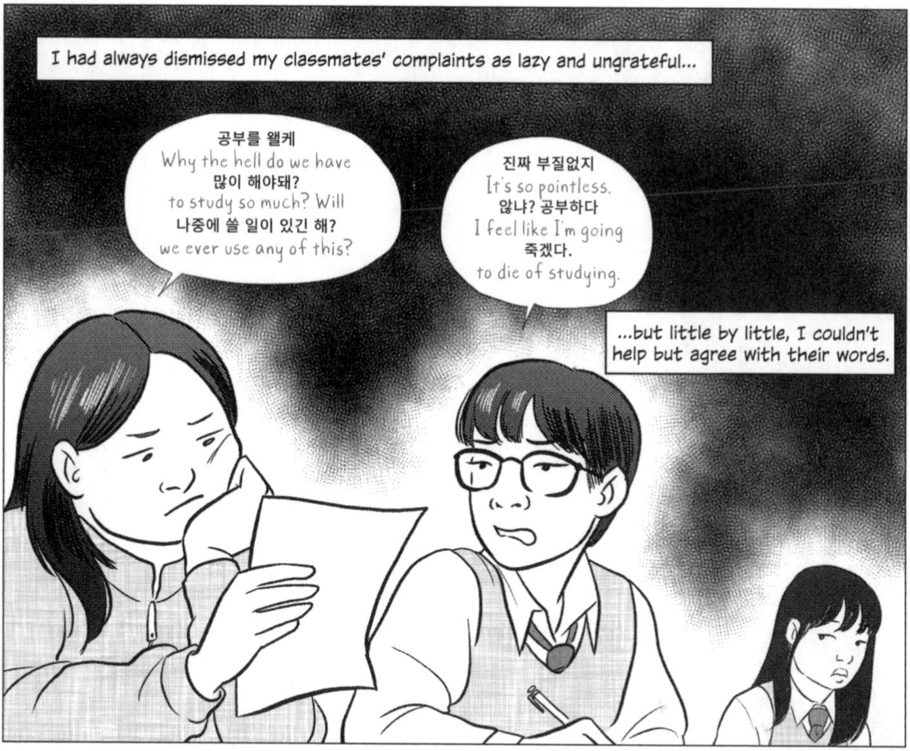
I had always dismissed my classmates' complaints as lazy and ungrateful...
공부를 왤케 Why the hell do we have 많이 해야돼? to study so much? Will 나중에 쓸 일이 있긴 해? we ever use any of this?
진짜 부질없지 It's so pointless. 않냐? 공부하다 I feel like I'm going 죽겠다. to die of studying.
...but little by little, I couldn't help but agree with their words.

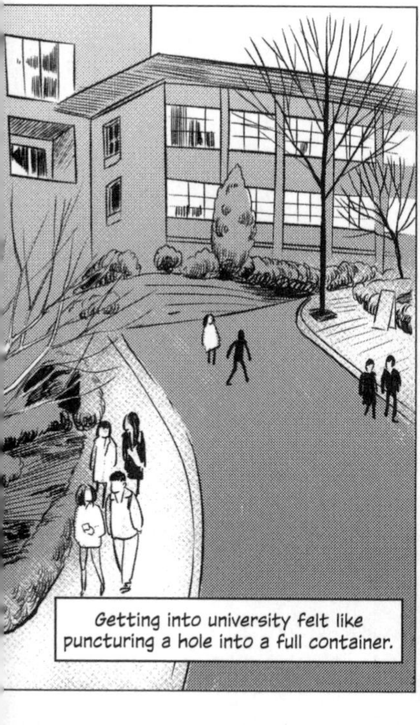
Getting into university felt like puncturing a hole into a full container.

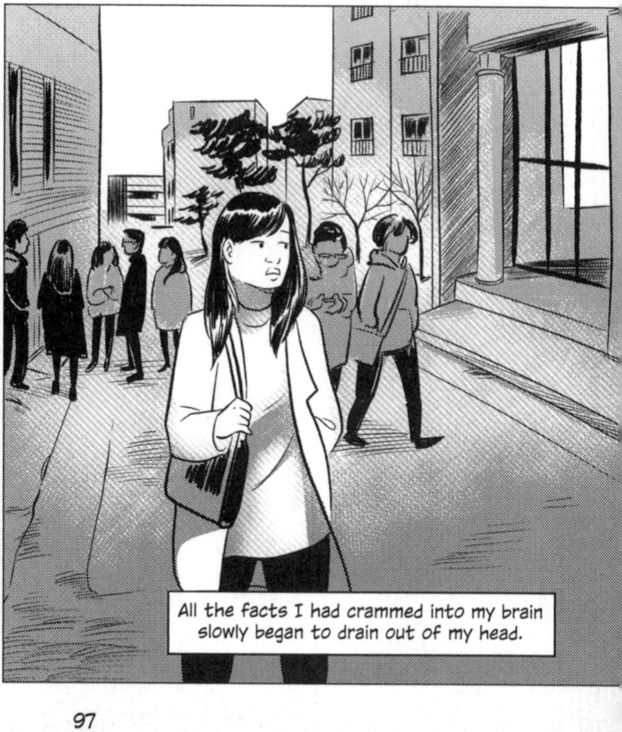
All the facts I had crammed into my brain slowly began to drain out of my head.

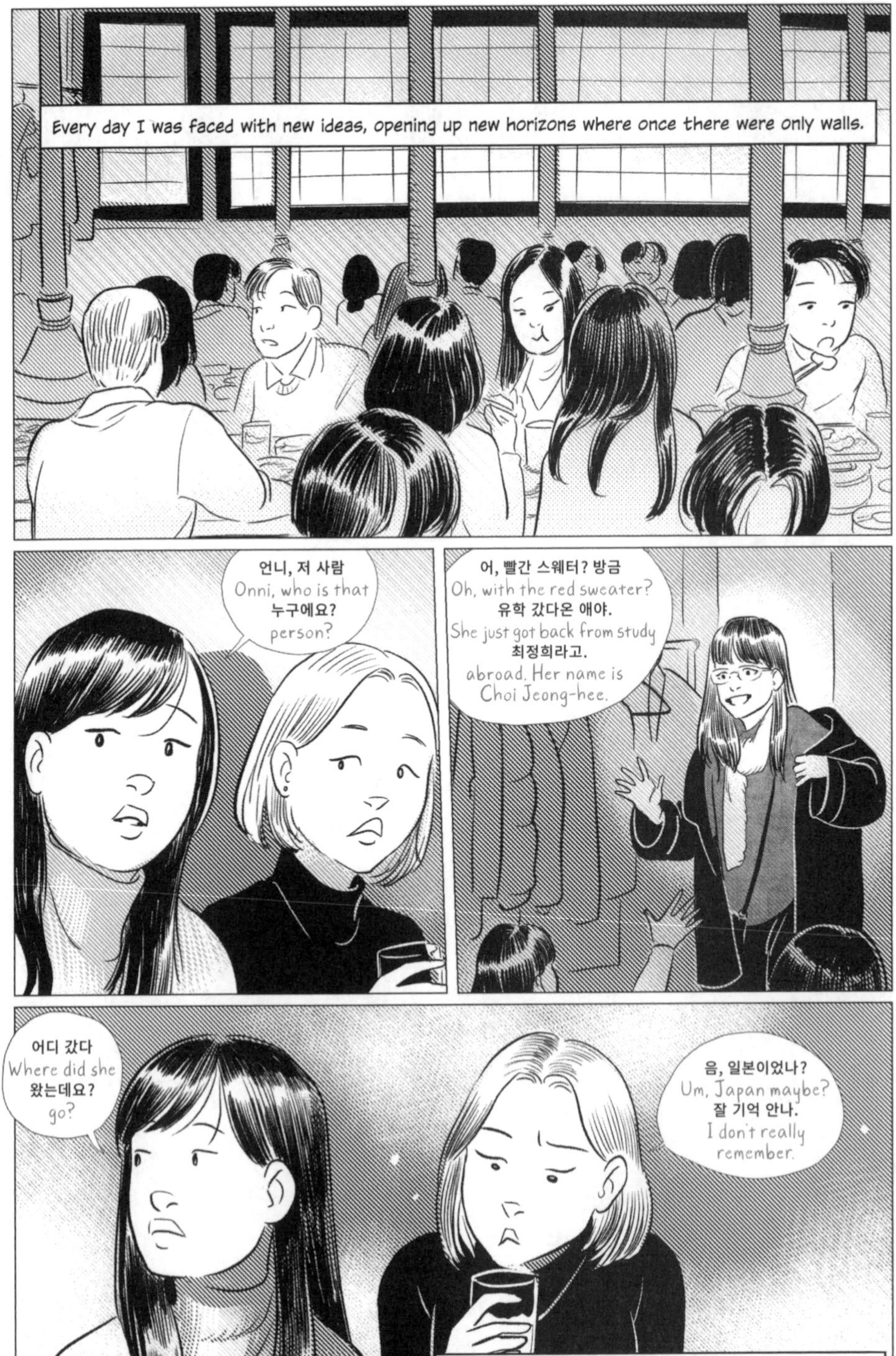

Every day I was faced with new ideas, opening up new horizons where once there were only walls.
언니, 저 사람 누구에요?
Onni, who is that person?
어, 빨간 스웨터? 방금 유학 갔다온 애야. 최정희라고.
Oh, with the red sweater? She just got back from study abroad. Her name is Choi Jeong-hee.
어디 갔다 왔는데요?
Where did she go?
음, 일본이었나? 잘 기억 안나.
Um, Japan maybe? I don't really remember.
Above all else was always that lingering question...

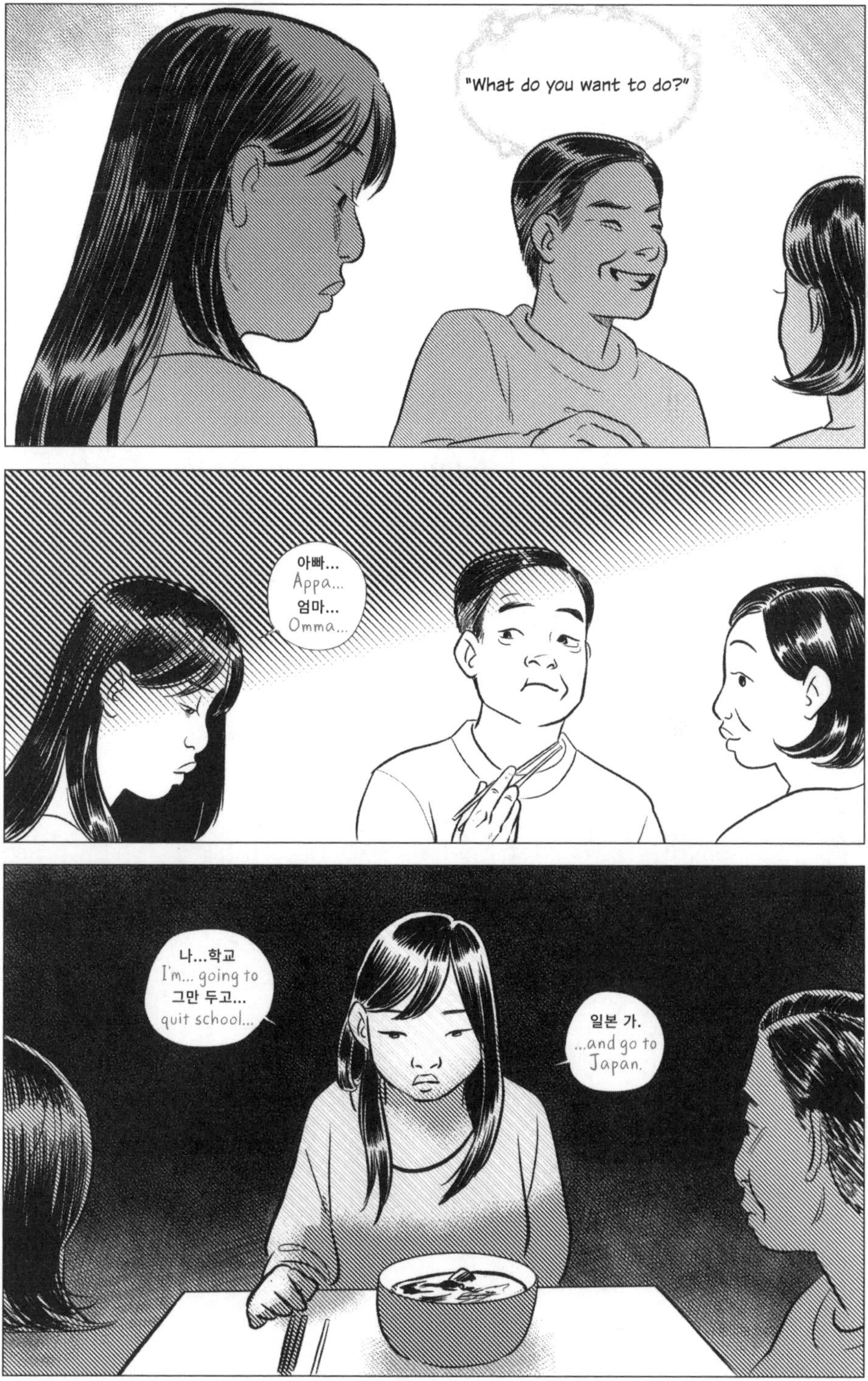
"What do you want to do?"
아빠...
Appa...
엄마...
Omma...
나...학교
I'm... going to
그만 두고...
quit school...
일본 가.
...and go to
Japan.

Chapter 6
Chuseok

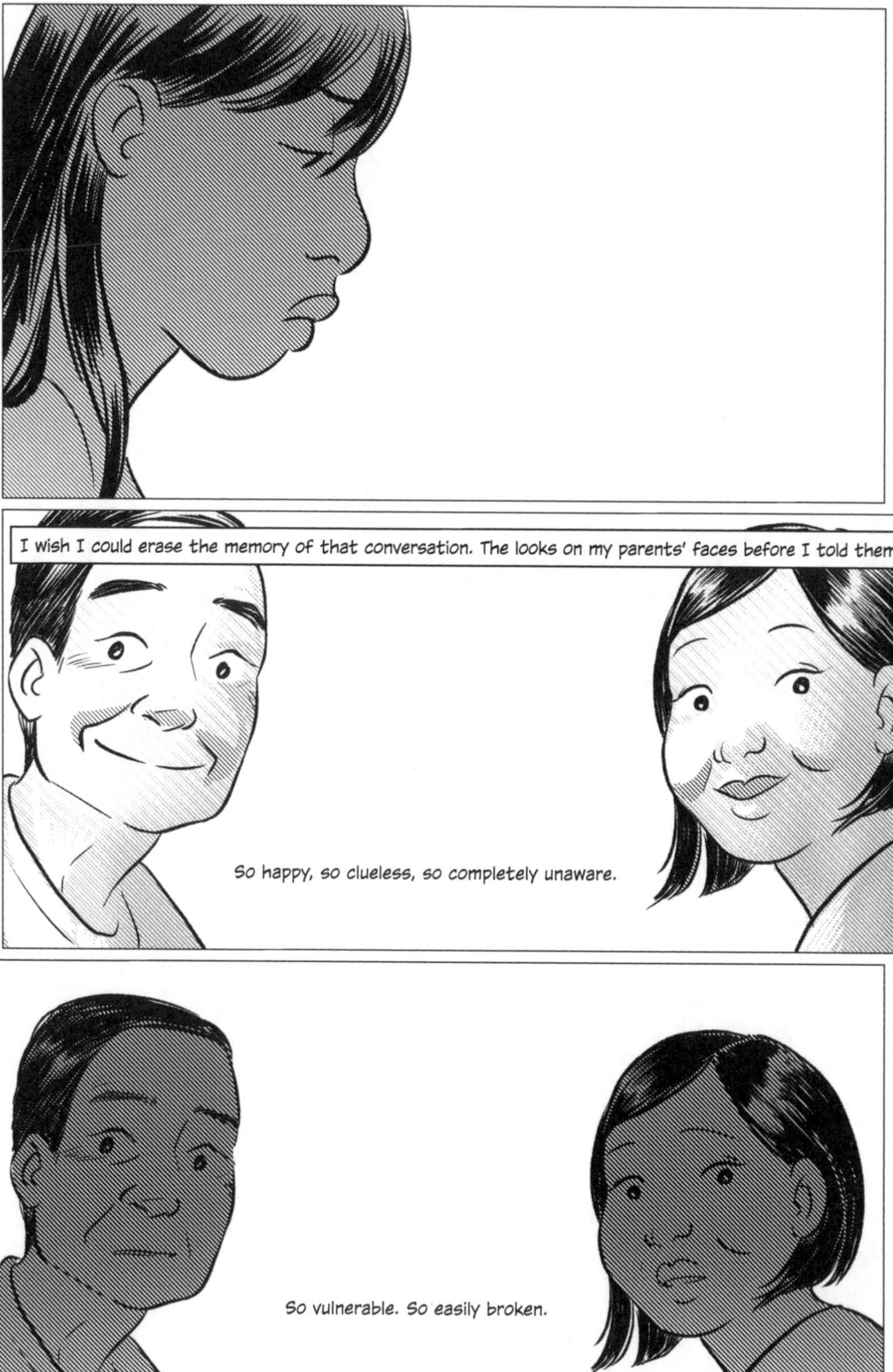
I wish I could erase the memory of that conversation. The looks on my parents' faces before I told them.
So happy, so clueless, so completely unaware.
So vulnerable. So easily broken.

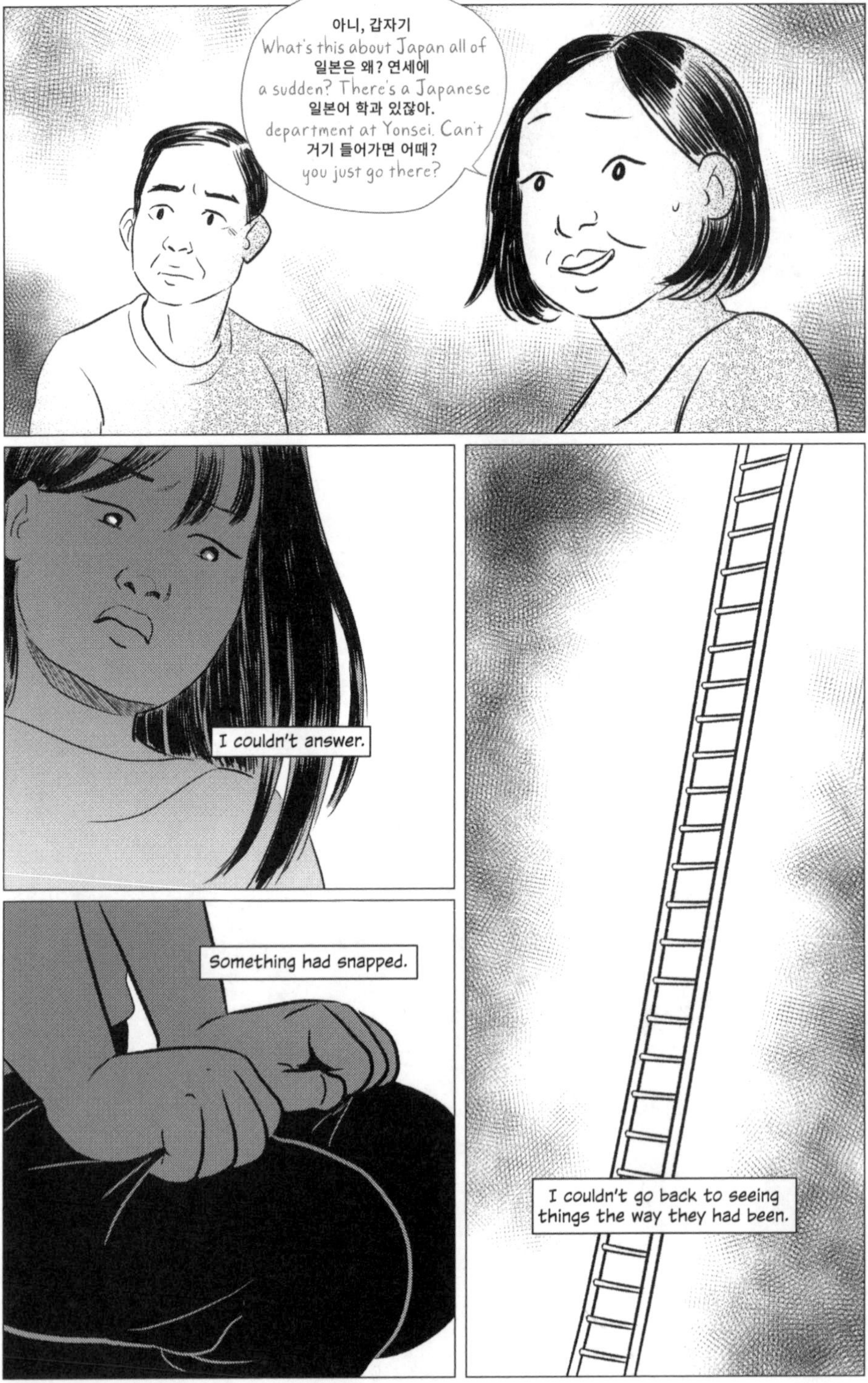
아니, 갑자기
What's this about Japan all of
일본은 왜? 연세에
a sudden? There's a Japanese
일본어 학과 있잖아.
department at Yonsei. Can't
거기 들어가면 어때?
you just go there?
I couldn't answer.
Something had snapped.
I couldn't go back to seeing things the way they had been.

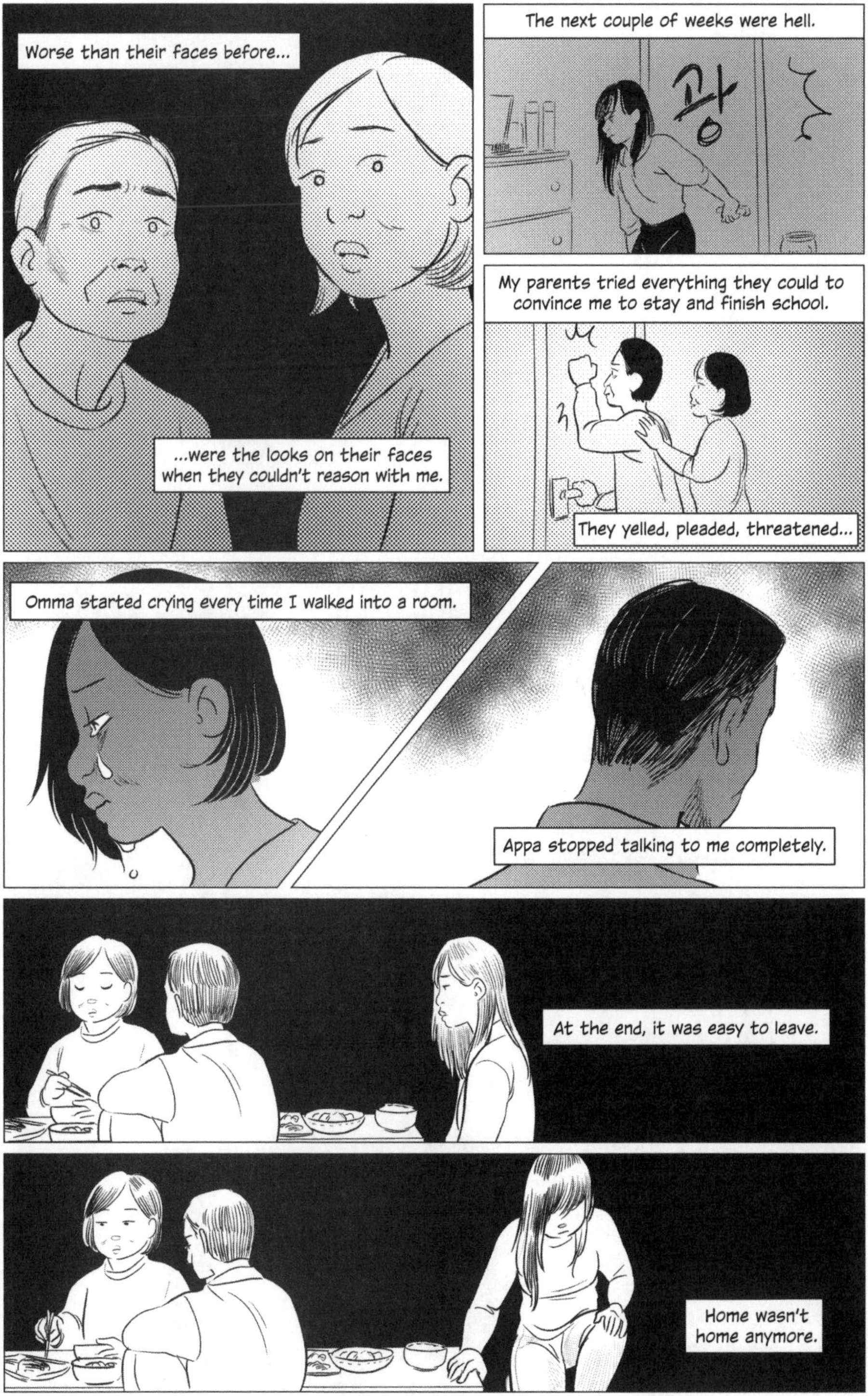
Worse than their faces before...
...were the looks on their faces when they couldn't reason with me.
The next couple of weeks were hell.
광
My parents tried everything they could to convince me to stay and finish school.
They yelled, pleaded, threatened...
Omma started crying every time I walked into a room.
Appa stopped talking to me completely.
At the end, it was easy to leave.
Home wasn't home anymore.

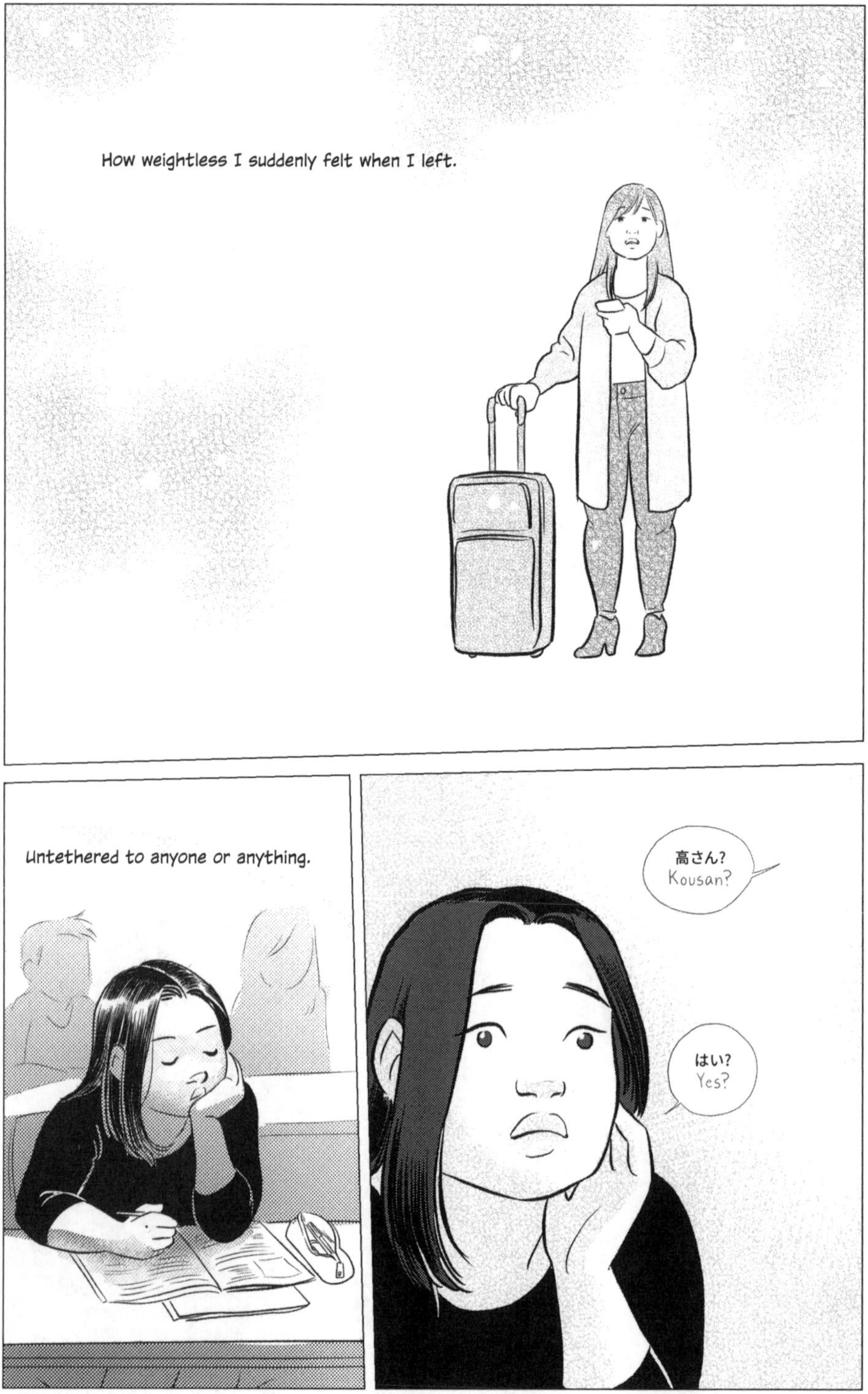
How weightless I suddenly felt when I left.
Untethered to anyone or anything.
高さん?
Kousan?
はい?
Yes?

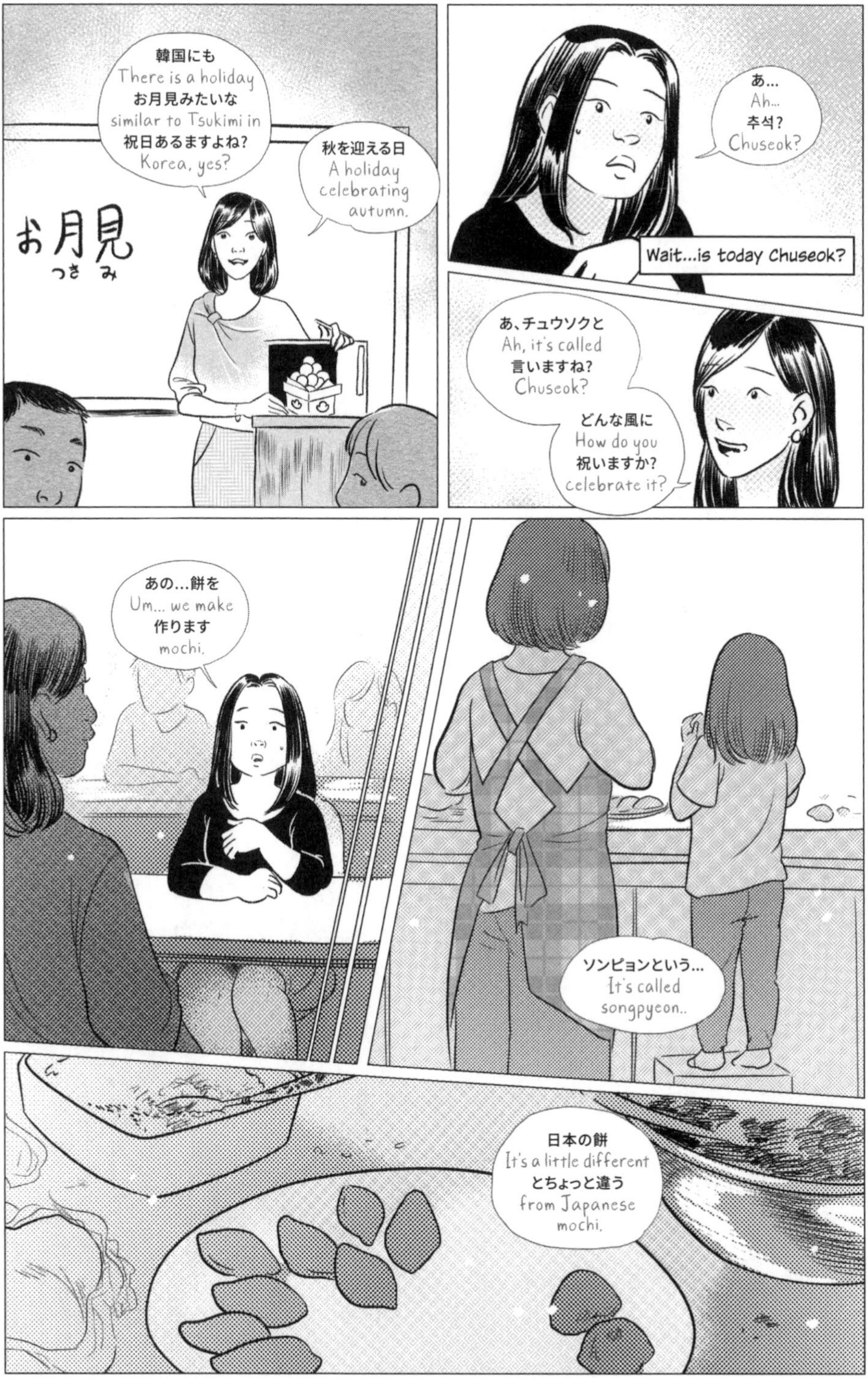

韓国にも
There is a holiday
お月見みたいな
similar to Tsukimi in
祝日あるますよね?
Korea, yes?
秋を迎える日
A holiday
celebrating
autumn.
お月見
つきみ
あ…
Ah...
추석?
Chuseok?
Wait...is today Chuseok?
あ、チュウソクと
Ah, it's called
言いますね?
Chuseok?
どんな風に
How do you
祝いますか?
celebrate it?
あの…餅を
Um... we make
作ります
mochi.
ソンピョンという…
It's called
songpyeon..
日本の餅
It's a little different
とちょっと違う
from Japanese
mochi.

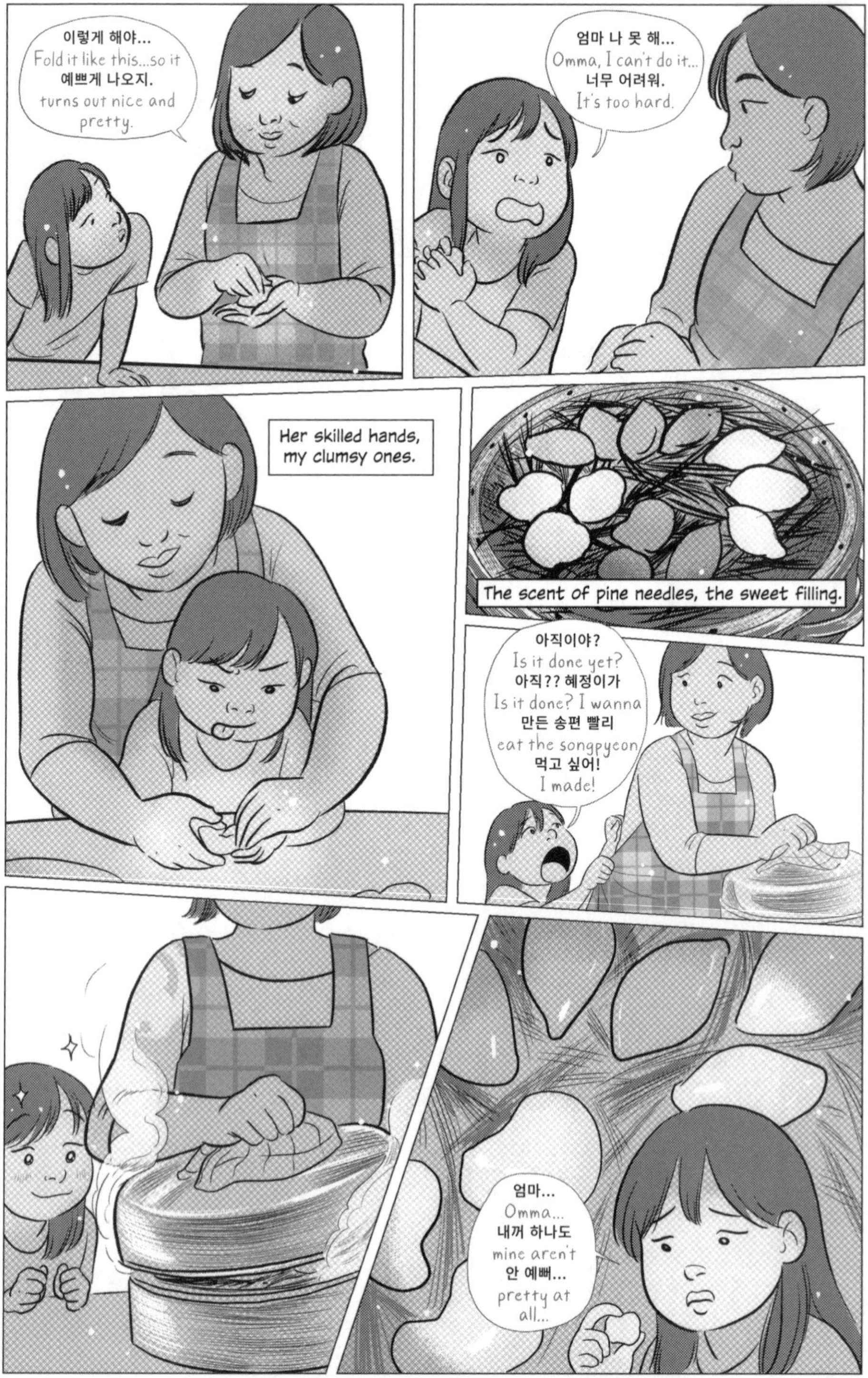
이렇게 해야...
Fold it like this...so it
예쁘게 나오지.
turns out nice and pretty.
엄마 나 못 해...
Omma, I can't do it...
너무 어려워.
It's too hard.
Her skilled hands, my clumsy ones.
The scent of pine needles, the sweet filling.
아직이야?
Is it done yet?
아직?? 혜정이가
Is it done? I wanna
만든 송편 빨리
eat the songpyeon
먹고 싶어!
I made!
엄마...
Omma...
내꺼 하나도
mine aren't
안 예뻐...
pretty at all...

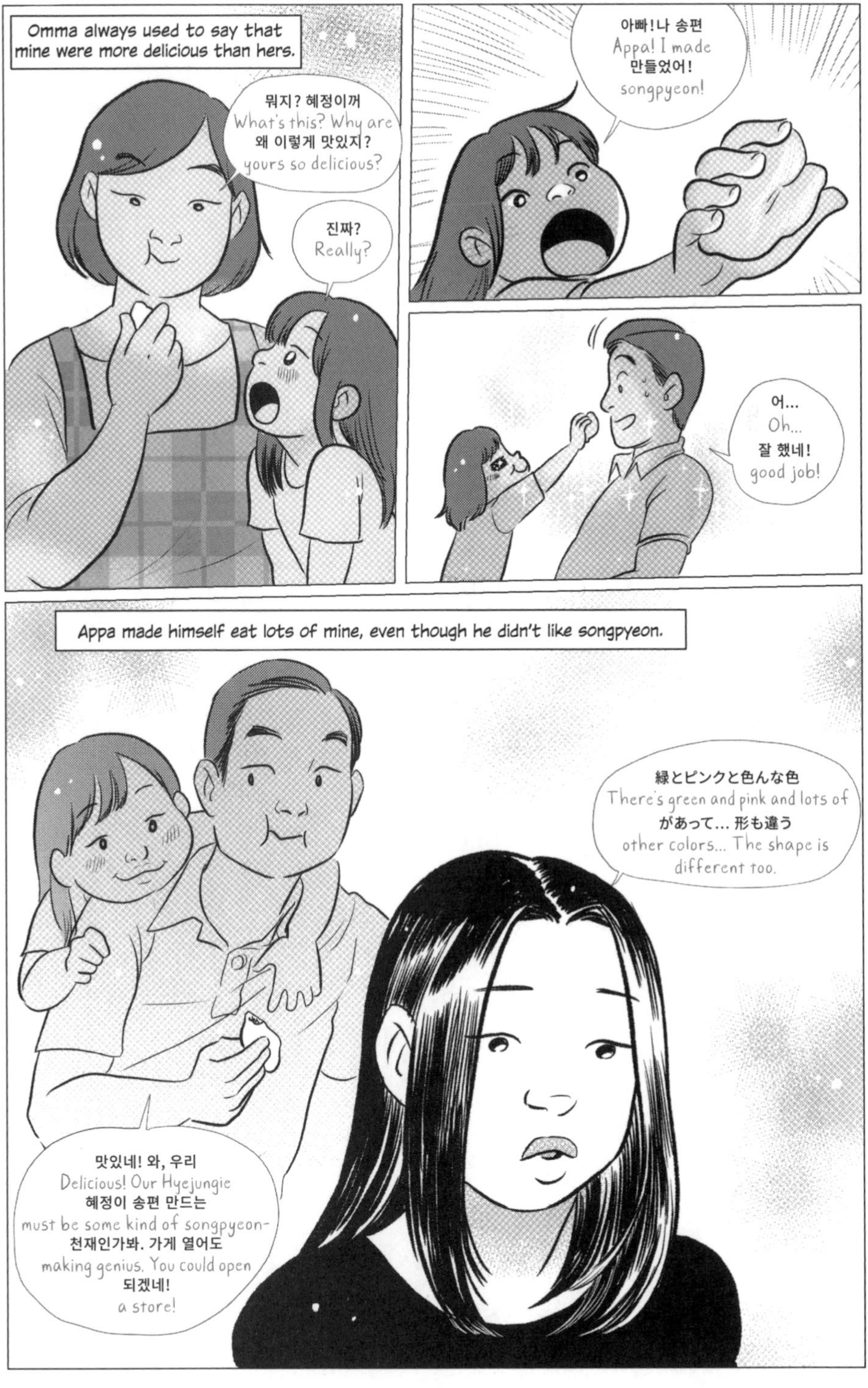
Omma always used to say that mine were more delicious than hers.
뭐지? 혜정이꺼 What's this? Why are 왜 이렇게 맛있지? yours so delicious?
진짜? Really?
아빠! 나 송편 Appa! I made 만들었어! songpyeon!
어... Oh... 잘 했네! good job!
Appa made himself eat lots of mine, even though he didn't like songpyeon.
緑とピンクと色んな色 There's green and pink and lots of があって... 形も違う other colors... The shape is different too.
맛있네! 와, 우리 Delicious! Our Hyejungie 혜정이 송편 만드는 must be some kind of songpyeon- 천재인가봐. 가게 열어도 making genius. You could open 되겠네! a store!

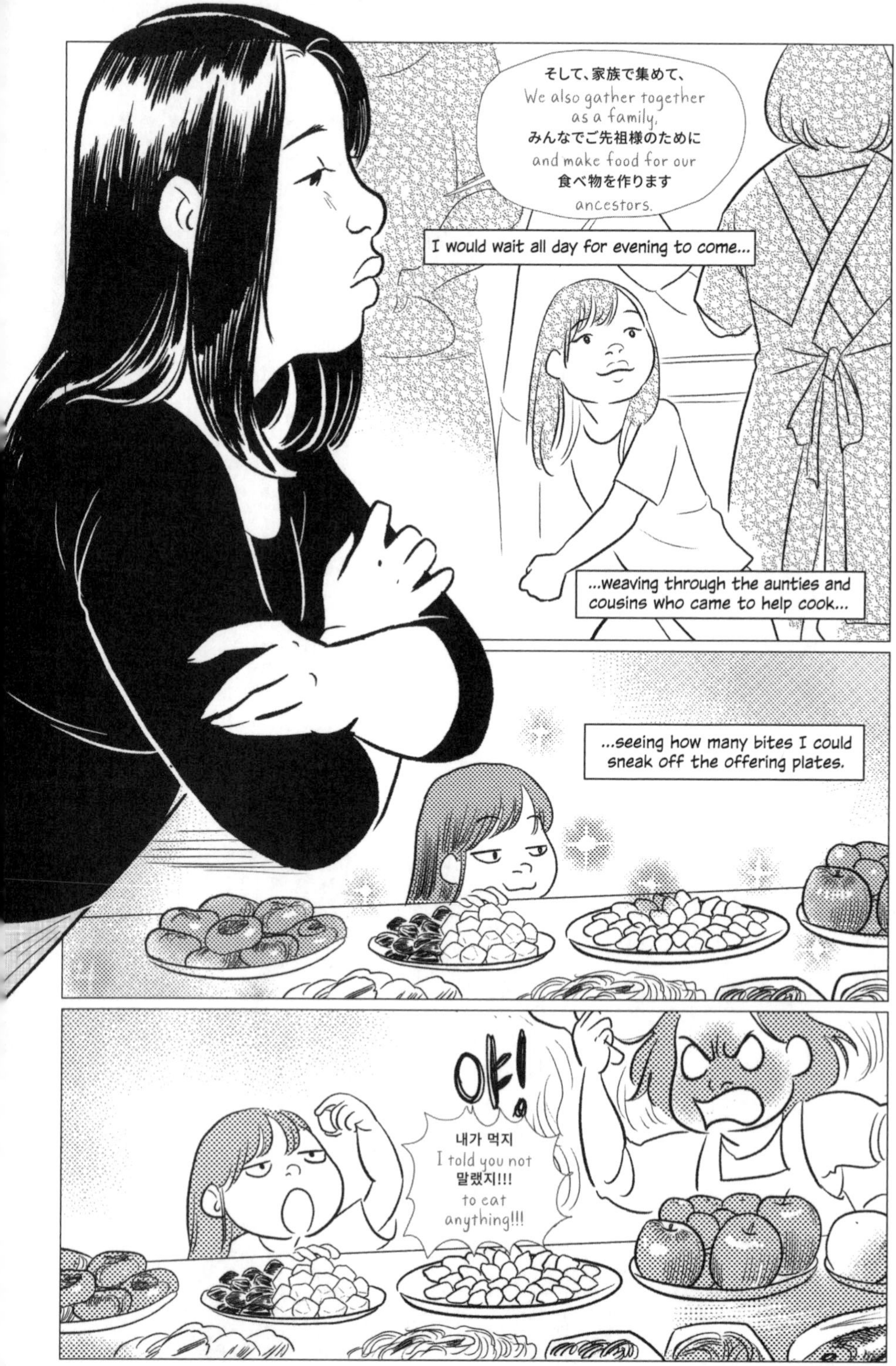

そして、家族で集めて、
We also gather together as a family,
みんなでご先祖様のために
and make food for our
食べ物を作ります
ancestors.
I would wait all day for evening to come...
...weaving through the aunties and cousins who came to help cook...
...seeing how many bites I could sneak off the offering plates.
야!
내가 먹지
I told you not
말랬지!!!
to eat anything!!!

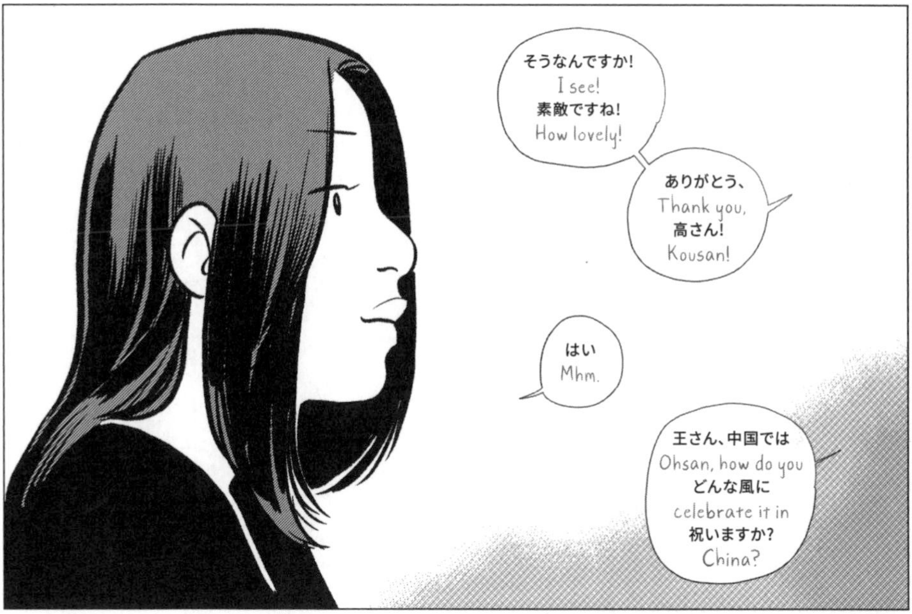
そうなんですか!
I see!
素敵ですね!
How lovely!
ありがとう、
Thank you,
高さん!
Kousan!
はい
Mhm.
王さん、中国では
Ohsan, how do you
どんな風に
celebrate it in
祝いますか?
China?

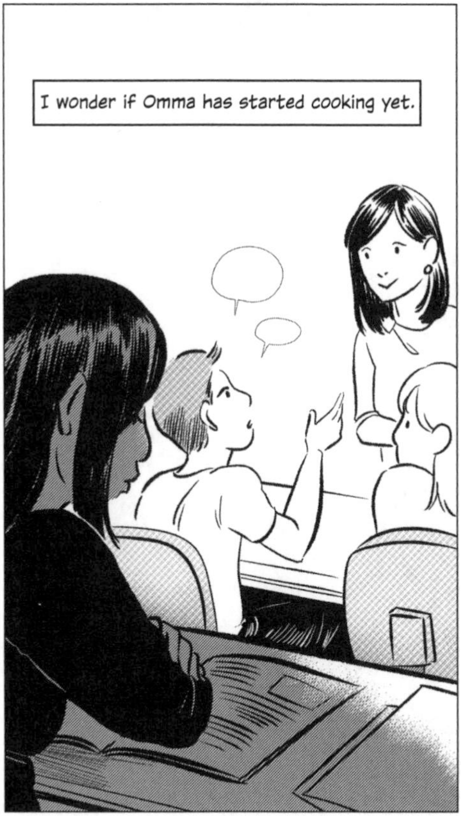
I wonder if Omma has started cooking yet.

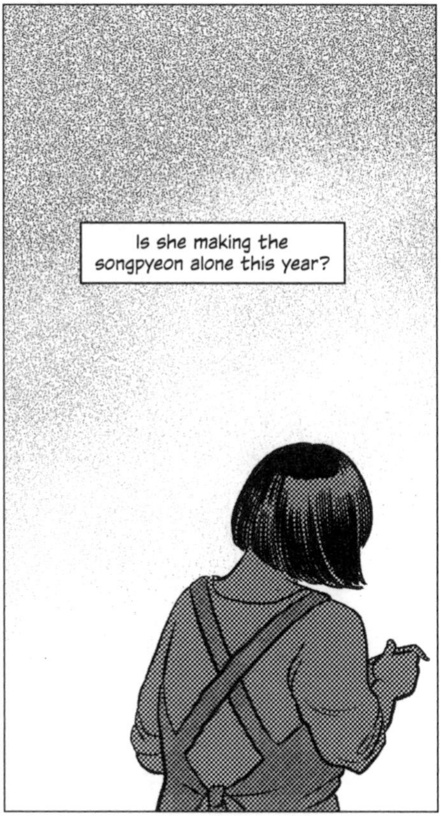
Is she making the
songpyeon alone this year?

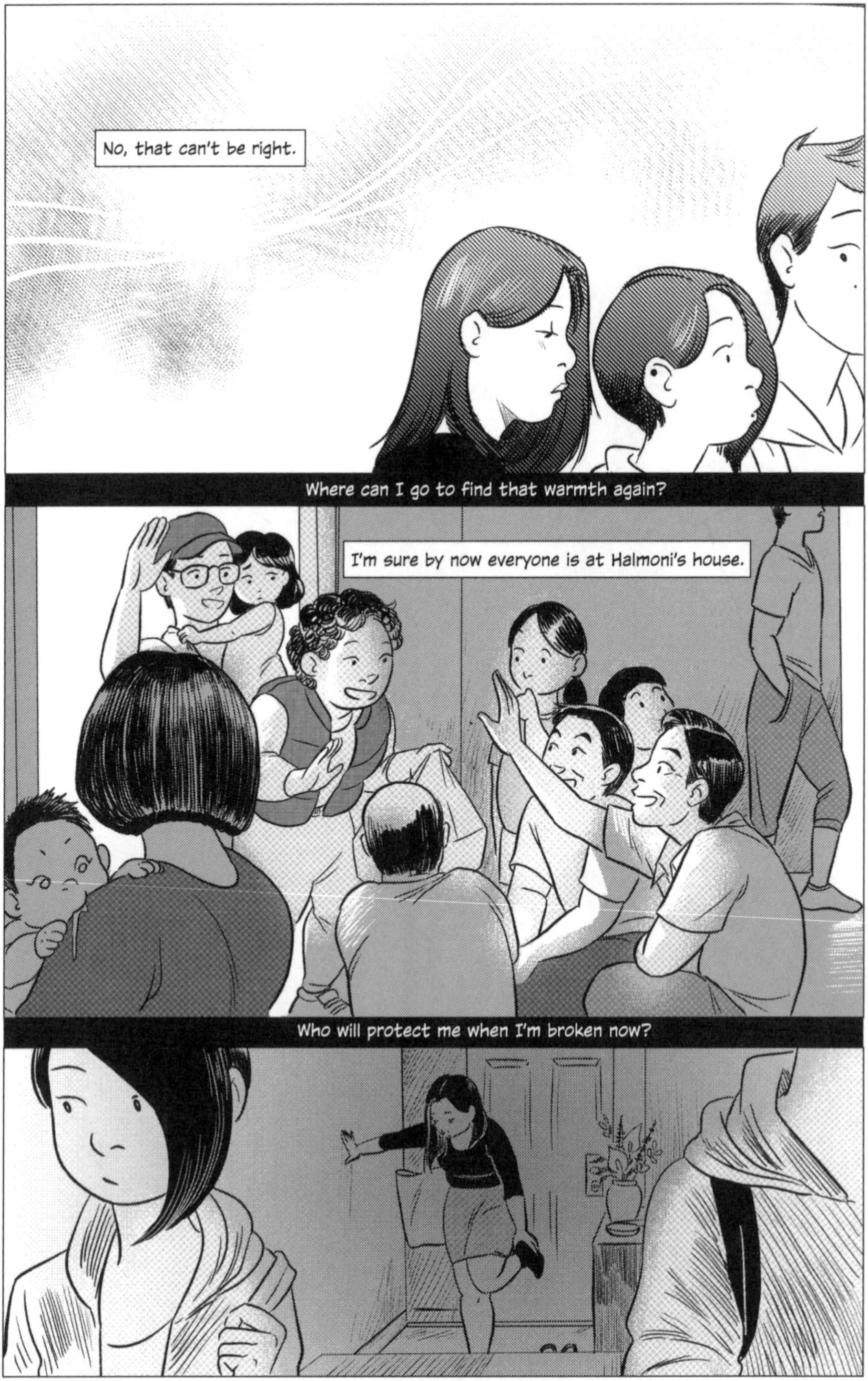
No, that can't be right.
Where can I go to find that warmth again?
I'm sure by now everyone is at Halmoni's house.
Who will protect me when I'm broken now?

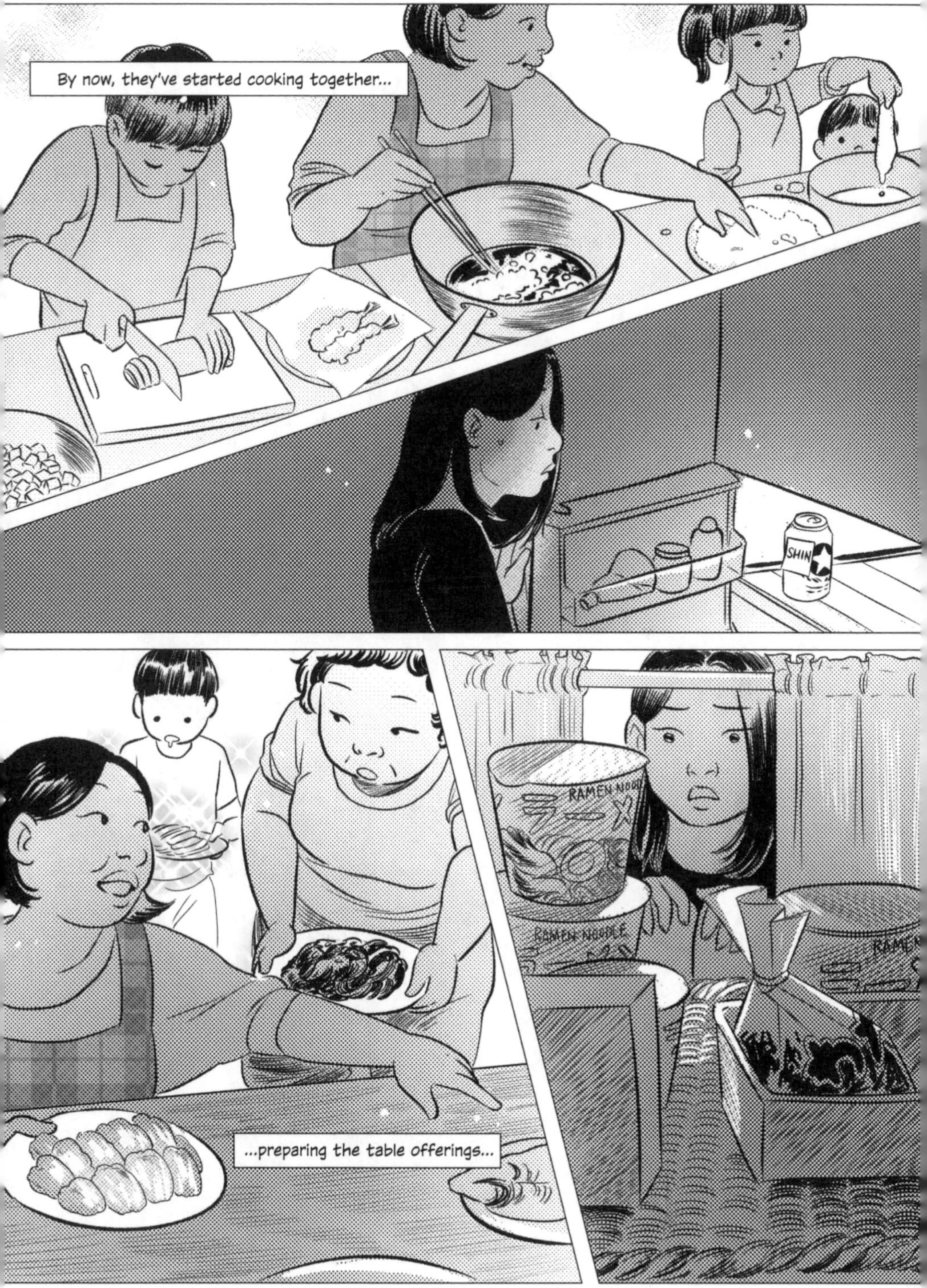

By now, they've started cooking together...
SHIN
...preparing the table offerings...
RAMEN NOODLE
RAMEN NOODLE

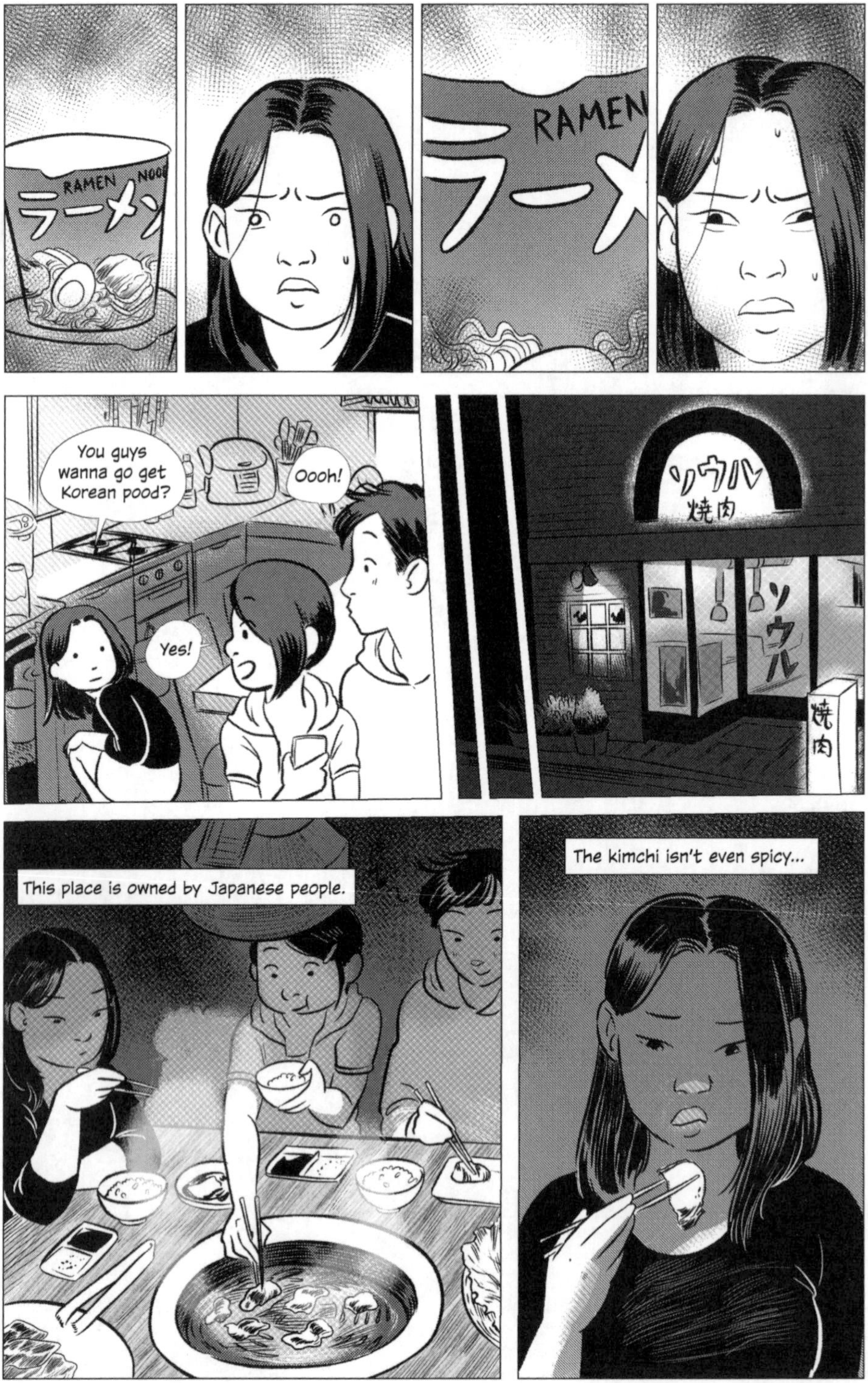

RAMEN NOO
ラーメン
RAMEN
ラーメ
You guys wanna go get Korean pood?
Oooh!
Yes!
ソウル
焼肉
ソウル
焼肉
This place is owned by Japanese people.
The kimchi isn't even spicy...

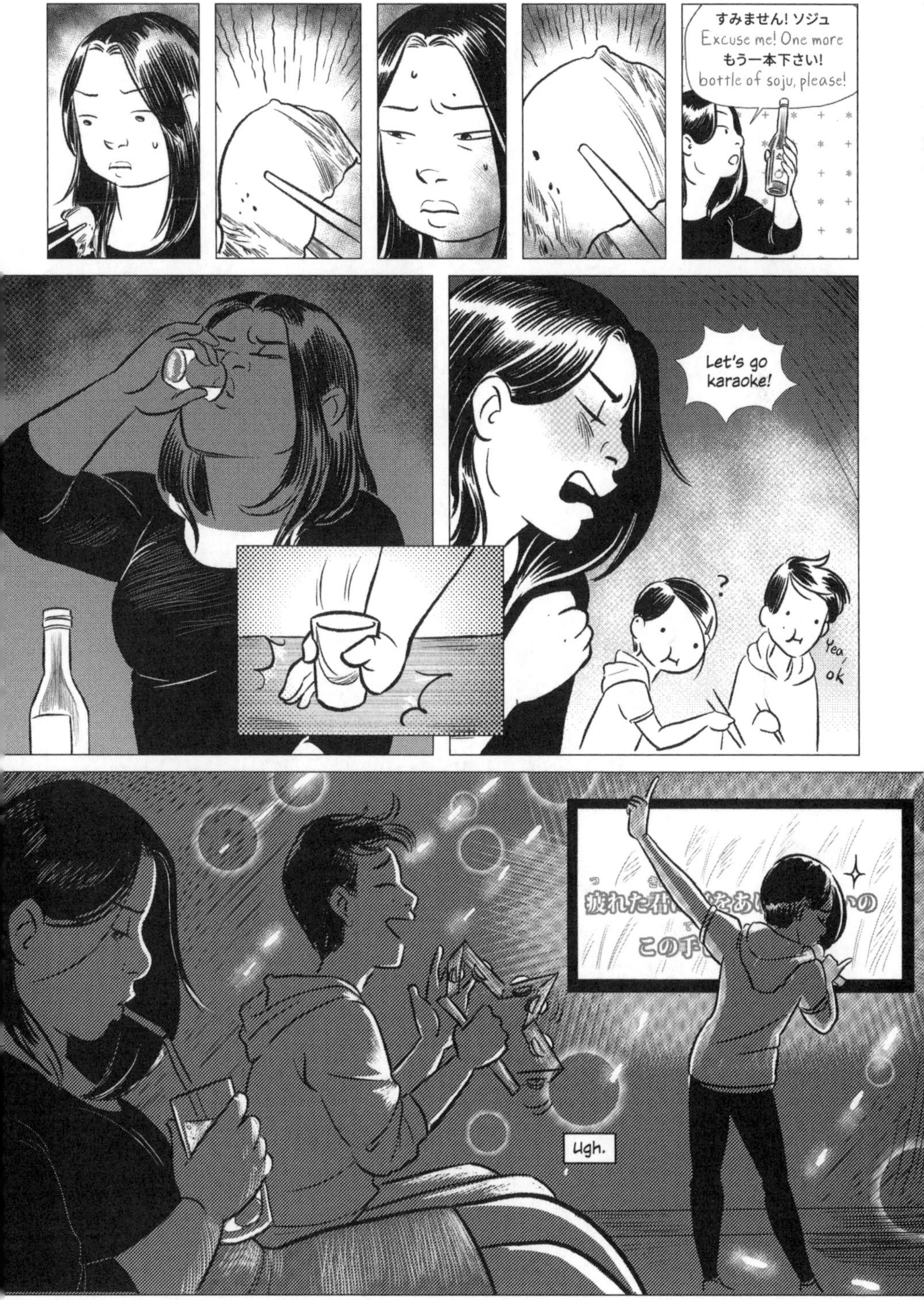
すみません! ソジュ
Excuse me! One more
もう一本下さい!
bottle of soju, please!
Let's go karaoke!
?
Yea, ok
Ugh.

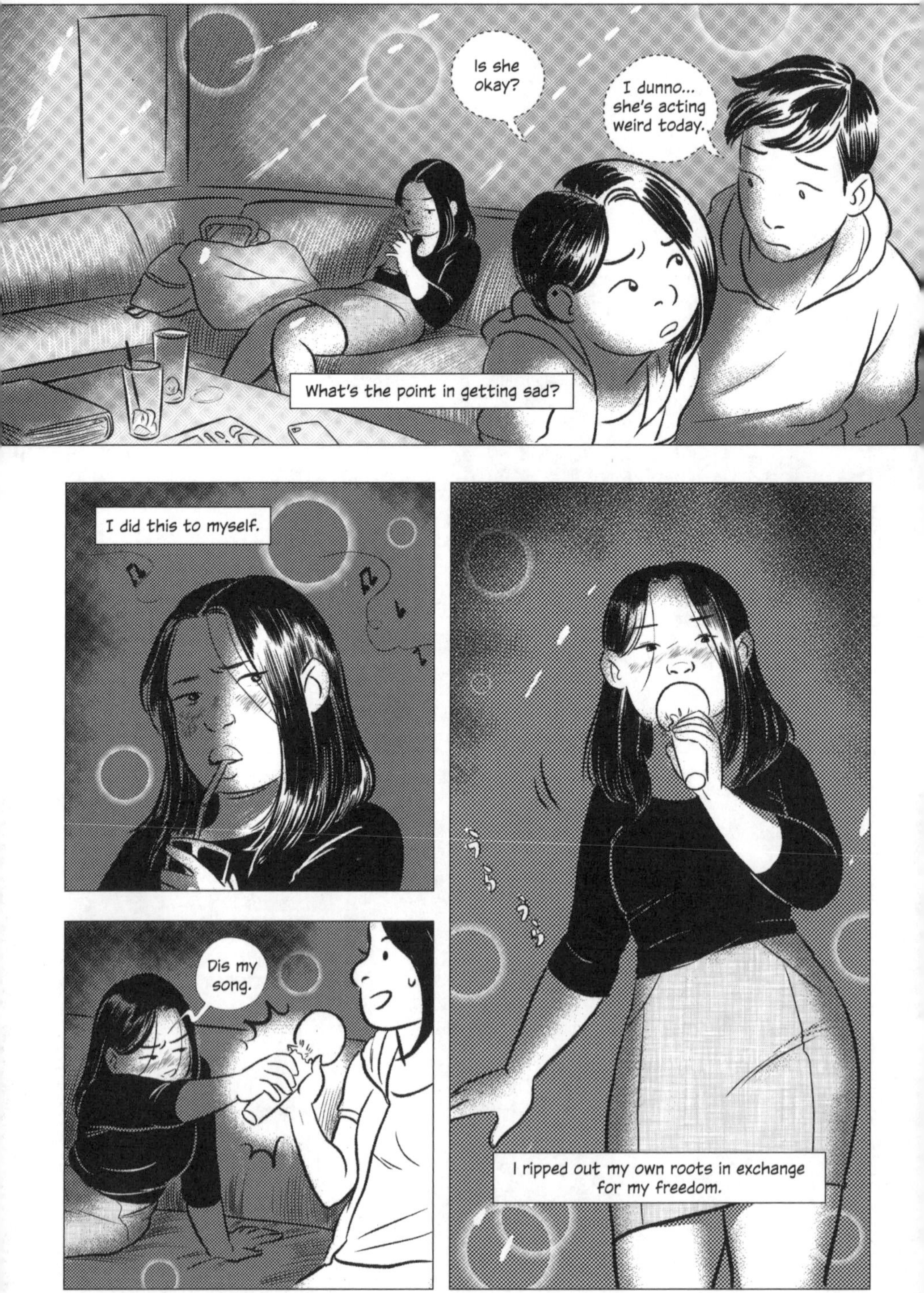
Is she okay?
I dunno... she's acting weird today.
What's the point in getting sad?
I did this to myself.
Dis my song.
I ripped out my own roots in exchange for my freedom.

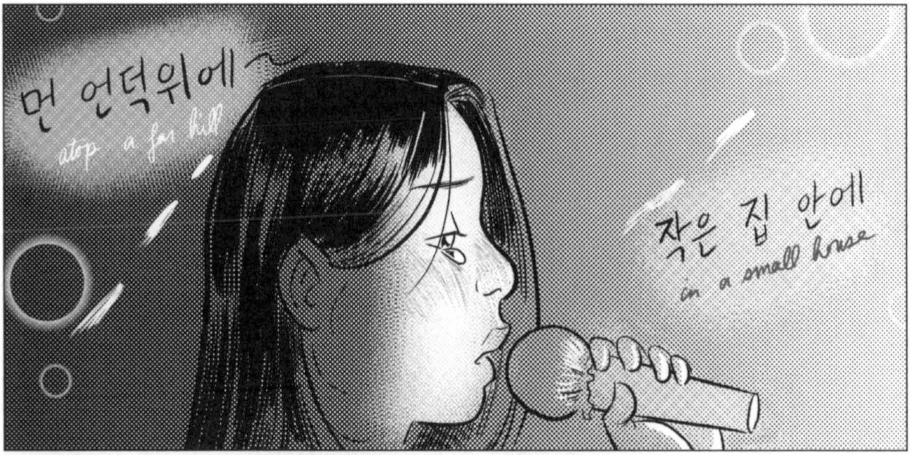
먼 언덕위에
atop a far hill
작은 집 안에
in a small house

What right do I have to miss my parents?

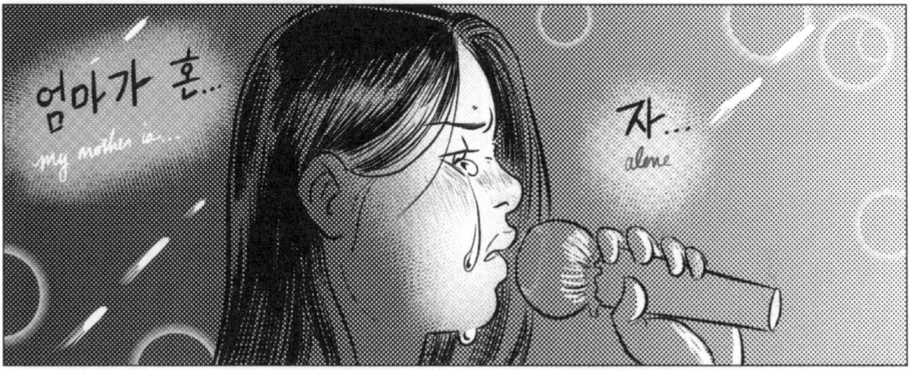
엄마가 혼…
my mother is…
자…
alone

I crushed their dreams with my own two hands.

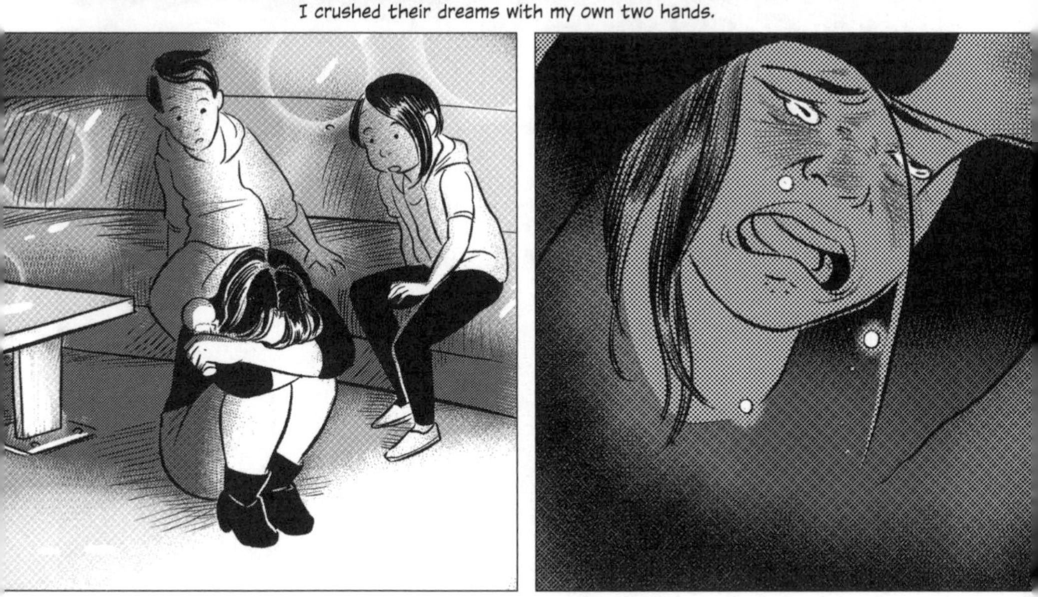

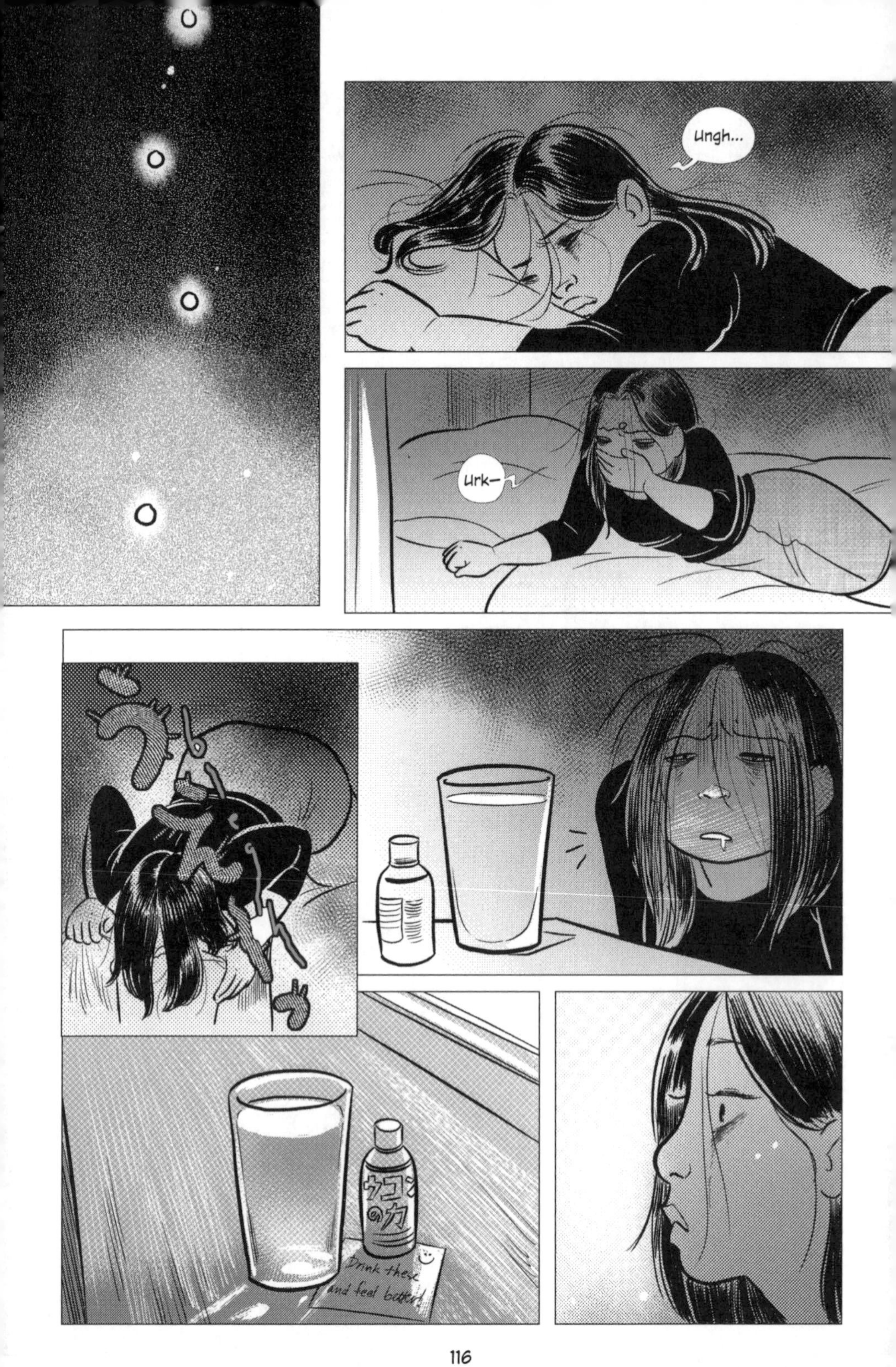
Ungh...
Urk—
ウコンの力
Drink these and feel better!

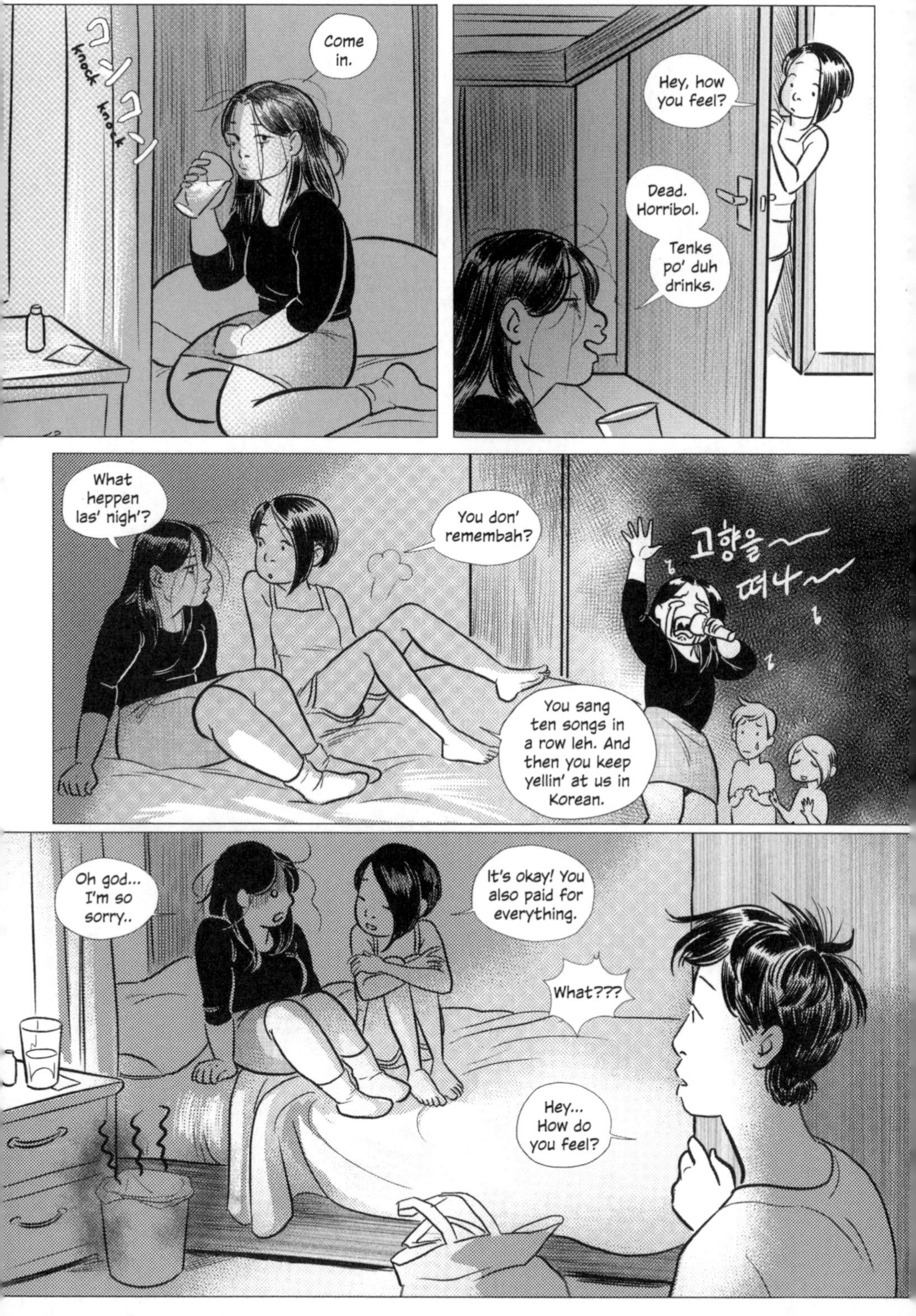

コンコン
knock knock
Come in.
Hey, how you feel?
Dead. Horribol.
Tenks po' duh drinks.
What heppen las' nigh'?
You don' remembah?
고향을~
떠나~
You sang ten songs in a row leh. And then you keep yellin' at us in Korean.
Oh god... I'm so sorry..
It's okay! You also paid for everything.
What???
Hey... How do you feel?

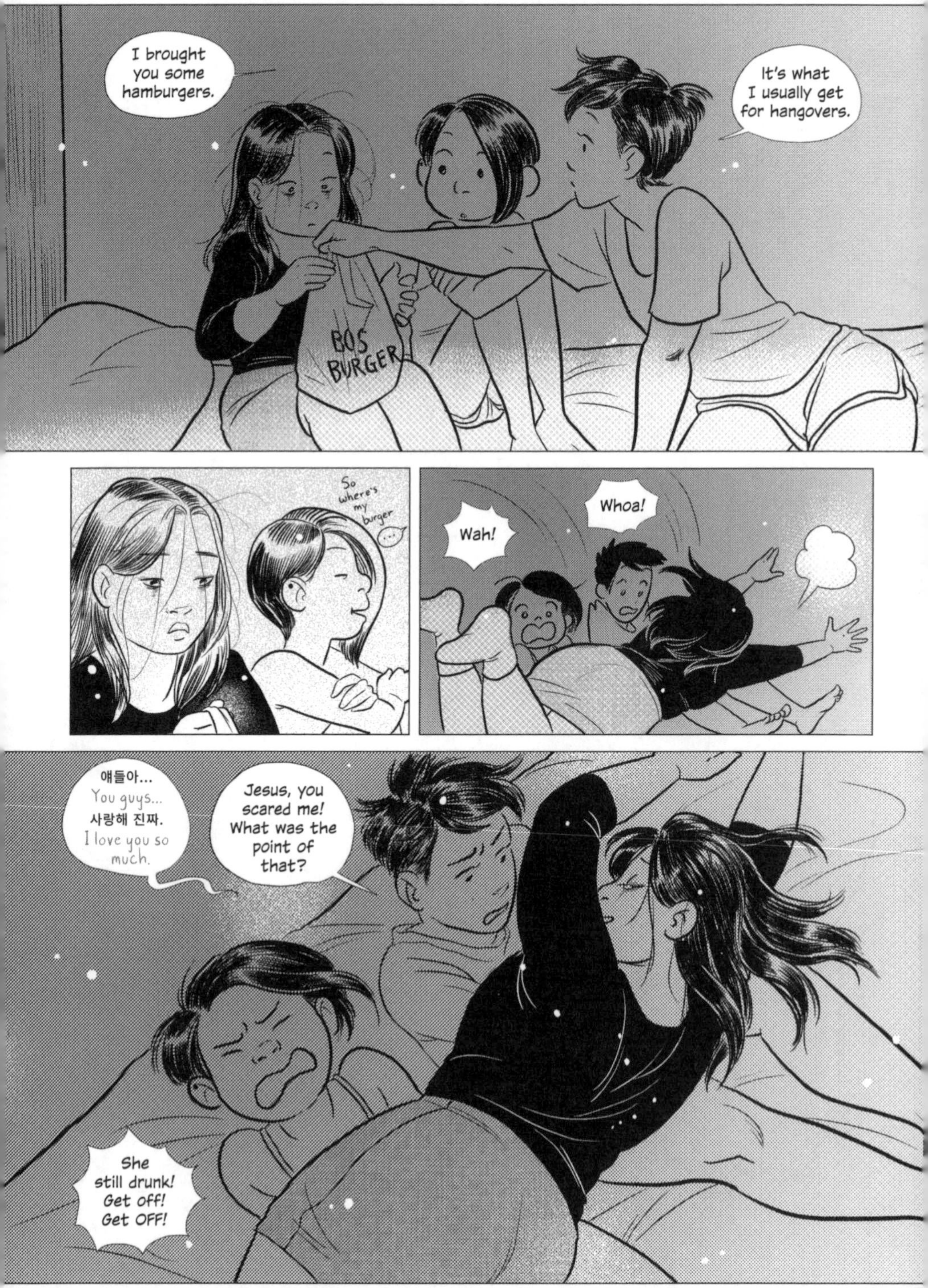
I brought you some hamburgers.
It's what I usually get for hangovers.
BOS BURGER
So where's my burger
...
Wah!
Whoa!
애들아...
You guys...
사랑해 진짜.
I love you so much.
Jesus, you scared me! What was the point of that?
She still drunk! Get off! Get OFF!

Chapter 7

Kaitenzushi

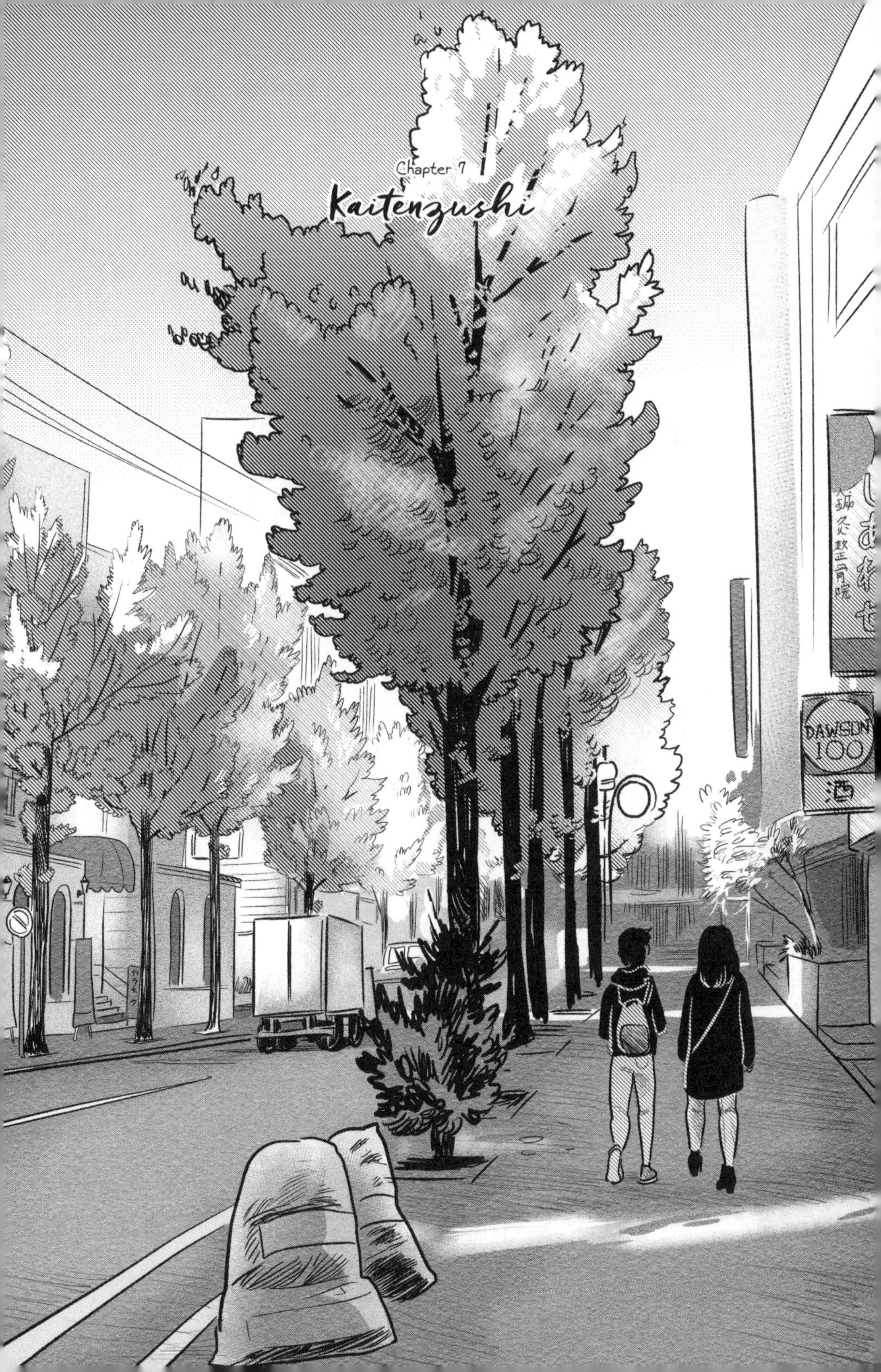
鍼灸整骨院
DAWSON
100
酒

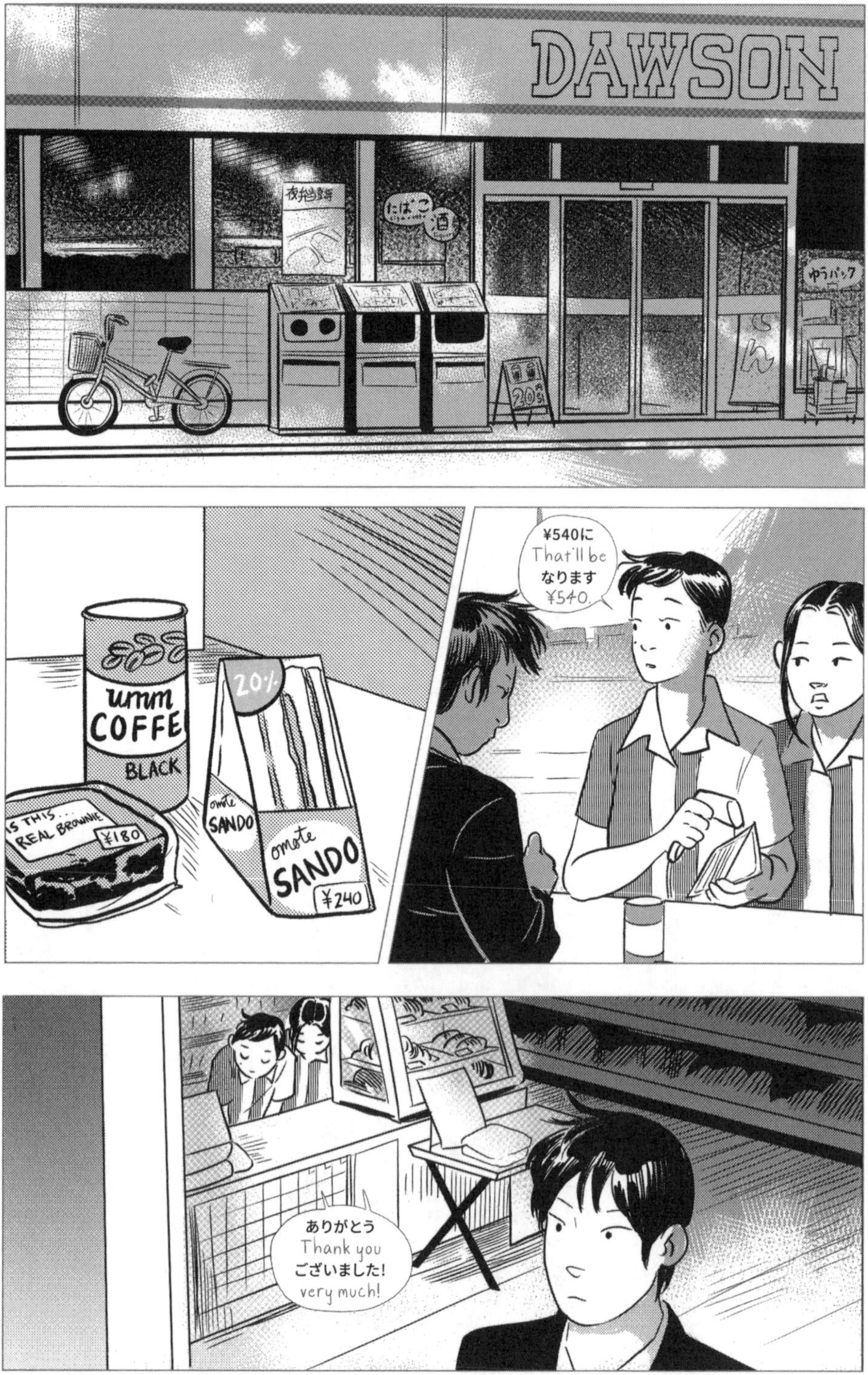
DAWSON
たばこ
酒
ゆうパック
umm
COFFE
BLACK
IS THIS...
REAL BROWNIE
¥180
20%
omote
SANDO
omote
SANDO
¥240
¥540に
That'll be
なります
¥540.
ありがとう
Thank you
ございました!
very much!

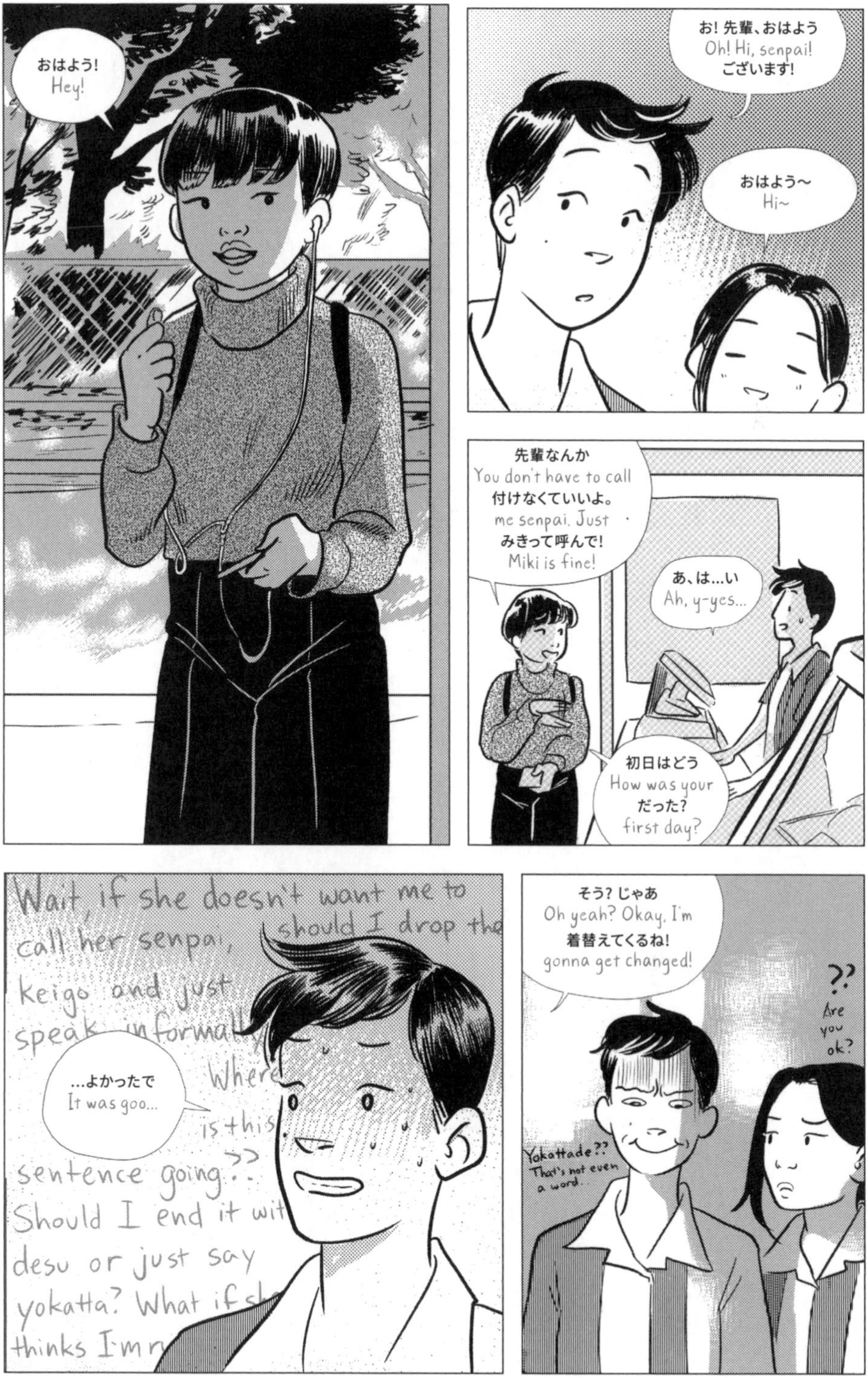
おはよう!
Hey!
お! 先輩、おはよう
Oh! Hi, senpai!
ございます!
おはよう~
Hi~
先輩なんか
You don't have to call
付けなくていいよ。
me senpai. Just
みきって呼んで!
Miki is fine!
あ、は...い
Ah, y-yes...
初日はどう
How was your
だった?
first day?
Wait, if she doesn't want me to call her senpai, should I drop the keigo and just speak informally? Where is this sentence going?? Should I end it with desu or just say yokatta? What if she thinks I'm r
...よかったで
It was goo...
そう? じゃあ
Oh yeah? Okay, I'm
着替えてくるね!
gonna get changed!
?? Are you ok?
Yokattade?? That's not even a word...

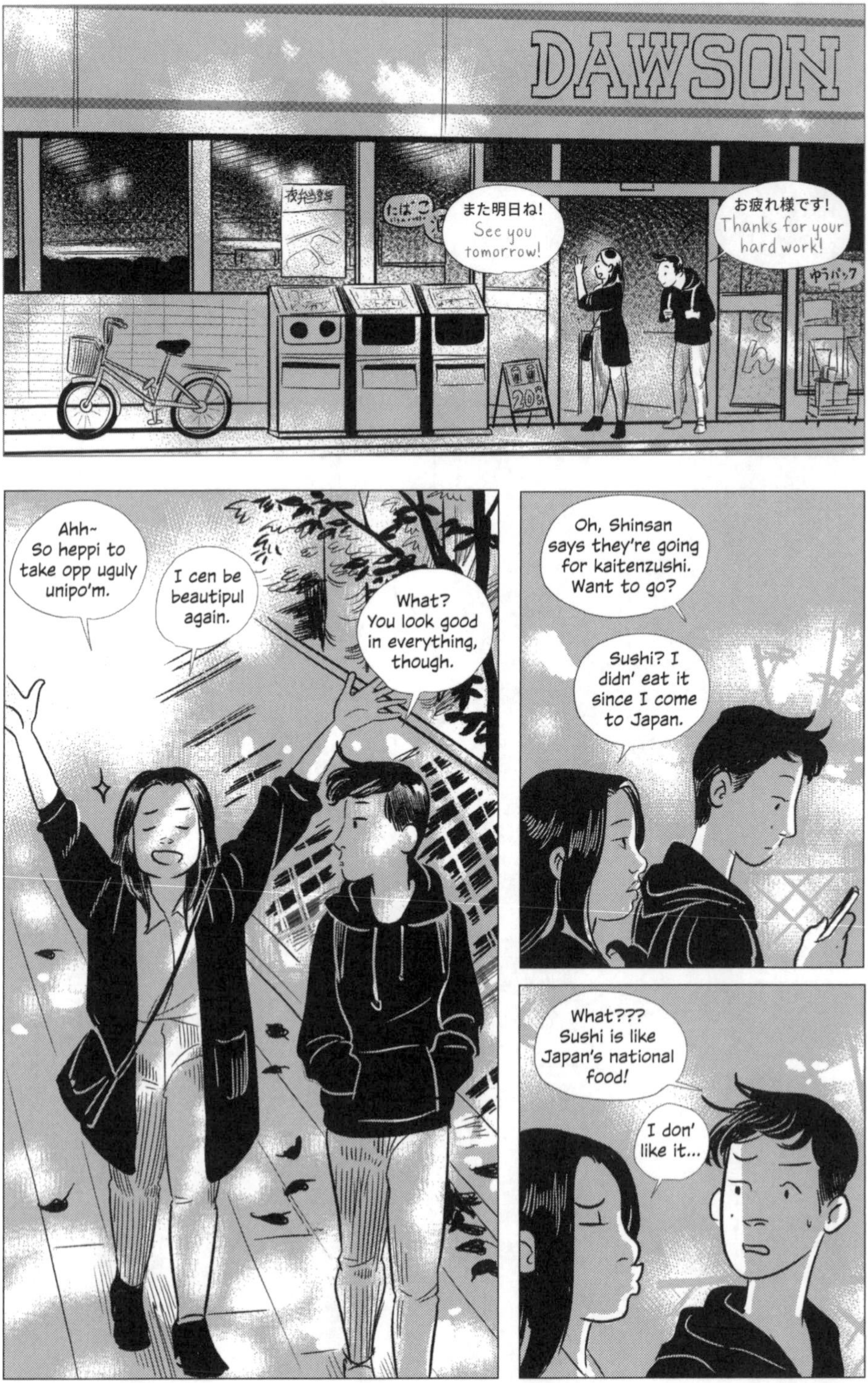
DAWSON
たばこ
また明日ね!
See you tomorrow!
お疲れ様です!
Thanks for your hard work!
ゆうパック
Ahh~ So heppi to take opp uguly unipo'm.
I cen be beautipul again.
What? You look good in everything, though.
Oh, Shinsan says they're going for kaitenzushi. Want to go?
Sushi? I didn' eat it since I come to Japan.
What??? Sushi is like Japan's national food!
I don' like it...

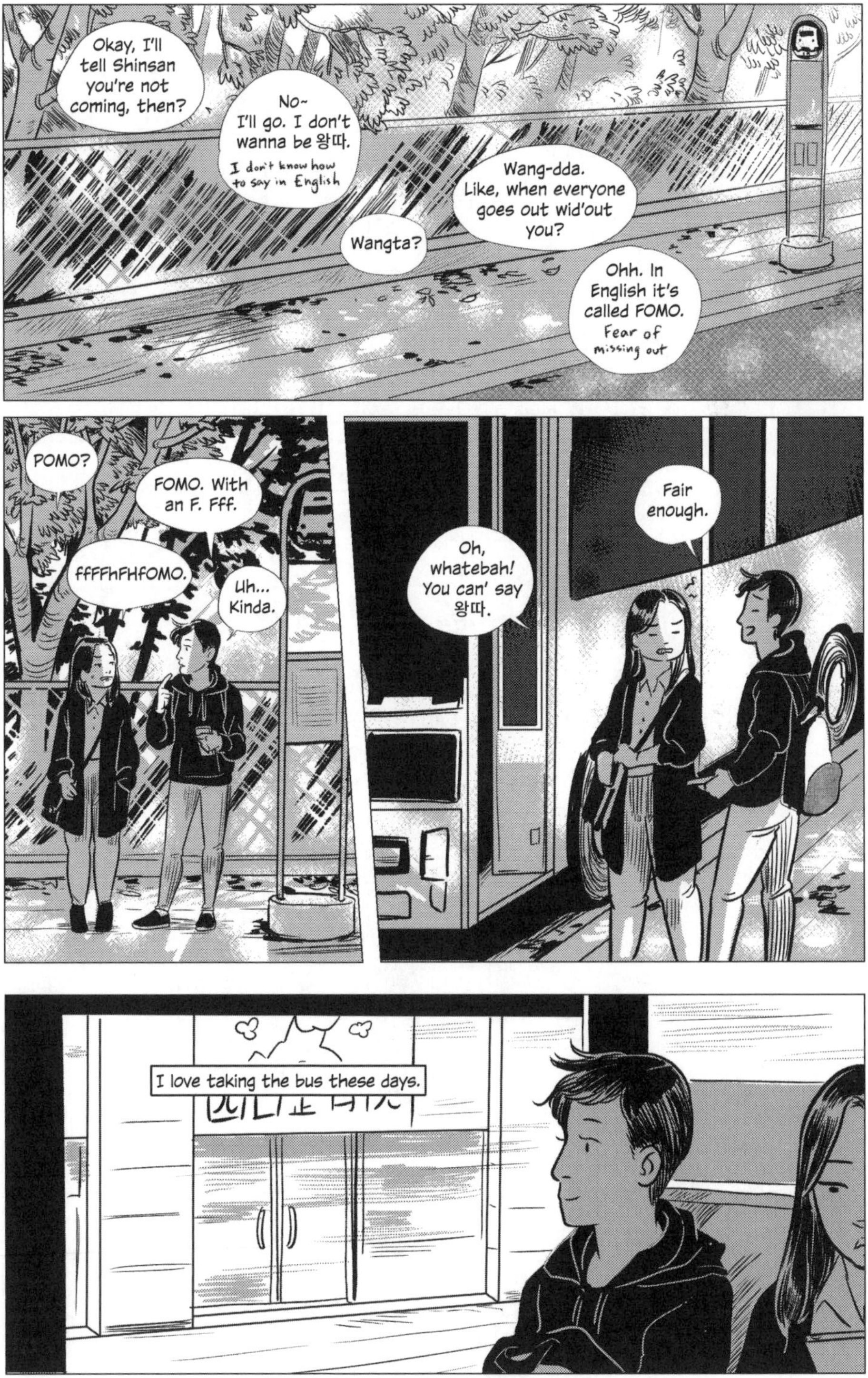
Okay, I'll tell Shinsan you're not coming, then?
No~ I'll go. I don't wanna be 왕따.
I don't know how to say in English
Wangta?
Wang-dda. Like, when everyone goes out wid'out you?
Ohh. In English it's called FOMO. Fear of missing out
POMO?
FOMO. With an F. Fff.
ffffhFHFOMO.
Uh... Kinda.
Oh, whatebah! You can' say 왕따.
Fair enough.
I love taking the bus these days.

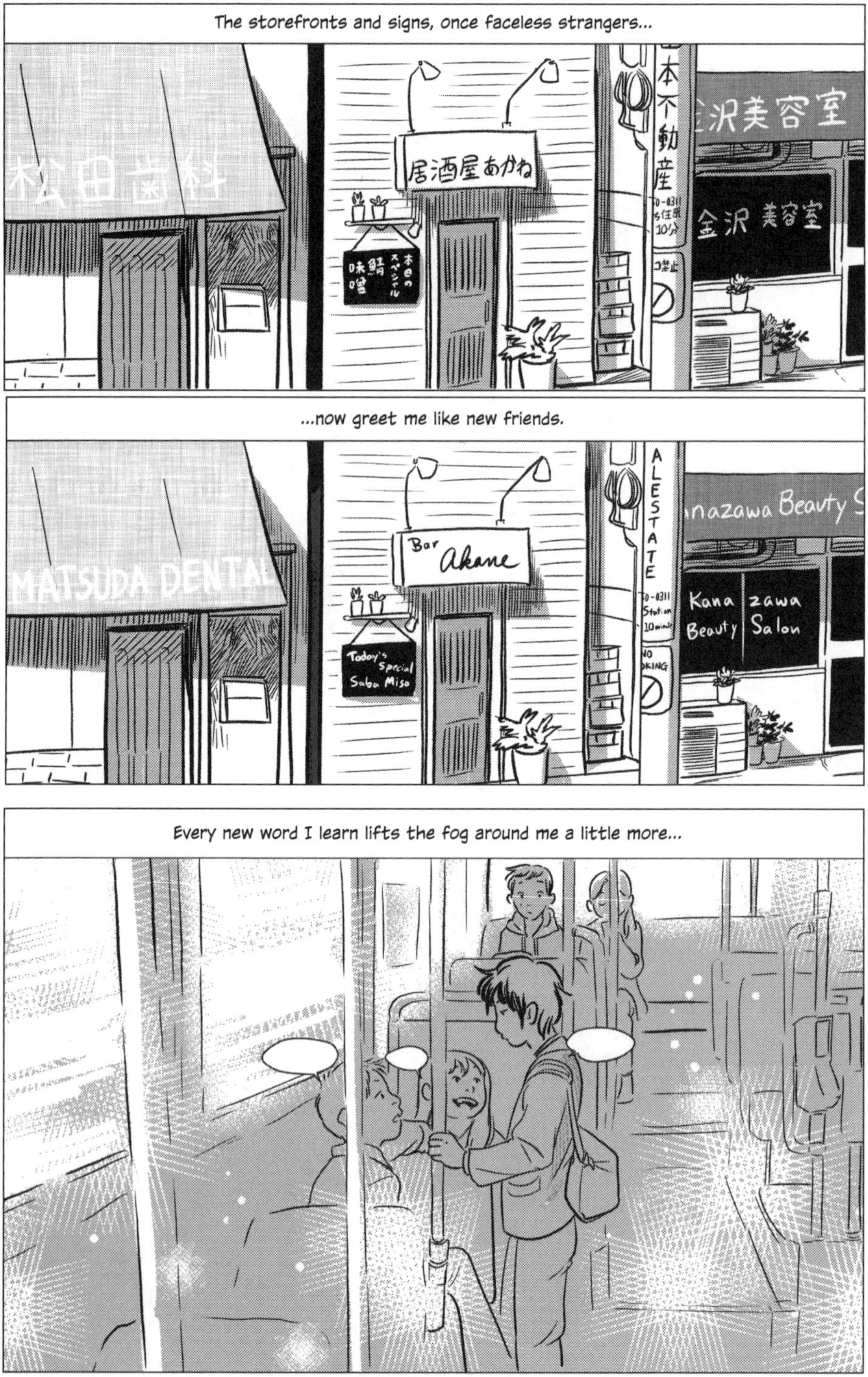
The storefronts and signs, once faceless strangers...
松田歯科
居酒屋あかね
本日のスペシャル
鯖味噌
金沢美容室
金沢 美容室
...now greet me like new friends.
MATSUDA DENTAL
Bar
akane
Today's Special
Saba Miso
ALESTATE
Kanazawa Beauty Salon
Every new word I learn lifts the fog around me a little more...

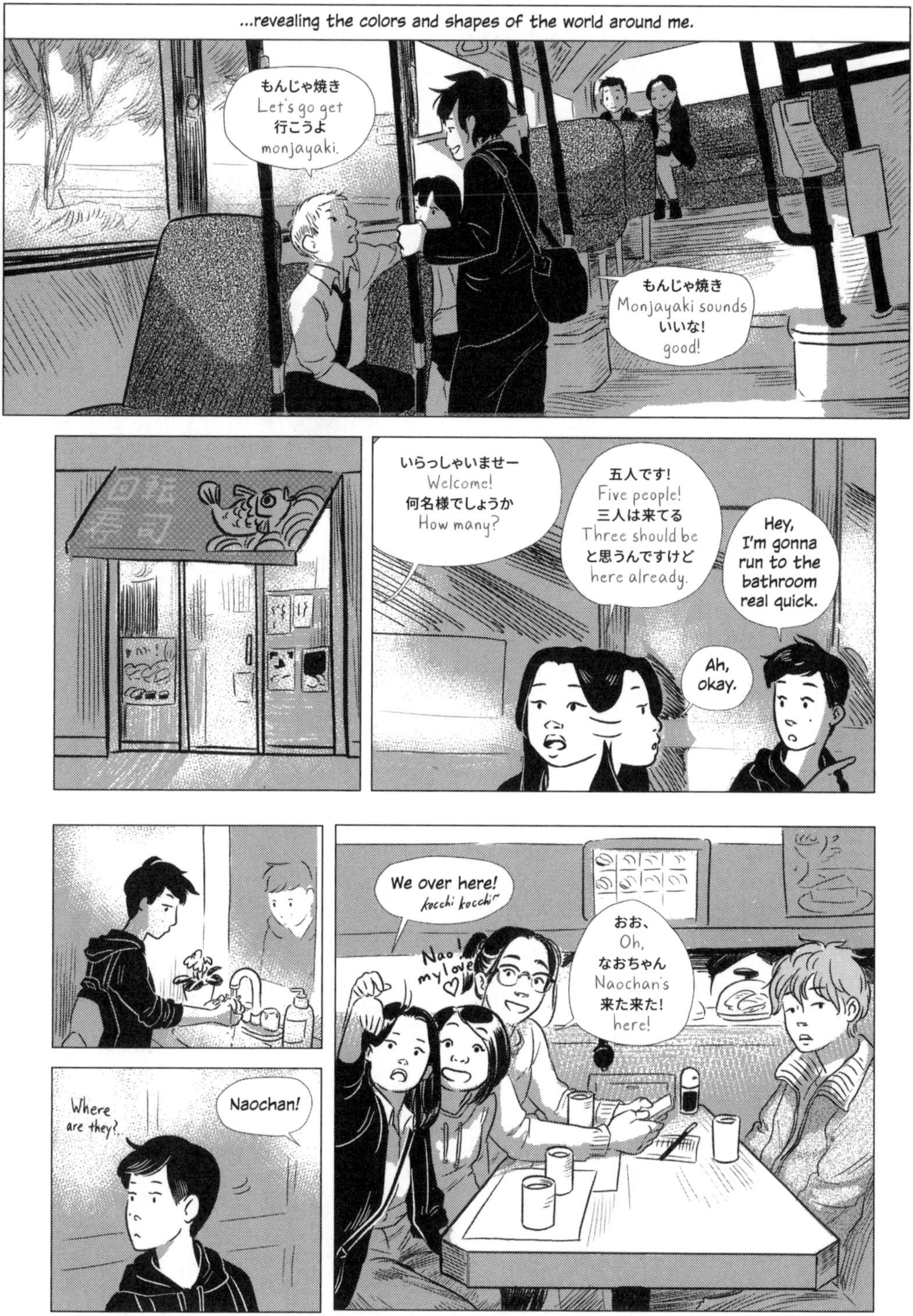

...revealing the colors and shapes of the world around me.
もんじゃ焼き Let's go get 行こうよ monjayaki.
もんじゃ焼き Monjayaki sounds いいな! good!
回転寿司
いらっしゃいませー Welcome! 何名様でしょうか How many?
五人です! Five people! 三人は来てる Three should be と思うんですけど here already.
Hey, I'm gonna run to the bathroom real quick.
Ah, okay.
Where are they?..
Naochan!
We over here! kocchi kocchi~
Nao! my love ♡
おお、 Oh, なおちゃん Naochan's 来た来た! here!

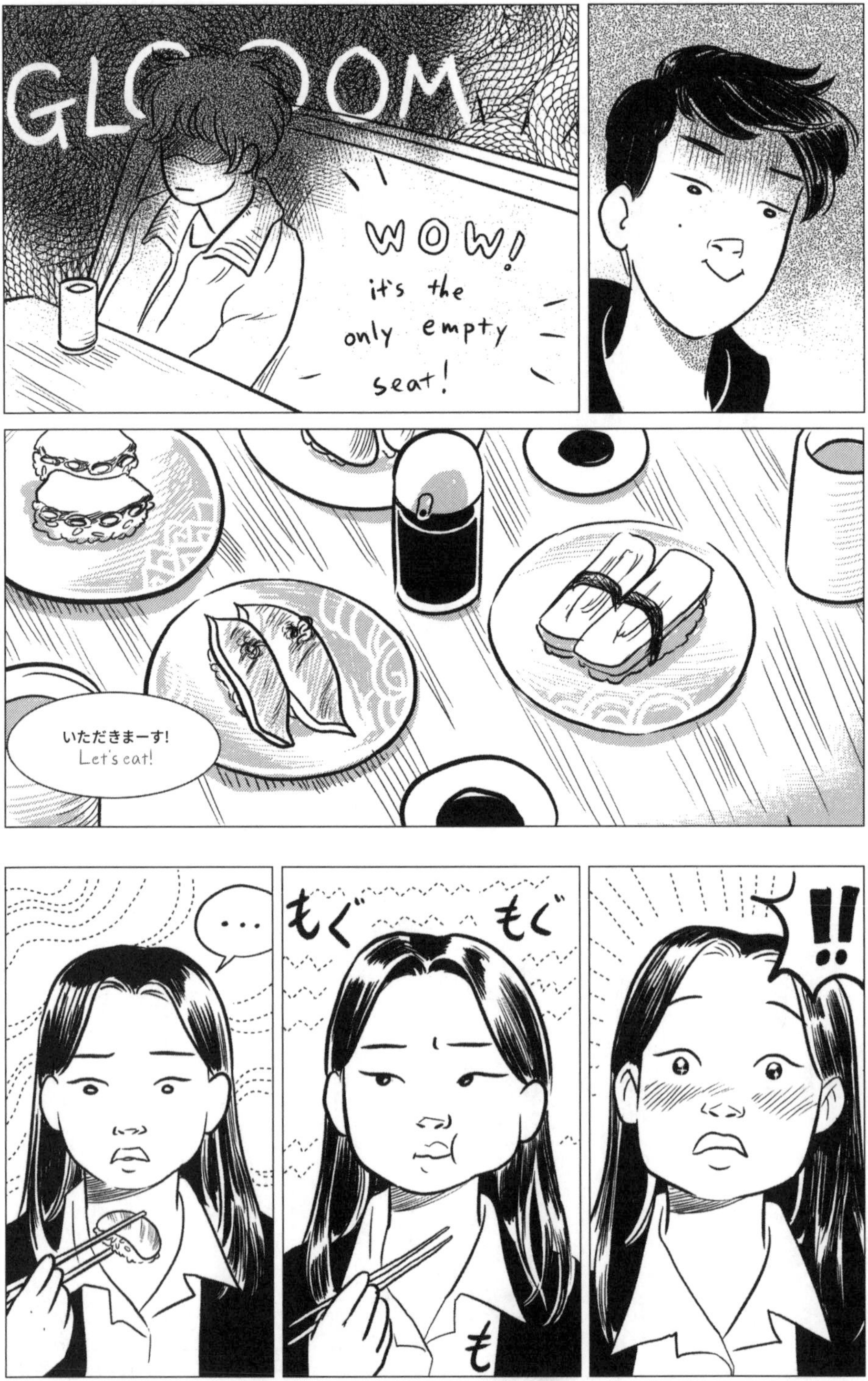
GLOOOM
WOW! it's the only empty seat!
いただきまーす!
Let's eat!
...
もぐ もぐ
も
!!

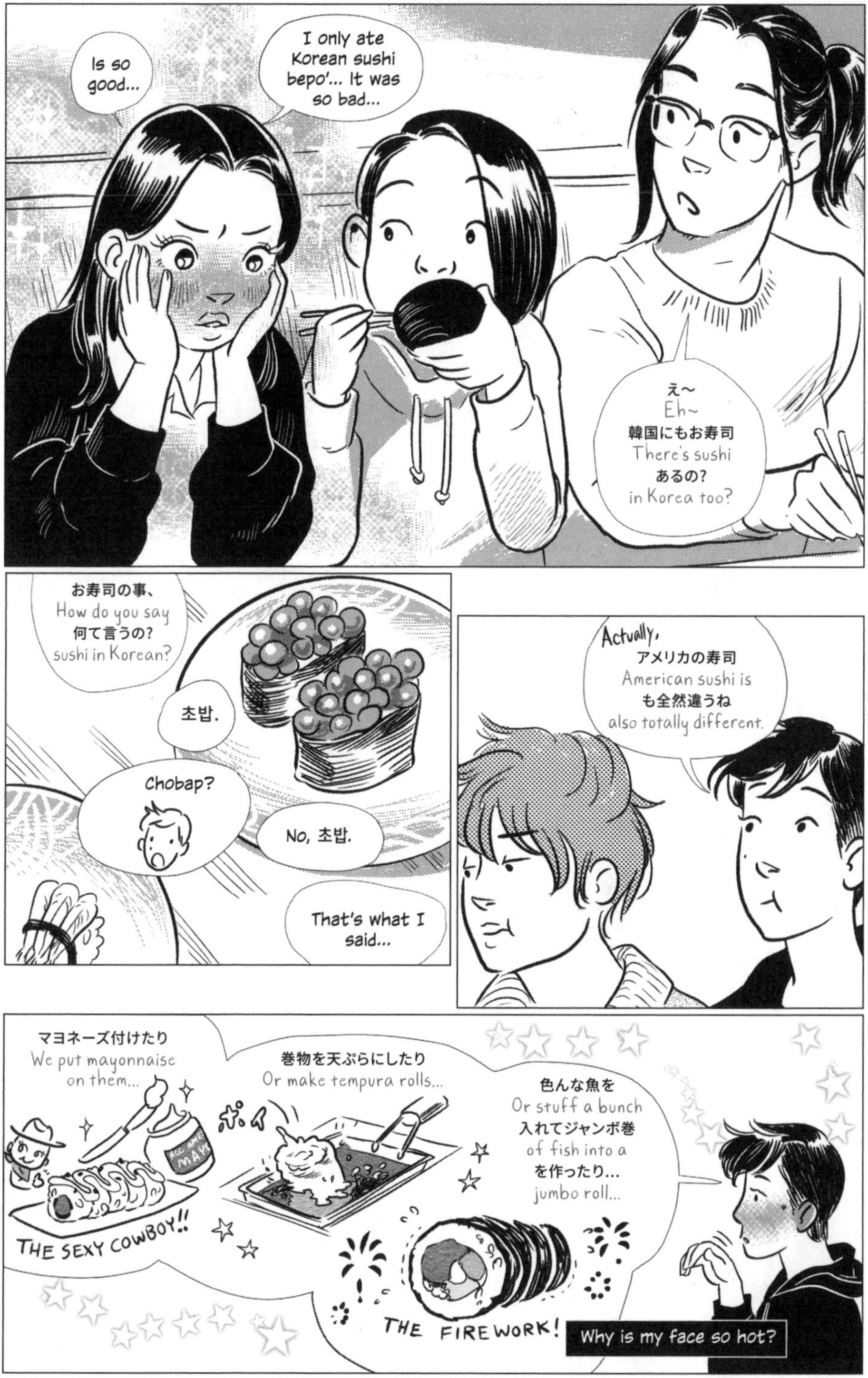
Is so good...
I only ate Korean sushi bepo'... It was so bad...
え~
Eh~
韓国にもお寿司
There's sushi
あるの?
in Korea too?
お寿司の事、
How do you say
何て言うの?
sushi in Korean?
초밥.
Chobap?
No, 초밥.
That's what I said...
Actually,
アメリカの寿司
American sushi is
も全然違うね
also totally different.
マヨネーズ付けたり
We put mayonnaise on them...
巻物を天ぷらにしたり
Or make tempura rolls...
色んな魚を
Or stuff a bunch
入れてジャンボ巻
of fish into a
を作ったり...
jumbo roll...
THE SEXY COWBOY!!
THE FIREWORK!
Why is my face so hot?

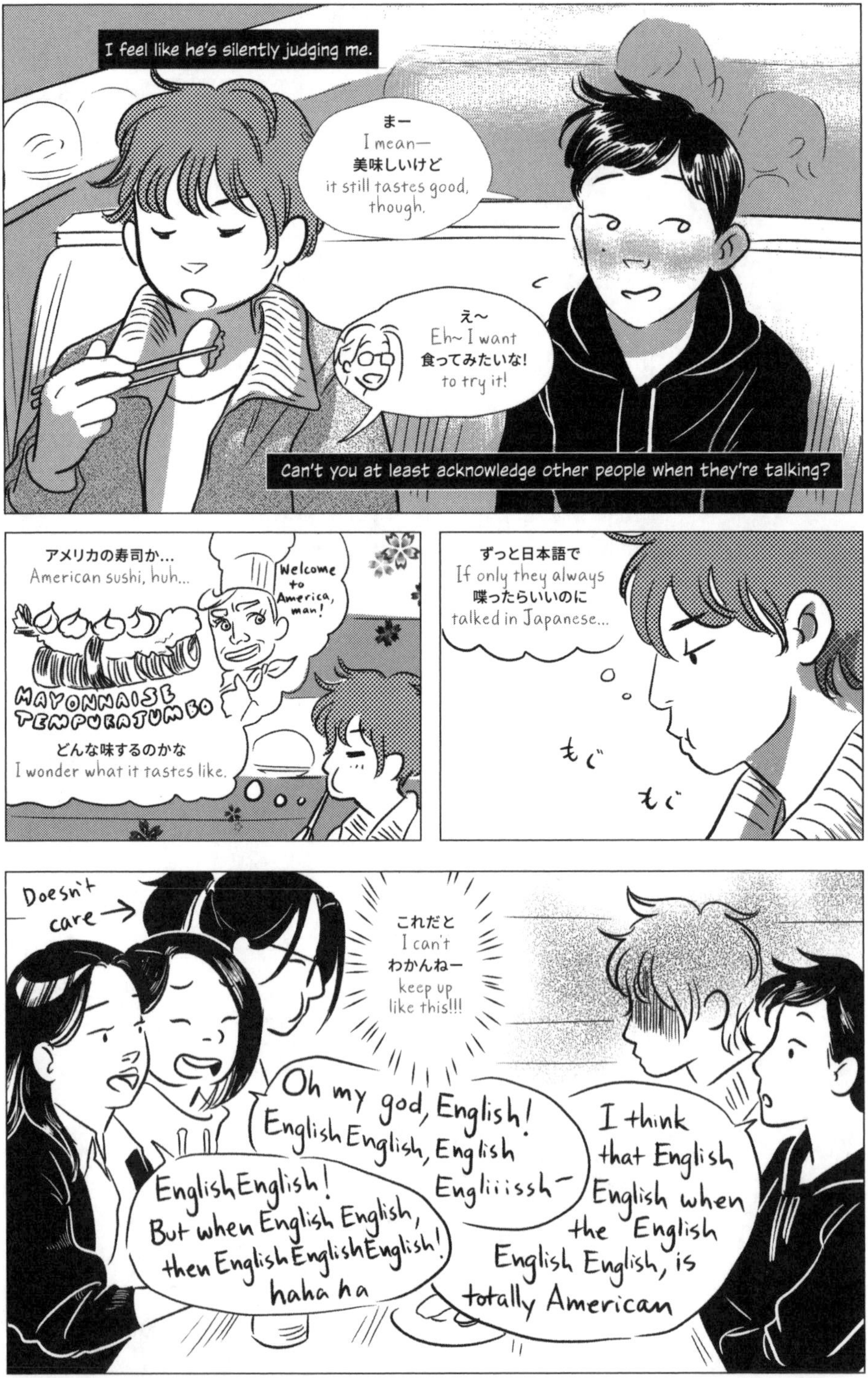
I feel like he's silently judging me.
まー
I mean—
美味しいけど
it still tastes good, though.
え~
Eh~ I want
食ってみたいな!
to try it!
Can't you at least acknowledge other people when they're talking?
アメリカの寿司か…
American sushi, huh...
Welcome to America, man!
MAYONNAISE TEMPURAJUMBO
どんな味するのかな
I wonder what it tastes like.
ずっと日本語で
If only they always
喋ったらいいのに
talked in Japanese...
もぐ
もぐ
Doesn't care →
これだと
I can't
わかんねー
keep up like this!!!
Oh my god, English! English English, English Engliiissh—
EnglishEnglish! But when English English, then EnglishEnglishEnglish! hahaha
I think that English English when the English English English, is totally American

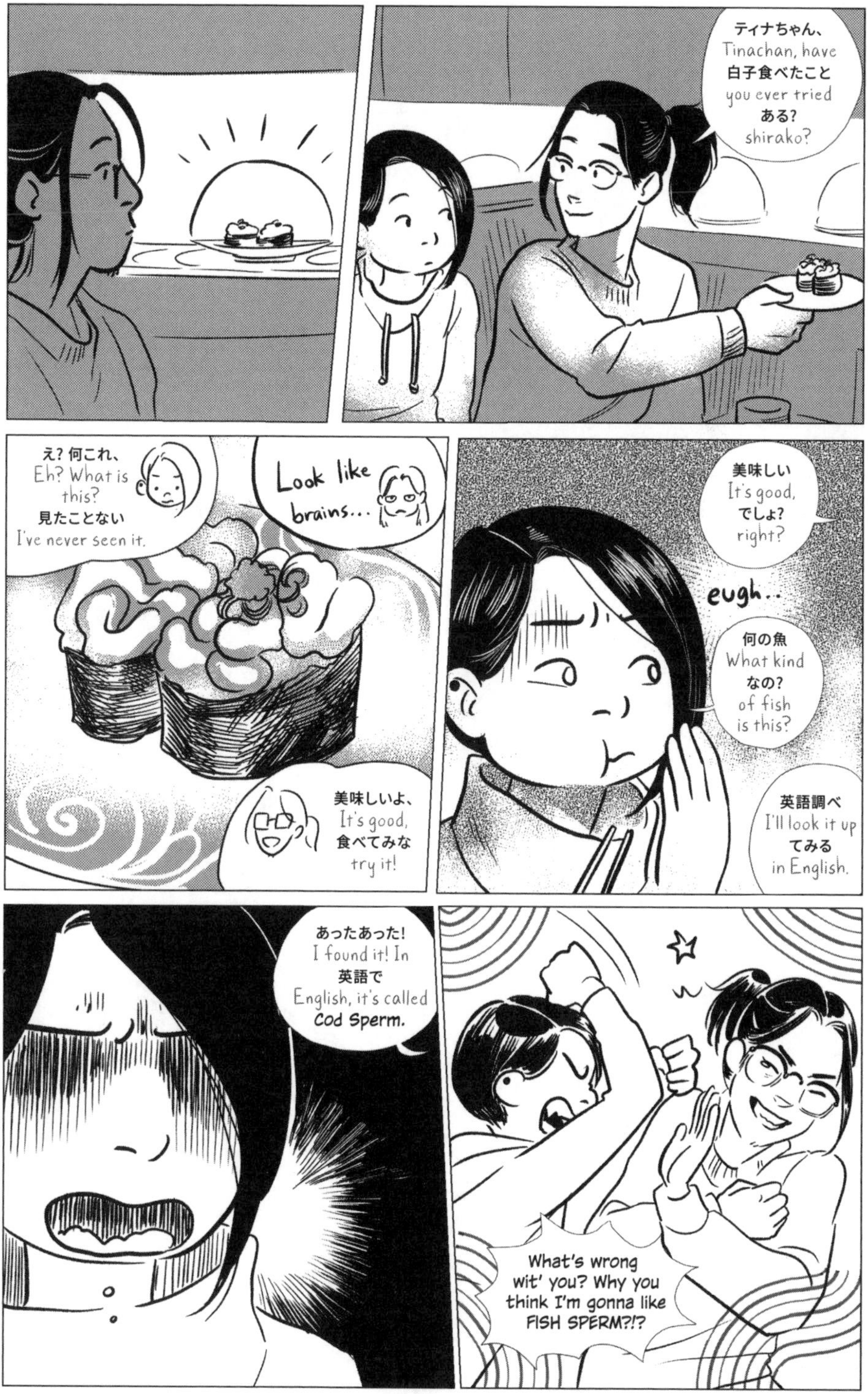

ティナちゃん、
Tinachan, have
白子食べたこと
you ever tried
ある?
shirako?
え? 何これ、
Eh? What is this?
見たことない
I've never seen it.
Look like brains...
美味しいよ、
It's good,
食べてみな
try it!
美味しい
It's good,
でしょ?
right?
eugh..
何の魚
What kind
なの?
of fish is this?
英語調べ
I'll look it up
てみる
in English.
あったあった!
I found it! In
英語で
English, it's called
Cod Sperm.
What's wrong wit' you? Why you think I'm gonna like FISH SPERM?!?

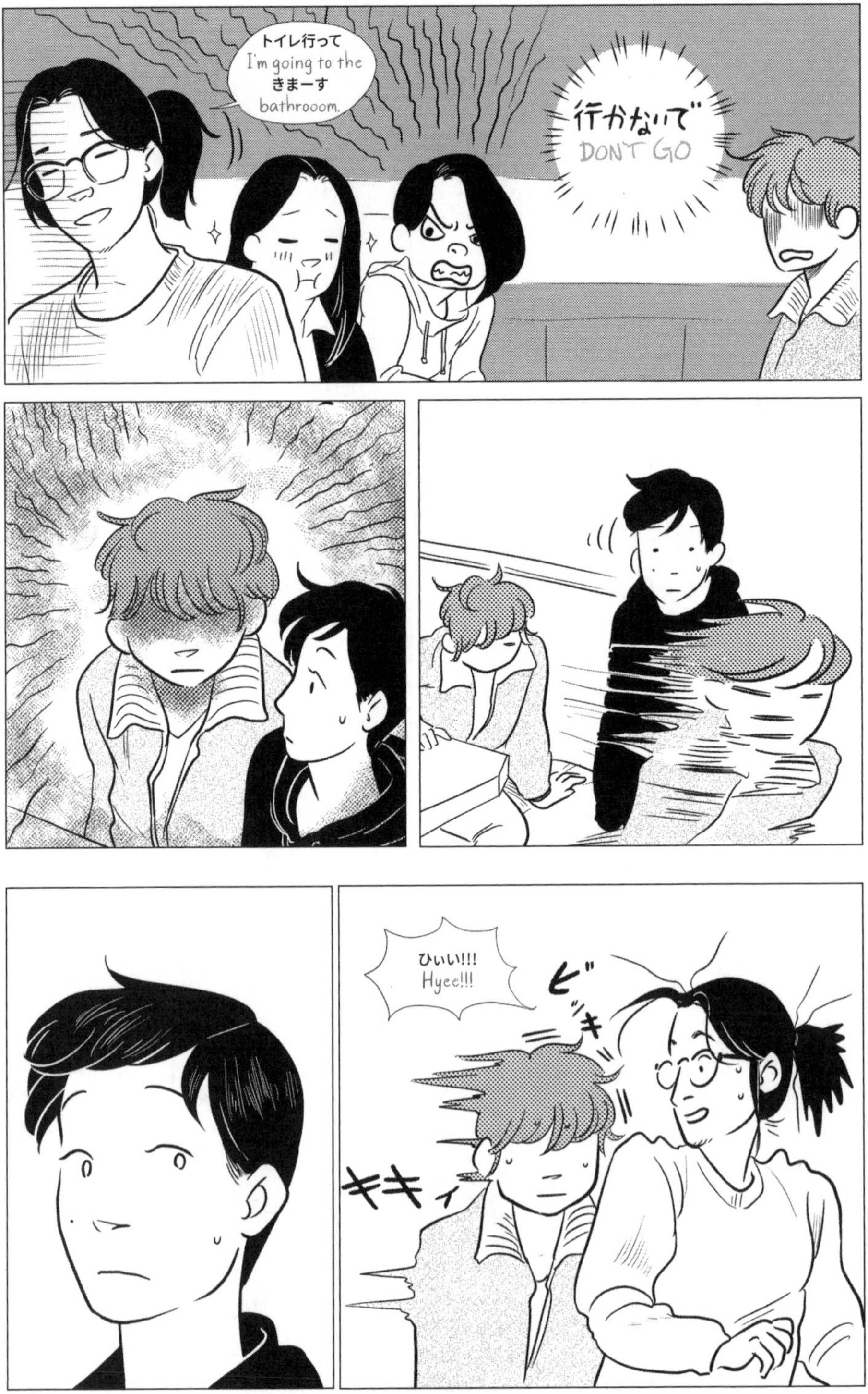
トイレ行って
I'm going to the
きまーす
bathrooom.
行かないで
DON'T GO
ひいい!!!
Hyee!!!
ビキ
キキィ

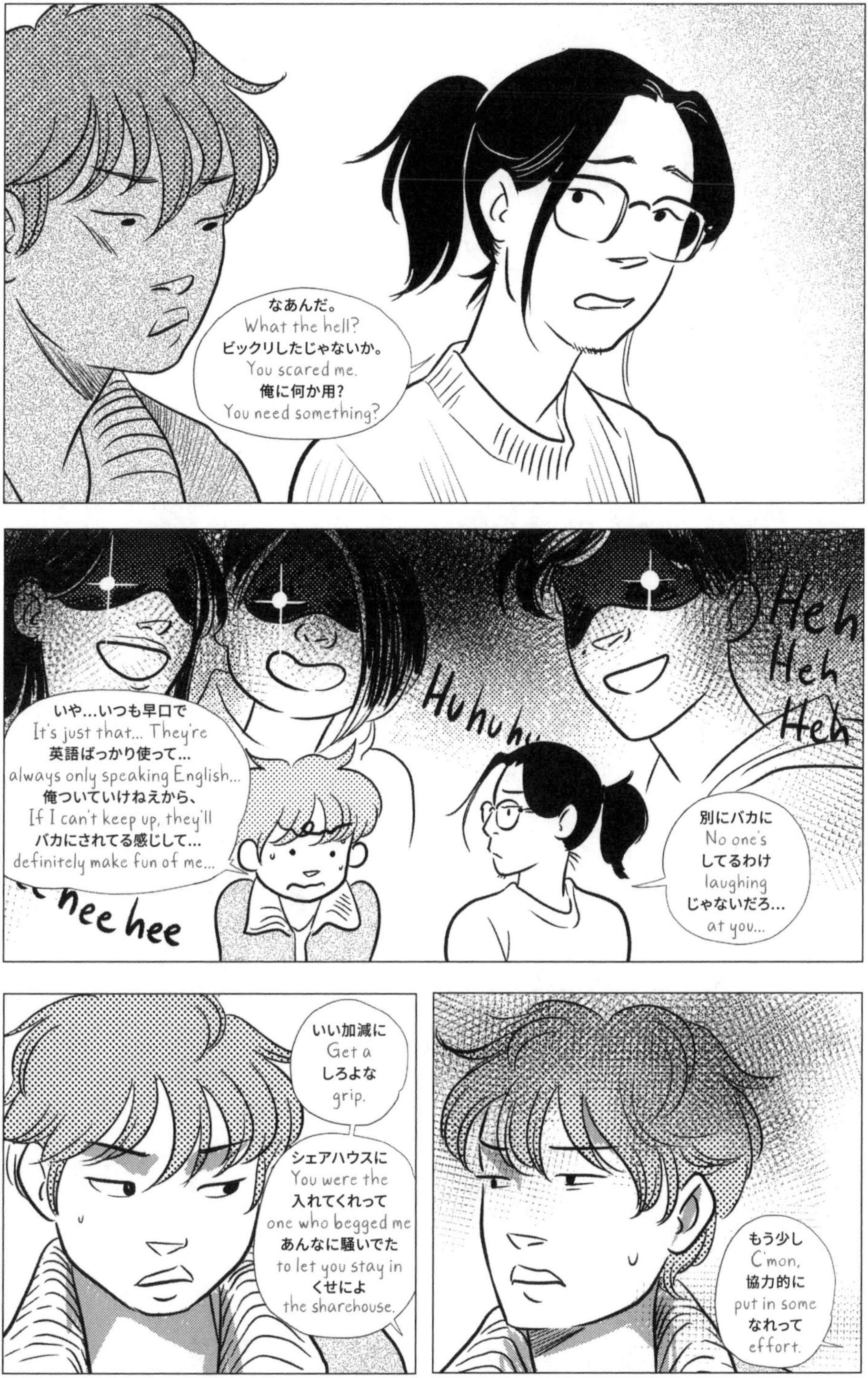
なあんだ。
What the hell?
ビックリしたじゃないか。
You scared me.
俺に何か用?
You need something?
いや…いつも早口で
It's just that... They're
英語ばっかり使って…
always only speaking English...
俺ついていけねえから、
If I can't keep up, they'll
バカにされてる感じして…
definitely make fun of me...
hee hee
Huhuh
Heh Heh Heh
別にバカに
No one's
してるわけ
laughing
じゃないだろ…
at you...
いい加減に
Get a
しろよな
grip.
シェアハウスに
You were the
入れてくれって
one who begged me
あんなに騒いでた
to let you stay in
くせによ
the sharehouse.
もう少し
C'mon,
協力的に
put in some
なれって
effort.

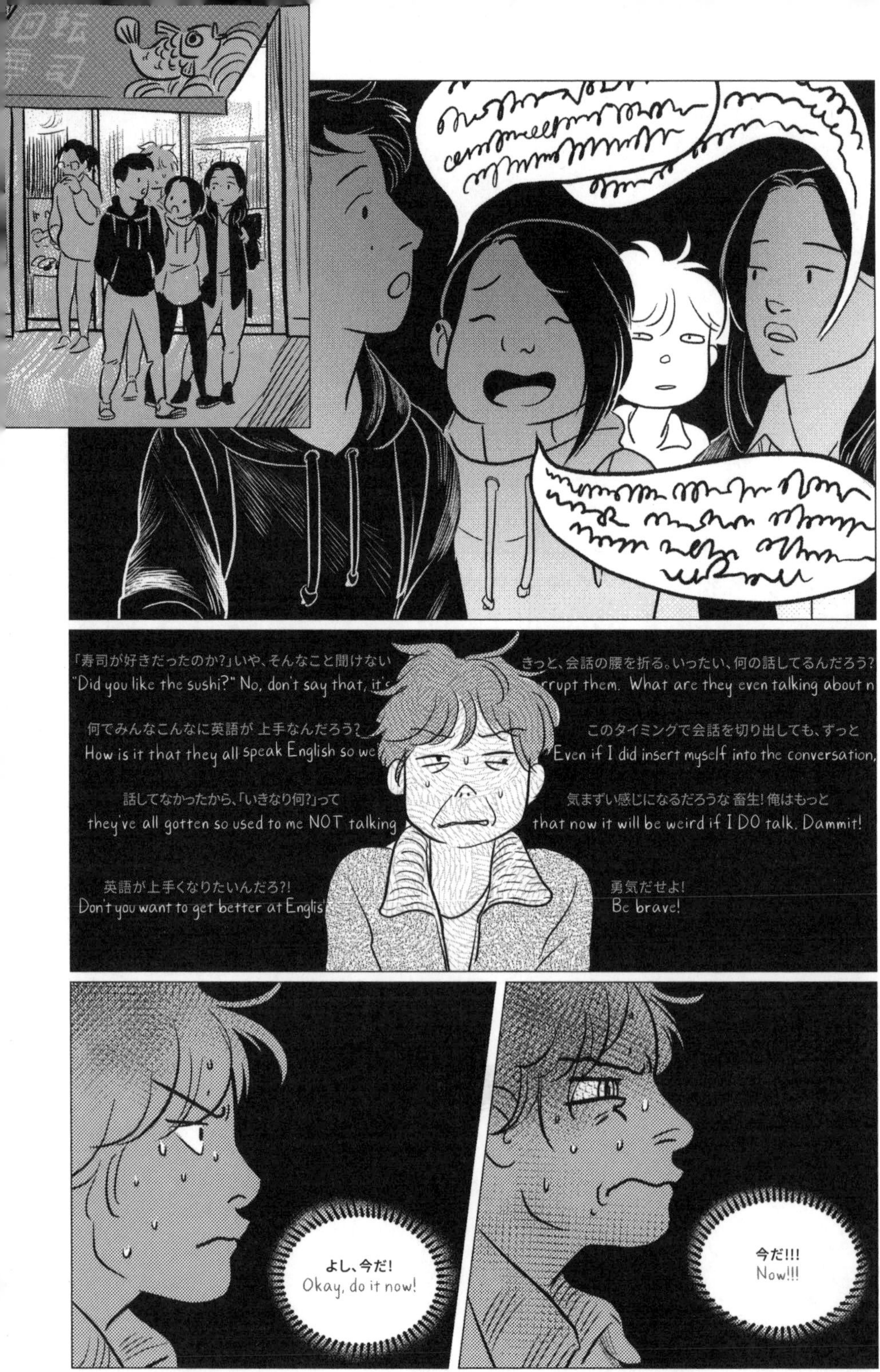

「寿司が好きだったのか?」いや、そんなこと聞けない
"Did you like the sushi?" No, don't say that, it's
きっと、会話の腰を折る。いったい、何の話してるんだろう?
rrupt them. What are they even talking about n
何でみんなこんなに英語が 上手なんだろう?
How is it that they all speak English so we
このタイミングで会話を切り出しても、ずっと
Even if I did insert myself into the conversation,
話してなかったから、「いきなり何?」って
they've all gotten so used to me NOT talking
気まずい感じになるだろうな 畜生! 俺はもっと
that now it will be weird if I DO talk. Dammit!
英語が上手くなりたいんだろ?!
Don't you want to get better at Englis
勇気だせよ!
Be brave!
よし、今だ!
Okay, do it now!
今だ!!!
Now!!!

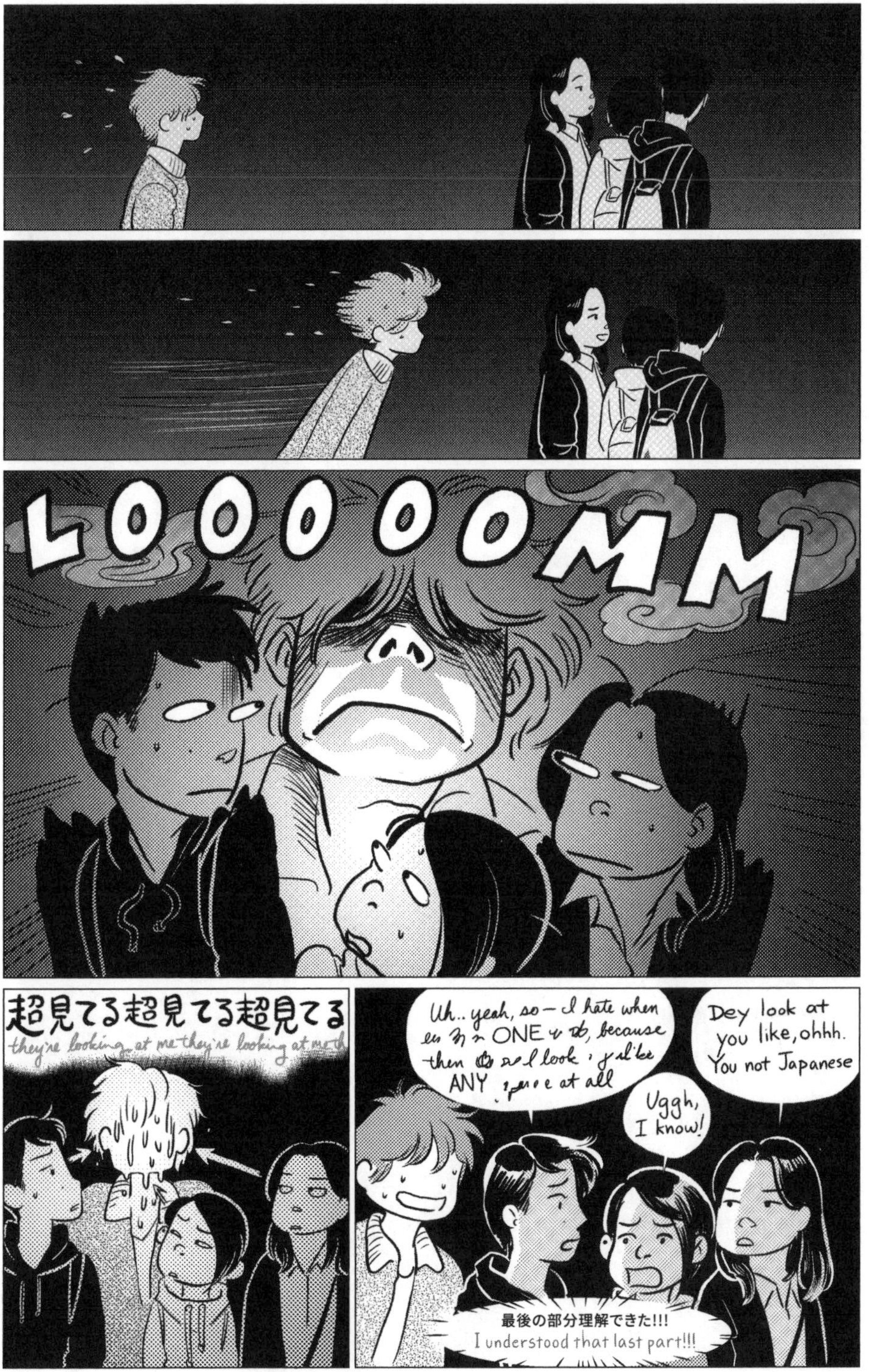
LOOOOOMM
超見てる超見てる超見てる
they're looking at me they're looking at me
Uh.. yeah, so— I hate when ONE because then look like ANY at all
Dey look at you like, ohhh. You not Japanese
Uggh, I know!
最後の部分理解できた!!!
I understood that last part!!!

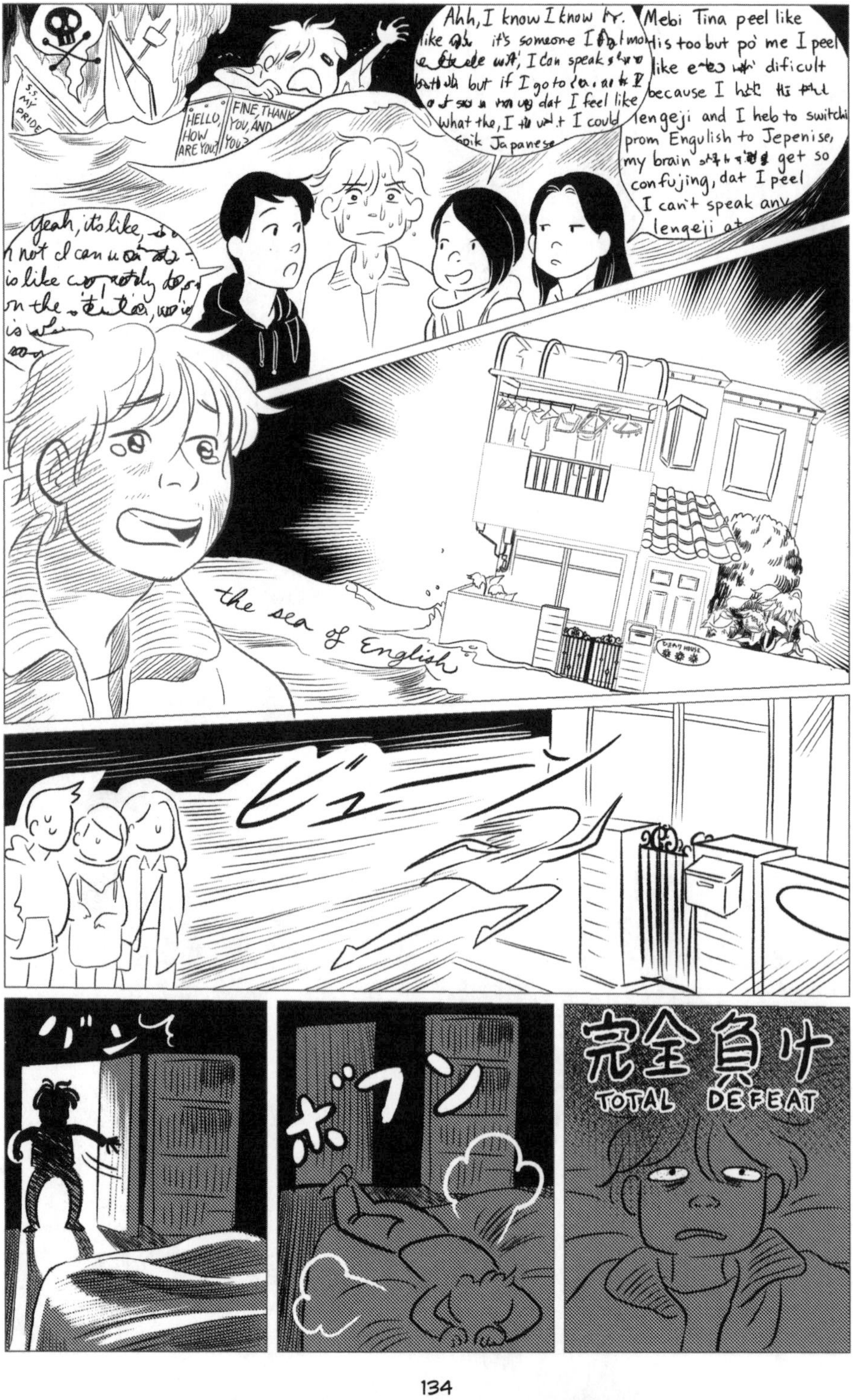

S.S. MY PRIDE
HELLO, HOW ARE YOU?
FINE, THANK YOU, AND YOU?
Ahh, I know I know. like it's someone I, I can speak but if I go to dat I feel like what the, I I could spik Japanese
Mebi Tina peel like dis too but po' me I peel like dificult because I lengeji and I heb to switchi prom Engulish to Jepenise, my brain get so confujing, dat I peel I can't speak any lengeji at
Yeah, its like,
the sea of English
ビューン
バン
ボフン
完全負け
TOTAL DEFEAT

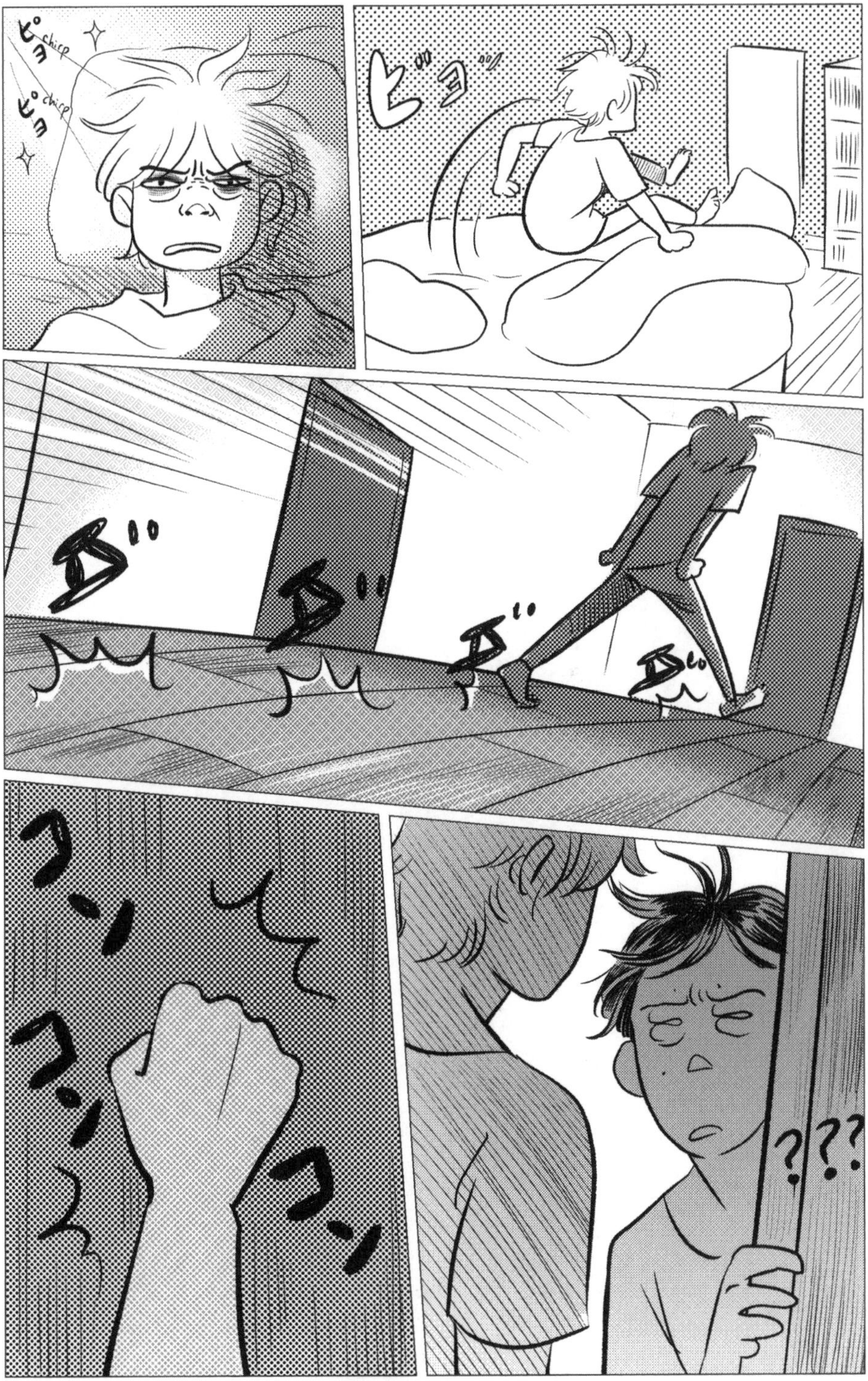
ピヨ chirp
ピヨ chirp
ピヨ
ダ"
ダ"
ダ"
ダ"
コン
コン
コン
???

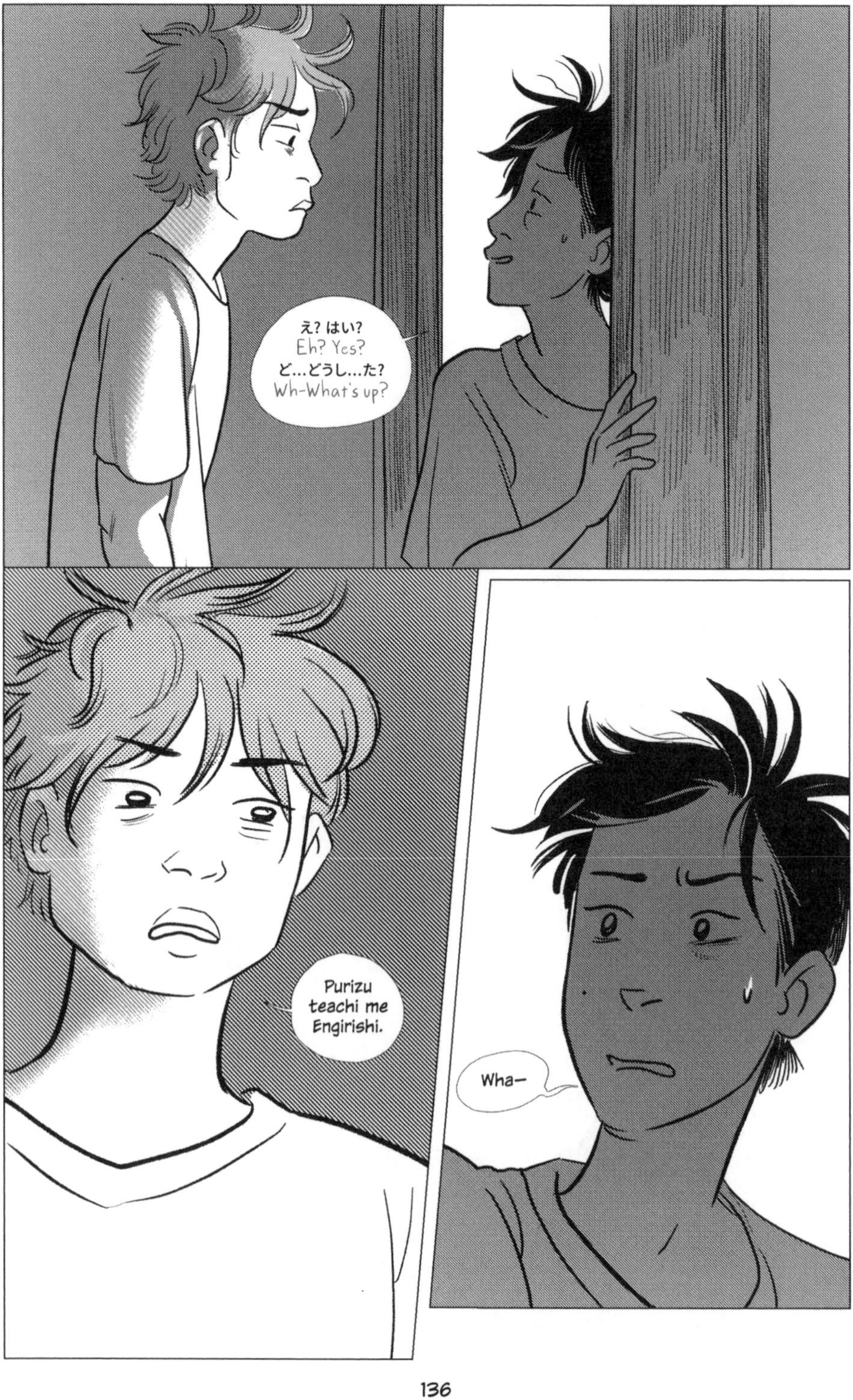
え? はい?
Eh? Yes?
ど…どうし…た?
Wh-What's up?
Purizu teachi me Engirishi.
Wha–

Chapter 8

Harajuku

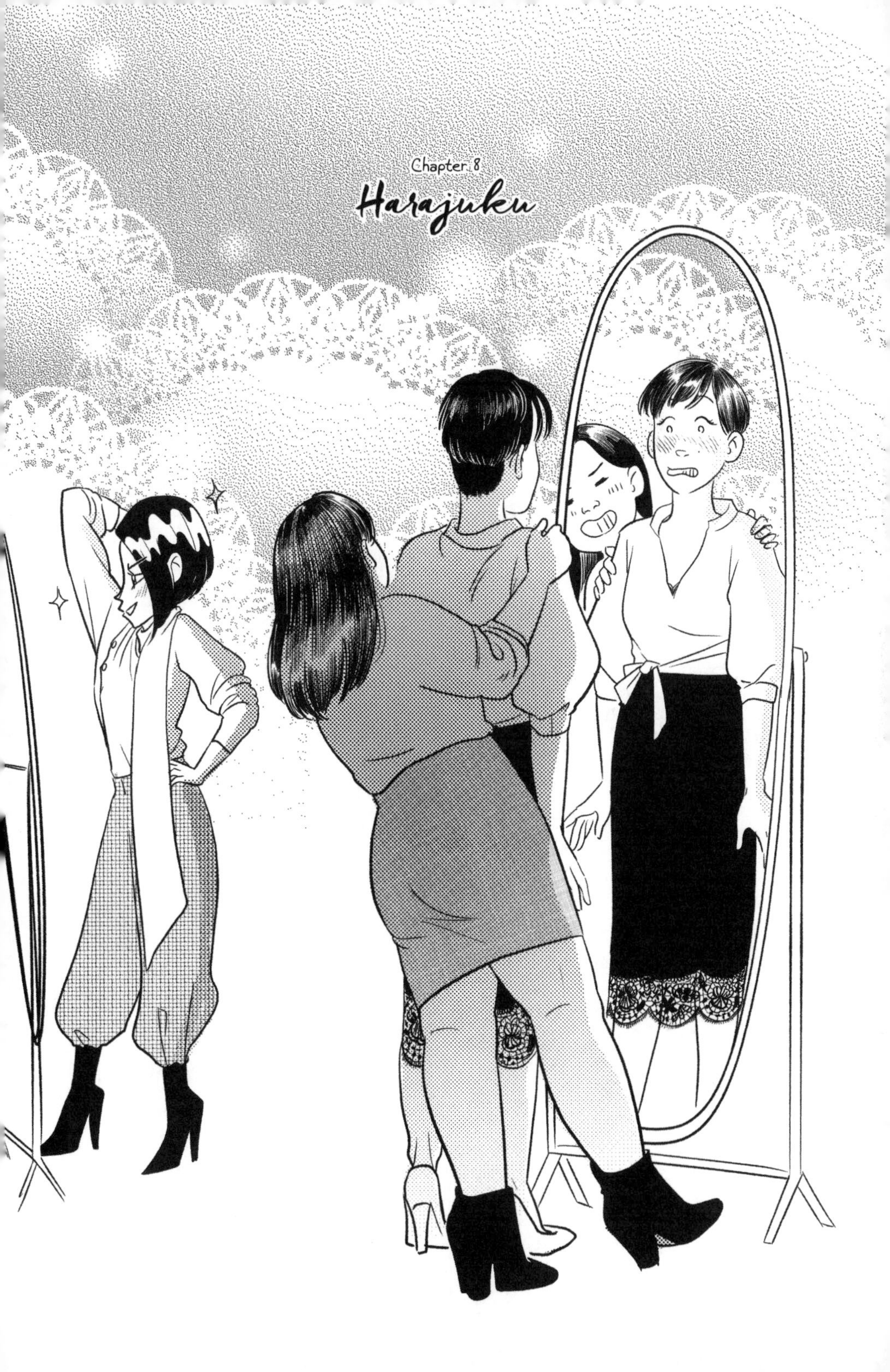

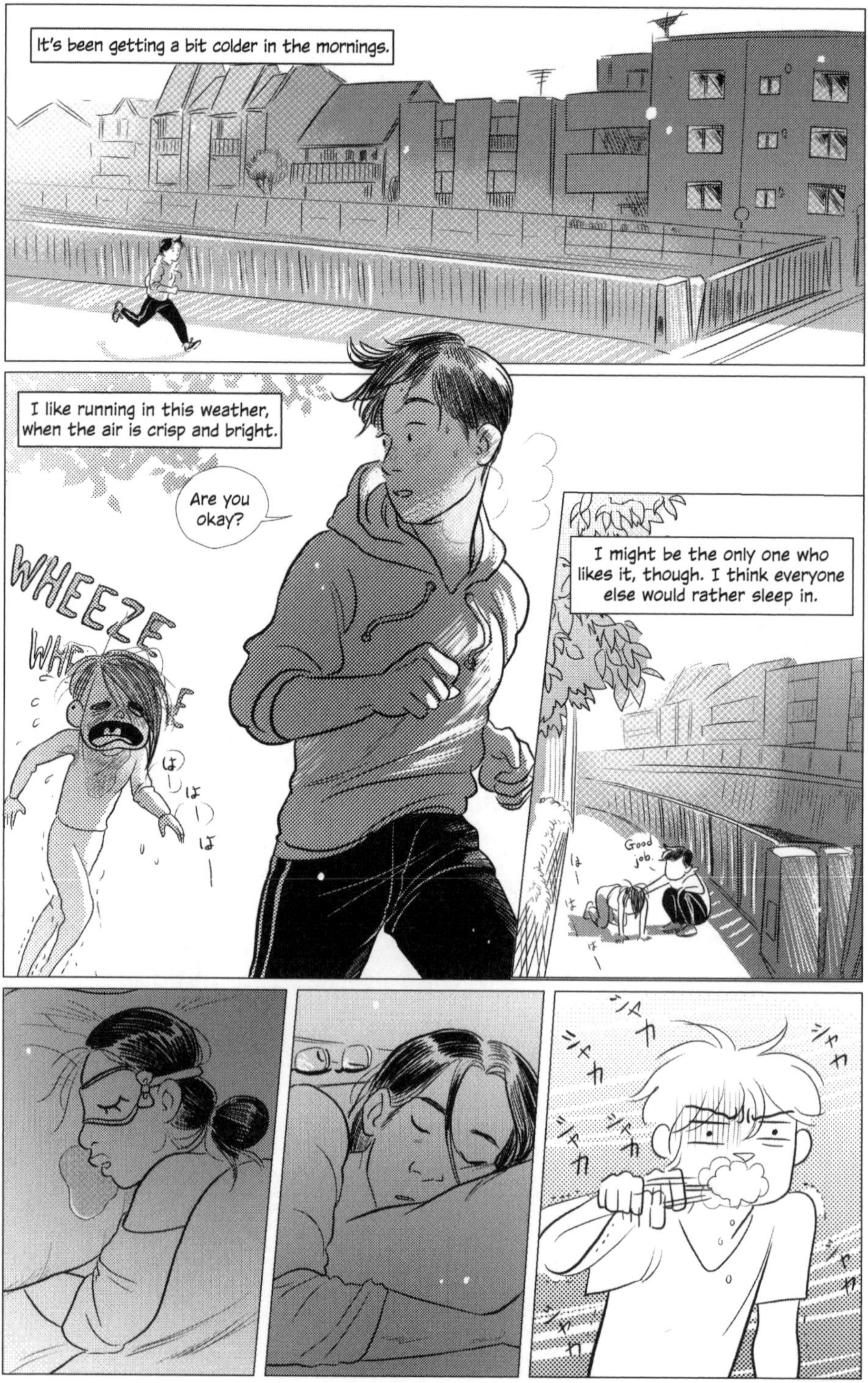

It's been getting a bit colder in the mornings.
I like running in this weather, when the air is crisp and bright.
Are you okay?
WHEEZE
はーはーはー
I might be the only one who likes it, though. I think everyone else would rather sleep in.
Good job.
はーはーはー
シャカ
シャカ
シャカ
シャカ
シャカ
シャカ
シャカ

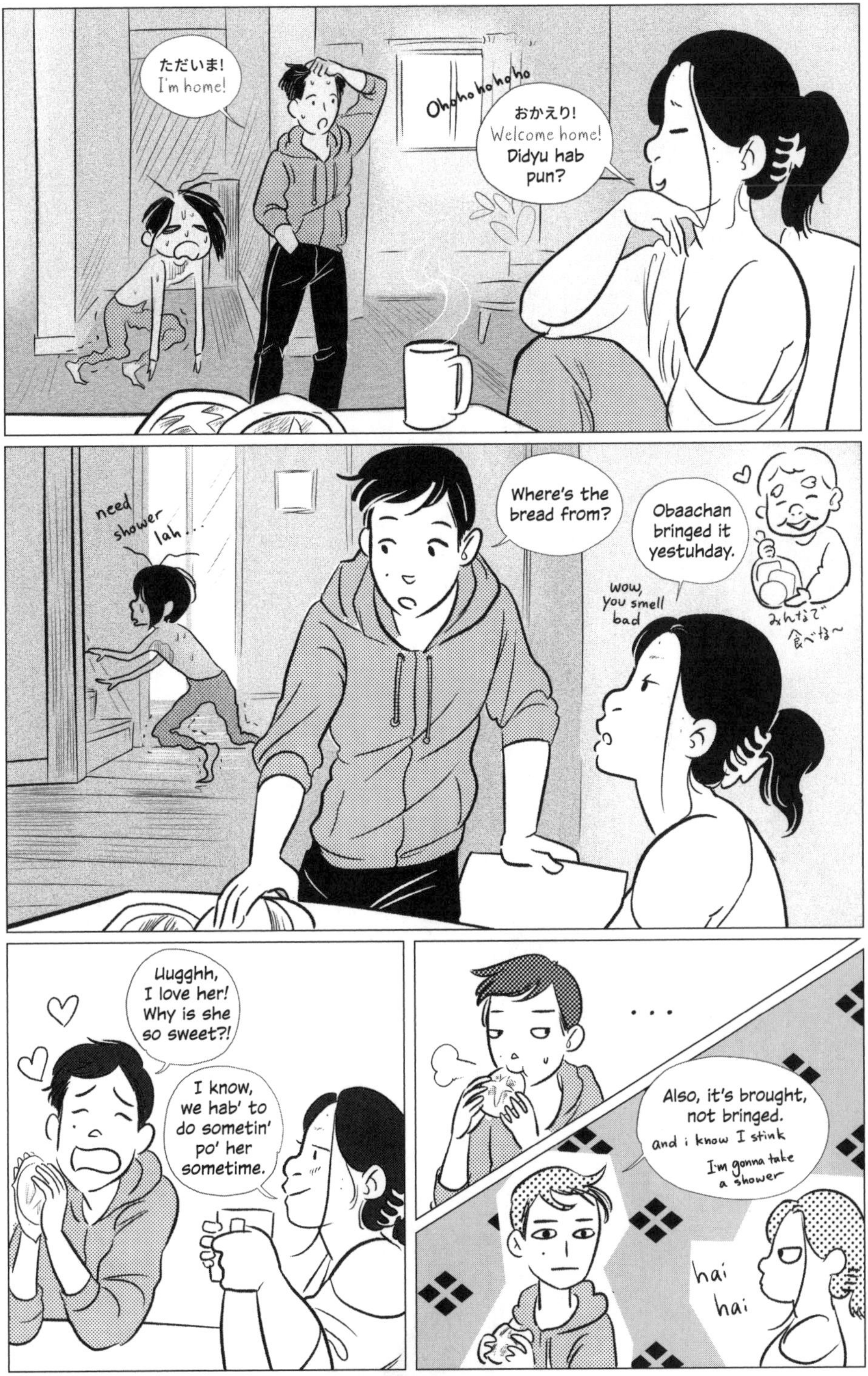
ただいま!
I'm home!
Ohohohohoho
おかえり!
Welcome home!
Didyu hab pun?
need shower lah...
Where's the bread from?
Obaachan bringed it yestuhday.
みんなで食べな~
wow, you smell bad
Uugghh, I love her! Why is she so sweet?!
I know, we hab' to do sometin' po' her sometime.
...
Also, it's brought, not bringed.
and i know I stink
I'm gonna take a shower
hai hai

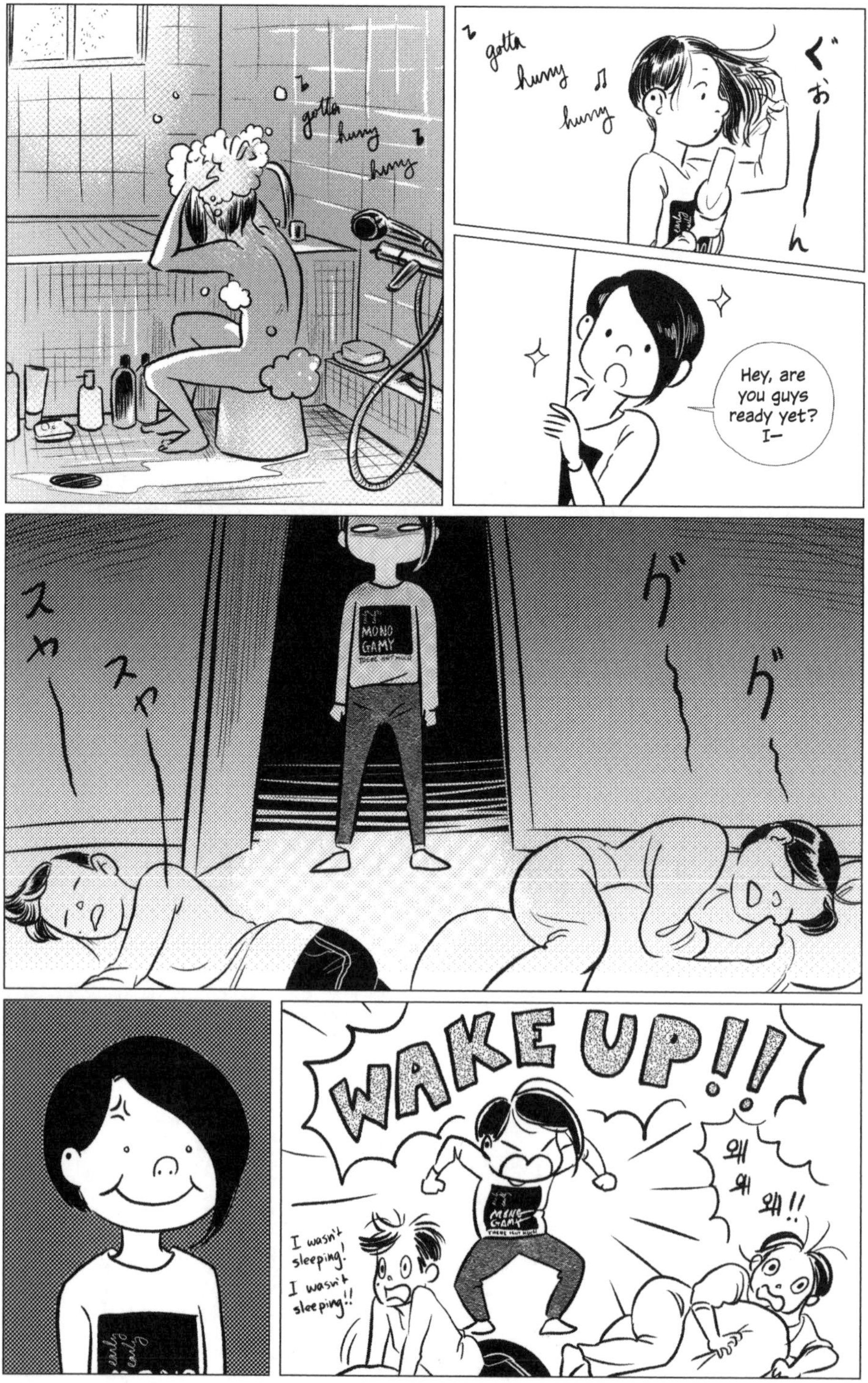
gotta hurry hurry
gotta hurry hurry
ぐおーん
Hey, are you guys ready yet? I–
スヤー
スヤー
グー
グー
WAKE UP!!
왜 왜 왜!!
I wasn't sleeping! I wasn't sleeping!!

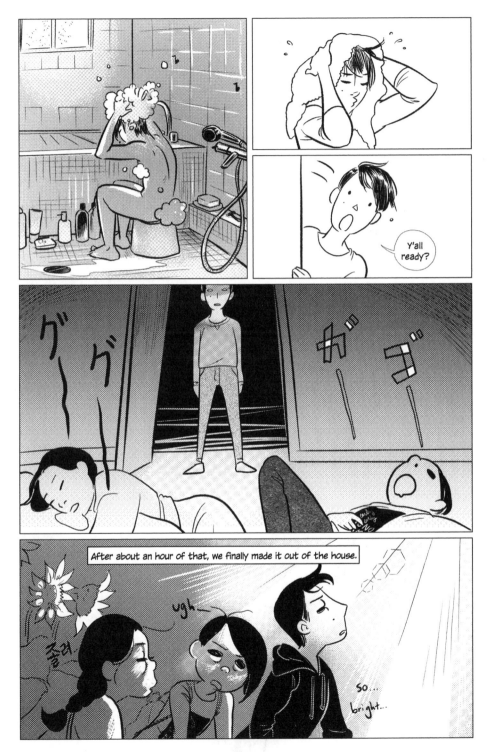

Y'all ready?

After about an hour of that, we finally made it out of the house.

ugh...

So... bright...

141

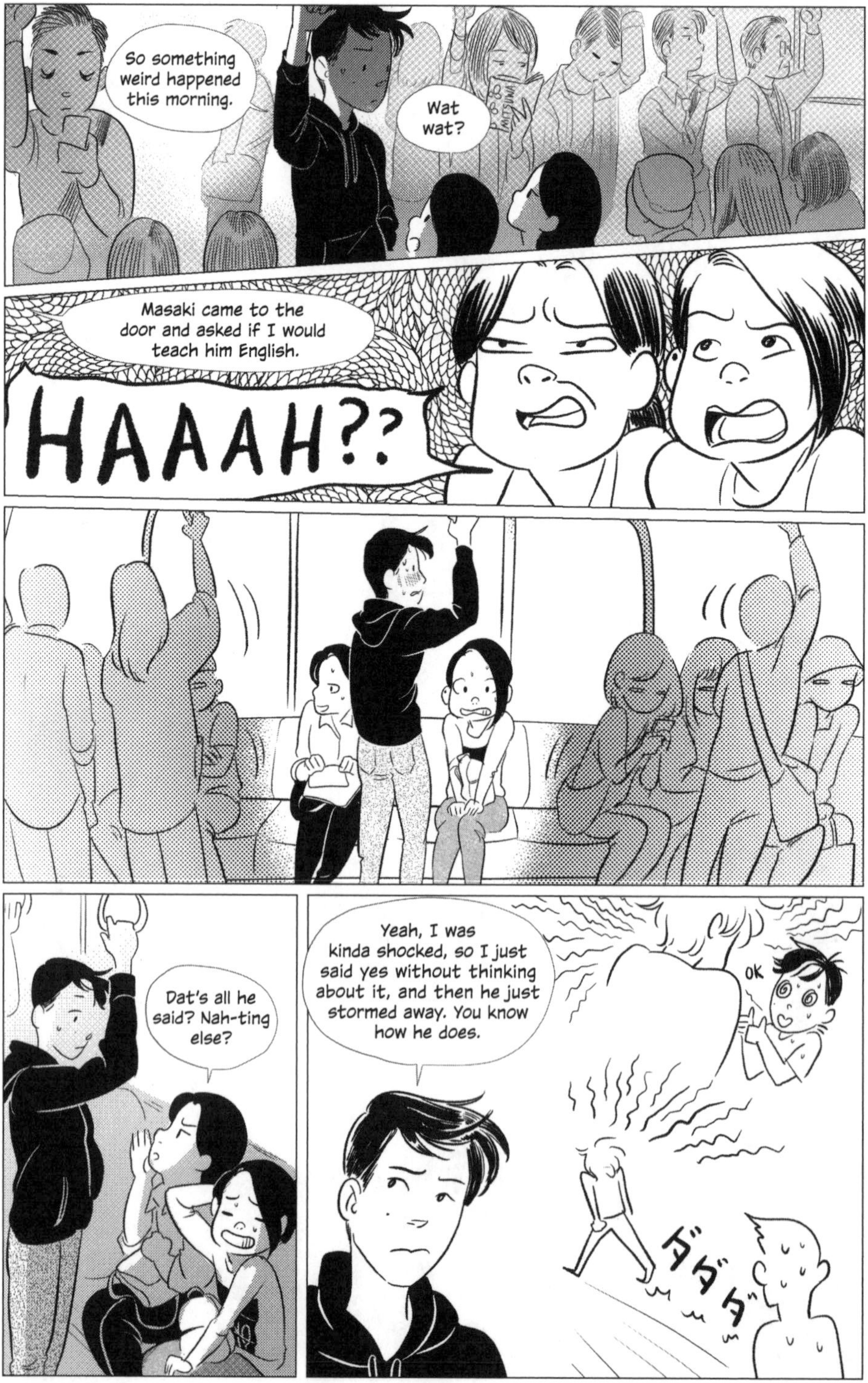

So something weird happened this morning.
Wat wat?
Masaki came to the door and asked if I would teach him English.
HAAAH??
Dat's all he said? Nah-ting else?
Yeah, I was kinda shocked, so I just said yes without thinking about it, and then he just stormed away. You know how he does.
OK
ダダダ

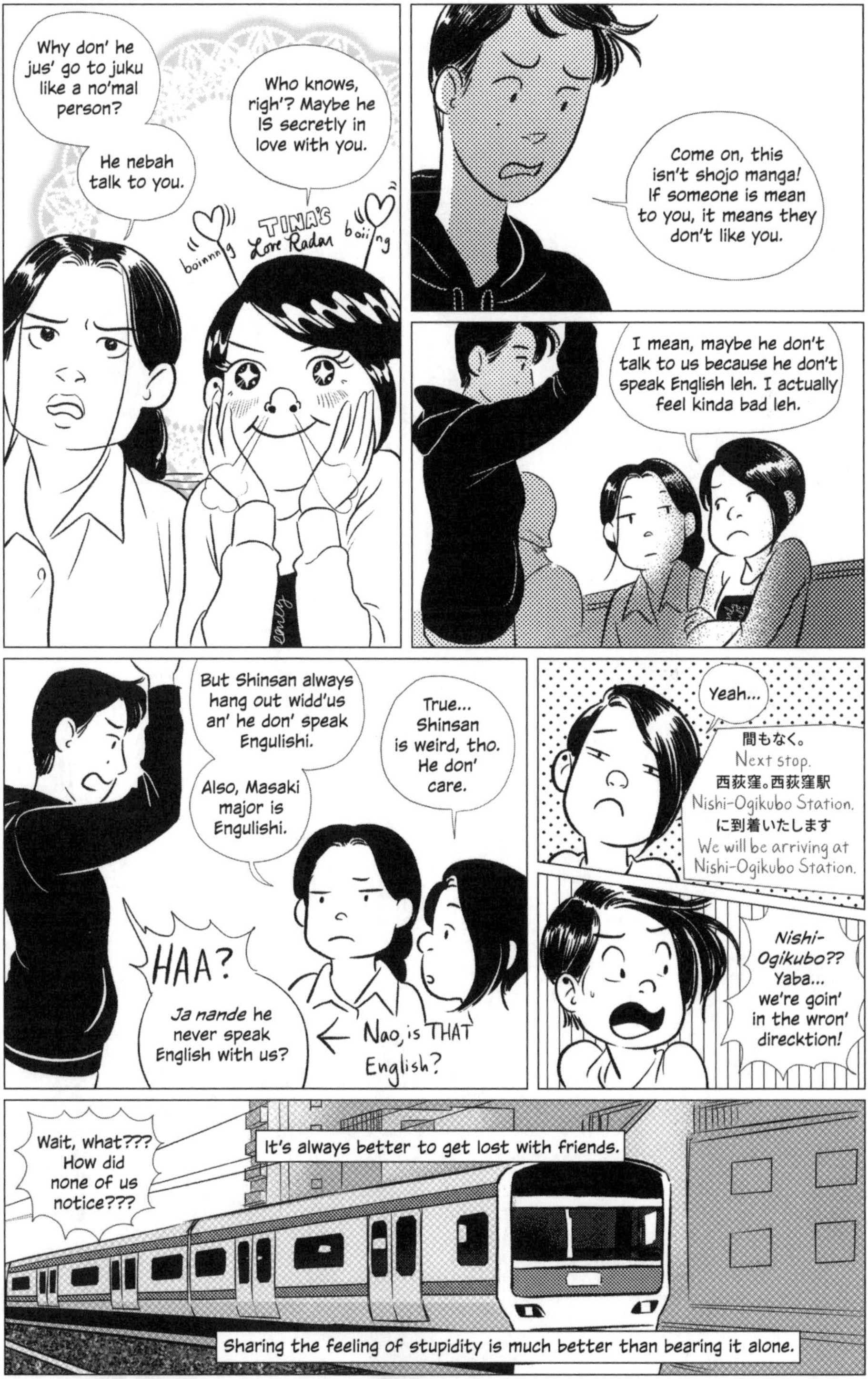

Why don' he jus' go to juku like a no'mal person?
He nebah talk to you.
Who knows, righ'? Maybe he IS secretly in love with you.
TINA'S Love Radar
boinnng
boiing
Come on, this isn't shojo manga! If someone is mean to you, it means they don't like you.
I mean, maybe he don't talk to us because he don't speak English leh. I actually feel kinda bad leh.
But Shinsan always hang out widd'us an' he don' speak Engulishi.
Also, Masaki major is Engulishi.
True... Shinsan is weird, tho. He don' care.
HAA?
Ja nande he never speak English with us?
Nao, is THAT English?
Yeah...
間もなく。
Next stop.
西荻窪。西荻窪駅
Nishi-Ogikubo Station.
に到着いたします
We will be arriving at Nishi-Ogikubo Station.
Nishi-Ogikubo?? Yaba... we're goin' in the wron' direcktion!
Wait, what??? How did none of us notice???
It's always better to get lost with friends.
Sharing the feeling of stupidity is much better than bearing it alone.

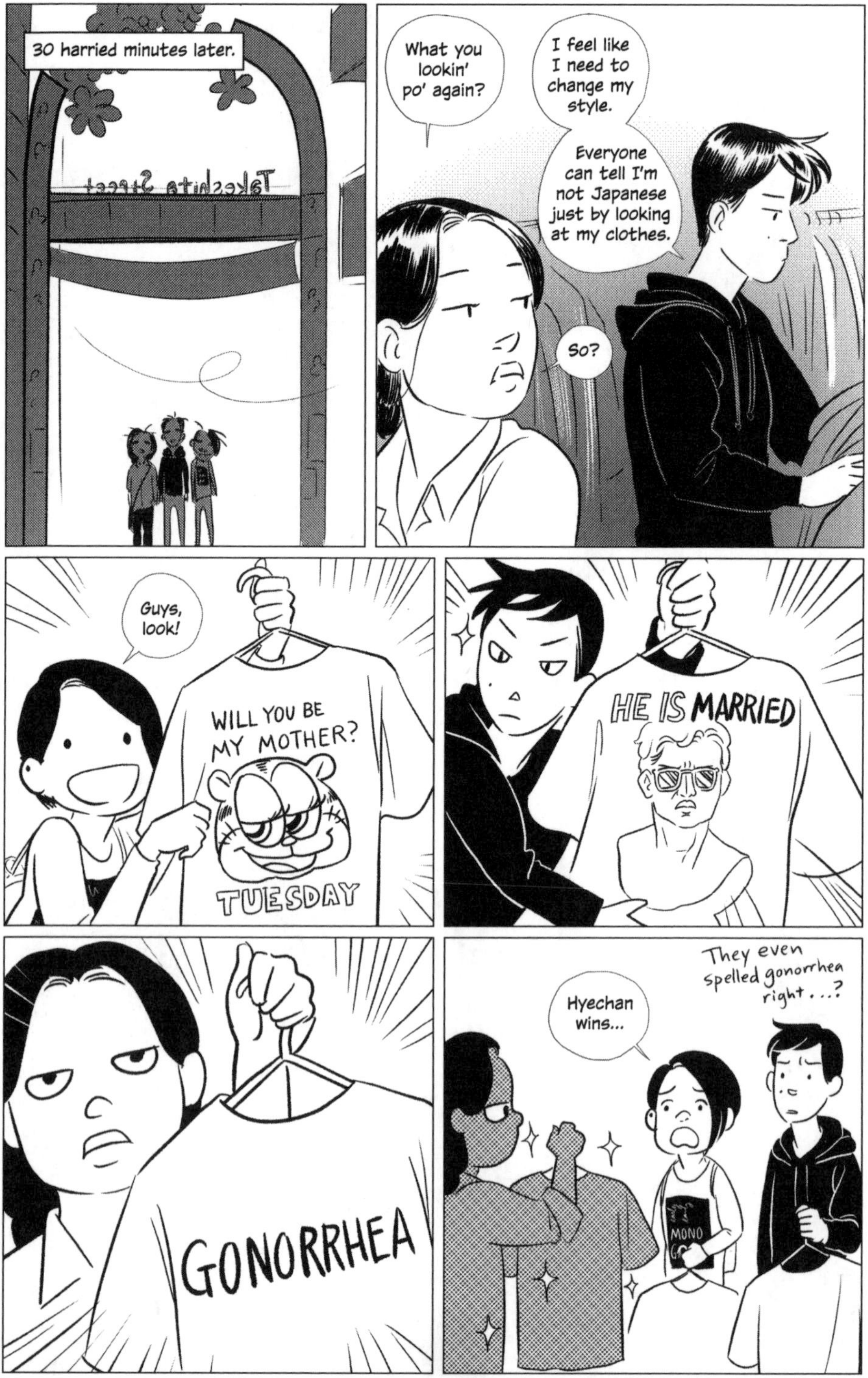
30 harried minutes later.
Takeshita Street
What you lookin' po' again?
I feel like I need to change my style.
Everyone can tell I'm not Japanese just by looking at my clothes.
So?
Guys, look!
WILL YOU BE MY MOTHER?
TUESDAY
HE IS MARRIED
GONORRHEA
Hyechan wins...
They even spelled gonorrhea right...?

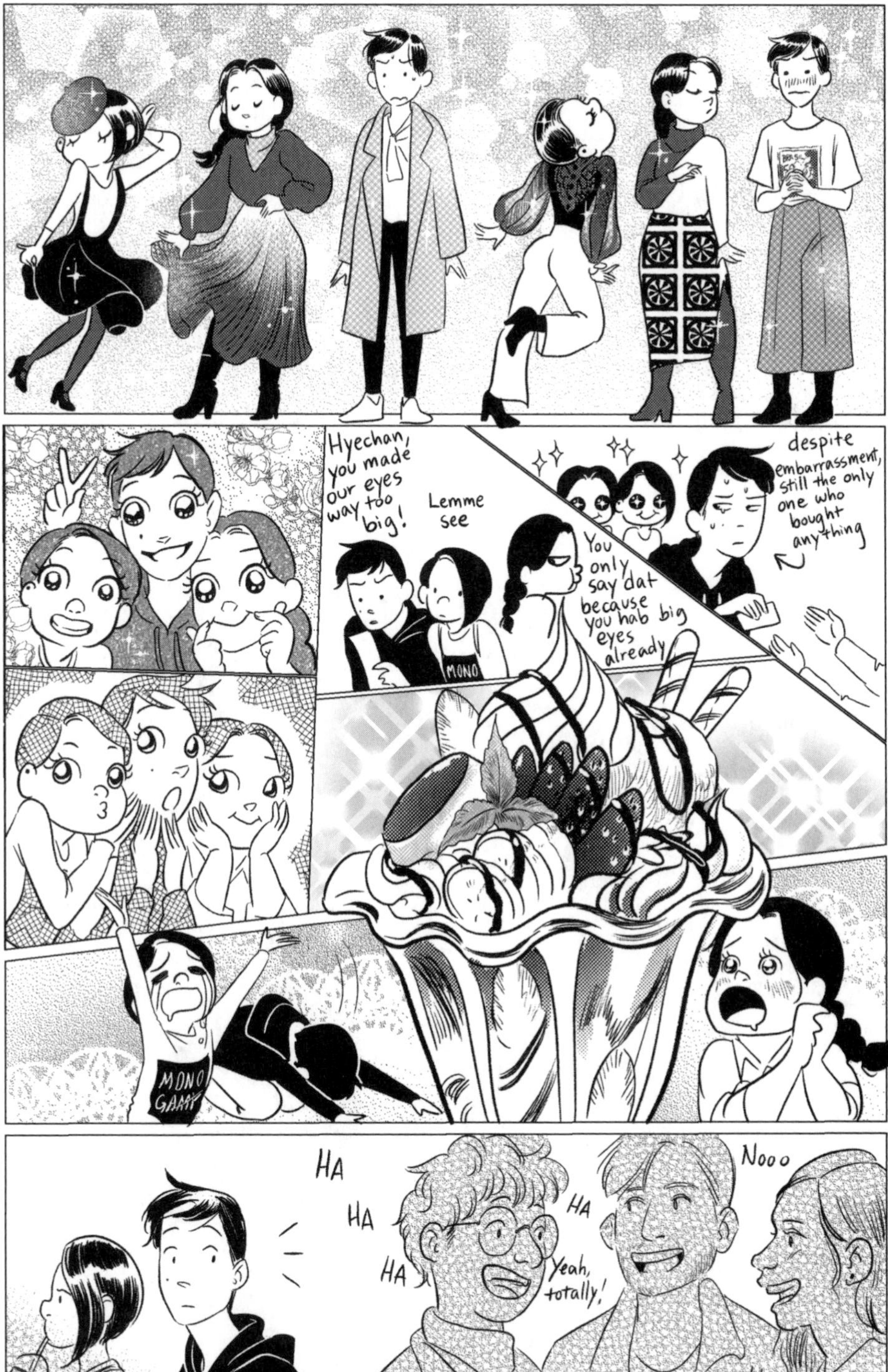
Hyechan, you made our eyes way too big!
Lemme see
You only say dat because you hab big eyes already
despite embarrassment, still the only one who bought anything
MONO
MONO GAMY
HA
HA
HA
HA
Yeah, totally!
Nooo
But, like,

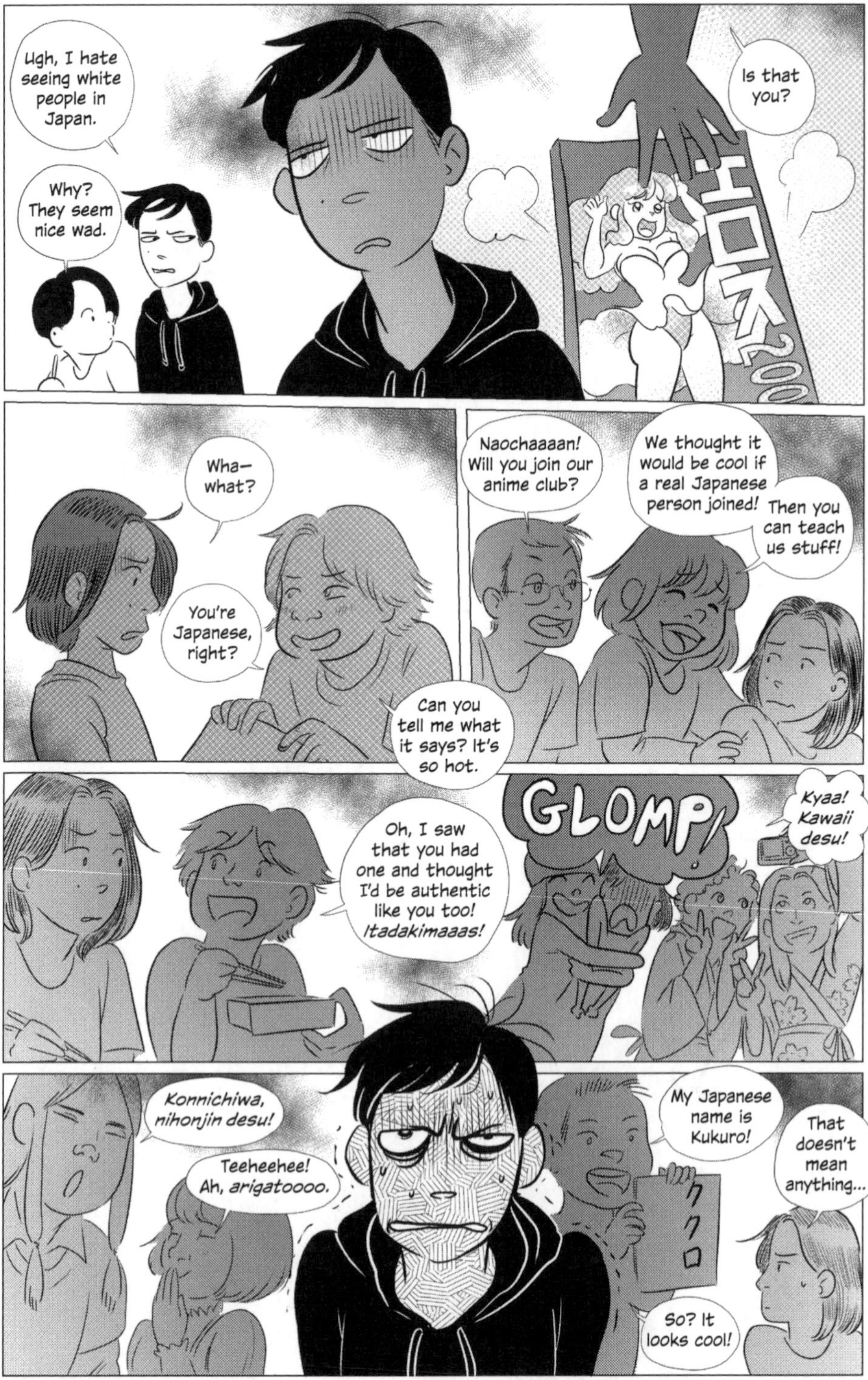
Ugh, I hate seeing white people in Japan.
Why? They seem nice wad.
Is that you?
エロス2000
Wha— what?
You're Japanese, right?
Can you tell me what it says? It's so hot.
Naochaaaan! Will you join our anime club?
We thought it would be cool if a real Japanese person joined!
Then you can teach us stuff!
Oh, I saw that you had one and thought I'd be authentic like you too! *Itadakimaaas!*
GLOMP!
Kyaa! Kawaii desu!
Konnichiwa, nihonjin desu!
Teeheehee! Ah, *arigatoooo.*
My Japanese name is Kukuro!
ククロ
That doesn't mean anything...
So? It looks cool!

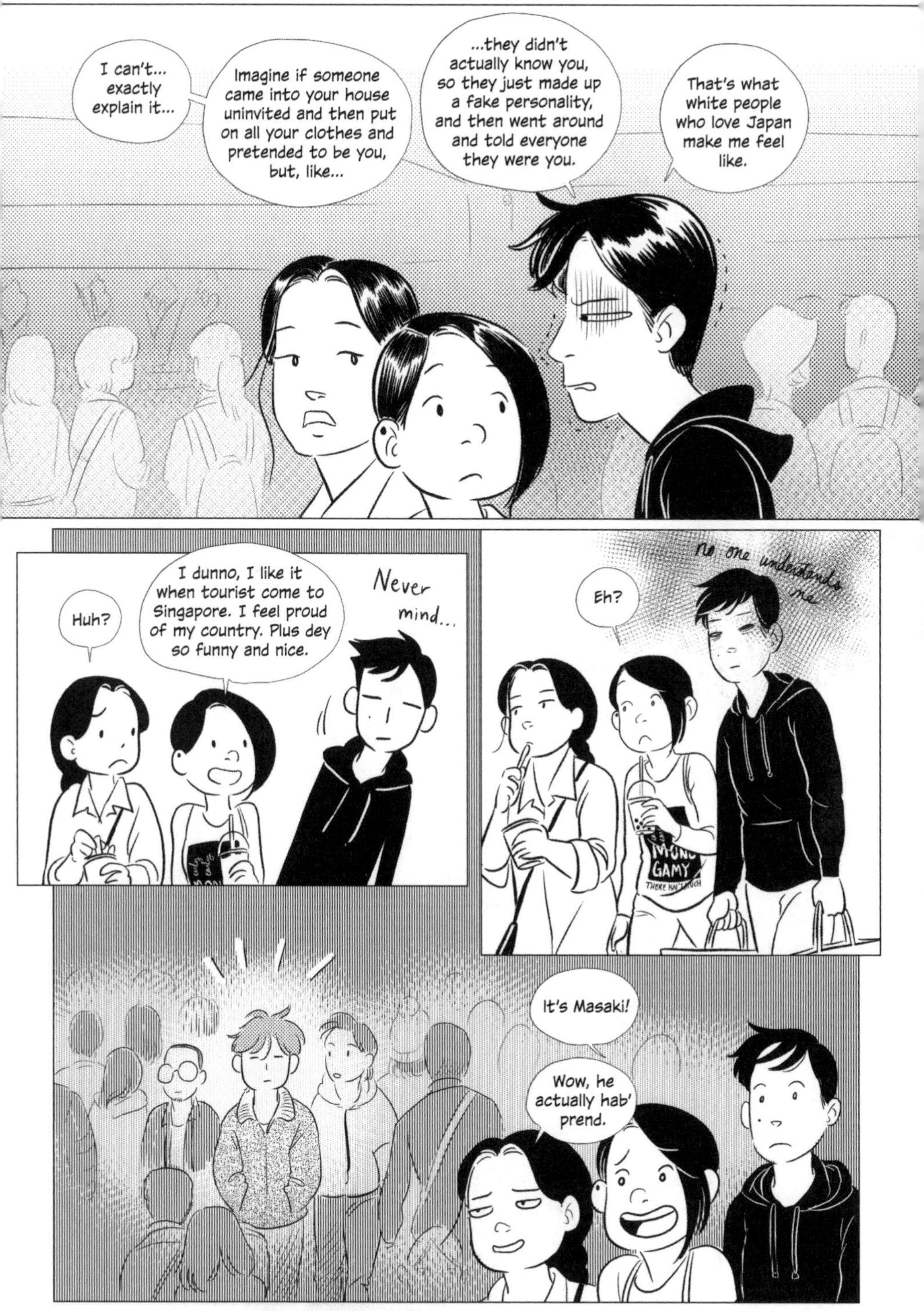
I can't... exactly explain it...
Imagine if someone came into your house uninvited and then put on all your clothes and pretended to be you, but, like...
...they didn't actually know you, so they just made up a fake personality, and then went around and told everyone they were you.
That's what white people who love Japan make me feel like.
Huh?
I dunno, I like it when tourist come to Singapore. I feel proud of my country. Plus dey so funny and nice.
Never mind...
Eh?
no one understands me
It's Masaki!
Wow, he actually hab' prend.

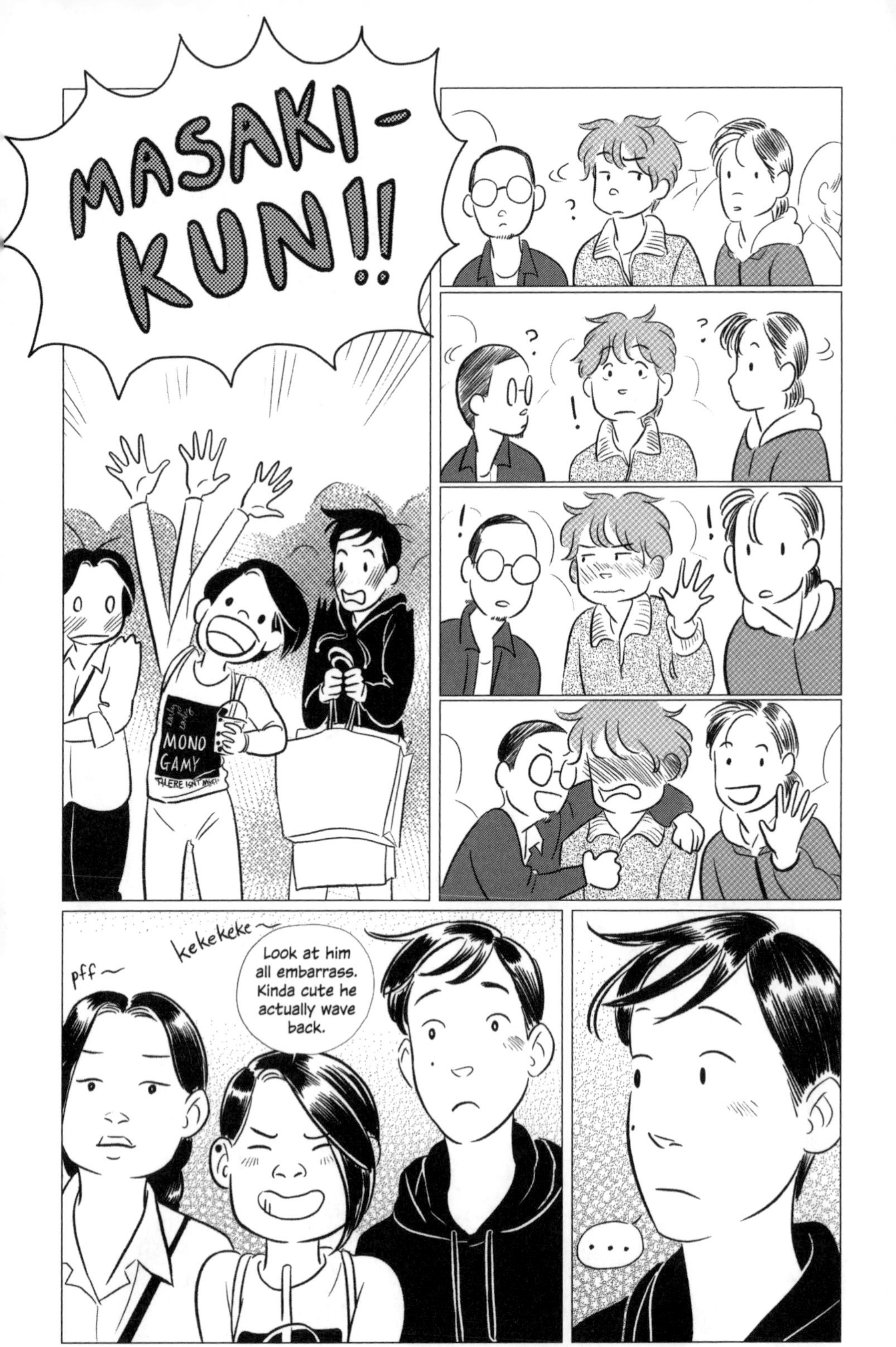
MASAKI-KUN!!
MONO GAMY
THERE ISN'T MUCH
pff~
kekekeke~
Look at him all embarrass. Kinda cute he actually wave back.
...

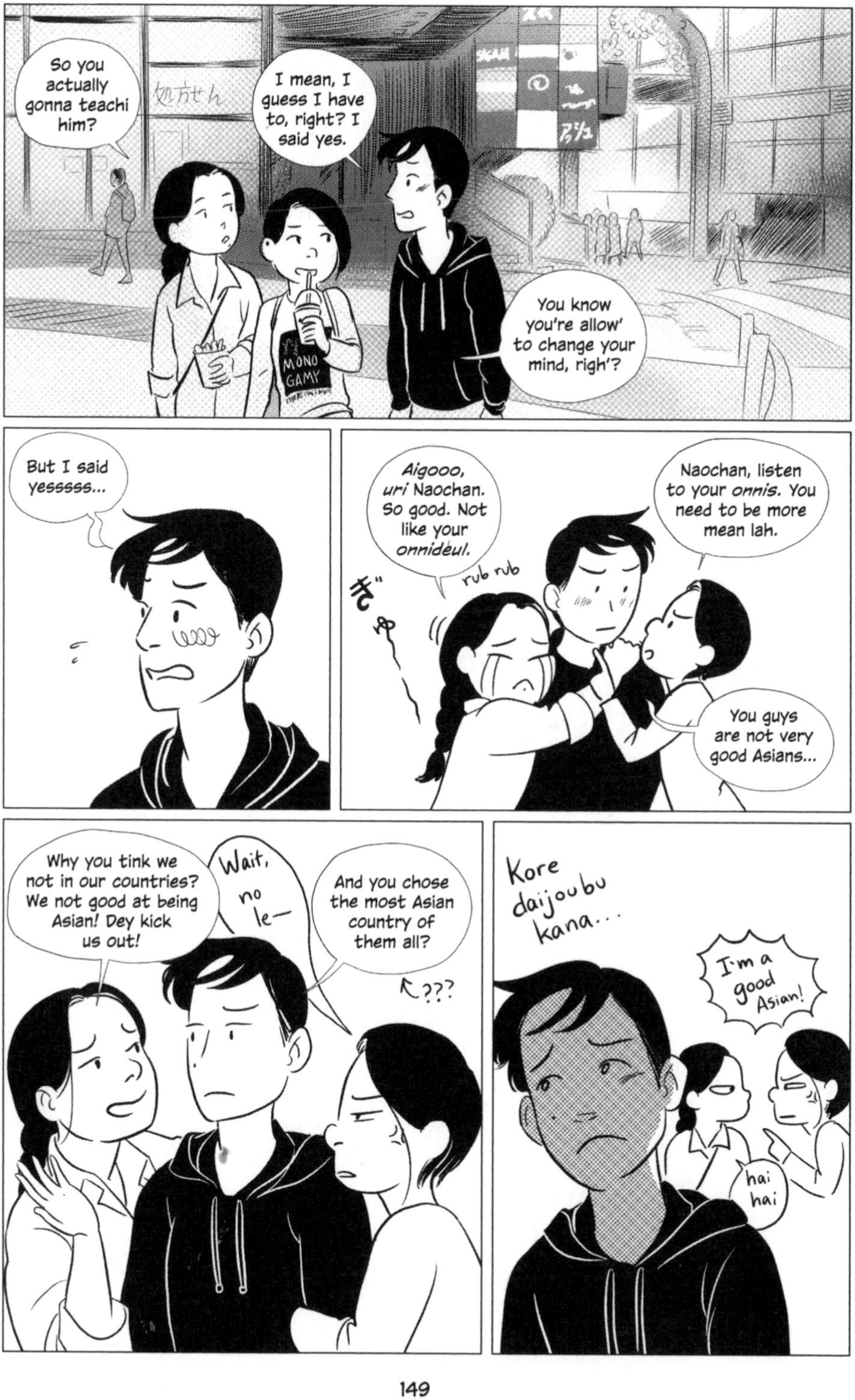
So you actually gonna teachi him?
I mean, I guess I have to, right? I said yes.
You know you're allow' to change your mind, righ'?
MONO GAMY
But I said yesssss...
Aigooo, uri Naochan. So good. Not like your *onnideul.*
rub rub
Naochan, listen to your *onnis.* You need to be more mean lah.
You guys are not very good Asians...
Why you tink we not in our countries? We not good at being Asian! Dey kick us out!
Wait, no le—
And you chose the most Asian country of them all?
???
Kore daijoubu kana...
I'm a good Asian!
hai hai

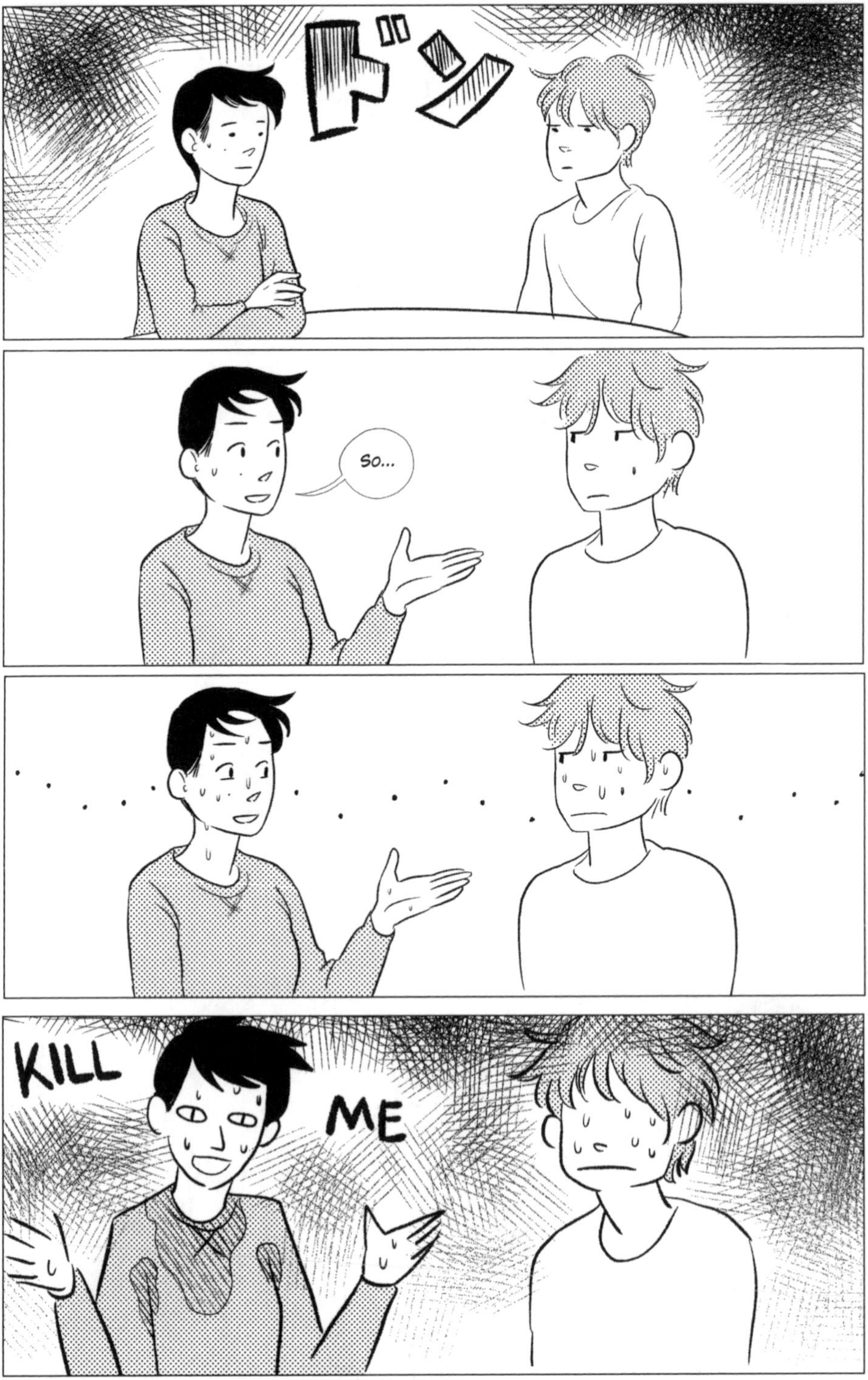
ドン
so...
KILL
ME

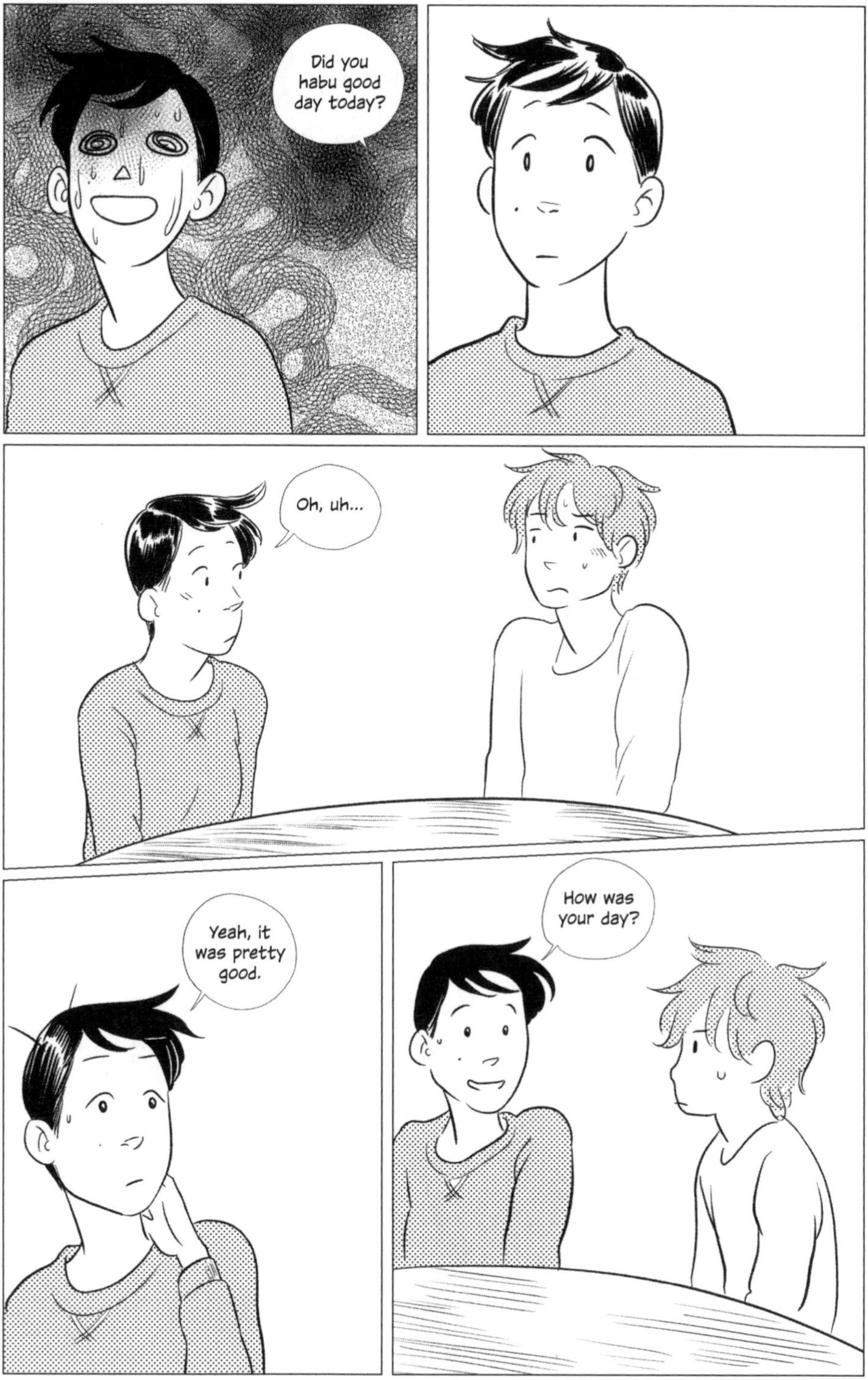
Did you habu good day today?
Oh, uh...
Yeah, it was pretty good.
How was your day?

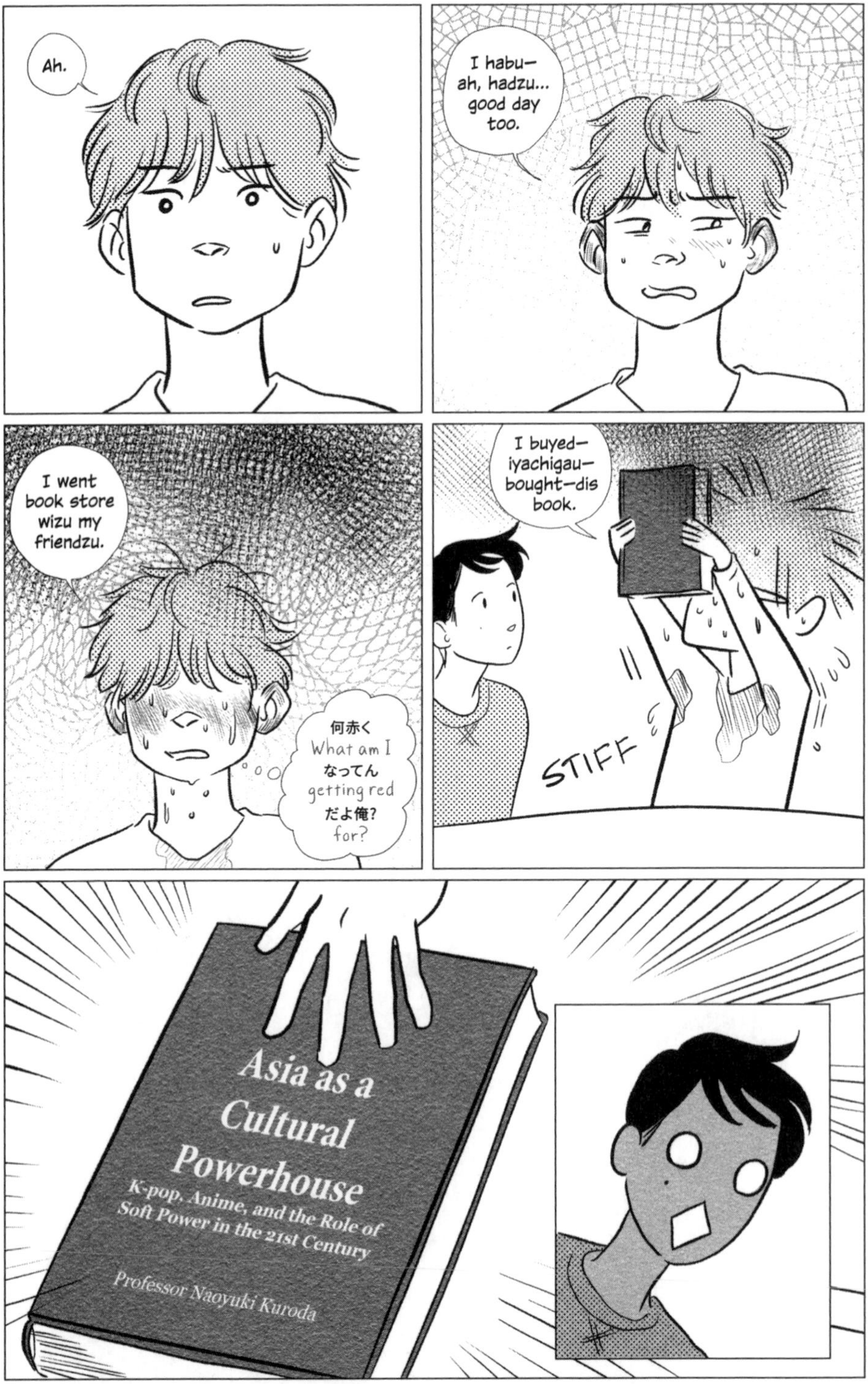
Ah.
I habu— ah, hadzu... good day too.
I went book store wizu my friendzu.
何赤く What am I なってん getting red だよ俺? for?
I buyed— iyachigau— bought—dis book.
STIFF
Asia as a Cultural Powerhouse
K-pop, Anime, and the Role of Soft Power in the 21st Century
Professor Naoyuki Kuroda

Can you purizu expurain me disu section?

ven just ten years ago, K-pop acts such as the Wonder Boys and 3PM drew only meager crowds outside of Korea, mostly made up of second neration Koreans and other diasporic Asians. JYT CEO Jin-Young Tak's plans of international fame seemed like nothing more than a pipe drear ite his many efforts to make the music more palatable overseas, includin sing an English version of every major track. Today, Poktan Sonyeondar TS as they're known to thei_____ational f_____ of the biggest and st influential musical acts_____rld_____ums not able to contain the masses of adori_____who_____o see them. usly, they do not perform a single song_____r the occasion Your Hands and You're My Girl that pep_____s. _____the wa lallyu (the term for the surge of Korean pop_____ra___ates to rrent'), K-pop stars have come to the very f_____t the international their Western counterparts in a way that has n_____e been seen in

Uh-huh.

OK.

つまり…
Basically…

$\sum + \zeta = \square / \sqrt{a}$

pitch / ₩ = famous?

KPOP

pipe dream

verbs

90°

Nao.

要するに…
In short…

You can expurain in Engurishu.

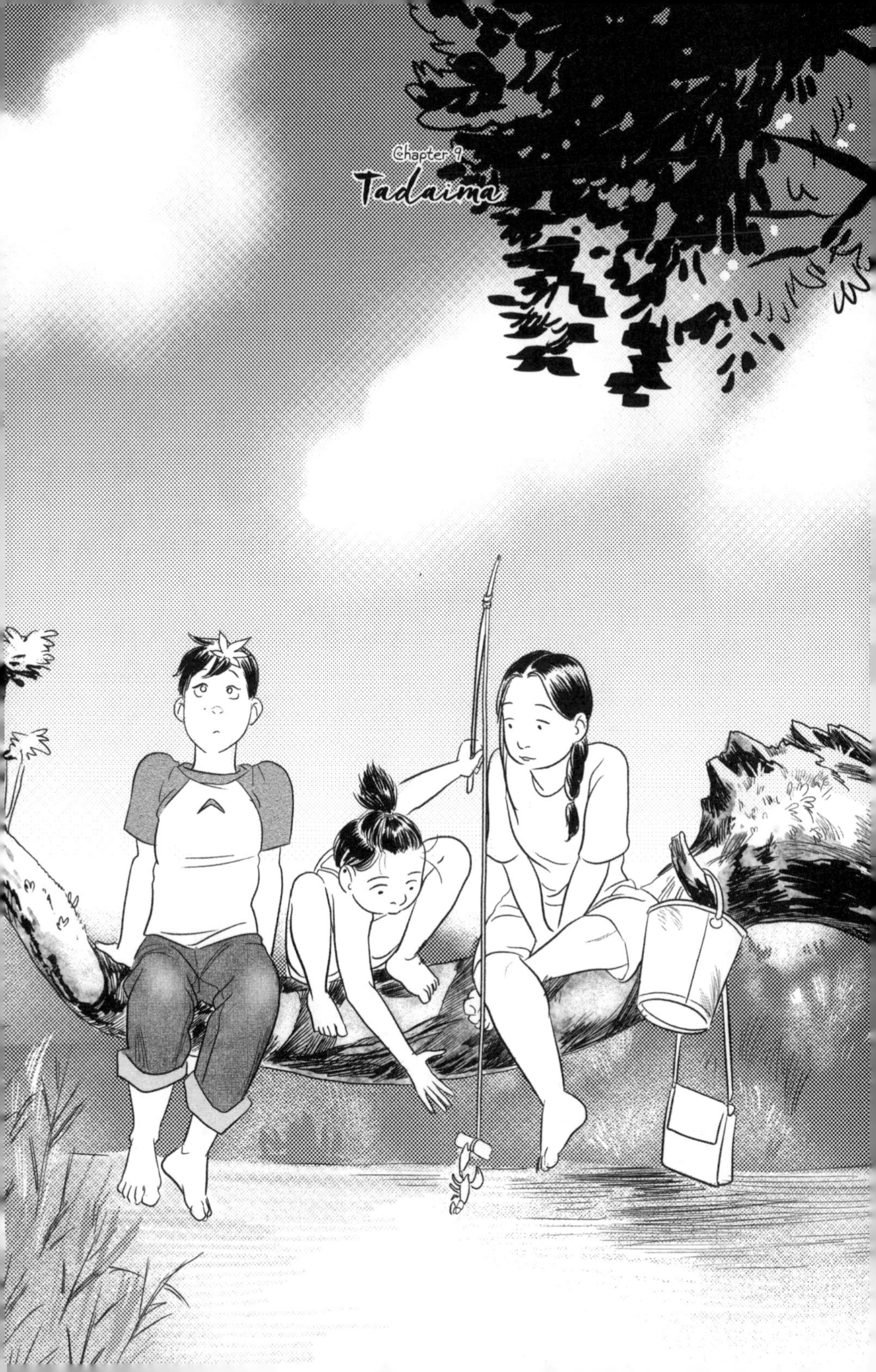
Chapter 9
Tadaima

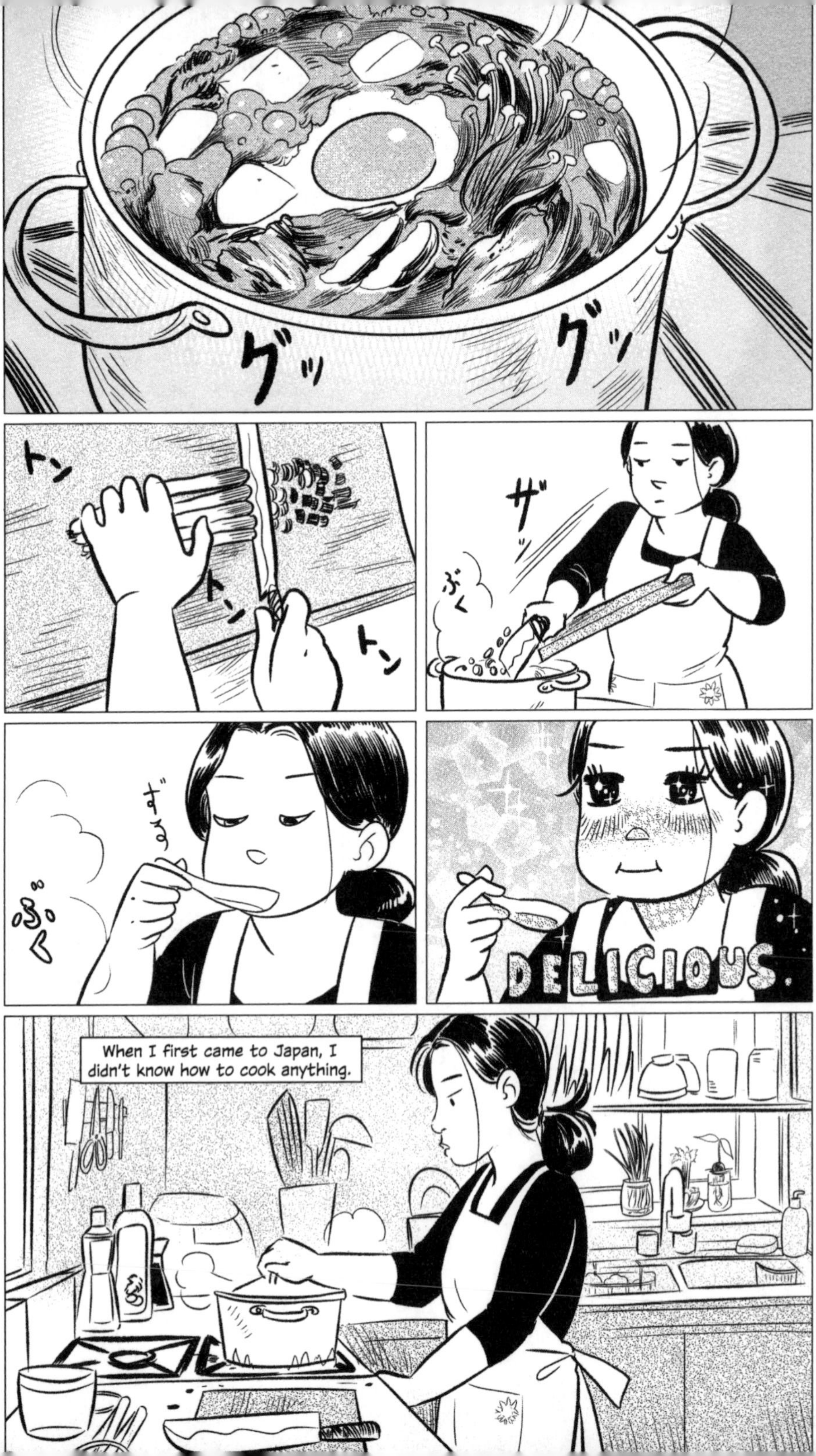
グツ
グツ
トン
トン
トン
ザ
ずず
DELICIOUS.
When I first came to Japan, I didn't know how to cook anything.

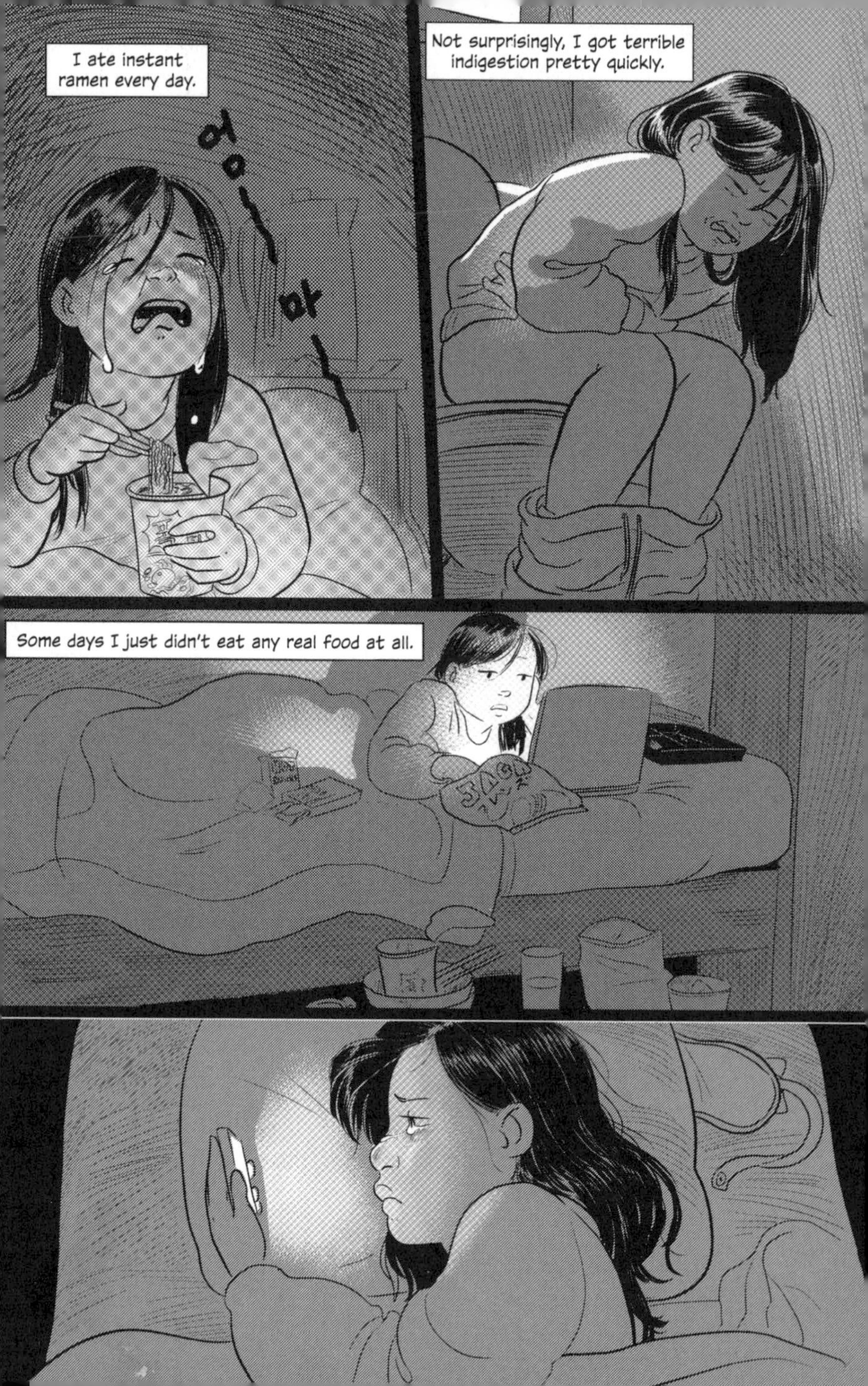
I ate instant ramen every day.
엉
아
Not surprisingly, I got terrible indigestion pretty quickly.
Some days I just didn't eat any real food at all.

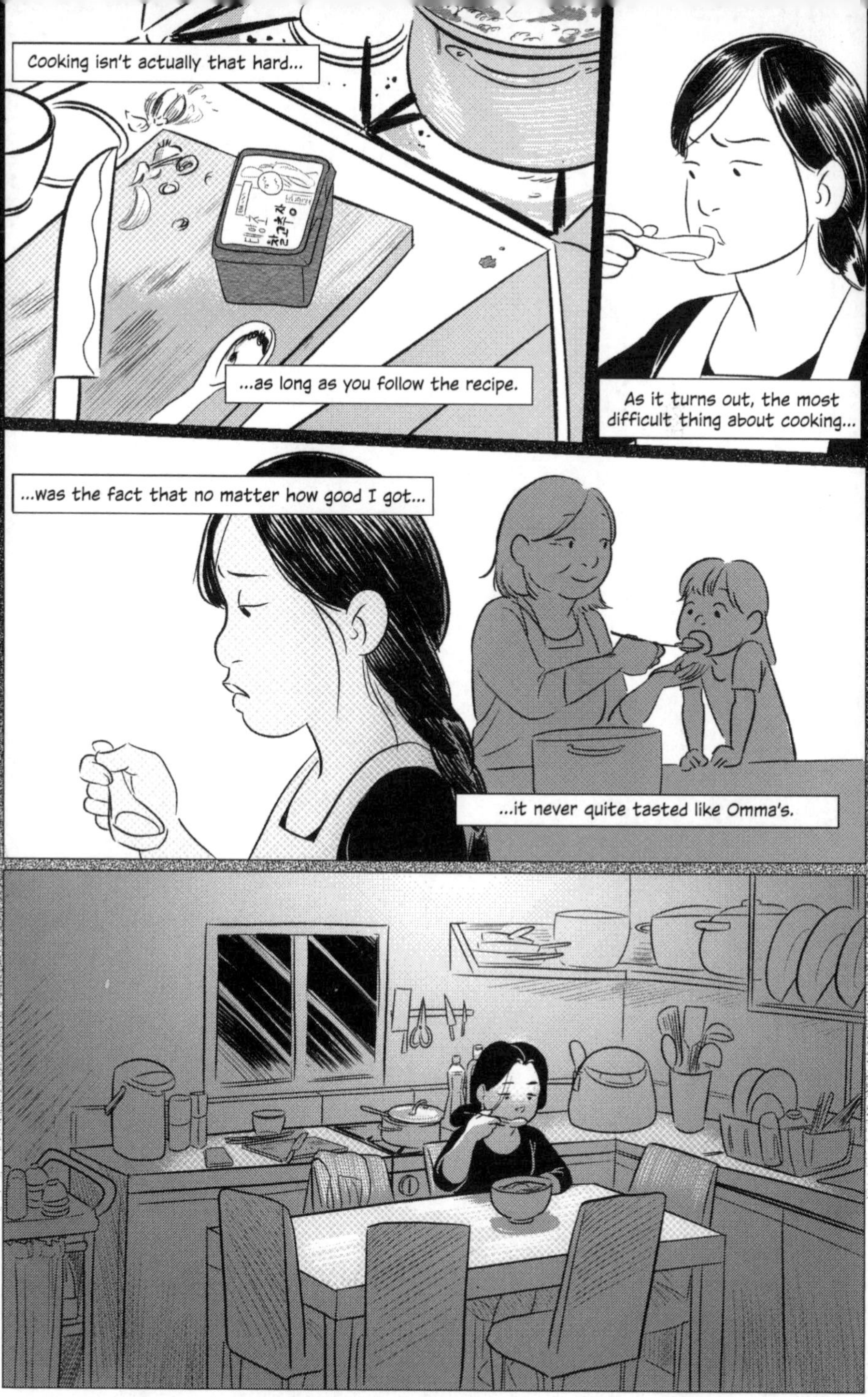
Cooking isn't actually that hard...
...as long as you follow the recipe.
As it turns out, the most difficult thing about cooking...
...was the fact that no matter how good I got...
...it never quite tasted like Omma's.

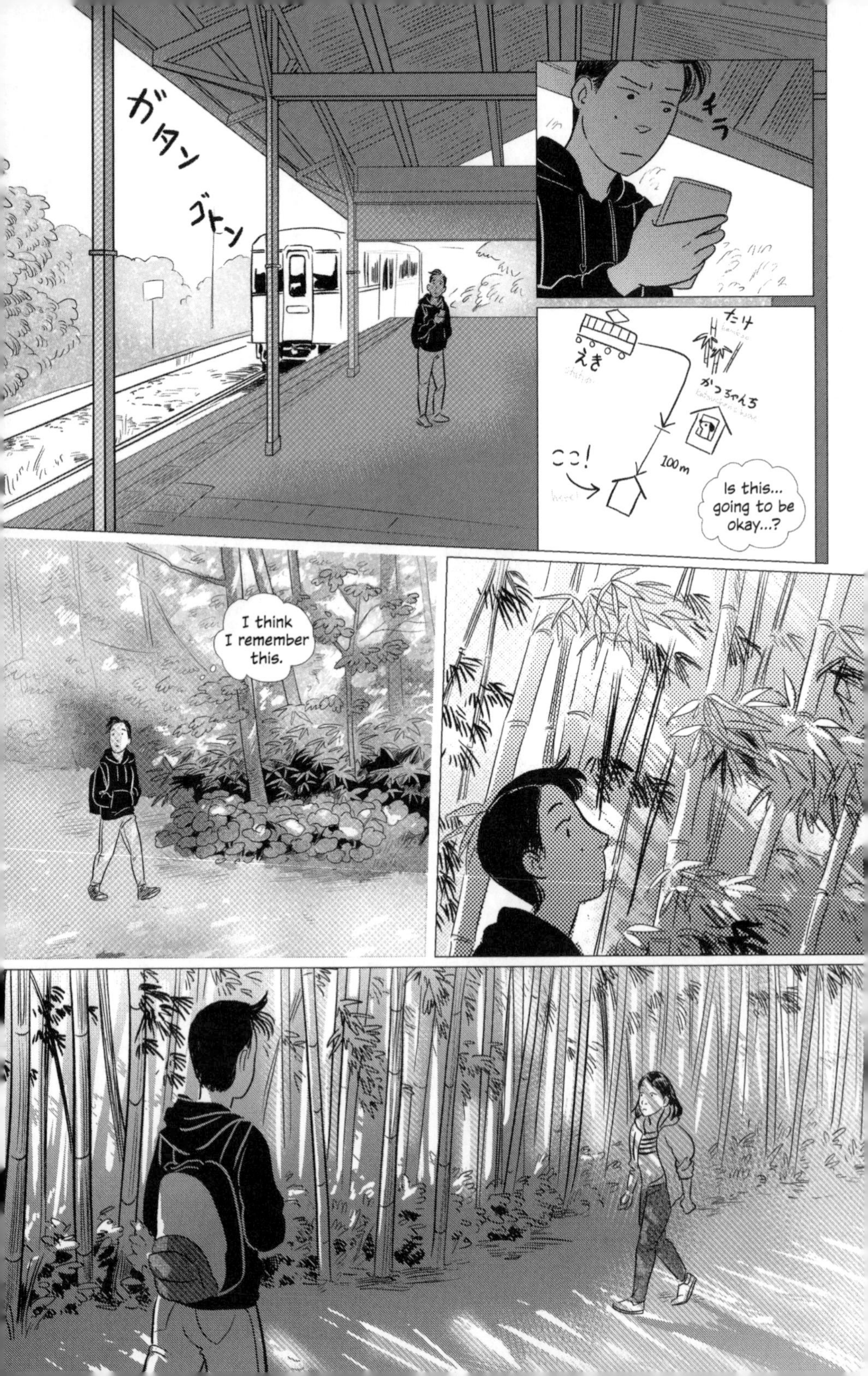
ガタン
ゴトン
キラ
たけ
えき
かつちゃんち
ここ!
100m
Is this... going to be okay...?
I think I remember this.

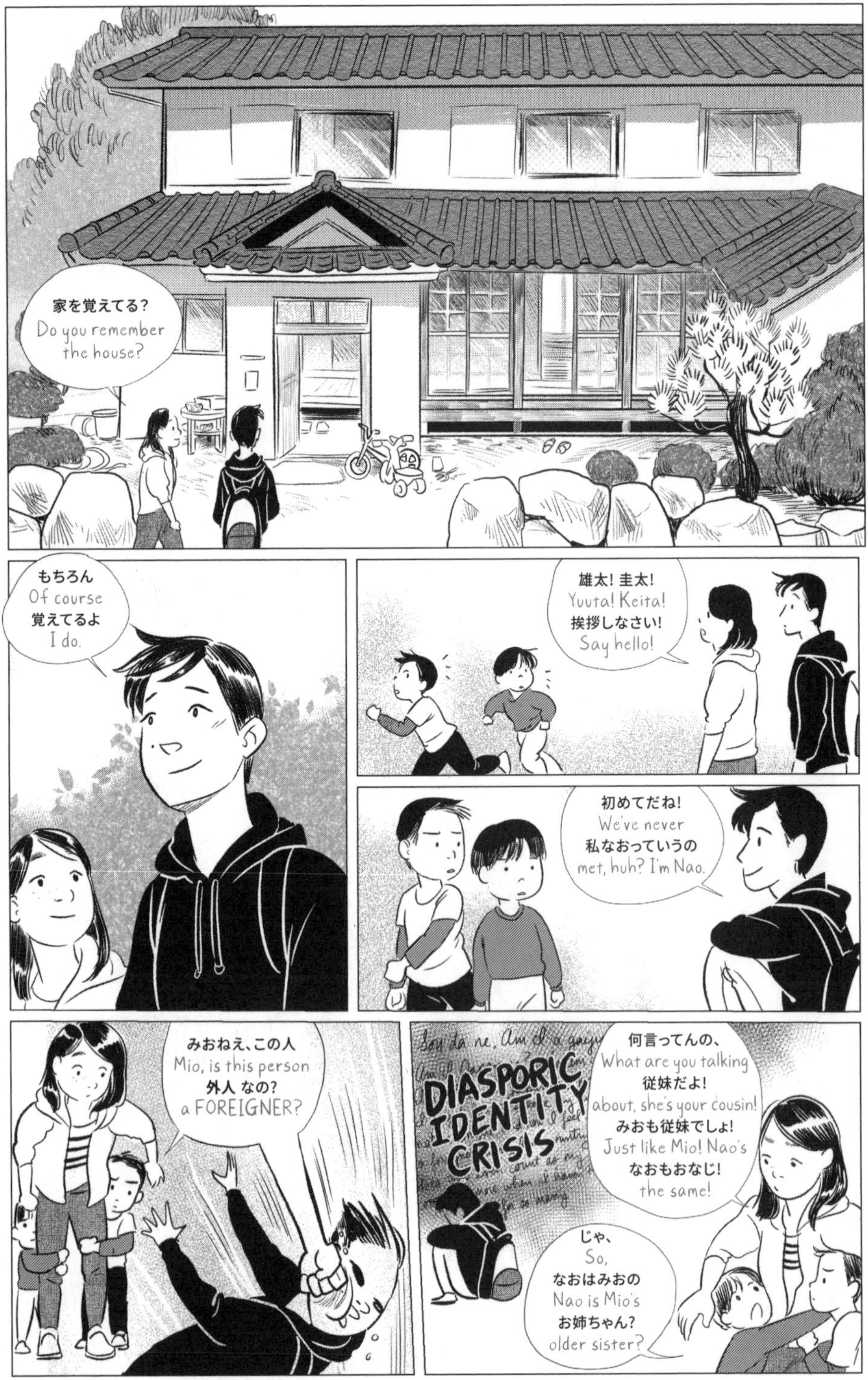
家を覚えてる?
Do you remember the house?
もちろん
Of course
覚えてるよ
I do.
雄太! 圭太!
Yuuta! Keita!
挨拶しなさい!
Say hello!
初めてだね!
We've never
私なおっていうの
met, huh? I'm Nao.
みおねえ、この人
Mio, is this person
外人 なの?
a FOREIGNER?
DIASPORIC IDENTITY CRISIS
何言ってんの、
What are you talking
従妹だよ!
about, she's your cousin!
みおも従妹でしょ!
Just like Mio! Nao's
なおもおなじ!
the same!
じゃ、
So,
なおはみおの
Nao is Mio's
お姉ちゃん?
older sister?

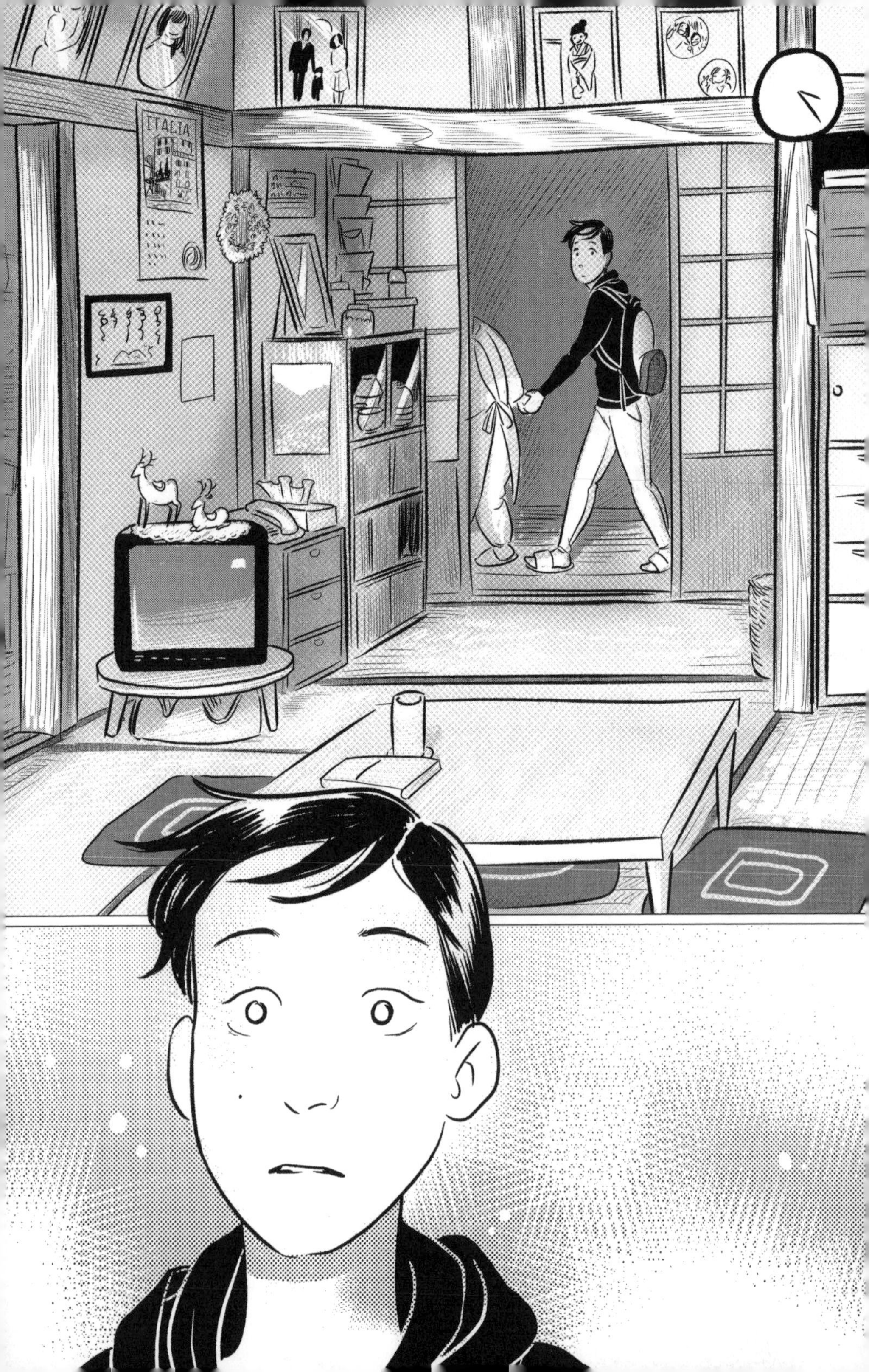
ITALIA

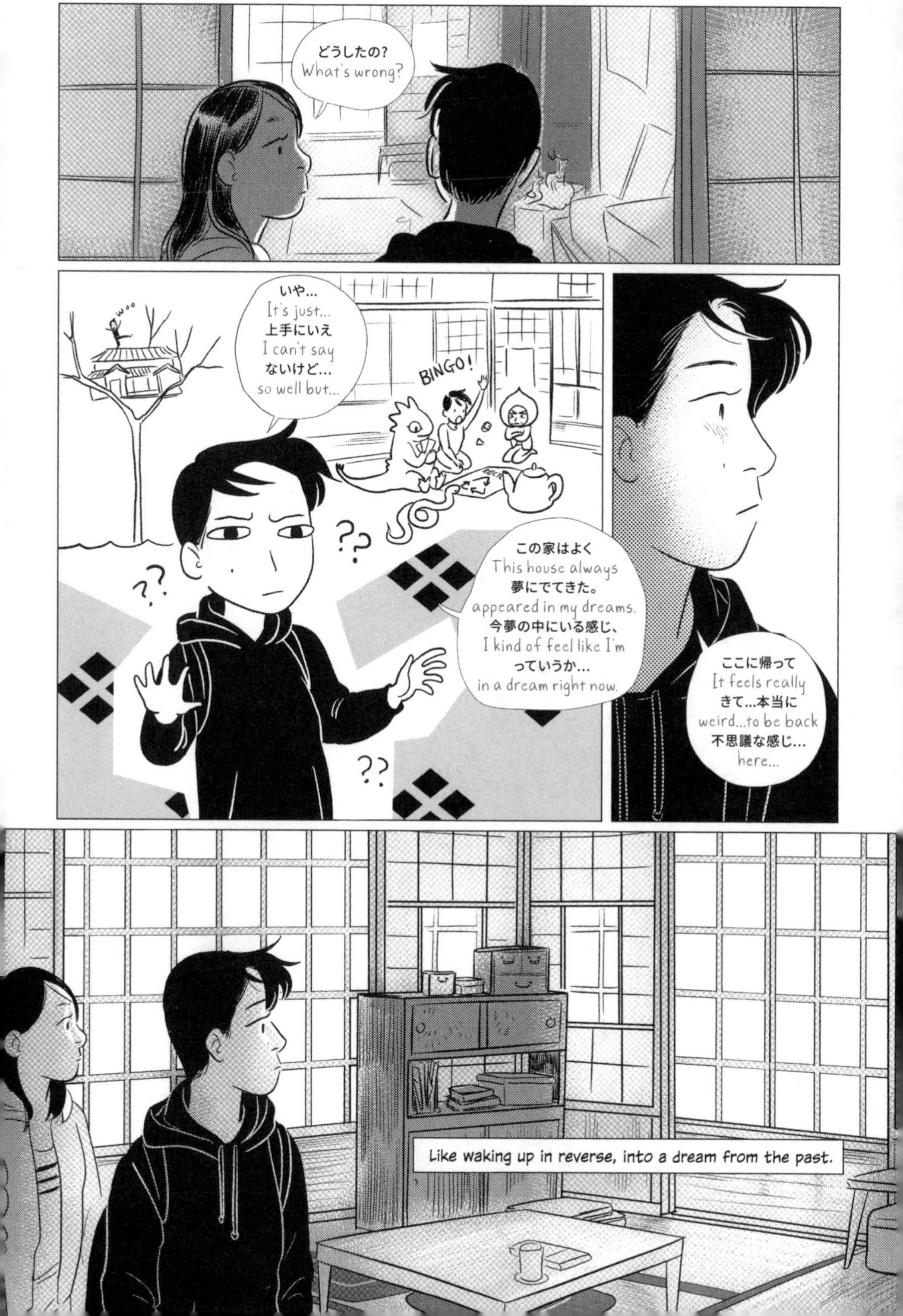

どうしたの? What's wrong?
いや… It's just… 上手にいえ I can't say ないけど… so well but…
BINGO!
この家はよく This house always 夢にでてきた。 appeared in my dreams. 今夢の中にいる感じ、 I kind of feel like I'm っていうか… in a dream right now.
ここに帰って It feels really きて…本当に weird…to be back 不思議な感じ… here…
Like waking up in reverse, into a dream from the past.

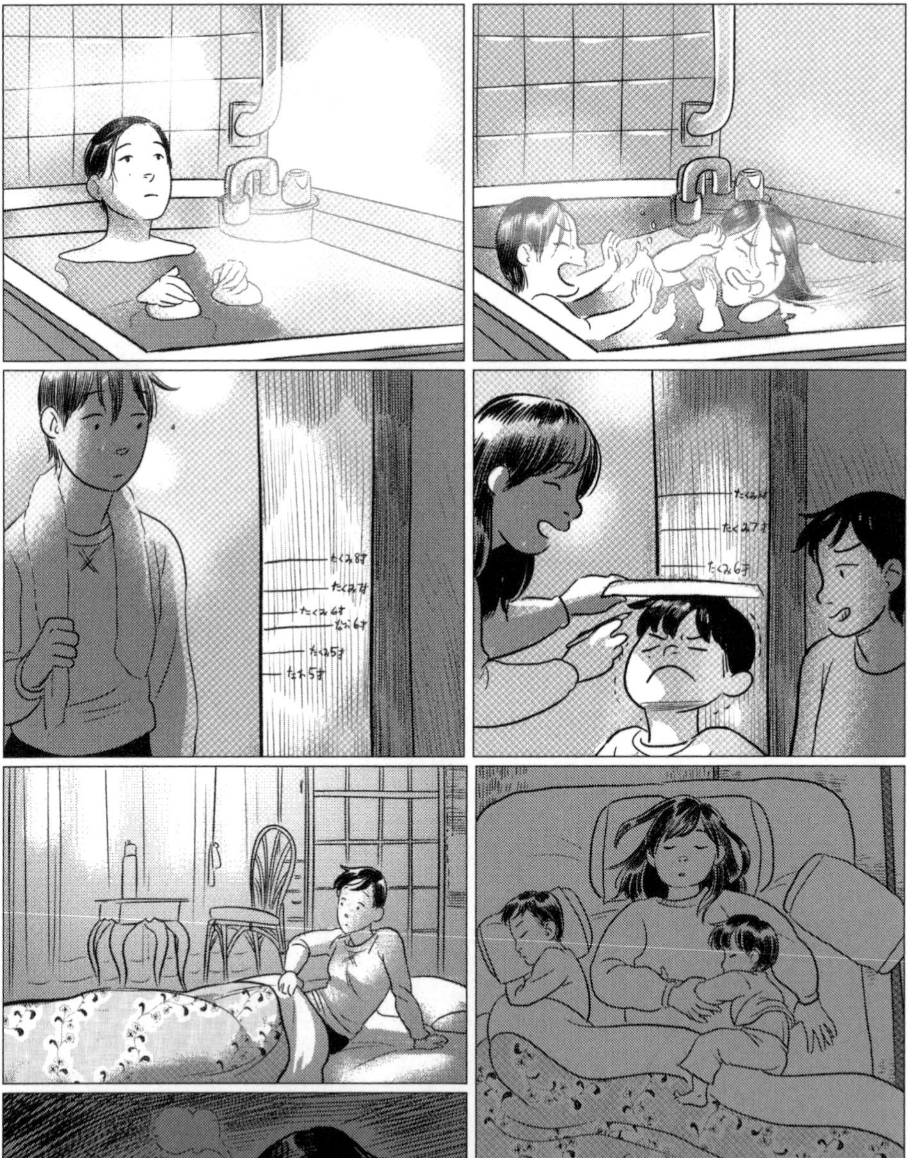
たくみ8才
たくみ7才
たくみ6才
なお6才
たくみ5才
なお5才
たくみ7才
たくみ6才
The futon is so heavy. It feels like being embraced.

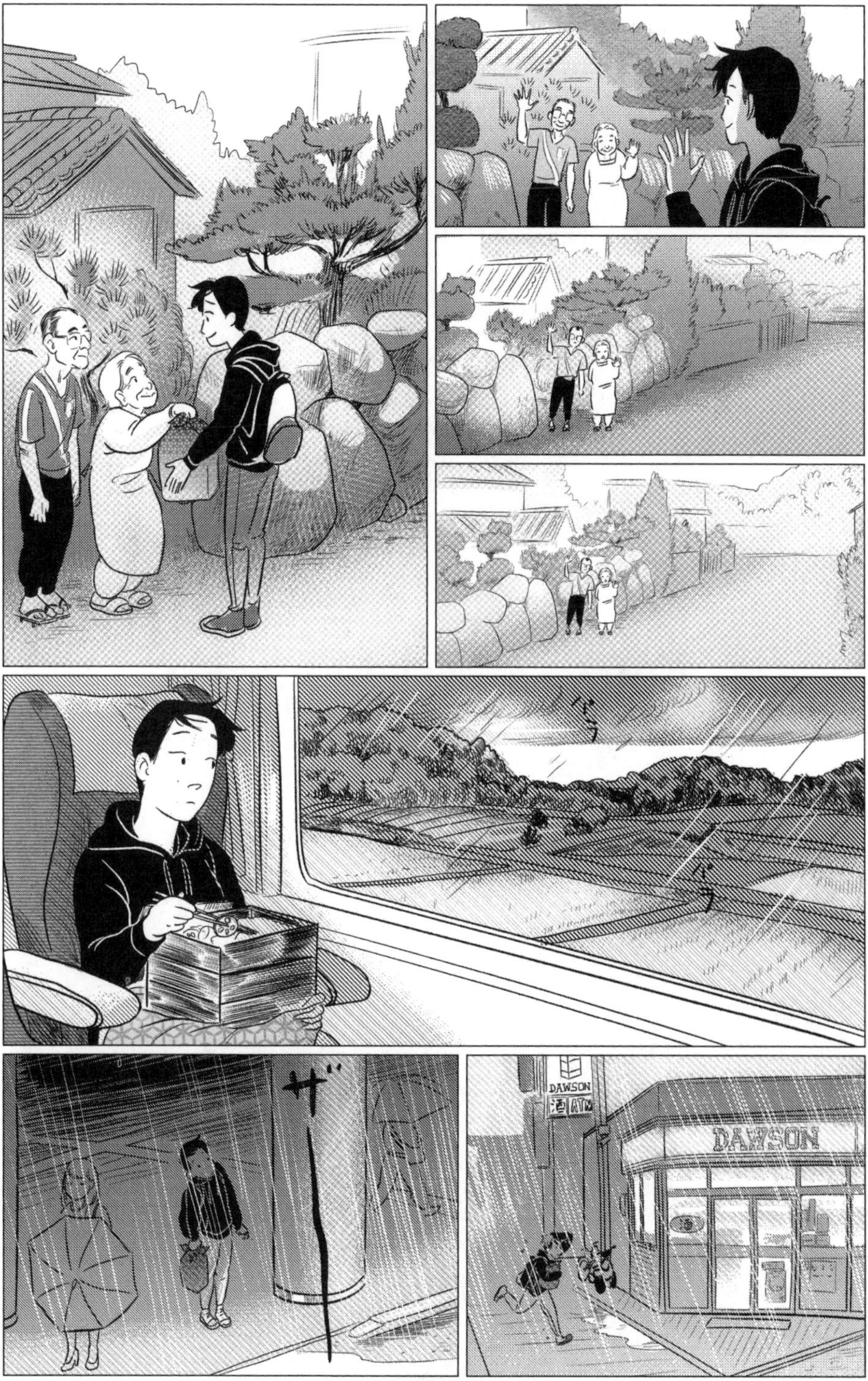
パラ
パラ
ザ
DAWSON
酒 ATM
DAWSON

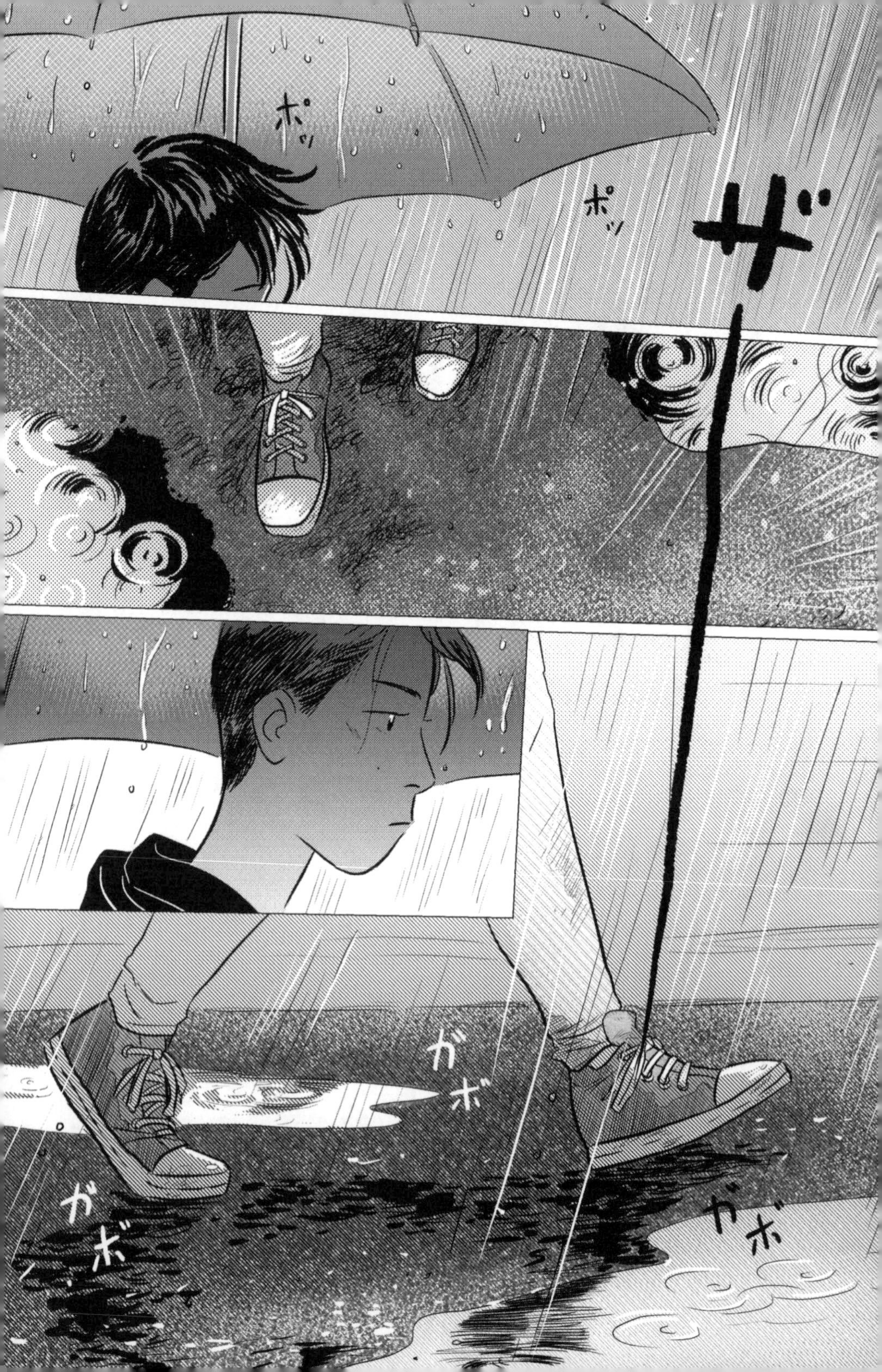
ポツ
ポツ
ザ
ガボ
ガボ
ガボ

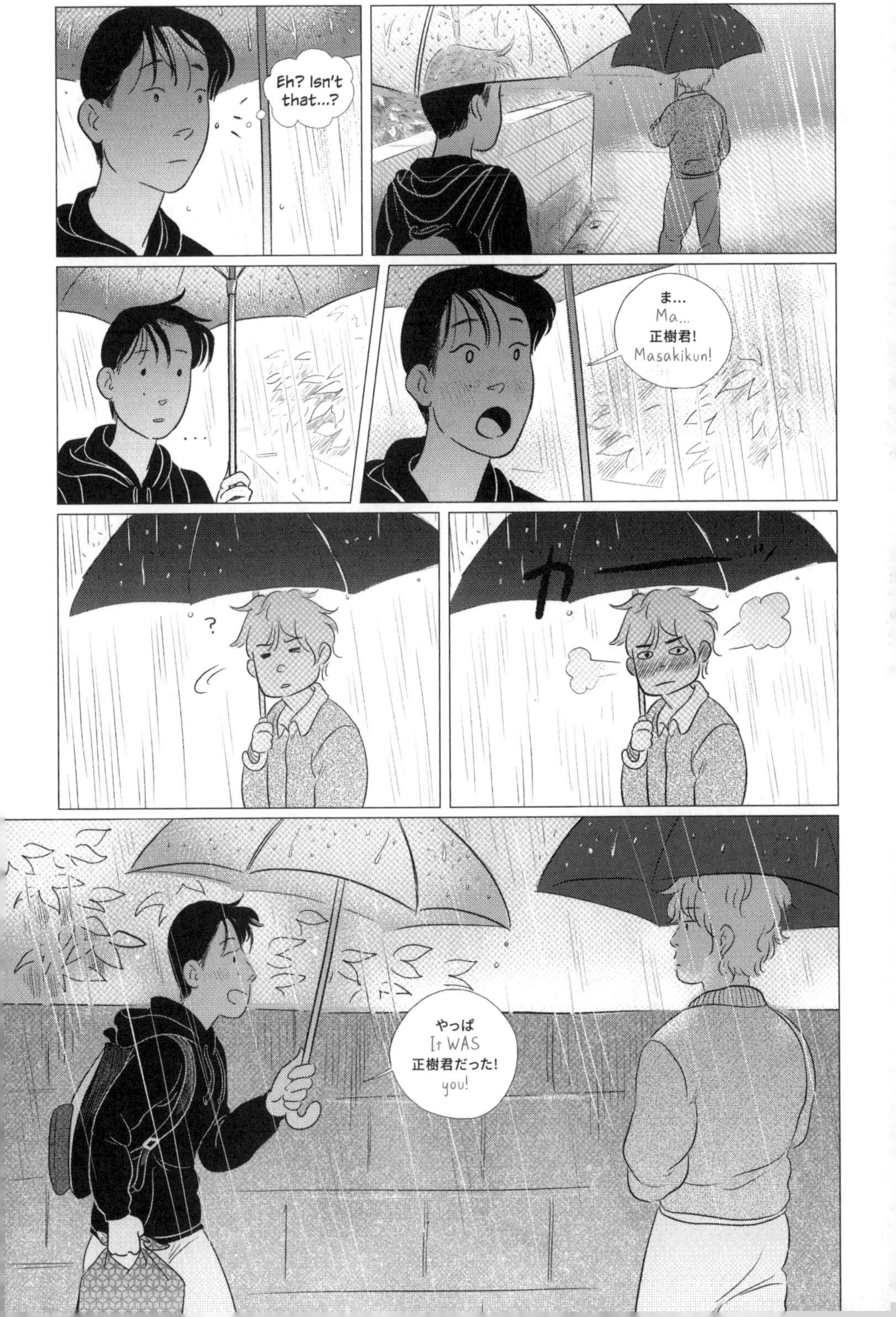

Eh? Isn't that...?
ま…
Ma...
正樹君!
Masakikun!
やっぱ
It WAS
正樹君だった!
you!

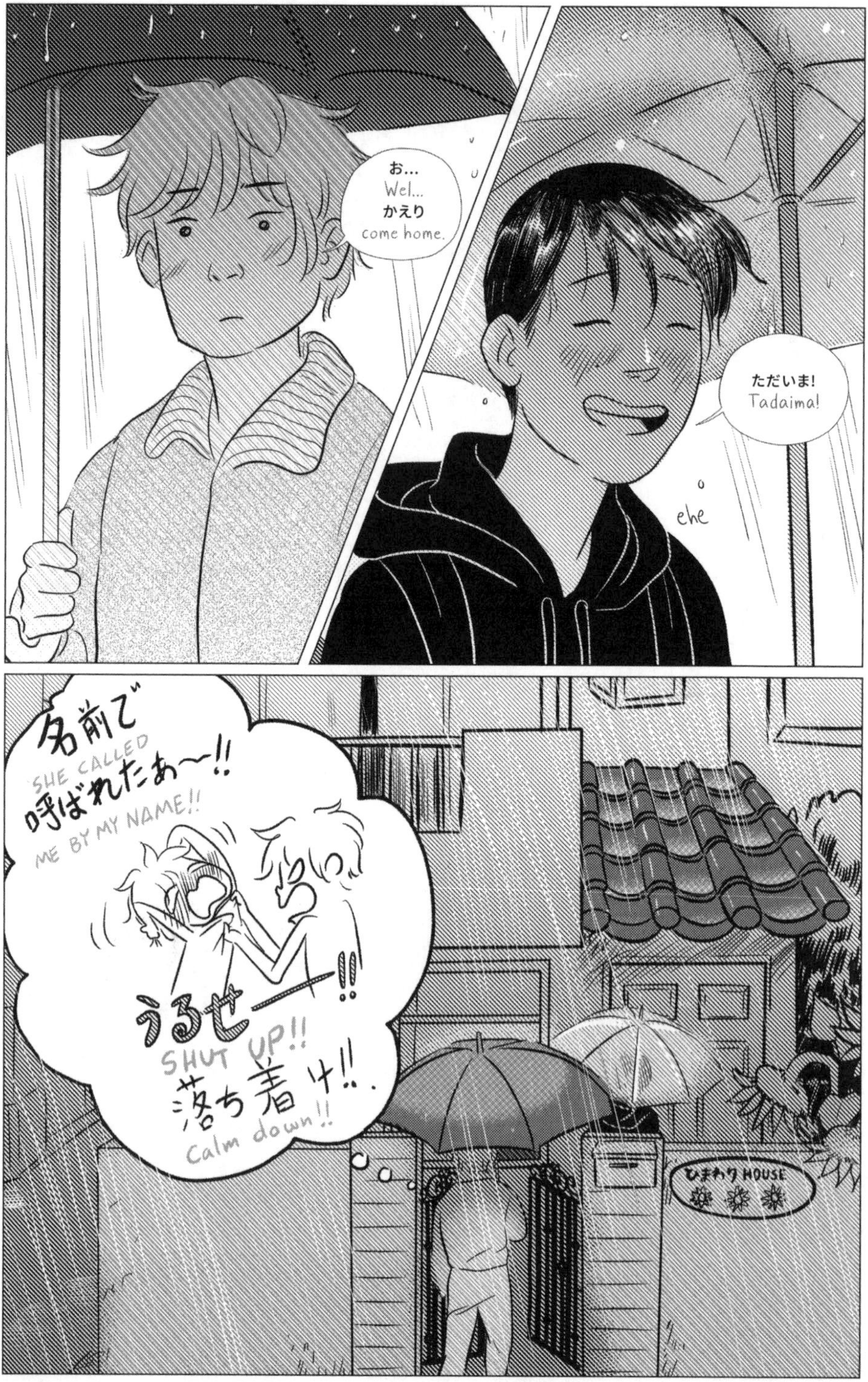
お… Wel…
かえり come home.
ただいま! Tadaima!
ehe
名前で呼ばれたあ~!! SHE CALLED ME BY MY NAME!!
うるせーー!! SHUT UP!!
落ち着け!! Calm down!!
ひまわりHOUSE

Chapter 10

Tetsuya Tachibana

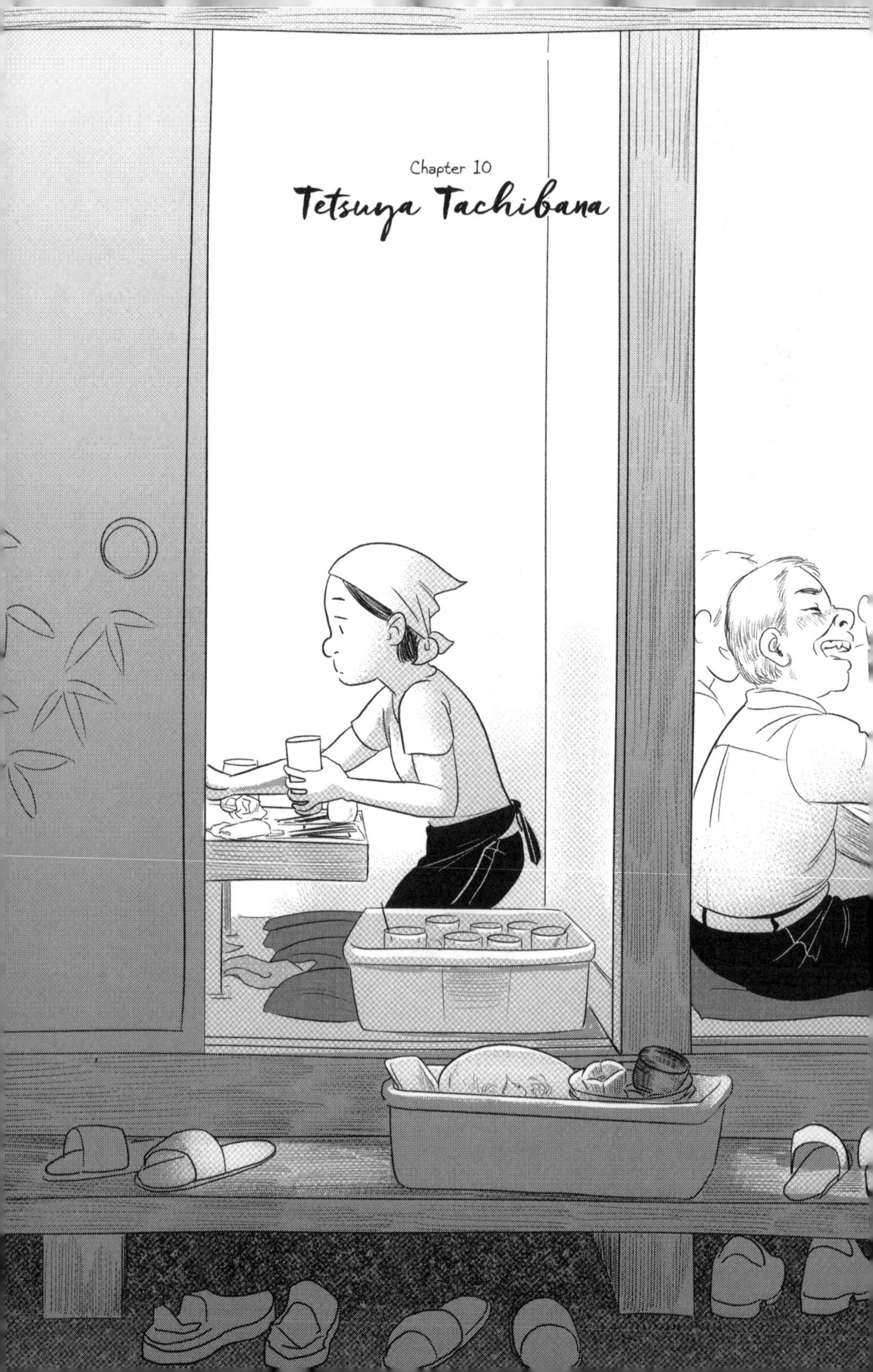

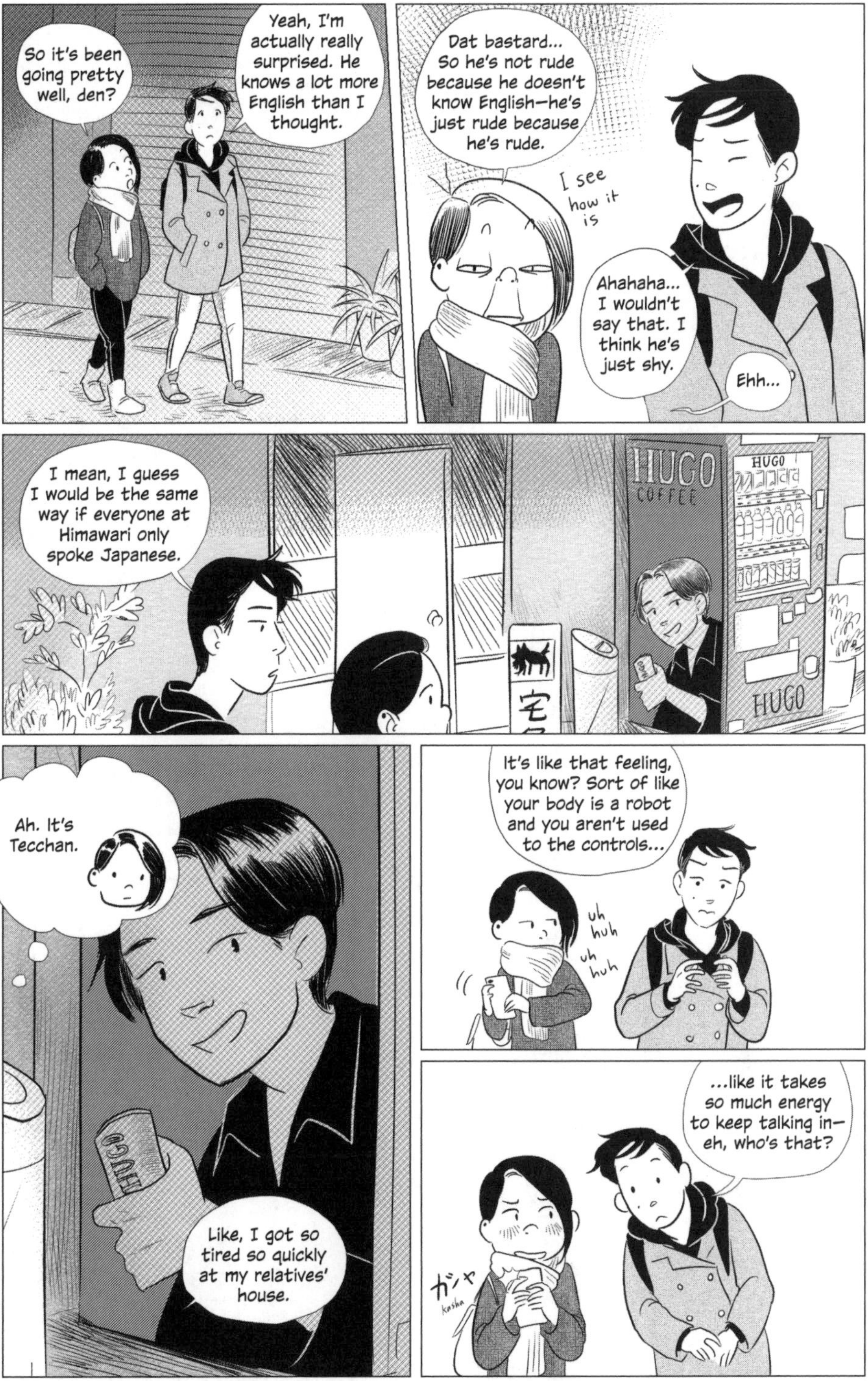
So it's been going pretty well, den?
Yeah, I'm actually really surprised. He knows a lot more English than I thought.
Dat bastard... So he's not rude because he doesn't know English—he's just rude because he's rude.
I see how it is
Ahahaha... I wouldn't say that. I think he's just shy.
Ehh...
I mean, I guess I would be the same way if everyone at Himawari only spoke Japanese.
HUGO COFFEE
HUGO
HUGO
Ah. It's Tecchan.
Like, I got so tired so quickly at my relatives' house.
It's like that feeling, you know? Sort of like your body is a robot and you aren't used to the controls...
uh huh
uh huh
...like it takes so much energy to keep talking in— eh, who's that?
ガシャ
kasha

If I can't connect to the people around me, why even bother trying?

この曲全部、一人で書いてたんです。
I was alone while writing each song.
音楽作る時はいつも一人でやってます。
I always make music alone. I'm actually
なんか、コラボレーションできる人って凄
quite jealous of people who are able to
く羨ましいけど、僕にはできないんですよ。
collaborate, because I can't do it. I get
意識しすぎて集中できなくなっちゃって
too self-conscious and lose
my concentration.

Why can't I have been born as someone in your life?

僕には一人が向いてるんですが、
I'm only able to make music alone,
やっぱり寂しく感じる事もあります。
but it is actually very lonely. The songs are always
曲を作る時は、最初に孤独感から始まるんです。
born out of a sense of loneliness, from this feeling
この気持ちを感じてるのって、
like I'm the only one in the world
この世界に僕だけなんじゃないかって
who is feeling this way.

I may not know how you fight, or how you kiss...

そこから曲作りが始まって、一つ一つの曲を磨いて、磨いて…
It starts from that feeling, and then throughout the process, as I polish
ずっとその流れで、一人なんですけど。
each song one by one, I'm always alone. If there was even just one listener
曲を聴いてくれた方の中で、たった一人でも、「あぁ、
who was able to think, "Ah, there's another person in the world
世界に自分以外にも同じような気持ちの人がいるんだなぁ」
who feels the same as me," I would be very happy.
って思ってくれる方がいてくれたらとっても嬉しいです

...but the things you said mattered to me.

They changed me.

まぁ、その、今度のアルバムには、
Well, anyway, as the album
そういう思いを込めて
was made with this feeling
作りたかったというか…
in mind... I would be
その思いが伝わると嬉しいなって…
very happy if people understood
what I felt...

Moved me.

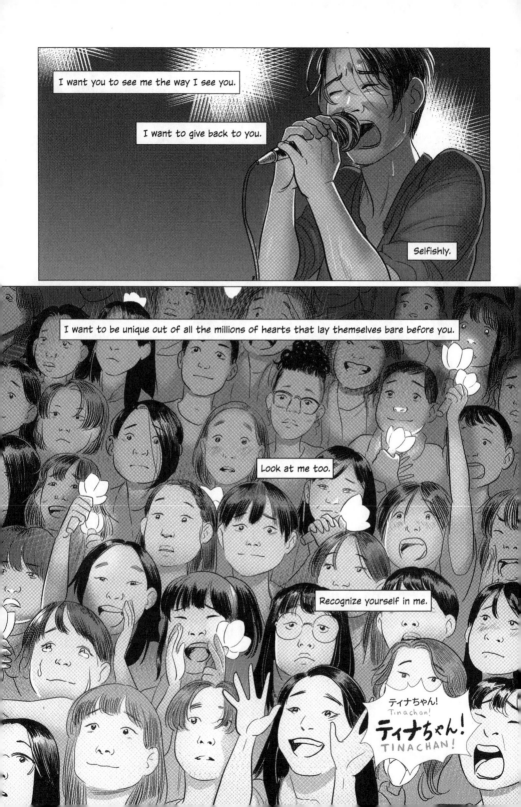

184

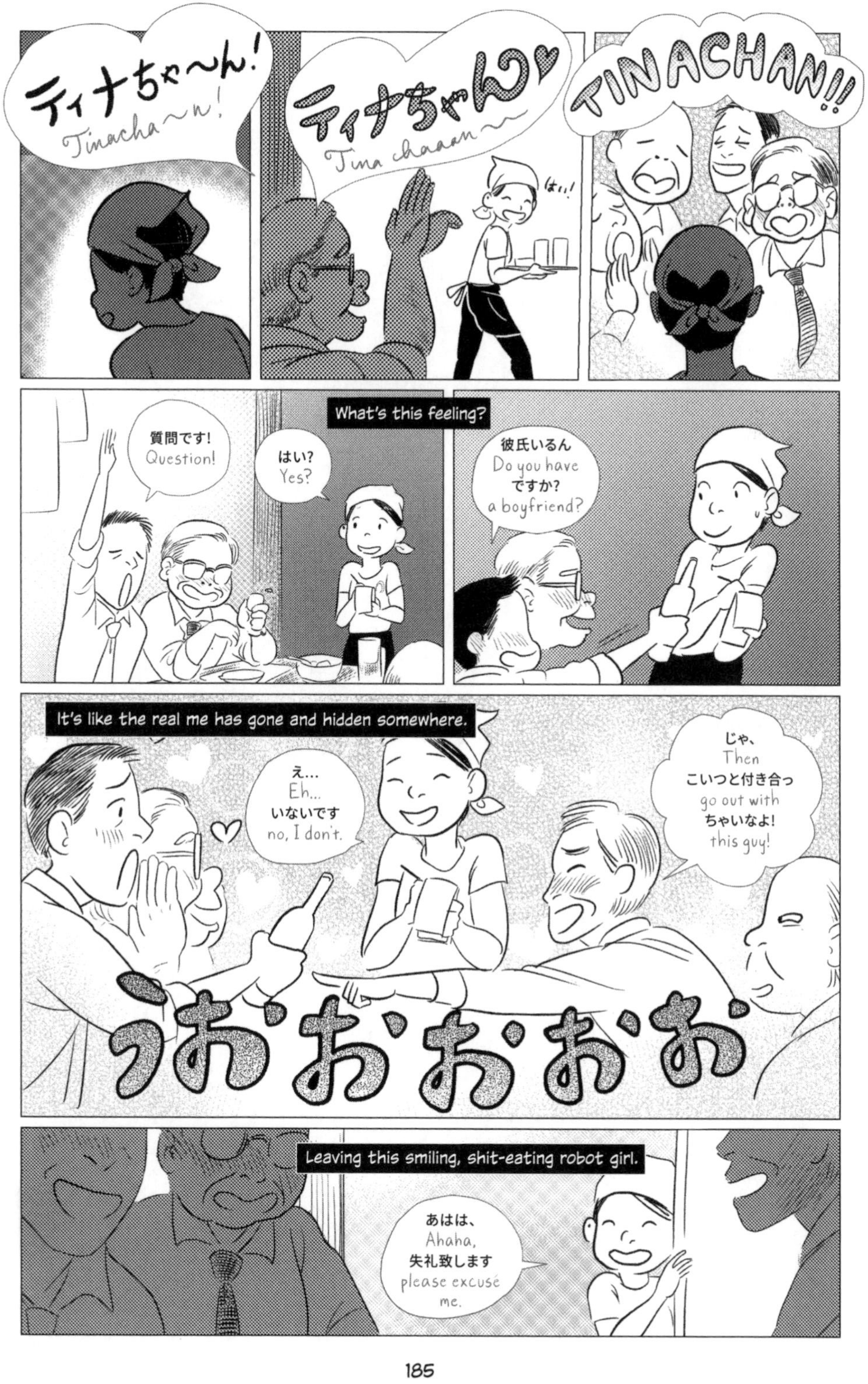

ティナちゃ〜ん!
Tinacha〜n!
ティナちゃん〜♥
Tina chaaan〜〜
はい!
TINACHAN!!
What's this feeling?
質問です!
Question!
はい?
Yes?
彼氏いるん
Do you have
ですか?
a boyfriend?
It's like the real me has gone and hidden somewhere.
え…
Eh...
いないです
no, I don't.
じゃ、
Then
こいつと付き合っ
go out with
ちゃいなよ!
this guy!
うおおおおお
Leaving this smiling, shit-eating robot girl.
あはは、
Ahaha,
失礼致します
please excuse
me.

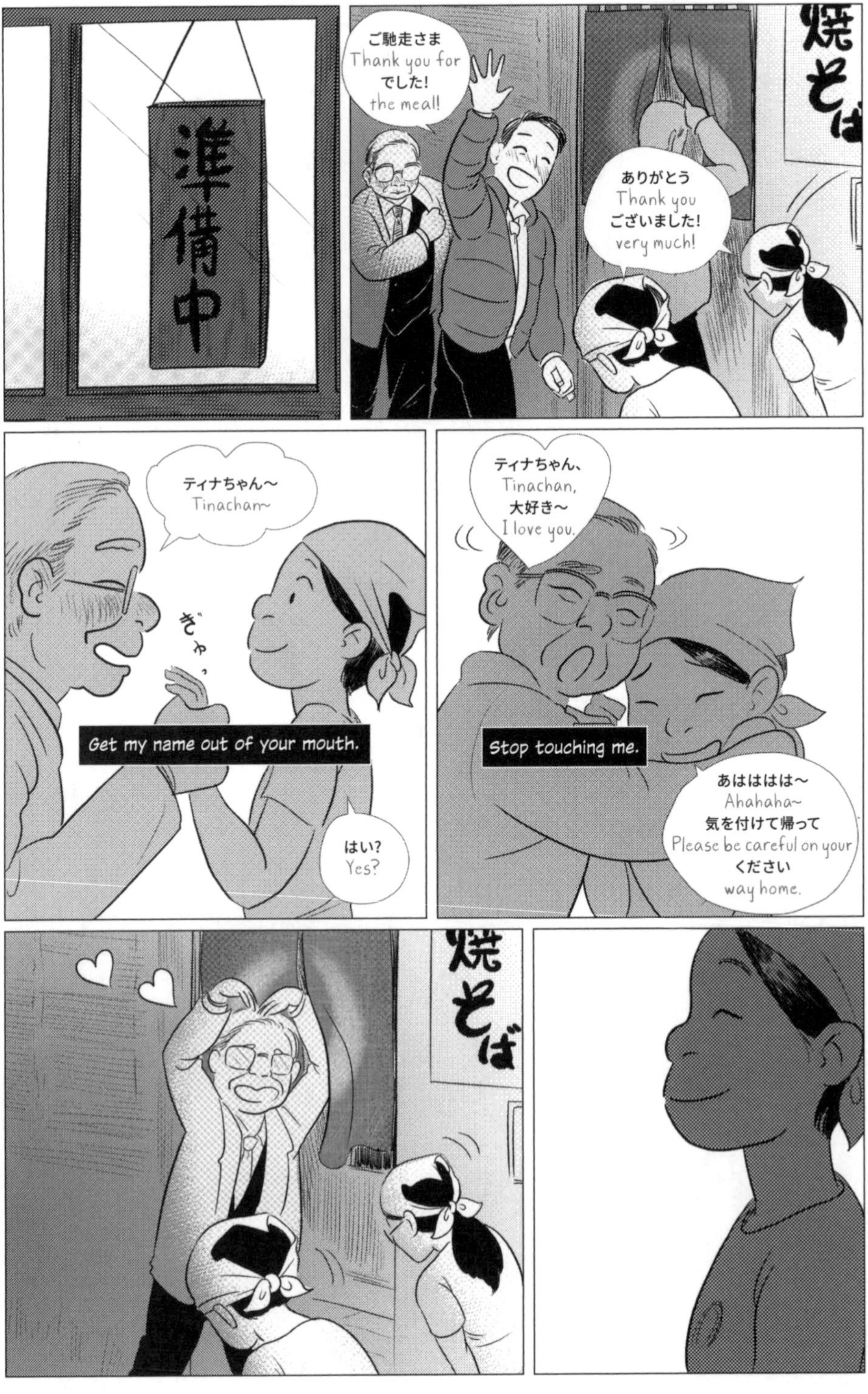
準備中
ご馳走さま Thank you for でした! the meal!
焼そば
ありがとう Thank you ございました! very much!
ティナちゃん～ Tinachan~
ぎゅ，
Get my name out of your mouth.
はい? Yes?
ティナちゃん、 Tinachan, 大好き～ I love you.
Stop touching me.
あはははは～ Ahahaha~ 気を付けて帰って Please be careful on your ください way home.
焼そば

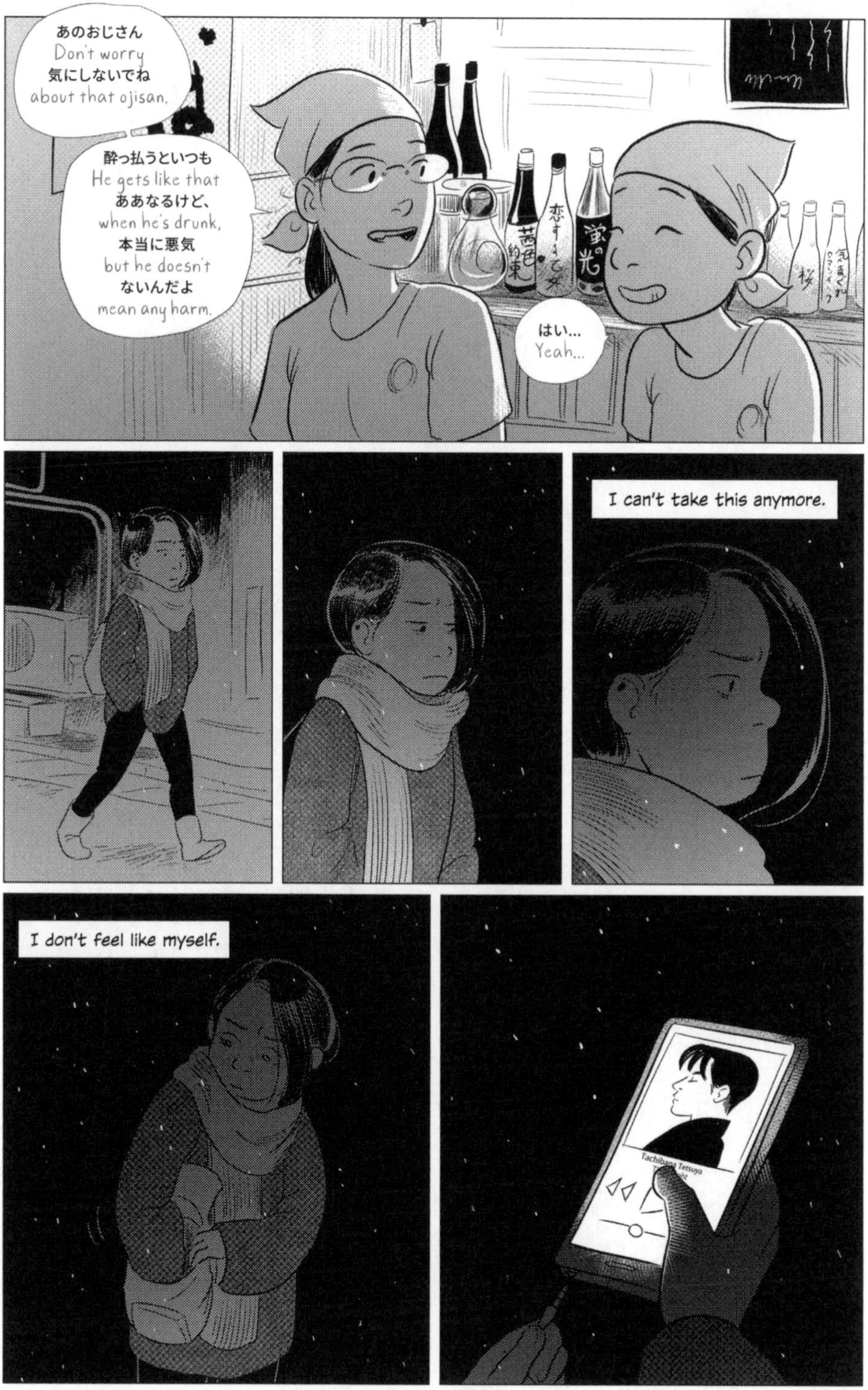

あのおじさん
Don't worry
気にしないでね
about that ojisan.
酔っ払うといつも
He gets like that
ああなるけど、
when he's drunk,
本当に悪気
but he doesn't
ないんだよ
mean any harm.
はい...
Yeah...
I can't take this anymore.
I don't feel like myself.
Tachibana Tetsuya

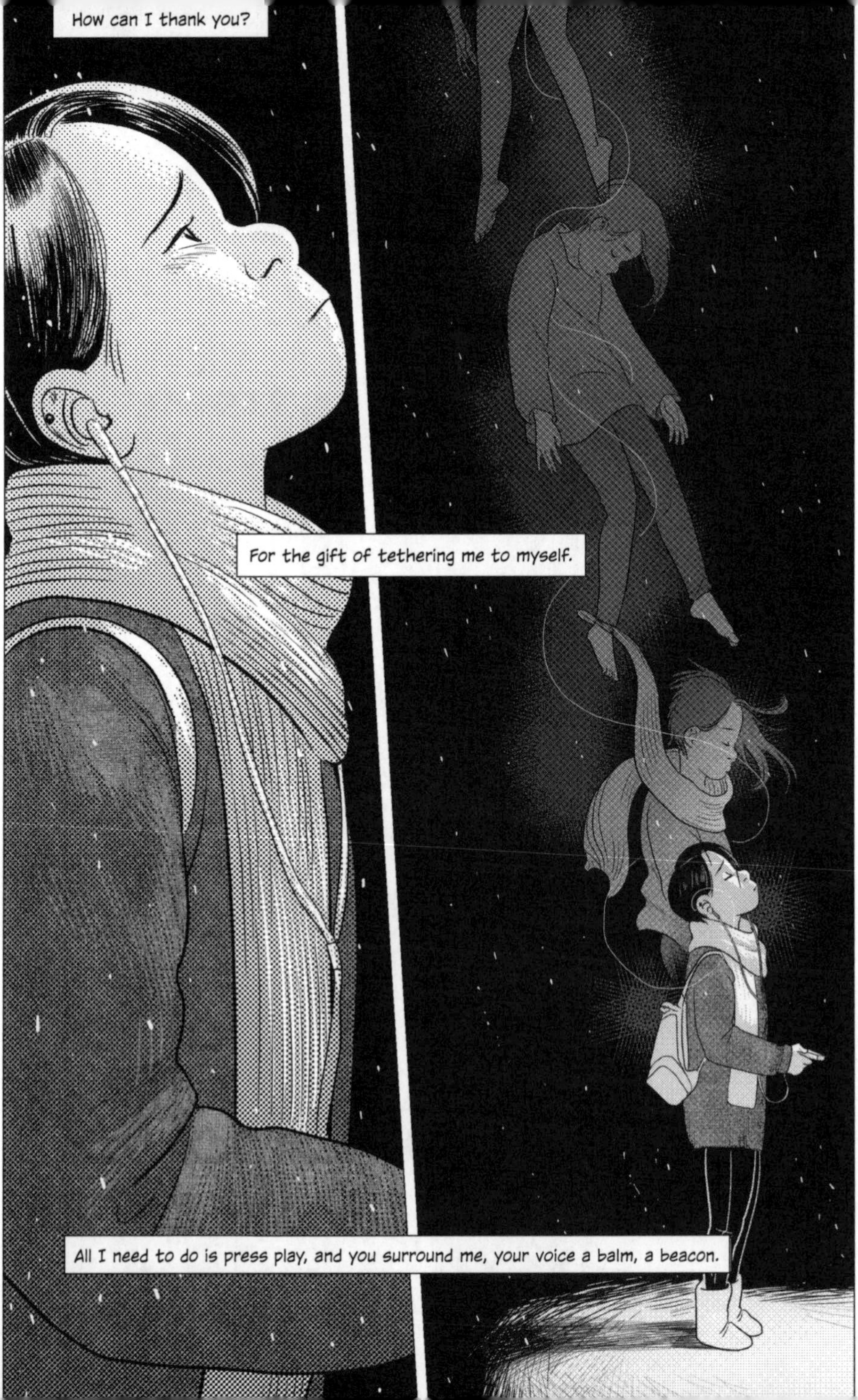
How can I thank you?
For the gift of tethering me to myself.
All I need to do is press play, and you surround me, your voice a balm, a beacon.

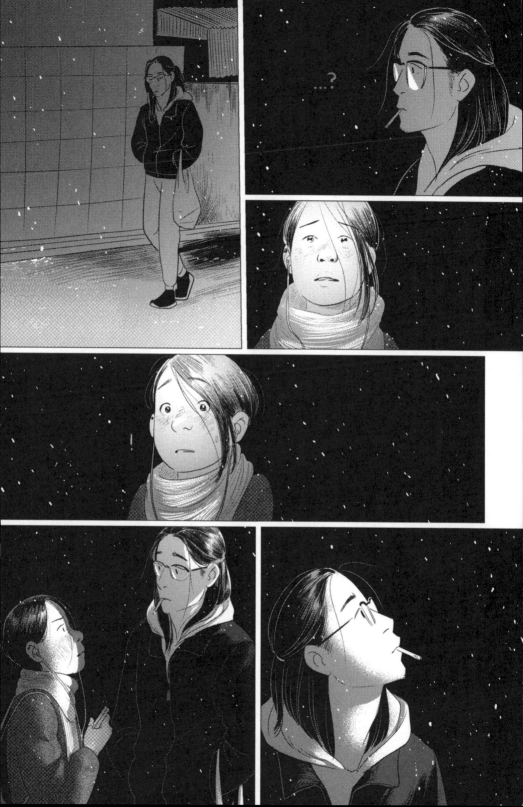

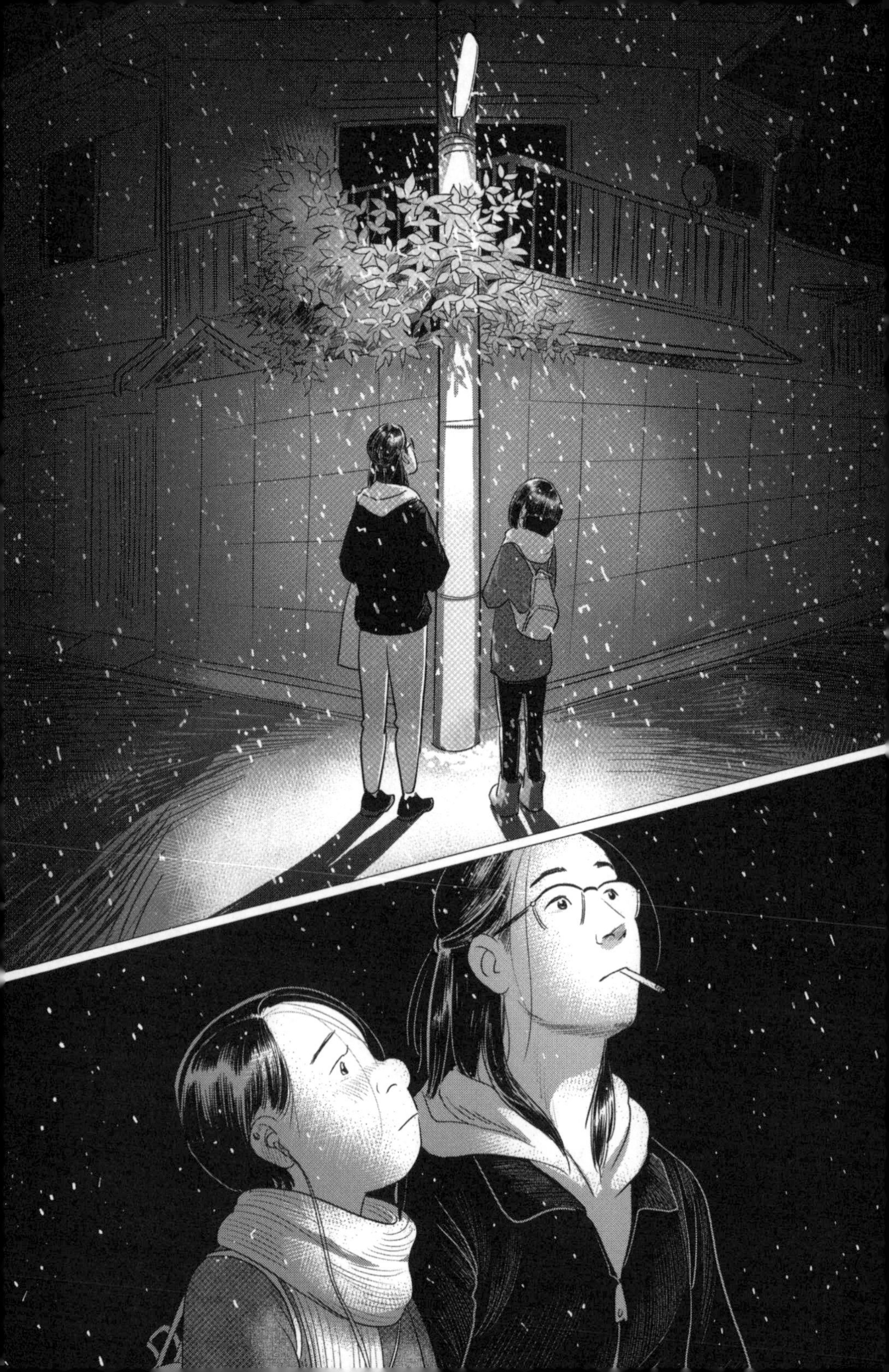

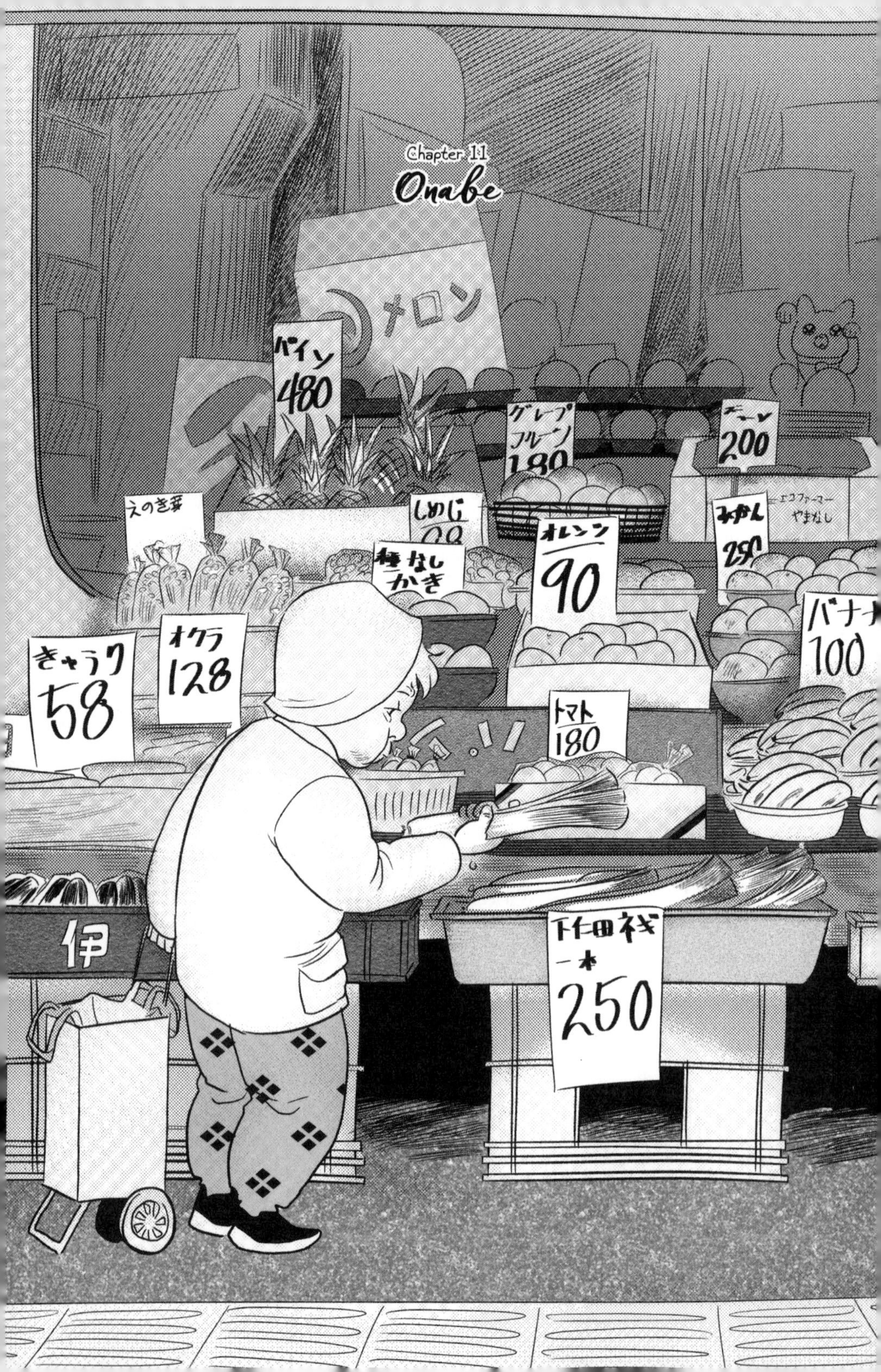
Chapter 11
Onabe
メロン
パイン
480
えのき茸
しめじ
グレープ
フルーツ
200
みかん
エコファーマー
やまなし
種なし
かき
オレンジ
90
バナナ
100
キャベツ
58
オクラ
128
トマト
180
伊
下仁田ネギ
一本
250

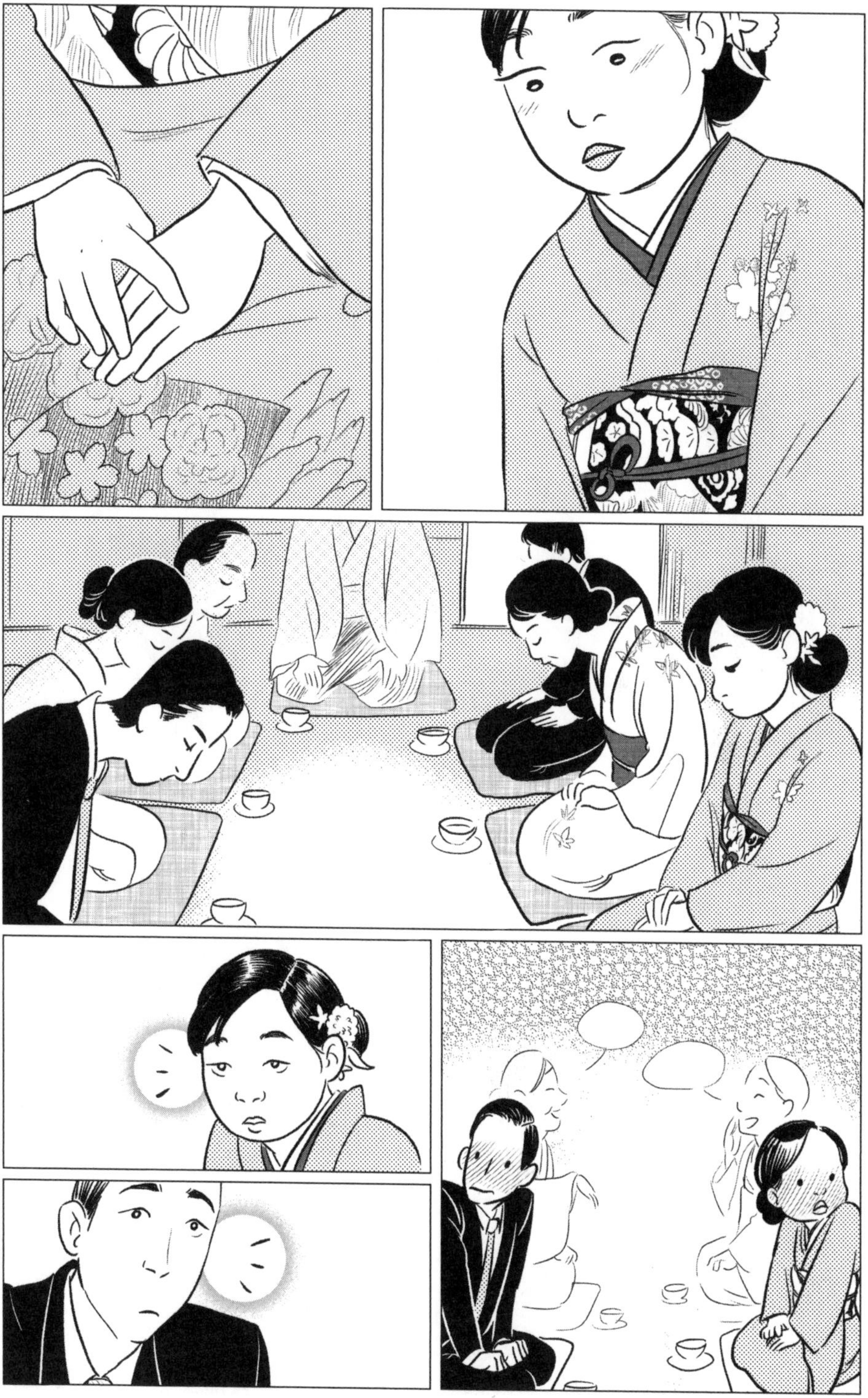

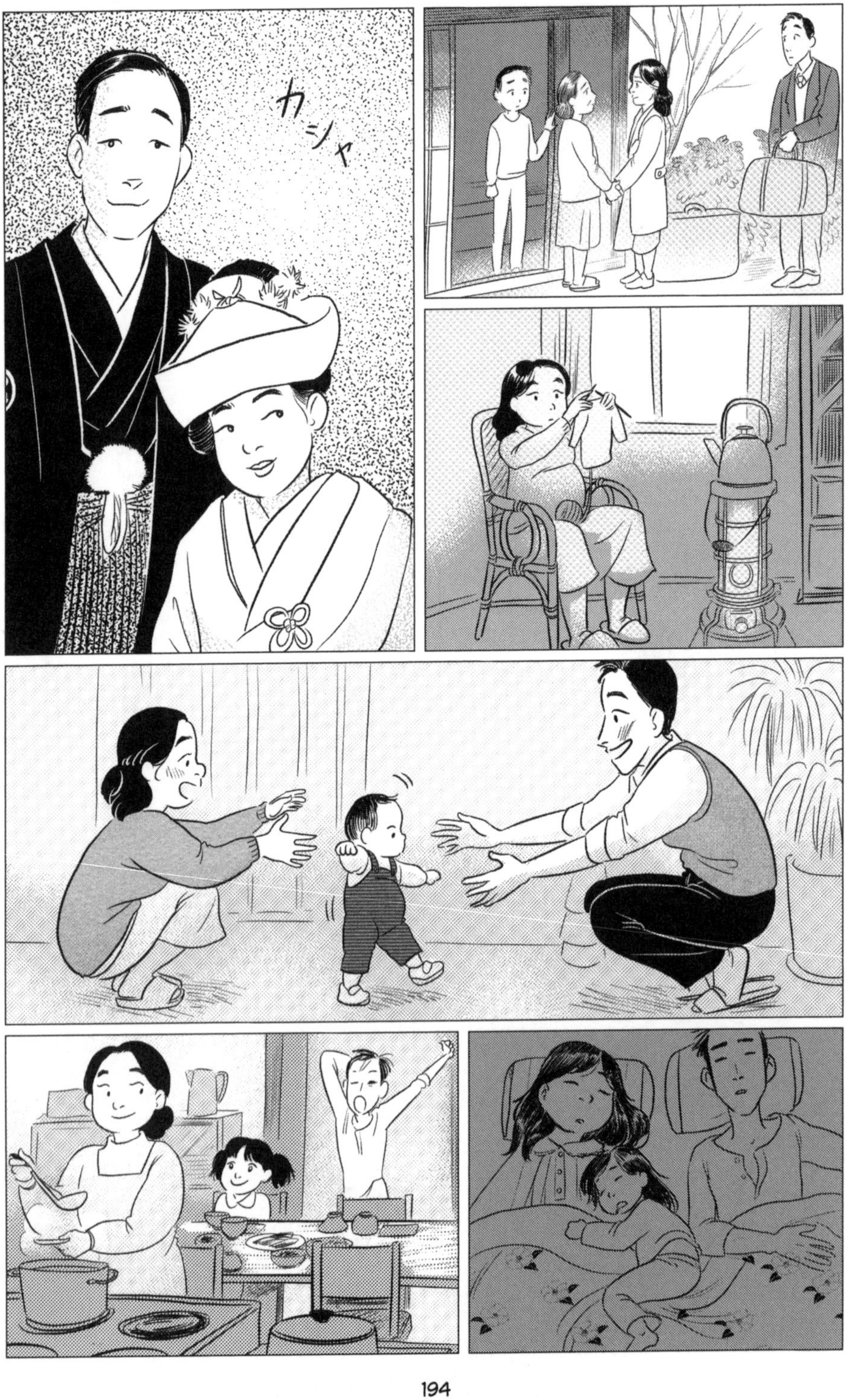
カシャ

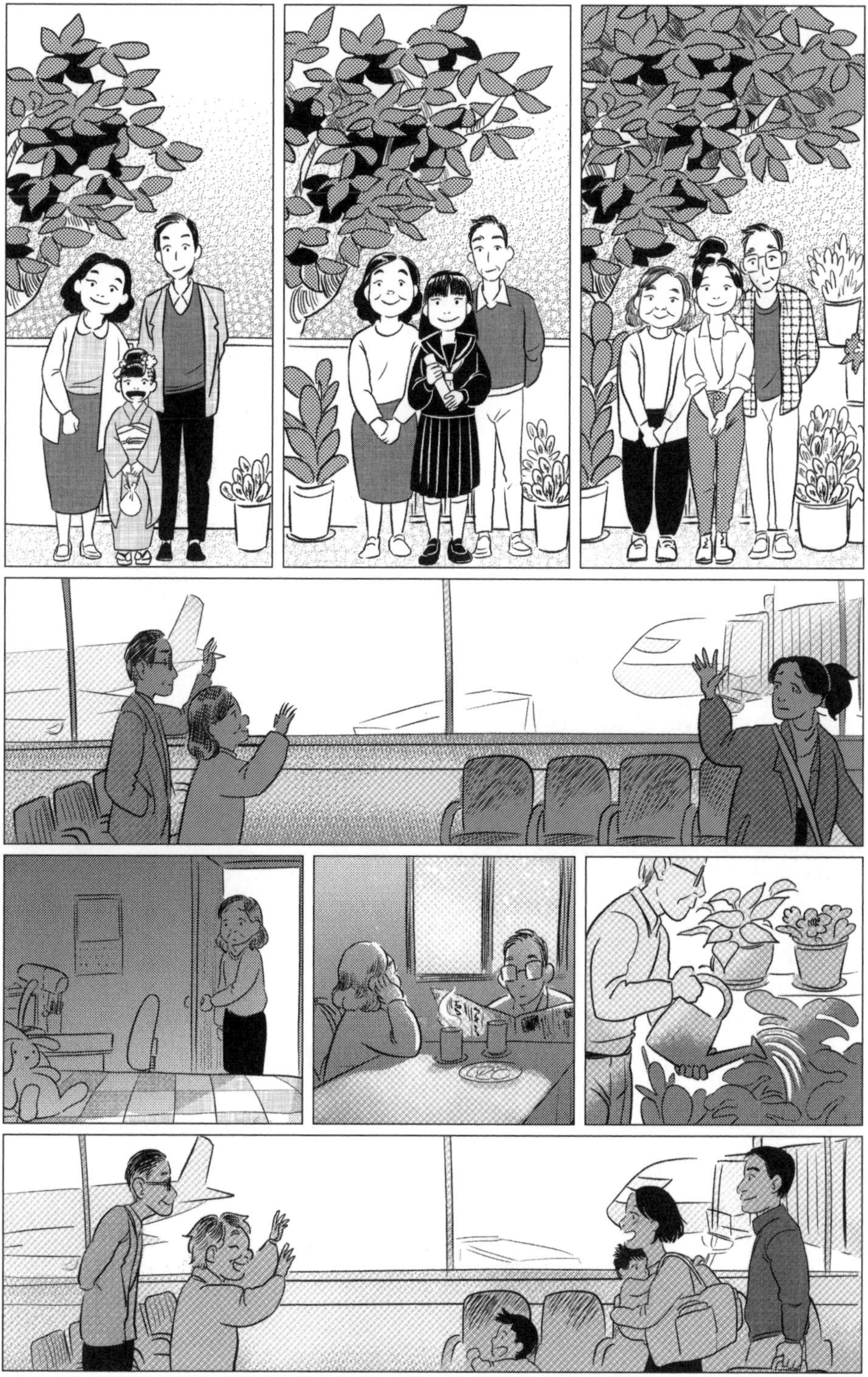

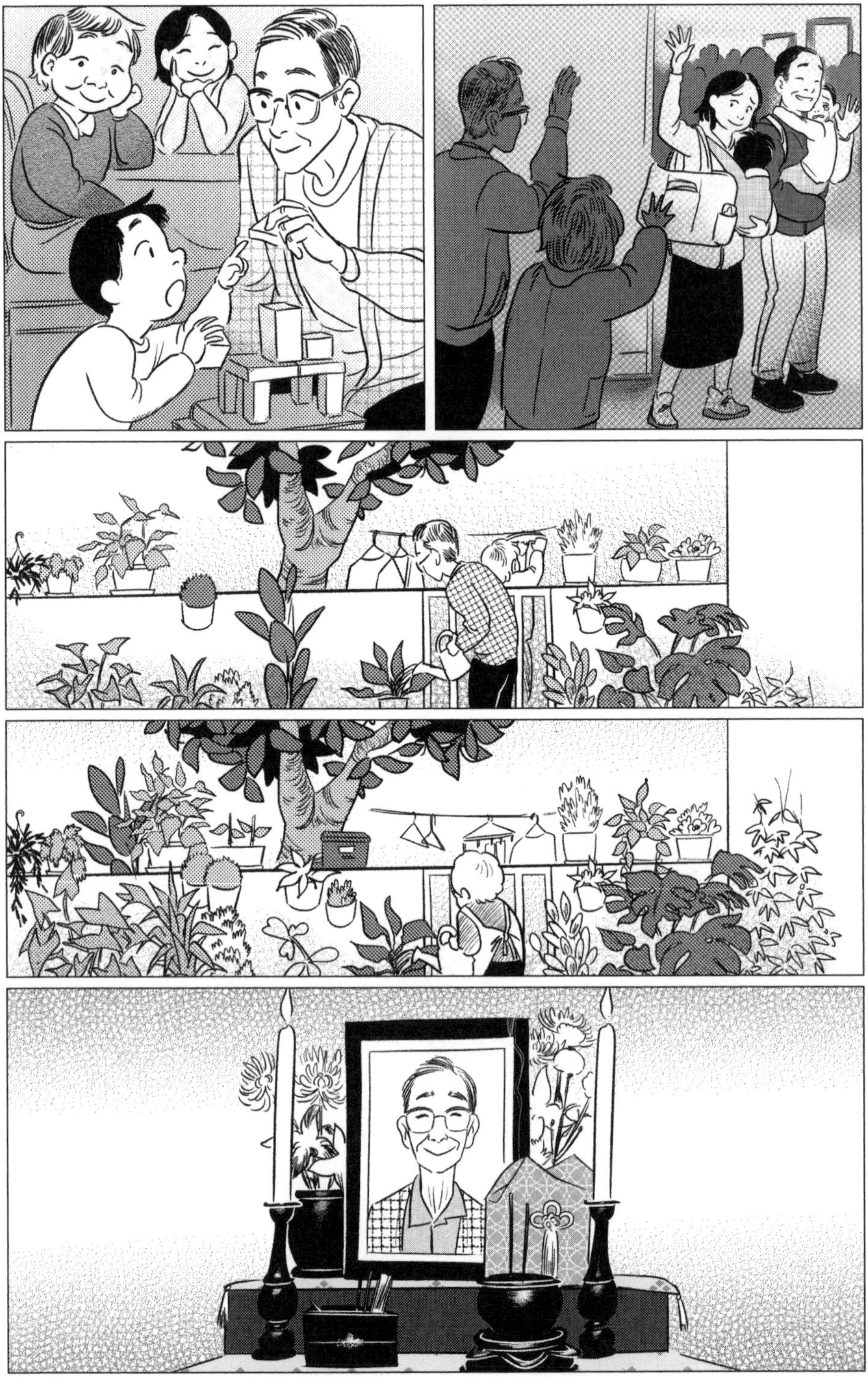

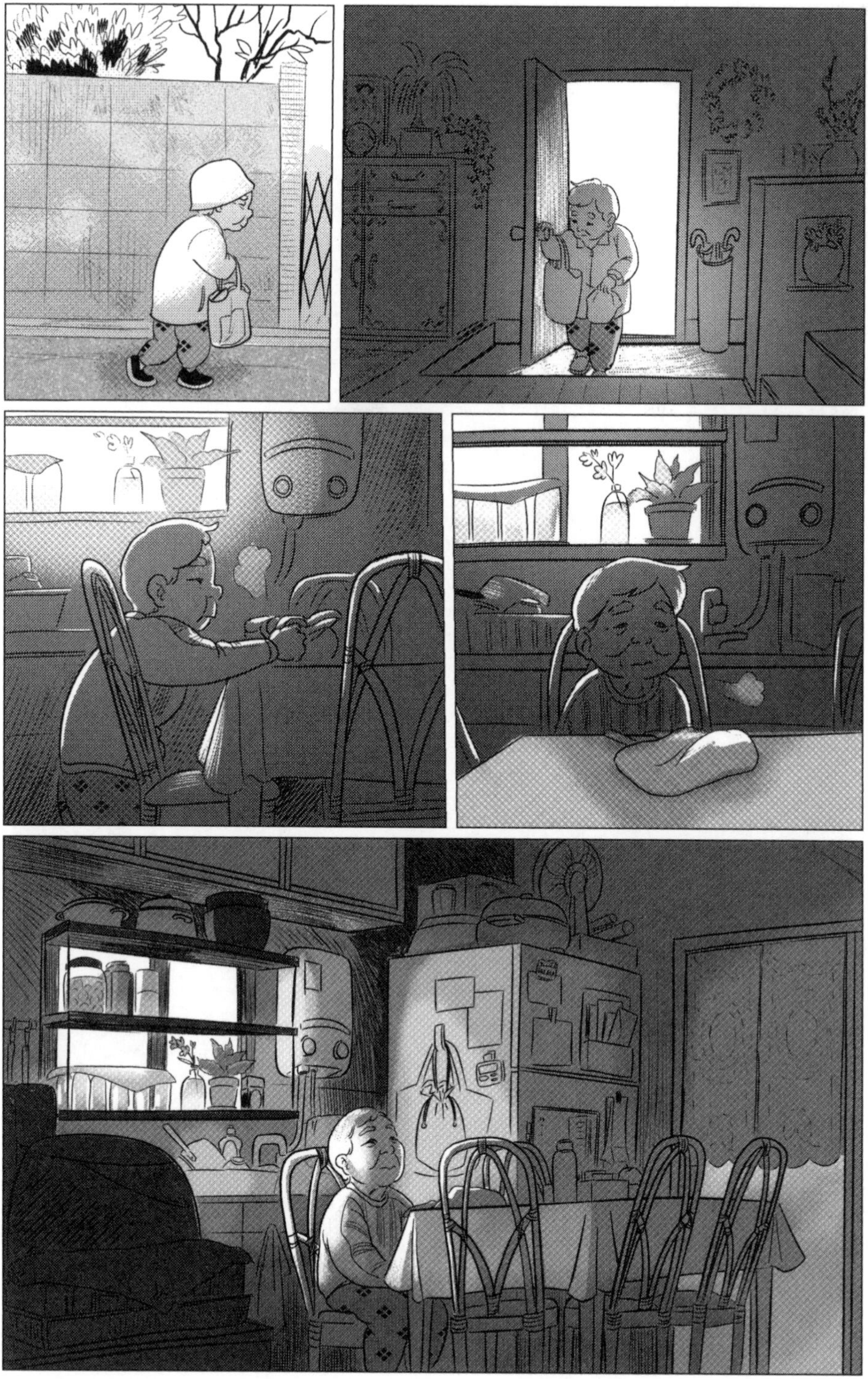

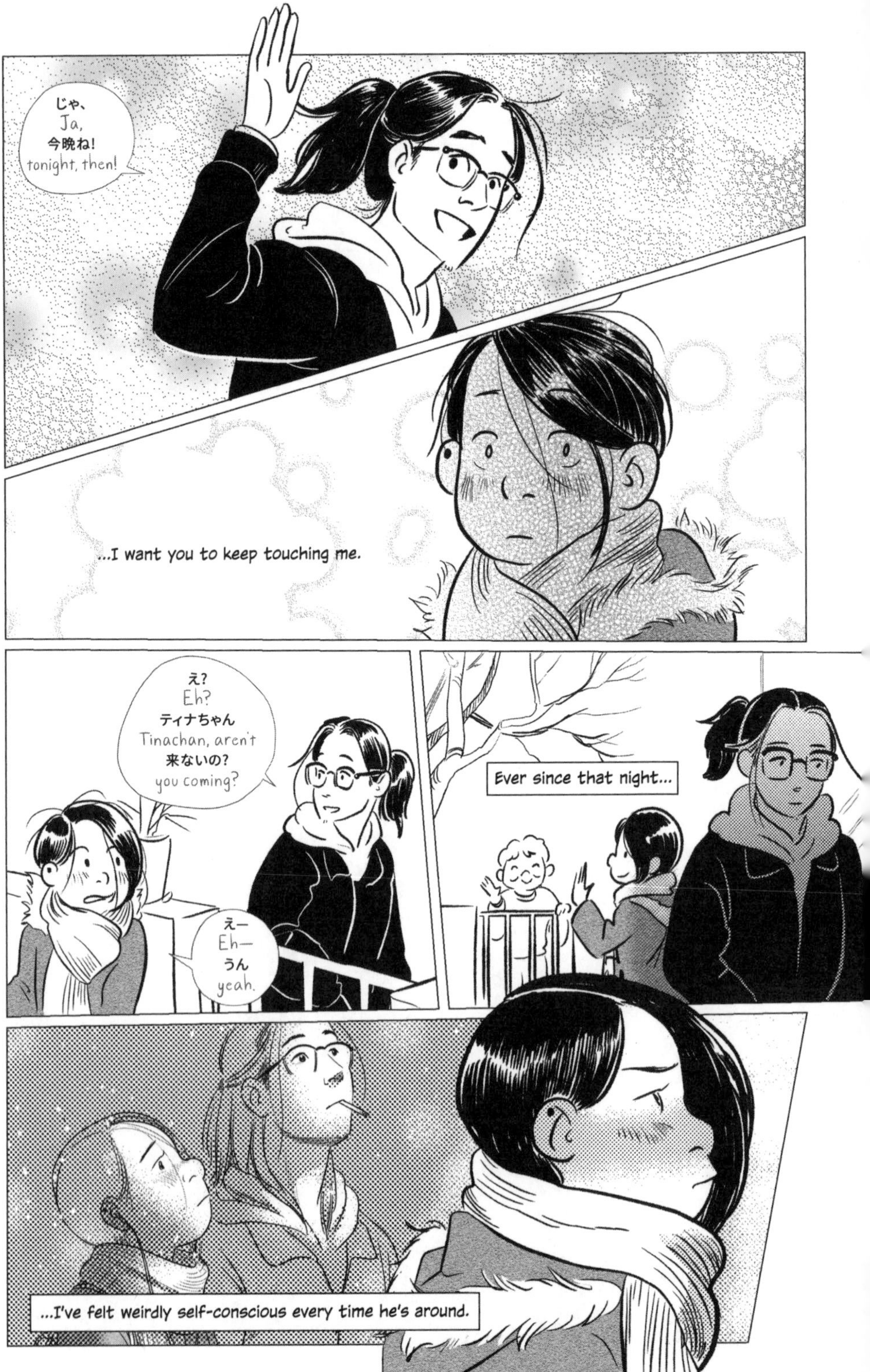
じゃ、
Ja,
今晩ね!
tonight, then!
...I want you to keep touching me.
え?
Eh?
ティナちゃん
Tinachan, aren't
来ないの?
you coming?
えー
Eh—
うん
yeah.
Ever since that night...
...I've felt weirdly self-conscious every time he's around.

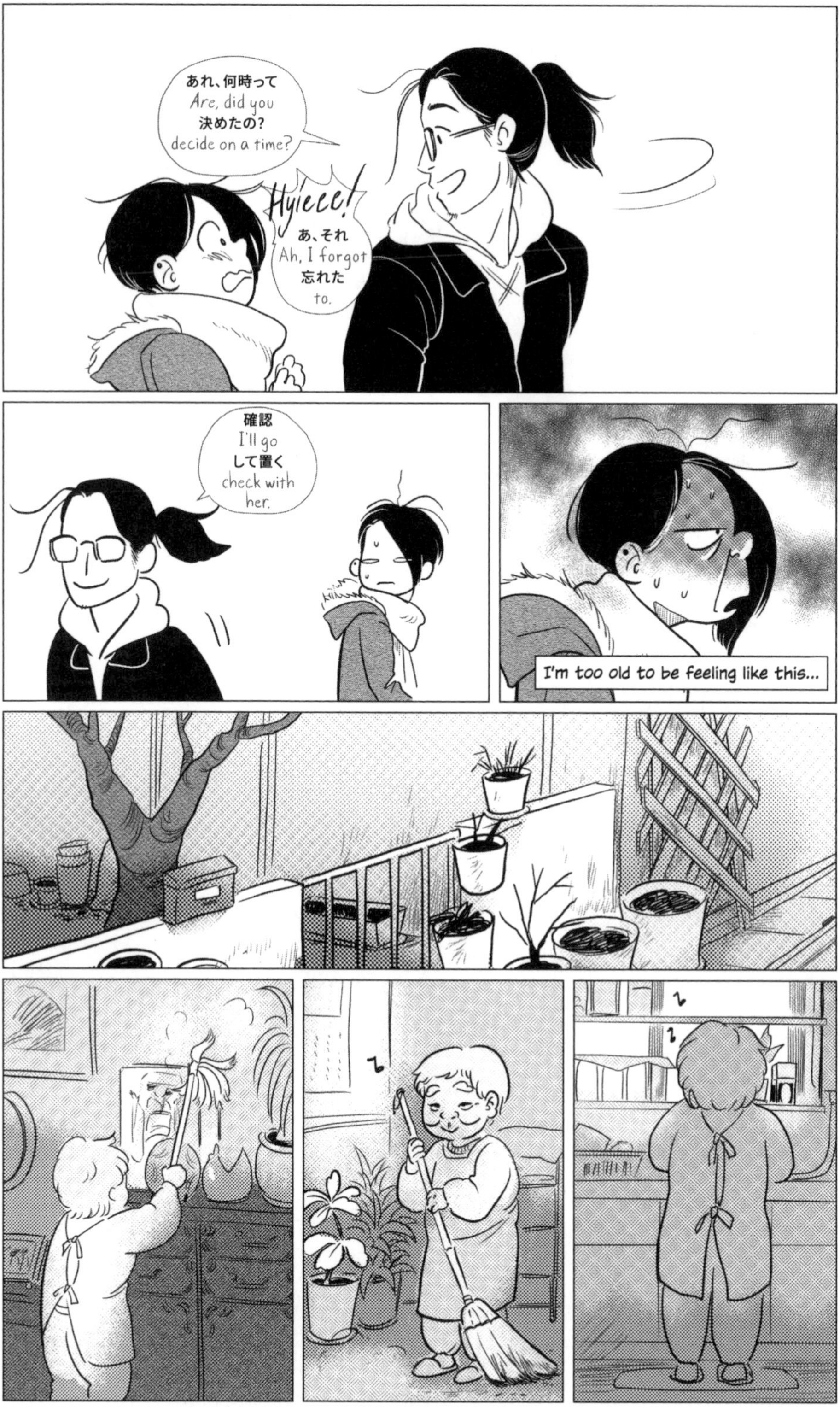
あれ、何時って
Are, did you
決めたの?
decide on a time?
Hyieee!
あ、それ
Ah, I forgot
忘れた
to.
確認
I'll go
して置く
check with
her.
I'm too old to be feeling like this...

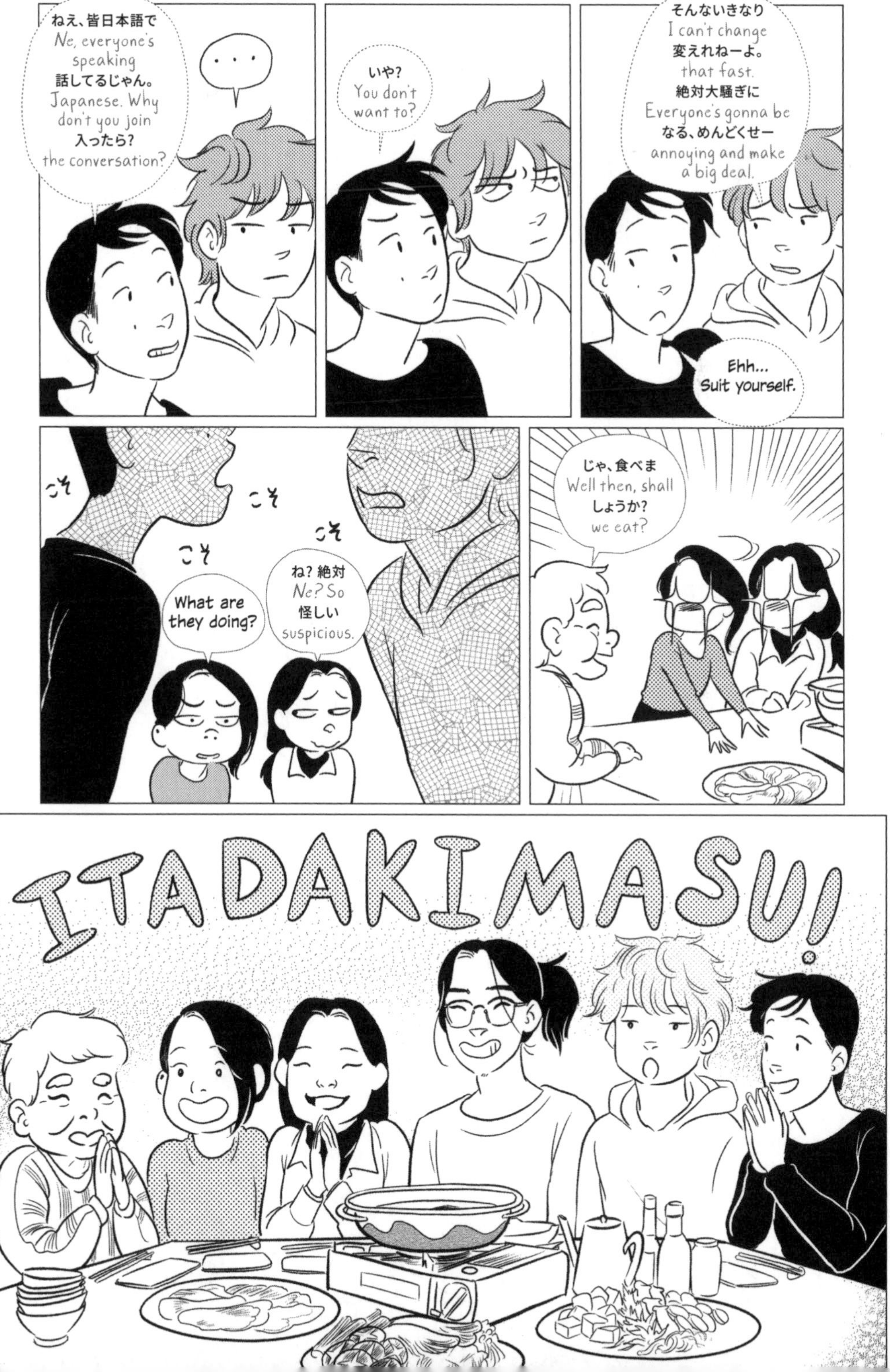

ねえ、皆日本語で
Ne, everyone's speaking
話してるじゃん。
Japanese. Why don't you join
入ったら?
the conversation?
. . .
いや?
You don't want to?
そんないきなり
I can't change
変えれねーよ。
that fast.
絶対大騒ぎに
Everyone's gonna be
なる、めんどくせー
annoying and make a big deal.
Ehh... Suit yourself.
こそ
こそ
こそ
こそ
What are they doing?
ね? 絶対
Ne? So
怪しい
suspicious.
じゃ、食べま
Well then, shall
しょうか?
we eat?
ITADAKIMASU!

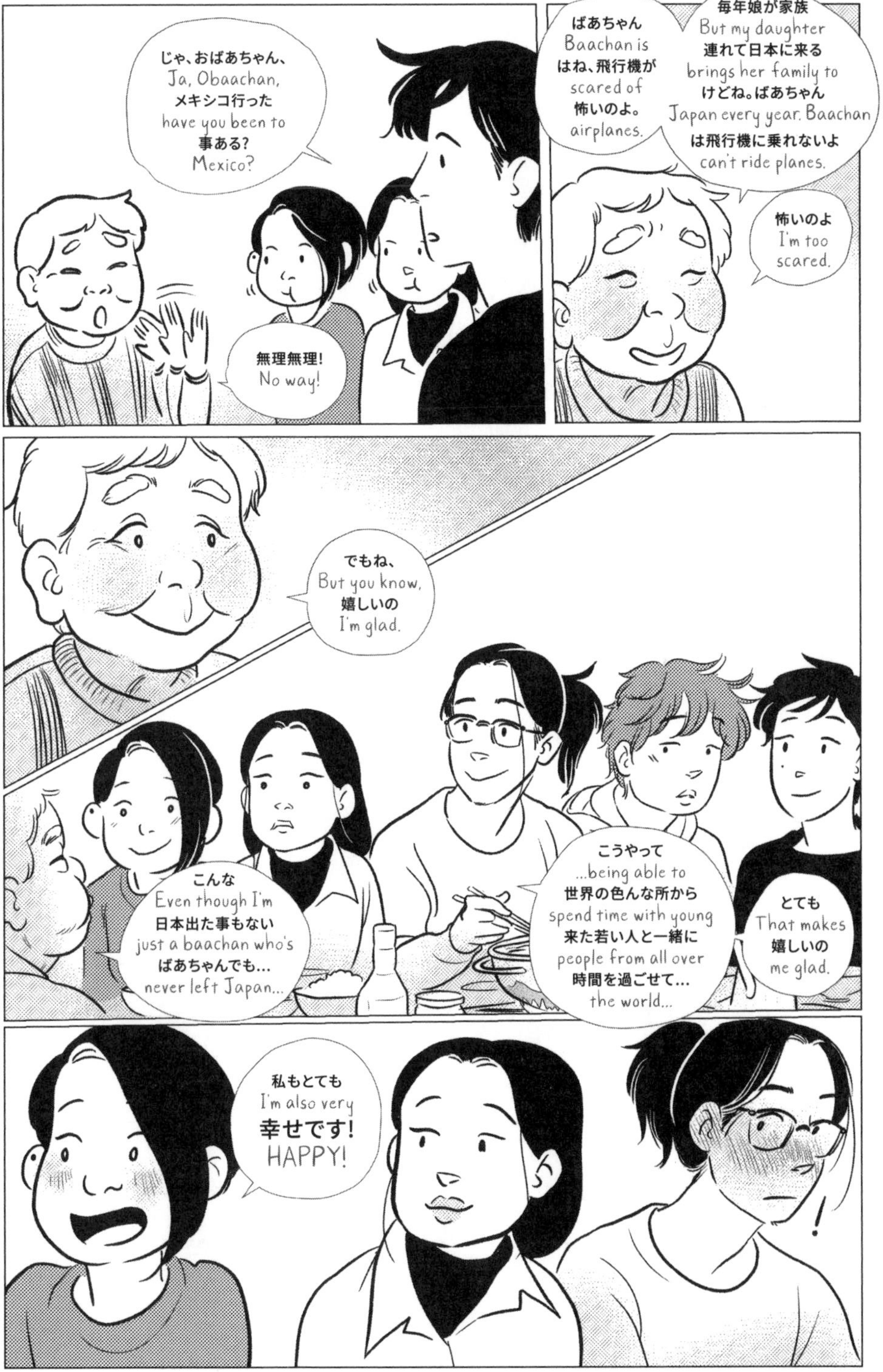
じゃ、おばあちゃん、
Ja, Obaachan,
メキシコ行った
have you been to
事ある?
Mexico?
無理無理!
No way!
ばあちゃん
Baachan is
はね、飛行機が
scared of
怖いのよ。
airplanes.
毎年娘が家族
But my daughter
連れて日本に来る
brings her family to
けどね。ばあちゃん
Japan every year. Baachan
は飛行機に乗れないよ
can't ride planes.
怖いのよ
I'm too
scared.
でもね、
But you know,
嬉しいの
I'm glad.
こんな
Even though I'm
日本出た事もない
just a baachan who's
ばあちゃんでも…
never left Japan...
こうやって
...being able to
世界の色んな所から
spend time with young
来た若い人と一緒に
people from all over
時間を過ごせて…
the world...
とても
That makes
嬉しいの
me glad.
私もとても
I'm also very
幸せです!
HAPPY!
!

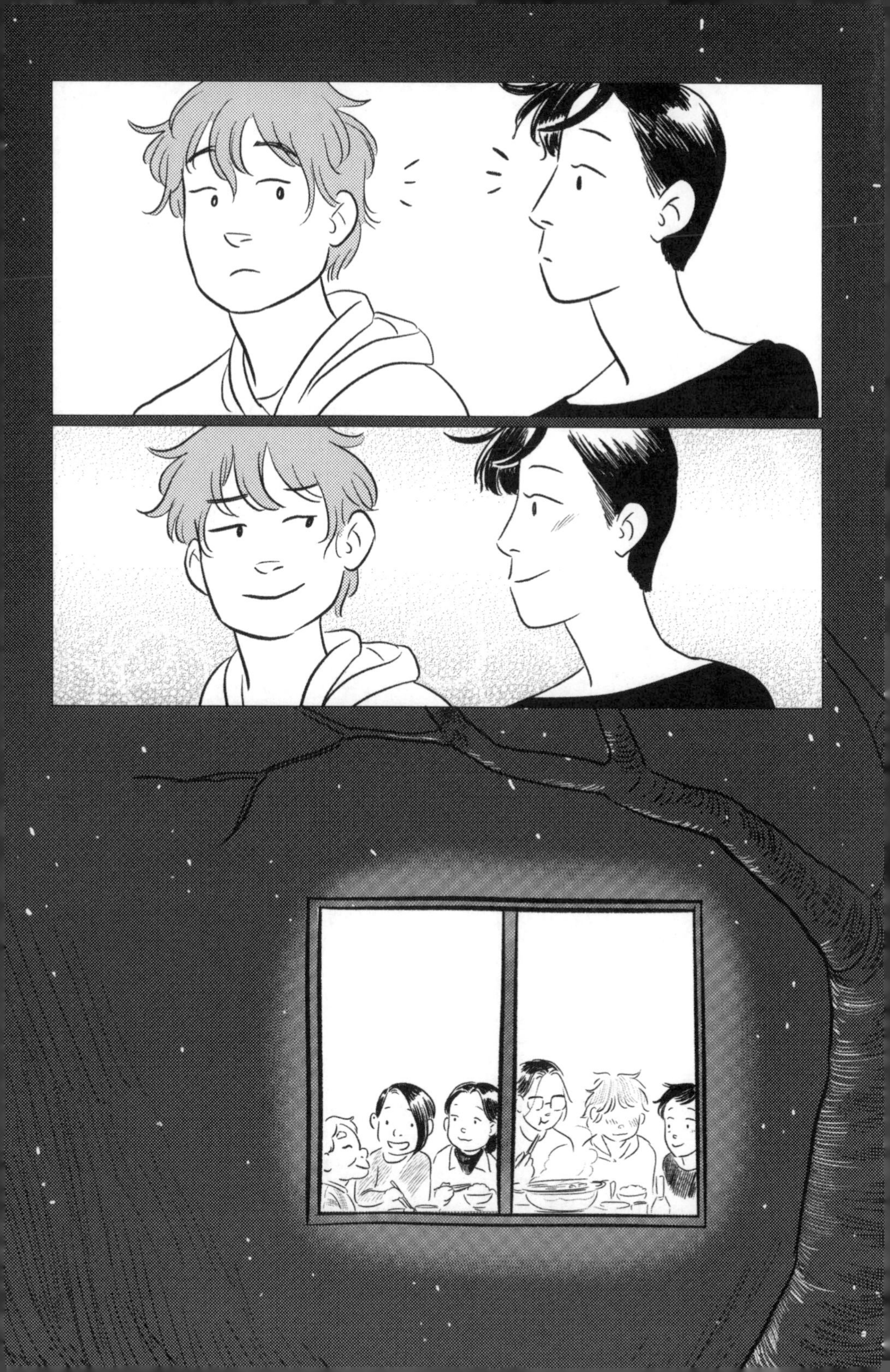

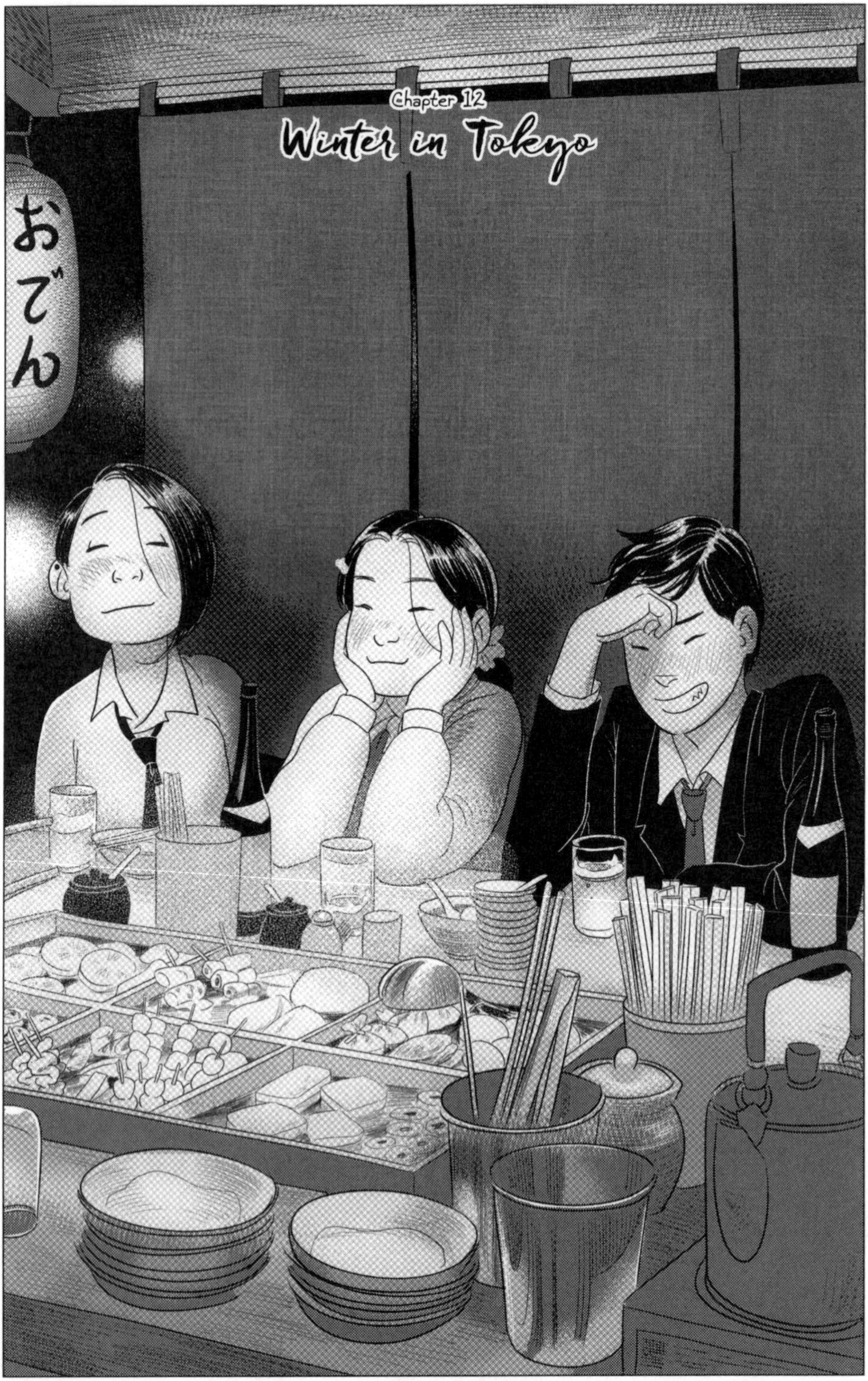
Chapter 12
Winter in Tokyo
おでん

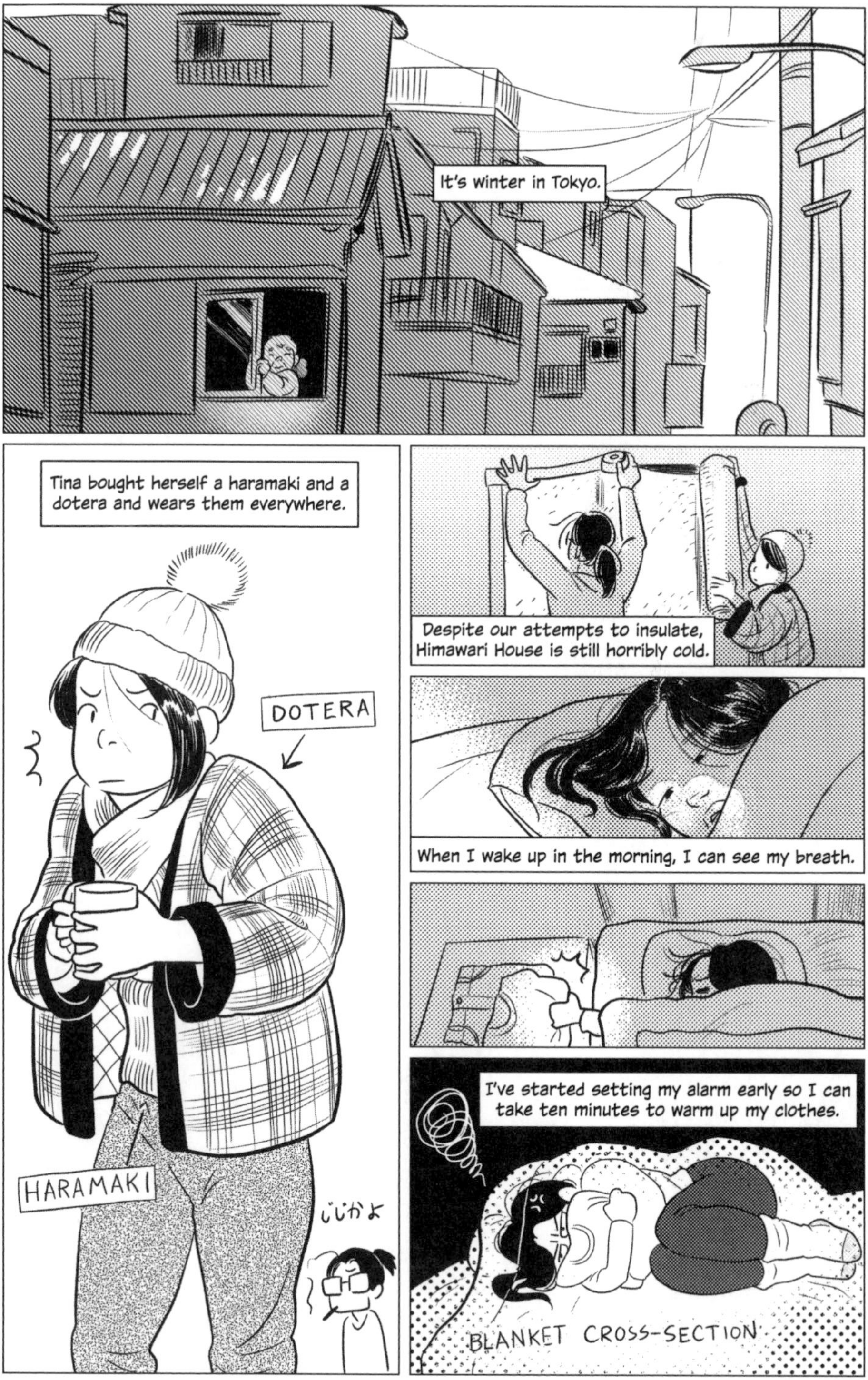
It's winter in Tokyo.
Tina bought herself a haramaki and a dotera and wears them everywhere.
DOTERA
HARAMAKI
じじかよ
Despite our attempts to insulate, Himawari House is still horribly cold.
When I wake up in the morning, I can see my breath.
I've started setting my alarm early so I can take ten minutes to warm up my clothes.
BLANKET CROSS-SECTION

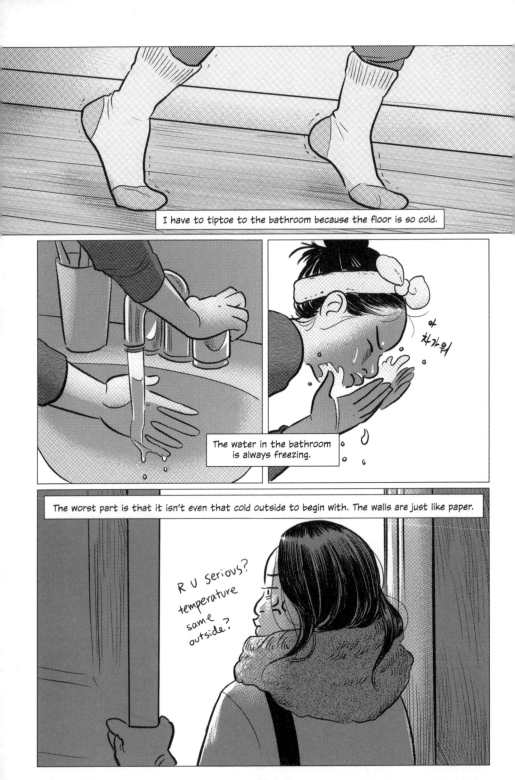

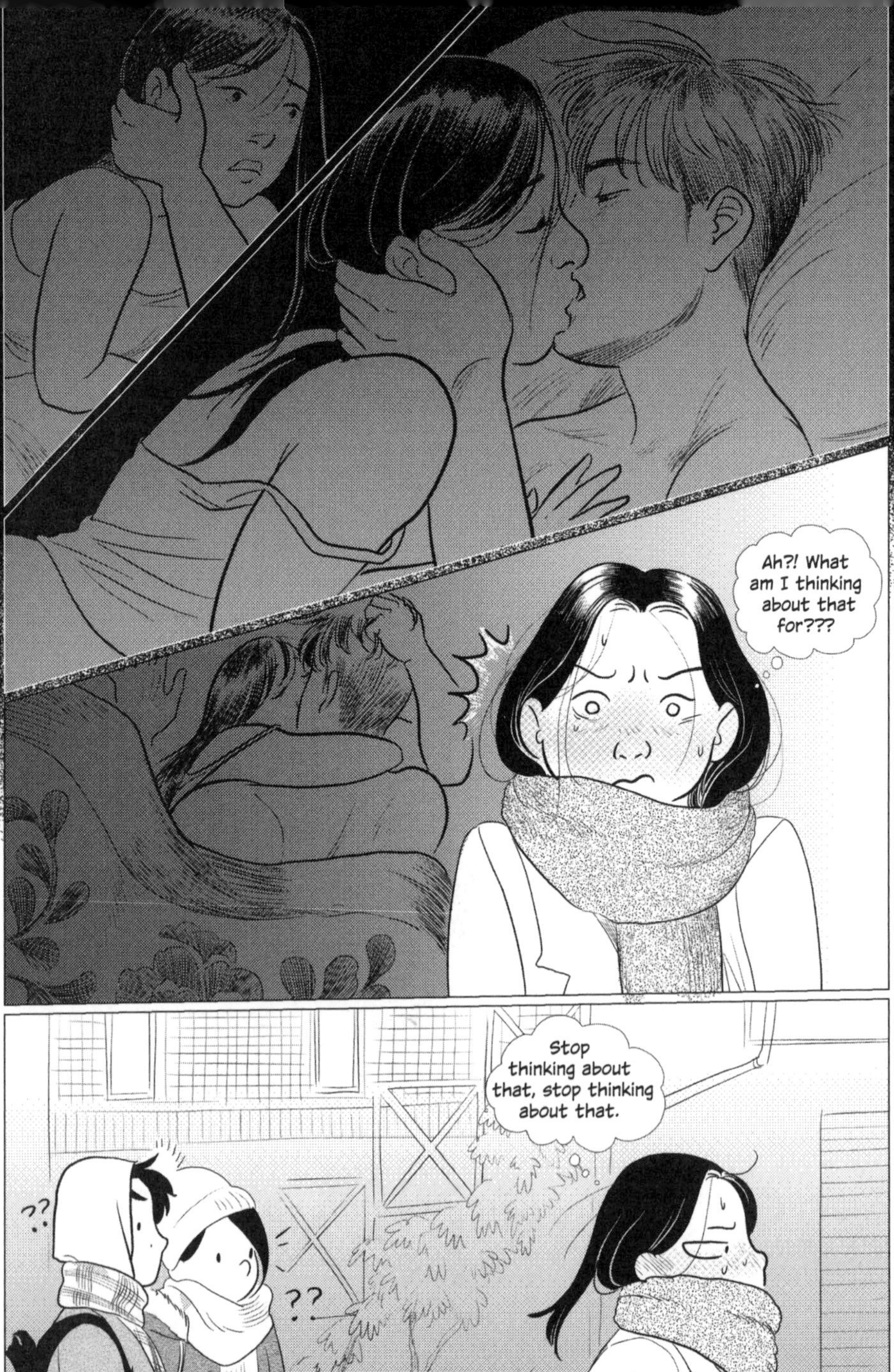
Ah?! What am I thinking about that for???
Stop thinking about that, stop thinking about that.
??
??

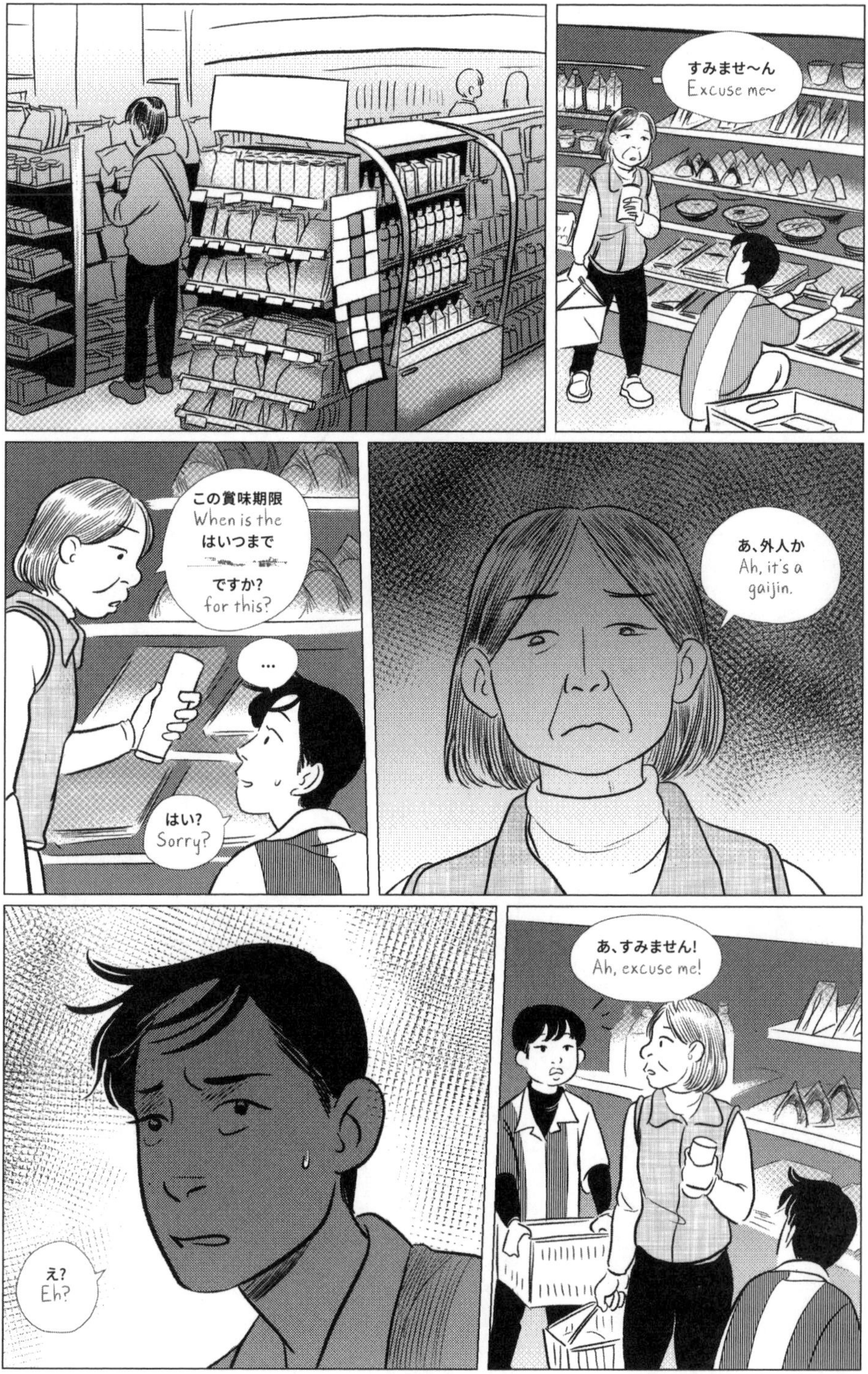
すみませ〜ん
Excuse me~
この賞味期限
When is the
はいつまで
ですか?
for this?
...
はい?
Sorry?
あ、外人か
Ah, it's a gaijin.
え?
Eh?
あ、すみません!
Ah, excuse me!

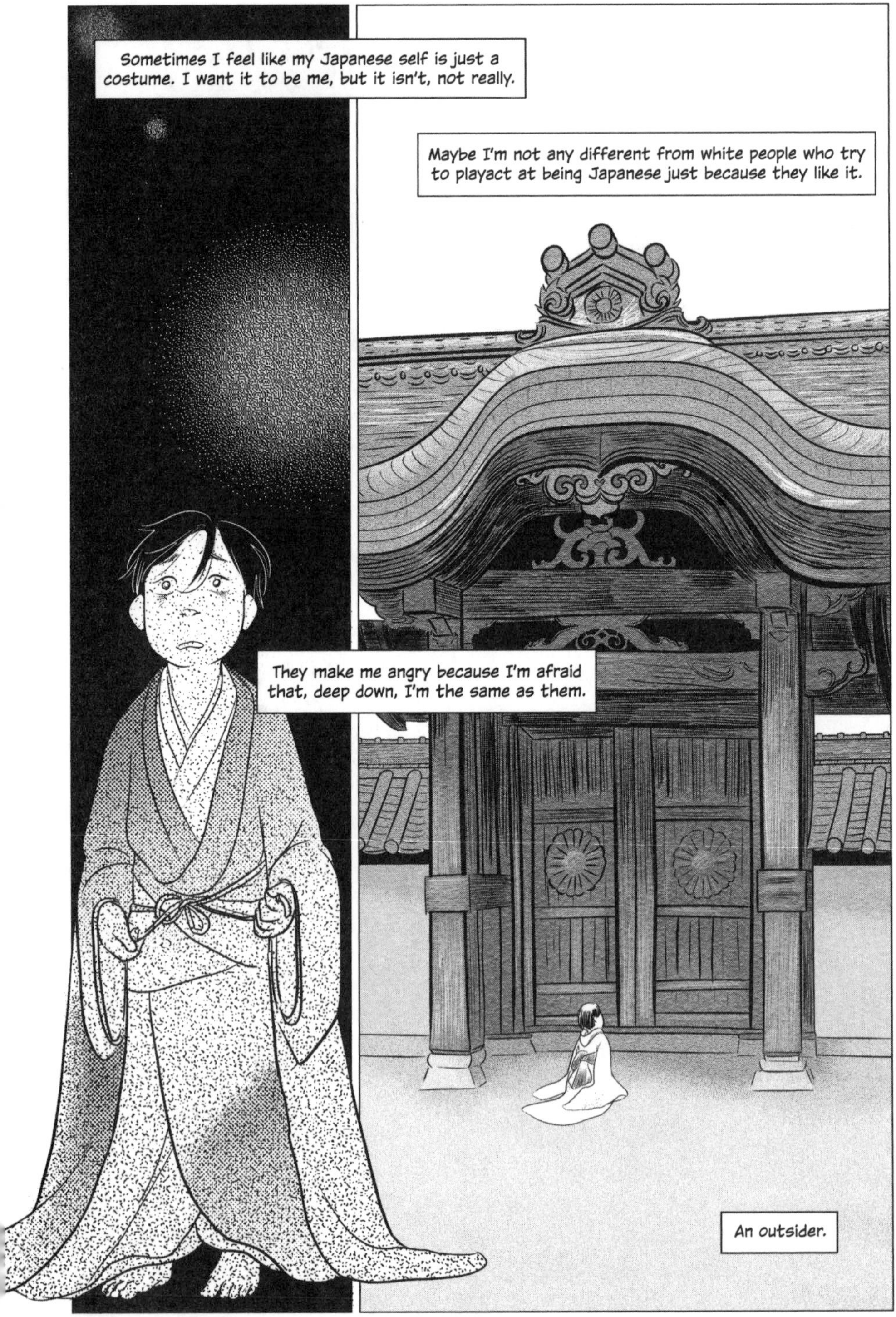
Sometimes I feel like my Japanese self is just a costume. I want it to be me, but it isn't, not really.
Maybe I'm not any different from white people who try to playact at being Japanese just because they like it.
They make me angry because I'm afraid that, deep down, I'm the same as them.
An outsider.

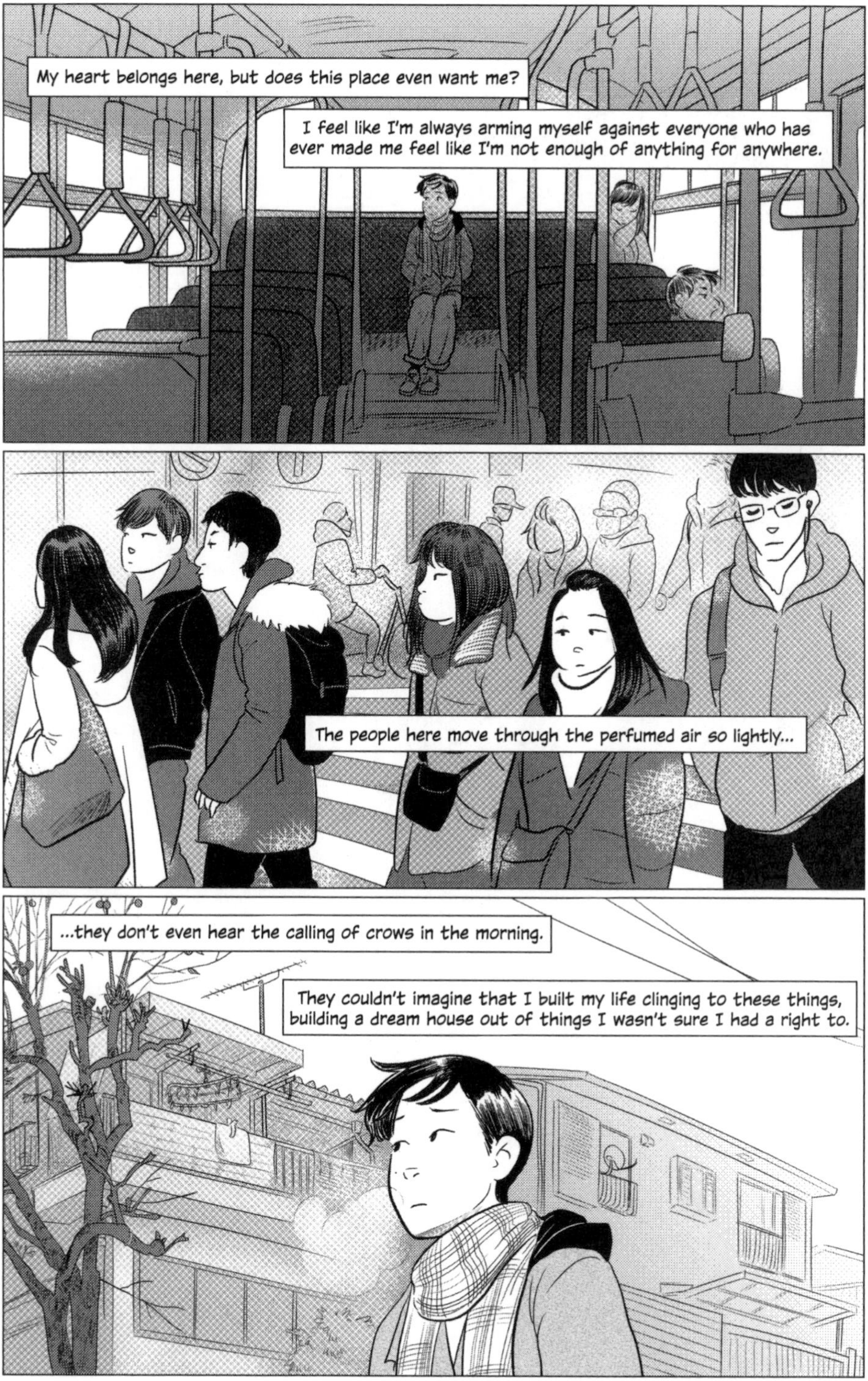
My heart belongs here, but does this place even want me?
I feel like I'm always arming myself against everyone who has ever made me feel like I'm not enough of anything for anywhere.
The people here move through the perfumed air so lightly...
...they don't even hear the calling of crows in the morning.
They couldn't imagine that I built my life clinging to these things, building a dream house out of things I wasn't sure I had a right to.

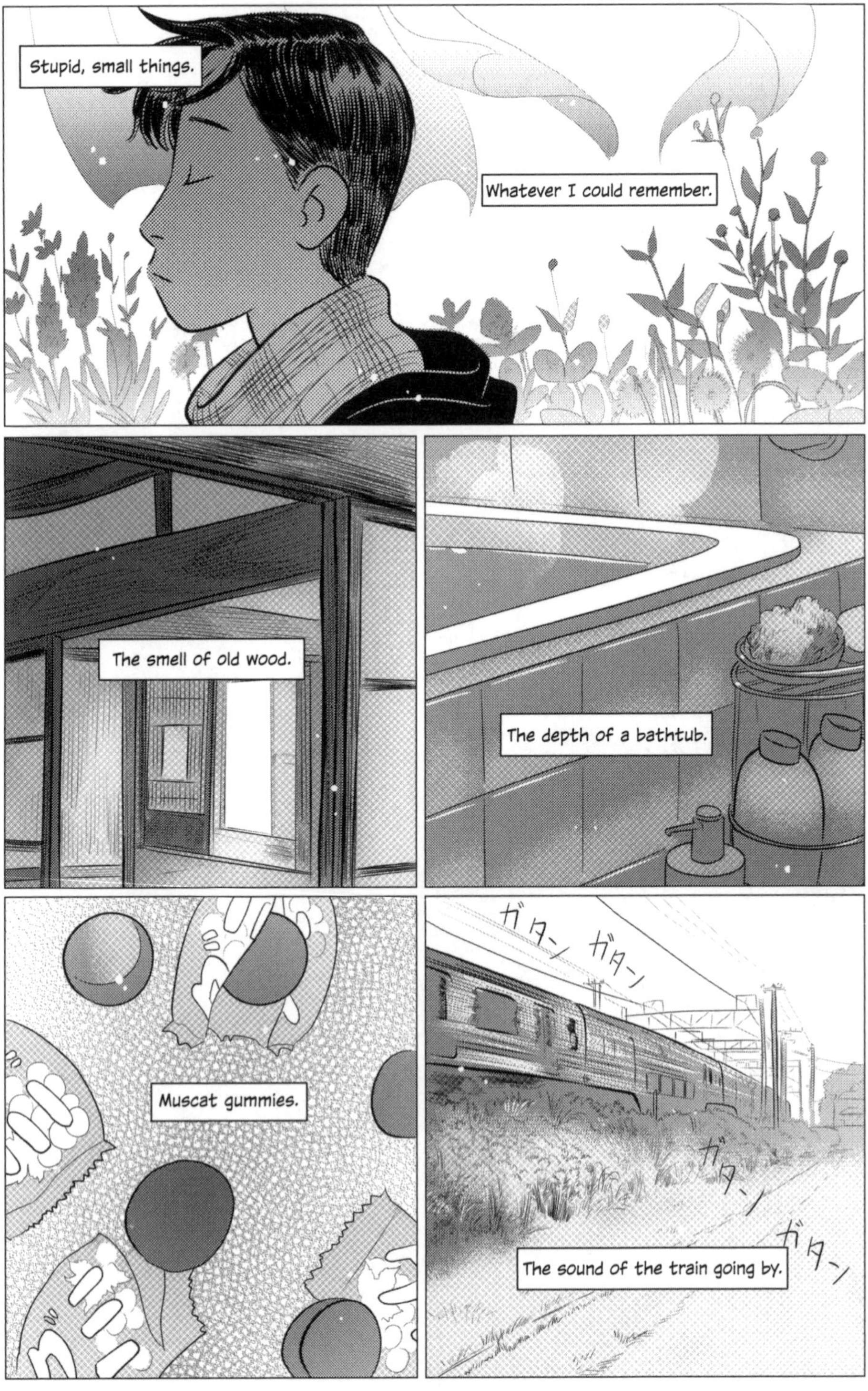
Stupid, small things.
Whatever I could remember.
The smell of old wood.
The depth of a bathtub.
Muscat gummies.
ガターン
ガターン
ガターン
ガターン
The sound of the train going by.

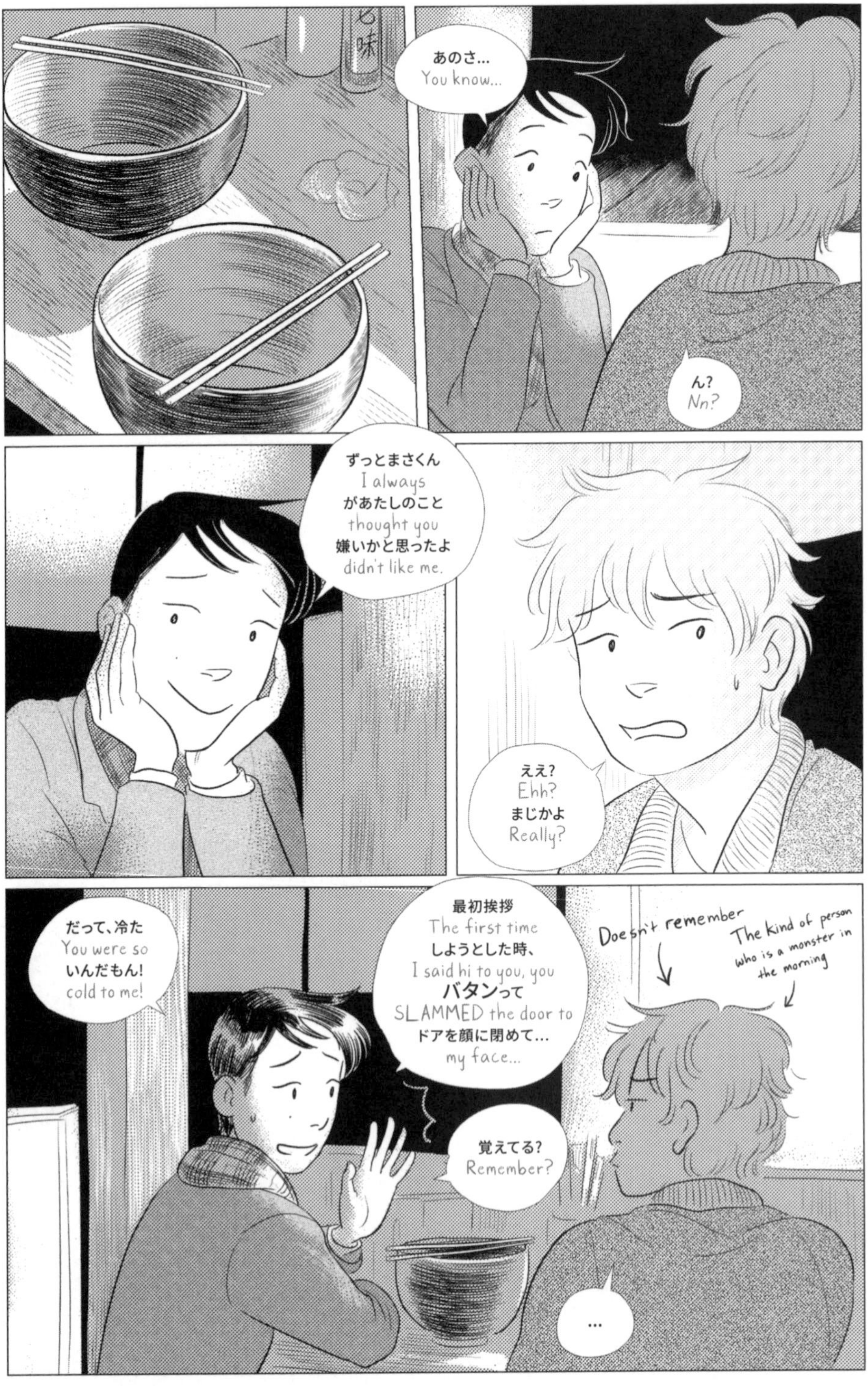

あのさ...
You know...
ん?
Nn?
ずっとまさくん
I always
があたしのこと
thought you
嫌いかと思ったよ
didn't like me.
ええ?
Ehh?
まじかよ
Really?
だって、冷た
You were so
いんだもん!
cold to me!
最初挨拶
The first time
しようとした時、
I said hi to you, you
バタンって
SLAMMED the door to
ドアを顔に閉めて...
my face...
覚えてる?
Remember?
Doesn't remember
The kind of person who is a monster in the morning
...

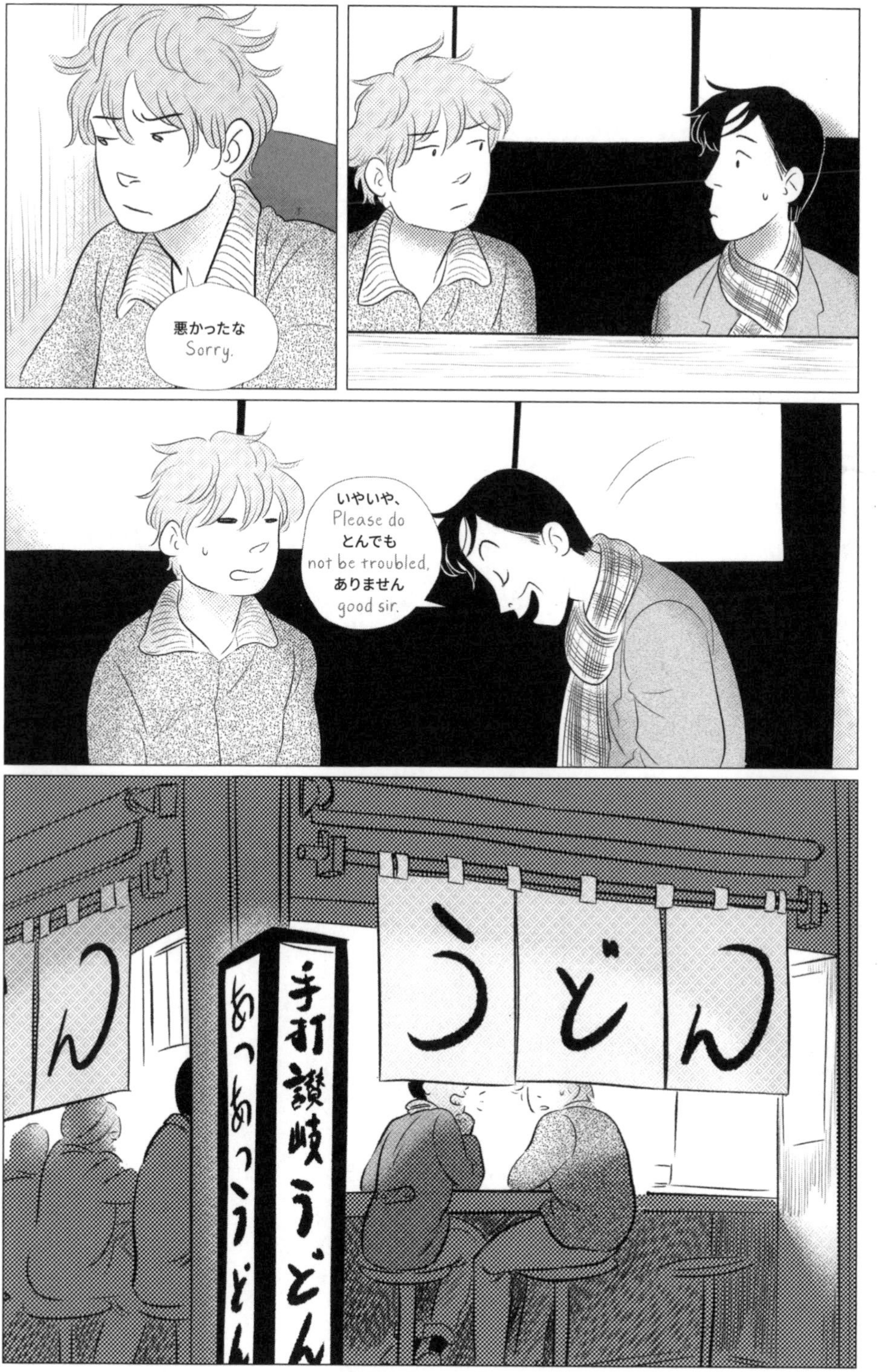
悪かったな
Sorry.
いやいや、
Please do
とんでも
not be troubled,
ありません
good sir.
手打讃岐うどん
あつあつうどん
うどん

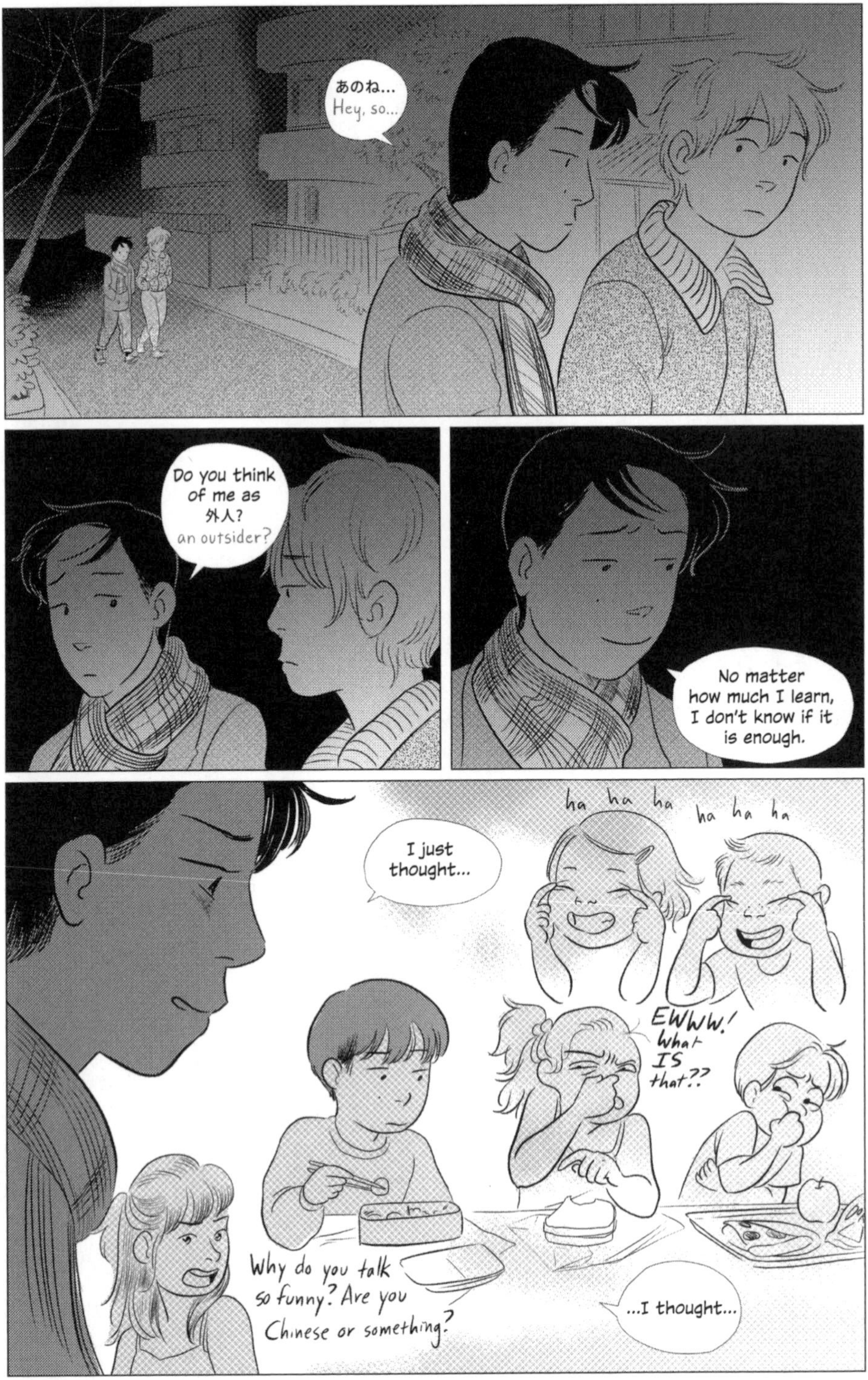
あのね...
Hey, so...
Do you think of me as 外人?
an outsider?
No matter how much I learn, I don't know if it is enough.
I just thought...
ha ha ha
ha ha ha
EWWW! What IS that??
Why do you talk so funny? Are you Chinese or something?
...I thought...

225

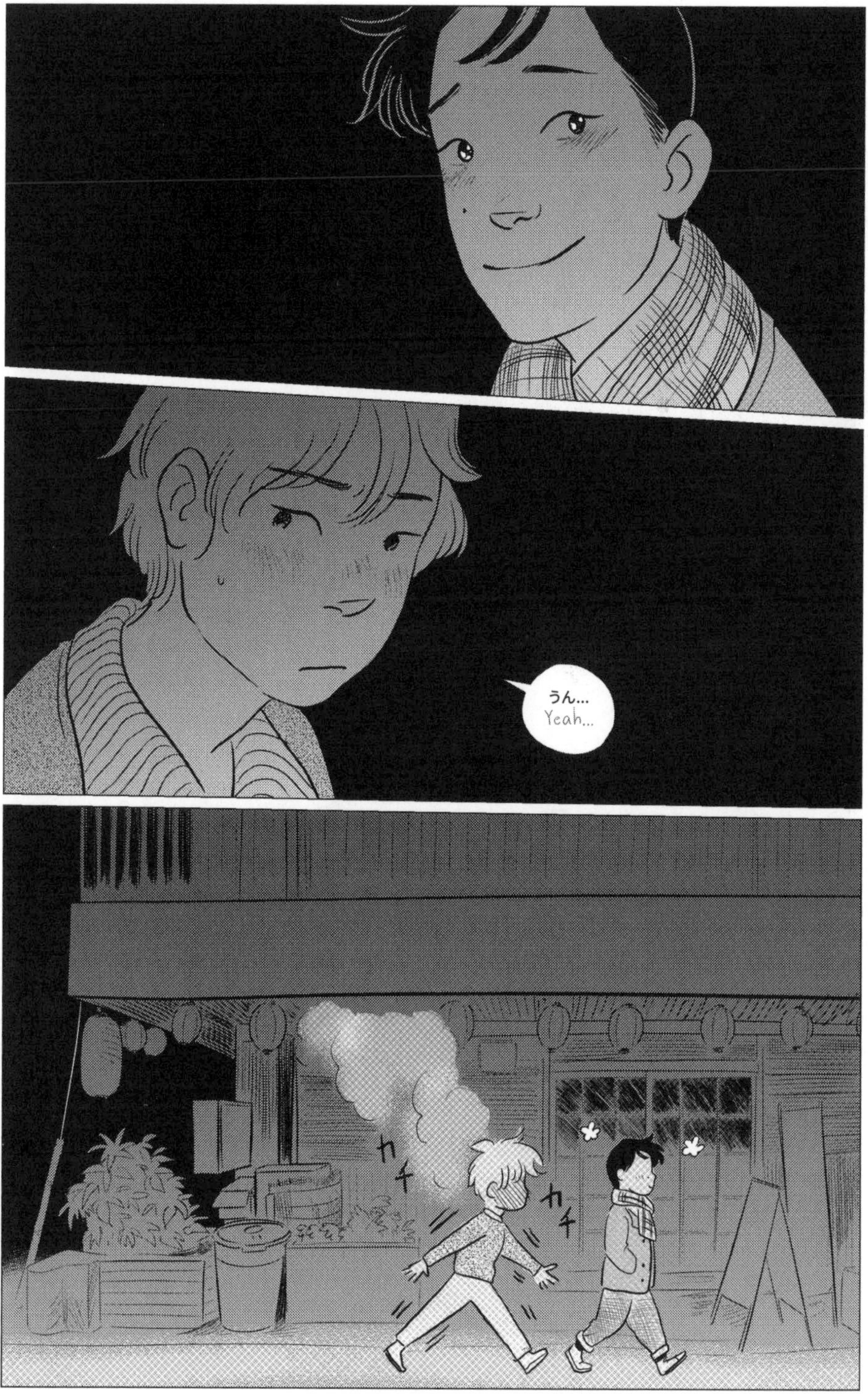
うん...
Yeah...
カチ
カチ

Chapter 13
Hatsumonde

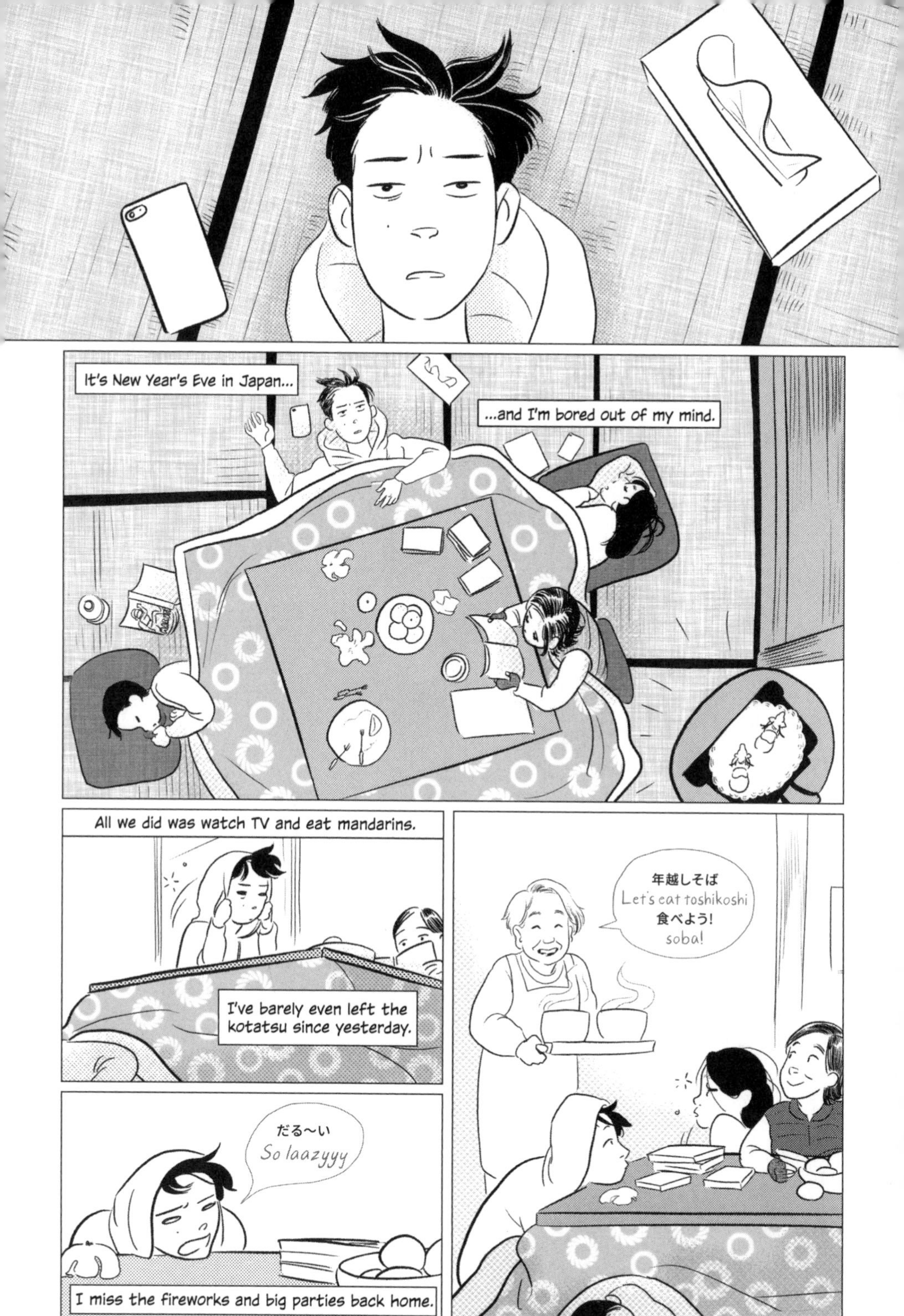
It's New Year's Eve in Japan...
...and I'm bored out of my mind.
All we did was watch TV and eat mandarins.
I've barely even left the kotatsu since yesterday.
だる〜い
So laazyyy
I miss the fireworks and big parties back home.
年越しそば 食べよう!
Let's eat toshikoshi soba!

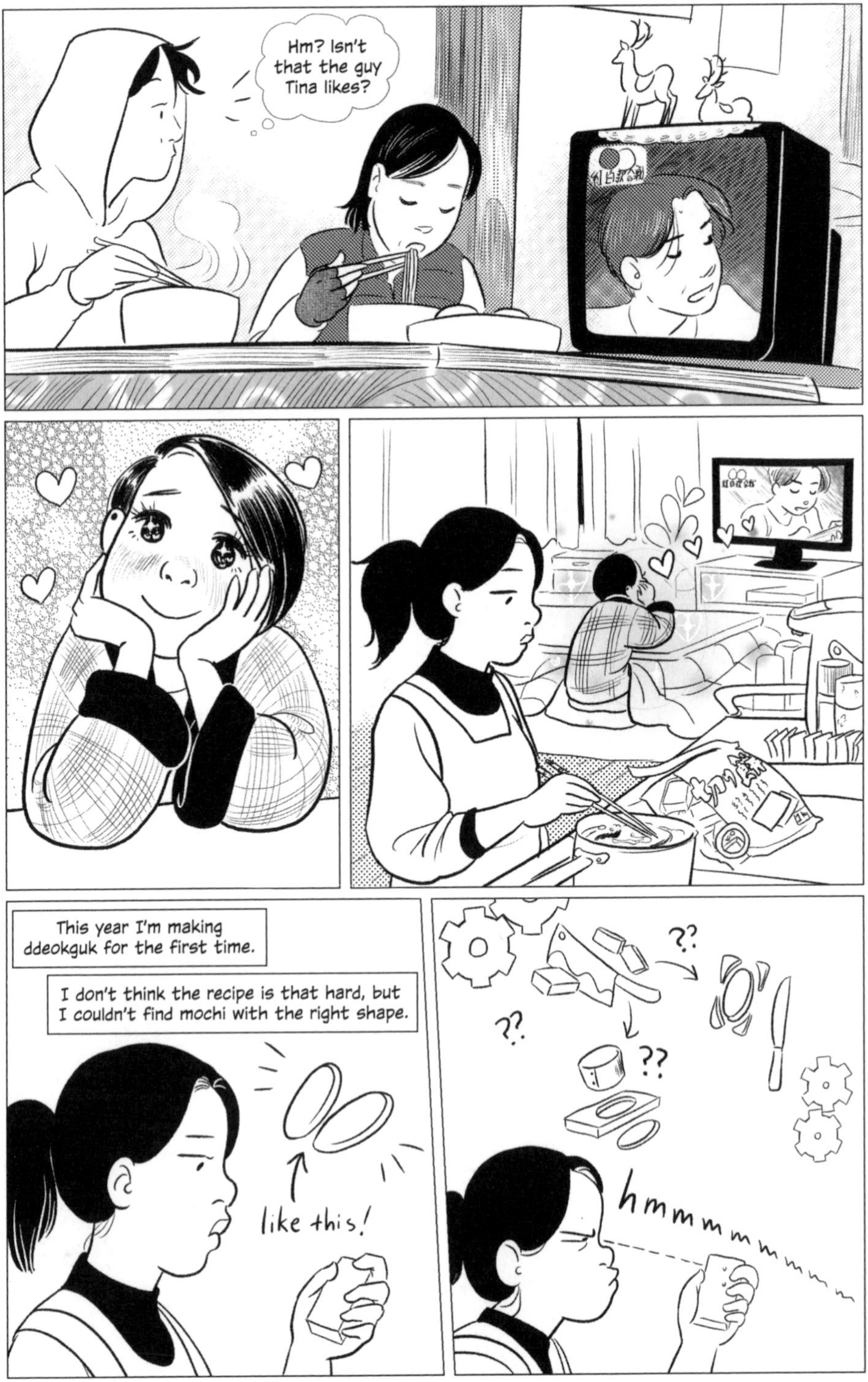
Hm? Isn't that the guy Tina likes?
This year I'm making ddeokguk for the first time.
I don't think the recipe is that hard, but I couldn't find mochi with the right shape.
like this!
??
??
??
hmmmmmmmmmmm

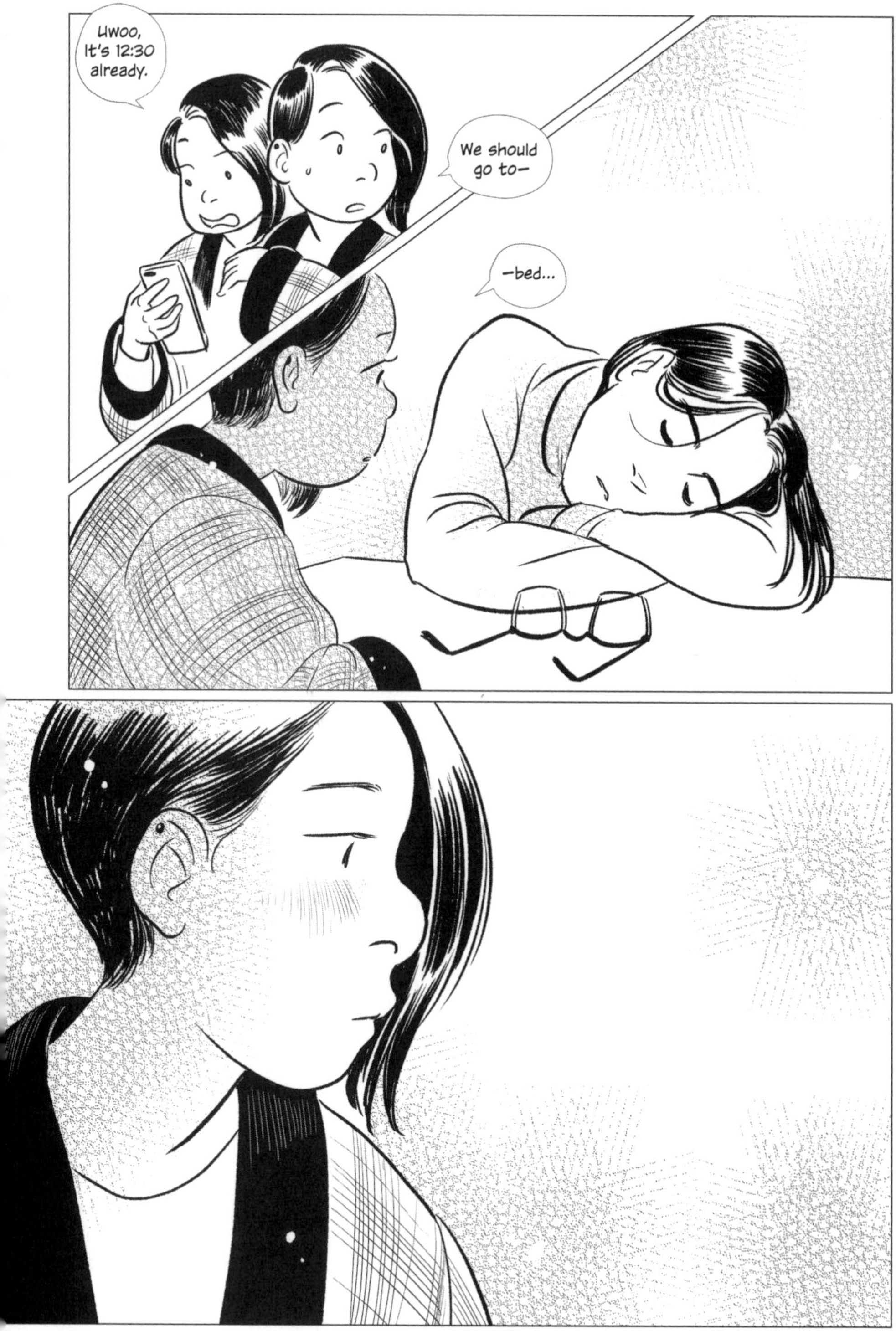
Uwoo, It's 12:30 already.
We should go to—
—bed...

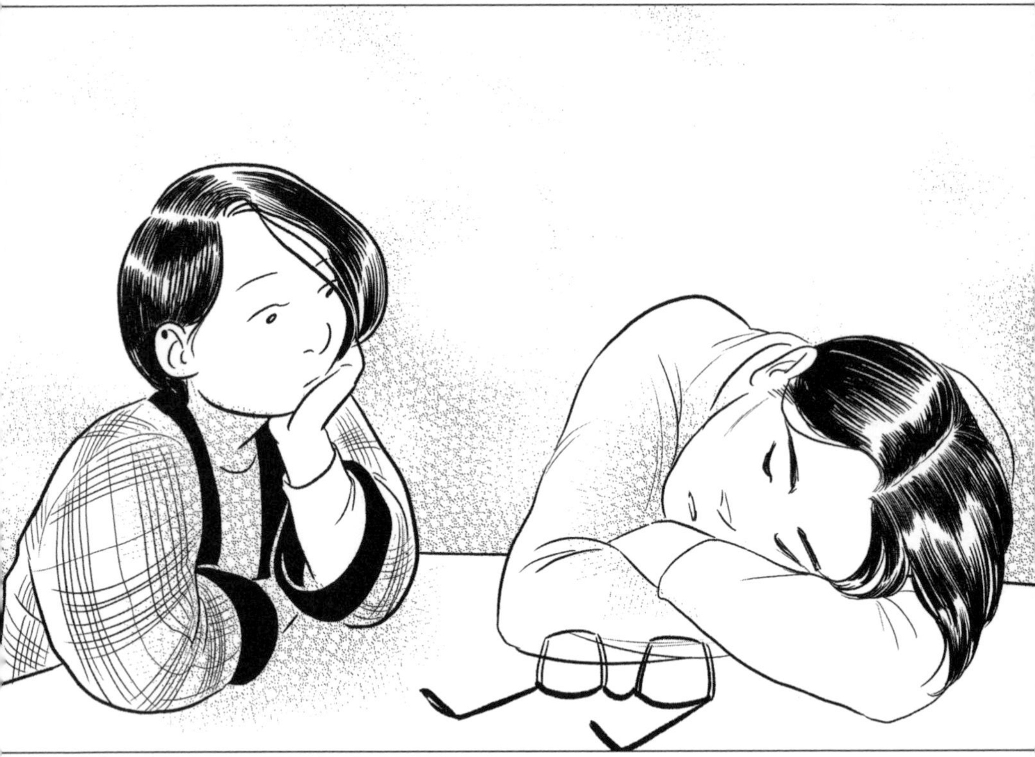

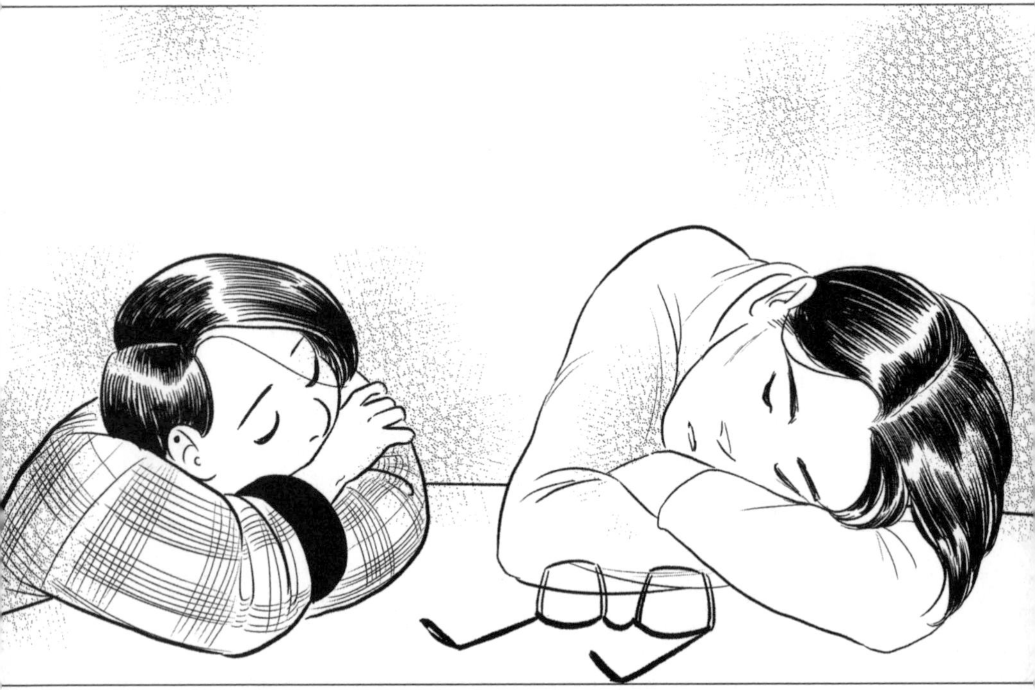

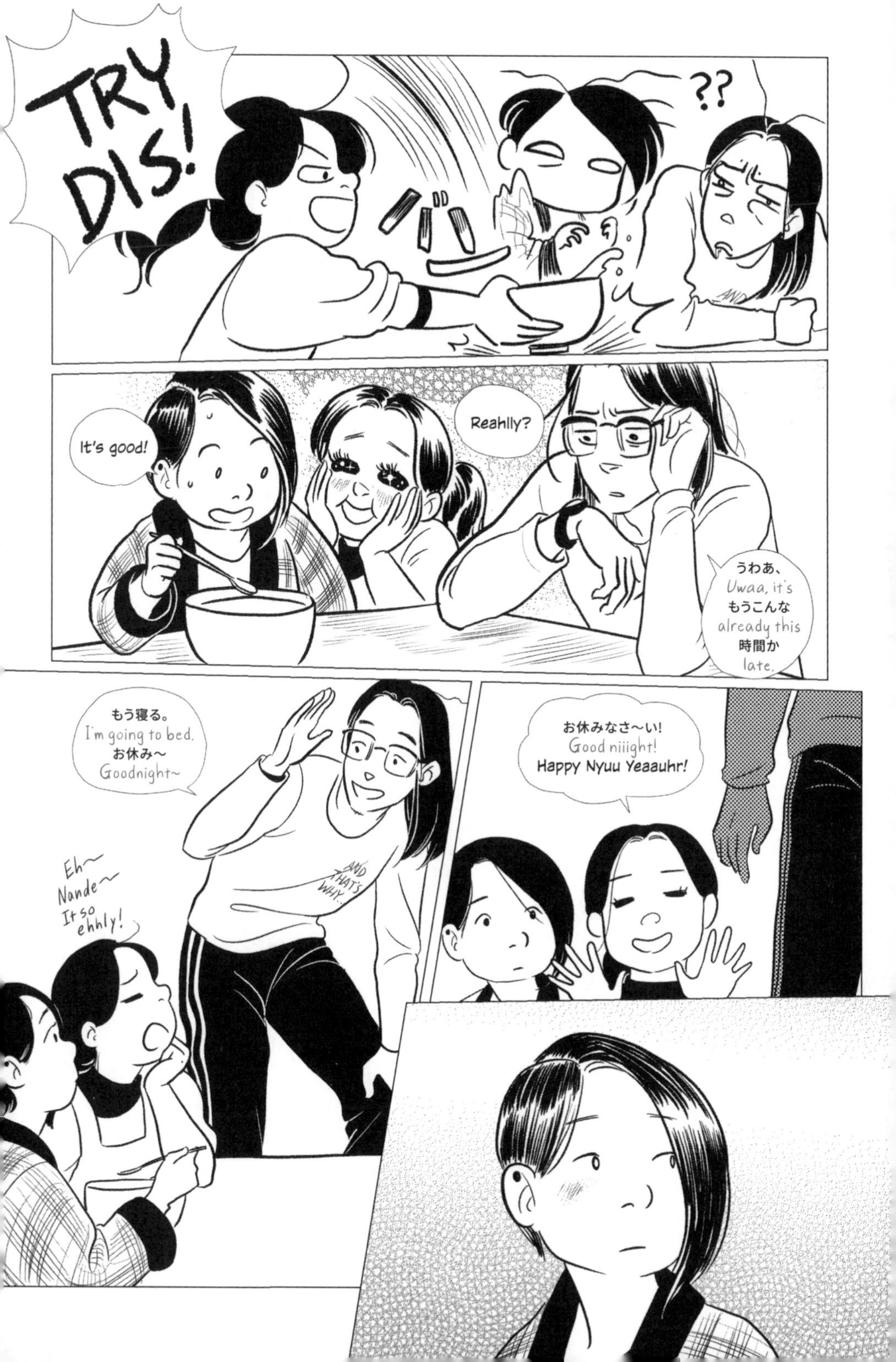
TRY DIS!
??
It's good!
Reahlly?
うわあ、
Uwaa, it's
もうこんな
already this
時間か
late.
もう寝る。
I'm going to bed.
お休み〜
Goodnight~
Eh~
Nande~
It so ehhly!
AND THAT'S WHY.
お休みなさ〜い!
Good niiight!
Happy Nyuu Yeaauhr!

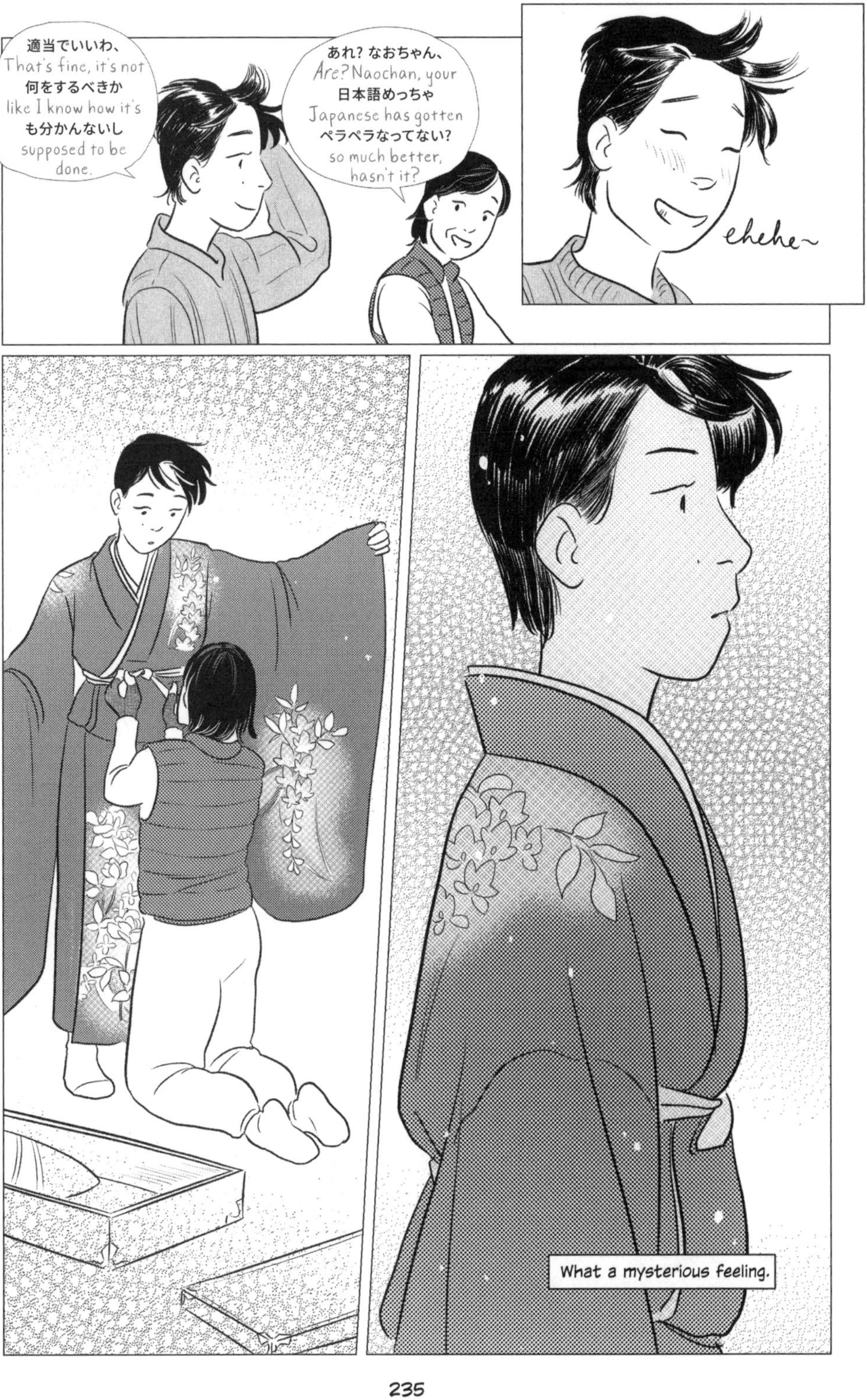
適当でいいわ、
That's fine, it's not
何をするべきか
like I know how it's
も分かんないし
supposed to be done.
あれ? なおちゃん、
Are? Naochan, your
日本語めっちゃ
Japanese has gotten
ペラペラなってない?
so much better, hasn't it?
ehehe~
What a mysterious feeling.

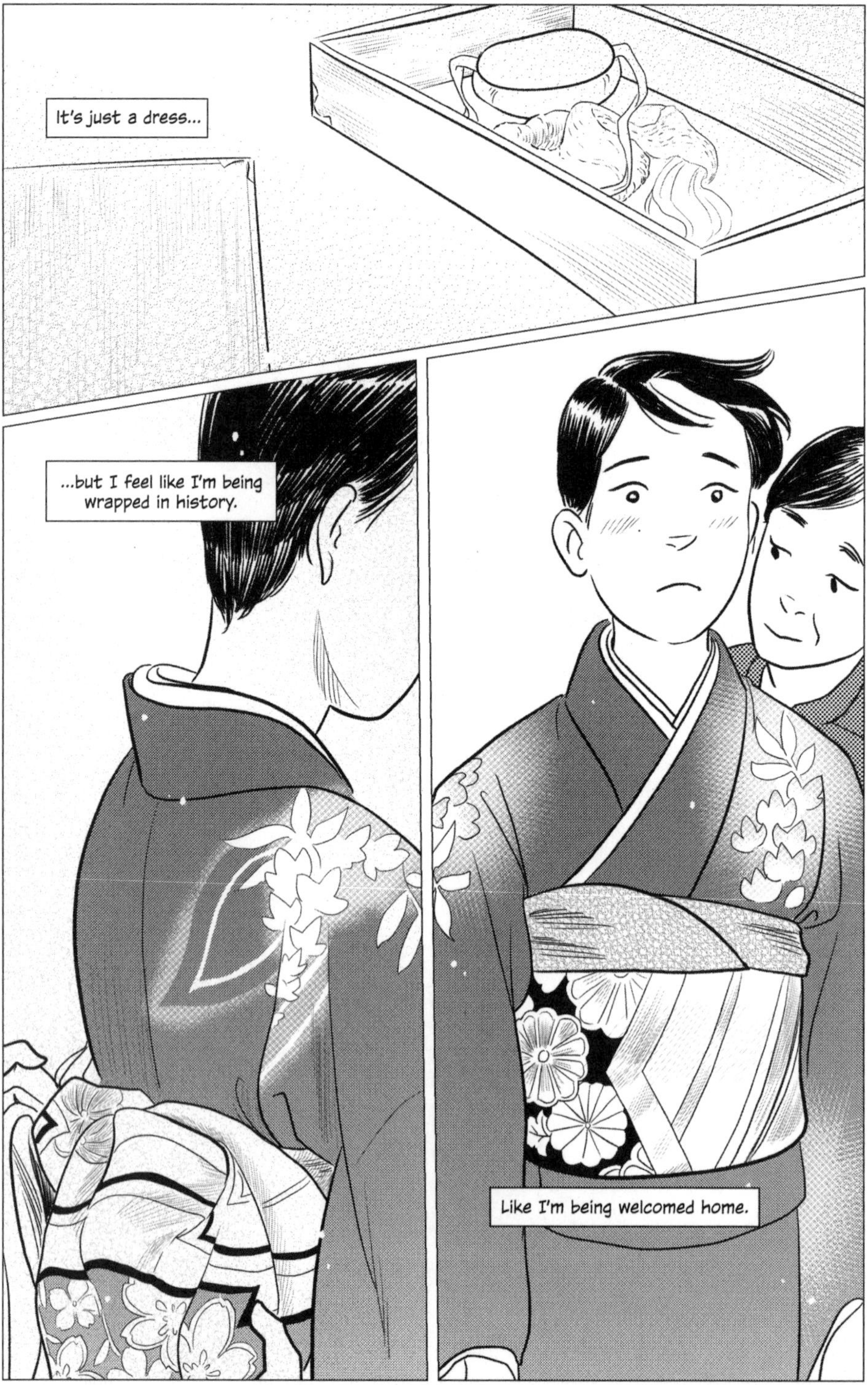
It's just a dress...
...but I feel like I'm being wrapped in history.
Like I'm being welcomed home.

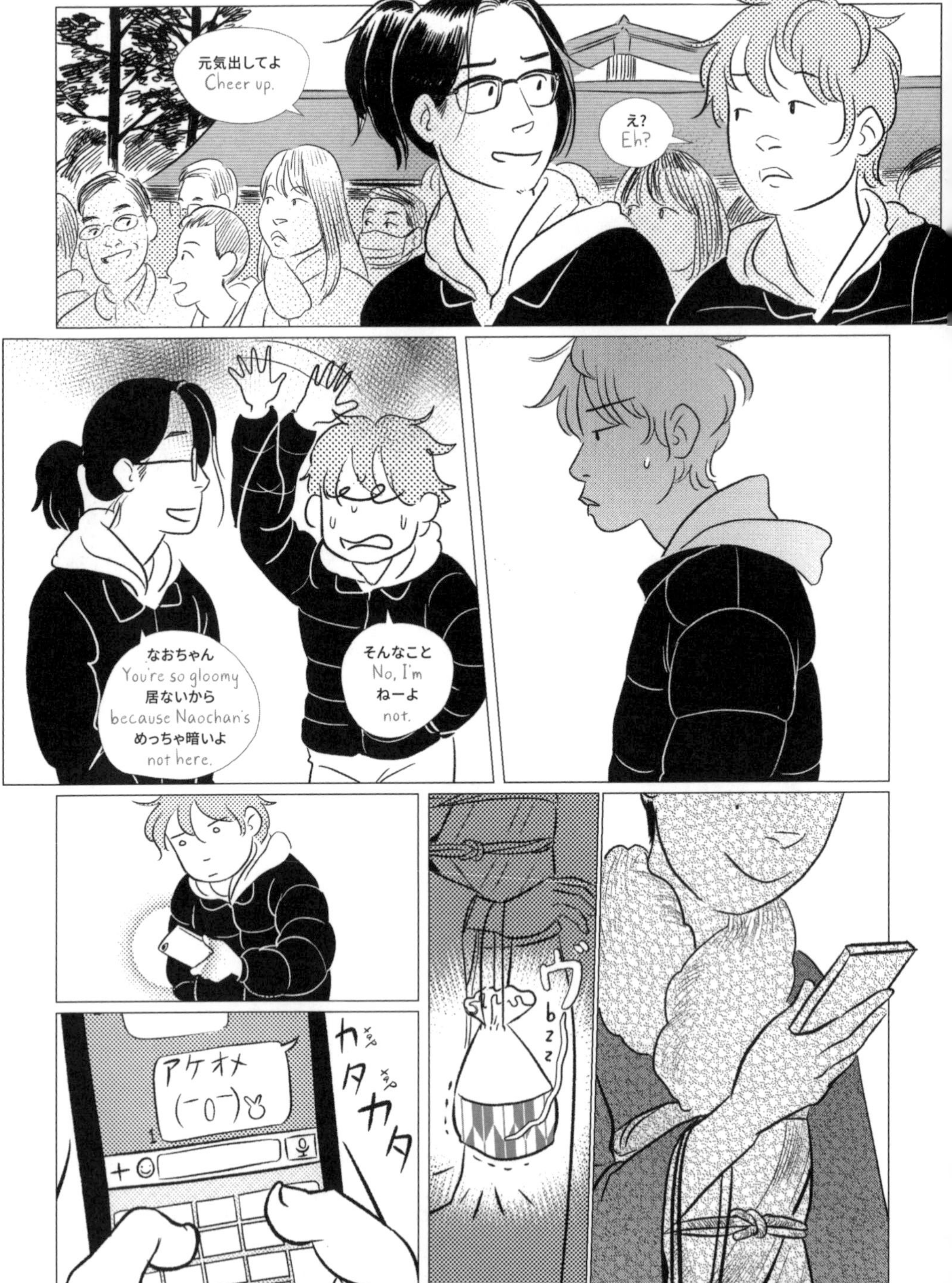
元気出してよ
Cheer up.
え?
Eh?
なおちゃん
You're so gloomy
居ないから
because Naochan's
めっちゃ暗いよ
not here.
そんなこと
No, I'm
ねーよ
not.
アケオメ
カタカタ
bzz

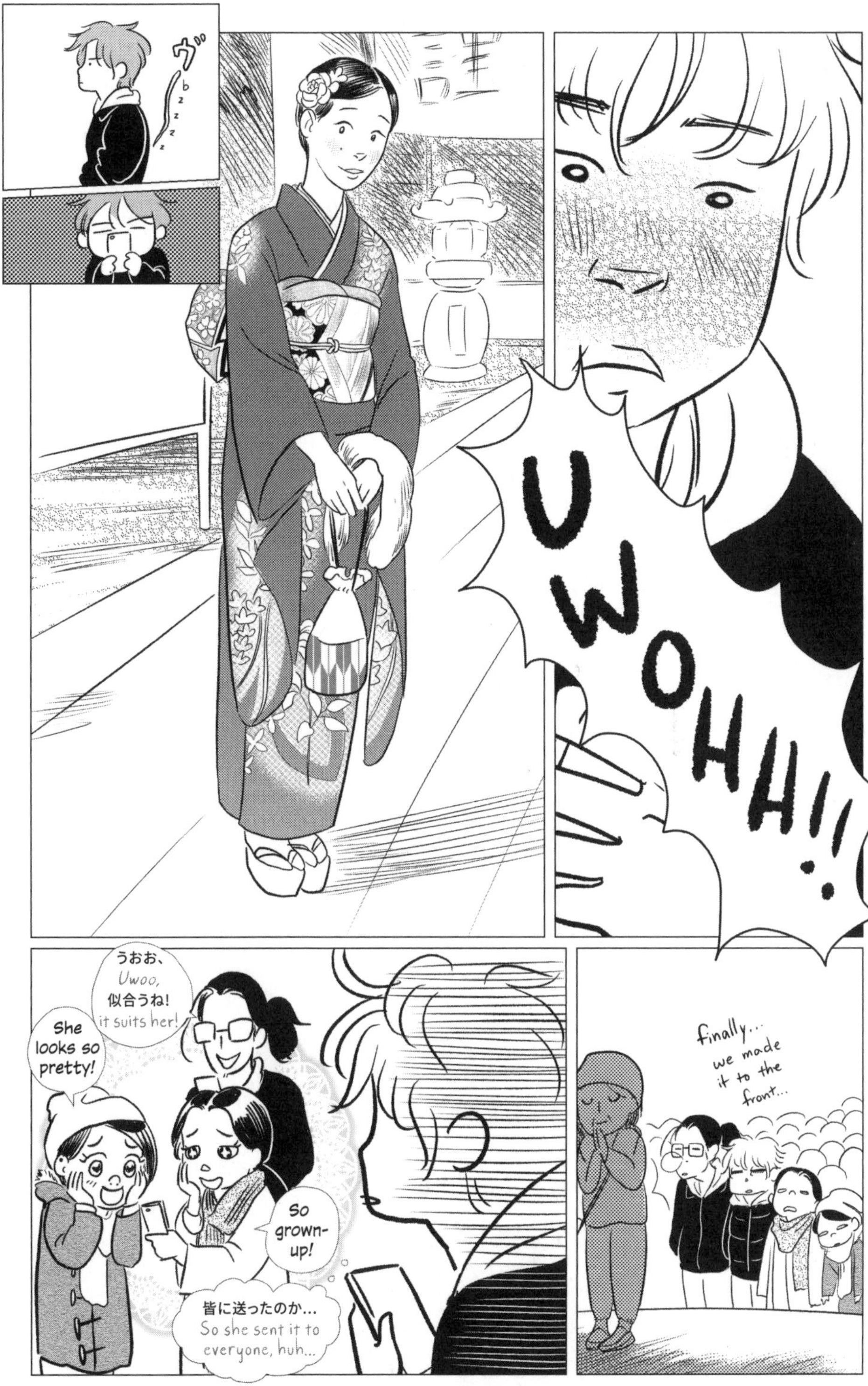
ヴ
bzzzz
UWOHH!!
うおお、
Uwoo,
似合うね!
it suits her!
She looks so pretty!
So grown-up!
皆に送ったのか…
So she sent it to everyone, huh...
finally... we made it to the front...

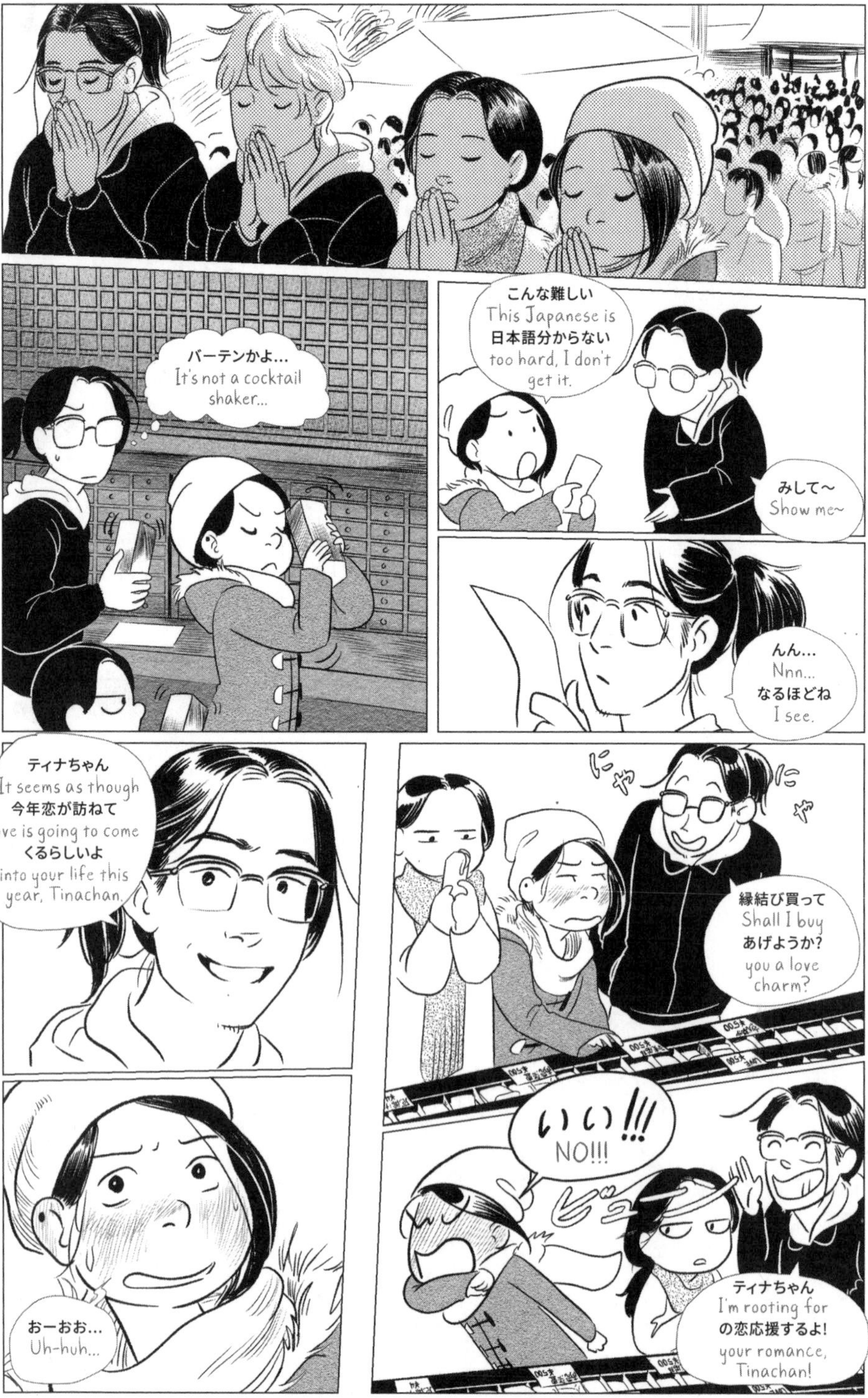
バーテンかよ…
It's not a cocktail shaker...
こんな難しい 日本語分からない
This Japanese is too hard, I don't get it.
みして~
Show me~
んん… なるほどね
Nnn... I see.
ティナちゃん 今年恋が訪ねてくるらしいよ
It seems as though love is going to come into your life this year, Tinachan.
にゃ にゃ
縁結び買ってあげようか?
Shall I buy you a love charm?
おーおお…
Uh-huh...
いい!!!
NO!!!
ティナちゃんの恋応援するよ!
I'm rooting for your romance, Tinachan!

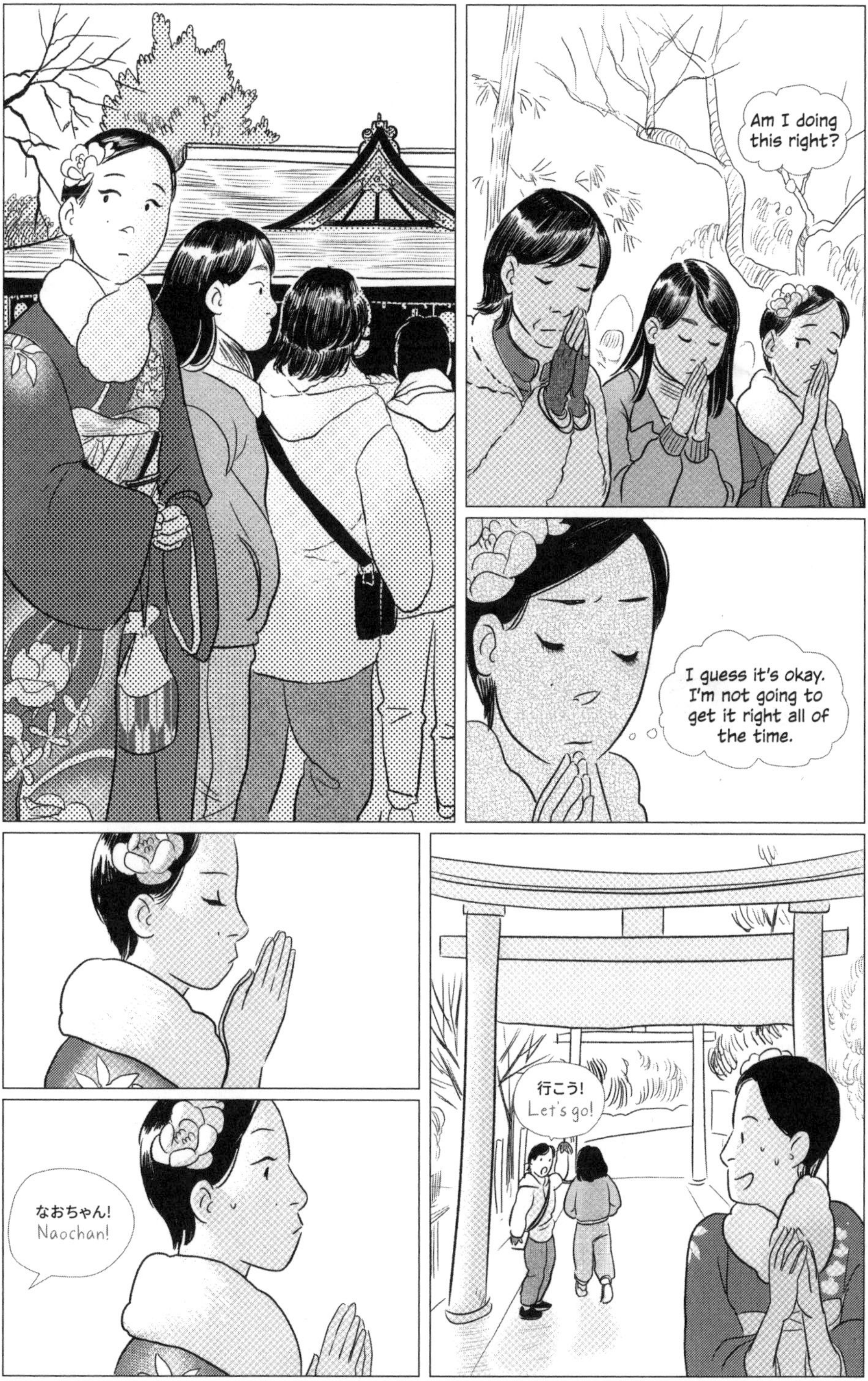

Am I doing this right?
I guess it's okay. I'm not going to get it right all of the time.
なおちゃん! Naochan!
行こう! Let's go!

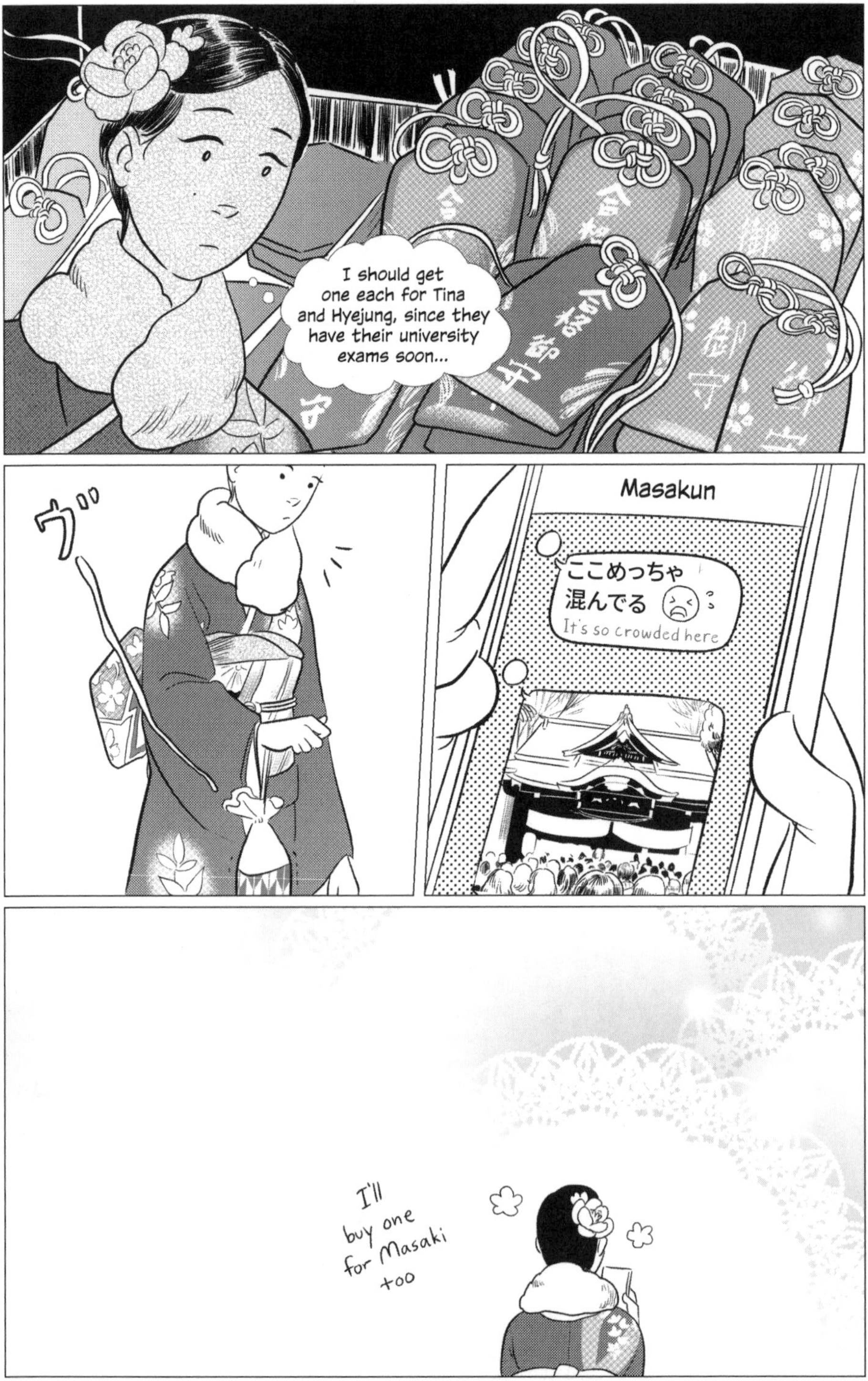
I should get one each for Tina and Hyejung, since they have their university exams soon...
ヴッ
Masakun
ここめっちゃ混んでる
It's so crowded here
I'll buy one for Masaki too

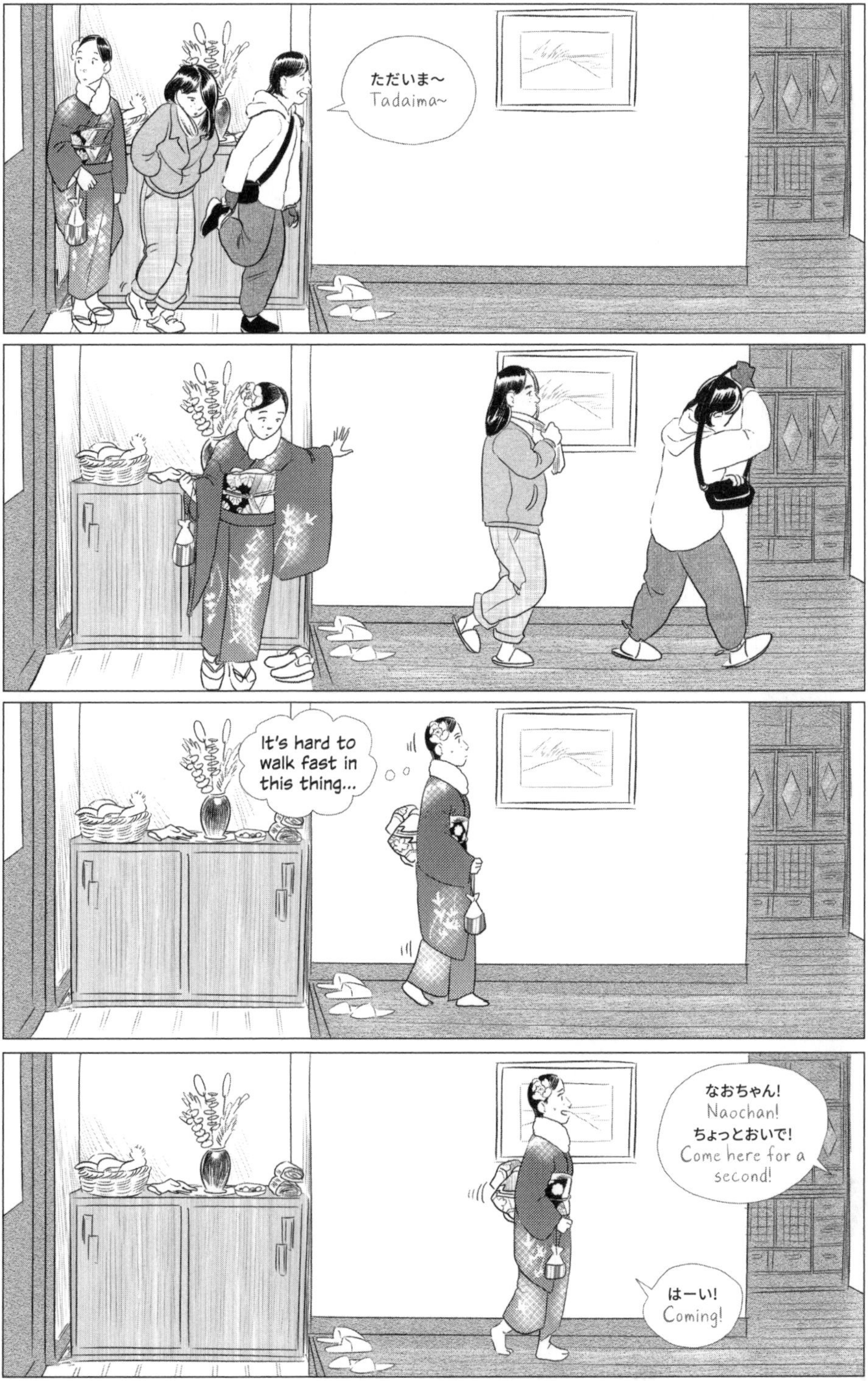
ただいま~
Tadaima~
It's hard to walk fast in this thing...
なおちゃん!
Naochan!
ちょっとおいで!
Come here for a second!
はーい!
Coming!

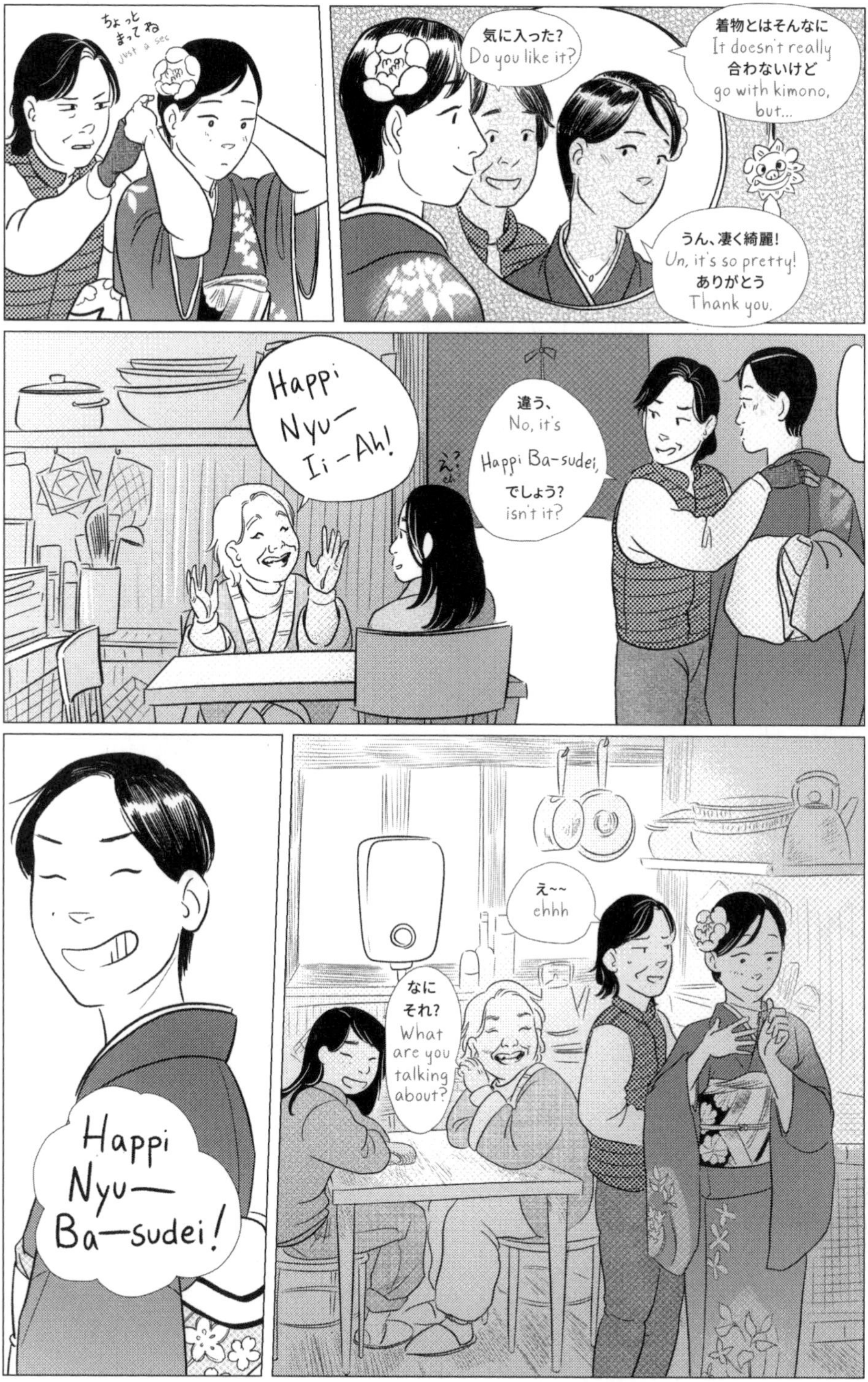
ちょっとまってね
just a sec
気に入った?
Do you like it?
着物とはそんなに
It doesn't really
合わないけど
go with kimono, but...
うん、凄く綺麗!
Un, it's so pretty!
ありがとう
Thank you.
Happi Nyu— Ii-Ah!
え?
eh
違う、
No, it's
Happi Ba-sudei,
でしょう?
isn't it?
Happi Nyu— Ba—sudei!
え~~
ehhh
なにそれ?
What are you talking about?

Chapter 14
Gong Xi Fa Cai

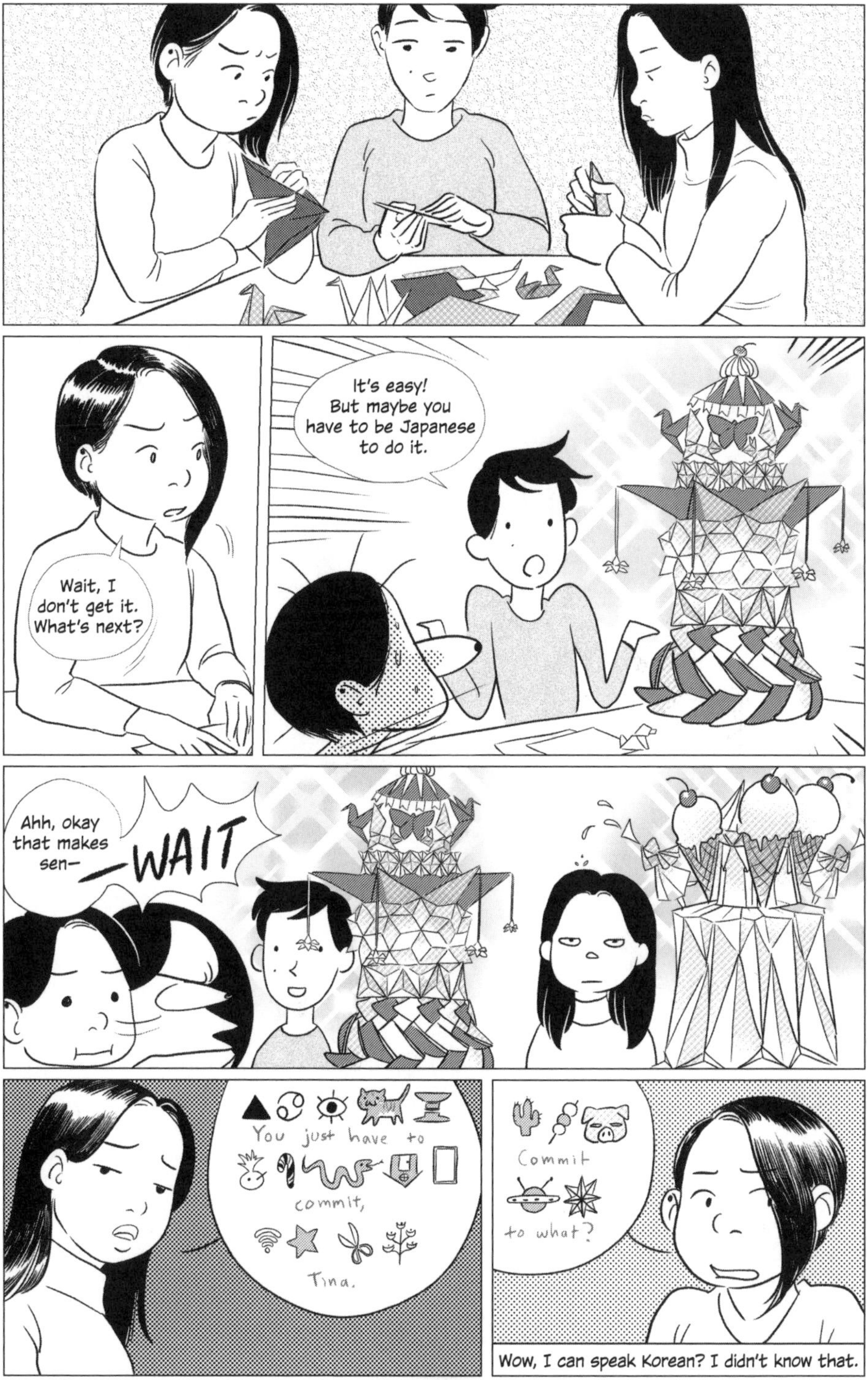

It's easy! But maybe you have to be Japanese to do it.
Wait, I don't get it. What's next?
Ahh, okay that makes sen—
—WAIT
You just have to commit, Tina.
Commit to what?
Wow, I can speak Korean? I didn't know that.

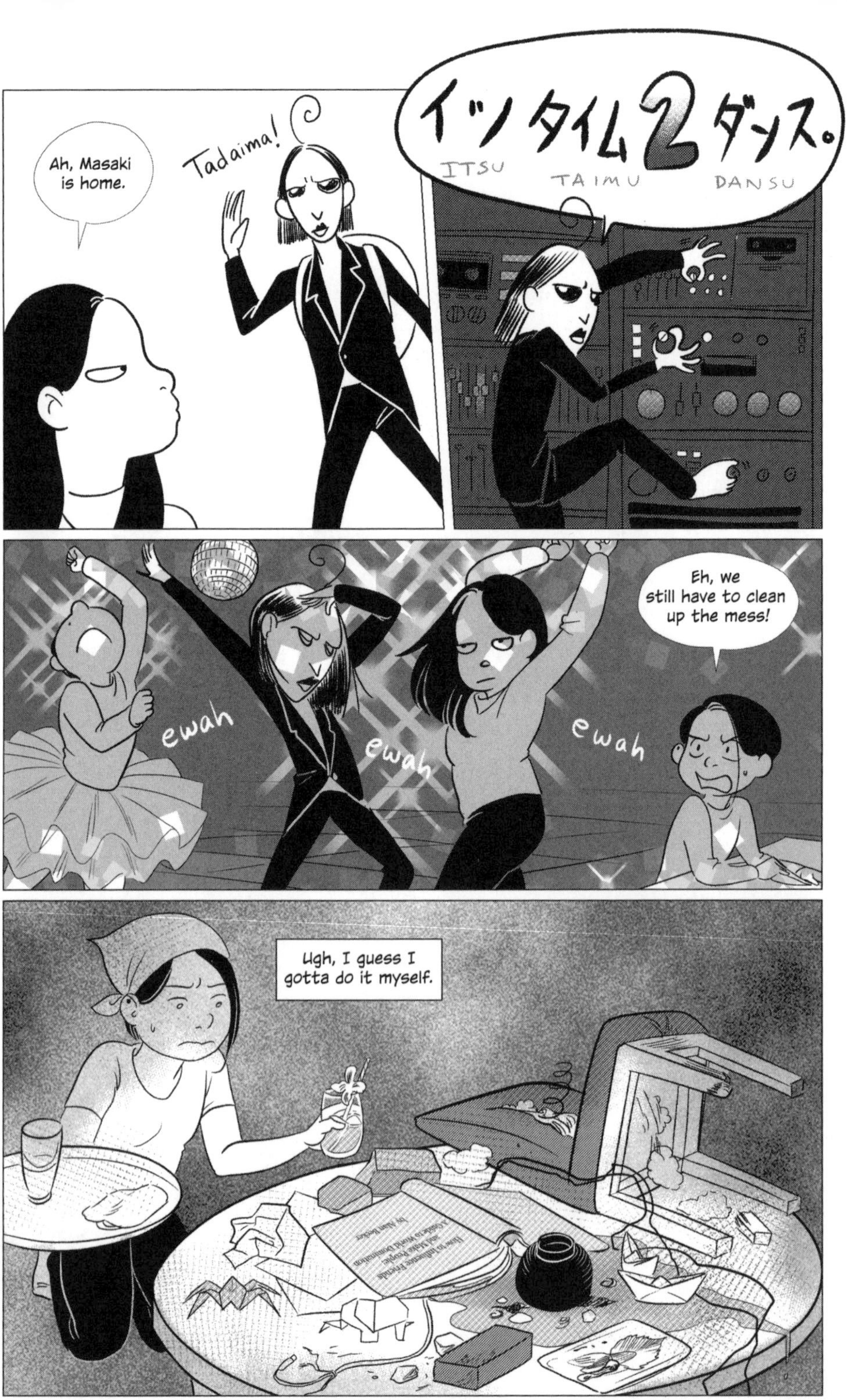
Ah, Masaki is home.
Tadaima!
イツタイム2ダンス。
ITSU TAIMU DANSU
ewah
ewah
ewah
Eh, we still have to clean up the mess!
Ugh, I guess I gotta do it myself.

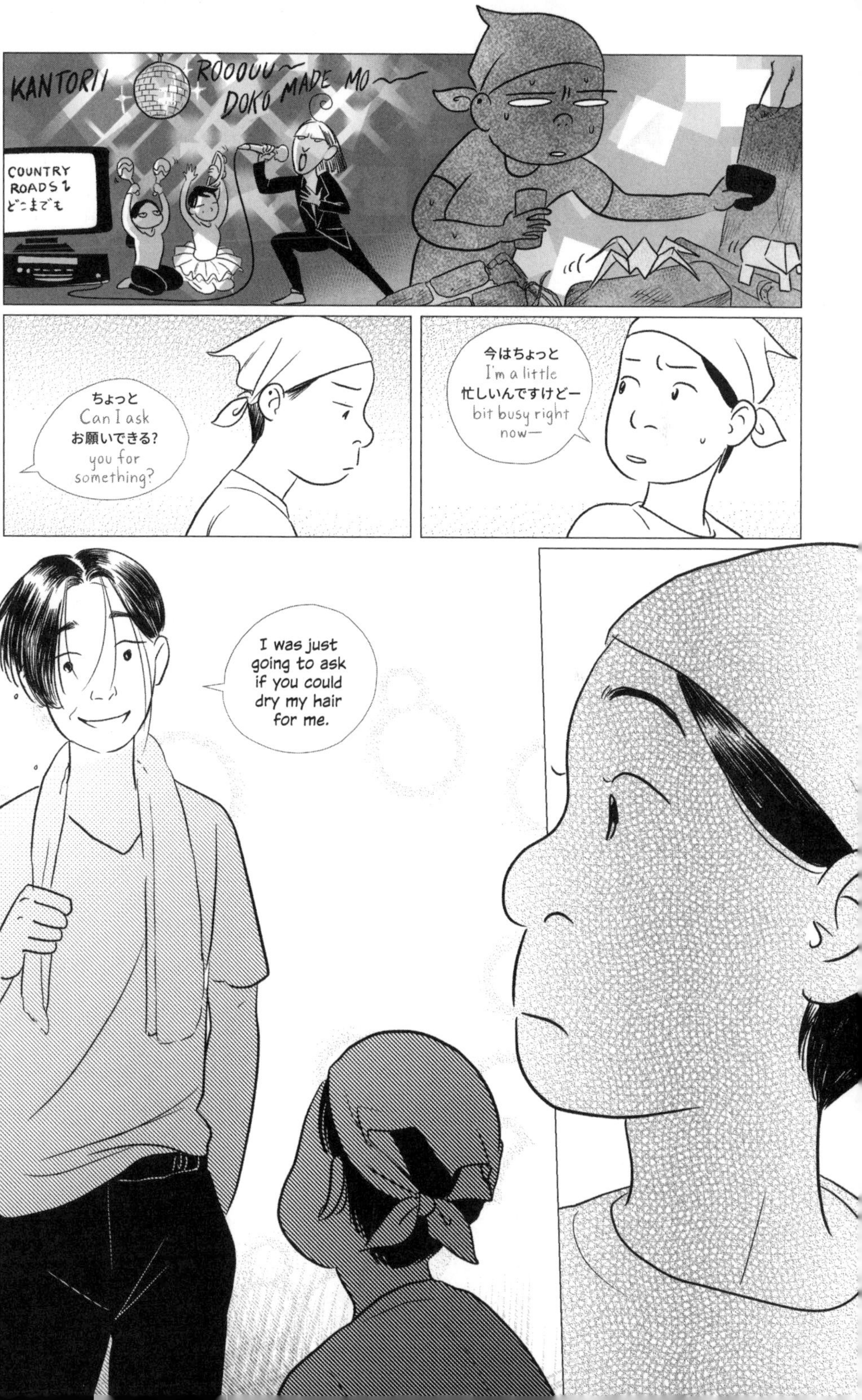
KANTORII ROOOUU~ DOKO MADE MO~~
COUNTRY ROADS♪ どこまでも
ちょっと Can I ask お願いできる? you for something?
今はちょっと I'm a little 忙しいんですけどー bit busy right now—
I was just going to ask if you could dry my hair for me.

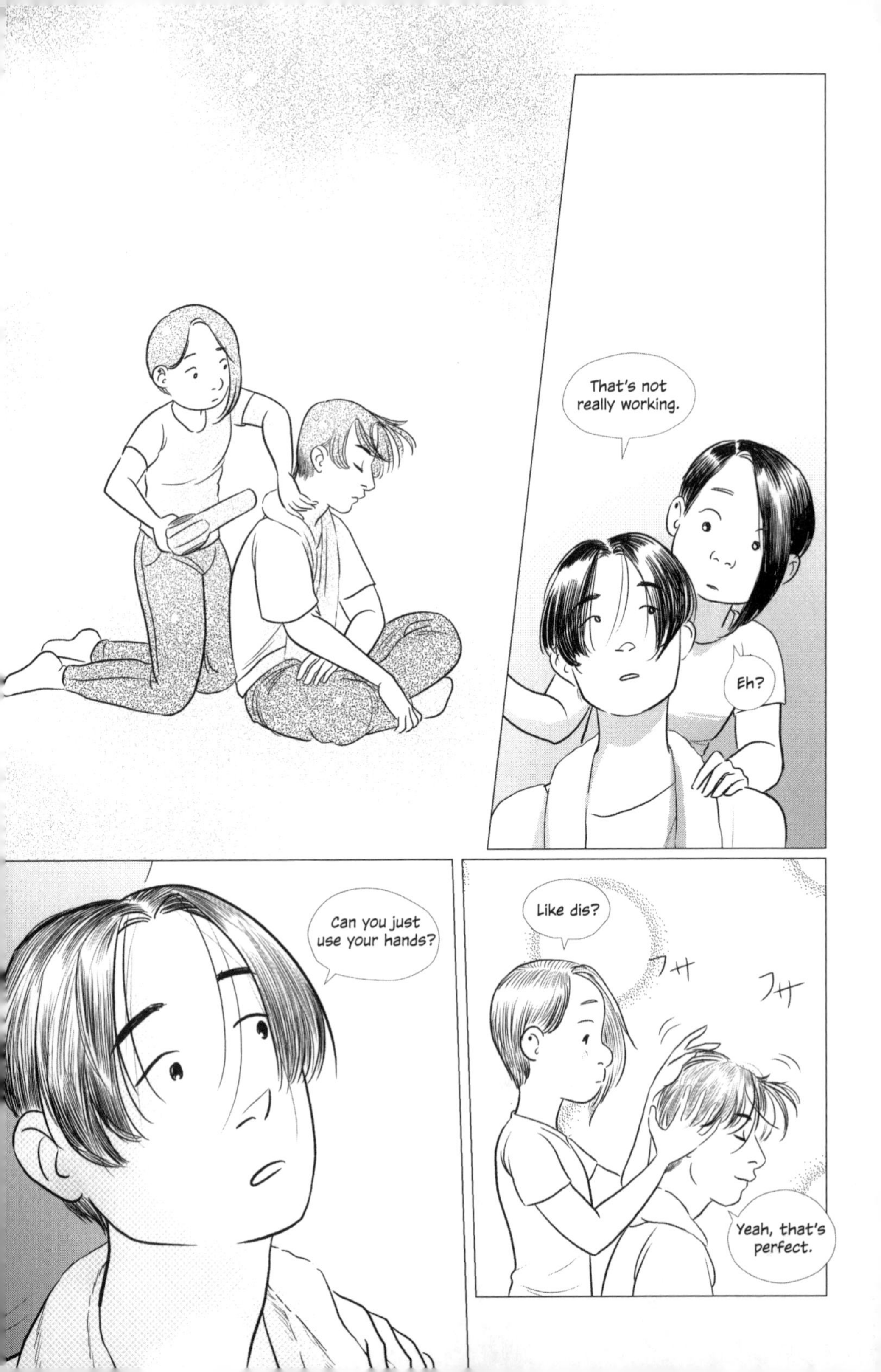
That's not really working.
Eh?
Can you just use your hands?
Like dis?
フサ
フサ
Yeah, that's perfect.

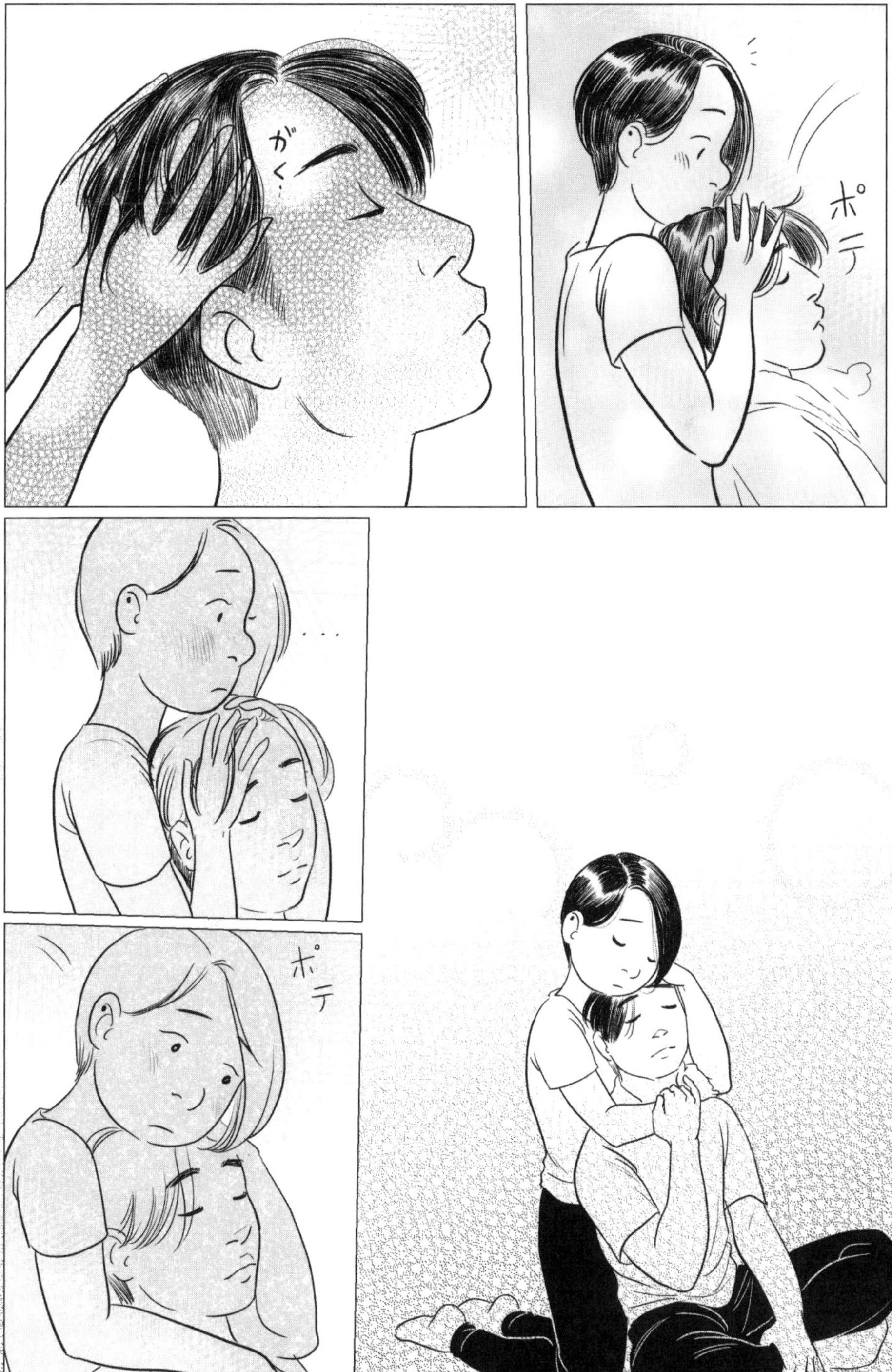
がく
ポテ
…
ポテ

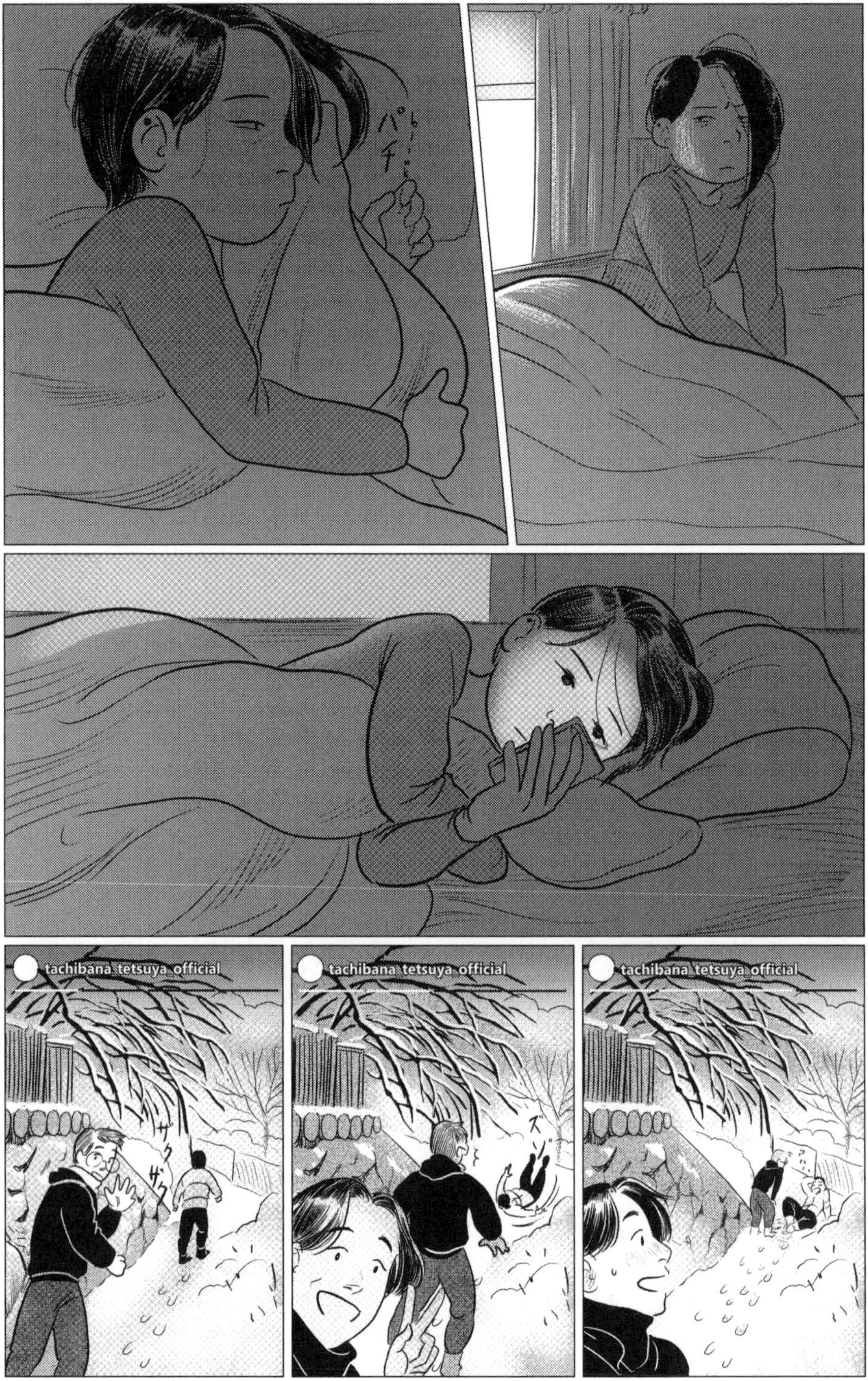
パチ
tachibana_tetsuya_official
ザク
ザク
tachibana_tetsuya_official
ズシン
tachibana_tetsuya_official
アハハ

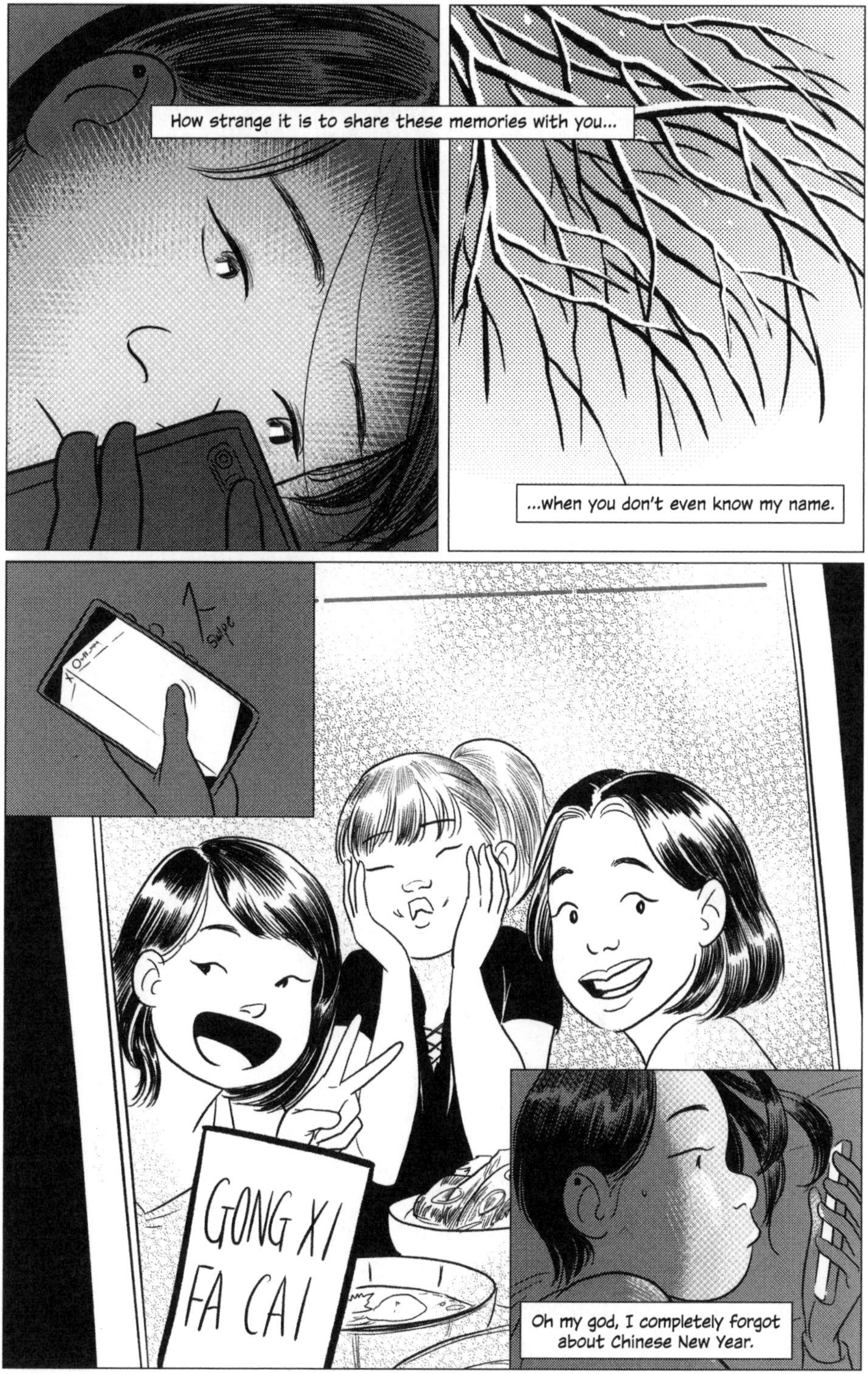
How strange it is to share these memories with you...
...when you don't even know my name.
GONG XI FA CAI
Oh my god, I completely forgot about Chinese New Year.

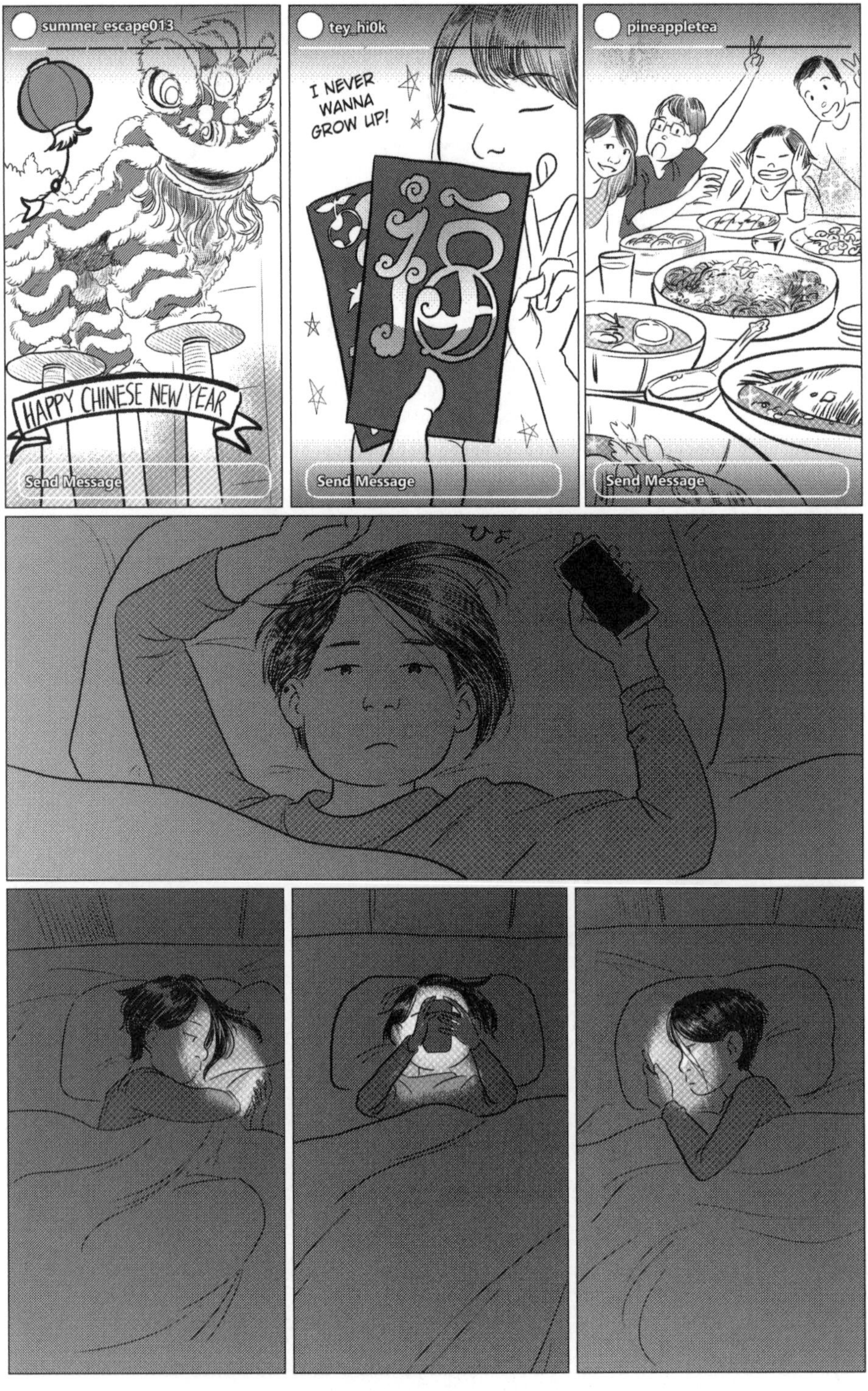
summer_escape013
HAPPY CHINESE NEW YEAR
Send Message
tey_hi0k
I NEVER WANNA GROW UP!
Send Message
pineappletea
Send Message

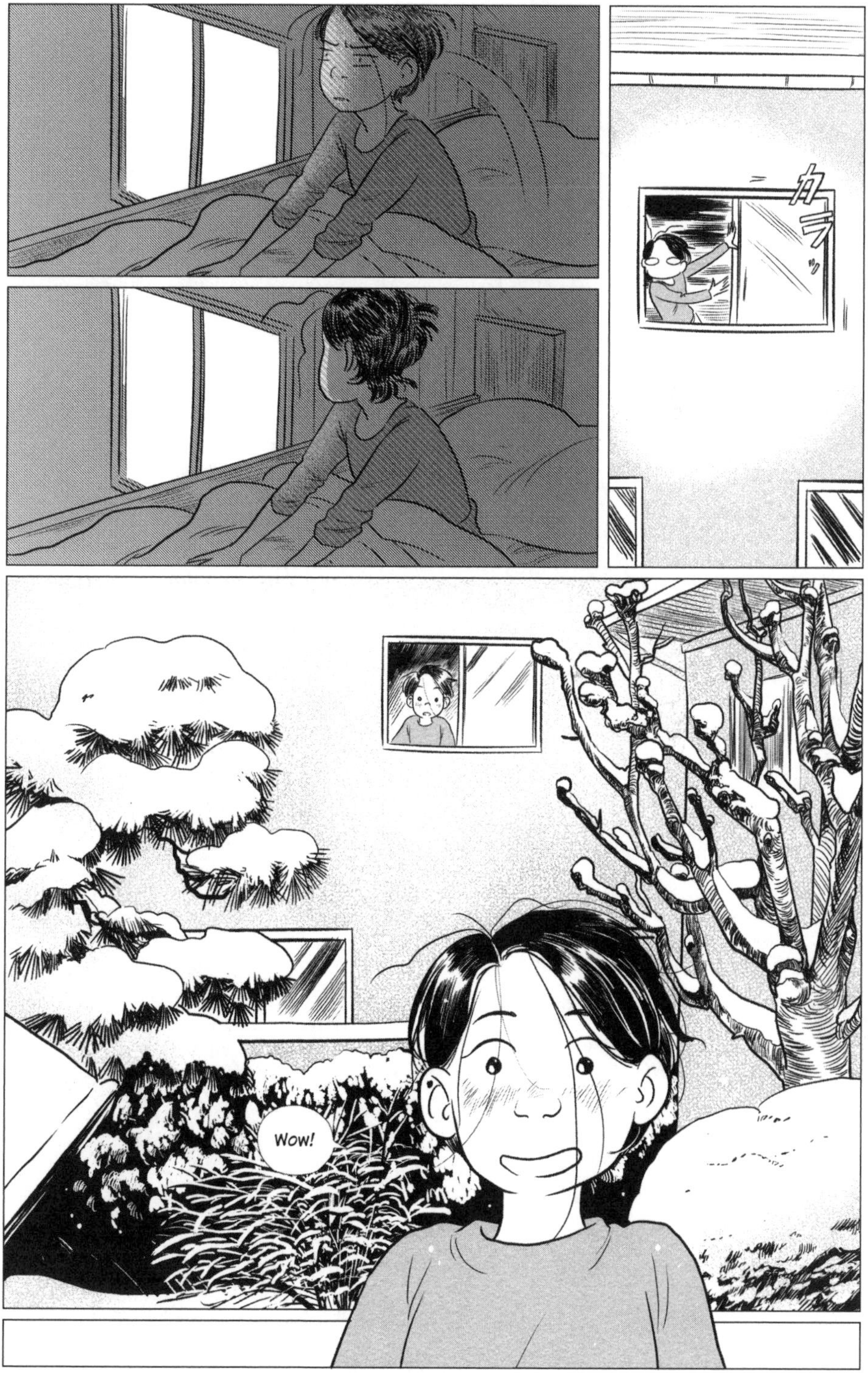
カラ
ッ
Wow!

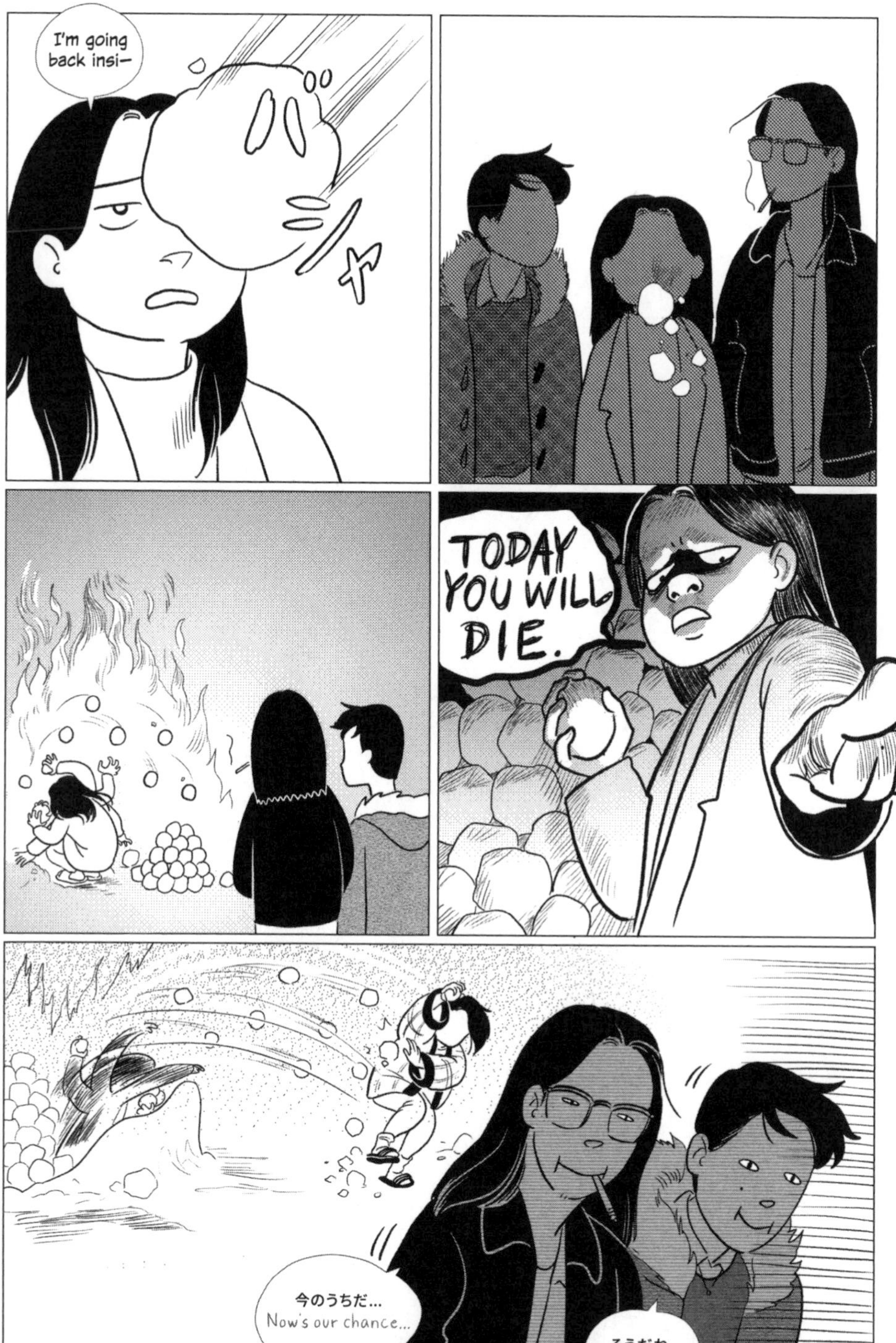
I'm going back insi—
TODAY YOU WILL DIE.
今のうちだ…
Now's our chance...
そうだね
Yup.

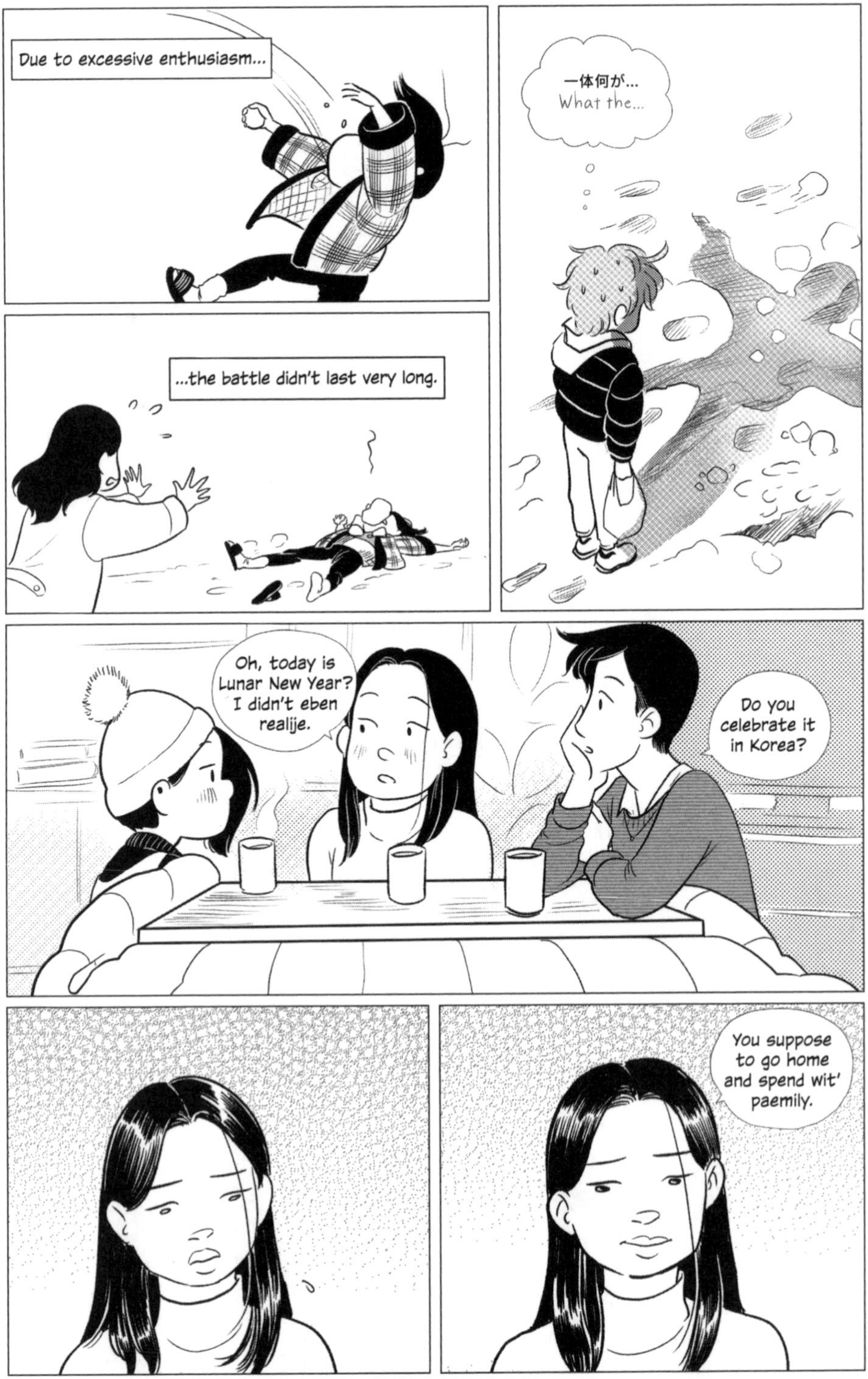
Due to excessive enthusiasm...
一体何が...
What the...
...the battle didn't last very long.
Oh, today is Lunar New Year? I didn't eben realije.
Do you celebrate it in Korea?
You suppose to go home and spend wit' paemily.

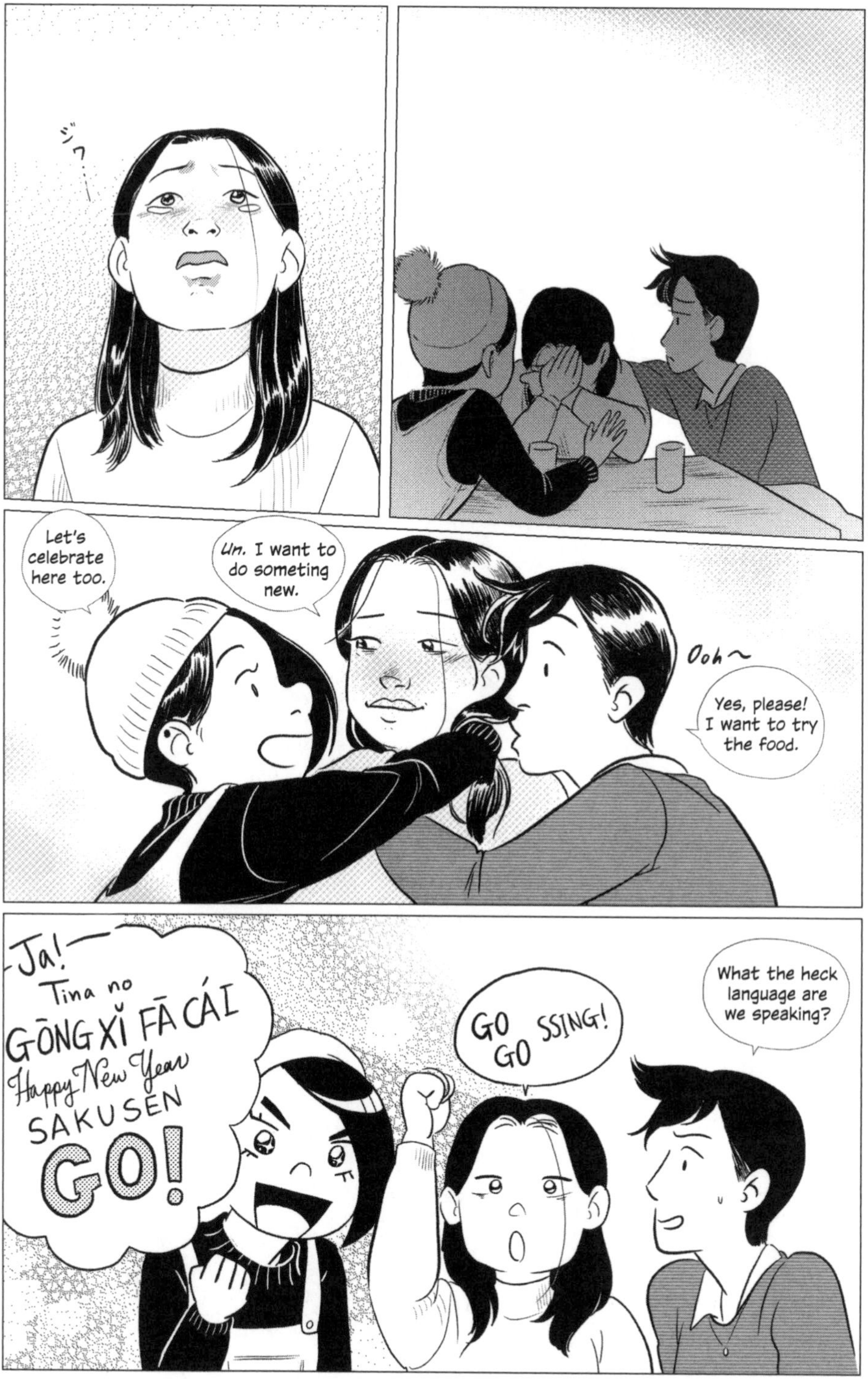
ジワ…
Let's celebrate here too.
Un. I want to do someting new.
Ooh~
Yes, please! I want to try the food.
Ja!— Tina no GŌNG XǏ FĀ CÁI Happy New Year SAKUSEN GO!
GO GO SSING!
What the heck language are we speaking?

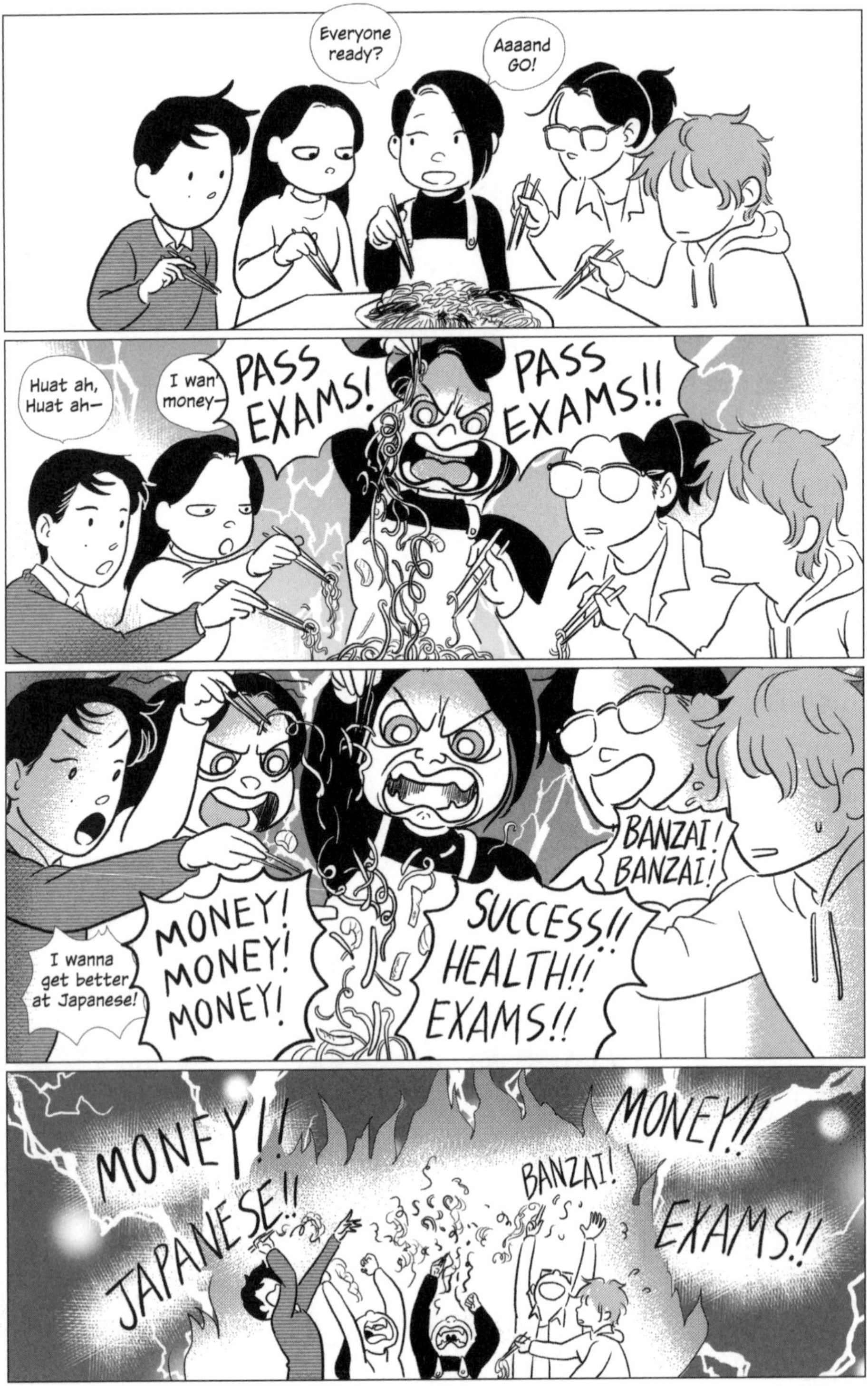
Everyone ready?
Aaaand GO!
Huat ah, Huat ah—
I wan' money—
PASS EXAMS!
PASS EXAMS!!
BANZAI! BANZAI!
I wanna get better at Japanese!
MONEY! MONEY! MONEY!
SUCCESS!! HEALTH!! EXAMS!!
MONEY!!
JAPANESE!!
BANZAI!
MONEY!!
EXAMS!!

Chapter 15

Yoojoon

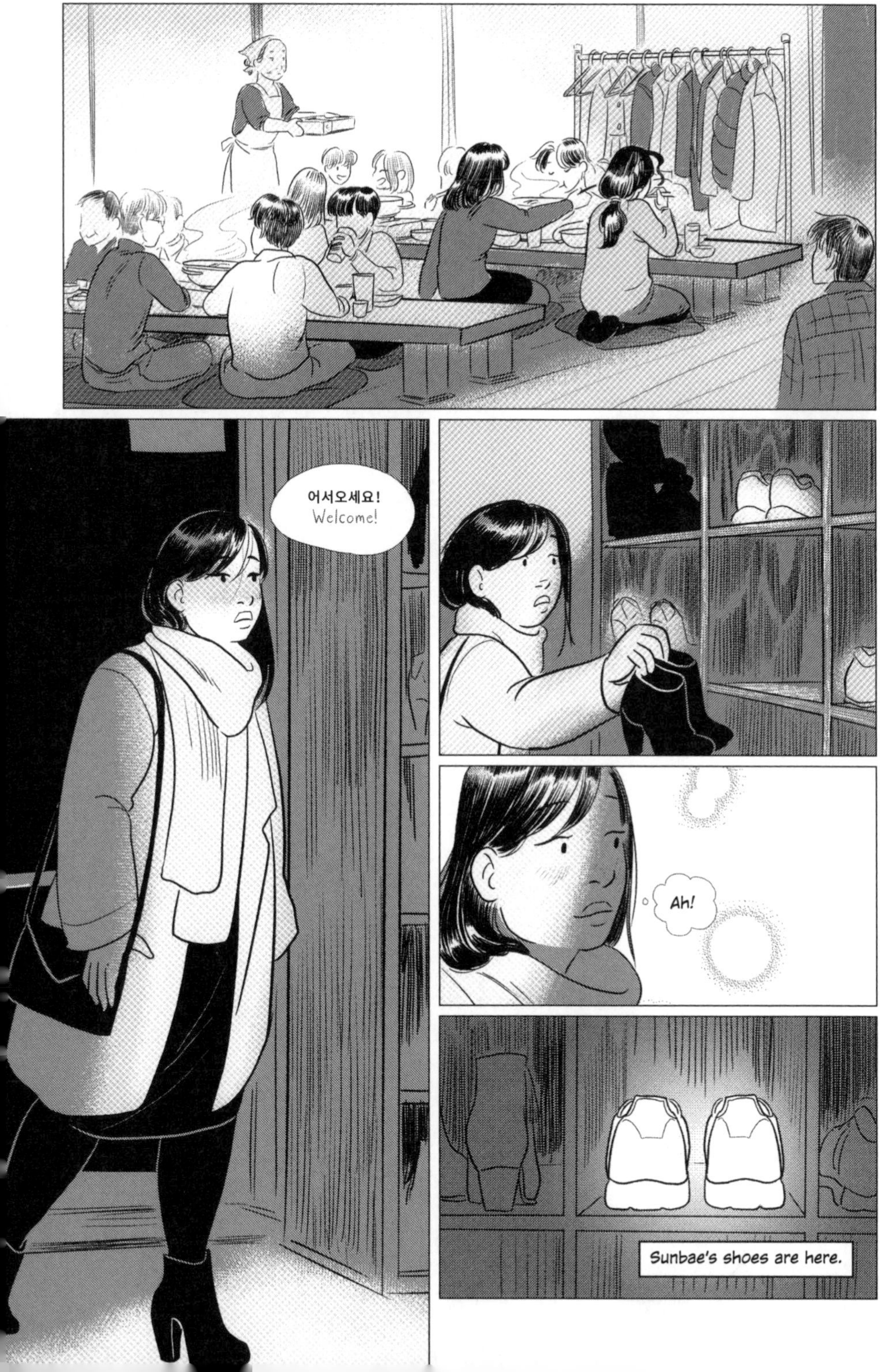
어서오세요!
Welcome!
Ah!
Sunbae's shoes are here.

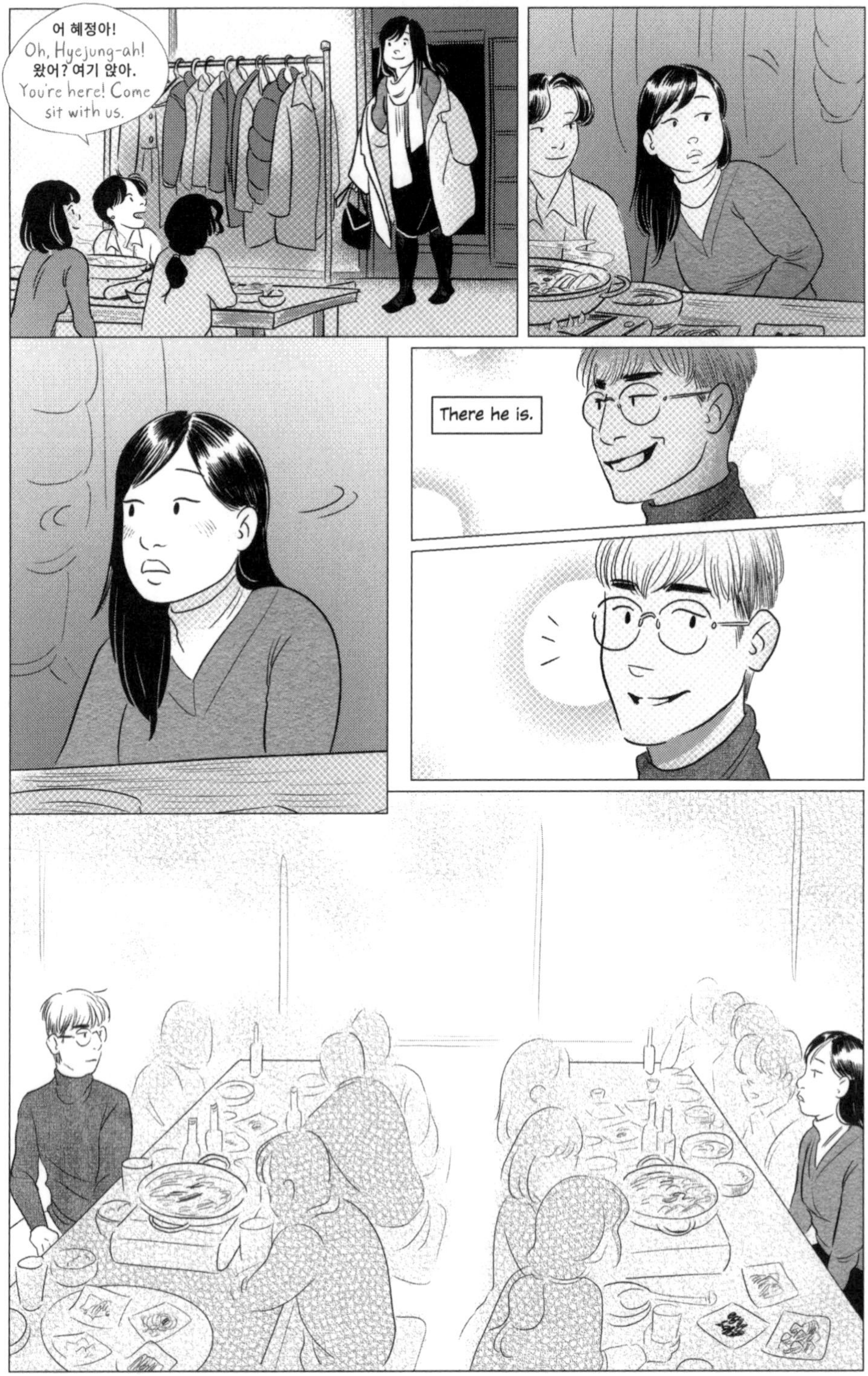
어 혜정아!
Oh, Hyejung-ah!
왔어? 여기 앉아.
You're here! Come sit with us.
There he is.

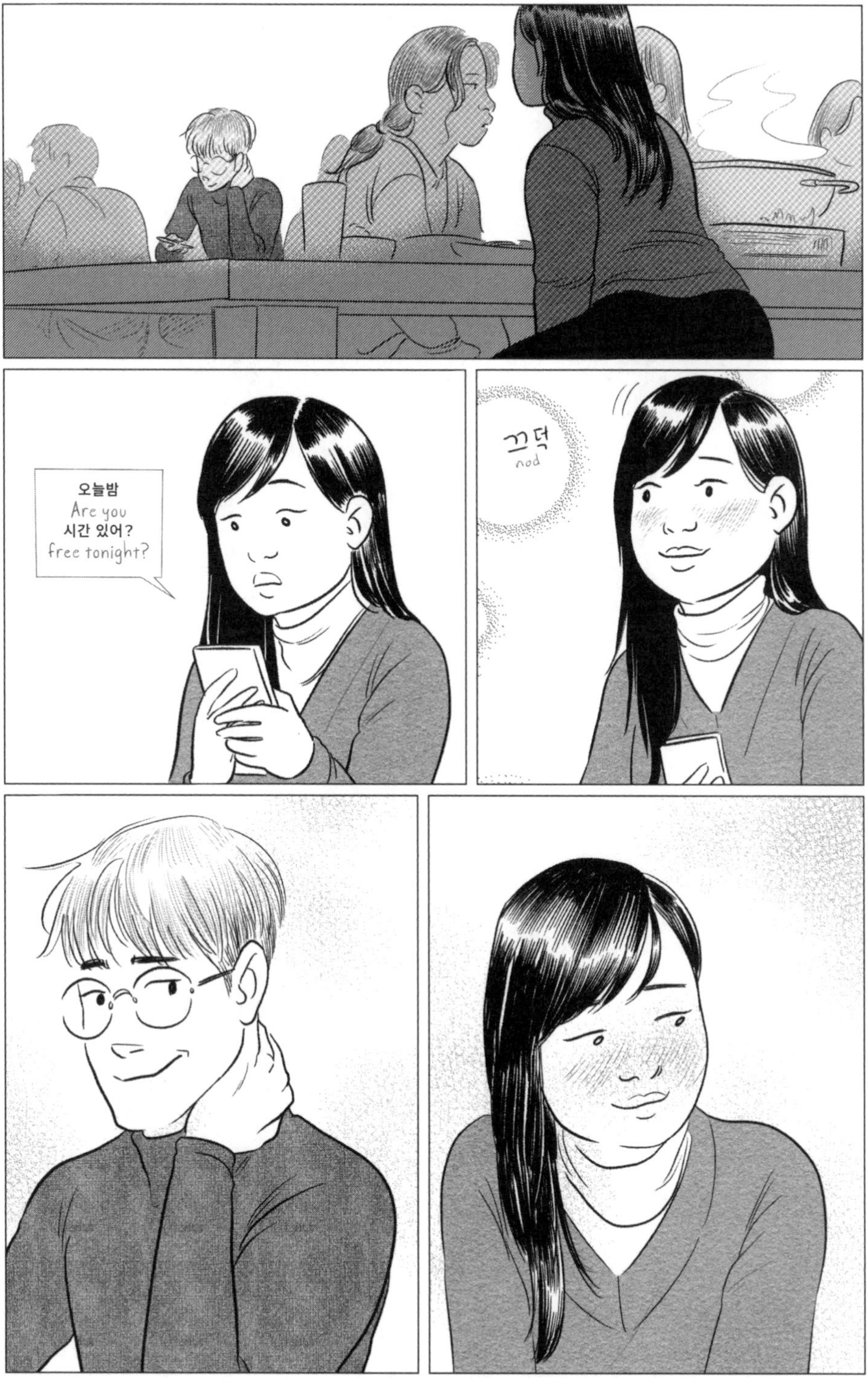
오늘밤
Are you
시간 있어?
free tonight?
끄덕
nod

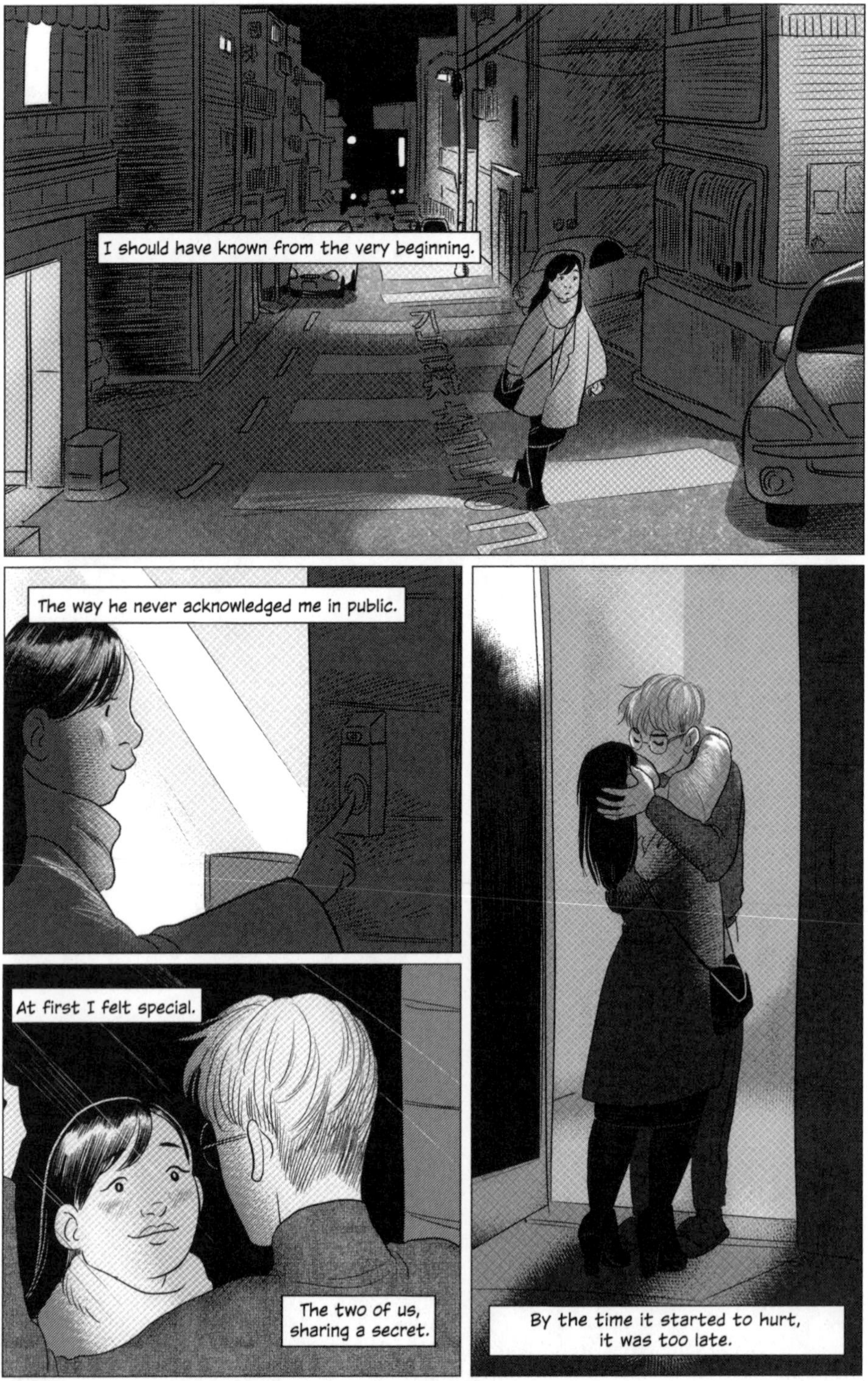
I should have known from the very beginning.
The way he never acknowledged me in public.
At first I felt special.
The two of us, sharing a secret.
By the time it started to hurt, it was too late.

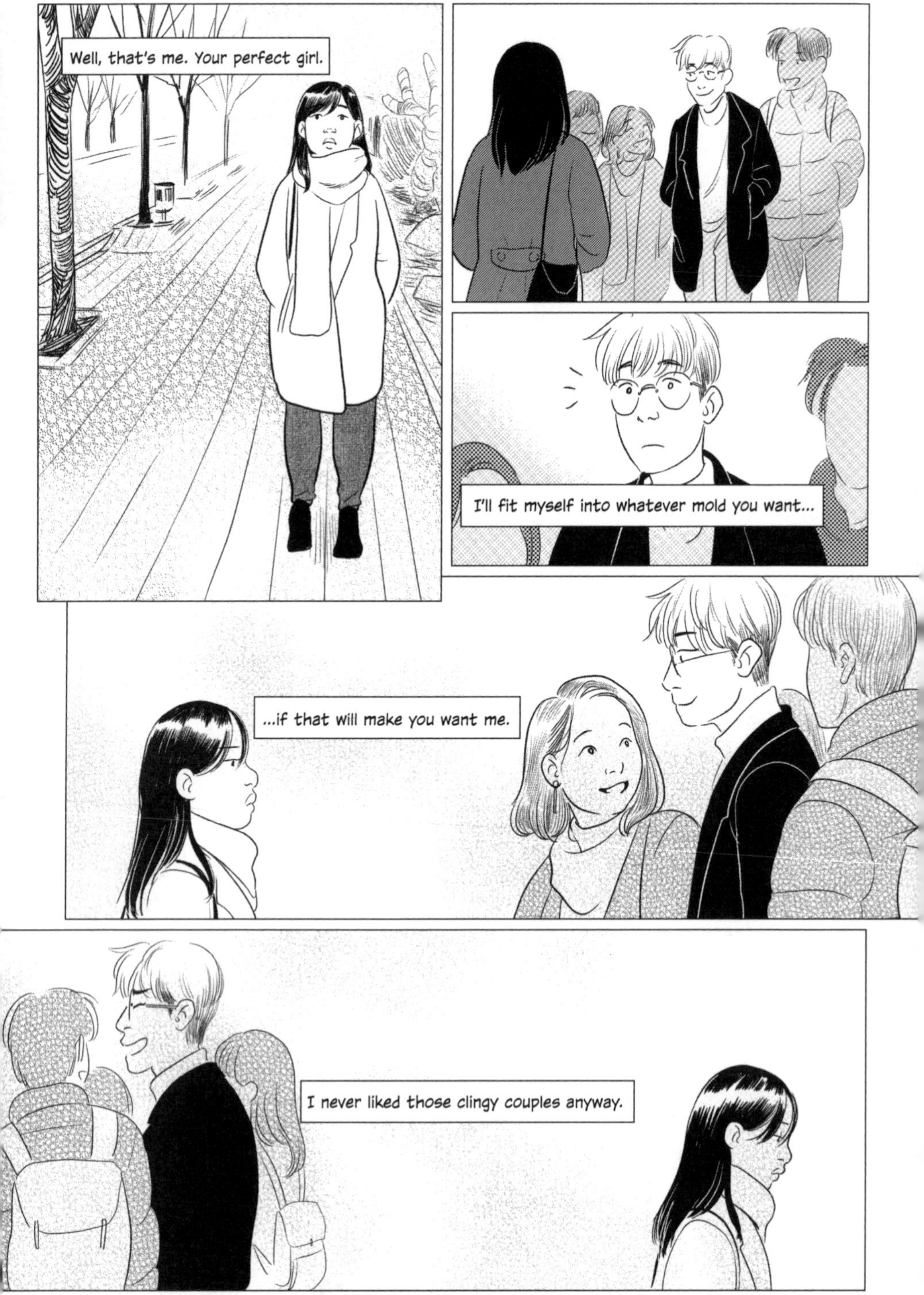
Well, that's me. Your perfect girl.
I'll fit myself into whatever mold you want...
...if that will make you want me.
I never liked those clingy couples anyway.

내일 보자!
see you tomorrow!

바이!
bye!

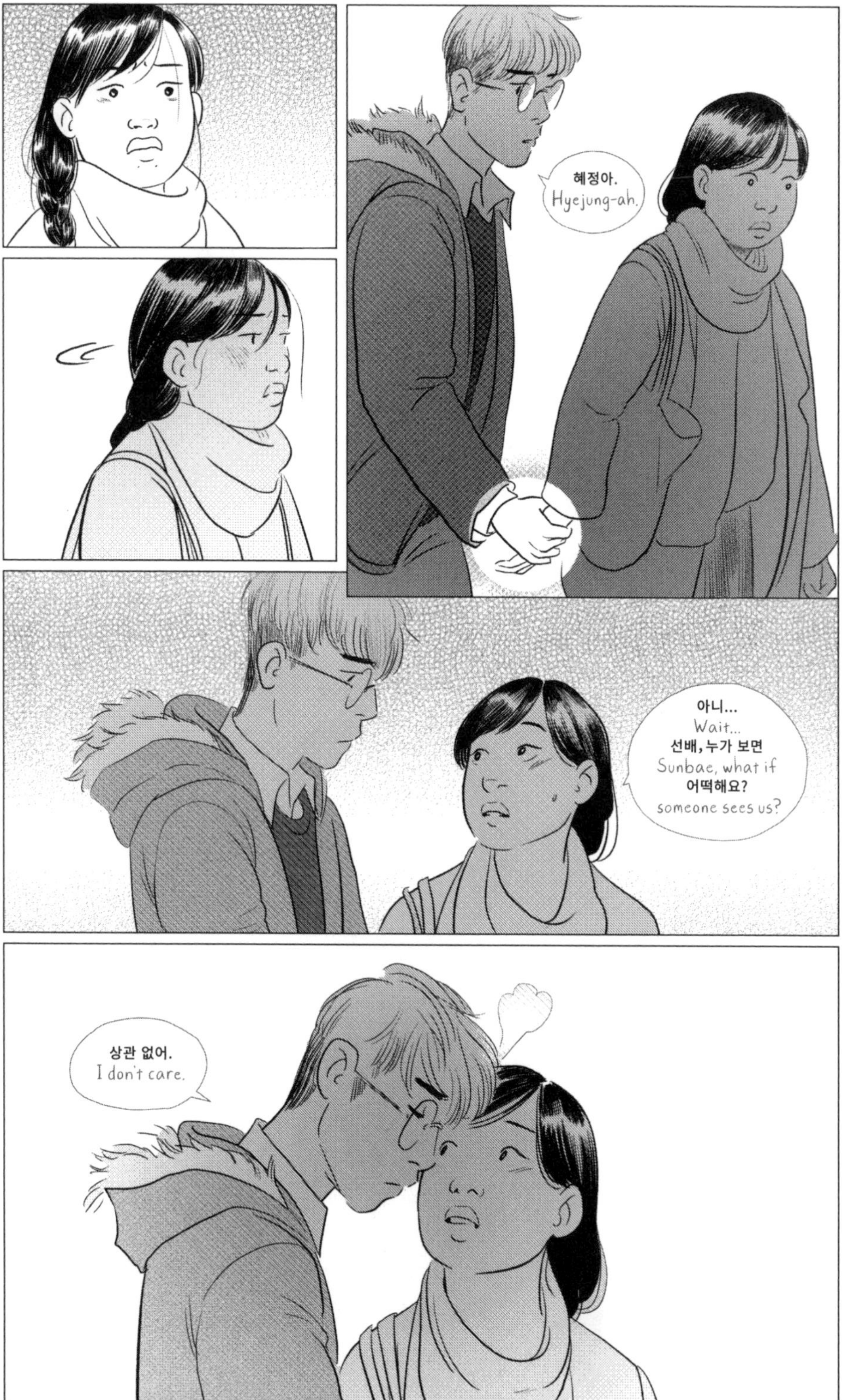
혜정아.
Hyejung-ah.
아니...
Wait...
선배, 누가 보면
Sunbae, what if
어떡해요?
someone sees us?
상관 없어.
I don't care.

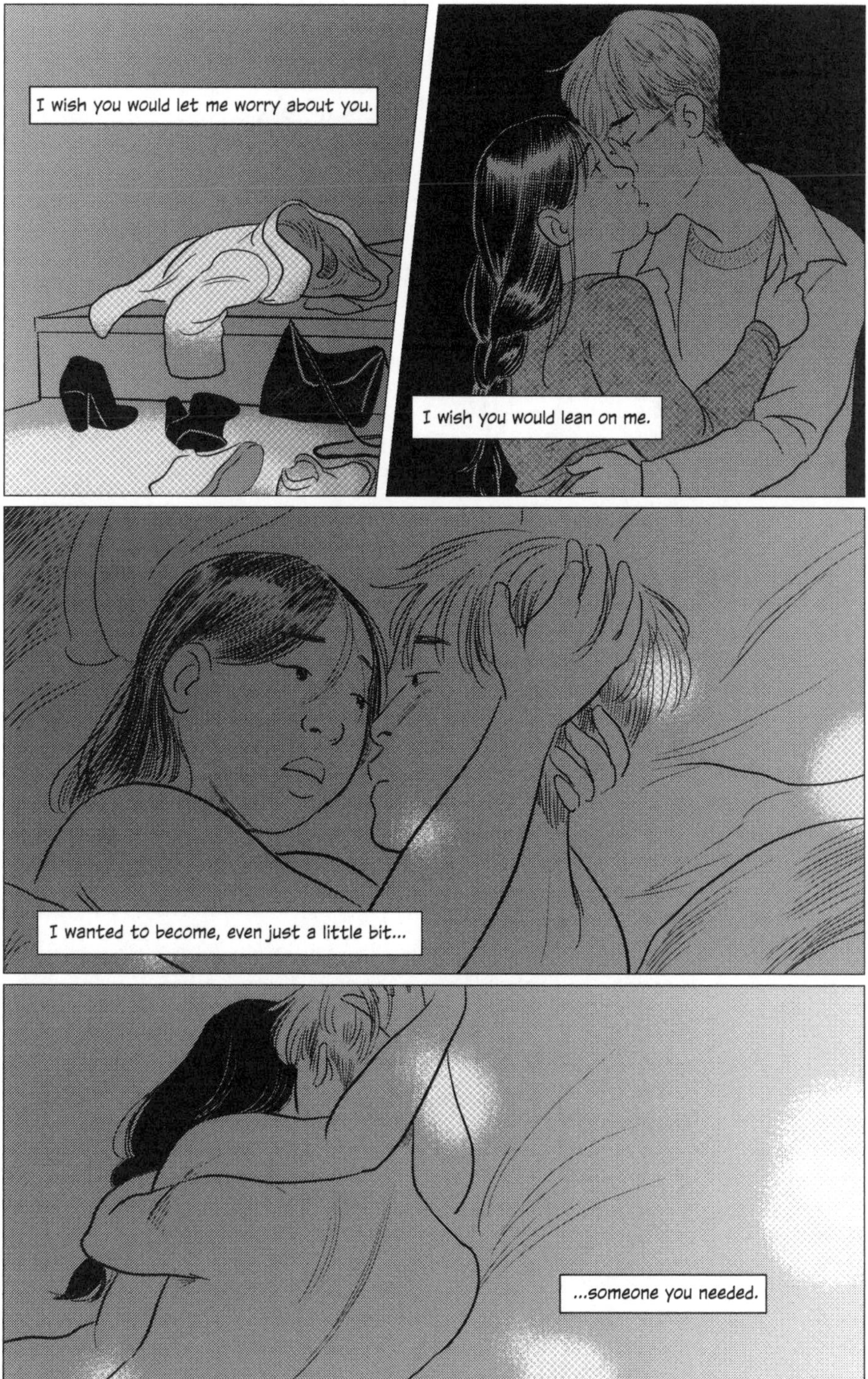
I wish you would let me worry about you.
I wish you would lean on me.
I wanted to become, even just a little bit...
...someone you needed.

276

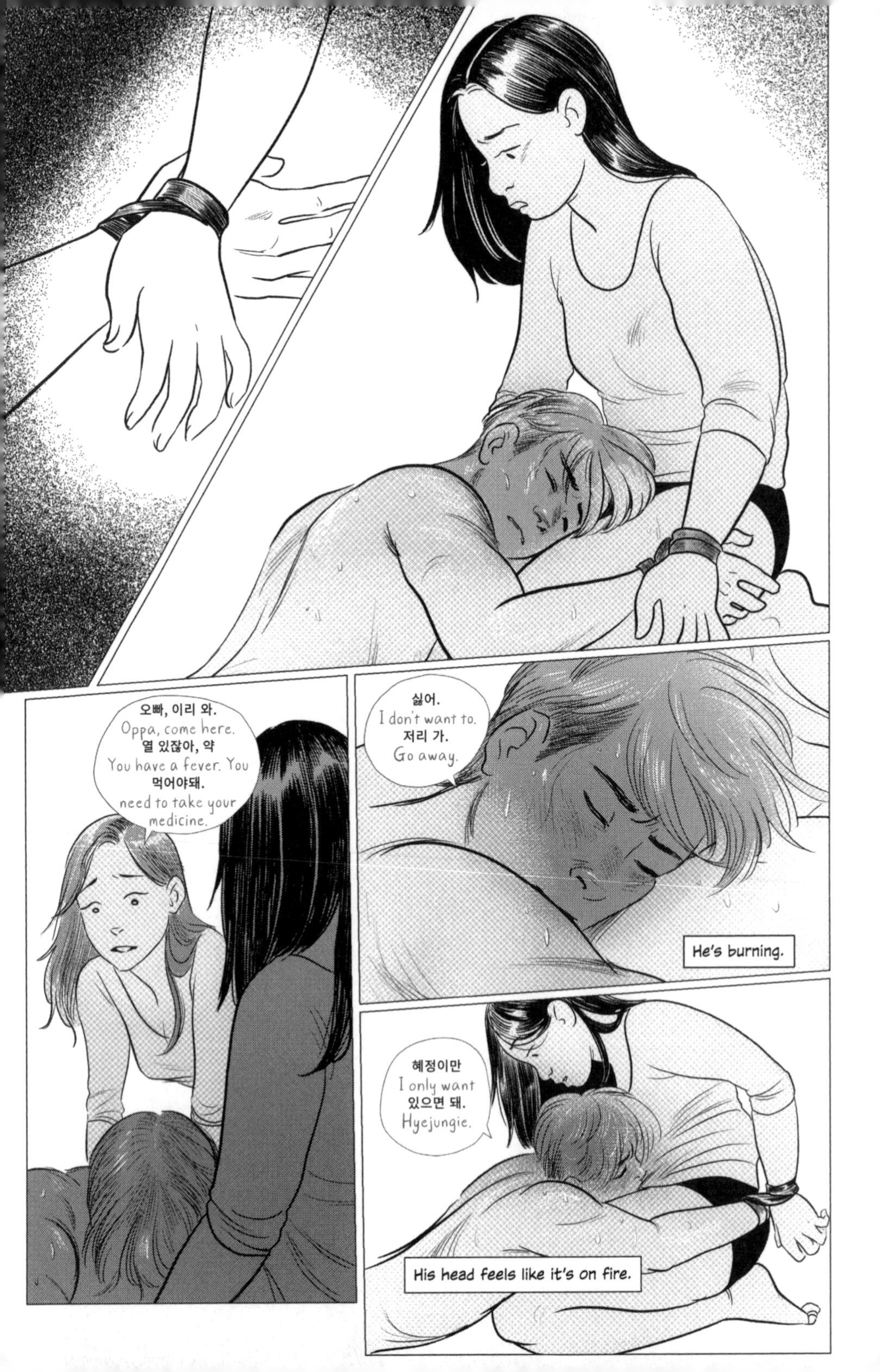

오빠, 이리 와.
Oppa, come here.
열 있잖아, 약
You have a fever. You
먹어야돼.
need to take your medicine.
싫어.
I don't want to.
저리 가.
Go away.
He's burning.
혜정이만
I only want
있으면 돼.
Hyejungie.
His head feels like it's on fire.

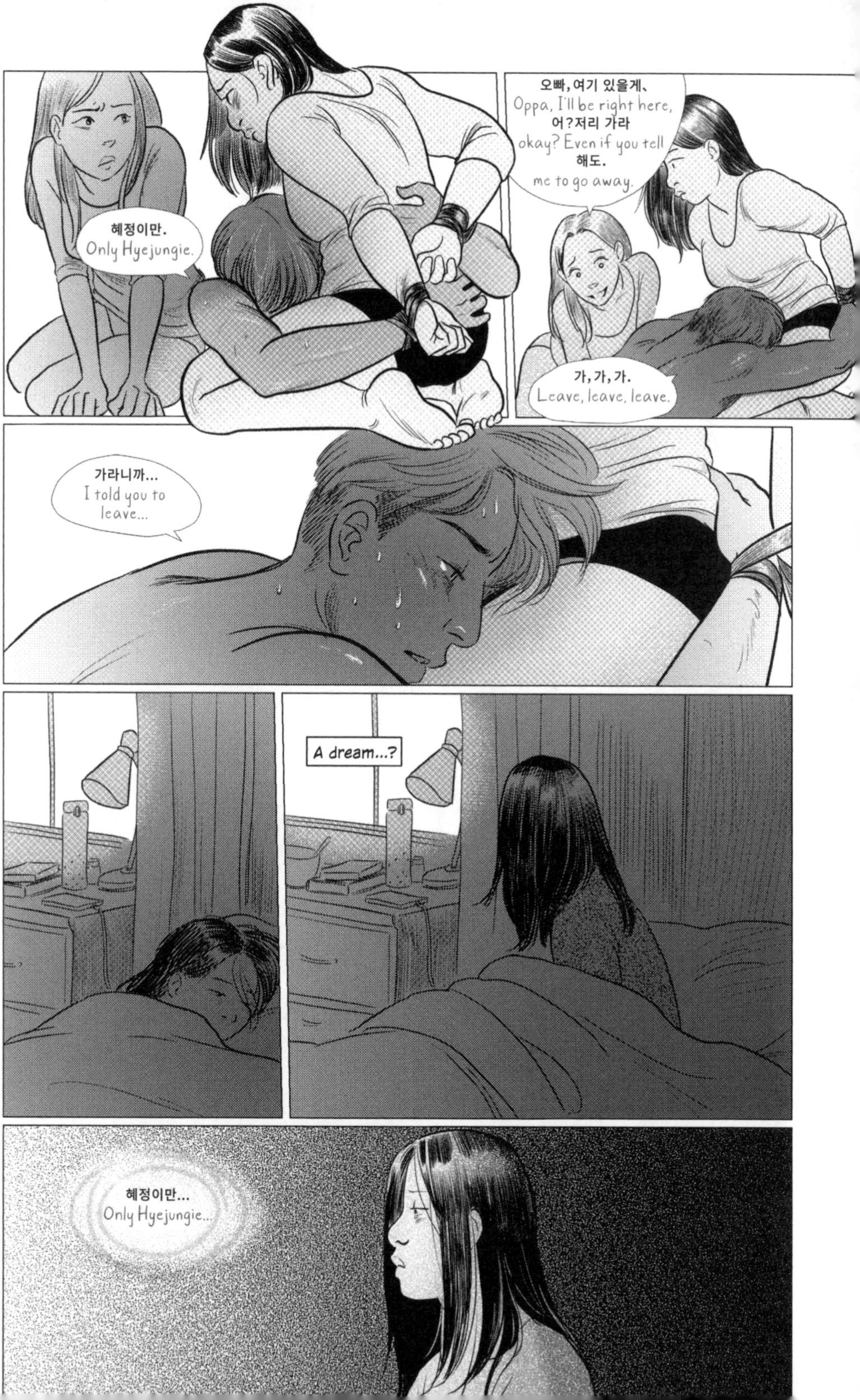
혜정이만.
Only Hyejungie.
오빠, 여기 있을게, 어?저리 가라 해도.
Oppa, I'll be right here, okay? Even if you tell me to go away.
가, 가, 가.
Leave, leave, leave.
가라니까...
I told you to leave...
A dream...?
혜정이만...
Only Hyejungie...

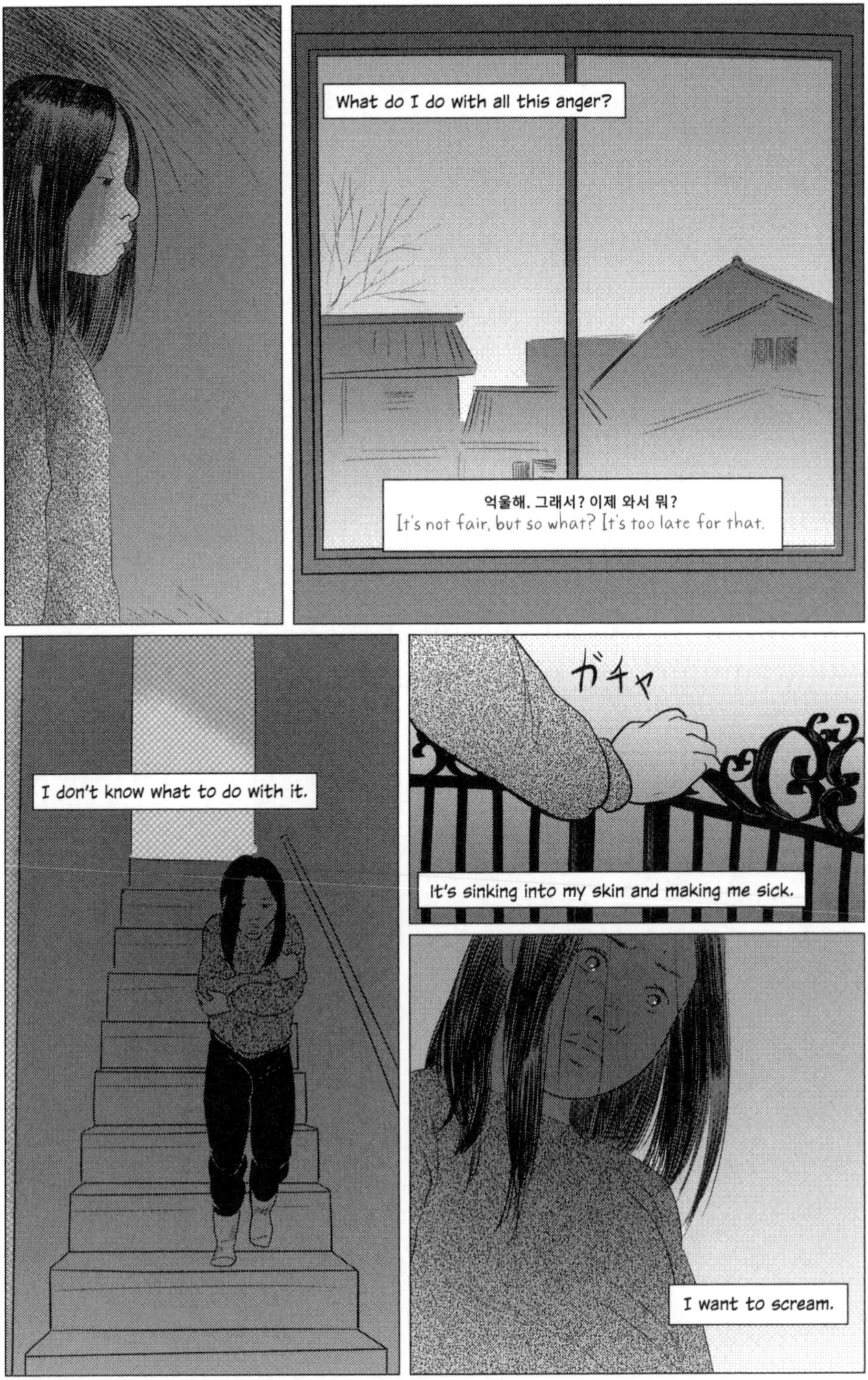
What do I do with all this anger?
억울해. 그래서? 이제 와서 뭐?
It's not fair, but so what? It's too late for that.
I don't know what to do with it.
ガチャ
It's sinking into my skin and making me sick.
I want to scream.

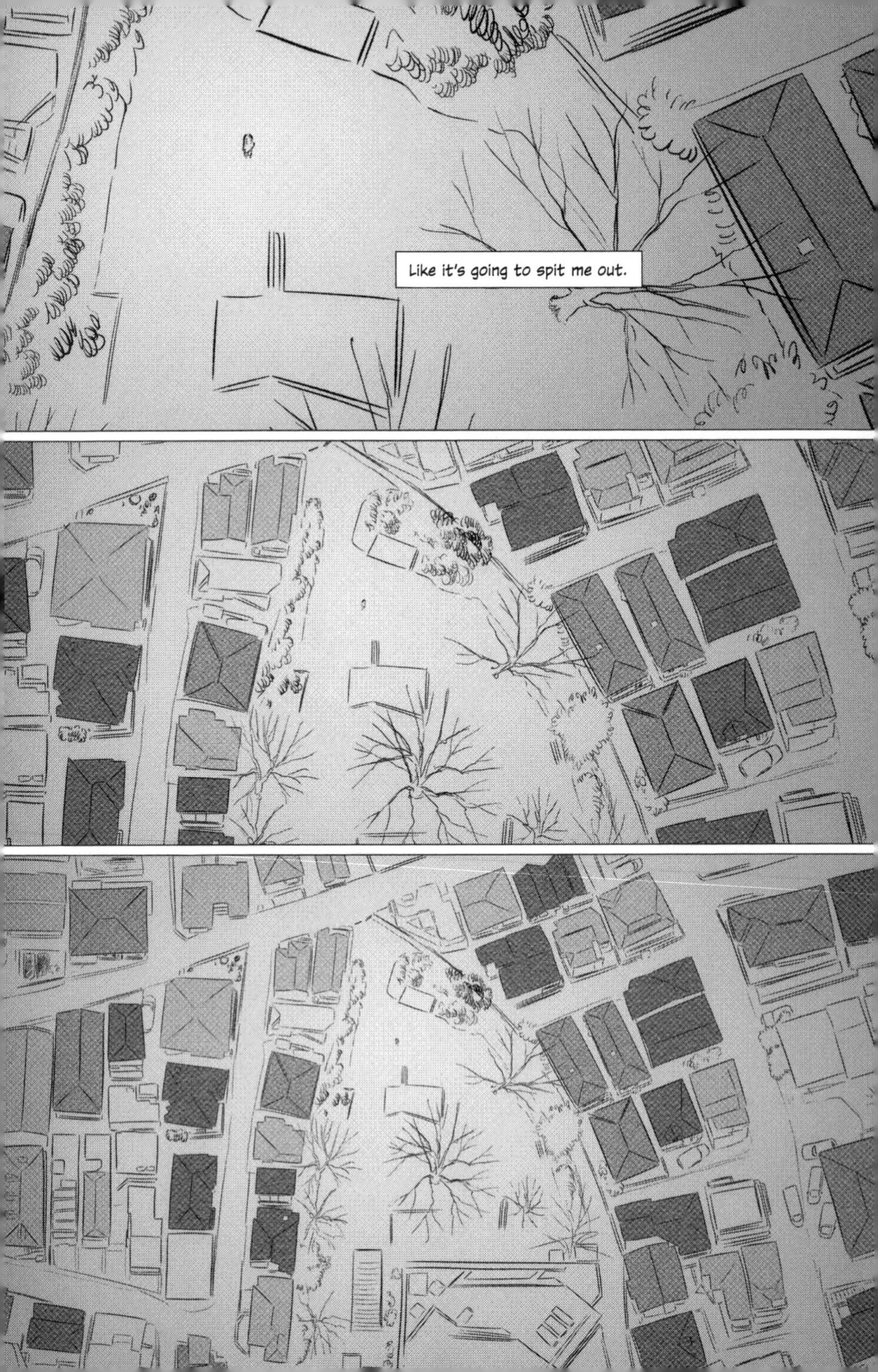
Like it's going to spit me out.

Chapter 16
Rakudai

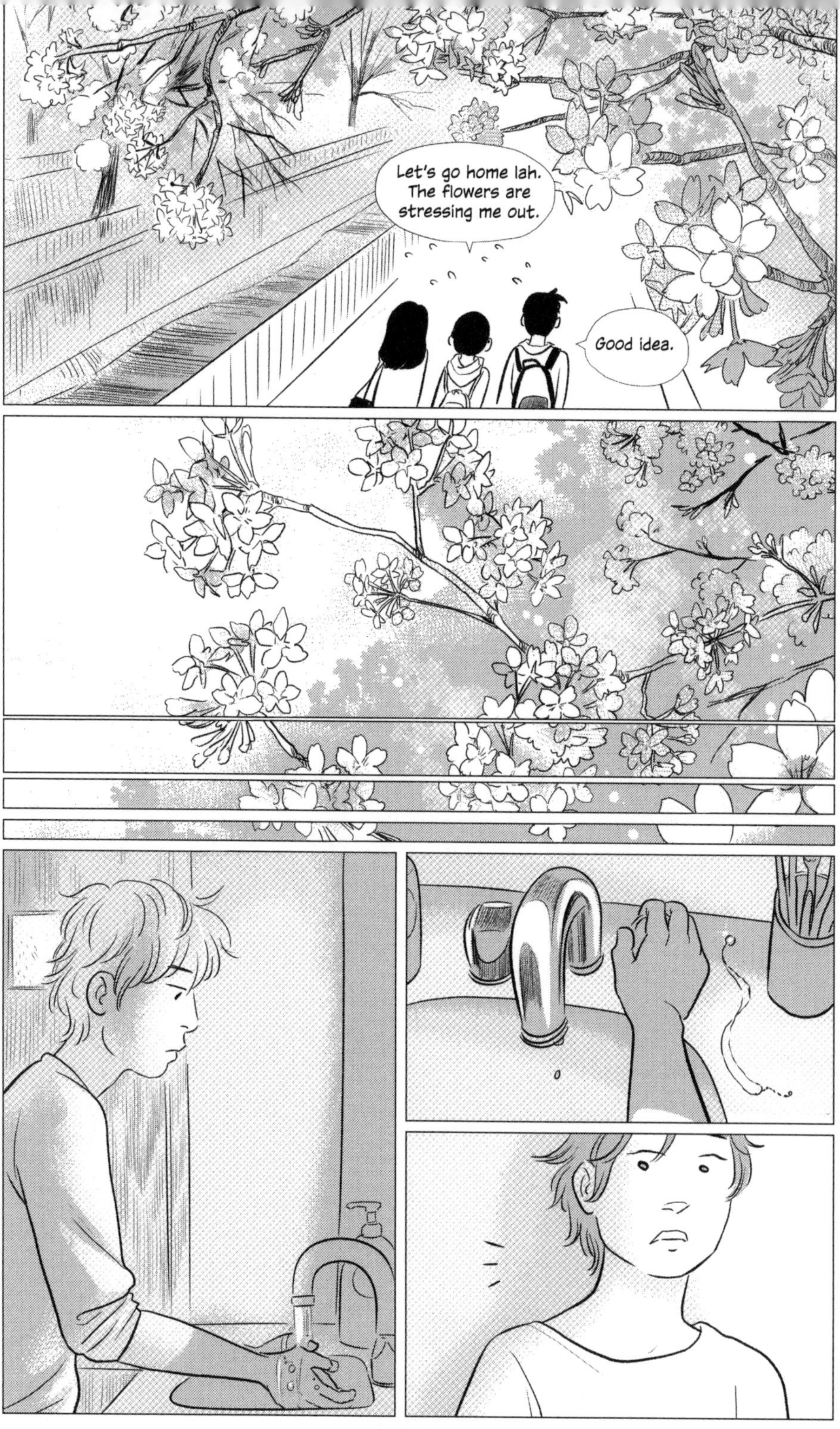
Let's go home lah. The flowers are stressing me out.
Good idea.

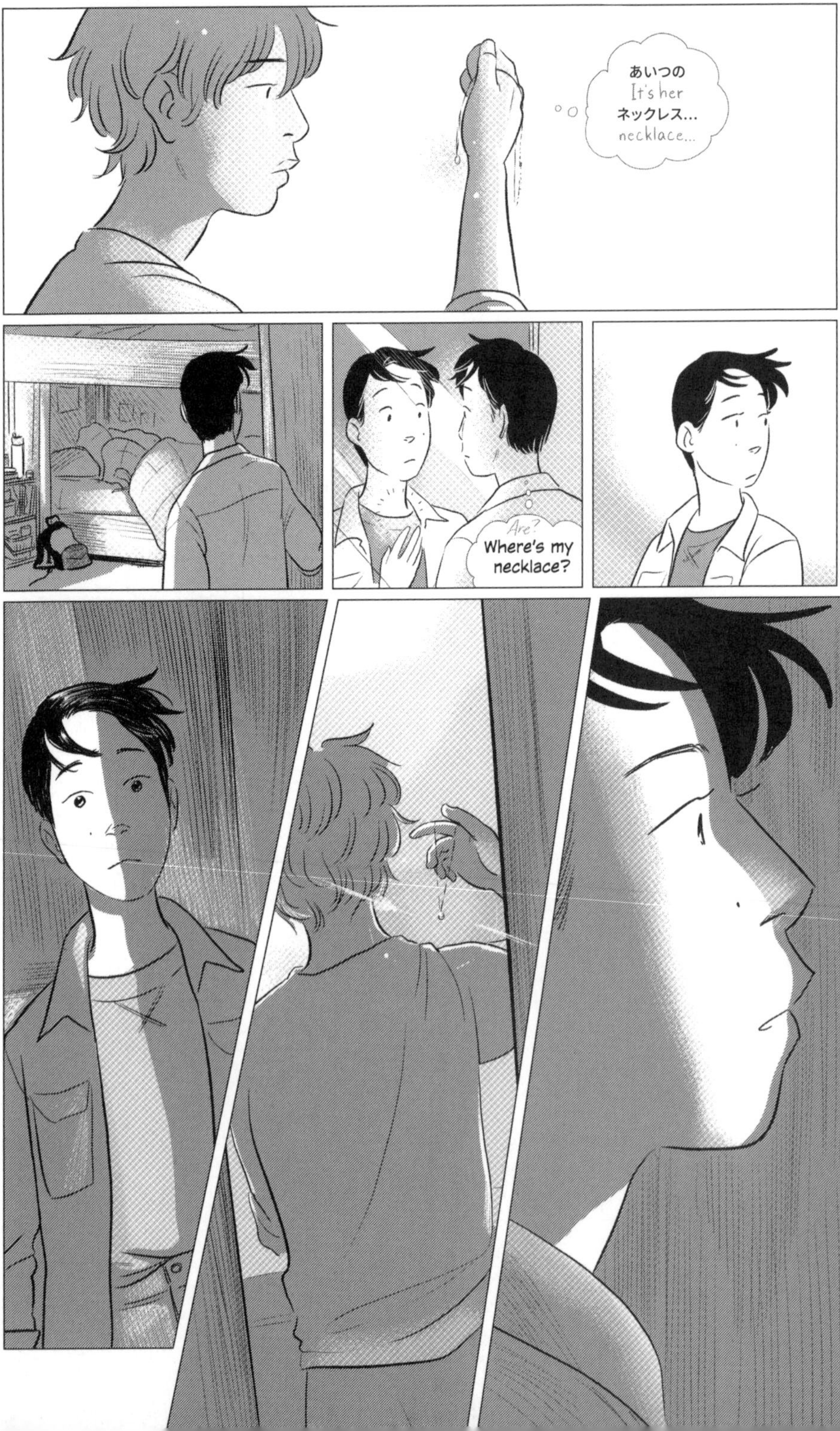

あいつの
It's her
ネックレス…
necklace...
Are?
Where's my necklace?

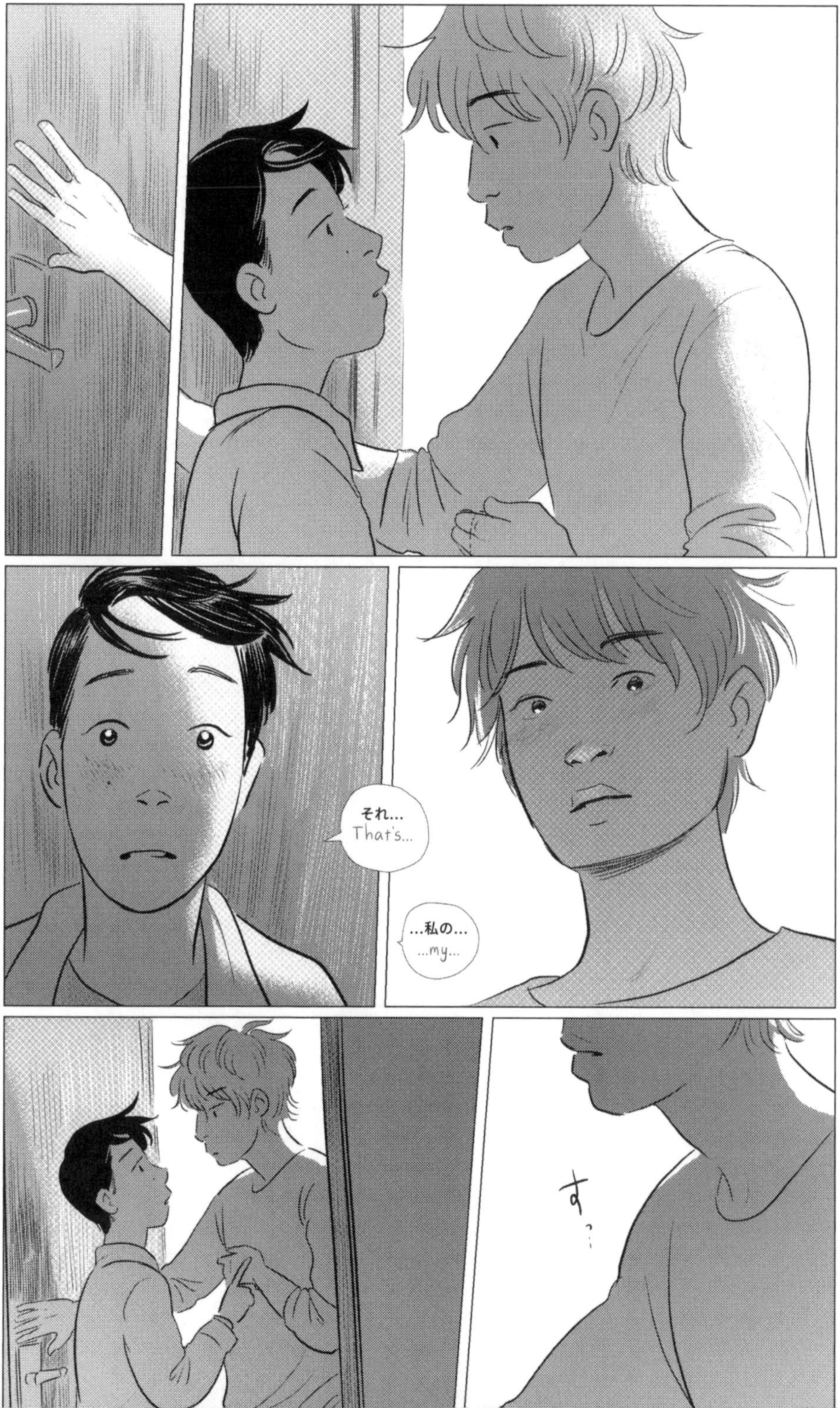
それ…
That's...
…私の…
...my...
す

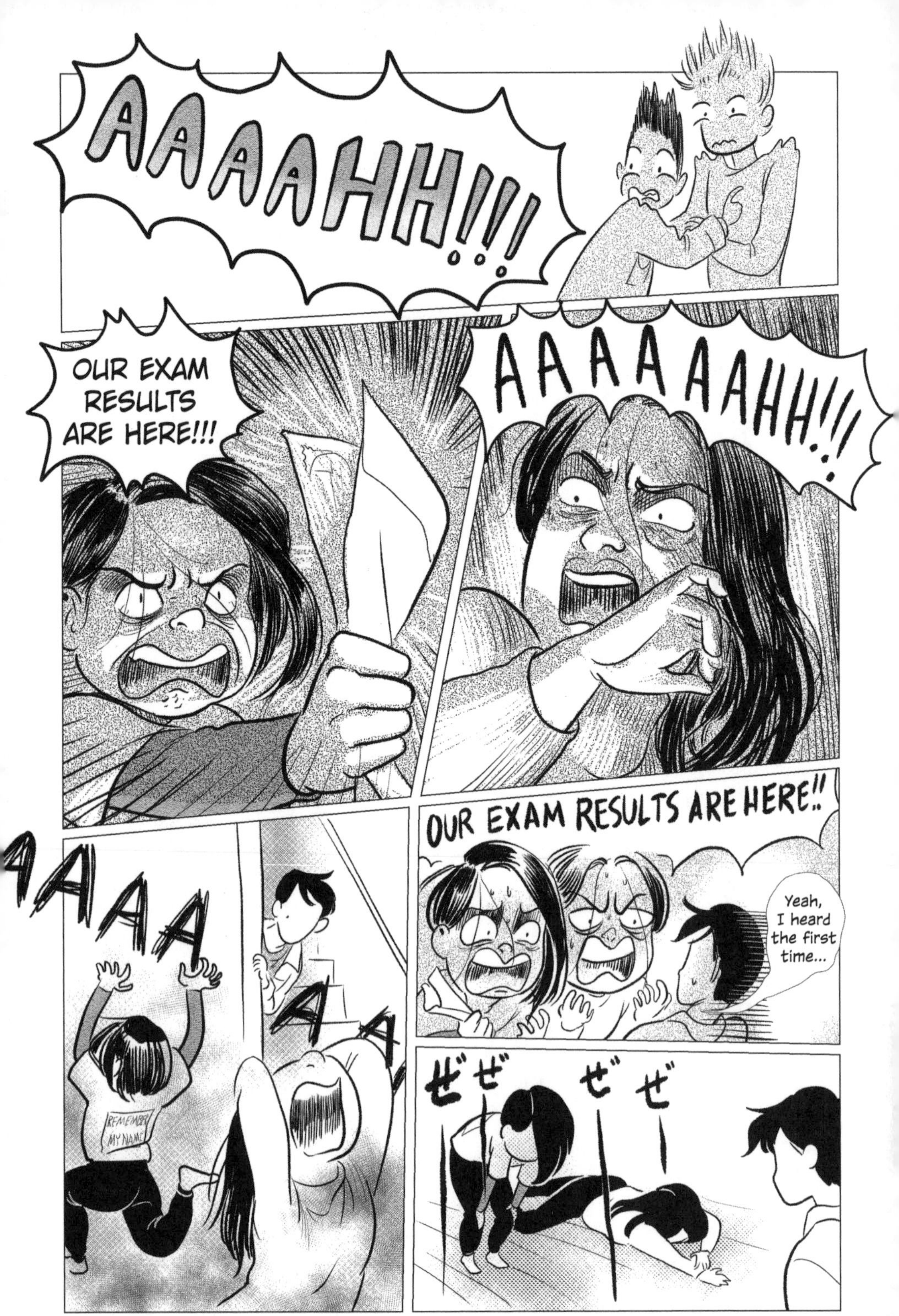
AAAAAHH!!!
OUR EXAM RESULTS ARE HERE!!!
AAAAAAAHH!!!
OUR EXAM RESULTS ARE HERE!!
Yeah, I heard the first time...
AAAAA
AA
REMEMBER MY NAME
ぜぜ
ぜぜー

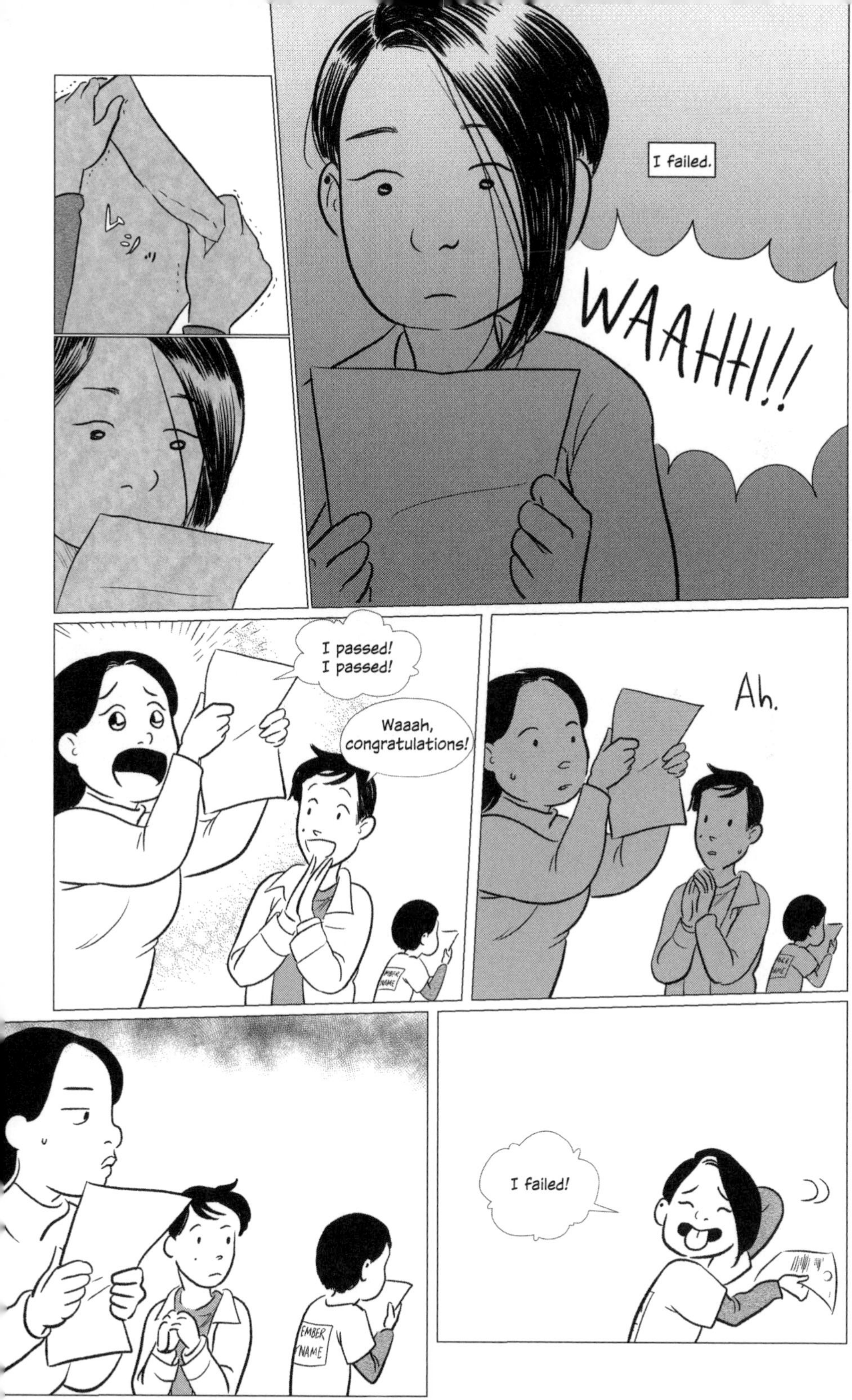
I failed.
WAAHH!!
I passed! I passed!
Waaah, congratulations!
Ah.
I failed!

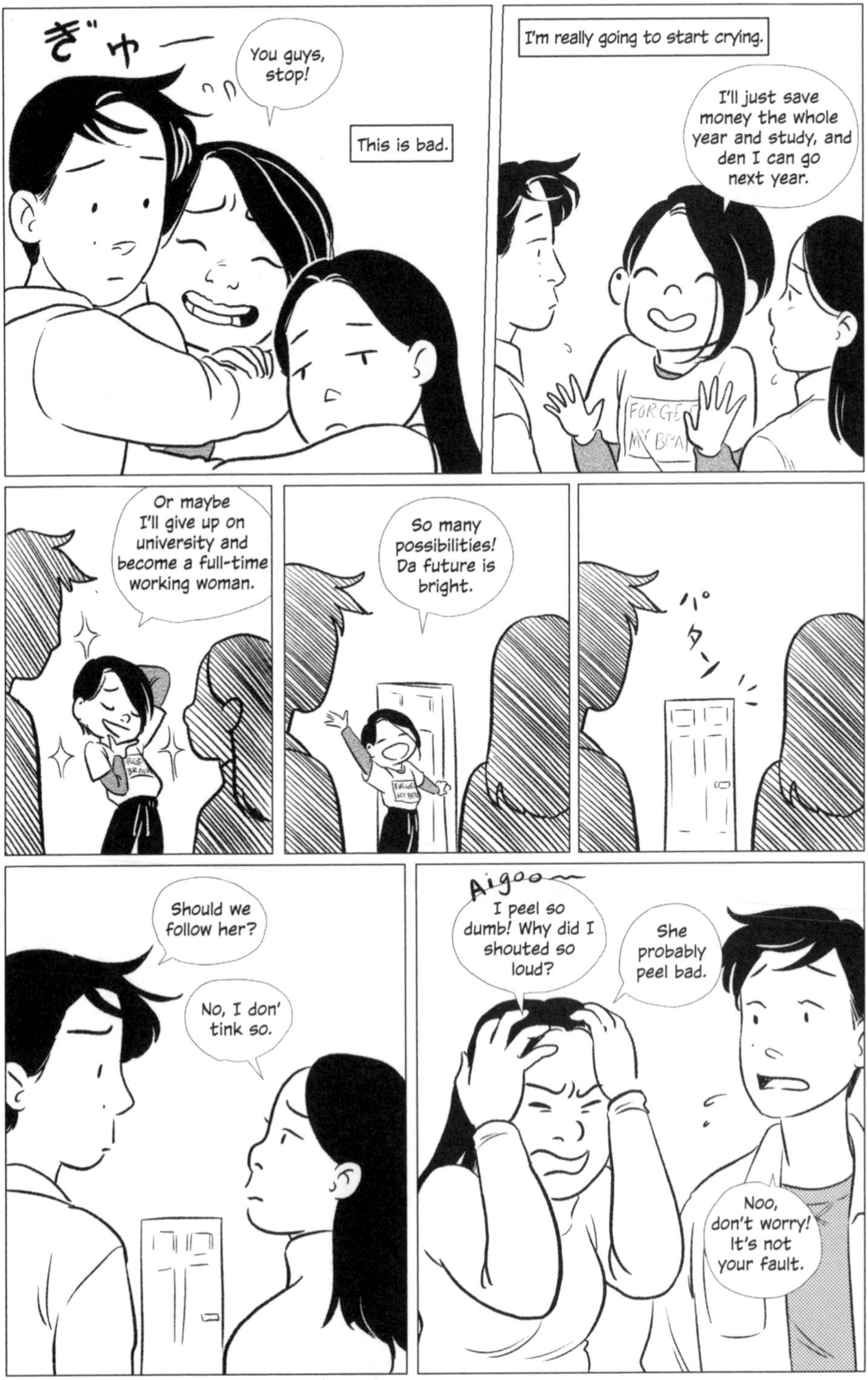

ぎゅー
You guys, stop!
This is bad.
I'm really going to start crying.
I'll just save money the whole year and study, and den I can go next year.
FORGET MY BRA
Or maybe I'll give up on university and become a full-time working woman.
So many possibilities! Da future is bright.
パターン
Should we follow her?
No, I don' tink so.
Aigoo~
I peel so dumb! Why did I shouted so loud?
She probably peel bad.
Noo, don't worry! It's not your fault.

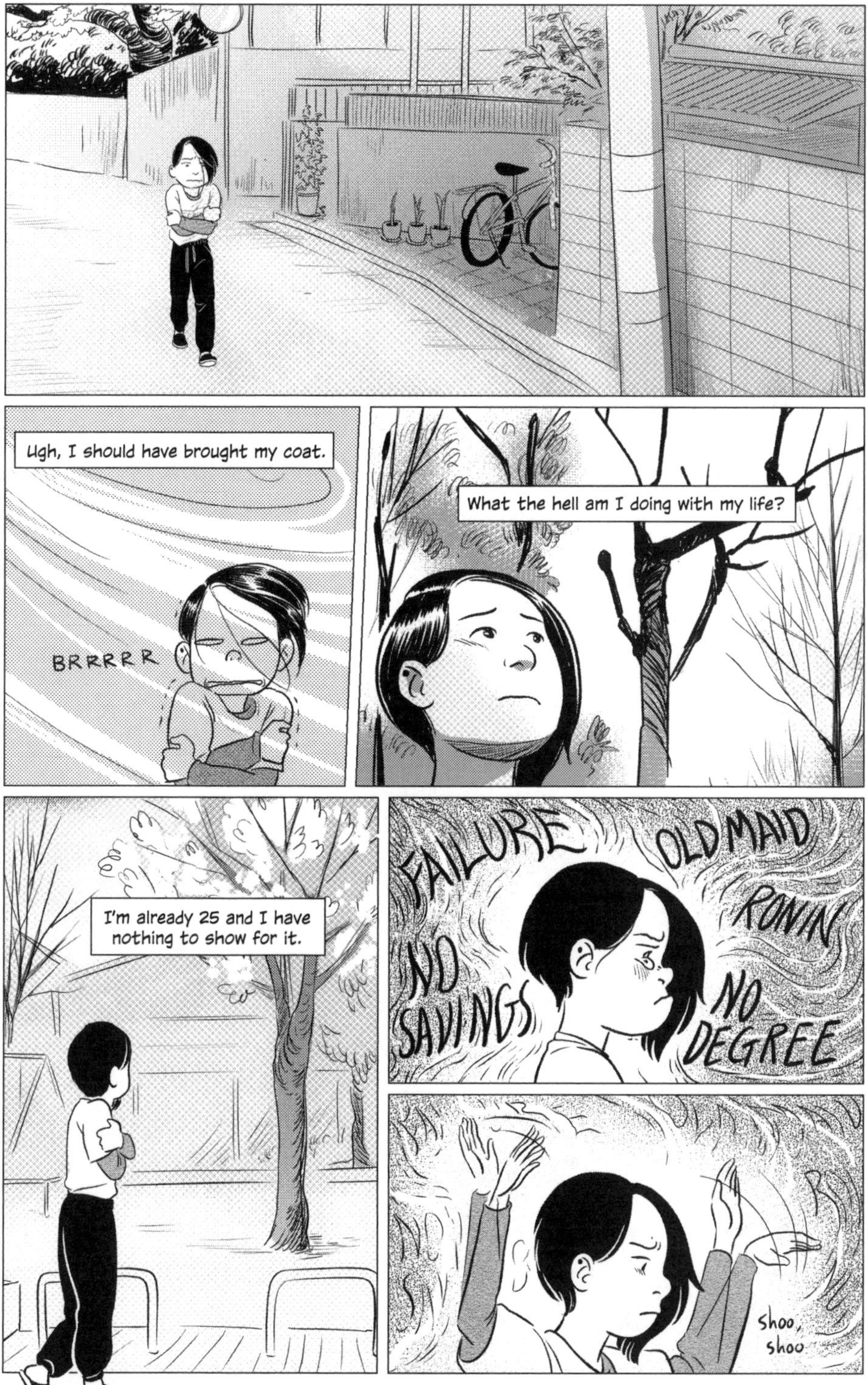
Ugh, I should have brought my coat.
BRRRRR
What the hell am I doing with my life?
I'm already 25 and I have nothing to show for it.
FAILURE
OLD MAID
RONIN
NO SAVINGS
NO DEGREE
Shoo, shoo

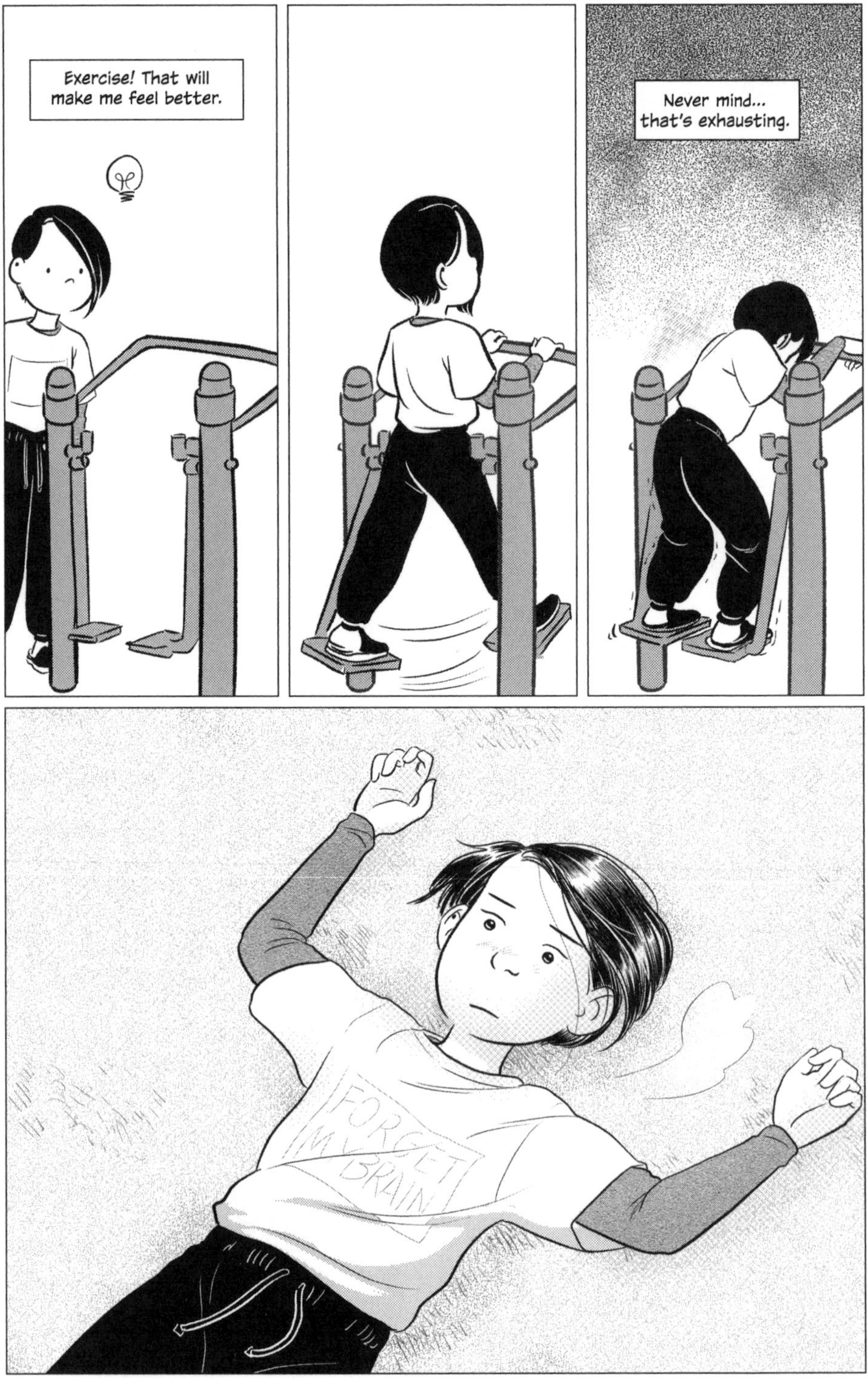
Exercise! That will make me feel better.
Never mind... that's exhausting.
FORGET MY BRAIN

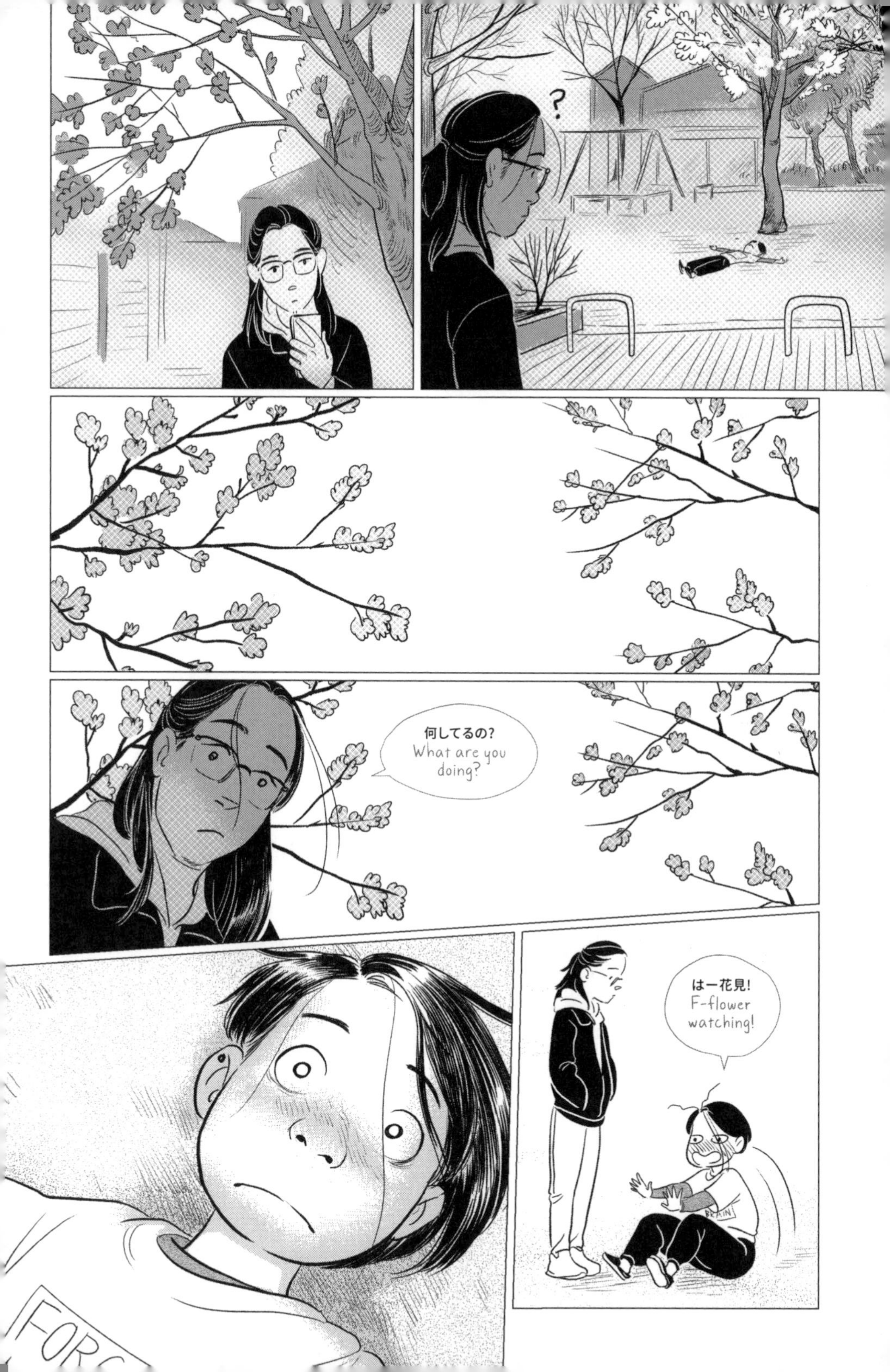
何してるの?
What are you doing?
はー花見!
F-flower watching!

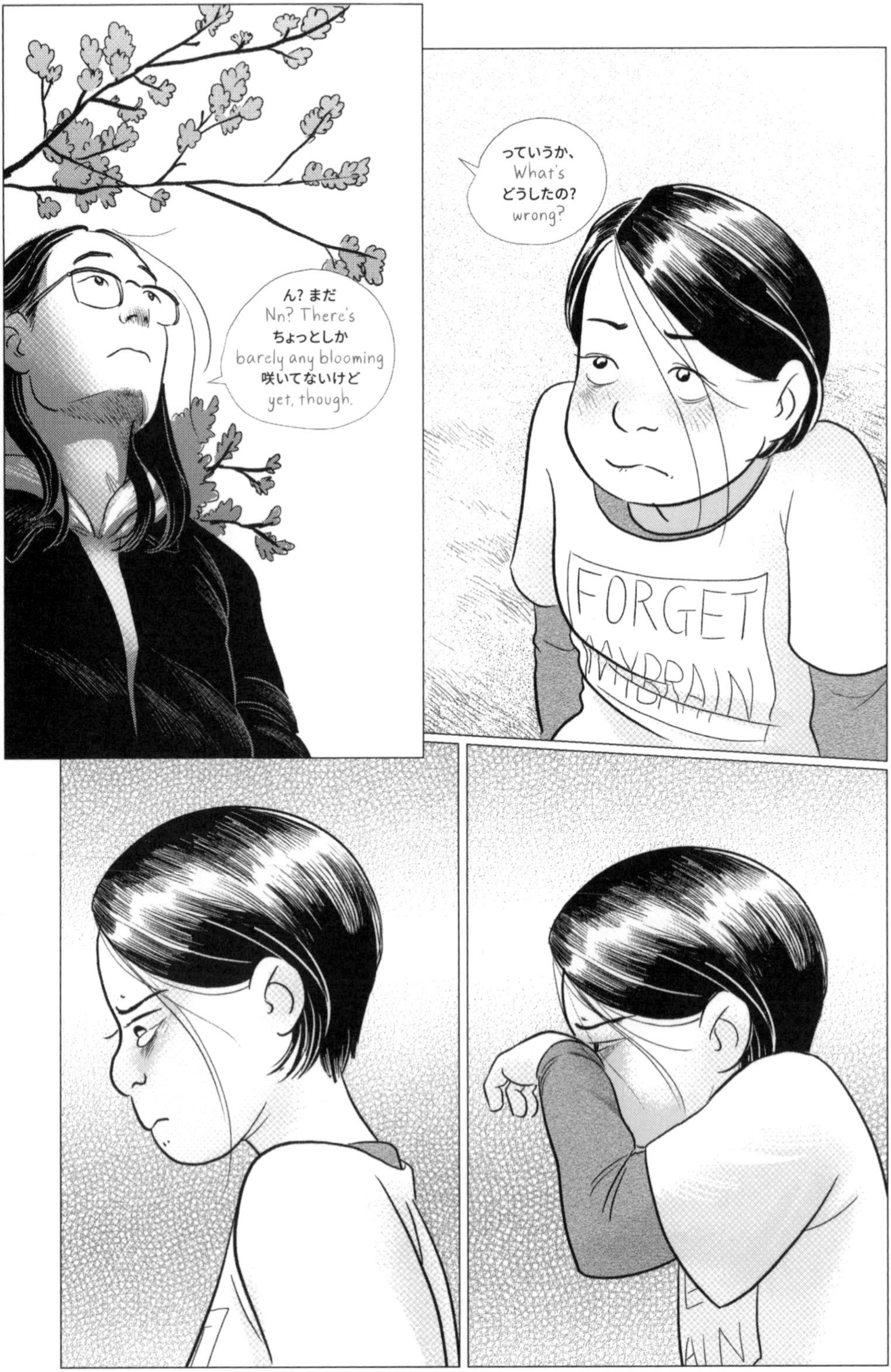
ん? まだ
Nn? There's
ちょっとしか
barely any blooming
咲いてないけど
yet, though.
っていうか、
What's
どうしたの?
wrong?
FORGET MYBRAIN

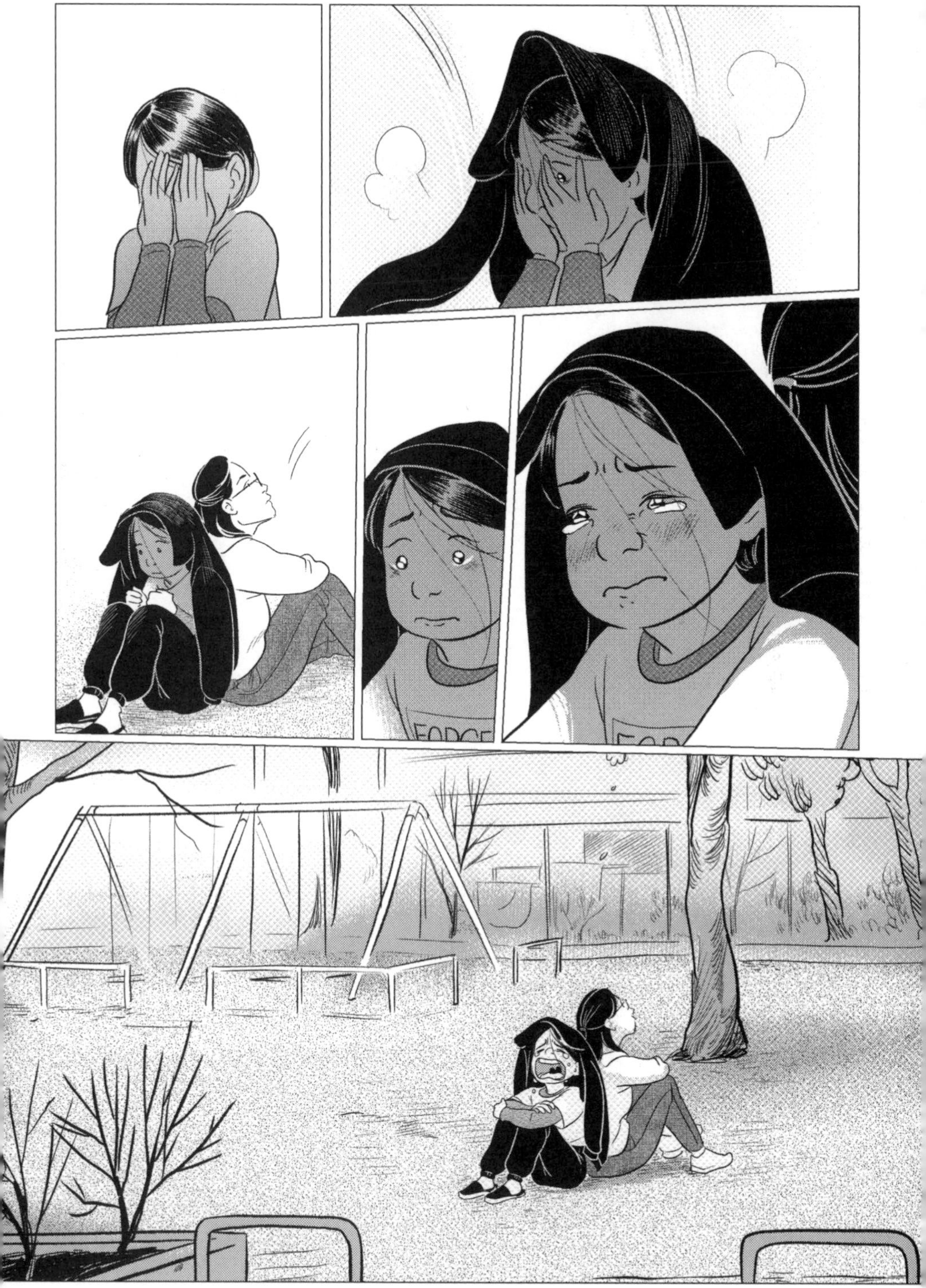

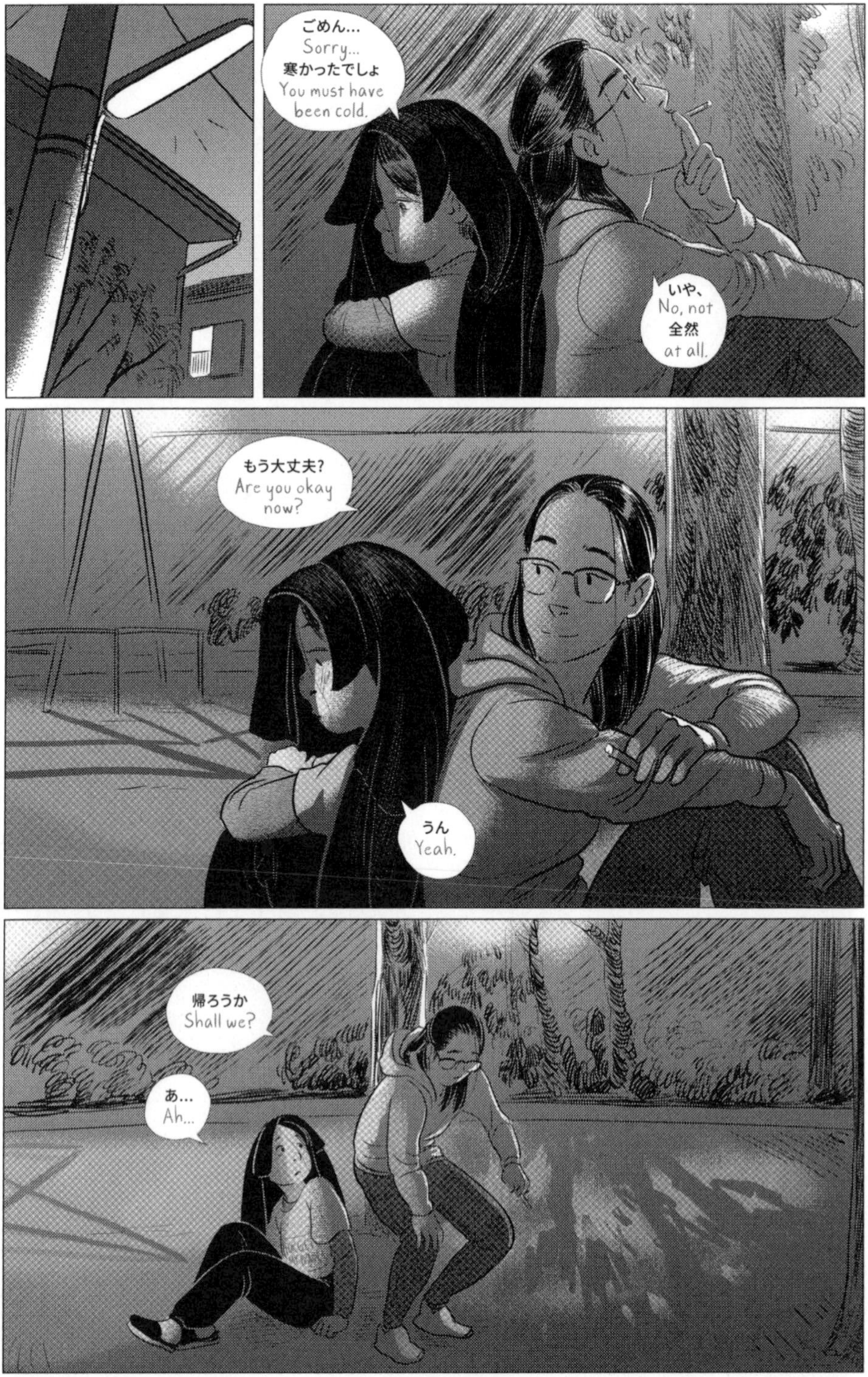
ごめん…
Sorry...
寒かったでしょ
You must have been cold.
いや、
No, not
全然
at all.
もう大丈夫?
Are you okay now?
うん
Yeah.
帰ろうか
Shall we?
あ…
Ah...

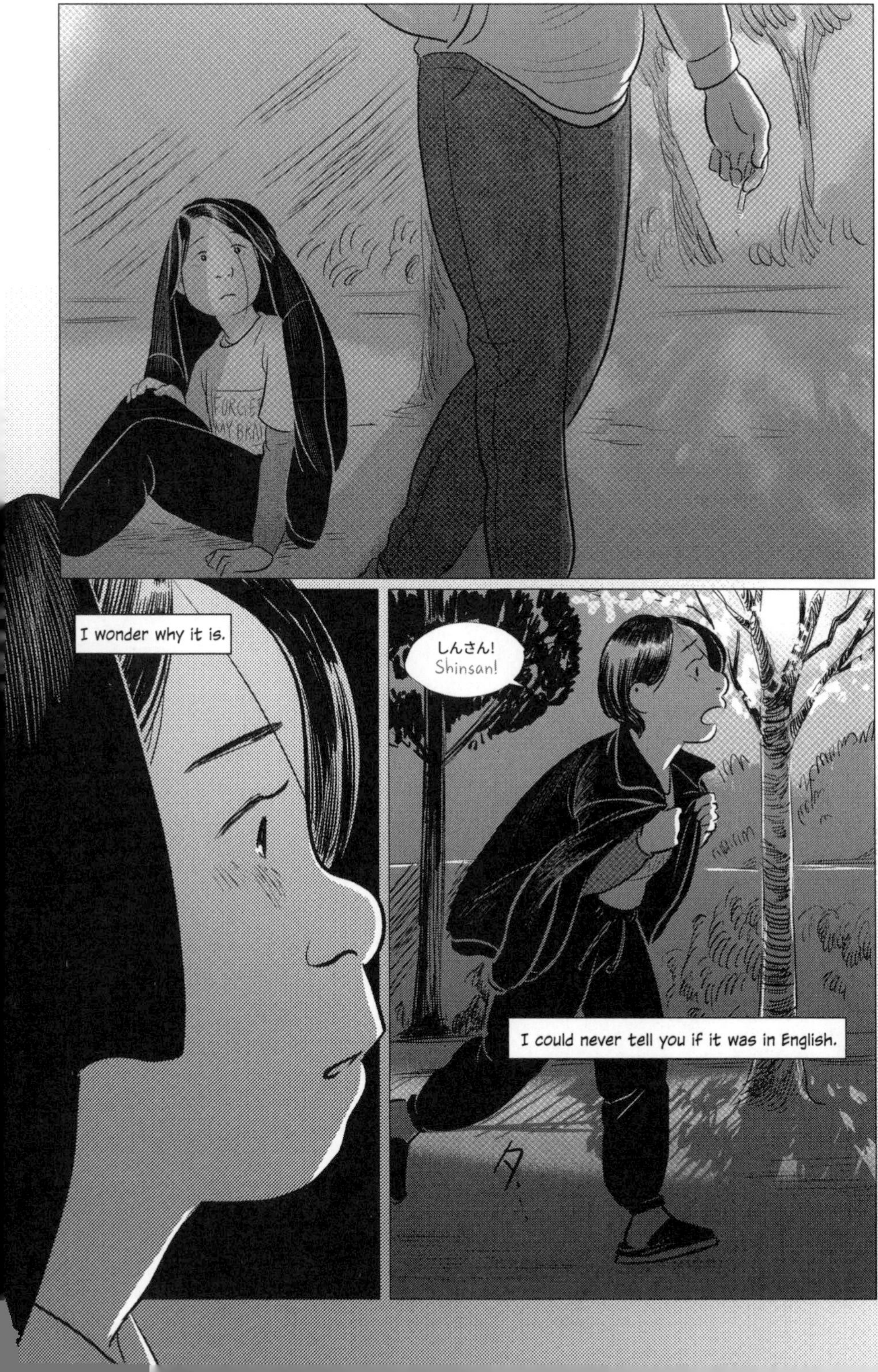
I wonder why it is.
しんさん!
Shinsan!
I could never tell you if it was in English.

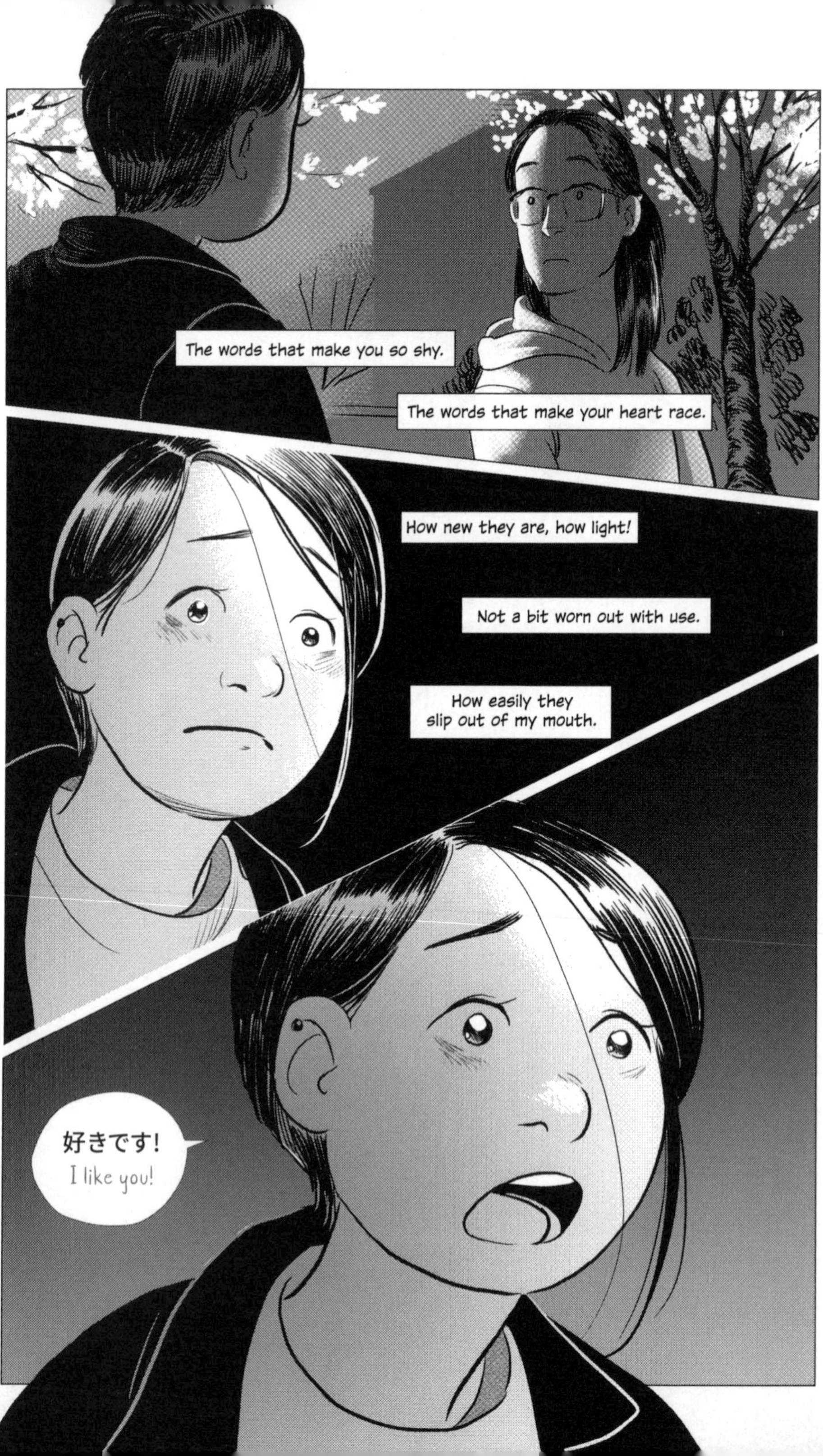
The words that make you so shy.
The words that make your heart race.
How new they are, how light!
Not a bit worn out with use.
How easily they slip out of my mouth.
好きです!
I like you!

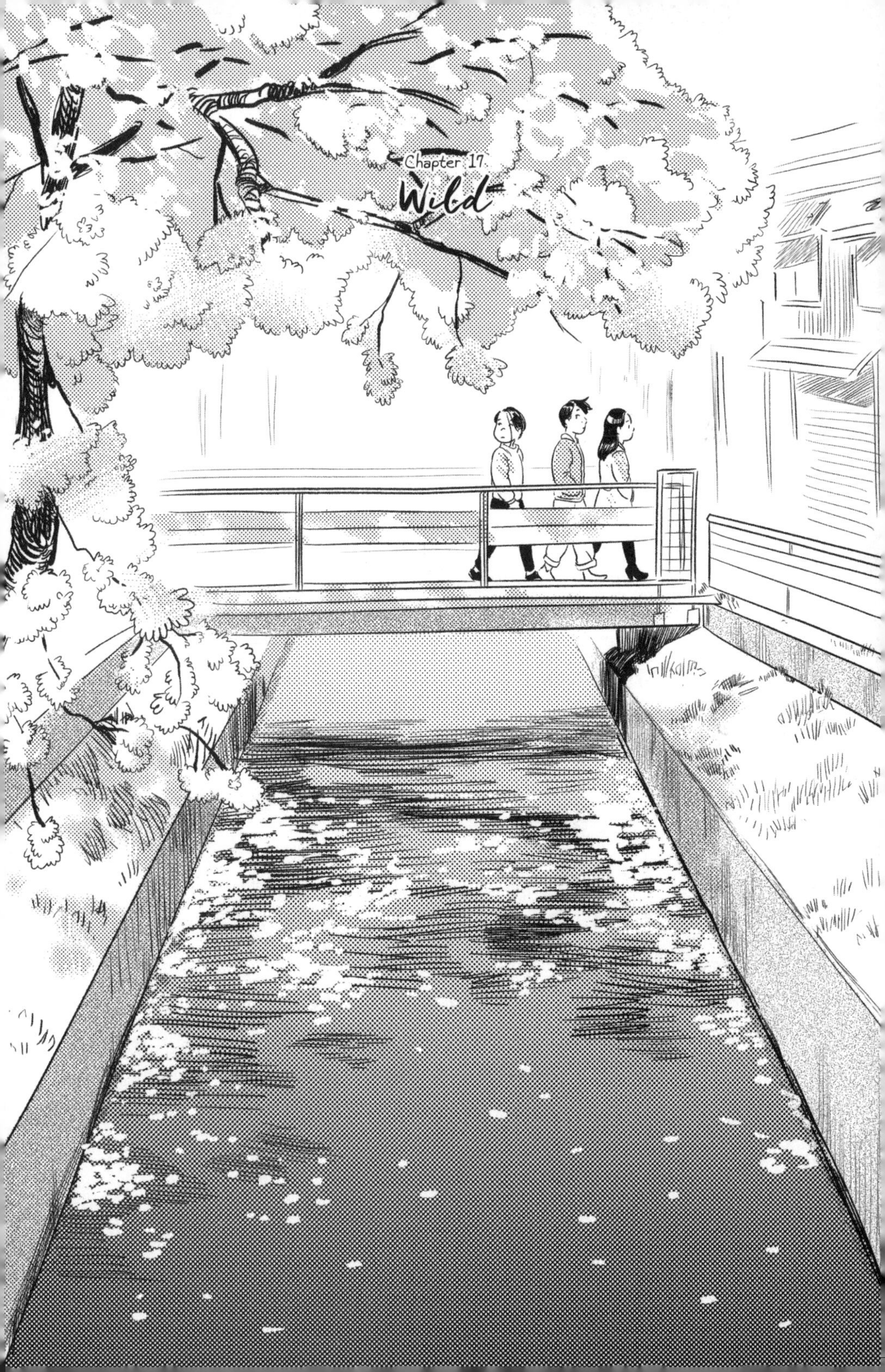
Chapter 17
Wild

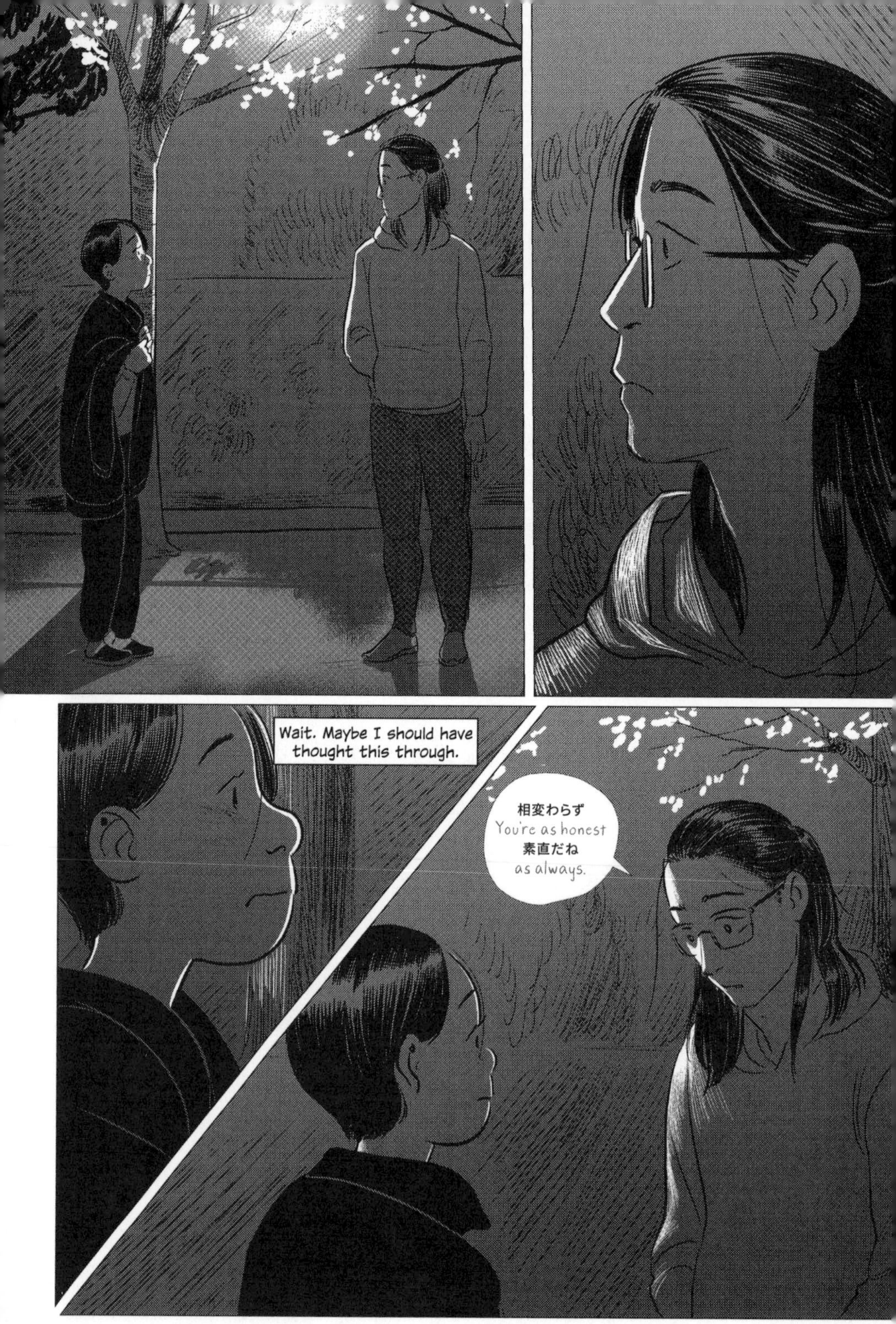
Wait. Maybe I should have thought this through.
相変わらず
You're as honest
素直だね
as always.

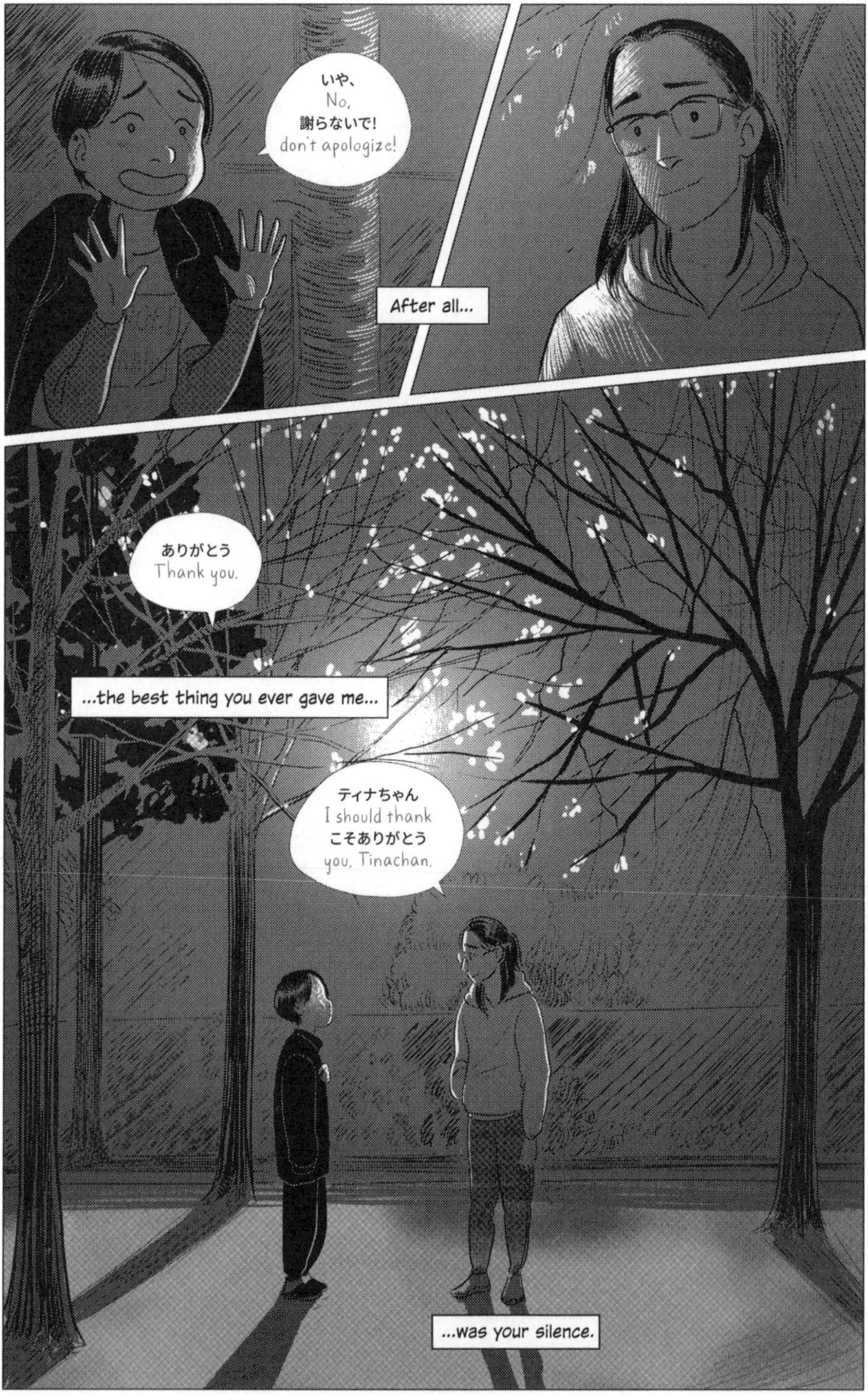
いや、
No,
謝らないで!
don't apologize!
After all...
ありがとう
Thank you.
...the best thing you ever gave me...
ティナちゃん
I should thank
こそありがとう
you, Tinachan.
...was your silence.

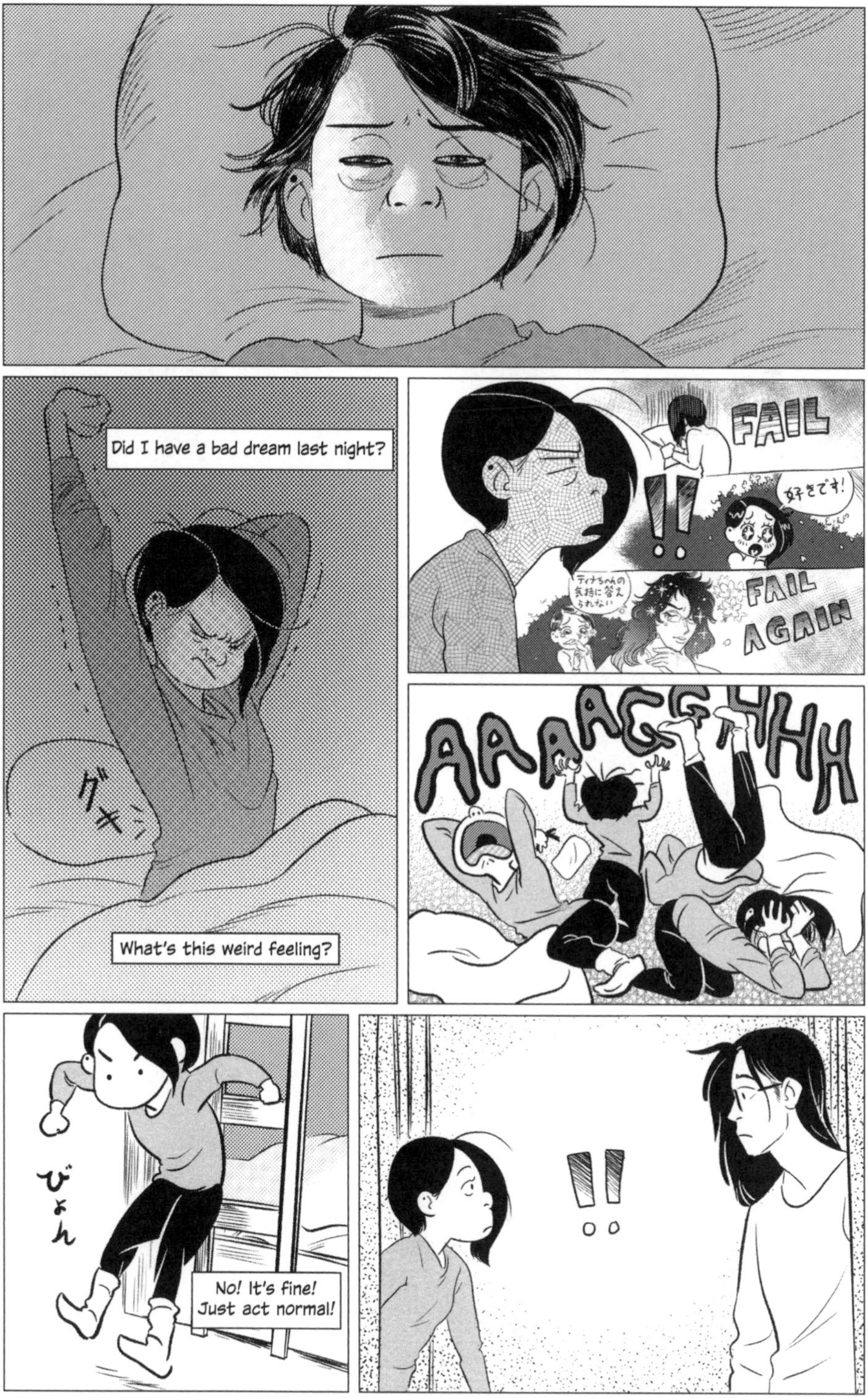

Did I have a bad dream last night?
グキ
What's this weird feeling?
FAIL
!!
好きです!
ティナちゃんの気持に答えられない
FAIL AGAIN
AAAAGGHHH
びょん
No! It's fine! Just act normal!
!!

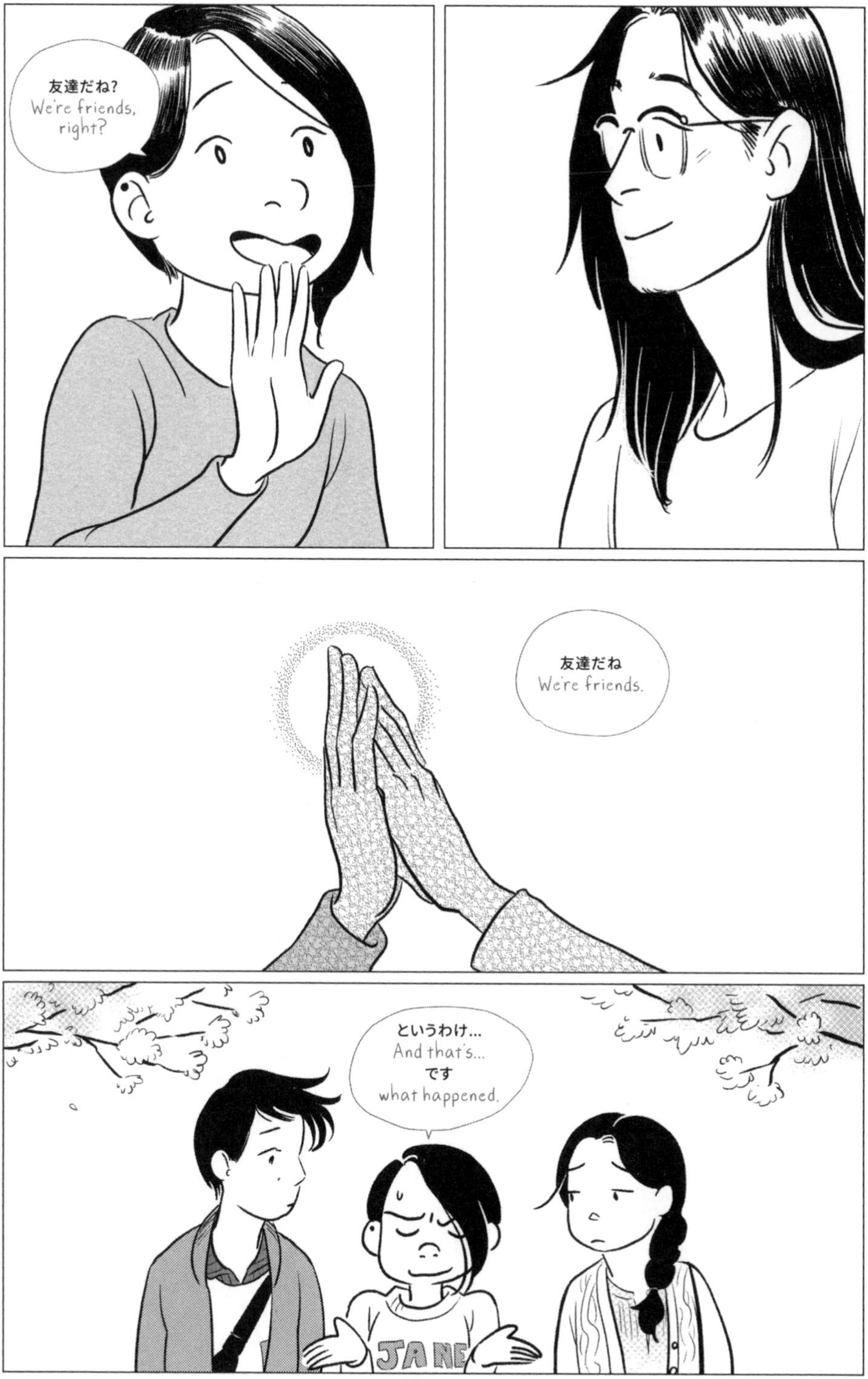
友達だね?
We're friends, right?
友達だね
We're friends.
というわけ...
And that's...
です
what happened.
JANE

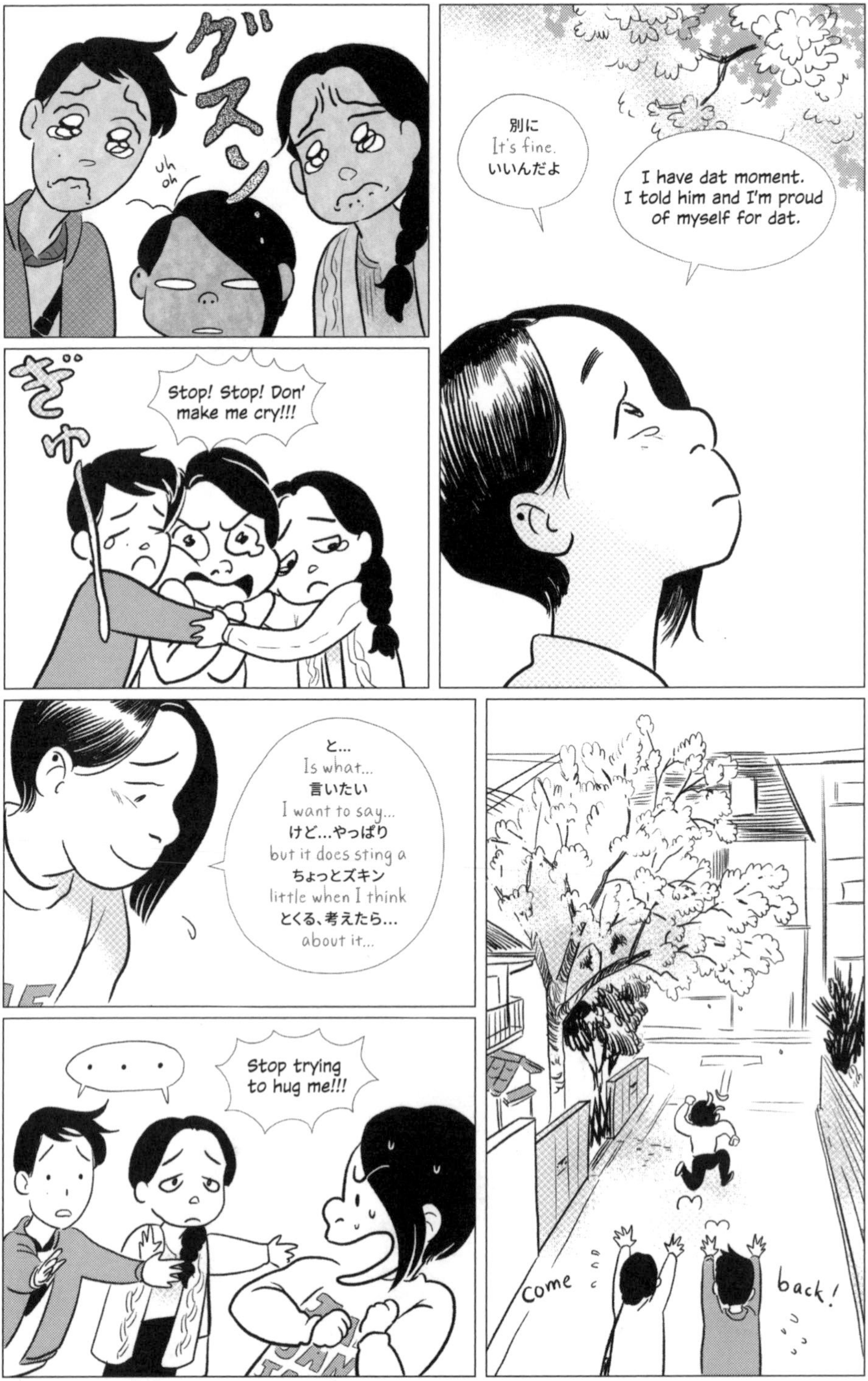

グスン
uh oh
ぎゅ
Stop! Stop! Don' make me cry!!!
別に It's fine. いいんだよ
I have dat moment. I told him and I'm proud of myself for dat.
と... Is what... 言いたい I want to say... けど...やっぱり but it does sting a ちょっとズキン little when I think とくる、考えたら... about it...
. . .
Stop trying to hug me!!!
come back!

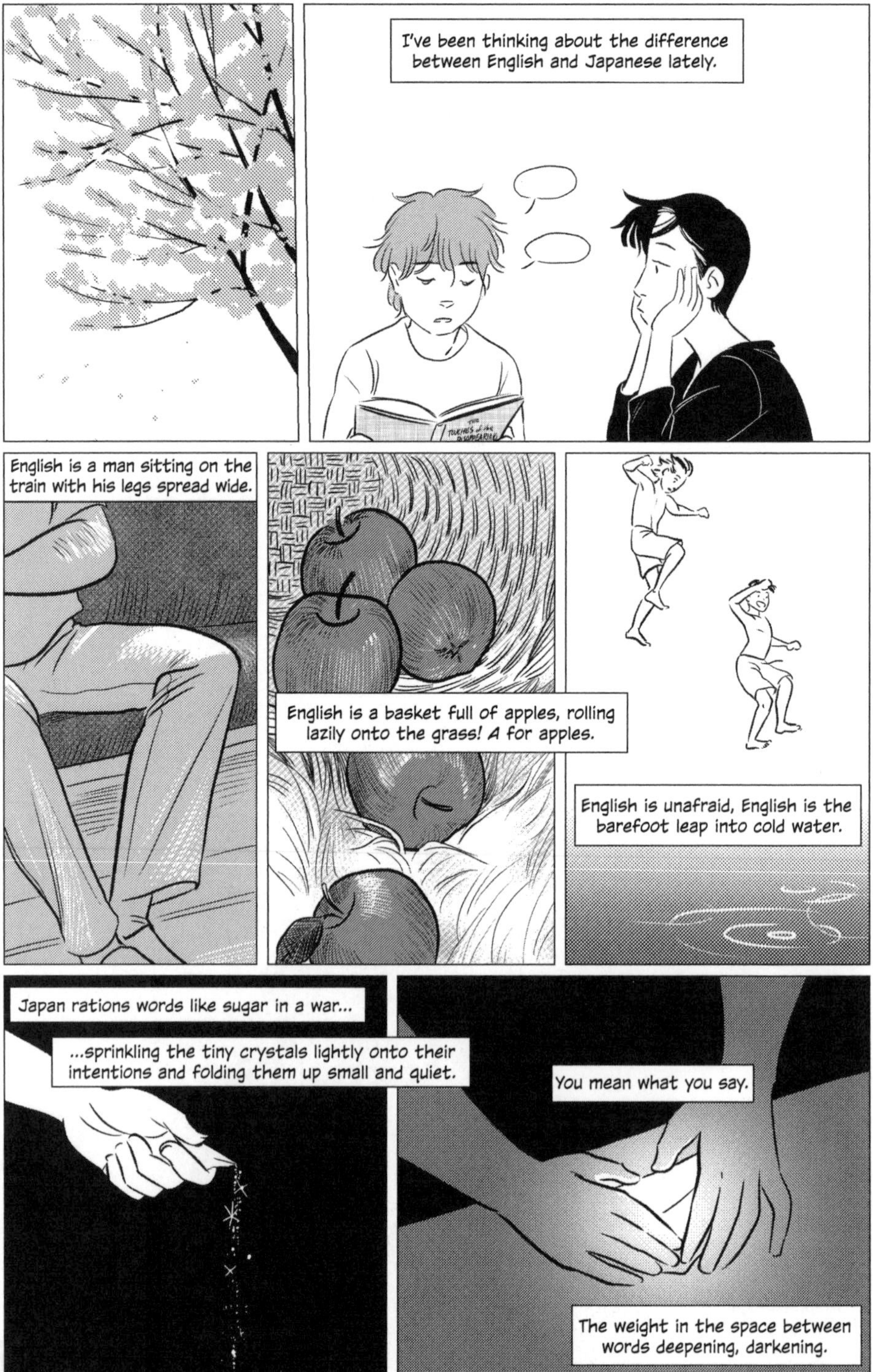
I've been thinking about the difference between English and Japanese lately.
English is a man sitting on the train with his legs spread wide.
English is a basket full of apples, rolling lazily onto the grass! A for apples.
English is unafraid, English is the barefoot leap into cold water.
Japan rations words like sugar in a war...
...sprinkling the tiny crystals lightly onto their intentions and folding them up small and quiet.
You mean what you say.
The weight in the space between words deepening, darkening.

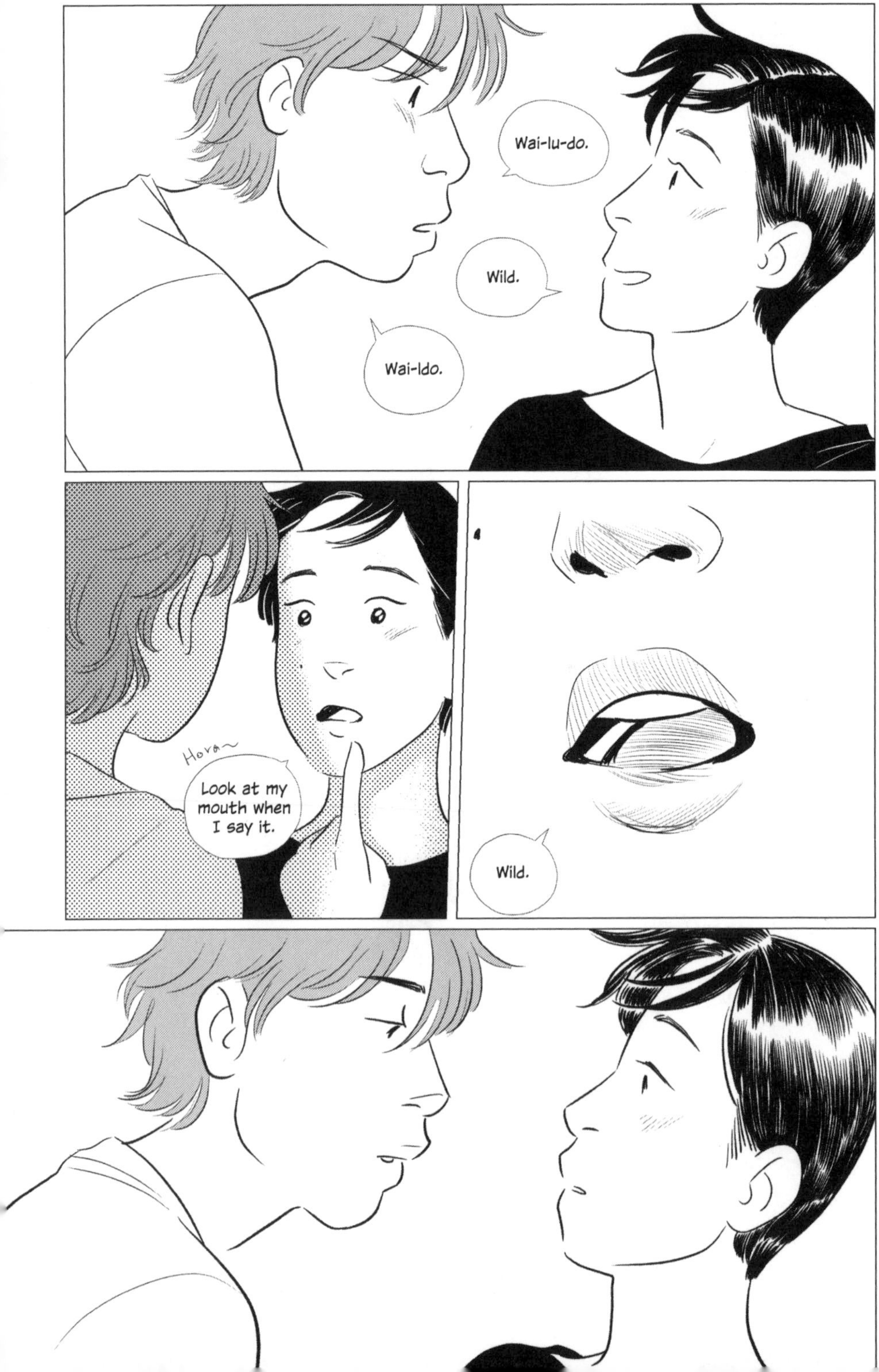
Wai-lu-do.
Wild.
Wai-ldo.
Hora~
Look at my mouth when I say it.
Wild.

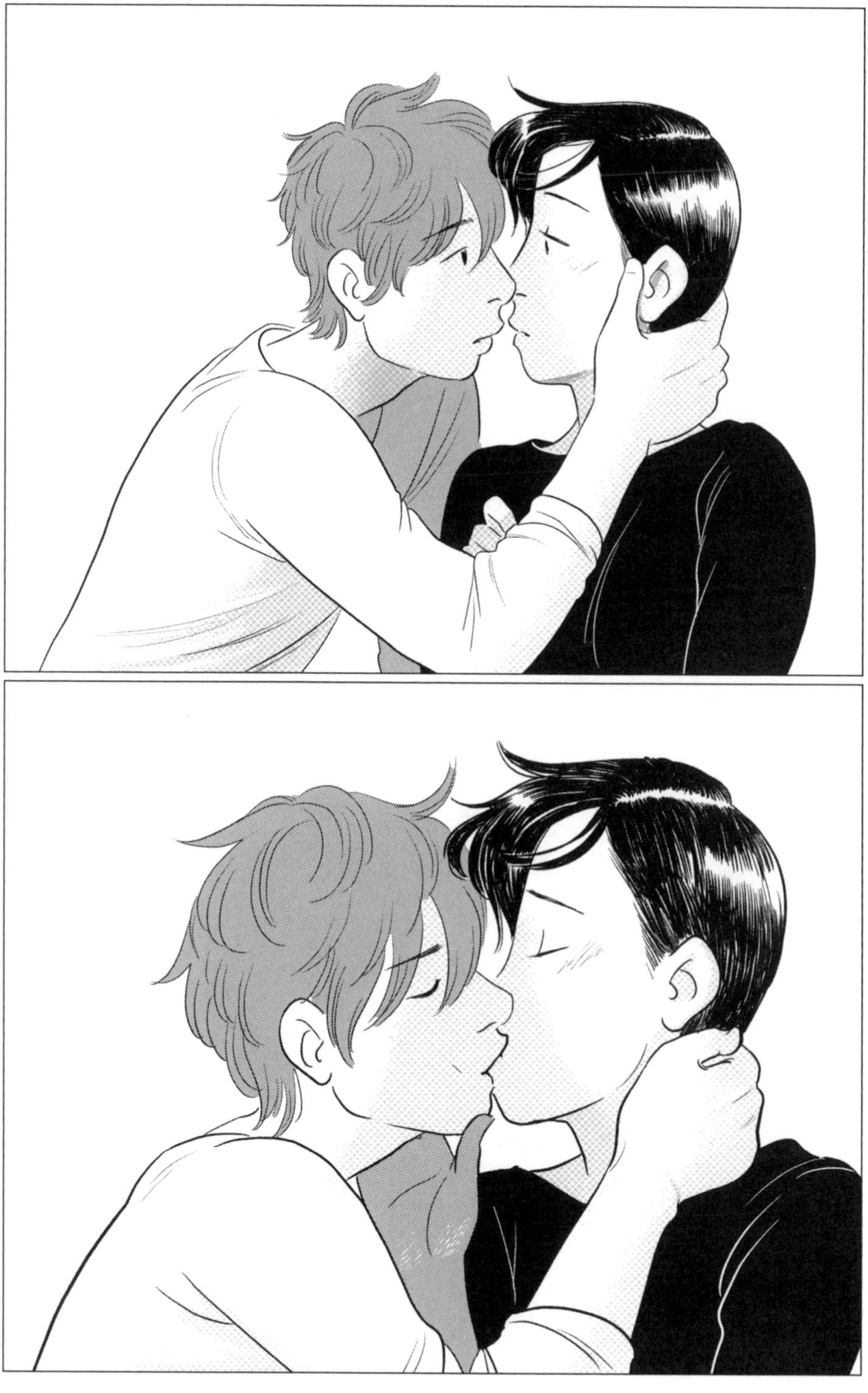

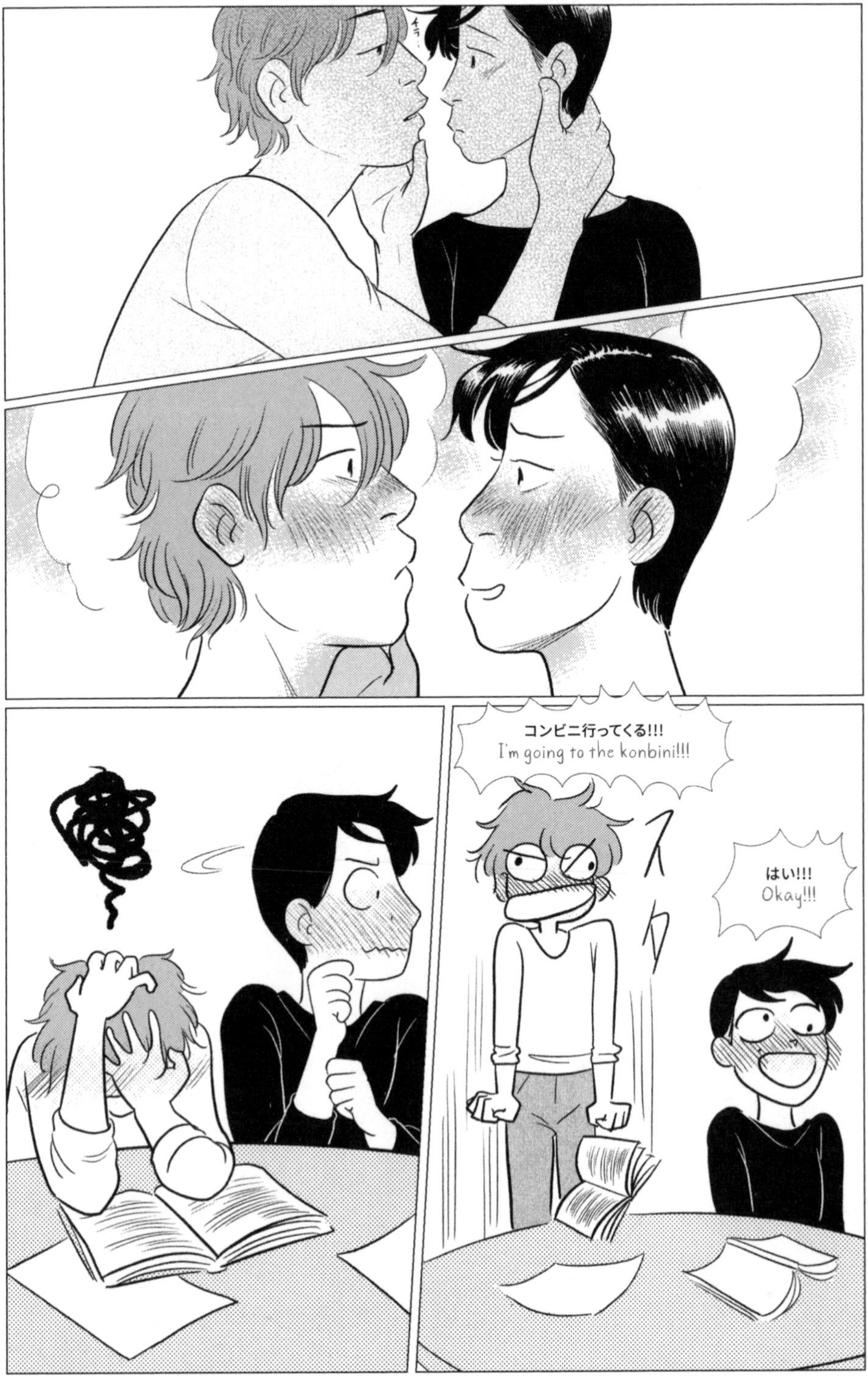
コンビニ行ってくる!!!
I'm going to the konbini!!!
はい!!!
Okay!!!

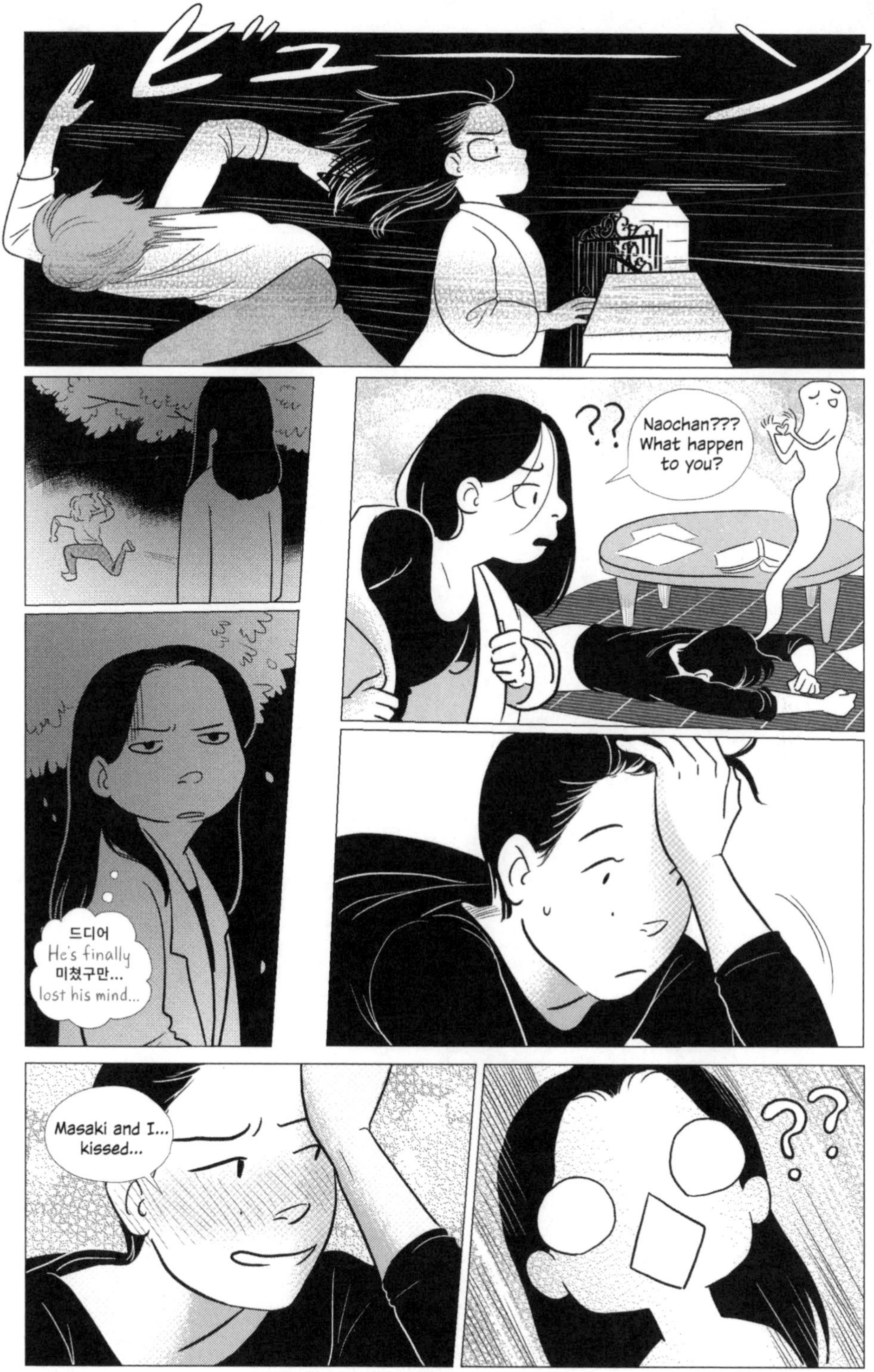
ビュ——ン
??
Naochan???
What happen
to you?
드디어
He's finally
미쳤구만...
lost his mind...
Masaki and I...
kissed...
??

Chapter 18

Hanami

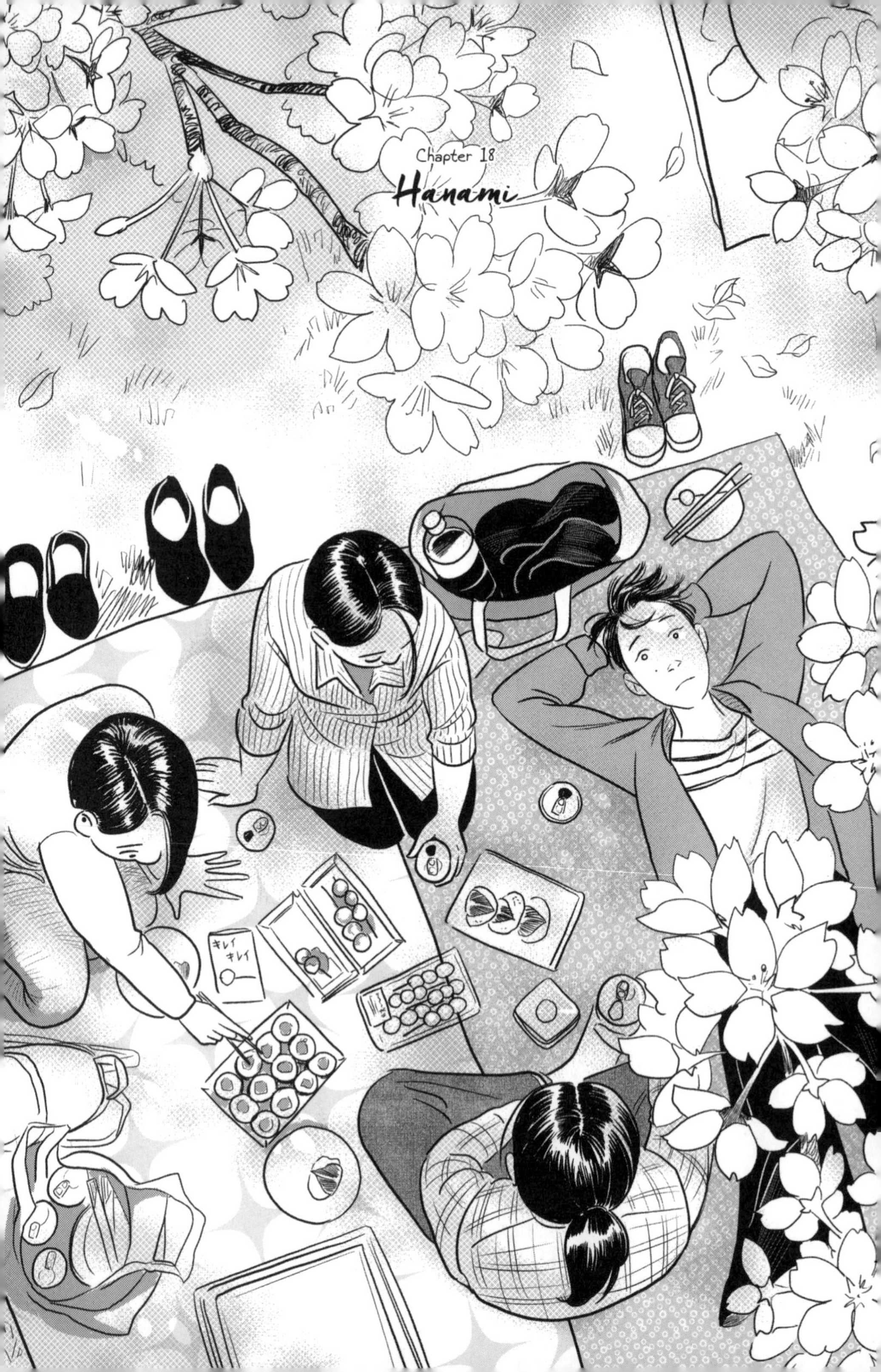
キレイ
キレイ

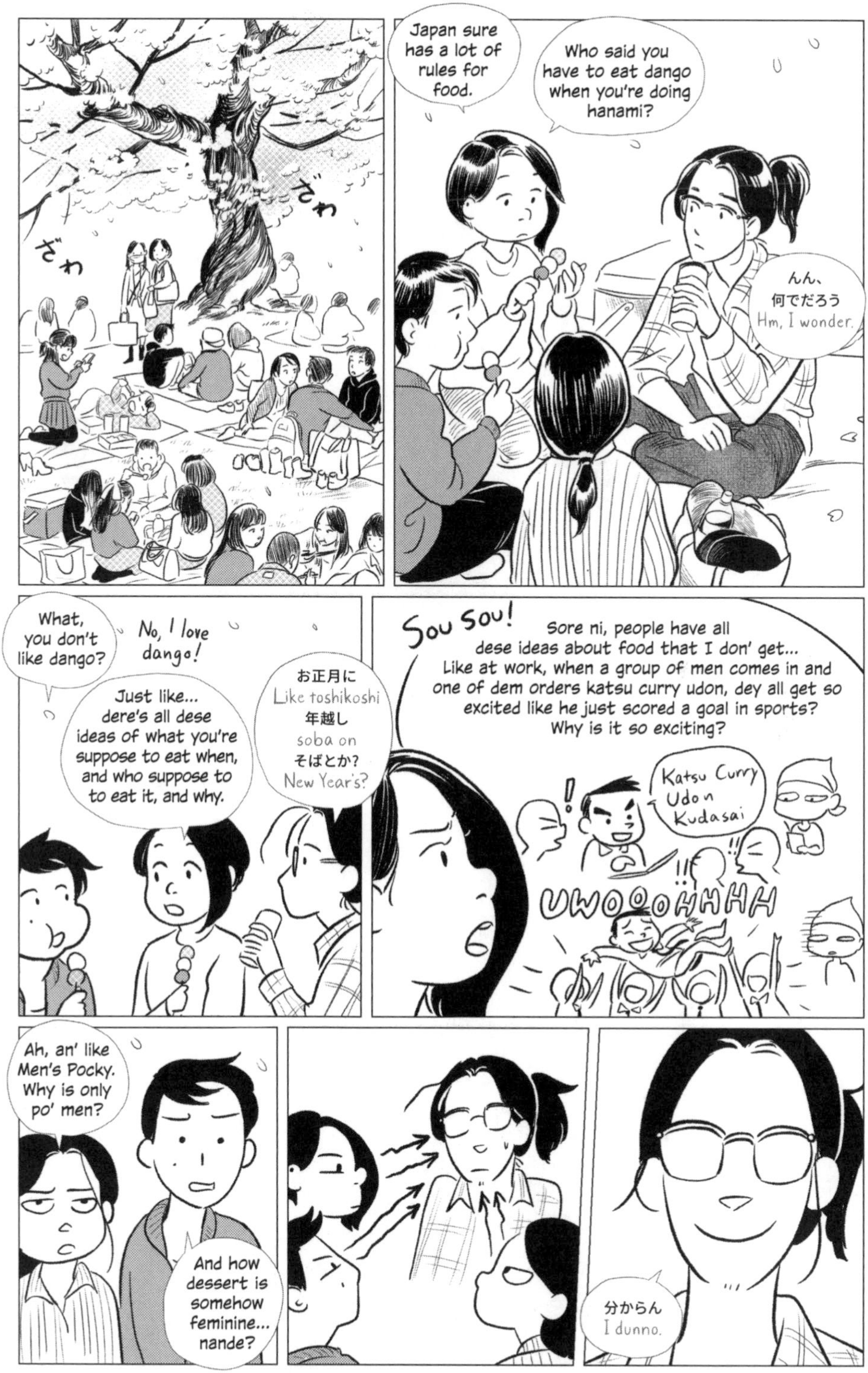
ざわ
ざわ
Japan sure has a lot of rules for food.
Who said you have to eat dango when you're doing hanami?
んん、何でだろう Hm, I wonder.
What, you don't like dango?
No, I love dango!
Just like... dere's all dese ideas of what you're suppose to eat when, and who suppose to to eat it, and why.
お正月に Like toshikoshi 年越し soba on そばとか? New Year's?
Sou Sou!
Sore ni, people have all dese ideas about food that I don' get... Like at work, when a group of men comes in and one of dem orders katsu curry udon, dey all get so excited like he just scored a goal in sports? Why is it so exciting?
Katsu Curry Udon Kudasai
UWOOOOHHHH
Ah, an' like Men's Pocky. Why is only po' men?
And how dessert is somehow feminine... nande?
分からん I dunno.

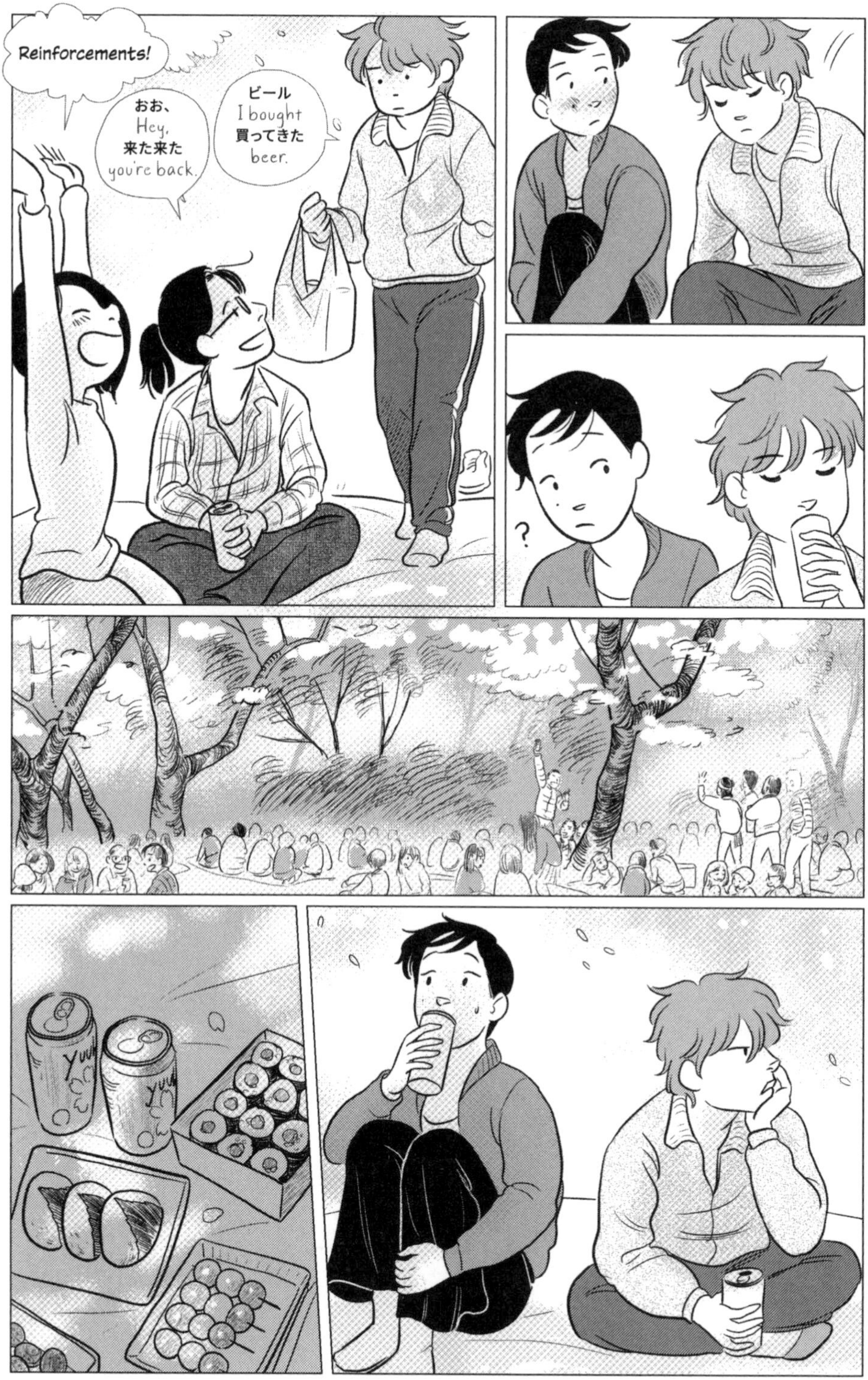
Reinforcements!
おお、Hey, 来た来た you're back.
ビール I bought 買ってきた beer.
?

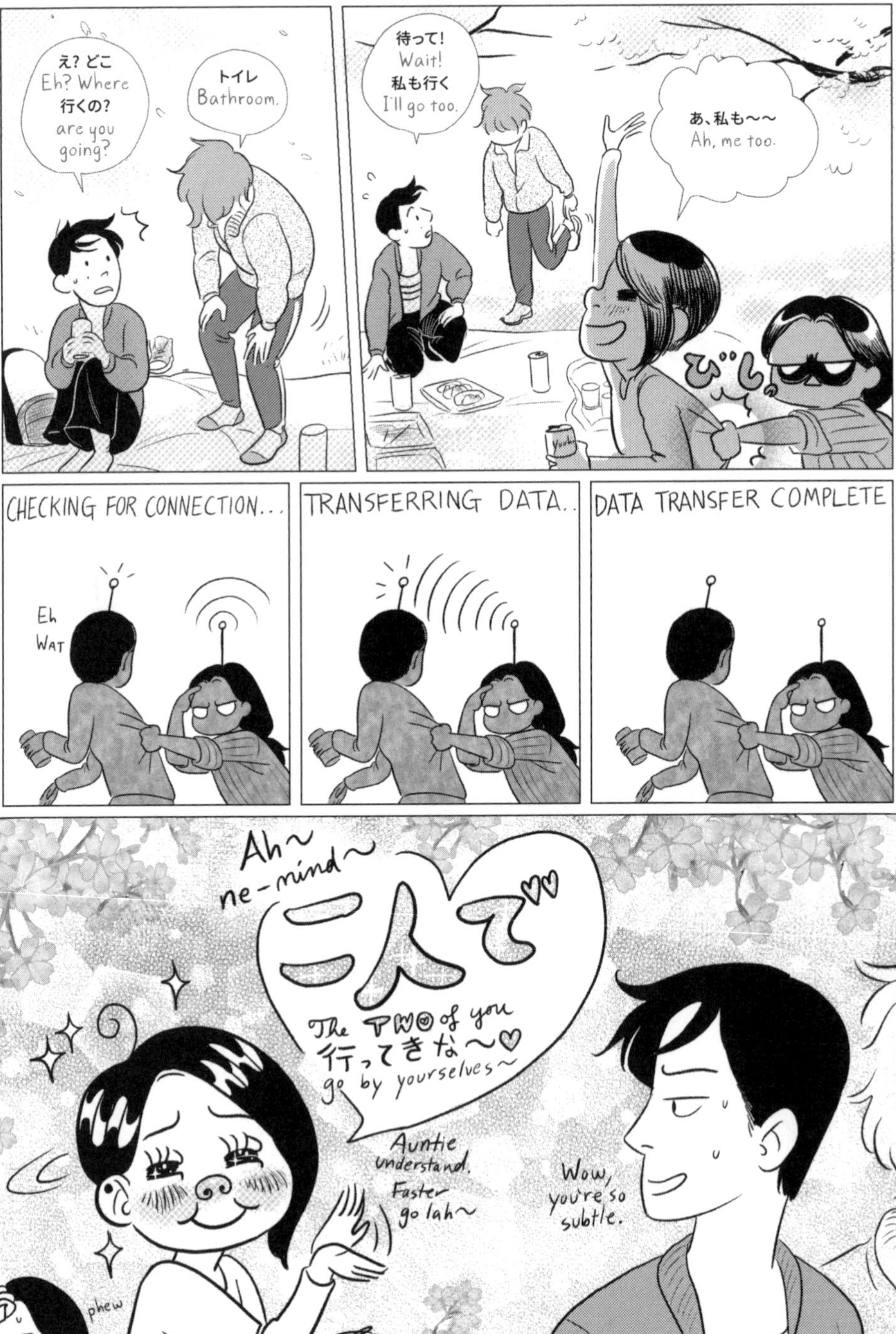

え? どこ
Eh? Where
行くの?
are you
going?
トイレ
Bathroom.
待って!
Wait!
私も行く
I'll go too.
あ、私も～～
Ah, me too.
CHECKING FOR CONNECTION...
Eh
WAT
TRANSFERRING DATA...
DATA TRANSFER COMPLETE
Ah~
ne-mind~
二人で
The TWO of you
行ってきな～
go by yourselves~
Auntie
understand.
Faster
go lah~
Wow,
you're so
subtle.
phew
Yuuhi

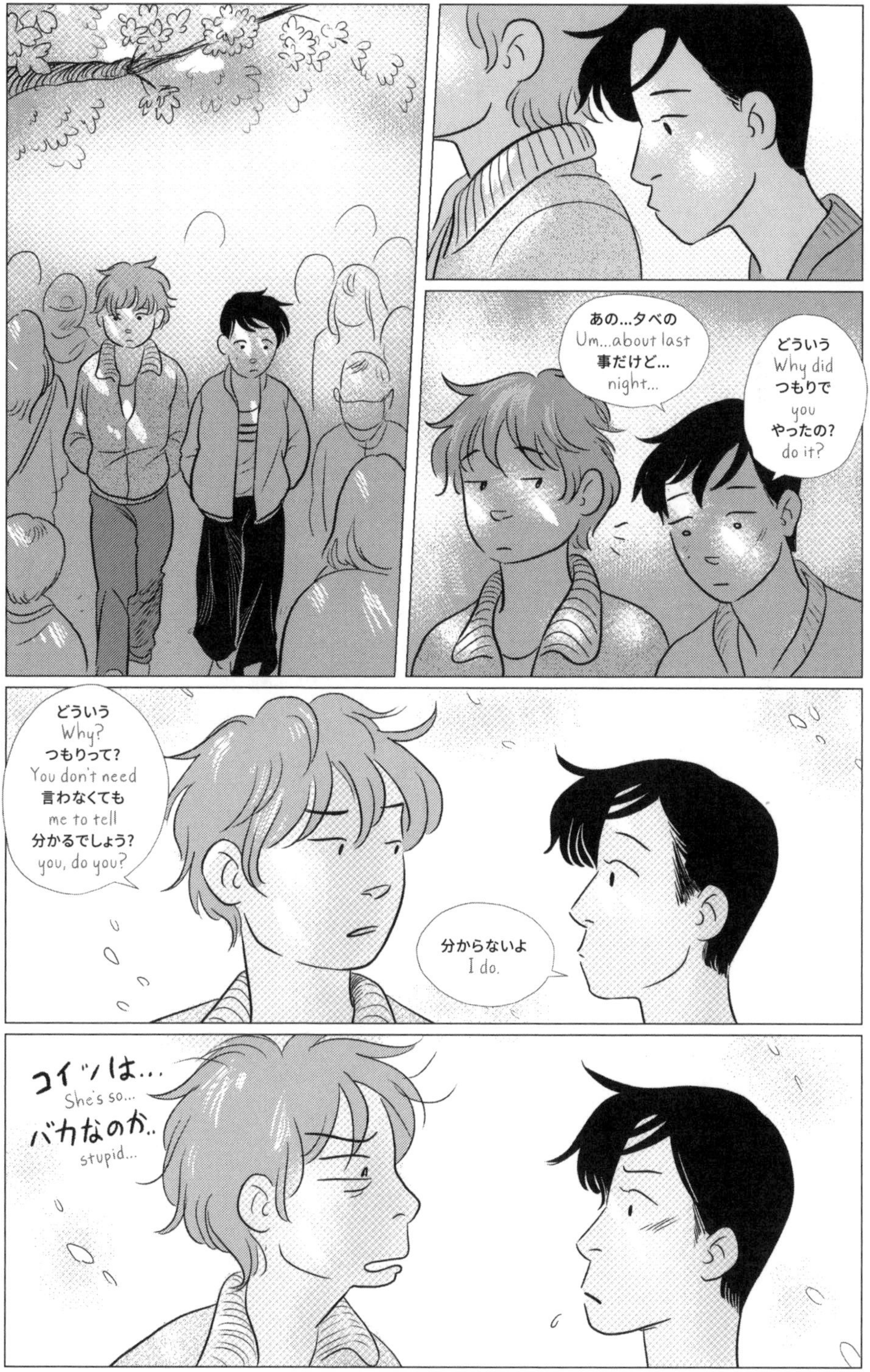
あの…夕べの
Um...about last
事だけど…
night...
どういう
Why did
つもりで
you
やったの?
do it?
どういう
Why?
つもりって?
You don't need
言わなくても
me to tell
分かるでしょう?
you, do you?
分からないよ
I do.
コイツは…
She's so...
バカなのか..
stupid...

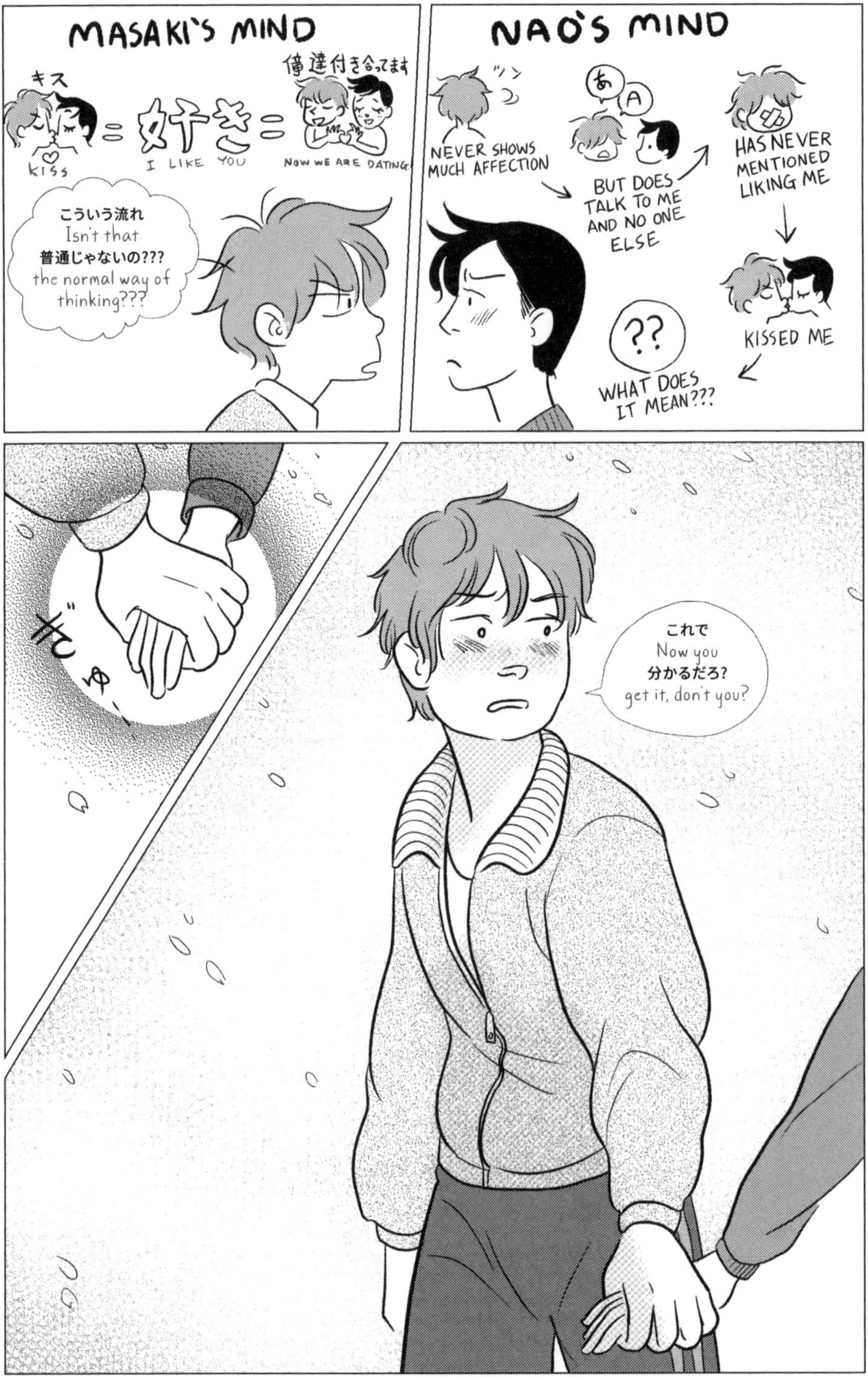
MASAKI'S MIND
キス
KISS
好き
I LIKE YOU
俺達付き合ってます
NOW WE ARE DATING!
こういう流れ
Isn't that
普通じゃないの???
the normal way of thinking???
NAO'S MIND
ツン
NEVER SHOWS MUCH AFFECTION
あ
A
BUT DOES TALK TO ME AND NO ONE ELSE
HAS NEVER MENTIONED LIKING ME
KISSED ME
??
WHAT DOES IT MEAN???
ぎゅ
これで
Now you
分かるだろ?
get it, don't you?

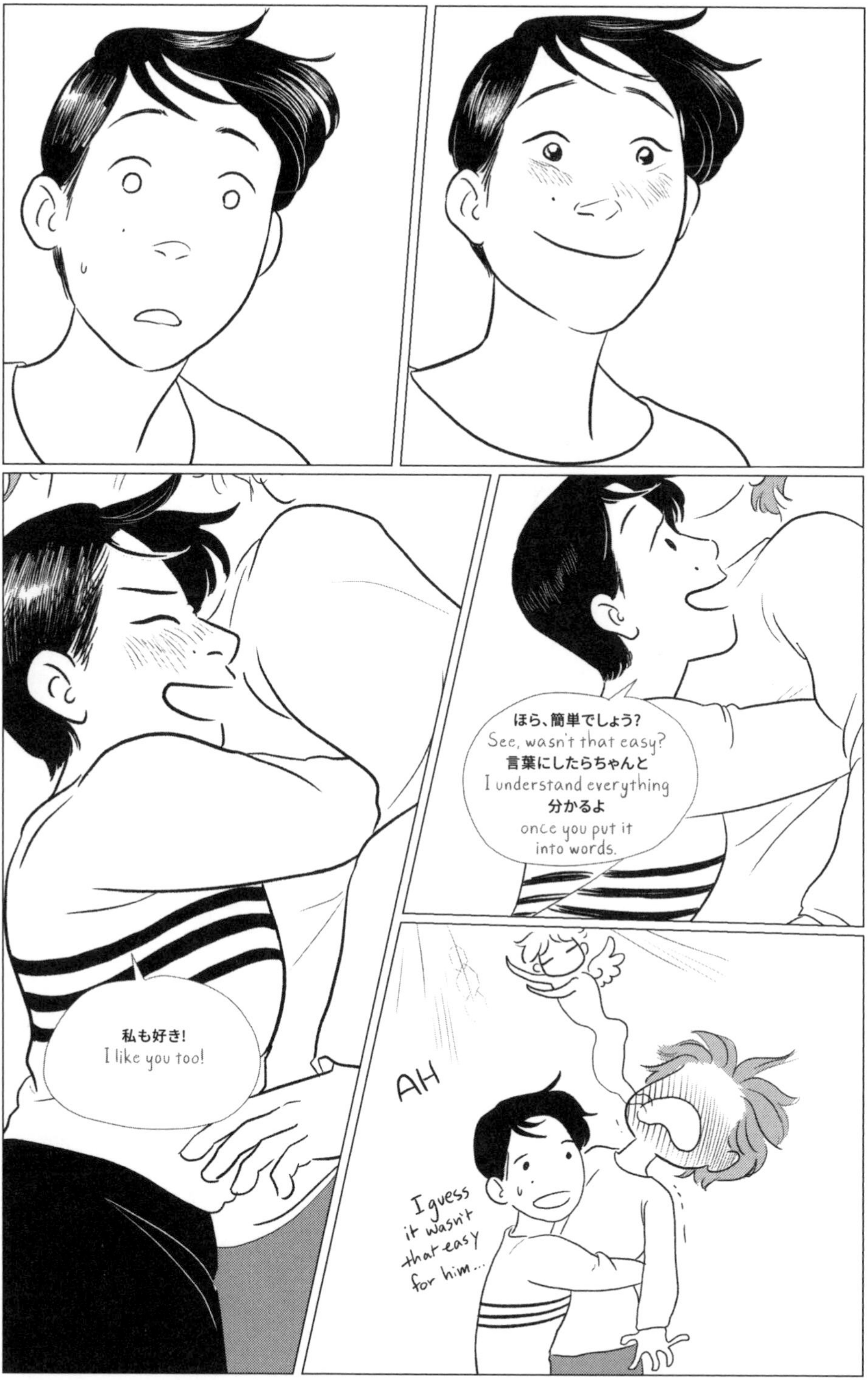
私も好き!
I like you too!
ほら、簡単でしょう?
See, wasn't that easy?
言葉にしたらちゃんと
I understand everything
分かるよ
once you put it into words.
AH
I guess it wasn't that easy for him...

Chapter 19

Omma

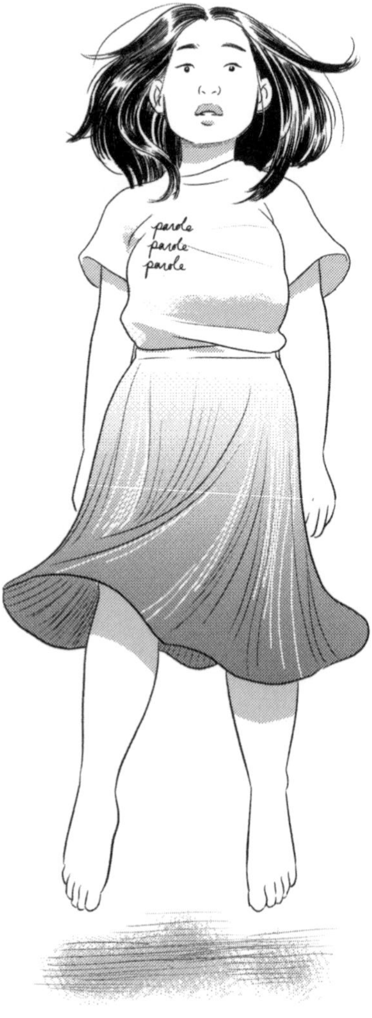
parole
parole
parole

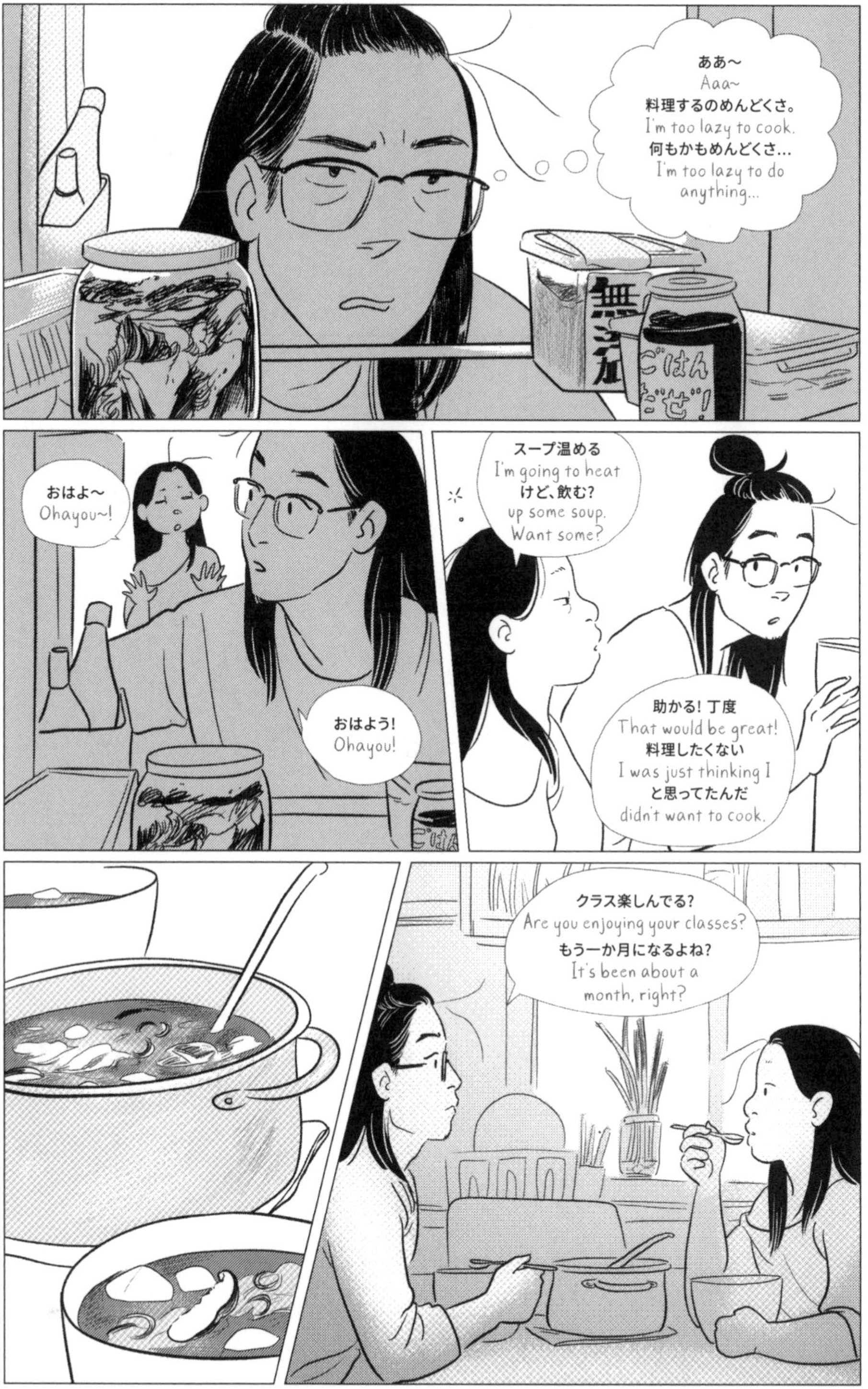

ああ～
Aaa~
料理するのめんどくさ。
I'm too lazy to cook.
何もかもめんどくさ…
I'm too lazy to do anything...
ごはんですよ!
おはよ～
Ohayou~!
おはよう!
Ohayou!
スープ温める
I'm going to heat
けど、飲む?
up some soup. Want some?
助かる! 丁度
That would be great!
料理したくない
I was just thinking I
と思ってたんだ
didn't want to cook.
クラス楽しんでる?
Are you enjoying your classes?
もう一か月になるよね?
It's been about a month, right?

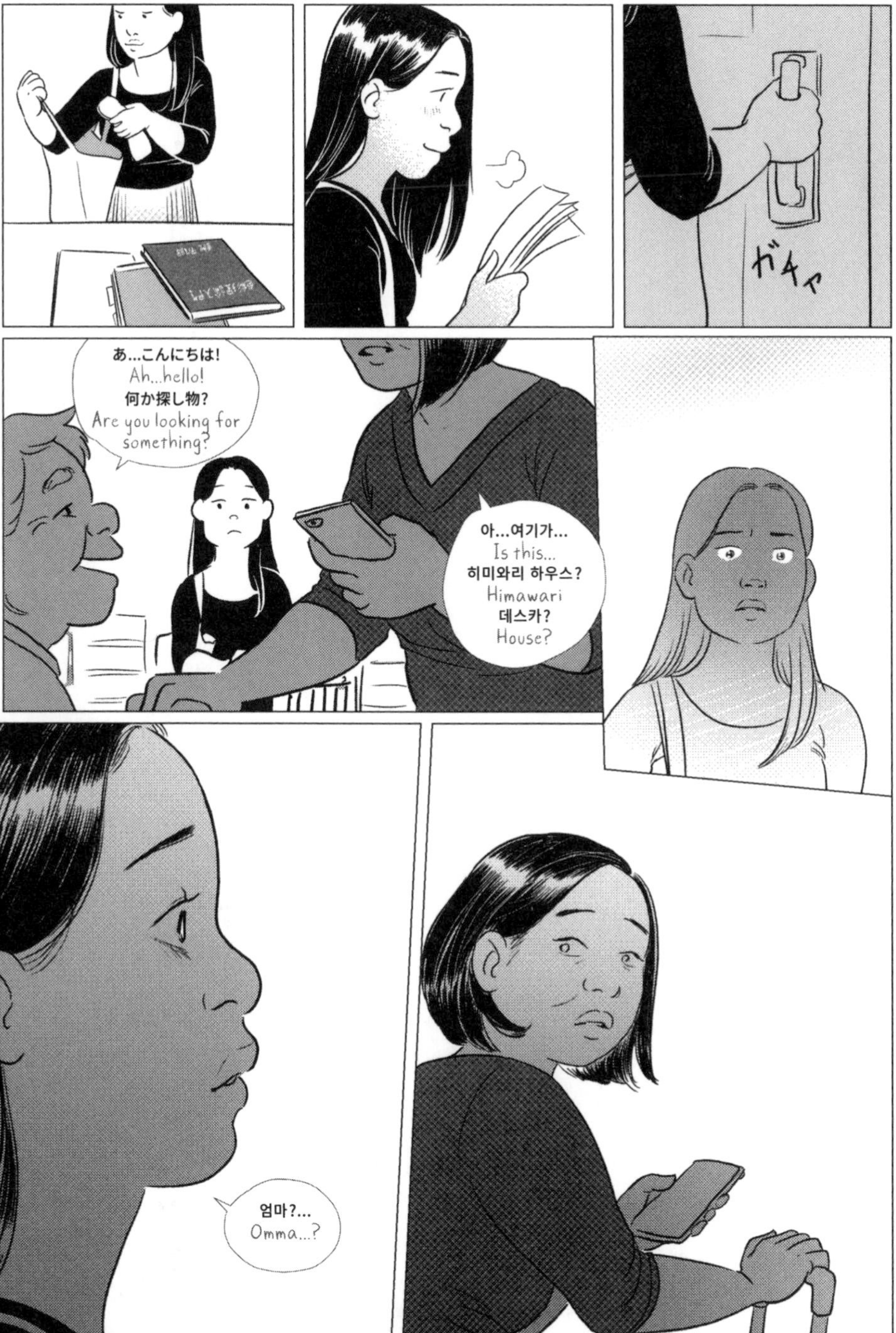
ガチャ
あ…こんにちは!
Ah...hello!
何か探し物?
Are you looking for something?
아…여기가…
Is this…
히미와리 하우스?
Himawari
데스카?
House?
엄마?…
Omma…?

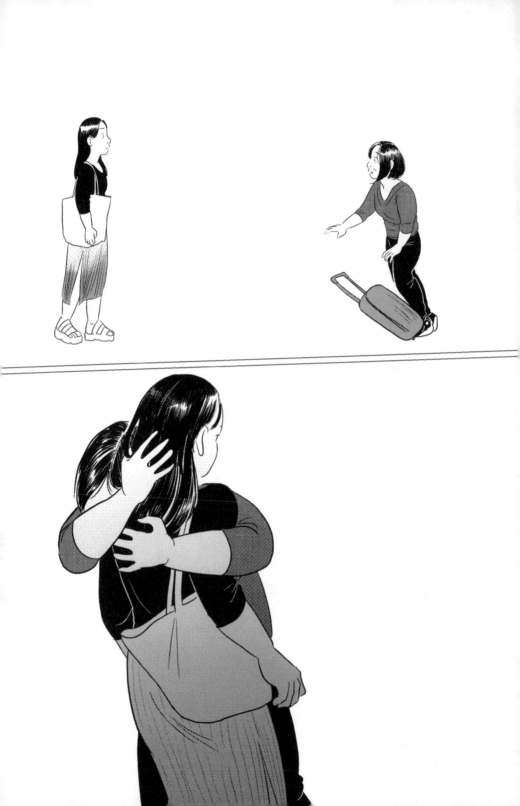

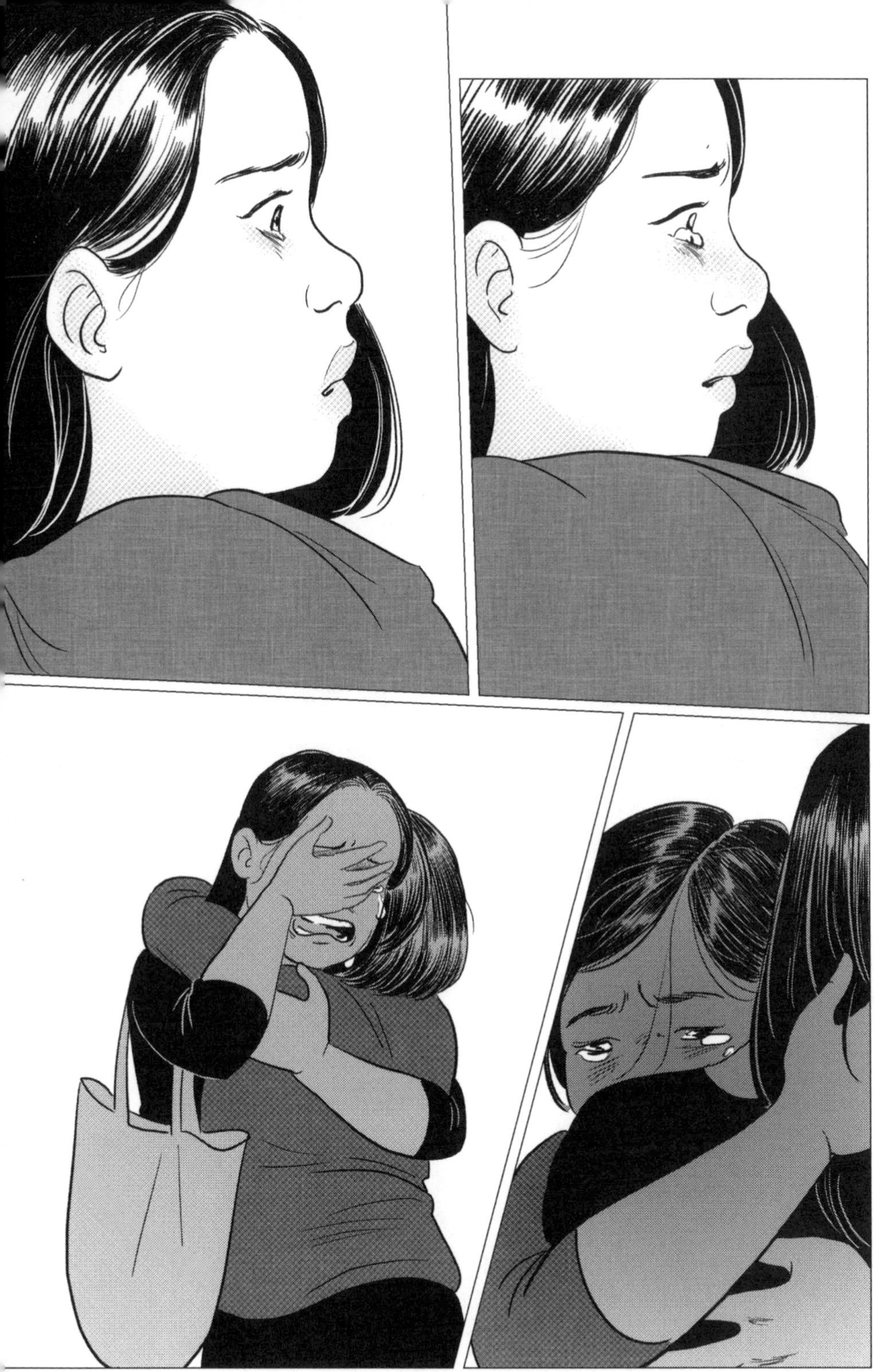

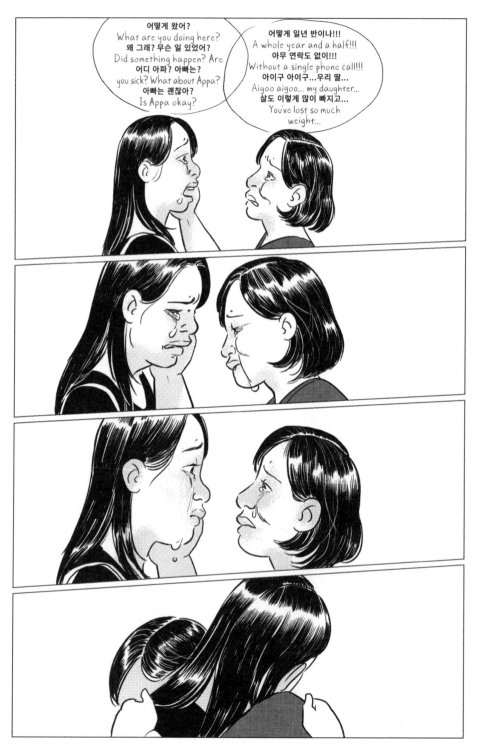

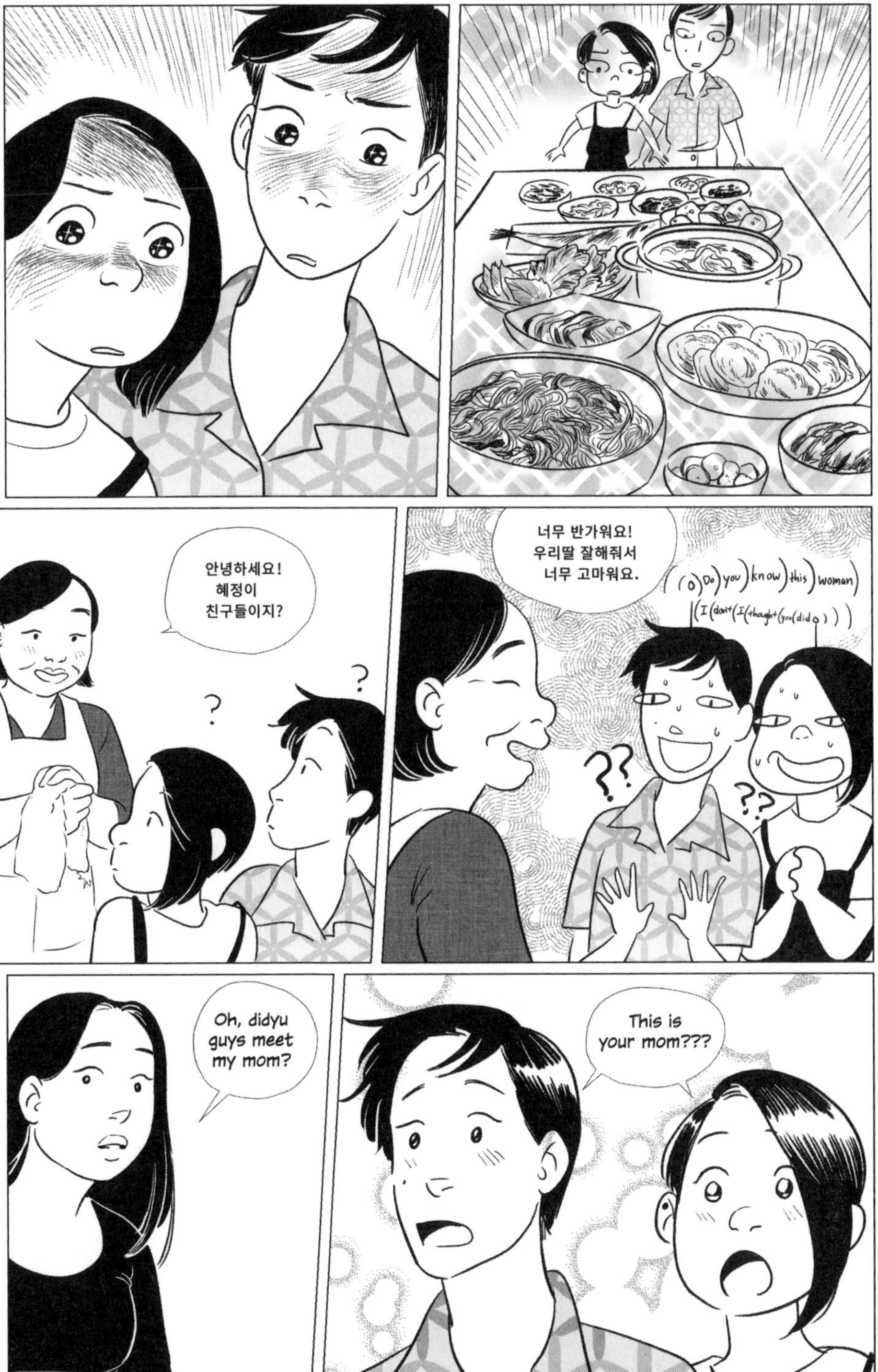
안녕하세요!
혜정이
친구들이지?
?
?
너무 반가워요!
우리딸 잘해줘서
너무 고마워요.
O Do you know this woman
I don't I thought you did
??
??
Oh, didyu guys meet my mom?
This is your mom???

334

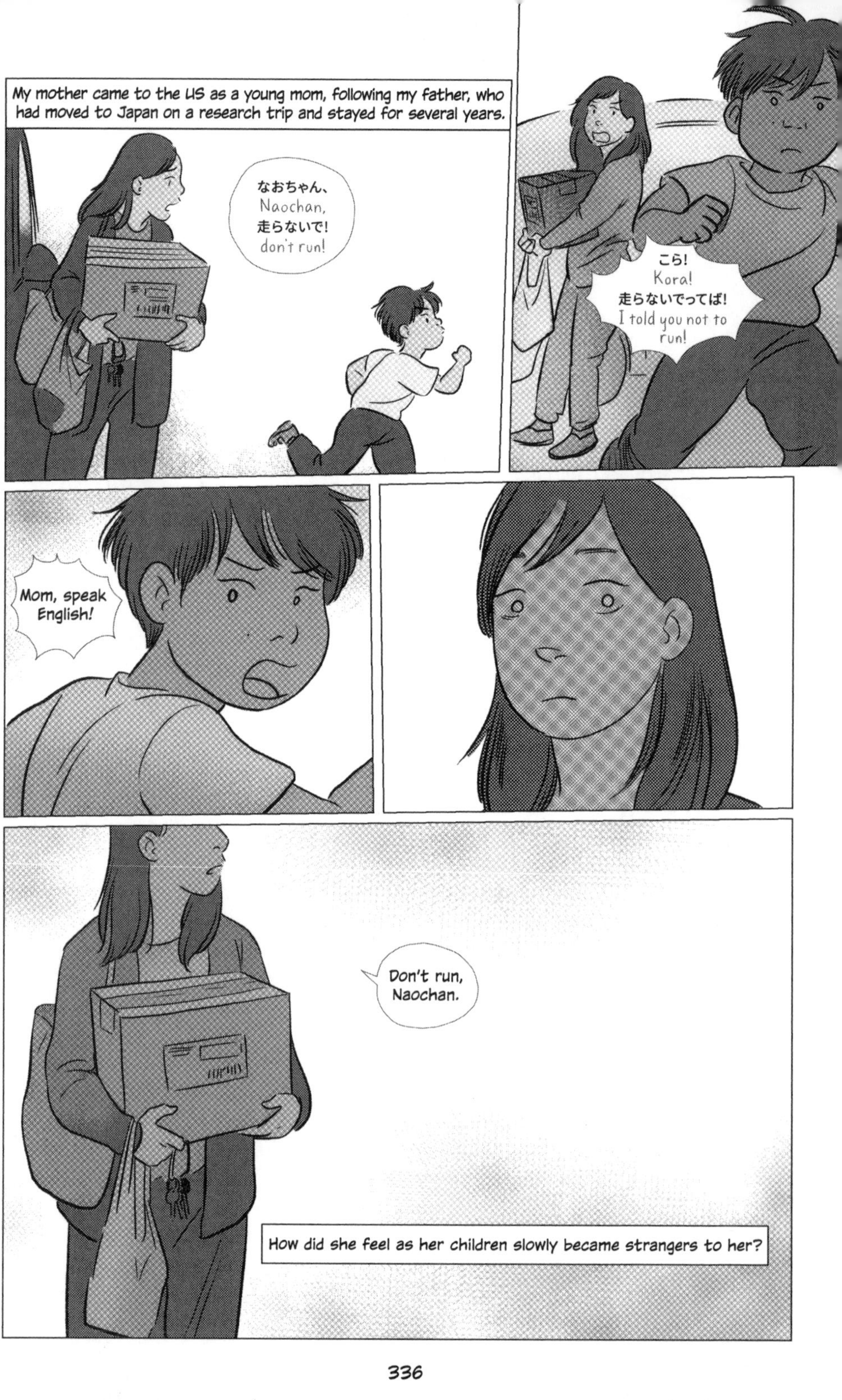
My mother came to the US as a young mom, following my father, who had moved to Japan on a research trip and stayed for several years.
なおちゃん、 Naochan, 走らないで! don't run!
こら! Kora! 走らないでってば! I told you not to run!
Mom, speak English!
Don't run, Naochan.
How did she feel as her children slowly became strangers to her?

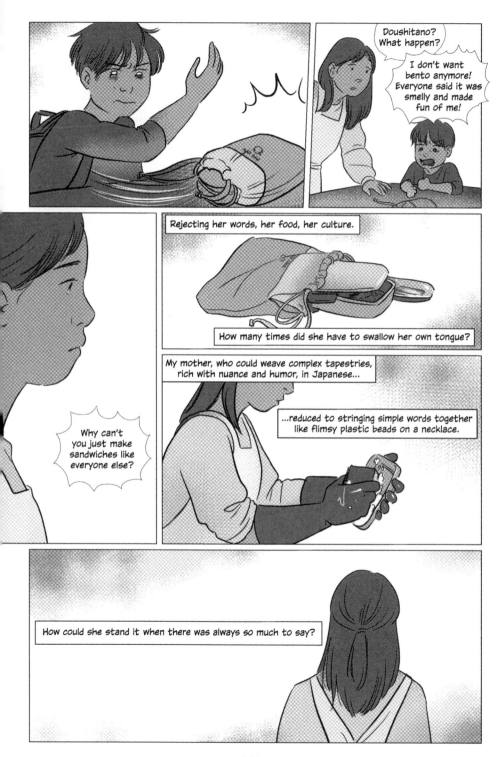

340

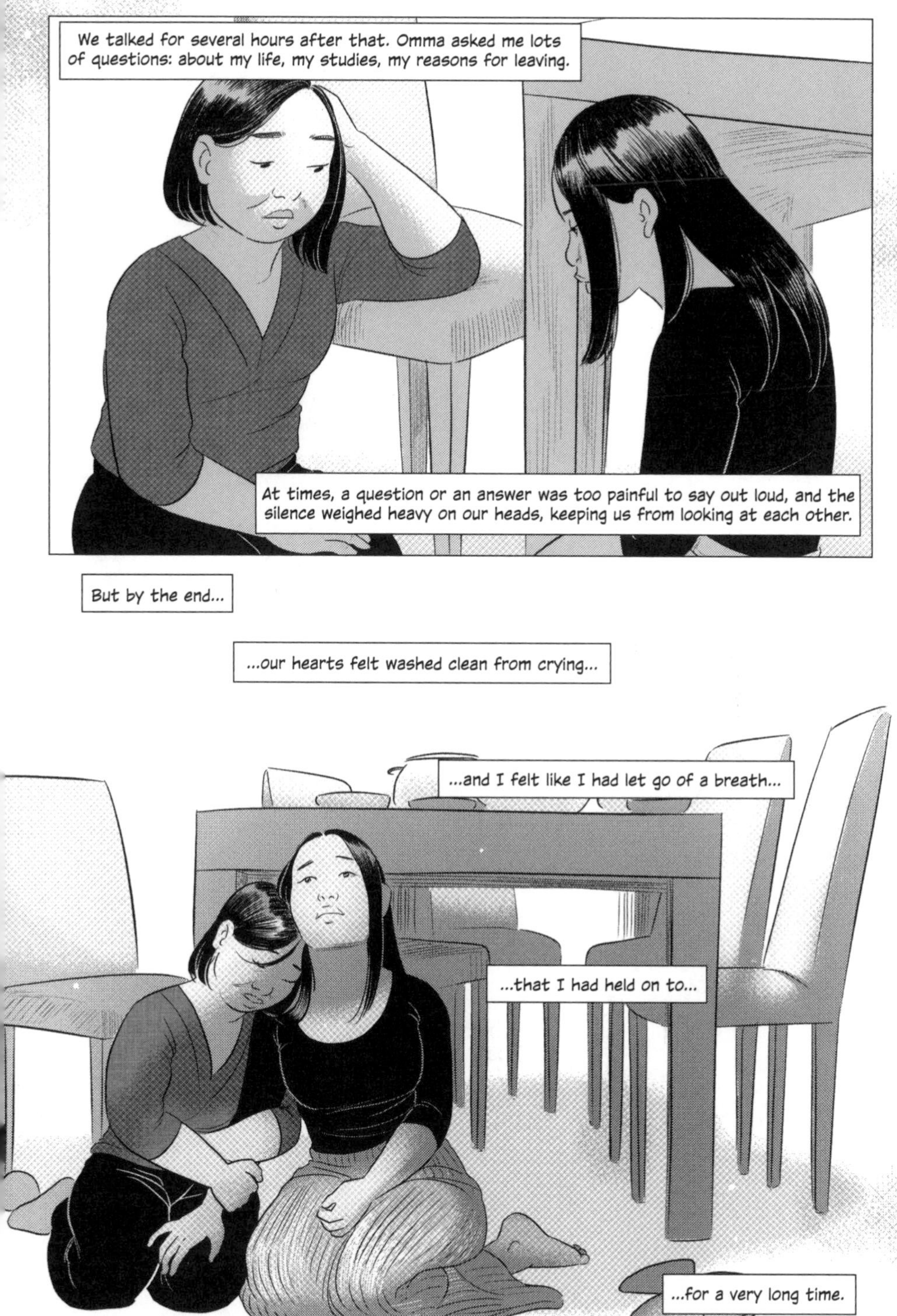
We talked for several hours after that. Omma asked me lots of questions: about my life, my studies, my reasons for leaving.
At times, a question or an answer was too painful to say out loud, and the silence weighed heavy on our heads, keeping us from looking at each other.
But by the end...
...our hearts felt washed clean from crying...
...and I felt like I had let go of a breath...
...that I had held on to...
...for a very long time.

Chapter 20

Forward

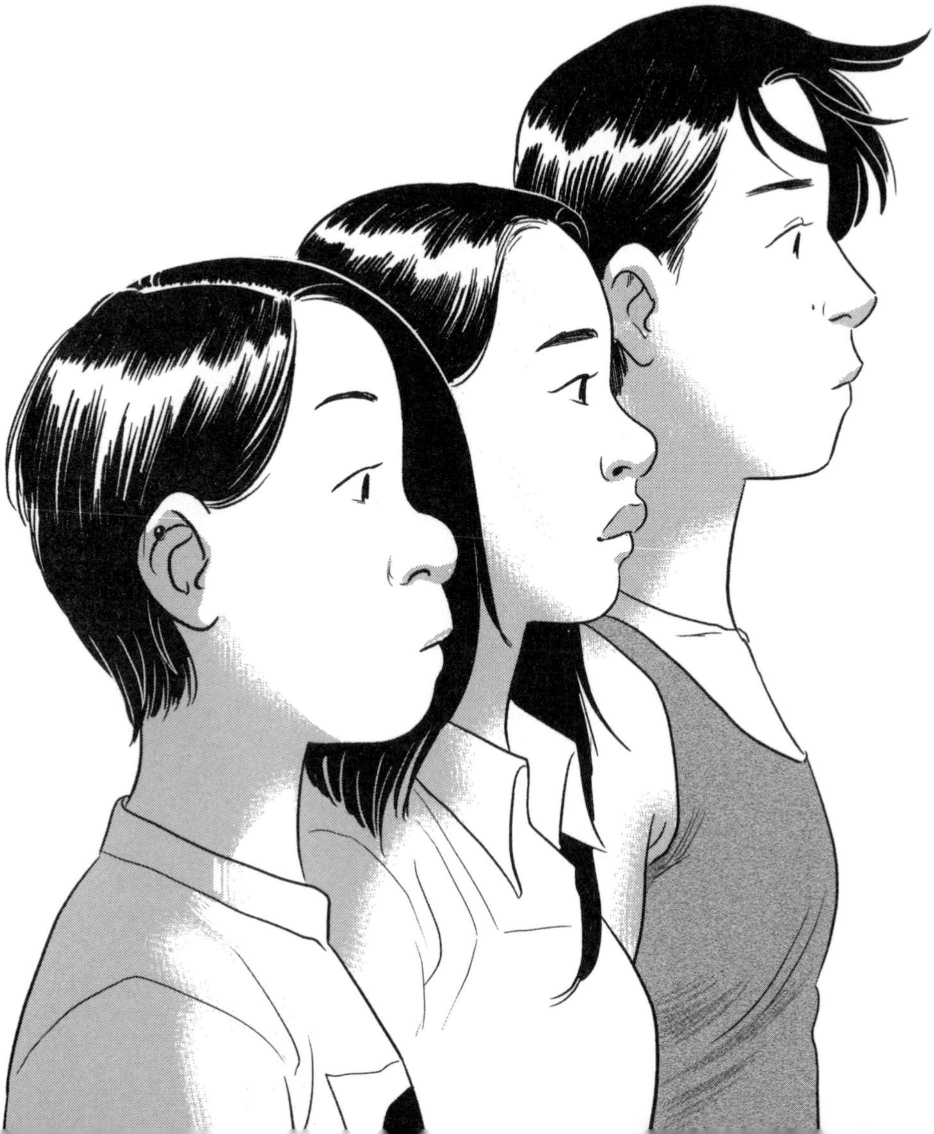

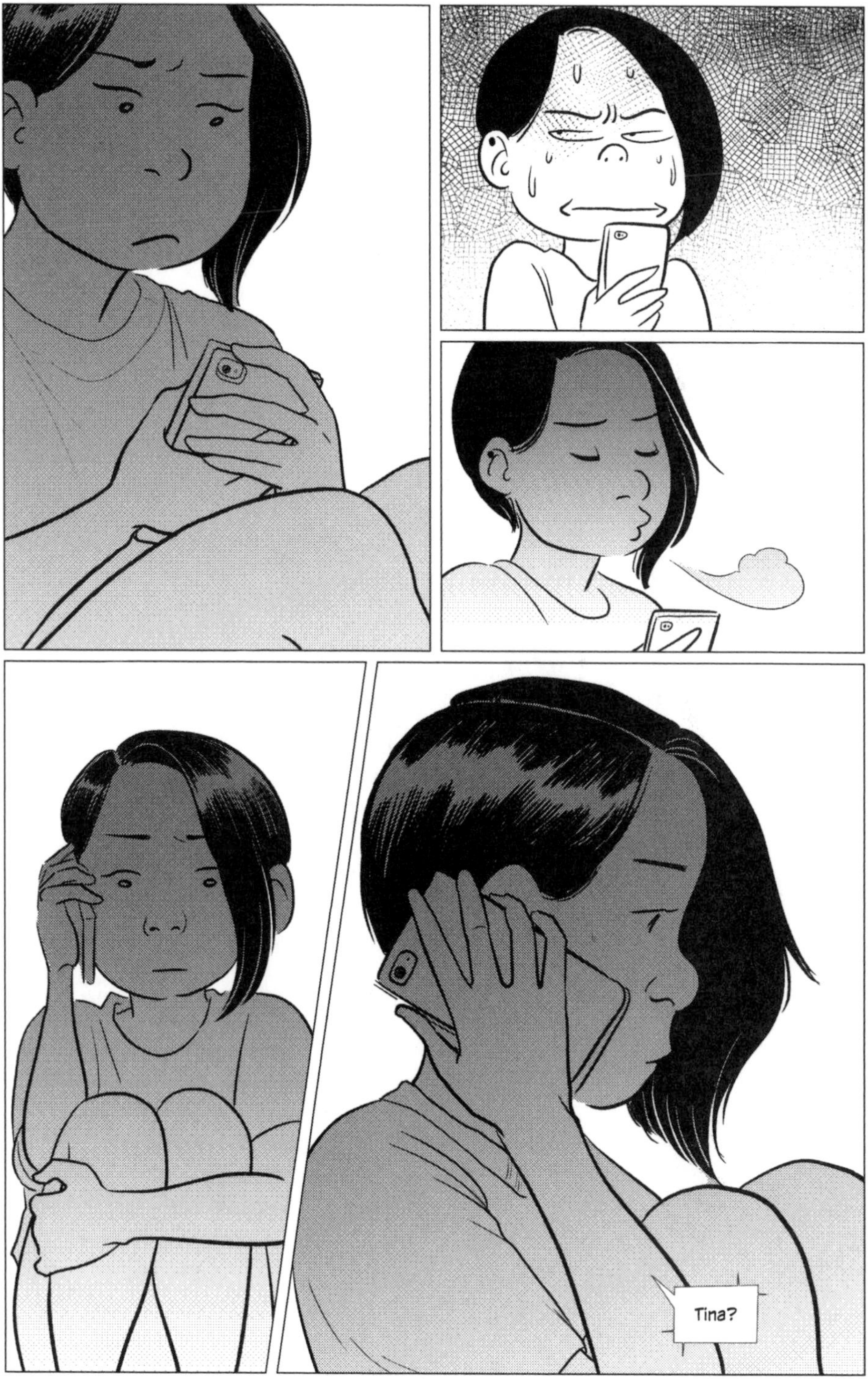
Tina?

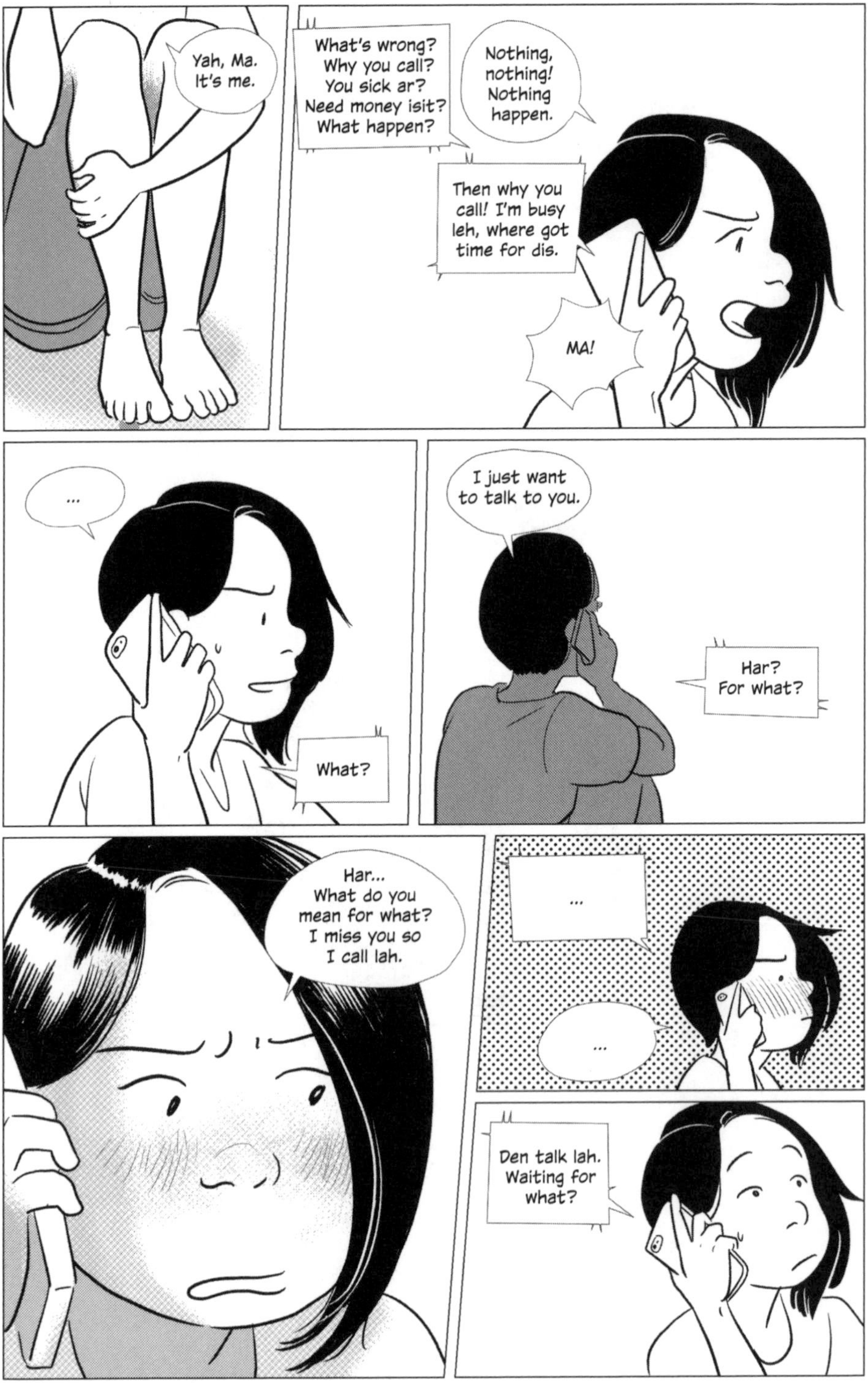
Yah, Ma.
It's me.
What's wrong? Why you call? You sick ar? Need money isit? What happen?
Nothing, nothing! Nothing happen.
Then why you call! I'm busy leh, where got time for dis.
MA!
...
What?
I just want to talk to you.
Har? For what?
Har... What do you mean for what? I miss you so I call lah.
...
...
Den talk lah. Waiting for what?

347

348

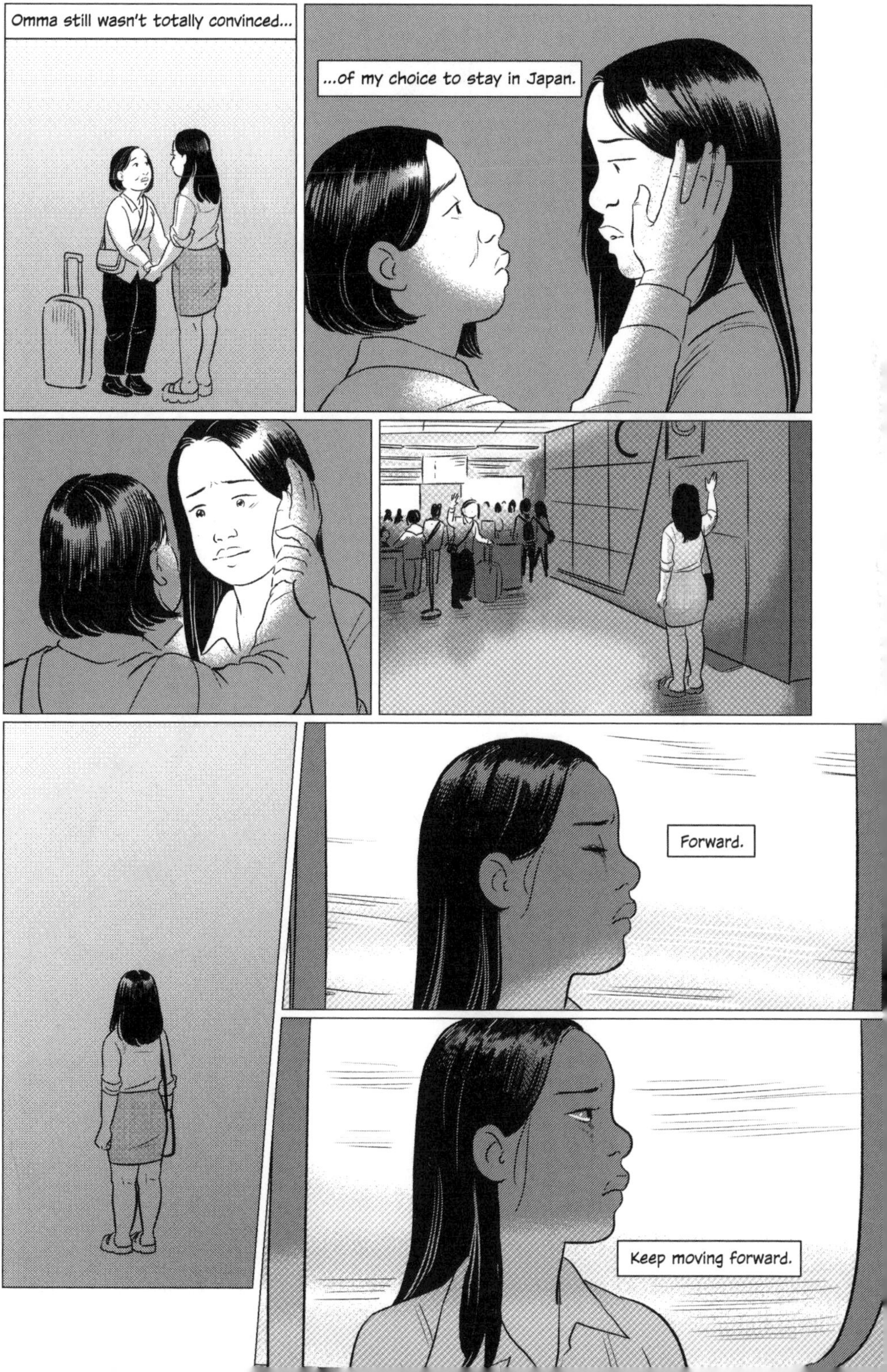
Omma still wasn't totally convinced...
...of my choice to stay in Japan.
Forward.
Keep moving forward.

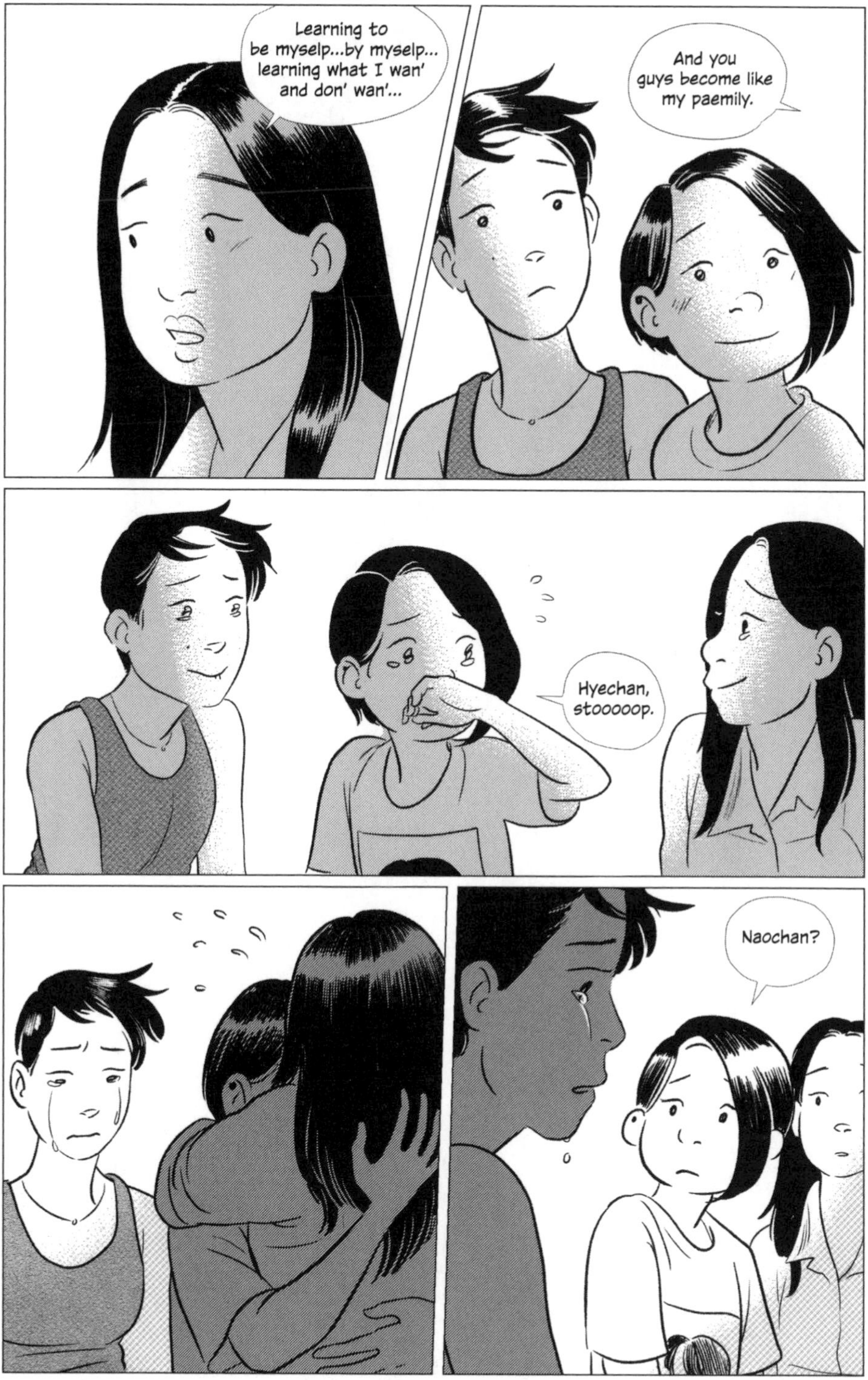

Learning to be myselp...by myselp... learning what I wan' and don' wan'...
And you guys become like my paemily.
Hyechan, stooooop.
Naochan?

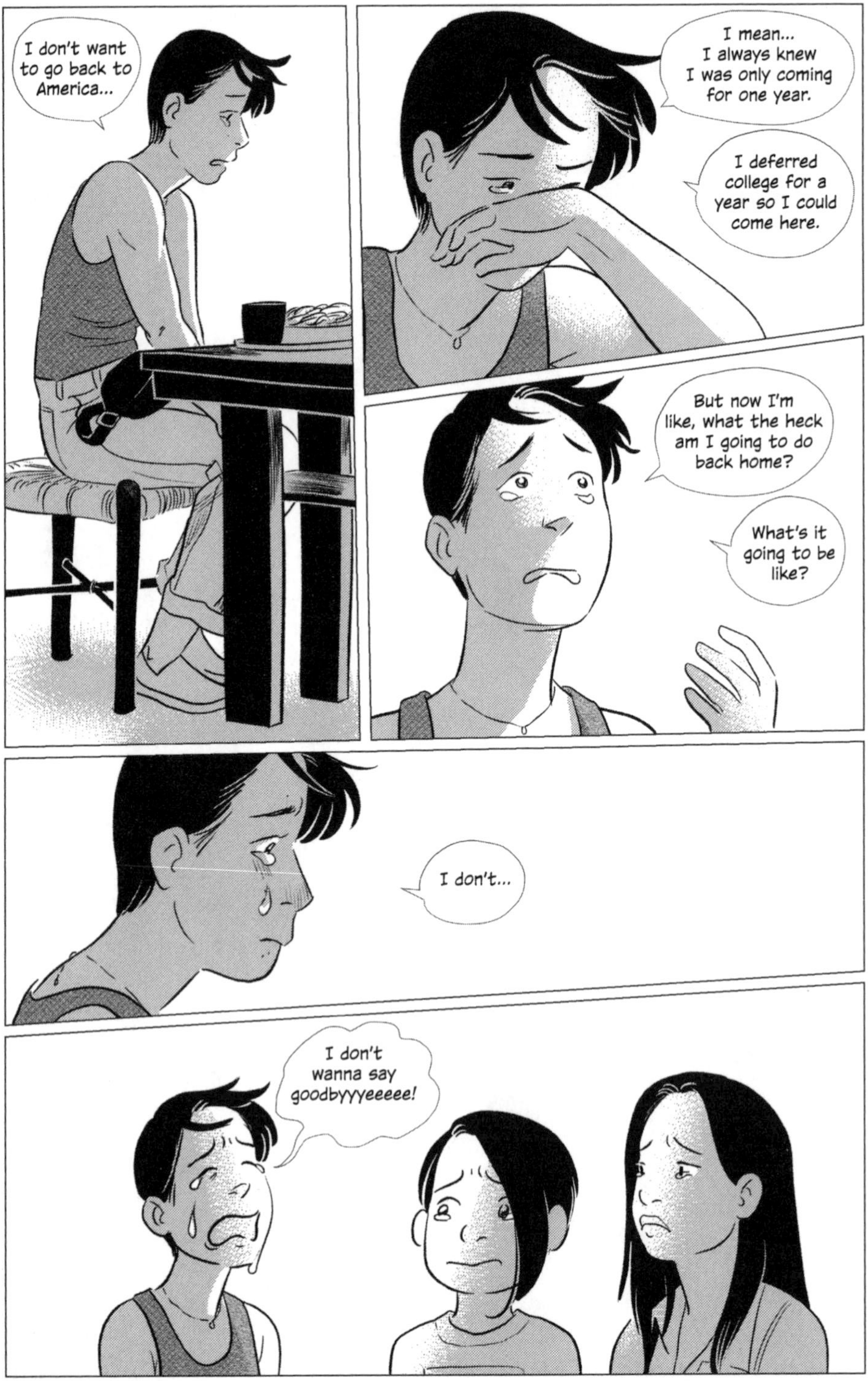
I don't want to go back to America...
I mean... I always knew I was only coming for one year.
I deferred college for a year so I could come here.
But now I'm like, what the heck am I going to do back home?
What's it going to be like?
I don't...
I don't wanna say goodbyyyeeeee!

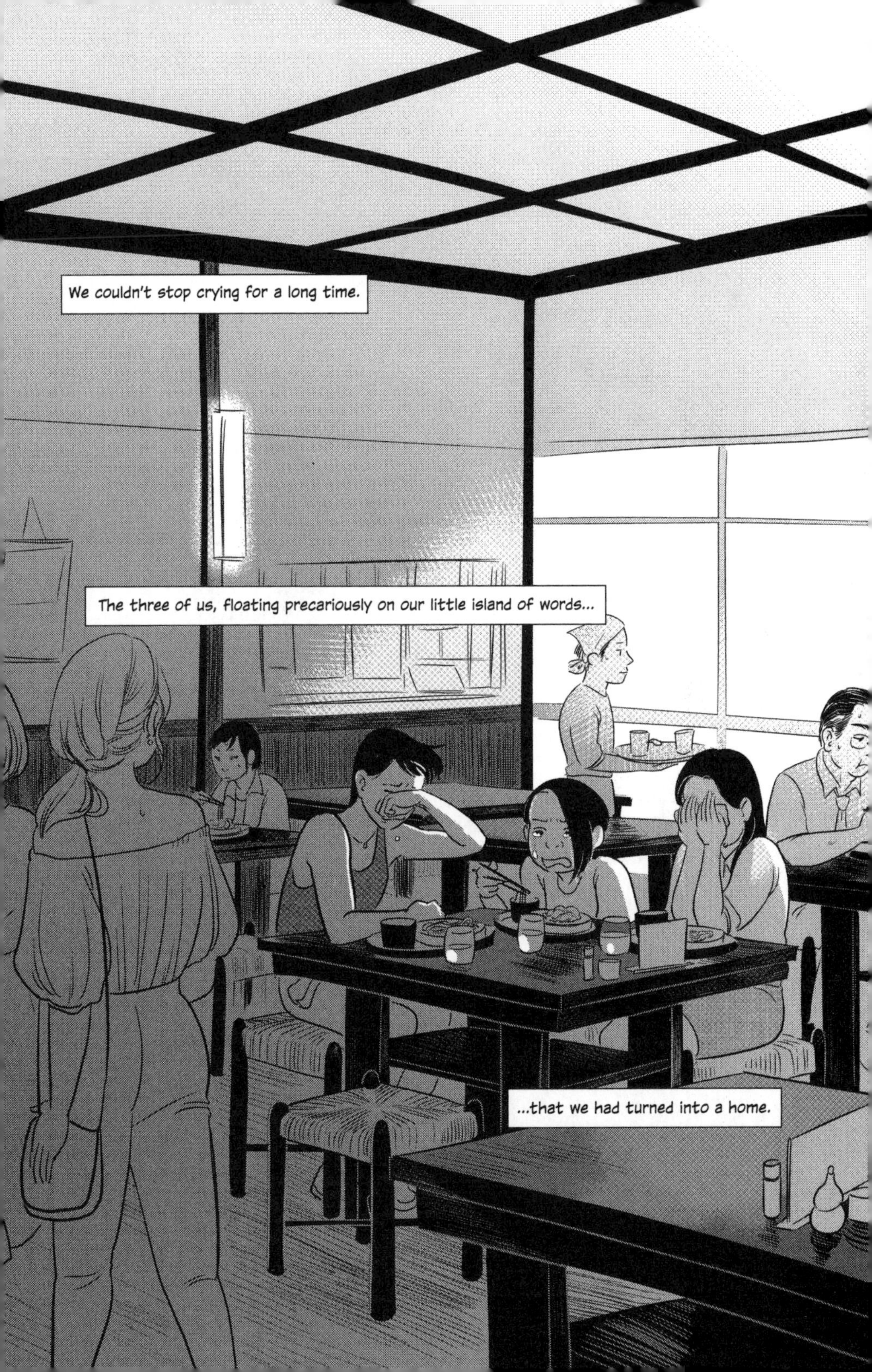
We couldn't stop crying for a long time.
The three of us, floating precariously on our little island of words...
...that we had turned into a home.

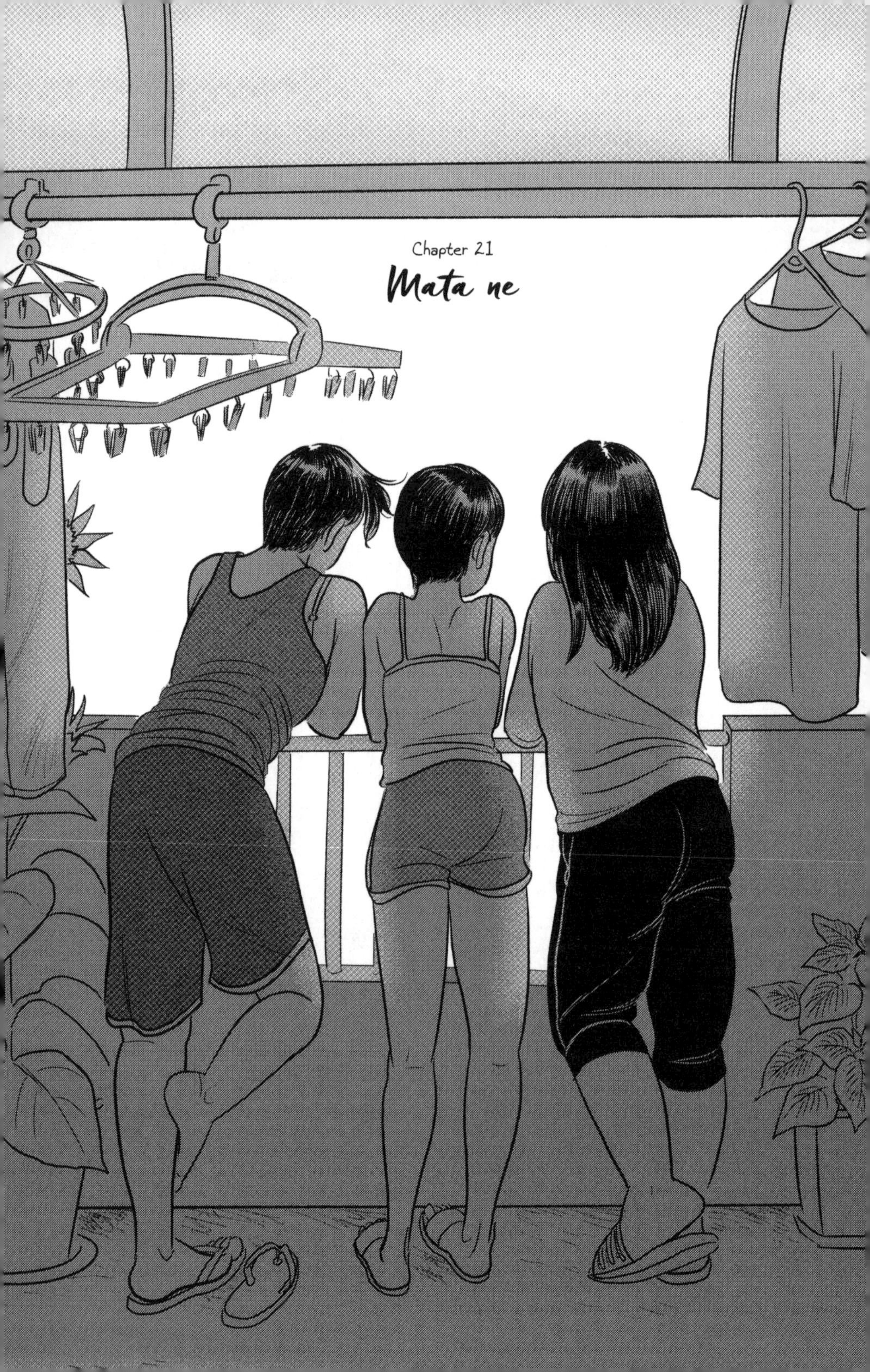
Chapter 21
Mata ne

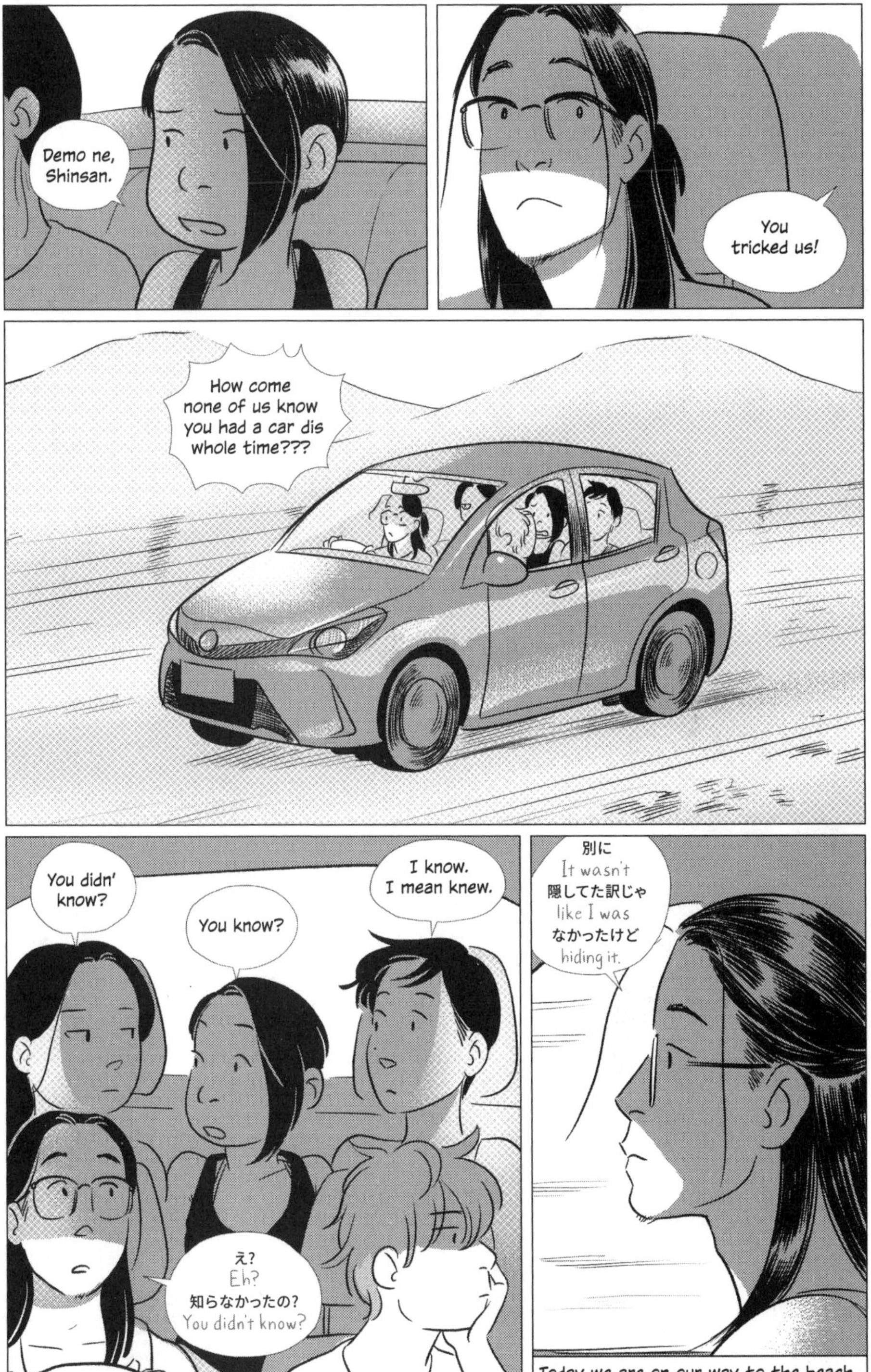

Demo ne, Shinsan.
You tricked us!
How come none of us know you had a car dis whole time???
You didn' know?
You know?
I know. I mean knew.
え? Eh? 知らなかったの? You didn't know?
別に It wasn't 隠してた訳じゃ like I was なかったけど hiding it.
Today we are on our way to the beach.

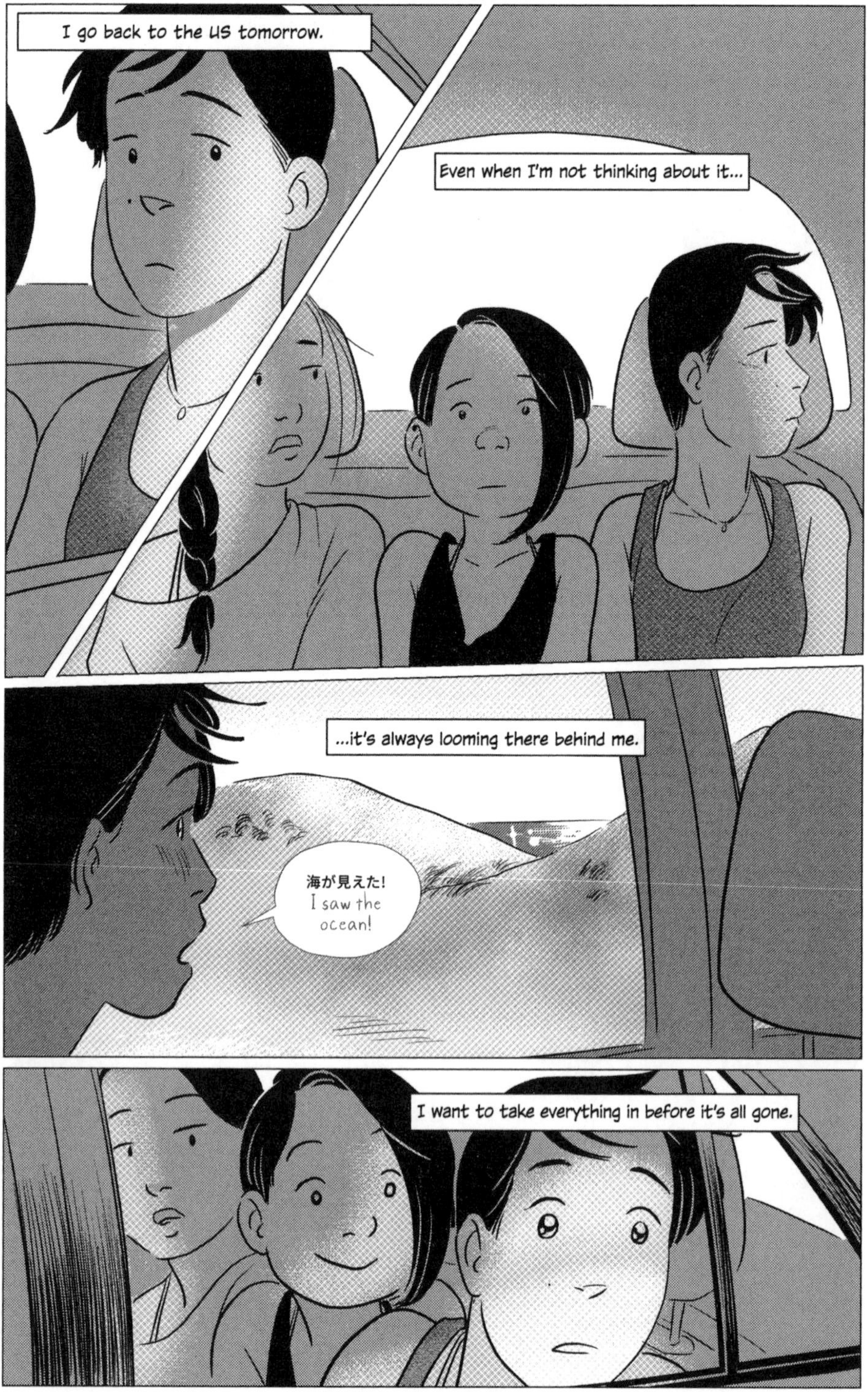
I go back to the US tomorrow.
Even when I'm not thinking about it...
...it's always looming there behind me.
海が見えた! I saw the ocean!
I want to take everything in before it's all gone.

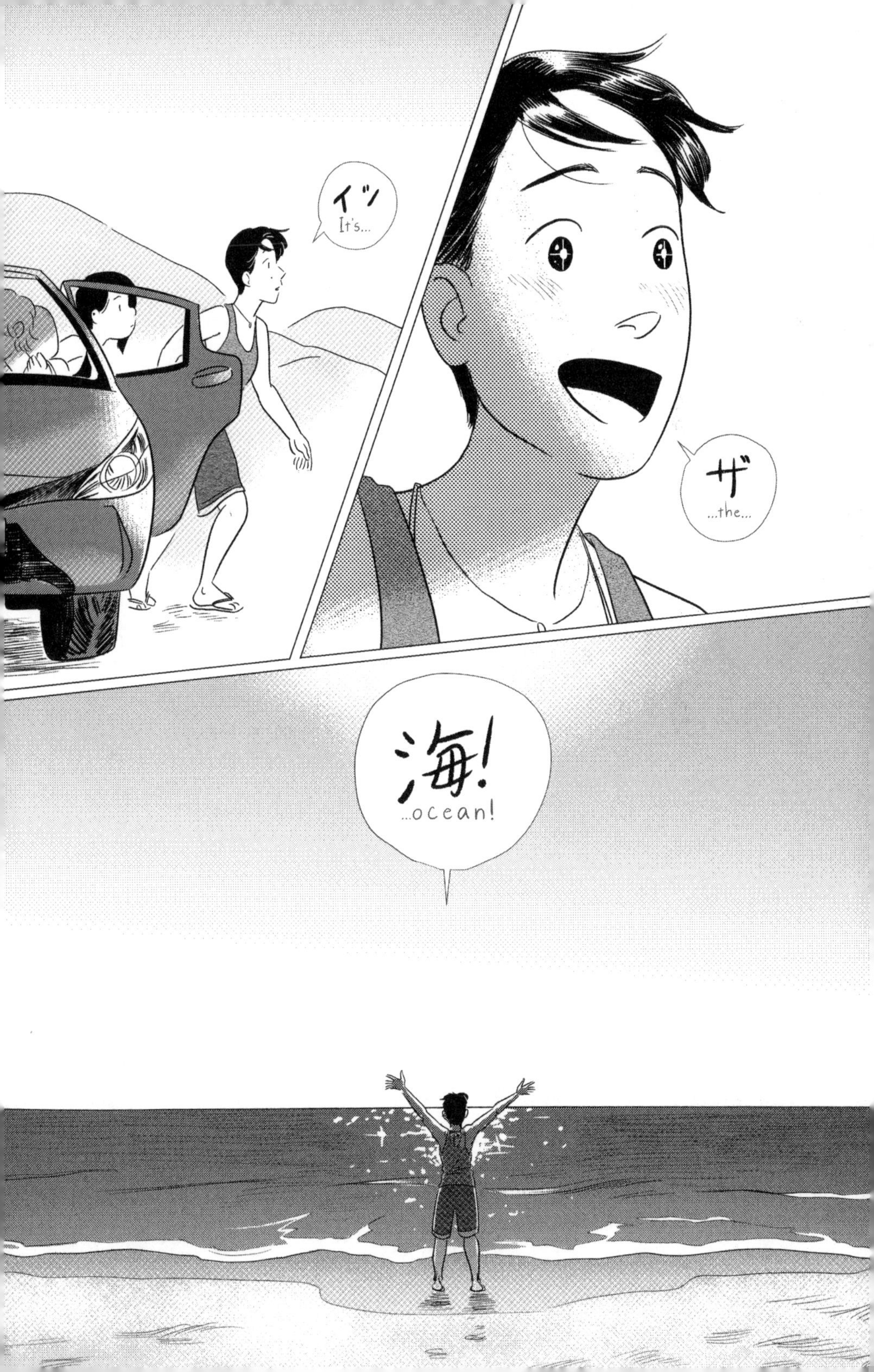
イッ
It's...
ザ
...the...
海!
...ocean!

362

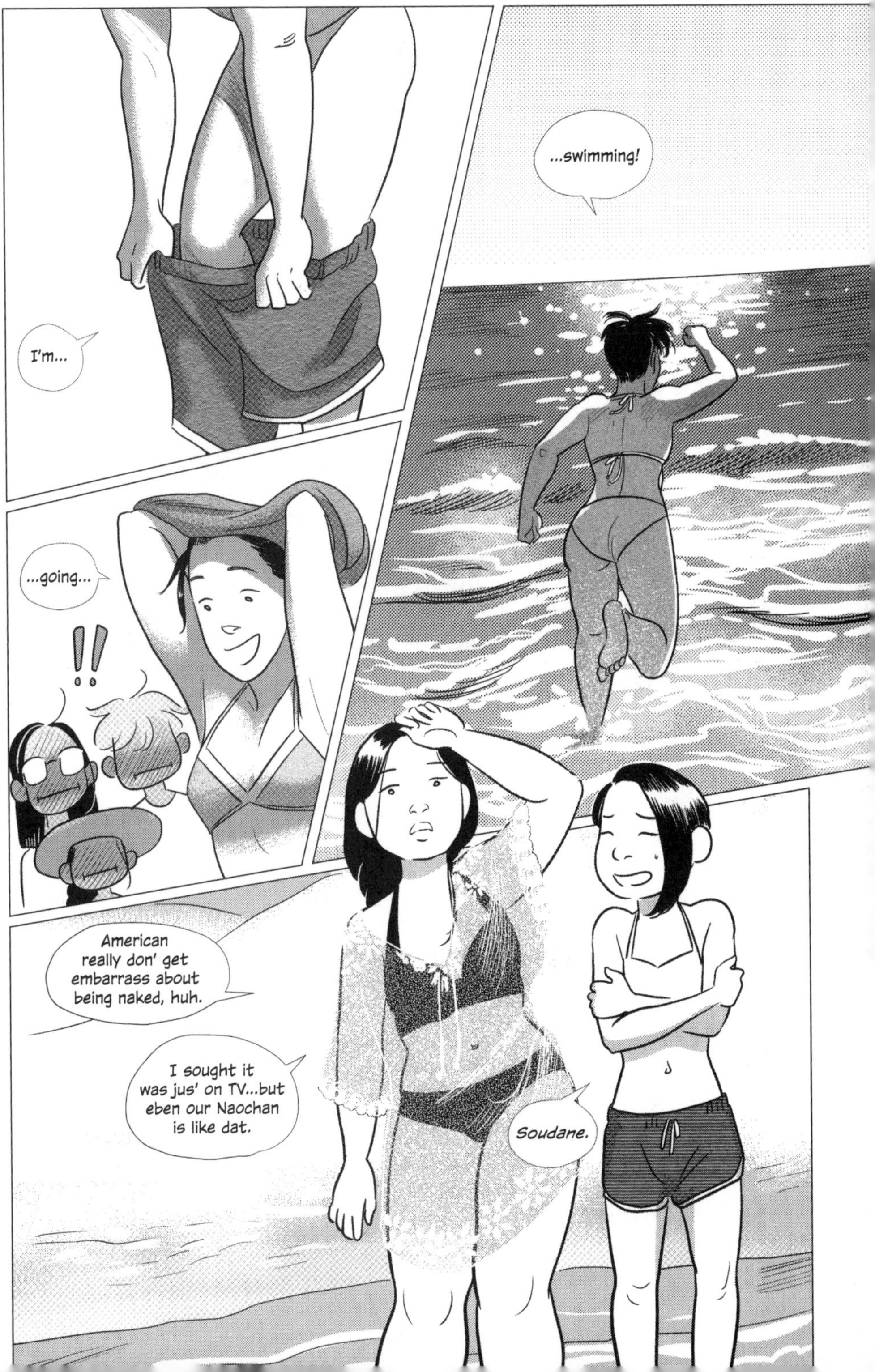
I'm...
...going...
!!
...swimming!
American really don' get embarrass about being naked, huh.
I sought it was jus' on TV...but eben our Naochan is like dat.
Soudane.

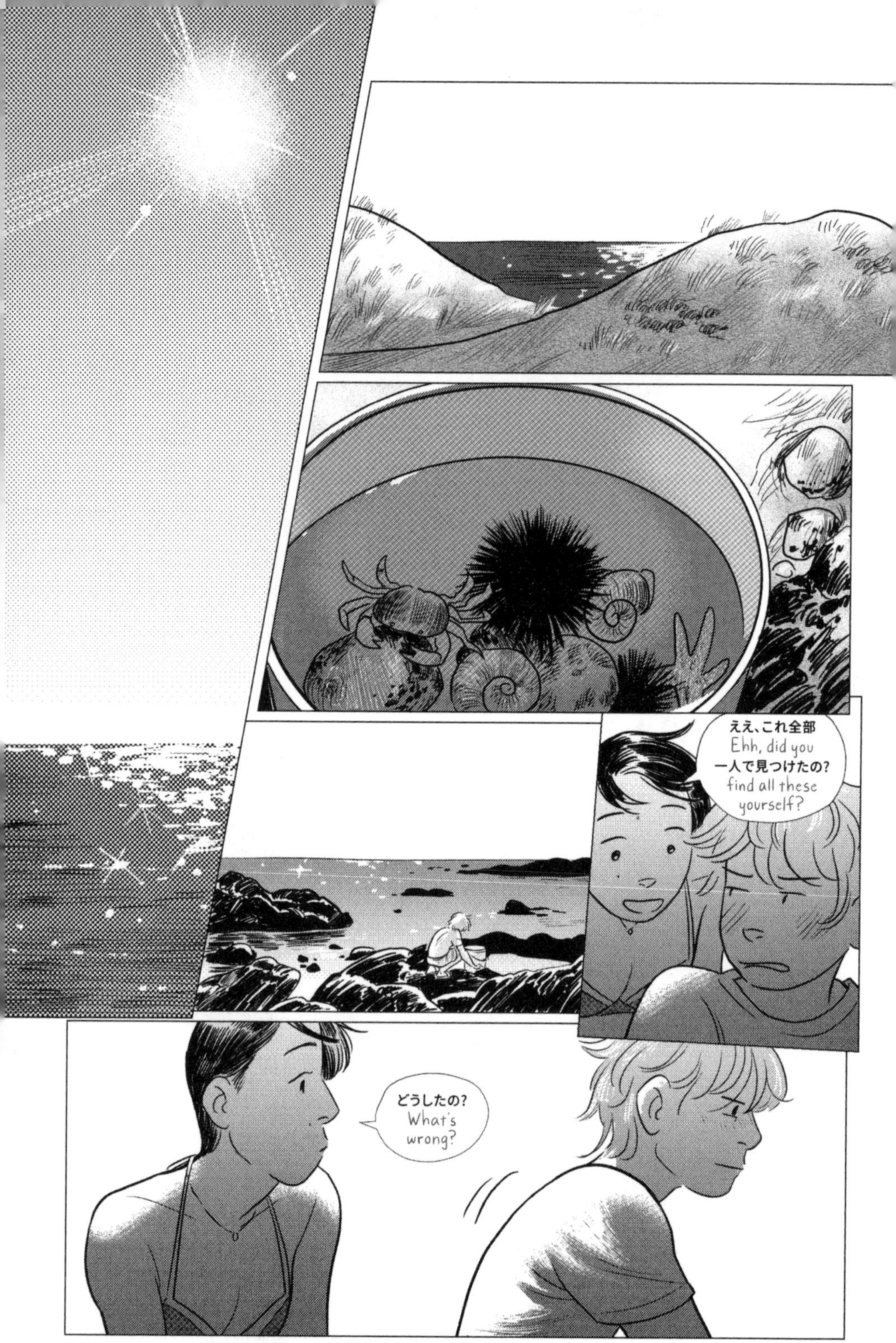
ええ、これ全部 Ehh, did you 一人で見つけたの? find all these yourself?
どうしたの? What's wrong?

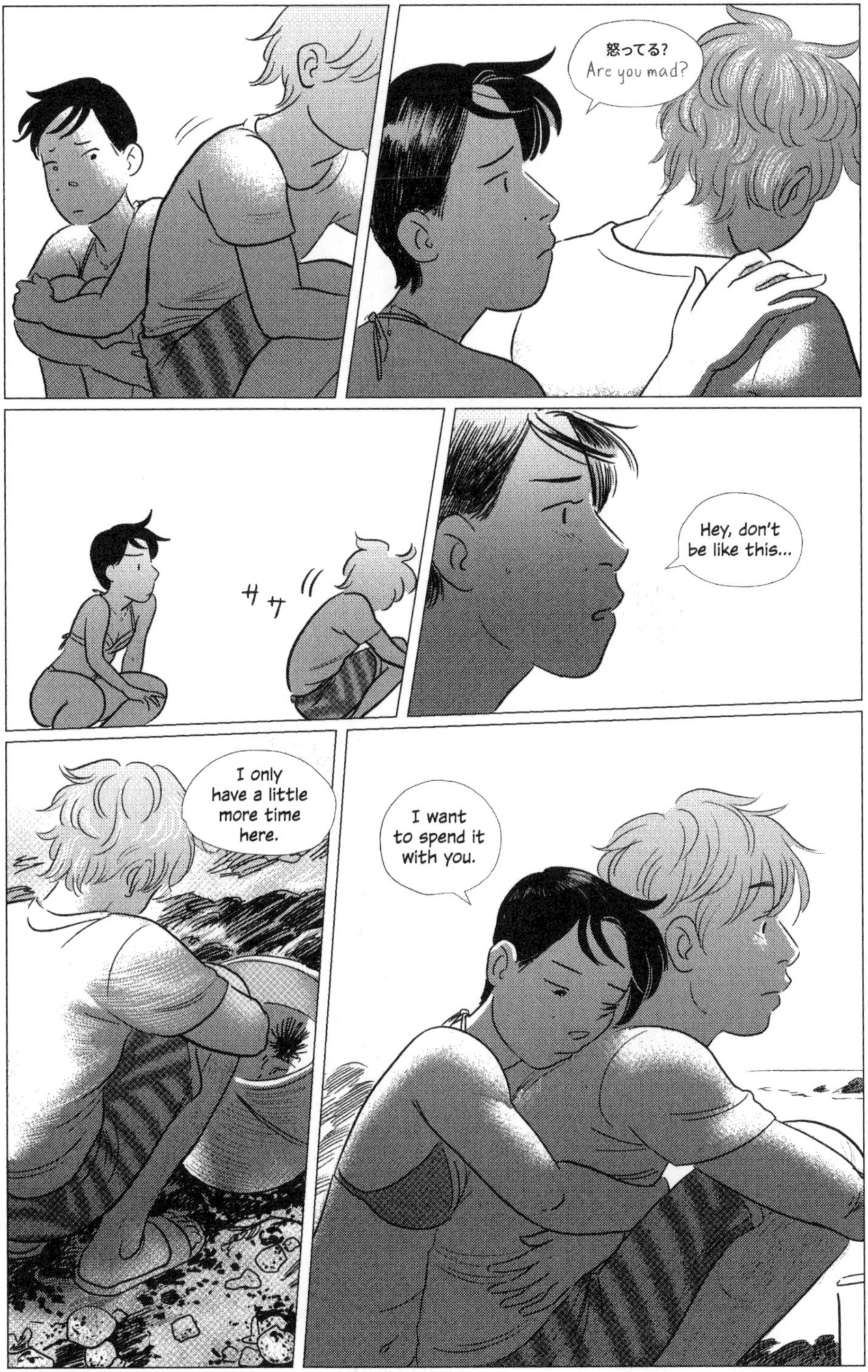

怒ってる?
Are you mad?
サッ
Hey, don't be like this...
I only have a little more time here.
I want to spend it with you.

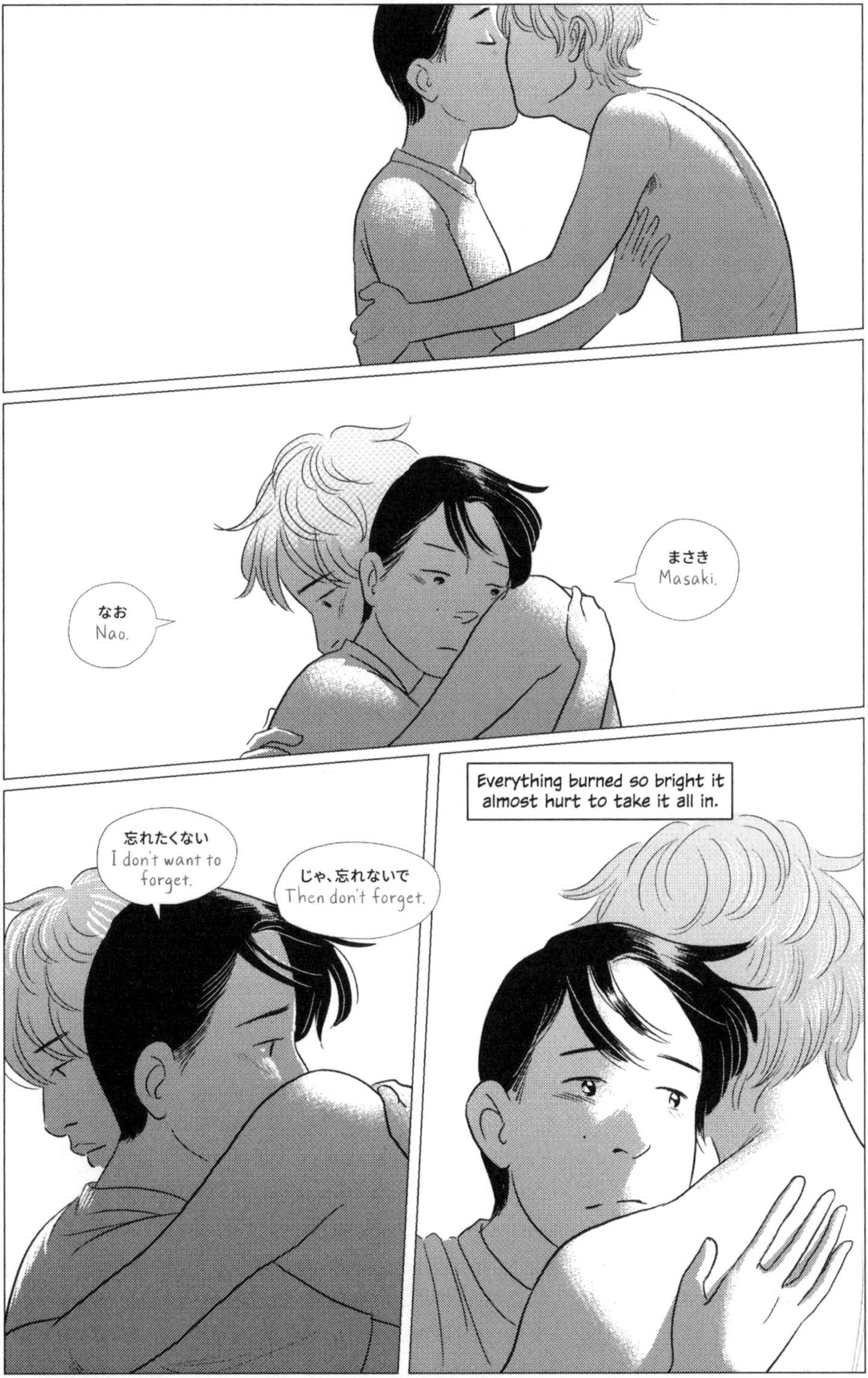

なお
Nao.
まさき
Masaki.
忘れたくない
I don't want to forget.
じゃ、忘れないで
Then don't forget.
Everything burned so bright it almost hurt to take it all in.

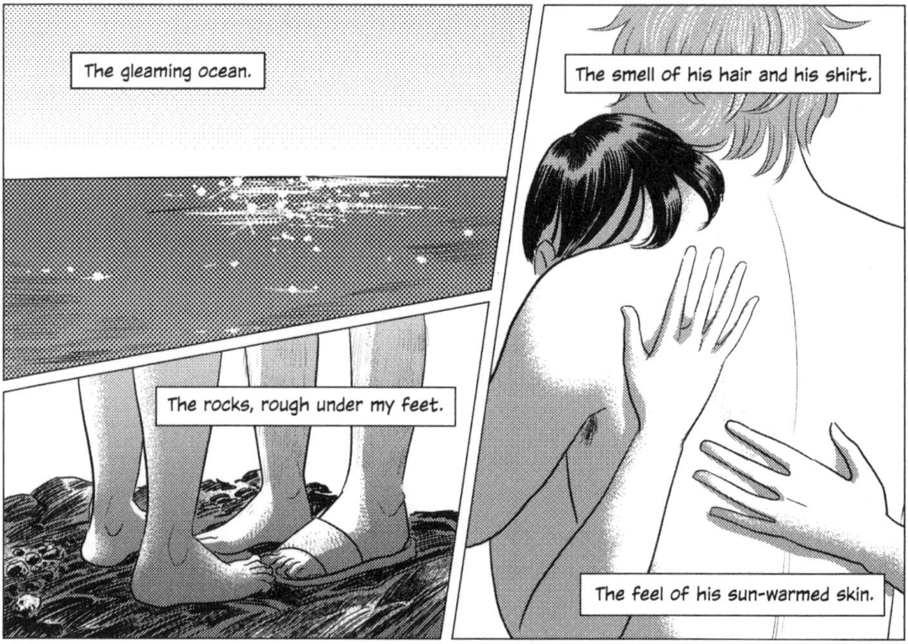
The gleaming ocean.
The rocks, rough under my feet.
The smell of his hair and his shirt.
The feel of his sun-warmed skin.

My heart felt so full I thought it would burst.

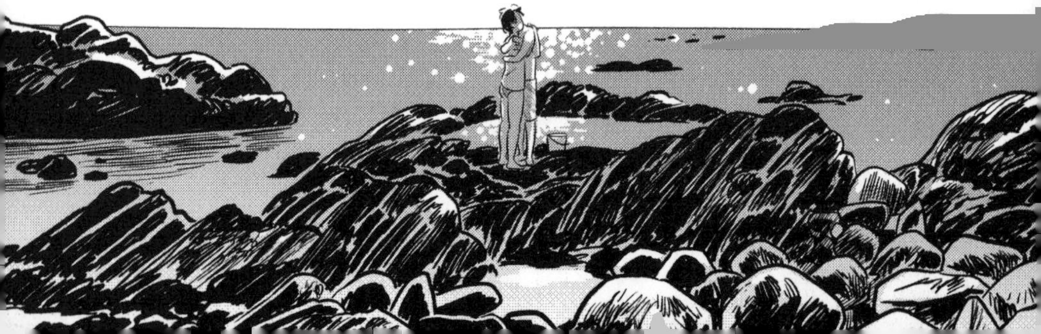

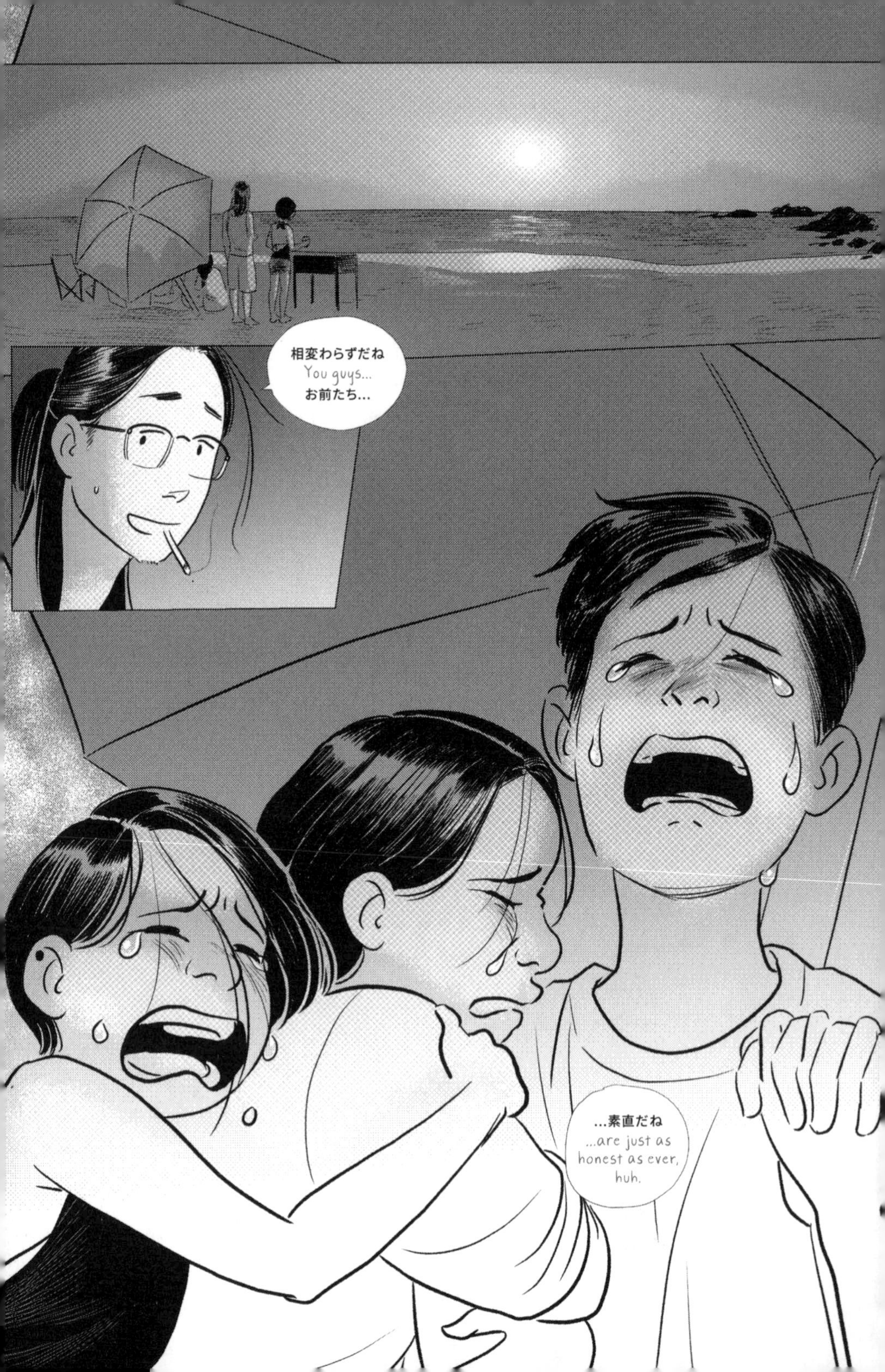
相変わらずだね
You guys...
お前たち...
...素直だね
...are just as honest as ever, huh.

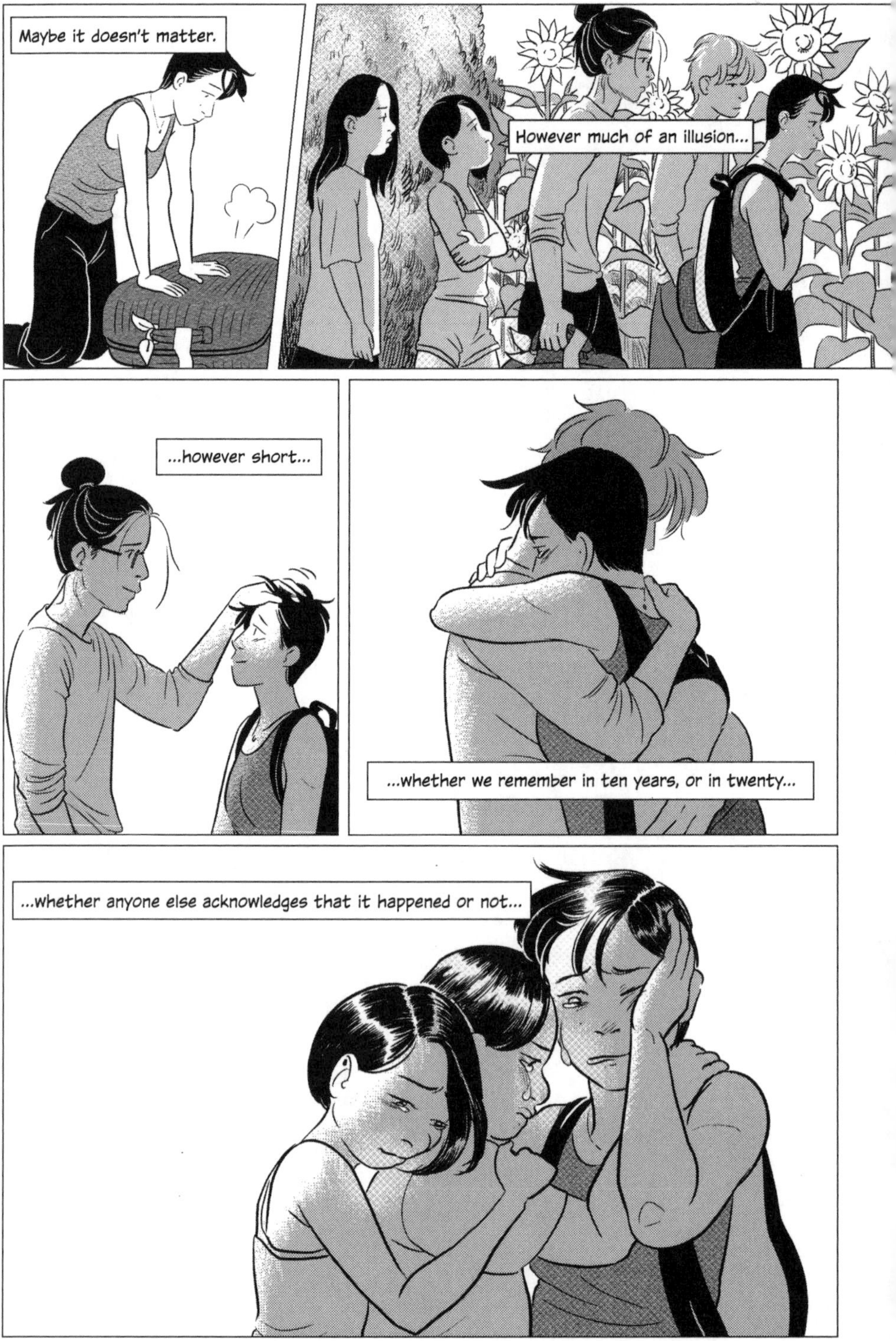
Maybe it doesn't matter.
However much of an illusion...
...however short...
...whether we remember in ten years, or in twenty...
...whether anyone else acknowledges that it happened or not...

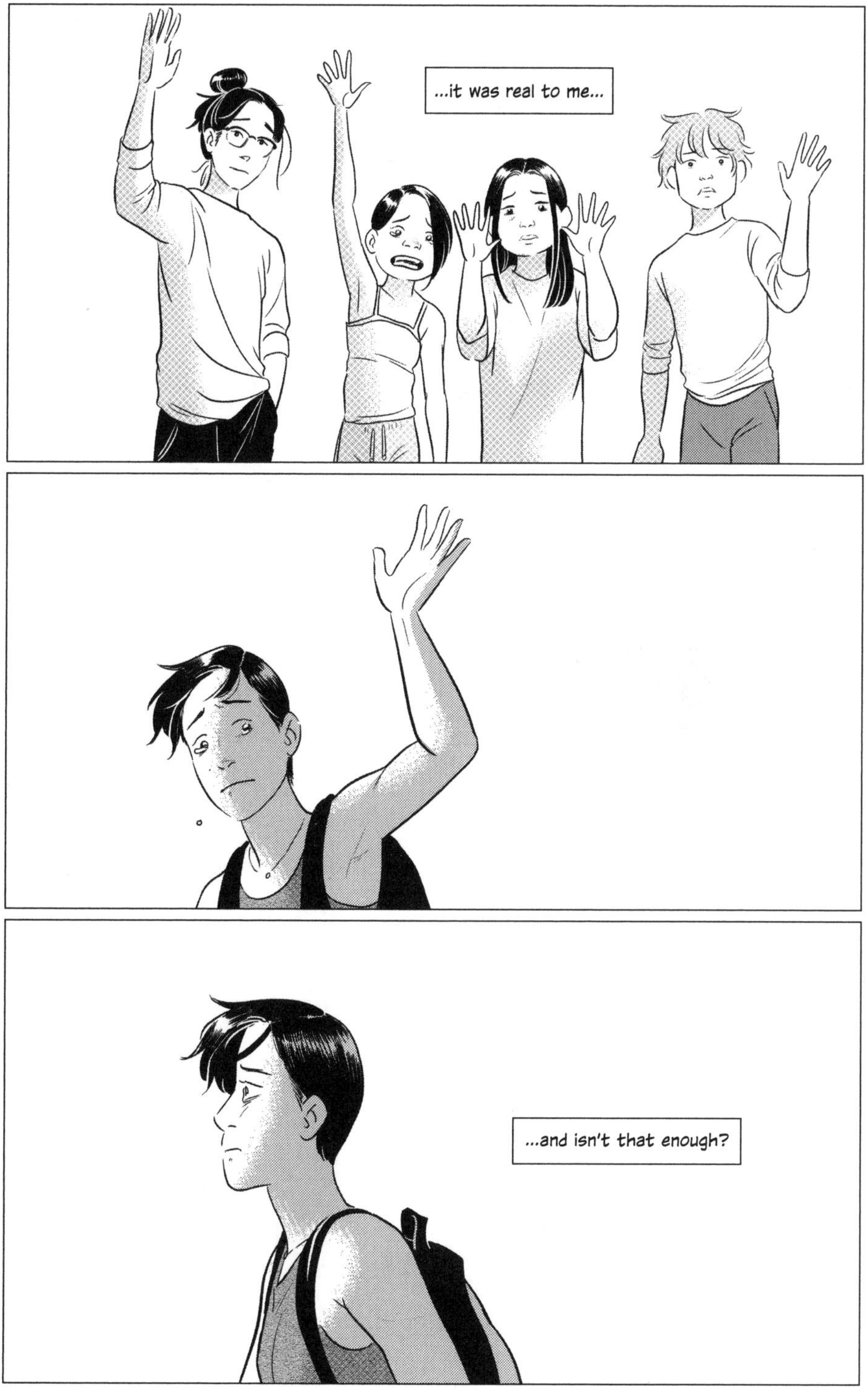
...it was real to me...
...and isn't that enough?

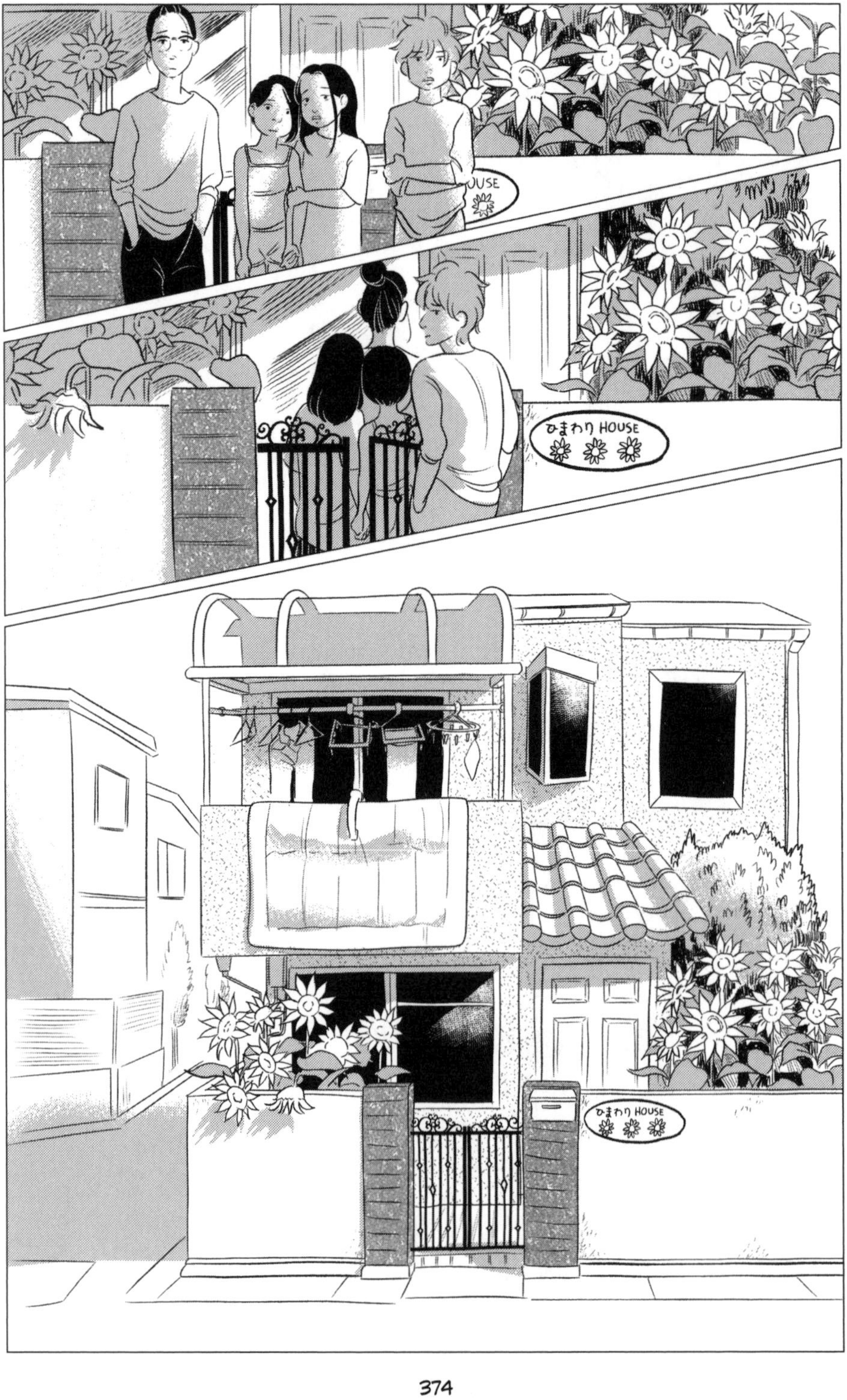
ひまわり HOUSE
ひまわり HOUSE

ON THE USE OF ACCENTS IN THIS BOOK

Western media has a long history of portraying Asian people in offensive, one-dimensional ways. So often characters are written with thick foreign accents for comic or exotic effect. I was surprised that even in movies celebrated for their good Asian representation, the only characters who had Asian accents were written as comic relief. This legacy has cemented the idea that to have an accent is to be laughable, to be stupid, to be "other."

I grew up listening to accented English in my home and community, and I have lived in several countries where I struggled with my own broken Japanese, Korean, and Spanish. My intent with *Himawari House* was to allow characters who spoke with accents, who occasionally stumbled over their grammar, to be fully actualized, three-dimensional people. I love accents, I think that they add depth and character to one's speech—a sense of place. I hope that this book can be a contribution to a different kind of legacy for Asian characters, one in which our accents are not a point of shame but a point of pride, because after all, what is an accent but proof of the ability to speak more than one language?

ACKNOWLEDGMENTS

I would like to thank Gracie, my first-ever reader, and the rest of my family, Mom, Dad, Alan, and Kaori. Thank you for your weirdness, your creativity, your love, and your warmth.

For their work as cultural and language consultants on this book, I want to thank Naoyuki Kuroda, Janelle Wong, Jonghee Choe, Heihachiro Shigematsu, and Yudori. I'd be lost without you!

I want to thank my editor, Kiara Valdez, my agent, DongWon Song, and all the wonderful staff at First Second for their hard work on making this book a reality.

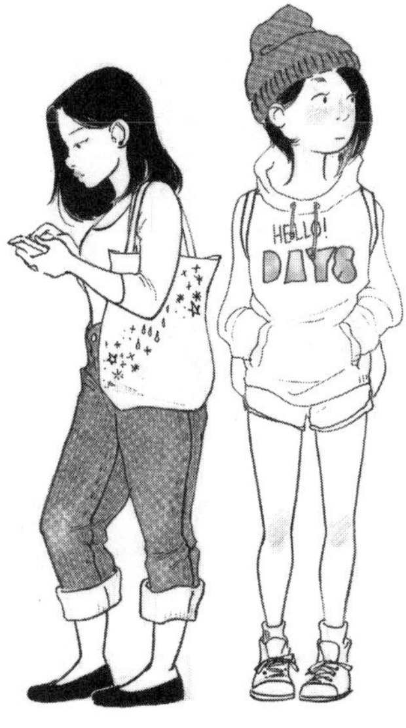
HELLO!
DAYS

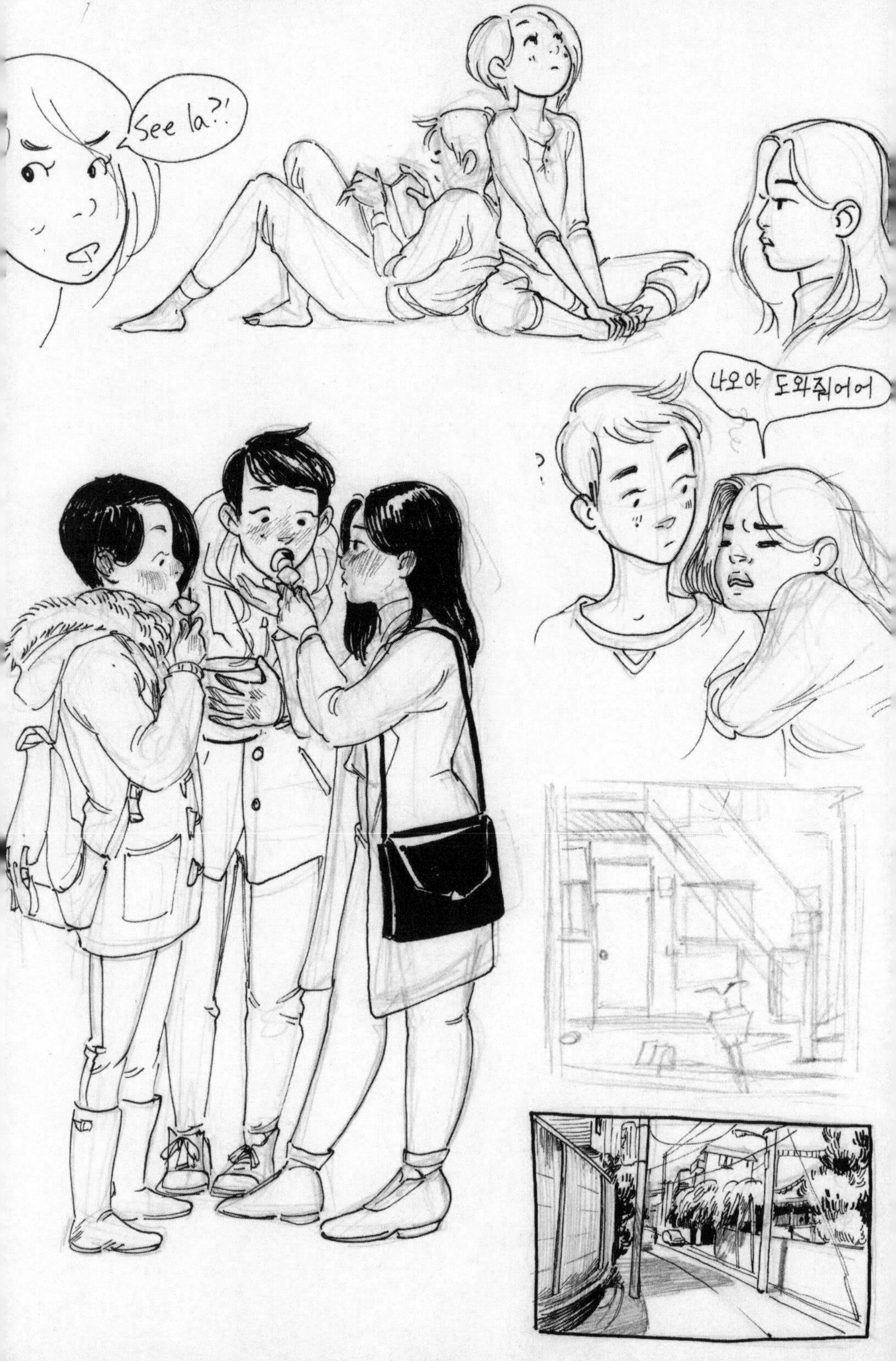
See la?!
나오야 도와줘어어

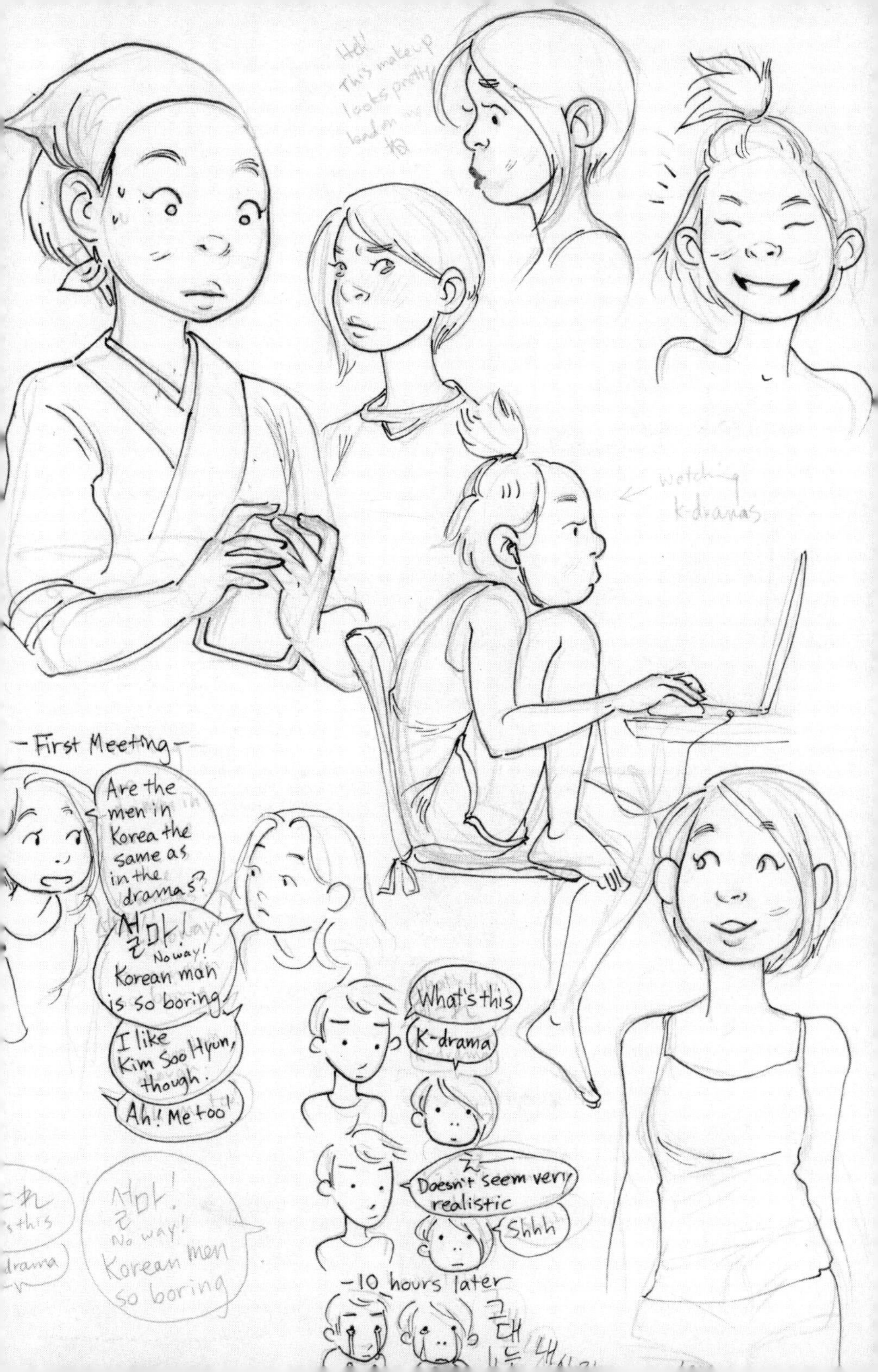
Watching k-dramas
-First Meeting-
Are the men in Korea the same as in the dramas?
설마! No way!
Korean man is so boring
I like Kim Soo Hyun, though.
Ah! Me too!
What's this
K-drama
Doesn't seem very realistic
Shhh
-10 hours later

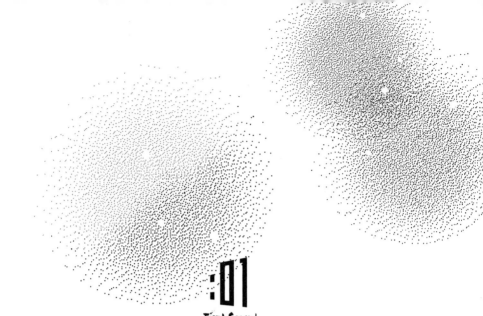

First Second

Published by First Second
First Second is an imprint of Roaring Brook Press,
a division of Holtzbrinck Publishing Holdings Limited Partnership
120 Broadway, New York, NY 10271
firstsecondbooks.com

Library of Congress Control Number: 2021906598

Our books may be purchased in bulk for promotional, educational, or business use.
Please contact your local bookseller or the Macmillan Corporate and Premium Sales Department
at (800) 221-7945 ext. 5442 or by email at MacmillanSpecialMarkets@macmillan.com.

FIRST

EDITION

First edition, 2021
Edited by Kiara Valdez
Cover design by Sunny Lee
Authenticity readers: Yudori and Anna Lee

Penciled, inked, and toned in Clip Studio Paint.

Printed in the United States of America

ISBN 978-1-250-23557-2 (paperback)
1   3   5   7   9   10   8   6   4   2

ISBN 978-1-250-23556-5 (hardcover)
1   3   5   7   9   10   8   6   4   2

Don't miss your next favorite book from First Second!
For the latest updates go to firstsecondnewsletter.com and sign up for our enewsletter.